"You wish to be a knife-dancer, Hekat of Et-Raklion?"

Her blue gaze shifted to his knife-dancers and their *hota*. "I wish to be a knife-dancer," she answered him. "I wish to be a charioteer. I wish to shoot an arrow, sling a shot-stone, bury my spear-point in an enemy's throat. I wish to be a warrior, warlord."

The calm declaration moved him. "And what are you now, Hekat of Et-Raklion?"

Her lips pursed in disgust. "I am a killer of chickens, I slaughter sheep."

She was scarred, her beauty destroyed. That did not matter either, though he mourned its loss. Warriors had no need for beauty in the face, a warrior's beauty was speed and strength, a lust for blood, the knack of survival.

"Why should I grant your bold request, Hekat? Why should I make you a warrior of Et-Raklion?"

She looked at him with those clear blue eyes, in their depths burned a fervent flame. "Because it is the will of the god, warlord. Hear it whisper in your heart. It whispers to you: *make Hekat a warrior*."

Praise for Karen Miller:

Books by Karen Miller

Kingmaker, Kingbreaker

The Innocent Mage
The Awakened Mage

The Godspeaker Trilogy

Empress
The Riven Kingdom
Hammer of God

Fisherman's Children

The Prodigal Mage

Writing as K. E. Mills

The Rogue Agent Trilogy

The Accidental Sorcerer
Witches Incorporated

EMPRESS

GODSPEAKER: BOOK ONE

KAREN MILLER

orbit

www.orbitbooks.net

Copyright © 2007 by Karen Miller
Excerpt from *The Riven Kingdom* copyright © 2008 by Karen Miller
All rights reserved. Except as permitted under the U.S. Copyright Act of 1976, no part of this publication may be reproduced, distributed, or transmitted in any form or by any means, or stored in a data base or retrieval system, without the prior written permission of the publisher.

Map by Mark Timmony

Orbit
Hachette Book Group
237 Park Avenue
New York, NY 10017
Visit our website at www.orbitbooks.net

Orbit is an imprint of Hachette Book Group, Inc. The Orbit name and logo is a trademark of Little, Brown Book Group Ltd.

Printed in the United States of America

Originally published by Voyager, Australia: 2007
First Orbit edition: April 2008

10 9 8 7 6

MIJAK

THE ANVIL

N

THE SAVAGE NORTH

✕ Hekat's Village

✕ Todorok Village

ET-JOKRIEL

✝

ET-MAMIKLIA

✝

Heart of Mijak

ET-TAKONA

✝

ET-NOGOLOR

✝

ET-ZYDEN

✝

ET-BAJADEK

✝

ET-RAKLION

✝

THE SAND RIVER

THE
GODLESS
LANDS

THE GODLESS LANDS

EMPRESS

PART ONE

CHAPTER ONE

Despite its two burning lard-lamps the kitchen was dark, its air choked with the stink of rancid goat butter and spoiling goat-meat. Spiders festooned the corners with sickly webs, boarding the husks of flies and suck-you-dries. A mud-brick oven swallowed half the space between the door and the solitary window. There were three wooden shelves, one rickety wooden stool and a scarred wooden table, almost unheard of in this land whose trees had ages since turned to stone.

Crouched in the shadows beneath the table, the child with no name listened to the man and the woman fight.

"But you promised," the woman wailed. "You said I could keep this one."

The man's hard fist pounded the timber above the child's head. "That was before another poor harvest, slut, before two more village wells dried up! All the coin it costs to feed it, am I made of money? Don't you complain, when it was born I could've thrown it on the rocks, I could've left it on The Anvil!"

"But she can work, she—"

"Not like a son!" His voice cracked like lightning, rolled like thunder round the small smoky room. "If you'd whelped me more sons—"

"I tried!"

"Not hard enough!" Another boom of fist on wood. "The she-brat goes. Only the god knows when Traders will come this way again."

The woman was sobbing, harsh little sounds like a dying goat. "But she's so young."

"Young? Its blood-time is come. It can pay back what it's cost me, like the other she-brats you spawned. This is my word, woman. Speak again and I'll smash your teeth and black your eyes."

When the woman dared disobey him the child was so surprised she bit her fingers. She scarcely felt the small pain; her whole life was pain, vast like the barren wastes beyond the village's godpost, and had been so since her first caterwauling cry. She was almost numb to it now.

"Please," the woman whispered. "Let me keep her. I've spawned you six sons."

"It should've been eleven!" Now the man sounded like one of his skin-and-bone dogs, slavering beasts who fought for scraps of offal in the stony yard behind their hovel.

The child flinched. She hated those dogs almost as much as she hated the man. It was a bright flame, her hatred, hidden deep and safe from the man's sight. He would kill her if he saw it, would take her by one skinny scabbed ankle and smash her headfirst into the nearest red and ochre rock. He'd done it to a dog once, that had dared to growl at him. The other dogs had lapped up its brains then fought over the bloody carcass all through the long unheated night. On her threadbare blanket beneath the kitchen table she'd fallen asleep to the sound of their teeth, and dreamed the bones they gnawed were her own.

But dangerous or not she refused to abandon her hate, the only thing she owned. It comforted and nourished her, filling her ache-empty belly on the nights she didn't eat because the woman's legs were spread, or her labors were unfinished, or the man was drunk on cactus blood and beating her.

He was beating her now, open-handed blows across the face, swearing and sweating, working himself to a frenzy. The woman knew better than to cry out. Listening to the man's palm smack against the woman's sunken cheeks, to his lusty breathing and her swallowed grunts, the child imagined plunging a knife into his throat. If she closed her eyes she could see the blood spurt scarlet, hear it splash on the floor as he gasped and bubbled and died. She was sure she could do it. Hadn't she seen the men with their proud knives cut the throats of goats and even a horse, once, that had broken its leg and was no longer good for anything but meat and hide and bleached boiled bones?

There were knives in a box on the kitchen's lowest shelf. She felt her fingers curl and cramp as though grasping a carved bone hilt, felt her heart rattle her ribs. The secret flame flickered, flared . . . then died.

No good. He'd catch her before she killed him. She would not defeat the man today, or tomorrow, or even next fat godmoon. She was too small, and he was too strong. But one day, many fat godmoons from now, she'd be big and he'd be old and shrunken. Then she'd do it and throw his body to the dogs after and laugh and laugh as they gobbled his buttocks and poked their questing tongues through the empty eye sockets of his skull.

One day.

The man hit the woman again, so hard she fell to the pounded dirt floor. "You poisoned my seed five times and whelped bitches, slut. Three sons you whelped lived less than a godmoon. I should curse you! Turn you out for the godspeaker to deal with!"

The woman was sobbing again, scarred arms crossed in front of her face. "I'm sorry—I'm sorry—"

Listening, the child felt contempt. Where was the woman's flame? Did she even have one? Weeping. Begging. Didn't she know this was what the man wanted, to see her broken and bleating in the dirt? The woman should die first.

But she wouldn't. She was weak. All women were weak. Everywhere in the village the child saw it. Even the women who'd spawned only sons, who looked down on the ones who'd spawned she-brats as well, who helped the godspeaker stone the cursed witches whose bodies spewed forth nothing but female flesh . . . even those women were weak.

I not weak the child told herself fiercely as the man soaked the woman in venom and spite and the woman wept, believing him. *I never beg.*

Now the man pressed his heel between the woman's dugs and shoved her flat on her back. "You should pray thanks to the god. Another man would've broke your legs and turned you out seasons ago. Another man would've plowed two hands of living sons on a better bitch than you!"

"Yes! Yes! I am fortunate! I am blessed!" the woman gabbled, rubbing at the bruised place on her chest.

The man shucked his trousers. "Maybe. Maybe not. Spread, bitch. You give me a living son nine fat godmoons from now or I swear by the village godpost I'll be rid of you onto The Anvil!"

Choking, obedient, the woman hiked up her torn shift

and let her thin thighs fall open. The child watched, un-moved, as the man plowed the woman's furrow, grunting and sweating with his effort. He had a puny blade, and the woman's soil was old and dusty. She wore her dog-tooth amulet round her neck but its power was long dead. The child did not think a son would come of this planting or any other. Nine fat godmoons from this day, or sooner, the woman would die.

His seed at last dribbled out, the man stood and pulled up his trousers. "Traders'll be here by highsun tomorrow. Might be seasons till more come. I paid the godspeaker to list us as selling and put a goat's skull on the gate. Money won't come back, so the she-brat goes. Use your water ration to clean it. Use one drop of mine. I'll flay you. I'll hang you with rope twisted from your own skin. Understand?"

"Yes," the woman whispered. She sounded tired and beaten. There was blood on the dirt between her legs.

"Where's the she-brat now?"

"Outside."

The man spat. He was always spitting. Wasting water. "Find it. When it's clean, chain it to the wall so it don't run like the last one."

The woman nodded. He'd broken her nose with his goat-stick that time. The child, three seasons younger then, had heard the woman's splintering bone, watched the pouring blood. Remembering that, she remembered too what the man did to the other she-brat to make it sorry for running. Things that made the she-brat squeal but left no mark be-cause Traders paid less for damaged goods.

That she-brat had been a fool. No matter where the Traders took her it had to be better than the village and the man. Traders were the only escape for she-brats.

Traders . . . or death. And she did not want to die. When they came for her before highsun tomorrow she would go with them willingly.

"I'll chain her," the woman promised. "She won't run."

"Better not," growled the man, and then the slap of goathide on wood as he shoved the kitchen door aside and left.

The woman rolled her head until her red-rimmed eyes found what they sought beneath the kitchen table. "I tried. I'm sorry."

The child crawled out of the shadows and shrugged. The woman was always sorry. But sorrow changed nothing, so what did it matter? "Traders coming," she said. "Wash now."

Wincing, breath catching raw in her throat, the woman clutched at the table leg and clawed herself to her knees, then grabbed hold of the table edge, panting, whimpering, and staggered upright. There was water in her eyes. She reached out a work-knotted hand and touched rough fingertips to the child's cheek. The water trembled, but did not fall.

Then the woman turned on her heel and went out into the searing day. Not understanding, not caring, the child with no name followed.

The Traders came a finger before highsun the next day. Not the four from last time, with tatty robes, skinny donkeys, half-starved purses and hardly any slaves. No. These two Traders were grand. Seated on haughty white camels, jangling with beads and bangles, dangling with earrings and sacred amulets, their dark skin shiny with fragrant oils and jeweled knife-sheaths on their belts. Behind them stretched the longest snake-spine of merchandise: men's inferior sons, discarded, and she-brats, and women. All naked, all chained. Some born to slavery, others newly sold. The difference was in their godbraids, slaves of long standing bore one braid of deep blood red, a sign from the god that they were property. The new slaves would get their red braids, in time.

Guarding the chained slaves, five tall men with swords and spears. Their godbraids bore amulets, even their slave-braids were charmed. They must be special slaves, those guards. In the caravan there were pack camels too, common brown, roped together, laden with baskets, criss-crossed with travel-charms. A sixth unchained slave led them, little more than a boy, and his red godbraid bore amulets as well. At his signal, groaning, the camels folded their calloused knees to squat on the hard ground. The slaves squatted too, silent and sweating.

Waiting in her own chains, the crude iron links heavy and chafing round her wrists and ankles, the child watched the Traders from beneath lowered lashes as they dismounted and stood in the dust and dirt of the man's small holding. Their slender fingers smoothed shining silk robes, tucked their glossy beaded godbraids behind their ears. Their fingernails were all the same neat oval shape and painted bright colors to match their clothing: green and purple and crimson and gold. They were taller than the tallest man in the village. Taller than the god-speaker, who must stand above all. One of them was even *fat*. They were the most splendid creatures the child had ever seen, and knowing she would leave with them, leave forever the squalor and misery of the man and the village, her heart beat faster and her own unpainted fingernails, ragged and shapeless, bit deep into her dirty scarred palms.

The Traders stared at the cracked bare ground with its withered straggle of weeds, at the mud brick hovel with its roof of dried grasses badly woven, at the pen of profitless goats, at the man whose bloodshot eyes shone with hope and avarice. A look flowed between them and their plump lips pursed. They were sneering. The child wondered where they came from, to be so clean and disapproving. Somewhere not like this. She couldn't wait to see such a place herself, to sleep for just one night inside walls that did not stink of fear and goat. She'd wear a hundred chains and crawl on her hands and knees across The Anvil's burning sand if she had to, so long as she reached it.

The man was staring at the Traders too, his eyes popping with amazement. He bobbed his head at them, like a chicken pecking corn. "Excellencies. Welcome, welcome. Thank you for your custom."

The thin Trader wore thick gold earrings; tattooed on his right cheek, in brightest scarlet, a stinging scorpion. The child bit her tongue. He had money enough to buy a protection like that? And power enough that a godspeaker would let him? *Aieee* . . .

He stepped forward and looked down at the man, fingertips flicking at her. "Just this?"

She was enchanted. His voice was deep and dark like the dead of night, and shaped the words differently from the man. When the man spoke it sounded like rocks grinding in the dry ravine, ugly like him. The Trader was not ugly.

The man nodded. "Just this."

"No sons, un-needed?"

"Apologies, Excellency," said the man. "The god has granted me few sons. I need them all."

Frowning, the Trader circled the child in slow, measured steps. She held her breath. If he found her unpleasing and if the man did not kill her because of it, she'd be slaved to some village man for beating and spawning sons and hard labor without rest. She would cut her flesh with stone and let the dogs taste her, tear her, devour her, first.

The Trader reached out his hand, his flat palm soft and pink, and smoothed it down her thigh, across her buttock. His touch was warm, and heavy. He glanced at the man. "How old?"

"Sixteen."

The Trader stopped pacing. His companion unhooked a camel whip from his belt of linked precious stones and snapped the thong. The man's dogs, caged for safety, howled and threw themselves against the woven goathide straps of their prison. In the pen beside them the man's goats bleated and milled, dropping anxious balls of shit, yellow slot-eyes gleaming.

"How old?" the Trader asked again. His green eyes were narrow, and cold.

The man cringed, head lowered, fingers knuckled together. "Twelve. Forgive me. Honest error."

The Trader made a small, disbelieving sound. He'd done something to his eyebrows. Instead of being a thick tangled bar like the man's they arched above his eyes in two solid gold half-circles. The child stared at them, fascinated, as the Trader leaned down and brought his dark face close to hers. She wanted to stroke the scarlet scorpion inked into his cheek. Steal some of his protection, in case he did not buy her.

His long, slender fingers tugged on her earlobes, traced the shape of her skull, her nose, her cheeks, pushed back her lips and felt all her teeth. He tasted of salt and things she did not know. He smelled like freedom.

"Is she blooded?" he asked, glancing over his shoulder at the man.

"Since four godmoons."

"Intact?"

The man nodded. "Of course."

The Trader's lip curled. "There is no 'of course' where men and she-flesh abide."

Without warning he plunged his hand between her legs, fingers pushing, probing, higher up, deeper in. Teeth bared, her own fingers like little claws, the child flew at him, screeching. Her chains might have weighed no more than the bangles on his slender, elegant wrists. The man sprang forward shouting, fists raised, face contorted, but the Trader did not need him. He brushed her aside as though she were a corn-moth. Seizing a handful of black and tangled hair he wrenched her to the tips of her toes till she was screaming in pain, not fury, and her hands fell limply by her sides. She felt her heart batter her brittle ribs and despair storm in her throat. Her eyes squeezed shut and for the first time she could remember felt the salty sting of tears.

She had ruined everything. There would be no escape from the village now, no new life beyond the knife-edged horizon. The Trader would toss her aside like spoiled meat, and when he and his fat friend were gone the man would kill her or she would be forced to kill herself. Panting like a goat in the slaughter-house she waited for the blow to fall.

But the Trader was laughing. Still holding her, he turned to his friend. "What a little hell-cat! Untamed and savage, like all these dwellers in the savage north. But do you see the eyes, Yagji? The face? The length of bone and the sleekness of flank? Her sweet breasts, budding?"

Trembling, she dared to look at him. Dared to hope . . .

The fat one wasn't laughing. He shook his head, setting the ivory dangles in his ears to swinging. "She is scrawny."

"Today, yes," agreed the Trader. "But with food and bathing and three times three godmoons . . . then we shall see!"

"Your eyes see the invisible, Aba. Scrawny brats are oft diseased."

"No, Excellency!" the man protested. "No disease. No pus, no bloating, no worms. Good flesh. Healthy flesh."

"What there is of it," said the Trader. He turned. "She is not diseased, Yagji."

"But she is ill-tempered," his fat friend argued. "Undisciplined, and wild. She'll be troublesome, Aba."

The Trader nodded. "True." He held out his hand and easily caught the camel whip tossed to him. Fingers tight in her hair he snapped the woven hide quirt around her naked legs so the little metal weights on its end printed bloody patterns in her flesh.

The blows stung like fire. The child sank her teeth into her lip and stared unblinking into the Trader's careful, watching eyes, daring him to strip the unfed flesh from her bones if he liked. He would see she was no weakling, that she was worthy of his coin. Hot blood dripped down her calf to tickle her ankle. Within seconds the small black desert flies came buzzing to drink her. Hearing them, the Trader withheld the next blow and instead tossed the camel whip back to its owner.

"Lesson one, little hell-cat," he said, his fingers untangling from her hair to stroke the sharp line of her cheek. "Raise your hand or voice to me again and you will die never knowing the pleasures that await you. Do you understand me?"

The black desert flies were greedy, their eager sucking made her skin crawl. She'd seen what they could do to living creatures if not discouraged. She tried not to dance on the spot as the feverish flies quarreled over her bloody welts. All she understood was the Trader did not mean to reject her. "Yes."

"Good." He waved the flies away, then pulled from his gold and purple pocket a tiny pottery jar. When he took off its lid she smelled the ointment inside, thick and rich and strange.

Startling her, he dropped to one knee and smeared her burning legs with the jar's fragrant paste. His fingers were cool and sure against her sun-seared skin. The pain vanished, and she was shocked. She hadn't known a man could touch a she-brat and not hurt it.

It made her wonder what else she did not know.

When he was finished he pocketed the jar and stood, staring down at her. "Do you have a name?"

A stupid question. She-brats were owed no names, no more than the stones on the ground or the dead goats in the slaughter-house waiting to be skinned. She opened her mouth to say so, then closed it again. The Trader was almost smiling, and there was a look in his eyes she'd never seen before. A question. Or a challenge. It meant something. She was sure it meant something. If only she could work out what . . .

She let her gaze slide sideways to the mud brick hovel and its mean kitchen window, where the woman thought she could not be seen as she dangerously watched the trading. The woman who had no name, just descriptions. *Bitch. Slut. Goatslit.* Then she looked at the man, shaking with greed, waiting for his money. If she gave *herself* a name, how angry it would make him.

But she couldn't think of one. Her mind was blank sand, like The Anvil. Who was she? She had no idea. But the Trader had named her, hadn't he? He had called her something, he had called her—

She tilted her chin so she could look into his green and gleaming eyes. "He—kat," she said, her tongue stumbling over the strange word, the sing-song way he spoke. "Me. Name. Hekat."

The Trader laughed again. "As good a name as any, and better than most." He held up his hand, two fingers raised; his fat friend tossed him a red leather pouch, clinking with coin.

The man stepped forward, black eyes ravenous. "If you like the brat so much I will breed you more! Better than this one, worth twice as much coin."

The Trader snorted. "It is a miracle you bred even this one. Do not tempt the god with your blustering lest your seed dry up completely." Nostrils pinched, he dropped the pouch into the man's cupped hands.

The man's fingers tore at the pouch's tied lacing, so clumsily that its contents spilled on the ground. With a cry of anguish he plunged to his knees, heedless of bruises, and began scrabbling for the silver coins. His knuckles skinned against the sharp stones but the man did not notice the blood, or the buzzing black flies that swarmed to drink him.

For a moment the Trader watched him, unspeaking. Then he trod the man's fingers into the dirt. "Your silver has no wings. Remove the child's chains."

The man gaped, face screwed up in pain. "Remove . . . ?"

The Trader smiled; it made his scarlet scorpion flex its claws. "You are deaf? Or would like to be?"

"Excellency?"

The Trader's left hand settled on the long knife at his side. "Headless men cannot hear."

The man wrenched his fingers free and lurched to his feet. Panting, he unlocked the binding chains, not looking at the child. The skin around his eyes twitched as though he were scorpion-stung.

"Come, little Hekat," said the Trader. "You belong to me now."

She followed him to the waiting slave train, thinking he would put his own chains about her wrists and ankles and join her to the other naked slaves squatting on the ground. Instead he led her to his camel and turned to his friend. "A robe, Yagji."

The fat Trader Yagji sighed and fetched a pale yellow garment from one of the pack camel's baskets. Barely breathing, the child stared as the thin Trader took his knife and slashed through the cloth, reducing it to fit her small body. Smiling, he dropped the cut-down robe over her head and guided her arms into its shortened sleeves, smoothed its cool folds over her naked skin. She was astonished. She wished the man's sons were here to see this but they were away at work. Snake-dancing, and tending goats.

"There," said the Trader. "Now we will ride."

Before she could speak he was lifting her up and onto the camel.

Air hissed between the fat Trader's teeth. "Ten silver pieces! Did you have to give so much?"

"To give less would be insulting to the god."

"Tcha! This is madness, Abajai! You will regret this, and so will I!"

"I do not think so, Yagji," the thin Trader replied. "We were guided here by the god. The god will see us safe."

He climbed onto the camel and prodded it to standing. With a muffled curse, the fat Trader climbed onto his own camel and the slave train moved on, leaving the man and the woman and the goats and the dogs behind them.

Hekat sat on the Trader's haughty white camel, her head held high, and never once looked back.

CHAPTER TWO

As the village and its splintered, weathered wooden godpost dwindled into the heat-hazed distance behind them the thin Trader Abajai said, his hand warm and secure on Hekat's shoulder, "The others we purchased. Do you know them?"

He and fat Yagji had bought four more villagers after leaving the man's holding. A woman, another she-brat and two boys. Unlike her, they walked with the rest of the slaves, chained to them and to each other, guarded by the five tall slaves with spears. Sitting before Abajai on his white camel, with its coarse hair tickling her bare legs, she shook her head. "No. Hekat knows man. Woman. Man's sons." A shiver rippled over her skin. "Godspeaker."

"No-one else? You had no friends?" said Abajai. "Who will you weep for tonight, Hekat?"

She shrugged. "Hekat not weep."

Riding beside them. Yagji sighed. "Must you talk to it, Aba? It's not a pet."

Abajai chuckled. "I've heard you talk to your monkey."

She looked over her shoulder at him. "Monkey?"

"An animal. Smelly, noisy, greedy." He smiled. "Yagji will introduce you when we reach Et-Raklion."

"I won't," said Yagji. "She will teach little Hooli bad manners. Abajai, you should sell this one before we get home." A red stone carved into a single staring eye dangled on a chain around his neck; he clutched it with plump fingers. "There is a darkness . . ."

"Superstition," Abajai grunted. "The god desired us to find this one, Yagji. You worry for nothing. We will reach Et-Raklion."

Hekat frowned. "Et-Raklion?"

"Our home."

"Where?"

Abajai pointed ahead, to where the ground met the sky. "Further than your eye can see, Hekat. Many godmoons traveling beyond the horizon."

She shook her head. That place was so far away she couldn't imagine it. Already she was lost. The barren land stretched on every side, dressed in all its hot colors: red, orange, ochre, brown. Spindle grass withered beneath the uncovered sun, dull purple, dying green. The sky was a heavy palm pressing her flat towards the slow-baked ground. Beneath the padding of camel-feet, the clanking of slave-chains, the clicking of rock against pebble, silence waited like a sandcat poised to smother and kill. If she wasn't careful, she'd forget how to breathe.

Abajai's hand returned to her shoulder. "Fear not, Hekat. You are safe with me."

"Safe?"

Beside them, Yagji tittered. "He may be a monkey but at least my little Hooli understands more than one word in five!"

Abajai ignored him. "Yes, Hekat. Safe. That means I will protect you." His fingers had tightened a little, and his voice was gentle. The wonder of that was as crushing as the sky. "No hurting. No hunger. Safe."

She became one with the silence. In the village no she-brat was safe. Not from the man, or his sons, or the god-speaker who stalked the streets like a vulture, always looking for sin to stone.

"Safe," she whispered at last. The white camel flicked its ear at her, grumbling softly as it walked. She looked back at the Trader. "Safe Et-Raklion?"

He smiled widely at her, teeth blinding. Tiny gemstones sparkled, blue and red and green. She gasped, and touched her own teeth in amazement. She had not noticed his gemstones in the village. Abajai laughed. "You like them?" She nodded. "You wish for some of your own?"

Fat Yagji moaned like a woman. "Aba, I beg you!

Protections in your teeth is one thing. It's proper. But in *her* mouth? The *waste*!"

"Perhaps," said Abajai, shrugging. "But I will buy her an amulet in Todorok. Other eyes are not blind, Yagji. They will see what you cannot."

"Yes, yes, they'll see," grumbled the fat Trader, like a camel. "They'll see you're godforsaken!"

Laughing, Abajai waved away an obstinate fly. "With this prize? Yagji, kiss your eye for blasphemy."

Yagji didn't kiss his red stone eye, but he touched it again. "You tempt the god to smiting, Aba. Boast less. Pray more."

Hekat sighed. Words, words, buzz buzz buzz. "Abajai." He'd said she could use his name. "Tell Hekat Et-Raklion."

"Don't," said Yagji. "She will see it soon enough."

"She can barely utter a civilized sentence, Yagji," said Abajai. "If I do not speak with her how will she learn?" He patted her shoulder. "Et-Raklion is a mighty city, Hekat."

"City?"

He held his arms wide. "A big, big, *big* village. You know big?"

She nodded. "Yes. Big not village. Hekat village small."

His sparkly teeth flashed again. "She is not stupid, Yagji. Underfed, yes, and starved of learning. But in no way is she stupid."

Yagji threw up his hands. "And this is good, Aba? Intelligent slaves are good? Aieee! May the god protect us!"

The talking stopped then. In silence they traveled away

from the sliding sun, chased the long thin shadows it cast down the red rock ground before them. Abajai was like the god, he knew where to ride even though the land was empty. Hekat felt her eyes drift closed, her head nod like a wilting weed on its stem. Abajai's hand rested on her shoulder. She would not fall. She was safe. She slept.

When he shook her awake the blue sky had faded. It was dusk, and little pricky stars sparkled like the gemstones in his teeth. The godmoon and his wife were risen, small silver discs against the deepening dark. The white camels lifted their heads, snuffling, then slowed, stopped and settled on the ground.

"This will do," said Abajai, sliding from his saddle. "Stake the slaves out, Obid," he ordered the oldest and tallest of the guards. "Food and water."

"How much, master?" said Obid. "That village was poor. Supplies are low and no hunting here."

Abajai looked around them at the sun-killed plain. "A fist of grain, a cup of water, night and dawn till my word changes. In twenty highsuns we'll reach Todorok village and trade for fresh supplies. What we have will last until then."

Hekat felt her eyes go wide. *Twenty* highsuns? So far away! Had any man in the village ever traveled so far? She did not think so.

While Obid and the other guards settled the slaves and camels for the night, Abajai and Yagji unpacked baskets and sacks. She watched for a moment, aware of a growing discomfort. She jiggled, looking around. There was nothing to squat behind. Yagji noticed. He stopped unpacking and tugged at Abajai's sleeve.

"Hekat?" said Abajai.

"Need lose water."

"Pish, you mean?"

Did she? Guessing, she nodded. "Need lose water *now*."

He went to his white camel, opened one of its carry baskets and pulled out a small clay pot. "Pish into this and give it to Obid."

To Obid? She stared. "Obid want body water?"

"I want it." When he saw she still didn't understand, he said, "Your village. Do the people keep body water?"

"For goat leather. No goats, Abajai."

"No, but we turn our body water into coin when other villages need more. Pish now, Hekat. We must make camp."

So she pished, and gave the sloshing pot to Obid. He did not speak to her, just poured her water into a big clay jar unstrapped from the sturdiest pack camel. As she walked away she felt the chained slaves' gazes sliding sideways over her skin, wondering and jealous.

Let them wonder. Let them hate. She did not care for them.

After pishing, tired and sore from camel-riding, she yawned cross-legged on the blanket Abajai gave her, amazed as the Traders produced rolls of colored cloth from the pack camels' baskets and turned them into little rooms.

"Tents," said Abajai, seeing her surprise. "You will sleep in mine."

There was food in the white camels' baskets, better than the slaves were eating. Better than any food she'd smelled in her life. Yagji made a fire with bricks of dried camel-dung and warmed the food in an iron pot over the flames, adding leaves she didn't recognize. He kept them in little shiny boxes and talked to himself as he pinched some from this one, some from that. Yagji was strange. As the food slowly heated, releasing such smells, her belly turned over and over and she almost choked on the juices flooding her mouth.

"Don't snatch," said Abajai as he handed her a pottery bowl filled halfway, and a spoon. His knuckles rapped hard on her head. "Dignity. Restraint. Conduct. You must learn these things."

She didn't know those words. All she knew was she'd displeased him. For the second time that day salty water stung her eyes.

"Tchut tchut tchut," he soothed her, no knuckles now, just a gentle pat to her cheek. "Eat. Slowly. I will fetch you drink. You know sadsa?"

Mouth stuffed full of meat, aieee, so wonderful, she shook her head, watching as he took an empty bronze cup and filled it from a leather flask. Yagji nodded. "Good idea," he said. "If you insist on having it in your tent, best it be well fuddled."

Abajai shook his head. "Hekat is no danger."

"You say."

"The god says," Abajai replied, frowning.

Yagji put down his own bowl and rummaged through the leather bag that held his little boxes of leaves. "Best be safe than sorry," he said, tossing him a small yellow pouch.

Abajai rolled his eyes, but he took some blue powder from the pouch, dropped it in the bronze cup and swirled. Then he tossed the pouch back to Yagji and gave her the cup. "Sadsa, Hekat. Drink."

No man had ever served her before. Women served

men, that was the way. Almost dreamy, she lifted the bronze cup to her nose. Sadsa was creamy white, and its sharp, sweet-sour smell tickled. There were tiny flecks of blue caught in its frothy surface. She looked at Yagji, not trusting him. "What?"

"Sadsa is camel's milk," said Abajai. "Good for you."

He didn't understand, so she pointed at the yellow pouch still caught in Yagji's fingers. "*What*?"

Abajai laughed. "I told you, Yagji. Not stupid." Bending, he patted her cheek again. "For sleeping, Hekat. It will not harm you. Drink."

He had saved her from the man. He did not chain her naked with the slaves, he clothed her and let her ride before him on his fine white camel. She drank. The sadsa flowed down her throat and into her belly like soft fire. She gasped, choking. The dancing flames blurred. So did Yagji's face, and Abajai's. She put down the bronze cup and ate more meat. Her fingers felt clumsy, wrapped around the spoon. Too soon the bowl was empty. Hopefully, she looked at Abajai.

"No," he said. "Your belly's had enough surprise. Finish your sadsa, then you must sleep."

By the time the cup was empty she could barely keep her eyes open. It slipped from her silly fat fingers to the ground, and rolled in little circles that made her laugh. Laughing made her laugh. What a stupid sound! The man didn't like it, he'd hit her when she laughed. Laughing was for secret. For almost never. But Abajai wasn't angry. He was smiling, his green eyes mysterious, and in the leaping firelight the jewels in his teeth were precious. The scarlet scorpion sat quietly in his skin, keeping him safe. She tried to stand but her legs had turned to grass. She lay on her back instead, staring at the pricky stars, and laughed even harder.

"Oh, put it to bed, Aba," said Yagji crossly. "If this is what we've got to look forward to on the long road to Et-Raklion I doubt you and I will be speaking by the end."

"Et-Raklion," she sang to the godmoon and his wife. "Hekat go Et-Raklion. La la la la . . ."

Strong arms slid beneath her shoulders and her knees. Abajai lifted her as the god's breath lifted dust. "See how the god smiles, Yagji?" he said. "She has a sweet song voice to match her face."

Yagji said something she couldn't understand, but it sounded rude. His upside-down face wore a rude look. Dangling backwards over Abajai's arm, she pointed at it. "Funny Yagji make goat talk. *Meh meh meh*."

Abajai lay her inside his tent on something soft and warm like a cloud of sunshine, and covered her in a blanket that didn't scratch her skin.

"Sleep, Hekat," he said.

"Abajai," she sighed, and felt her lips curve as she fell headfirst into the warm dark. "Abajai."

She woke in daylight from a bad dream about the man's dogs, needing to lose water so badly her belly was cramping. Abajai snored, a long still shape beneath his striped wool blankets. Heart pounding from the dream she fumbled the tent-flap open and stumbled outside, where Obid and the other guards walked up and down the snake-spine of slaves, taking away their dirty wool blankets, making sure none had died in the night. They carried pots, and one by one the slaves squatted over them, losing water. Making coin for Abajai.

There was no time to ask for a pot of her own, hot trickles were tickling her thighs, so she moved away from the tent, hiked up the yellow robe Abajai had given her and let her own water flow. Obid saw her. Shoving the pot he carried at another guard he loped towards her, arms waving, lips peeled back over teeth like knife points, all stained red.

She staggered backwards, fingers clawed. "*Abajai!*"

He came out of the tent as Obid reached her with his hand swinging to smack her face. "Obid!" he shouted. "*Hunta!*"

Obid dropped to his knees like an axed goat, and pressed his forehead to the dirt. "Master."

Abajai wore a dark green robe and carried a club with a knot on one end and plaited thongs at the other. He tossed it in the air, caught it again just above the knot and brought the thongs down hard across Obid's bowed shoulders. Obid was wearing nothing but his loincloth. His light brown skin welted at once and he whimpered. Four more times Abajai struck him. Obid's fingers spasmed, but he didn't cry out.

"Stand," said Abajai. He sounded calm, but stern. "See this one?"

Standing again, Obid looked at her. "Master."

"This one may not be touched without my nod."

Obid struggled for words. "Master, this one spilled its water on the ground."

"Ah." Abajai dropped to a crouch before her, the scarlet scorpion flexing its claws as he grimaced. "What did I tell you, Hekat?"

"Use pot."

"If you don't use a pot, you waste your water. That is the same as stealing my coin. You understand?"

She felt the cool newsun air catch in her throat. The godspeaker saved his second-sharpest rocks for stealers. "No steal, Abajai," she said jerkily. "No time for pot. Need pish *now*."

Abajai sighed. Behind him, Obid's face was flat as stone. Only his pale blue eyes were alive, they were full of questions. "Hekat, you are precious. But if you close your ears to my word again I will give Obid my nod and he will beat you. Just like you were one of the slaves he guards. You understand?"

Hekat, you are precious. The words burst inside her like a rain cloud, rare and hardly looked for. She nodded, drenched with pleasure. "Yes, Abajai. Water in pot."

His lips twitched. "*All* my words must be obeyed, Hekat. You understand?"

"Yes, Abajai."

Supple as a snake, he rose to his feet. "Good. Obid?"

Obid stepped forward. "Master."

Abajai rested a fingertip on her head. "Unless you receive my nod, this one is hidden from you."

Now the questions in Obid's eyes writhed like maggots in old meat. "Yes, master."

"Go back to your business. We leave soon."

Obid bowed. "Master."

She watched Obid lope back to the slave line, where his fellow guards pretended not to watch. "Obid not like Hekat."

Abajai looked down at her, faintly smiling. "Does Hekat care?"

She grinned. "No. Hekat not care."

"Good," he said. "It is foolish to care for the feelings of a slave. Now come."

She returned with him to their camp, where Yagji was brewing tea and cooking corncakes in a pan. He was dressed in a white robe shot through with gold threads. All his godbraids were gathered in a tail at the base of his neck and he'd taken off his red stone eye. Now a green coiled snake dangled round his neck. The stone it was carved from was shiny, she'd never seen anything like it before.

"More trouble, Aba?" he said sourly as she settled on a blanket and watched Abajai portion out food and drink for two.

"No," said Abajai, handing her a plate and cup. Then he picked up a jug and held it over her corncakes. "Honey?"

"What honey?"

"What *is* honey," he corrected. "You must learn proper Mijaki, Hekat. Fluent, pleasing speech. Not this cobbled-together grunting of yours."

"What Mijaki?"

"What *is* Mijaki. It is the tongue of our people. We are Mijaki. This land is Mijak, gift of the god." When she looked at him, not understanding, he shook his head. "He never taught you that much, your father?"

Father. He meant the man? She shrugged. "She-brats like goats. Who want teach goats?"

"Only godforsaken fools," muttered Yagji.

Abajai shot him a dark look. "What of your mother?"

She sniggered. "Woman not teach. Man beat woman if she talk she-brats." She sipped from the cup carefully, not

sadsa this time, but tea. It was cool enough to drink. She
gulped, suddenly thirsty. "Woman try. Talk a little, when
man gone."

"Did anybody else talk to you?"

"Sometimes." She shrugged. "Man not like. But Hekat
listen to man. To man's boys. To men visit man. Hekat
learn words. Learn counting."

Abajai smiled. "Clever Hekat." He lifted the jug again.
"Honey is sweet. You know sweet?"

She shook her head, staring as Abajai poured a sticky
gold stream onto her corncakes. "Eat," he said, still smiling. "Use your fingers."

"I thought you wanted it civilized," protested Yagji.

"That will come," said Abajai, as she put down the cup
and balanced the plate more firmly in her lap. "For now
let her touch the world with her fingers. Let it become
real. Something to be embraced, not feared. If she is to
make my fortune, she—"

"*Our* fortune," said Yagji, and pointed at her plate.
"You heard Aba, monkey. Eat! If you don't eat there'll be
no meat on your bones and the good coin we paid for you
will have been wasted!"

More goat words from Yagji. She would listen to Abajai. She folded a corncake in half and shoved it into her
mouth. Her eyes popped as the sticky gold *honey* melted
on her tongue. *This* was sweet? This—this—

Abajai and Yagji were laughing at her. "So? You like
honey, Hekat?" said Abajai.

She chewed. Swallowed. Looked down at the other
honey-soaked corncakes. Cold now, but she didn't care
about that. "Hekat like."

"You should say thank you," said Yagji, sniffing.

"Only savages and monkeys have no manners. Say: Thank you, Yagji and Abajai."

Her tongue yearned for more sweet. "Thank you, Abajai and Yagji." She smiled, for Abajai alone. "Thank you for honey."

Abajai patted her cheek. "You are welcome, Hekat. Now eat. The sun flies up. We must go."

As she obeyed his word, stuffing sweet corncakes into her mouth, Yagji took the honey jar from Abajai and poured it over his own food. "Educate it if you must, Aba, but do refrain from fondling. As slaves go it might be quick-witted but your pet does not understand as much as you think."

Abajai laughed, and drank his tea.

After breakfast they climbed onto the white camels and the caravan continued, traveling slowly but steadily beneath the hot blue sky. Every highsun Abajai taught Hekat proper Mijaki speech, and Yagji grumbled. Soon after newsun on the sixteenth day the land changed from flat to uneven, with ravines and steep hillsides. Four fingers after the nineteenth highsun they reached a road that twisted and turned like a snake, then plunged downward over a sharp jutting edge. Tall spindly trees with whippy branches crowded close on either side, flogging their faces and arms and legs. The camels complained with every step, and Abajai tightened his arm around Hekat's middle, leaning back, as they shuffled to the bottom.

She gasped when they reached it. Here was *green* land spread before them! Thick grass wherever she looked, and more flowering bushes than ever grew in the village. Springs of water, bursting from underground. Aieee! She wished they could stop, she wanted to touch the bubbling water, to run with bare feet in all the growing grass, but lowsun was casting its long thin shadows. They would have to camp soon. Yagji was asleep already, trusting his camel to keep pace with Abajai.

Abajai woke him. "We have reached the lands of Jokriel warlord, Yagji. The savage north is left behind."

Grunting, snuffling, Yagji straightened from his sleeping slouch. "At last. I never wish to travel there again, Aba. Make a note."

"We travel where the god desires," said Abajai. "Now let us do our duty to the godpost, then seek a pleasant place to camp."

There was a godpost, Hekat saw, a little further along the road. Tall and grim and scorpion-carved, with a white stone crow at its top. No godbowl for offerings at its base, but a craggy lump of blue crystal. Abajai and Yagji halted their camels and the slave train, and Hekat watched as Abajai went to the godpost, took two small carved cylinders from his robe's pocket and pressed them to the unremarkable stone. Bright light flared, brief as a falling star. Surprised, she looked at Yagji.

"The warlord guards the borders of his lands," said Yagji. "Traders travel wherever they please, but still we must announce our presence and prove we have paid our road-right taxes."

She did not know what a warlord was, or understand what Yagji meant or how Abajai had made the light flare from the stone.

"Tchut tchut," Yagji said, impatient with her not knowing. "Let Aba explain if he wishes. I couldn't care less what you know and what you do not."

But Abajai wasn't interested in talking of stones and warlords when he returned to his camel. He only cared for making camp. As they rode on, looking for the best place to spend the night, she saw small grey animals with long ears in the grass on either side of them. Abajai gave his word and Obid killed the bounding creatures with a slingshot. Every time he stuffed a limp body into the sack slung over his shoulder he flashed Abajai a broad smile.

"Rabbits," said Abajai, seeing her confusion. "You do not know rabbits?"

She shook her head. "No rabbits village."

"You are far from your village now, Hekat. Forget that place, it does not exist."

She nodded. "Yes, Abajai. How far Todorok village?"

"We will reach it a finger or two past highsun tomorrow."

"More honey there?" she asked him hopefully.

That made him laugh. "Perhaps. Slaves, too."

She felt a moment's prickling. If he found a she-brat more precious than her . . . "Many slaves now."

"There is no such thing as too many slaves, Hekat."

They should talk of something else. She frowned, and carefully put her words together in the way he told her she must. "How far is Et-Raklion?"

He made a pleased sound in his throat. "Many god-moons caravanning still. Your village lies at the doorstep of The Anvil, Hekat. The Anvil. You know it?"

She nodded. The Anvil was the fierce forever desert one highsun's ride from the village godpost. She'd never seen it, of course, but knew of men and boys lured into it hunting sandcats, who were never seen again. She used to wish the man would be so foolish.

"Et-Raklion sits at the far side of Mijak. Et-Raklion city, where the warlord lives, where we live, lies close to the Mijaki border, half a godmoon's swift travel from the Sand River."

Bewildered, she wriggled around to look at him. "Border? Sand River?"

He shook his head. "Your world would fit in a stunted nutshell, Hekat. The border is where Mijak ends. The Sand River is a desert, like The Anvil, though not as vast. You understand?"

Beside them, Yagji roused. "Save your breath, Aba. It doesn't need geography. Teach it a dozen ways to spread its legs and it'll know more than enough for our purpose."

She struggled to untangle his meaning. "Mijak ends?"

"Yes." Abajai rested his warm hand on the back of her neck. "At the Sand River. Beyond the Sand River lie other lands. We do not go to those places, the people there are dead to us."

"Why?"

Abajai shrugged. "Because the god has said it."

"Why?"

Yagji squealed and kissed his lizard-foot amulet. Abajai's fingers closed around her neck, painted nails biting her throat, and his lips touched her ear. "You wish to live, Hekat?"

Heart pounding, she nodded. Abajai's voice had turned dark and cold. He was angry. What had she done? His harsh breath scoured her cheek.

"Never ask the god why. Not in your heart and never with your mouth. You understand?"

No, but he was hurting her. Again, she nodded.

"Good," he said, and let her go. "That is all you learn today."

Yagji had kissed his amulet so hard the carved yellow stone had split his flesh. A thin thread of blood dribbled down his chin. He touched the small wound, stared at the blood, then leaned over to thrust his wet red finger into Abajai's face.

"See this, Aba! The god *bites* me! It gives a sign! Dream no more of fortune. Sell your precious Hekat in Todorok, I beg you!"

Abajai gave him a square of white cloth. "The god does not punish sideways, Yagji. You bleed for your own sin, or by accident. Hekat is not for sale in Todorok."

Hekat let out a deep breath and waited for her heart to slow. She didn't want Abajai to know she'd been so frightened. For a long time Yagji rode in silence, the white cloth held to his cut lip with trembling fingers. His eyes were wide and staring far ahead, into the gathering dusk.

"We'll talk on this again, Abajai," he said at last, very softly. "Before we reach Et-Raklion."

"We'll talk of many things, Yagji," said Abajai, as softly. "Before we reach Et-Raklion."

CHAPTER THREE

They reached Todorok village a half-finger after highsun next. Hekat stared and stared, so much strangeness to see.

First was Todorok's godpost. It looked new, untouched by harsh sunshine, unsplintered by windstorms. Twice as tall as the godpost she'd left behind in the village, it was painted bright godcolors: purple and green and gold. Scorpions carved from shiny black crystal crawled around and around to the white crow at its top, carrying messages to the god. The god-bowl at its base was a scorpion too, heavy black iron, tail raised, claws outstretched, and its belly was full of coin. Abajai dropped gold into it as they passed and pressed his knuckles to his breast in respect. So did Yagji show respect. So did she, after Abajai pinched her shoulder and growled.

Barely had she stopped marveling over the godpost than her breath was stolen a second time. Todorok village was *big*. It had wide streets covered in smooth stones and houses painted white. Their roofs weren't made of grass, they had *scales*, like a snake, many different colors. The air was clean, it did not stink of goats and men.

The villagers waving as the caravan passed wore bright clothes all over and coverings on their heads. *Strange*. They had flesh on their bones. Their skin was shiny and smooth, not baked into cracked leather by endless sun. Some of them were *she-brats*, not chained in secret but walking freely beneath the sky, no man close to poke and strike.

How could *that* be?

Abajai and Yagji led the caravan to the center of the village, where the road opened into a large square. White buildings lined every side. One was a godhouse, its door and windows bordered with stinging scorpions and striking snakes. Here were scattered clumps of colorful flowers and water bubbling inside a ring of white rocks to splash *unused* on the ground.

Hekat couldn't believe it. If she had ever once wasted so much the man would not have waited for the godspeaker, he would have broken her body himself and tossed it to his dogs.

The villagers gathered to greet them, smiled and laughed, they were pleased to see the Trader caravan. A smiling godspeaker stepped forward as Abajai and Yagji halted their camels. Not stooped and skinny, this one. His arms weren't stringy, his robes were clean. The scorpion-shell bound to his forehead was uncracked and shiny. He had all his teeth and fingers.

"Welcome, Trader Abajai, Trader Yagji," said the godspeaker. "It is many seasons since you were seen in Todorok."

Abajai ordered his camel to kneel, climbed down, and snapped his fingers. Hekat climbed down after him and stood a little to one side, silent and wide-eyed. As Yagji's camel folded its legs so the fat Trader might stand on the ground, Abajai said, "The god sends us where and when it desires, Toolu godspeaker. This far north good slaves grow thin on the ground, like grain without nourishment. But we are here this highsun, to trade for supplies and buy such flesh from you as promises us profit. If you have flesh to sell?"

"I am certain there will be some," said the godspeaker. "Let us wait in the godhouse as word is sent to bring merchandise for your inspection. I will make sacrifice for your arrival."

Abajai bowed. "The god sees you, godspeaker. And as we wait . . ." He took Hekat's arm, tugging her forward. "You see this one?"

The godspeaker nodded, his curiosity almost hidden. "I see that one, Trader Abajai."

"I wish it bathed and fed and dressed in cotton, with shoes upon its feet and charm-beads in its godbraided hair, for health and beauty and obedience. You will please me and the god to grant my desire. I will make an offering in return."

The godspeaker's hooded gaze lingered on Abajai's scarlet scorpion, quiet in his cheek. Then he raised a sharp hand, so the snake-bones bangled round his wrist chattered. "Bisla."

A short plump woman stepped forward from the watching crowd. Ivory amulets dangled from her ears and her nakedness was hidden beneath robes too fine for *any* female, surely. "Godspeaker."

"Abajai wishes this one bathed and fed and dressed in cotton, with shoes upon its feet and charm-beads for health and beauty and obedience in its godbraided hair," the godspeaker said, not looking at the woman. "You and your sisters may honor him so."

"Yes, godspeaker." The woman held out her hand. "Come, child."

Hekat looked up at Abajai. "Go with her," he said. "Obey her wishes but hold your tongue. There is nothing to fear, you will return to me before we leave."

"Yes, Abajai," she said, trusting him. His word was his word, he kept her safe.

The woman and two others took her to a white house two streets away from Abajai. Its lizard roof had scales of blue and yellow. Inside, the floor was made of wood—did so many trees grow anywhere, to be cut down and turned into houses?—and on top of the wood were large squares of colored wool, soft beneath her feet. The women hurried her to a room with no windows. Sunk into its floor was a deep round hole maybe six man-paces across, lined with smooth stones. Stone steps led down into it. The woman Bisla rang a bell. A moment later a large slave appeared at the door. He was bare-chested, sewn with beads across his breast. He wore loose green trousers and red cloth shoes with pointy toes.

"Mistress," he said, his hairless head bowed.

"Hot water," said the woman Bisla. "Fresh soap. Cloths. Brushes and combs. My bead box. My hand mirror. Tunic and pantaloons from Dily's room, cotton, not linen or wool. And shoes."

"Mistress," the slave said again, and withdrew.

A wide wooden bench ran the length of one wall. The woman Bisla and her sisters pushed Hekat onto it. Then they stripped off the yellow robe Abajai had given her. Hekat would have shouted and snatched it back again, slapped the women for daring to touch Abajai's gift. But Abajai had told her his word so she just pinched her lips and let them take it.

"Skinny! Skinny!" the woman Bisla exclaimed, pointing at her ribs. "Does Abajai not feed you, child?"

Abajai had told her not to talk. She shrugged.

"Is that yes or no?"

Another shrug.

"She's afraid, poor thing," said one of the other women. "I wonder who she is? Not Abajai's get!" She arched her thin eyebrows at the others and giggled.

As slaves led by the hairless beaded man entered the room bearing leather buckets of steaming water, the woman

Bisla frowned and shook her head. "Tcha! It is not needful to know these things."

The hairless beaded slave put down the items the woman Bisla had ordered him to bring, then watched as one by one the other slaves emptied their buckets into the stone-lined hole. They left and returned many times until the hole was filled almost to the top. They placed four full wooden buckets to one side, bowed, and withdrew. The woman Bisla spread a large cloth beside the hole and on it placed a brush, a comb, a pile of smaller cloths and a pale pink jar. She took off its lid. Inside was something soft and slippery, smelling like flowers.

Amazed, Hekat stared at the hole full of water. Stared even more amazed as the woman Bisla stripped off her clothes and trod down the stone steps into it. The water reached up to her waist. Bisla held out her hand. "Come, child. Into the bath."

She shook her head. It was a stoning sin to put your body into water. Seasons and seasons ago, when she'd been a tiny she-brat, a boy in the village had lost his wits and put himself into the largest of the village's four wells. The godspeaker stoned him slowly, one small rock at a time, and he left the boy's face till last. The god's wrath was terrible, it opened so many screaming mouths in that boy's flesh, wept so many blood tears over that boy's sin, it only took one stone in the eye to finish him. That dead boy was hung from the village godpost until he turned to leather. Then every dwelling in the village had to keep him under their roof for a godmoon. Once every dwelling had housed him that boy was given back to his family, and his family was driven onto The Anvil.

Only a fool put his body into water.

"Come, child!" Bisla said again, sounding impatient. "You are dirty and wretched and the godspeaker will punish us if you are not made presentable for Abajai."

Hekat shook her head. Bisla snapped her fingers at the other women, they lifted her by the arms and dropped her shrieking and kicking into the water. It closed over her head as though the god was swallowing her alive, rushed up her nose and down her throat. A haze as scarlet as Abajai's tattooed scorpion rose behind her screwed-shut eyes. She thrashed to the surface, opened her mouth to scream and the water poured in . . .

"Aieee, you stupid child!" the woman Bisla shouted, smacking. "Spit it up! *Spit it up!*"

Hekat spat and retched and could breathe again. Making her legs strong she stood up straight. The water stopped at her shoulders. Her unbraided hair was a wet mat plastered to her skin, she coughed and spluttered and her chest was on fire, but she wasn't dead. Bisla dragged the sopping hair away from her eyes and dug long fingernails into her cheeks.

"This is Abajai's word! You must do as Abajai commands!"

Yes. Yes. The woman Bisla was right. Above all things she must obey Abajai.

"It is a bath, child," the woman said crossly. "Surely you've had a bath before?"

"I don't think she has, Bisla," said the shorter of her sisters. "The poor thing's terrified."

"No wonder she's so filthy if she's never had a bath," said the other one. "Be gentle, Bisla. If you frighten her she might complain to Abajai or Toolu godspeaker."

The woman Bisla loosened her fingers, and managed a

smile. "Do not be afraid, child. The water will not hurt you, and neither will we. You want to be clean, don't you?"

Still breathing hard, Hekat shrugged. The water sloshed against her skin, warm and comforting. All the tight places in her body, the muscles in her legs, her back, that had knotted like goathide rope with the camel-riding, they were starting to unknot. She'd wanted to walk some days, to run beside Abajai on the ground to ease her aching body, but he wouldn't let her. She hadn't complained, had never once whimpered, but with every newsun her body had hurt just a little bit more.

This hot water was . . . was . . .

Good? No. Good was a small word. She didn't have a big enough word for what this was.

She smiled.

"There!" said the woman Bisla, and pinched the end of her nose, but not meanly. "Soon you will feel wonderful, I promise!"

With her sisters' help, Bisla poured the pink flower-smelling stuff onto cloths and scrubbed Hekat all over, even between her toes. More pink stuff was poured into her hair, so Bisla could scrub that too. The pink stuff turned frothy like sadsa, but not white. Grubby brown, it floated on the water and stung her eyes. But that was only a small pain and it was what Abajai wanted, so Hekat didn't protest or fight. She gasped when the woman Bisla poured a whole bucket of water over her head, was astonished when her hair was scrubbed again, then again, until the froth at last was sadsa white.

By then the hot water was cool and she was feeling so soft, so floppy, it was all she could do to keep her legs strong and straight. If she wasn't careful she'd slide right back under the water again. Her wet hair was so heavy her head wanted to tip backwards. If she let that happen it might snap off altogether. That was how heavy her hair felt.

"There, child. You are properly clean," said the woman Bisla. "Does it please you?"

Hekat nodded. Properly clean was something else bigger than good. What had the woman said? *Wonderful.*

"Now we must somehow untangle that rat's nest you call hair. Aieee! Let's hope Abajai and Yagji are in a haggling mood today or you'll never be godbraided before they finish their business!"

The woman Bisla helped her climb up the stone steps on her wobbly legs. Then the other two women wrapped her in a large thick cloth and pressed the water from her heavy hair with more cloths as the woman Bisla dried and dressed herself. After that, all three women sat her on the floor. They seated themselves around her and began to tease at her damp hair. It hurt. Their busy fingers tugged and twisted, they made sharp sounds of annoyance and asked the god over and over to help them.

"Has it ever been brushed?" grumbled the shortest sister. "I don't think it has."

She was wrong. The woman had brushed her hair sometimes, when the man wasn't looking. Not often, though, and not for long.

"How many godbraids does Abajai want?" said the other sister, tchut-tchutting as her comb caught in another knot. Hekat swallowed a cry of pain. She-brats who made noises like that were always sorry. "Even with the god's help we won't manage more than fifteen before the haggling's done. Will that be enough?"

"If you waggle your fingers as fast as your tongue there'll be plenty of godbraids when we give her back!" snapped the woman Bisla.

Hekat yawned and closed her eyes. The hot water had left her sleepy, all her nagging pains lulled to silence. The knots were gone from her hair now, the women's fingers whispered through it. Their light touches on her scalp prickled over her warm clean sweet-smelling skin. The woman Bisla and her sisters chattered as they worked, talking of people and secrets, village business. She let herself drift away from it, wondering about Abajai and what he was doing.

"There!" the woman Bisla said at last, jerking her back to the room. "You are godbraided. See?" She waggled her fingers, and the shorter sister gave her a polished silver disc attached to a carved wooden handle. Hekat had never seen anything like it. "Look!" said the woman Bisla. "The god has blessed you, child."

Hekat looked and saw a face. Even though it was against Abajai's word, she cried out. "Aieee! Demon! *Demon*!"

The woman Bisla grabbed her wrist. "Demon? Silly child! That is no demon, that is *you*." She held up the silver disc. "This is a mirror. Have you never seen a mirror?"

Mirror? Heart pounding, all the warmth and softness in her body turned cold and hard with fear, Hekat shook her head.

"She is a savage, Bisla," the other sister said.

"Where are you from, child?" said the woman Bisla, still holding her wrist. "Where did Abajai find you?"

She'd spoken too many words, against Abajai's want. She shook her head again, lips pinched shut. The woman Bisla sighed, and held up the mirror again.

"Look," she said, her voice coaxing now, like the man's sons to the shy goats. "It will not harm you. How can it? The face in the mirror is yours."

She had never seen her face before, never dreamed there was a way anyone could see their own face or imagined why they would want to. She looked.

Two blue eyes, big and frightened. Thick black lashes, long enough to brush her skin. High cheekbones. Hollow cheeks. A wide mouth with plump pink lips. A softly pointed chin. All these face-parts the woman had shown her, touching her own and saying the words over and over until she remembered. She could see the woman's face in the mirror and the man's too, muddled together to make Hekat.

Framing Hekat's face were her godbraids. Fascinated, she watched her fingers touch the bright red and green beads the women had woven into her thick black hair. Her godbraids weren't like Abajai's, they were fatter and looser and they didn't hold as many charms. When they reached Et-Raklion she would ask him to give her godbraids like his. He would do that for her, she was precious.

The woman Bisla's finger stroked her cheek. "You are very beautiful, child. Do you understand?"

No, but the woman was smiling. Did that make beautiful a good thing? She wanted to know. Abajai had said no speaking, but these words were in service of him, so . . . "Beautiful please Abajai?"

"Yes," said the woman Bisla. "Of course. Beautiful pleases every man."

She let herself smile. Pleasing Abajai was all that mattered. In the mirror she saw her teeth, pure white in her clean and beautiful face.

"Now you must dress, child," said the woman Bisla. "Abajai will be waiting."

The tunic and pantaloons they put on her weren't soft and silken slippery like Abajai's yellow robe but they felt good all the same. They were colored dark green, with gold and crimson threads sewn around the neck and the wrist and the ankles. They sat upon her scented skin lightly, and rustled when she moved.

"Look at her feet," said the older sister, frowning. "The soles are like leather! Does she even need shoes?"

"Shoes are Abajai's word," said the woman Bisla. "In shoes her soles will soften over time. She has pretty, slender feet. They must be protected."

In the village only men had clothed their feet. Hekat wriggled as her toes were imprisoned.

"Tchut tchut," said the woman Bisla, and tapped her on the shoulder. "Would you disobey Abajai?"

Never. Abajai had saved her from the man. He was more real to her than the god itself.

The women led her out of the white house with the blue and yellow lizard roof, back to the open place where the caravan waited. The villagers had gone away, now it was just Obid and his guards keeping close watch on the merchandise. A group of Todorok slaves waited in the village space, naked and chained. Hekat stared hard at them as she waited for Abajai to return, but none of these slaves looked precious or beautiful.

Not like me.

She counted two men slaves, three women and four boys. No she-brats. They were taller than the people of her own village. Their faces were wider. All were darker colored, save one man whose skin was dark and pale, faded patches like an ancient goatskin. *Strange*. One boy slave was fat. She had never seen a fat boy before. The man beat his sons with the goat-stick if he thought their flesh was gaining. Fat boys ran too slowly after goats and couldn't do the snake-dance properly. That angered the god.

The fat boy's hair was tightly godbraided and all black, no single scarlet slave braid. Not like the others standing with him. There was water on his cheeks. He was *crying*. Hekat shook her head, amazed. Here there was so much water, he must be used to wasting it. Here there was so much water, maybe it couldn't be wasted. But he was still stupid to cry. Water could not melt the chains from his wrist and ankles. Better to stand up straight and show Abajai he was worthy of coin.

The fat boy stared at her, and she stared back. Then Abajai came out of the godhouse with Yagji and the god-speaker Toolu and she didn't stare anywhere but at Aba-jai's stern face. When he saw her, Abajai smiled and crossed the open village space. His long fingers dipped inside his robe and dropped three bronze coins into the woman Bisla's palm.

"You have pleased me and the god."

"Go now, Bisla, you and your sisters. Tend your men-folk and your hearths," said the godspeaker. The woman and her sisters nodded, and walked away.

Abajai looked to Yagji, who went to one of the pack camels and from its panniers pulled a stout wooden box criss-crossed with leather lacings. Strung on the lacings were so many charms and amulets the box looked infested. Yagji carried the heavy box to Abajai, who beckoned one of the slave guards to him. Without having to be told, the guard knelt on the ground, making himself into a table.

Yagji put the box on the guard's back and together, with great care, he and Abajai began to unlace it.

Each charm and amulet had to be touched, with fingertip or lip or tongue or a charm pulled from a pocket or set into a ring. With every touch a wisp of godsbreath puffed into the air. Only when the godsbreath had been blown away was the charm or amulet safe to unstring from its leather thong and only then if the right man had touched it, in the right order. If the wrong man tried to unlace the box, he would die a horrible death.

This was how the Traders protected their wealth, Abajai had explained on the road. Even though Traders were beloved of the god, men were sometimes foolish and thought they could steal from Trader caravans. Or sometimes Traders fell into misfortune so they perished and their money was found beside their bodies. That money by the god's law must be returned to the Traders' city but if it was not protected by godsworn Trader charms a man might not do his duty. He might keep that money and spend it for himself.

Hekat marveled that men could be so wicked.

The godspeaker Toolu had brought a large woven basket with him from the godhouse. When the godsbreath was blown from the last amulet, and all the box's leather lacings unlaced to show its burden of coin, Abajai poured silver and bronze coins into the basket. Last of all he took a single black purse from the box and added three gold coins to the silver and bronze. When he was finished there was more air than money in the unlaced wooden box.

The godspeaker Toolu nodded, and carried his laden basket back into the godhouse. Yagji closed the box's lid and relaced all the leather lacings, threading them with the charms and amulets. His fingers moved swiftly, surely. Hekar marveled at how he remembered every charm and amulet's proper position. Abajai stood quietly watching, a small smile curving his lips.

Just as Yagji finished, the godspeaker returned carrying a large scorpion carved from some shiny black stone banded with thin strips of bronze.

Yagji stood back. The godspeaker placed the carved scorpion on top of the leather-laced wooden box and closed his eyes. It seemed to Hekar that the whole world went silent.

"*Breathe, god,*" said the godspeaker Toolu, in a voice like distant thunder. "*Breathe, god. Breathe, god.*"

A thick black mist oozed from the carved stone scorpion and onto the charms laced over the wooden box, soaking into them and swiftly disappearing. The guard who was a table shuddered and groaned, but did not collapse. Blood dripped from his open mouth to splash on the ground beneath him.

"The god has breathed," said the godspeaker once the mist stopped oozing, and picked up the carved stone scorpion. "Merchandise has passed between us. Payment is given, payment is taken. Our business is done."

"Our business is done," said Abajai, as Yagji put the wooden box back into its pannier on the pack camel. "It has been a good Trading."

The godspeaker nodded. "Travel well, Trader Abajai. I will not ask where next you buy and sell, for this I know is Traders' business not fit for a village-bound man to know, even if he is the godspeaker."

Abajai's small smile grew wider. "Well do you know the ways of Trading, Toolu godspeaker."

"But be wary as you travel through Et-Jokriel," said the godspeaker, frowning. "The times are grown uneasy. Green fields turn brown and where water flowed freely, in places now it trickles. Where there was water now is dirt. The sky is blue, crops wither in the sun. Jokriel warlord dreams of grain within his empty barns. He sends his warriors over the borders to raid and fight his brother warlords. He is not the only warlord so afflicted. Hammers ring on anvils, Abajai. Bloodshed rides the wind."

Abajai bowed. "We will be wary. The god see you, Toolu godspeaker. The god see you in its eye."

They left the village, then, with the handful of new slaves chained to the tail of the snake and poked into walking by Obid's sharp spear. Once Todorok was behind them, Yagji turned to Abajai in fright.

"You heard him, Aba! Bloodshed rides the wind! How bad have things become since we began our caravan?"

"The god knows," said Abajai. "Hold your tongue, Yagji. We will talk of this beneath the stars, when only you and I are listening."

"Abajai—' said Hekat, wanting to know, but he pressed his hand on her shoulder, then dropped a loop of leather over her head. Dangling from it was a beautiful amulet, a carved snake's eye in deepest blue.

She snatched it up. "*Abajai!*"

"You must wear this always," Abajai told her. "While you wear it the god will see you in its eye."

Never in her life had she possessed her own amulet. "Yes, Abajai," she whispered, and pressed the snake-eye against her lips.

"Such extravagance!" Yagji scolded. "And after we were paid too little for the pish, and charged too much for

Todorok's slaves! With all your spare coin it would he better had you paid the godspeaker to give it a slave-braid, not—"

"No," said Abajai. "The god does not desire that."

Yagji made a gobbling sound. "And does the god desire us reduced to seven bronze coins and a single camel? Aieee, you try me, Aba, you try me sorely! I will bargain next time, you are growing soft in your old age . . ."

Buzz, buzz, buzz. Yagji had more words than the sky had stars, and none of them as pretty. Hekat didn't listen. Abajai had paid coin to give her an amulet, to keep her in the god's eye. She was precious. He cared for her. She cared for him, too. A new feeling, strange, unfurling shyly like a seed in dry dirt. He was the only breathing thing she had ever cared for. She was his, for ever and ever.

No matter what that Yagji said.

CHAPTER FOUR

That night, after dinner, Hekat curled up by the camp fire and listened, eyes closed, as Abajai and Yagji talked Trader business in soft urgent voices.

"It is unwise not to heed a godspeaker's warning," said Abajai. "From newsun we will travel straight through Et-Jokriel to Thakligar in Et-Mamiklia, and from there over the border into Et-Nogolor. Nogolor warlord's treaties with Et-Raklion will keep us safe. Until then we are prey for raiding warbands."

"That is true," Yagji sighed. "But surely we can do a *little* Trading along the way, Aba? Remember we were blessed by Nagarak himself. The god sees us in its eye."

Abajai hissed air between his teeth. "Being blessed does not make us untouchable. Demons can take us, and so can fighting warlords with no love for Et-Raklion."

Demons. Hekat clutched her snake-eye amulet. The village godspeaker shouted loud against demons. Demons sickened goats. They spoiled the snake-dance so the young men died fangstruck. They dried up the well-water, or made it bitter. Demons dressed in plague and pestilence. Women who spawned she-brats only were demon-ridden. They had opened their legs to a demon so their man's seed was poisoned. That was why such women were stoned. Only stoning could drive out a demon and afterwards sacrifice, because demons had power where the people did not love the god enough.

I love the god, she promised, as her snake-eye amulet bruised her fingers. *Do not let the demons prick me.*

"I know, I know we must travel swiftly," moaned Yagji, and tugged his godbraids. "But so much lost money, Aba!"

Abajai growled. "What is money to a dead man in the grass? We are no match for a warlord's raiding party."

"No, but perhaps we will not see one!"

"That is not a risk I am prepared to take," said Abajai, sounding grim. "You have eyes, Yagji, you see Et-Jokriel is turning brown. It is not alone, you saw how changed are Et-Bajadek and Et-Takona since last we caravanned through them. Those warlords will soon be at each other's throats, spilling blood."

"Each other's throats, Aba," Yagji wheedled. "Not ours. We are Traders, no part of their squabbles."

"When the bloodlust is on them they will not care!" Abajai's voice was cold and hard. "And we are from Et-Raklion. Raklion warlord's lands are still lush and green. That alone is cause for hate."

Yagji sighed again. "True."

"Et-Raklion is like a fat lamb cast before a pack of starving dogs. When the other warlords have stolen all they can from each other *there* is where they will turn their envious eyes. They might even think to defy the god and band together in a single attack. We must be home before that happens. You do not believe me?" Abajai added, as Yagji fidgeted. "Then I will read the godbones, and the god will tell you."

Through slitted eyes Hekat watched Abajai study his godbones. The scarlet scorpion in his cheek was restless as he rolled the painted pieces of snake-spine, read them, and rolled them some more. She had never seen godbones painted like that, blood red and venom green and blue like the sky at highsun. The man had godbones, small, chipped and bare of paint. He'd made them himself after a snake-dance and was never pleased with what they told him. The racing lizards he bet on always lost.

But neither was Abajai pleased with his fine godbones. His scarlet scorpion leapt and writhed. In the flickering firelight it looked like it was stinging Abajai. His forehead sweated, his breathing rasped.

"Well? Well? What do they say?" Yagji demanded.

"They say what I have said already," Abajai whispered harshly. "We must caravan hard to Et-Nogolor city, sell the merchandise there and seek the swiftest way home to Et-Raklion."

"Aieee!" said Yagji, pressing his palms to his plump cheeks. Then he flicked a sideways, hopeful glance. "Sell *all* the merchandise?"

Hekat stopped pretending to sleep, she threw herself to the edge of Abajai's blanket. "Abajai not sell Hekat!" Her teeth chattered with fear. "Hekat belong to Abajai!"

"There, Aba, you see what you've done?" said Yagji, outraged. "It's got attached! You made a pet of it and it's got attached!" He took her by the shoulders and shook her till her eyes rolled. "You be quiet! Shall I beat you? Shall I give you to the god? Be quiet with your howling, you wretched monkey!"

"Be still, Hekat," said Abajai. "You also, Yagji." The scorpion in his cheek was sleeping now, his fingers plucked up the godbones one by one and slipped them into their snakeskin pouch. When it was full he closed his eyes and pressed it to his lips.

Yagji released her. She sat on the cold ground and waited as Abajai gave thanks to the god for its teachings in the bones. She had no fear of a beating. Yagji told Abajai all the time he should beat her, and Abajai never listened. She knew he never would. Abajai would never hurt her.

"You belong to Abajai, Hekat," he said when he was finished, slipping the godbone pouch into his robe pocket. His face was grave, but his eyes were warm. "I will not sell you in Et-Nogolor city."

Silly pricky burning in her eyes. They traveled through a land of water but she wouldn't waste any of hers. "Hekat belong to Abajai," she whispered.

Muttering crossly, Yagji withdrew to his tent. Abajai ignored him, and raised a finger so she would pay close attention.

"Yes. She does. Now go to bed, Hekat. From tomorrow you will walk as well as ride my camel. You are stronger now, there is meat on your bones. You have shoes on your feet. Walking will be good for you."

She gifted him with her widest smile. "Yes, Abajai! Thank you, Abajai!"

Tucked beneath her blankets, she held her beautiful blue snake-eye and waited for sleep to claim her. She was not afraid of squabbling warlords, or of demons, or Yagji. Abajai was here, Abajai would protect her. Abajai, and the god.

It gave me to Abajai. It sees me in its eye. The god sees Hekat, it knows she is precious.

So the caravan continued, but she did not walk. She ran. She danced. She darted ahead, then back to Abajai, sometimes with flowers to give him, other times just a smile. She felt like a snake that had shed its skin, all scaled and wrinkled, tattered, torn. Hekat was the new snake, with cotton clothes and shoes on her feet and charms woven through her godbraided hair.

Yes. She was a beautiful snake.

Following many highsuns travel they left the lands of Jokriel warlord and entered the lands ruled by the warlord Mamiklia. There they were told of warbands on the prowl, of fighting fierce and bloody and not far away. They came across burning bodies and slaughtered horses twice. The stink made Yagji vomit. Once they were nearly caught in a warrior raid.

After that, Abajai and Yagji made their white camels jog as well as walk. The pack-camels jogged too, and the long chained snake-spine of slaves, with Obid and his fellow guards poking and hitting and scolding with vulture voices. Abajai wouldn't let Hekat run, he kept her on the camel with him. All the camel-jogging made Yagji sick, like the dead rotting horses had made him sick. He clutched his fat belly, moaning and spitting. Abajai wouldn't stop for him to get off and spew into the grass so he spewed up his insides over the side of his camel, or when they paused to water the slaves.

Hekat lost count of the highsuns that followed. One day blurred into the next, and the next. Even the countryside lost its charm. There were trees, she'd seen trees. There were flowers, she'd seen flowers. And villages, and crops, and orchards, and horses, and cattle, and wild hawks flying. The water flowing deep beneath the land of Mijak, Abajai said, rose to the surface where the god desired, in streams and rivers. Creatures called *fish* swam in them, good for eating, she had seen fish now. Once there was a small blue lake, there were things called *boats* on it, she could not get excited. Water was water, it had lost its power to amaze.

She was tired of traveling. She wanted to rest.

They crossed the border into Et-Nogolor, and four fingers after acknowledging the godpost met a band of hard-riding warriors, men and women wearing shells of hardened leather on their upper bodies. In the middle of their leather chests was a hunting bird picked out in stones of lowsun fire, and plaited into their charm-heavy godbraids waved long red feathers banded thickly with black. Leather thongs dangled round their necks, threaded with rattling, bouncing fingerbones. They were fierce men and women with cold eyes and cruel months. Their horses' eyes were angry. They carried arrows on their backs and a bow looped onto their saddles. Long curved blades belted at their waists flashed silver in the sunlight.

The warriors belonged to Nogolor warlord, Abajai said, and those curved blades were scimitars. A scimitar could cut a camel's head right off its neck. Never cross a man with a scimitar, said Abajai. Sell him a sharpstone instead.

Hekat stared as the warband drummed towards Et-Mamiklia on their dusty, sweat-streaked horses. They were beautiful, those warriors. As beautiful as she was, in their way.

"If all we see are Et-Nogolor's warriors we need not be afraid," Abajai told Yagji. "Or even the warriors of Raklion warlord. But if we see warriors of Bajadek, or Mamiklia, or one of the other warlords . . ."

Yagji whimpered and was sick again down the side of his unhappy camel.

On and on and on they caravanned, and slowly the road grew crowded with other travelers, ox-carts and slave-litters and plain men on horses. Farms and fenced cattle pastures stretched on either side of them. Eleven high-suns after crossing the border they reached Et-Nogolor city. It rose from the plain like a rock on green sand.

"So *big*," said Hekat to Abajai, astonished.

"Not as big as Et-Raklion city," said Yagji, and shifted on his camel. "Or as fine. Aba, I hope this means we are out of trouble. I hope we see no more galloping warriors.

Are you certain you read the godbones right? We will be safe in Et-Nogolor city?"

Hekat knew Abajai well, now. She knew he wanted to shout at Yagji or smackck him till his godbraids clattered their charms. But she knew Yagji, too. Shouting at the fat man only made him sulk and when he sulked his cooking was bad.

So did Abajai know Yagji. "I have told you ten times, Yagji, they say we are safe here."

Yagji fumbled in his pocket and pulled out a cloth. "The godbones will never speak to me," he fretted, dabbing sweat from his face. "I wish I had the ears to hear them. Aba, we should spend coin to make sacrifice in Et-Nogolor's godhouse. If the warlords squabble it is because demons prick them. We must make an offering against their wicked wiles."

Abajai said, "Sacrifice is a good idea, Yagji. Deaf to the godbones you may be, but never deaf to the god."

Yagji's miserable face brightened. He always smiled when Abajai told him good about himself. "Never."

So many others now traveled the road with them it was three fingers past highsun before they reached the tail-end of wagons and horses waiting to be allowed through the enormous city gates. Et-Nogolor rose up and up above their heads, ringed by a wooden wall, tall cut-down trees as wide as three Abajais, standing side by side by side, no space between. Each tree was carved and painted with the god's eye, with snakefangs and centipedes, with scorpions and the same bird face that shrieked on the leather shells of Et-Nogolor's warriors. Real skulls there were, too, glaring blind at the spreading plain. Horse. Goat. Bird. Man. Painted with god colors, dangled with amulets, jangled with charms. Godbells sang silver-tongued on the breeze.

With her head tilted back so her godbraids tickled the camel's shoulder, Hekat looked past the city's climbing buildings to the godhouse at its very top. The godhouse's godpost was so tall that even from so far below she could see its stinging scorpion, tail raised to strike the wicked sinner.

She felt her voice shrivel in her throat. This place . . . this *city* . . .

"You are right to be awed," said Abajai. He always knew what she was thinking. "Et-Nogolor is a mighty city. Only the city Et-Raklion is greater, because once it was Mijak's ruling city."

She looked at him over her shoulder. "Ruling city, Abajai?"

He nodded. "When Mijak was ruled by a single warlord, before the god decreed one must be seven. The city Et-Raklion was his home. It was not called Et-Raklion then, but still. It is the same."

Warlords. She had been thinking about them. "Abajai, what is a warlord?"

"A man of power," he said. "Appointed by the god to rule lands and villages and the people who live there."

She frowned. "No warlord rules Hekat's village, Abajai. Only godspeaker."

"The savage north is different. Long ago it had warlords to rule it. It was part of what is now Et-Jokriel and Et-Mamiklia. But the land is harsh there. With every season, grain by grain, the sands of The Anvil creep closer. Those long-ago warlords abandoned the north. Its villages are in the god's eye, Hekat. The god is their warlord."

"*Tcha*," said Yagji, pulling a face. "First geography, now history. To what end, Aba, there is no point."

Abajai patted her shoulder. "Yagji is right. The past does not matter, or the savage north. Rest your tongue, Hekat. We move again."

So they did, but slowly. She could see the city gates, they had long iron teeth to bite off the heads of the unwary, and tall men with bladed spears to guard them. Snakes and scorpions were carved in the wood, and the sign for godsmite. Any demon who tried to pass these gates would die.

At last they reached the Gatekeeper, a monstrous tall man like a tree made flesh. His body was clothed in red and black striped horsehide. On his head he wore a horse skull with horns, around his neck a scarlet scorpion. His belt was green snakeskin threaded with snake-skulls, each winking eye a crimson gem. He wore no godbraids, his head was bald. His skin was hidden beneath writhing tattoos. Hekat was pleased to see not one was as fine as Abajai's scarlet scorpion.

"Business!" the Gatekeper barked, like a dog. He had so many protections set in his teeth his lips wouldn't close properly over them.

Abajai put his hand in his pocket, then held out a piece of carved green stone, round like a thin branch and as long as his palm was wide. "Trader business, Gatekeeper. Abajai and Yagji of Et-Raklion, brother city of Et-Nogolor. There you have our seal stamped by Raklion warlord himself." His hand dipped again into his pocket, to pull out another stone cylinder. This one was blue.

"And here is proof of road-rights fully paid. We come to trade our merchandise and give the god sacred blood in the godhouse."

The Gatekeeper examined both carved stones, then nodded to one of the tall city guards. The guard walked with his bladed spear all the way to the end of the merchandise and back again. When he returned he nodded to the Gatekeeper and took his place at the gate.

"And what is this?" said the Gatekeeper, jerking his chin.

Hekat shrank from the Gatekeeper's gaze. His eyes were hot, they had no whites, they glowed yellow in the shade beneath the dagger-tooth gates. Abajai's finger touched the small of her back. "A bauble," he said, his voice soft and calm.

She didn't know what a bauble was but she sensed he was trying to make the hot-eyed Gatekeeper cool. That was good, she wanted him cool. Something about him reminded her of the man, he hated she-brats, she could tell. His hot eyes frightened her. She hated being frightened, it made her angry. She stared at the white camel's neck so he wouldn't see her anger.

The Gatekeeper growled in his throat. He sounded like a dog again. "For sale?"

"Alas, this one is sold already," said Yagji, and his voice was pouty. "To a very special client. We would not dare to sell it twice, Gatekeeper Et-Nogolor. Not and keep our name as honest Traders."

Hekat held her breath and risked a look through her lowered lashes.

The Gatekeeper grunted. His hot yellow eyes were

disappointed. He handed back the two carved stones and jerked his thumb. "Pass."

"*Thank* you, Gatekeeper," said Yagji. "The god sees you in its eye."

"Well done, Yagji," Abajai murmured as they entered Et-Nogolor. "Your tongue is as persuasive as ever."

"And my brain is upside down," said Yagji, sour as goat-milk. "What a chance to get rid of the brat, Aba. Aieee, the god see me in its eye. The foolish things I do for you . . ."

Hekat said nothing, just pressed her blue snake-eye against her lips and breathed a sigh of happiness.

Et-Nogolor city's godpost stood just inside the open gates, grim and glorious as the god itself. Not wood, but solid shiny black stone. All its carved scorpions were purple and crimson. Abajai gave its huge godbowl more than gold, he gave it amulets and godbells and tiny snake-skulls bound with charms. Yagji gave it a fistful of gem-stones, and they both bowed their heads to the ground before it.

The god appeased, Abajai and Yagji climbed back on their camels and led the slave-train along a crowded narrow street lined with buildings made of stone and brick and wood. Hekat stared at the buildings and the men and the women and the brats and the skinny dogs running free around their feet. The hot air of Et-Nogolor city was thick with man stink, animal stink, smoke fires and cooking meat. No trees. No grass. The street was stony, lots and lots of little stones jammed and crammed together, black and grey and white and red. The camels groaned as they walked and their ears flicked crossly. The buildings unwinding above them to the sky shut out the light, it was as dim as lowsun at the bottom of Et-Nogolor.

Hekat didn't like it.

The narrow street curved around the base of the city. At last they reached an open place divided into pens. Most of them were full of goats and sheep and cattle, the air was ripe with pish and dung. There were huge black dogs chained at the front of each pen, as mean as the man had ever owned. But these dogs didn't bark, they just climbed growling to their feet, the hair on their massive backs standing stiff like the spiny collar of the deadly striped lizards that sometimes crawled in from The Anvil.

A man sat on a stool nearby. He stood as they approached and shouted at the growling dogs. The dogs dropped to their haunches but didn't hide their teeth and their shiny white eyes stayed open.

Abajai made his camel kneel five paces before the man and got down. Behind him the slave-train stopped too, in a clanking of chains and a grumbling of pack-camels.

"Penkeeper," Abajai said, his purse in his hand. "I am Trader Abajai. How much to pen these slaves and the camels?"

The penkeeper was old and bent over. One arm stuck out from his body strangely, as though the bone had broken and never knew its right place after. He wore amulets in his saggy ears and on a thong around his scrawny neck. His grubby clothes were brown and white goathide, rubbed bare and shiny in big patches. Around his sunken middle was strapped a leather purse, its laces strung with charms. Staring up into Abajai's face he hawked, and spat.

"Two silver coins till this time next highsun."

The look on Yagji's face said that was a lot of money. Hekat thought it sounded a lot. But Abajai nodded undismayed and counted silver into the penkeeper's hand. As the penkeeper put the money away, Abajai turned.

"Obid!"

Obid came, dirty and tired. "Put the merchandise in the large pen there," said Abajai. "Take off its chains, give it feed and water. Camels in the other pen." He pointed. "There is Hekat on my camel, you see her now. She goes in the pen, she does not leave it."

Obid looked at her. His eyes still writhed with maggot questions but the rest of his face was quiet. "Yes, master."

As Obid withdrew to do his master's bidding, Abajai crooked a finger. "Hekat."

She slid off the camel and joined him. "Yes, Abajai?"

"Yagji and I go to do Trader business. You will stay here. You will attend Obid. That is my nod."

She didn't want to wait in a pen, or be told what to do by a dirty slave. She wanted to see this city Et-Nogolor, and a godhouse so big its godpost could be spied from a distance in the road. But Abajai's word was his word. Like dirty Obid, she must obey.

"Yes. Abajai."

With pricky eyes she watched him and Yagji walk away. When they were gone from sight she turned. The penkeeper was watching her, she could feel his hungry gaze.

"You not stare at Hekat," she said, making her voice hiss like a snake. "Hekat belong to Abajai."

The penkeeper's wrinkled face went still, and his eyes rolled like a goat's when the knife approaches. He shook his fist at her, then went to help Obid and the guards prod the merchandise into a large empty pen.

Hekat smiled, and folded her arms.

The pen's black guard dog stood quietly, its white eyes watching, but did nothing to stop them. When all the slaves had shuffled in, and the guards had taken off their chains and dropped them outside the pen with a clanking thud, Obid crooked his finger at her.

"I see you now," he said. "I see you in this pen."

Scuffing her shoes on the tiny colored stones she walked past the staring dog and the penkeeper and Obid to join the naked slaves. They stared at her in wondering silence, standing as though they still wore chains. Obid pulled the pen's gate shut and the penkeeper fastened its lock. She heard the penkeeper say to Obid, "Your master's a mad one, keeping that. Don't you see its evil eye?"

"I do not speak of my master," said Obid. He sounded sullen. Hekat thought he wanted to agree with the penkeeper but did not dare.

"My eye not evil," she said, loud enough for them to hear her. "My eye beautiful. Hekat beautiful. So the mirror say, and the woman Bisla, and Abajai when he look at me."

The black dog with white eyes growled, and Obid said, "I see you no talking. I say the word. Abajai's nod."

If she made trouble he'd tell Abajai, and Abajai would be angry. So, no making trouble. She pulled a face at Obid because that was not talking. Obid slitted his eyes at her, then went with the other guards to unpack supplies from the pack-camels so she and the merchandise could eat and drink. The penkeeper returned to his stool and made sure he didn't look anywhere near her.

The floor of the pen was dirt, not colored stones like the road. She'd had too many highsuns of sitting on the camel, her legs itched to run. But the pen was crowded, no room for running, instead she walked around its inside edge and smiled to see Abajai's slaves cringe as though they were goats and she a prowling sandcat. Like a sandcat she bared her teeth, laughing aloud as they remembered their chains were gone and fought each other to get away.

It was a good feeling, to see them fall over in their fear.

Obid and the guards fed and watered themselves first. After that they watered the camels, then they carried bowls and cups, bags of food and jars of water into the pen with the merchandise. "Sir!" said Obid, and all the slaves bumped their skinny haunches to the ground and held out their hands for a bowl and a cup. The bowls were filled with bread, cheese and cold roasted corn. Each cup received a ladle's worth of water. The slaves' eyes were greedy, their tongues licked their lips, but they could not eat or drink until Obid gave his nod.

Hekat did not sit. She could see Obid wanted to make her but did not dare. He knew if he could make trouble for her she could make it for him, too. He shoved a bowl and cup at her, his face angry.

"Eat," he said, and the merchandise obeyed him.

She stared at the bowl, letting her face show her distaste. She had not eaten slave food once since Abajai saved her from the man. She did not want to eat it now, it reminded her of that life she no longer lived, the nameless she-brat she'd left behind in that village. But her belly was empty and her mouth was parched.

She drank the water, then put dry bread in her mouth

and chewed, and chewed, and swallowed. Outside the pen the penkeeper told Obid and the other guards to help him clean up pish and dung. Obid's eyes showed he did not want to, but he could not say no. He was a slave, the penkeeper was free.

Hekat smiled, and ate her food.

On the other side of the pen she heard a scuffle. Grunting. Still chewing, she went to see. One of the slaves had dropped its bowl. Its bread and cheese and corn were in the dirt. Other slaves were stealing them. They would never dare to steal from a bowl, Obid beat slaves who sinned like that. But food in the dirt belonged to whoever picked it up fastest.

The slave who'd lost its food was on its hands and knees, it was trying to cover its bits of bread and cheese so the other slaves' sneaking fingers couldn't snatch them. Its face was wet, it was wasting water.

"No! Mine! You've eaten your food, this is mine!"

She leaned against the pen's railings and watched. The slaves were so busy growling and snatching and pinching they didn't care or try to run away.

Very soon there was no bread or cheese or corn kernels left to steal. The hungry slave sat in the dirt with its empty bowl, its face muddy because its eye-water had mixed with the pen's dust.

Surprised, she realized she knew this one. This one was the fat boy from the lizard-roofed village Todorok where the woman Bisla had called her beautiful. But it wasn't fat anymore. It had used up its fat running on the road behind Abajai and Yagji's white camels.

Beneath the fat, this slave was beautiful.

He said, "You could have helped me."

She chose a piece of sticky white cheese and pushed it between her teeth. "Why?"

The slave was maybe five seasons older than she was. He looked at her, his beautiful eyes dull with hunger and hurt, then dragged his fingers through the dust, searching for any corn kernels the others had missed.

"Slaves should help each other."

She spat out cheese-rind. "*Tcha*! Slave? Hekat is not slave. I have name. I wear clothes. I ride with Abajai."

"I have a name too," the slave said. His voice was low, and unhappy. "My name is Vortka."

She nodded at the chafed places on his wrists and ankles. "You wear chains, not clothes. You run on the road behind the white camels. Your name far behind you."

The slave's scabby fist struck his chest. "Not in here! In here I am Vortka. I was sold because my father died and the god gave my mother to another man. He had his own sons. He did not want my mother's son. He wanted gold. He got gold and I got chains. Why do you have clothes? Why do you ride with Abajai?"

She shrugged. "I am beautiful."

"You are not so beautiful," the slave muttered.

"The god not see you!" she said, scorched with rage. "The god not see you, stupid slave!"

"The god already not see me," he said, sounding sad again. "The god not see me when it blew out my father's godspark." He squeezed water from his eyes with a dirty finger, then smiled at her. "I lied. You are beautiful. What are you called?"

There was one piece of bread in the bottom of her bowl, and one piece of cheese. All the corn was eaten. She picked out the bread and threw it at the slave's feet.

"I am called Hekat."

The slave Vortka snatched up the bread and crammed it into his mouth. "The god see you, Hekat," he said, his lips smeared with dirt.

She turned her back and walked away. She did not know why her fingers had picked out the bread and thrown it at that slave. Give her food to a slave? *Talk* to a slave? Had a scorpion stung her, to do such a thing?

She swallowed the last lump of cheese, threw her empty bowl to the ground, then sat down, far from the merchandise, to wait for Abajai's return.

CHAPTER FIVE

He came at last, with Yagji and a godspeaker and two other men. Behind them panted a young male slave harnessed to an empty cart. The slave unstrapped itself from the cart's leather traces, then went away.

The men with Abajai wore plain dark robes and Trader charms around their necks. They were maybe a little younger than Abajai, their eyes were sharp. They didn't seem like men who were easily fooled, or foolish.

The godspeaker was young and her robe was the finest Hekat had ever seen, sewn all over with gold amulets and bronze charms and singing silver godbells. Stitched into the robe's hem were lumps of the blue stone her snake-eye amulet was carved from, that Abajai had told her was lapis lazuli. The scorpion-shell bound to the godspeaker's forehead was white. Its claws were painted crimson, its sting banded purple and gold. She had never seen a scorpion-shell so fine.

Around her neck the godspeaker wore a chunk of green crystal, large as a fist and threaded onto a leather thong. She pulled it over her head and held it in her hands. When the crystal touched her flesh it flared into life. Abajai's slaves cried out then, pressing against each other and the pen's railings. Yagji and the two Traders snatched at their amulets and closed their eyes, trembling. Abajai stood quietly, his gaze calm upon the godspeaker.

The godspeaker said, "The godstone sees the hearts of those known to the god."

Abajai bowed his head. "What slaves the god sees I gladly gift to its godspeaker and the godhouse of Et-Nogolor. Come into the pen with me, that the godstone might seek for hearts known to the god."

The godspeaker nodded, then released the crystal to dangle from its leather thong on the end of her finger. There it swung gently, all its blaze dead like a cold fire. Abajai opened the pen's gate. The black dog cowered as the godspeaker passed by, it did not growl or bite.

"Hekat," Abajai said, not looking at her. "Leave this pen and stand with Yagji."

The godspeaker said, "The god looks at all offerings, Trader Abajai."

"Forgive me, godspeaker," said Abajai. "This one is not mine to offer."

The godspeaker nodded, and Hekat went to Yagji. For once he touched her, his fingers taking hold of her shoulder. He felt frightened.

Abajai clapped his hands. "Obid!"

Obid came and poked the slaves with his spear until they stood in a line around the pen's edge. The godspeaker walked to the nearest one and held up the leather thong so the crystal was in easy reach.

"The god sees you," she said. "Take the crystal."

Panting with fear, the boy clutched the crystal but nothing happened.

"The god sees you," said the godspeaker. "But not your heart."

She took back the crystal and gave it to the next slave. "The god sees you," she said. "Take the crystal."

Whimpering, the woman took it. For the second time, the crystal did not wake.

"The god sees you, but not your heart," said the godspeaker, and moved to the next slave.

Hekat had counted, there were thirty-seven slaves in Abajai's caravan. One by one the godspeaker gave them the crystal and said her words and waited. One by one, the god did not see any hearts. If the godspeaker was angry or disappointed her face did not show it.

She gave the crystal to the slave calling himself Vortka. When that slave's fingers closed around the rock it came alive in a blaze of light. The slave Vortka gasped, and stared without words at the godspeaker.

"The god sees you," said the godspeaker. "The god sees your heart." She took back the crystal. "Stand apart from the unseen. You belong to the god until it strikes you dead in its eye."

Dazed, the slave Vortka stumbled away from the others. Hekat looked at Abajai, to see how he felt about the god taking one of his slaves. She couldn't tell. His face was quiet, and so was the scarlet scorpion in his cheek.

Yagji's face she could tell like the open sky. He was pleased to please the god, he was sorry to lose more coin.

The godstone saw no other slave's heart after Vortka's. The godspeaker put the leather thong with its threaded green crystal around her neck and clicked fingers at the chosen slave Vortka. He followed her out of the pen and waited, looking only at the ground.

"The god sees your gift, Trader Abajai," said the godspeaker. "The god is pleased. Ask one thing of the god and that one thing shall be granted."

As Yagji gasped, Abajai bowed to the godspeaker. "The god is good. The one thing I ask, for myself, my fellow Trader and our possessions, is passage from Et-Nogolor to Et-Raklion in a godspeaker caravan."

The godspeaker nodded. "Granted. Go to the godgate wayhouse when you are ready to travel. You must wait there until the next godspeaker caravan departs."

Abajai bowed again. "The god see you in its eye, godspeaker."

"The god see you also, Trader Abajai," the godspeaker replied. She walked away then, with the slave Vortka a pace behind her.

"Obid," said Abajai. "Fetch your fellow guards and the camel-boy."

As Obid did as he was told, Abajai turned to the two Traders waiting silently for the god's business to be done. "Trader Ederog, Yagji will show you our camels." Yagji and Trader Ederog went to haggle over the beasts, and Obid returned with the other guards and the camel-boy. Abajai nodded to him and one other, almost as tall and strong as Obid. "Stand away," he said. "You remain in my possession. You others stand with the merchandise."

Watching the guards Abajai no longer wanted, Hekat saw their eyes go wet with fear and sorrow. But they said nothing to Abajai, they obeyed his nod. They were slaves.

"Trader Rogiv?" said Abajai. "Here is our merchandise. Inspect it. I invite you."

Trader Rogiv looked at the waiting slaves, then turned and pointed. "Trader Abajai, what about that one?"

Hekat held her breath, she stared at Abajai. Trader Rogiv's pointing finger was a stab in the heart.

"That one belongs to me," said Abajai. "She is not for sale." His deep dark voice was cool, and strong. In his face a warning not to argue.

Hekat felt herself melt inside. *I will not sell you in Et-Nogolor.* So he had told her, and so it was proved. He was Abajai, his word was his word.

Then it was Trader haggling, as the camels and the slaves were sold. When it was over and the Et-Nogolor Traders had departed to fetch for Abajai the promised coin, Obid and the other slave began unloading the camels and packing all their goods into the empty cart. Yagji supervised them for a small time, then returned to Abajai.

"Aieee, Aba," he said, pouting with displeasure. "Must we travel with a godspeaker caravan? There are so *many* of them in a caravan. You know what it will be like. They live and breathe and sweat out the god. To be close like that, it makes me frightened! I lose my appetite, I cannot eat. Would you have me skin and bone by the time we reach Et-Raklion?"

"Better skin and bone in Et-Raklion than dead on the road between here and there with all your plumpness bleeding," said Abajai. "The god saw us, Yagji, when it sent us that chosen slave. No other price would buy us the protection of a godspeaker caravan. If the other warlords should send warriors against Et-Nogolor only godspeakers will be safe on the road to Et-Raklion. You know it, we have seen trouble like this before."

"And had hoped to never see it again!" cried Yagji. "Warlords fighting are bad for business!"

"Yes," said Abajai, and patted his shoulder. "But do not dwell on that. We have good profit from this caravan, and business at home that must be tended, remember. We have been many godmoons on the road."

Yagji sighed. "Yes. I know. Our villa is likely a tumbled ruin, that Retoth cannot care for it properly without my strict supervision."

"You know he can," said Abajai, laughing. "He always does. But we will both be relieved to see it again."

The Et-Nogolor Traders returned with their payment. When the sale was completed and the money safely added to the coin box, Abajai nodded to Obid and the other slave. They harnessed themselves to the heavy cart, and followed Abajai and Yagji away from the slave pens.

Walking between the Traders, Hekat looked up. "Abajai, why did the god see that slave?"

"So it might serve in the godhouse."

She frowned. "Serve how?"

"That is not our business."

"That slave," she said, after a moment. "He had a name. He told me."

Abajai tugged her godbraids. "Slaves have no names, Hekat. Not until a master gives one, with the giving of the scarlet slave-braid."

She smiled inside. She had given herself a name, and she wore no scarlet slave-braid. She was as special as the slave

Vortka, gone to serve the god. "If I held the godstone, Abajai. Would it see me? See my heart? Tell the god?"

Yagji snorted. "Your heart, monkey? My Hooli's heart will be seen by the god before yours."

"The god sees all hearts," said Abajai. "Godstones are for godspeakers, who are less than the god. Now be silent, Hekat. It is a long walk to Et-Nogolor's godgate."

She was silent because he had said she must be silent, but she still didn't understand. She wanted to know how the godstone knew to burn, or stay dead. To know what would happen to that special slave Vortka who had gone to serve in Et-Nogolor's godhouse. How he would serve, and what the god wanted from him.

That slave Vortka had called her Hekat. He had called her beautiful. She had given him bread.

Surprised, she realized she felt sorry, that she would not see him again.

They made their slow way along the crowded streets towards the godgate, which Abajai said was on the far-distant other side of Et-Nogolor city. Hekat walked close beside him, she had never seen so many people in one place before, the noise of them battered her ears, their stink clogged her nose.

They walked and they walked, and came across an open place where there were tall red wooden godposts set into the cobbled ground. A skinny slave was nailed alive to one of them with his belly cut open and all his gizzards spilling free. His ankles were broken, his eyes were put out. He wore no clothes, just a blanket of flies. Hekat knew he lived only because of his horrible moaning, his begging for the god to let him die.

She felt her belly clutch tight, she tasted muck in her mouth. This was worse than the boy who put his body in the village well. This was the worst thing she had ever seen.

"He tried to run away," said Abajai. "The god abhors wicked runaway slaves. This is their fate, Hekat. The godspeakers smite them for the god."

She nodded, she had no words for the dying slave in his tunic of flies. They kept on walking.

Et-Nogolor's godgate was an anthill place, with wagons and carts and oxen and slaves and godspeakers coming and going without cease, and pens for many complaining animals. The air was heavy with smells and smoke and sounds. The gates themselves stayed shut, huge black scorpions towering over the tallest man. They looked like they could sting. They would not open until the caravan was ready to leave for Et-Raklion.

The wayhouse for travelers intending to journey with the godspeaker caravan was small and spare, with no-one wanting to travel except Abajai, Yagji and Hekat. There was nothing to do there but eat, and sleep, and wait. Each day at highsun they stood by its godpost to watch a god-speaker ask the god if the time had come for the caravan to leave Et-Nogolor. The question was asked by sacrific-ing a golden cockerel, burning its entrails in a scorpion bowl and breathing deep of the sacred smoke. If the god's answer was no, the godspeaker fell to the ground twitch-ing and foaming and drumming bare heels on the ground.

Three times now they had witnessed the asking. Three times the god had answered no.

The godspeaker who came to make sacrifice on the

fourth highsun was naked except for a loincloth and the scorpion-shell bound to his brow. His scorpion sting marks were all on show, angry red welts covering the dark skin of his belly and back. Many of them looked fresh. Hekat remembered the village godspeaker with only five, so old they'd turned dull and muddy. The village godspeaker was nothing, a dried-up husk, compared to the godspeakers of Et-Nogolor. She was angry to think such a shrunken, unbitten old man had frightened her so much . . . and surprised the god would accept him as its speaker.

Although, to be fair, the god had not had many men to choose from in the village.

The Et-Nogolor godspeaker sprinkled his circle of sacred sand. It was crimson, the color of golden cockerel blood, and it sparkled strangely on the stony ground in front of the wayhouse. At the circle's completion the sand burst into life, leaping black tongues of night-cold flame. Though he'd seen the god wake over and over, Yagji swallowed a little shriek and kissed his snake-fang amulet.

The godspeaker picked up the golden cockerel and his sacrifice knife. Like the others before it the beautiful bird died soundless, slit from crop to tail in a single blow. Its entrails slipped into the waiting scorpion bowl and became hot fire. As the sacred circle's black flames danced around him the godspeaker fell to his knees and plunged his face into the offering's greasy blue smoke, breathing deeply, his eyes rolled back in his head.

He did not fall twitching and foaming to the ground.

"Aieee!" squealed Yagji. "The god has answered!"

"The god always answers," Abajai scolded. But he was smiling.

"I know, I know," said Yagji, impatient. "But this time it has answered *yes*!"

The godspeaker breathed in the last of the sacrifice smoke, breathed it out, and stood. From his left hand dangled the gutted golden cockerel, from his right the bloodied knife.

"The god speaks!" he cried to the distant sky. The whites of his eyes had turned a greasy blue and the scorpion bites on his body glowed like living coals. "The caravan to Et-Raklion departs at newsun!"

He threw the sacrifice into the air. As the golden cockerel's feathers caught fire, burning it into nothingness, the sacred circle's black flames roared higher than the godspeaker's head, then vanished, the last of the sacred sand consumed.

"And a good thing too," said Yagji, watching the almost naked godspeaker walk away carrying his knife and his scorpion bowl. "If I pray hard I might survive one more night in that dreadful wayhouse. But only one. And only if the god is good!"

Hekat hid her face so Yagji wouldn't see her disgust. She had a bed in the wayhouse too. It was the most wonderful thing she'd ever slept on, with softness beneath her and too many blankets. She'd never dreamed there could be too many blankets. Let Yagji sleep on a baked earth floor under a table, or chained to a wall where dogs could sniff him, dogs that longed to devour his bones, and a man to beat him if he was so cold and stiff on waking he could hardly walk. Let Yagji sleep like that and then complain of blankets and a bed.

He was a stupid, stupid man.

Abajai patted him on the shoulder. "Hush yourself, Yagji. It is known the god is always good."

As the god desired, the godspeaker caravan left Et-Nogolor next newsun. Hekat rode with Abajai and Yagji at the rear, in an open wagon pulled by a team of stolid oxen. Behind them, Obid and his fellow slave hauled the cart carrying Abajai and Yagji's possessions and wealth. She watched Obid sweat and strain and smiled so he could see it. No more jabby spear, Obid. No more eyes full of maggot questions. He was just a slave now, while she was still precious and beautiful.

There were ten Et-Nogolor godspeakers in the carvan. Six drove covered carts laden with mysterious godspeaker goods, one drove an open cart full of caged birds for each newsun sacrifice. The other three walked. The sun climbed higher, the caravan passed the high-walled barracks where Abajai said Nogolor warlord's warriors lived, it passed farms, and orchards, and pastures full of grazing cows. Hekat thought the land looked fat but Abajai and Yagji frowned at each other and called it sad.

Two fingers past highsun they came upon a band of warriors riding towards Et-Nogolor city. Some wore red-and-black feathers in their hair and hunting birds on their leather chests, but others covered their godbraids with caps of spotted grey catskin, long tails bouncing down their straight backs, and on their leather chests brilliant green stones picked out a snarling cat face.

Hekat shifted on her wagon seat to watch the straight-backed warriors ride by. They did not yield the road to the godspeakers like the other few travelers they had encountered, but they did drop into single file and slow from a canter to a trot. So fierce, so proud, she thought they were beautiful.

Yagji leaned close. "Aba, Aba, what can this mean? The falcon and the woodcat riding together? Et-Nogolor and Et-Bajadek are not friends!"

"Shhh," hissed Abajai, glaring. "Wait until we are alone!"

Hekat counted sixty riders, half were birds and half were cats. When the last warrior had trotted sedately past them and they were once more cantering towards distant Et-Nogolor city, Abajai let out a sigh.

"Here is a tangle, Yagji."

"A *tangle*?" said Yagji, and clutched his green snake amulet. "Aba, it's *disaster*. Why do warriors of Bajadek and Nogolor warlords ride together? Bajadek warlord is a sworn enemy to Et-Raklion, and Raklion warlord is to mate with Et-Nogolor's Daughter! Nogolor warlord must not smile at Bajadek warlord, their warriors must not ride shoulder to fist along the road!"

Pinch-faced, Abajai toyed with a beaded godbraid. "Bajadek warlord has two sons and bears no love for either," he said slowly, as though thinking aloud. "He is a lusty man, he could yet sire a third son worth loving, but—"

"The god took his wife and besides, she was old," said Yagji. "*Aba!*" His voice was a shocked whisper. "*No!* Surely not!"

The scorpion in Abajai's cheek rippled. "I think so."

"But *Aba*—"

Abajai smoothed his robe. "If Raklion warlord dies sonless, Bajadek warlord can make a claim on his lands. I suspect he does not trust that a son sired by Raklion

upon Et-Nogolor's Daughter will die, like all his other
sons have died. I suspect Bajadek warlord reasons it is
better that Raklion does not mate with the Daughter at all.
Better that *he* have her, kill Raklion when the Daughter's
theft leads to war, claim Et-Raklion lands as his own and
afterwards sire a son worth loving." He nodded. "It is a
sound strategy."

"But Aba, Et-Nogolor's Daughter is *godpromised* to
Raklion. Nogolor warlord *cannot* give her to Bajadek."

"No?" said Abajai, and tugged his godbraids. "I wonder, Yagji. Truly, I wonder."

Confused, Hekat slid along the wagon seat towards
him and touched his sleeve. "Abajai? What is godpromised?"

"Promised in the presence of the god," Yagji snapped.
"In the godhouse of Et-Raklion. Et-Nogolor's high godspeaker himself sealed the oath with sacrifice before the
warlords and Et-Raklion's high godspeaker Nagarak and
selected witnesses." He preened a little. "Aba and I repre-
sented the Traders."

She was not interested in Yagji's silly boastings.
"What is *high* godspeaker?"

Yagji rolled his eyes. "Stupid monkey. *Abajai* . . ."

Abajai lifted his hand, frowning. Yagji fell silent, his
feelings hurt. Hekat said nothing but inside she smiled.
Yagji had lost, and she had won. She always won. She
was precious and beautiful.

Abajai said, "A high godspeaker rules all the godspeakers of a warlord's lands."

"Who rules high godspeaker?"

Yagji tittered. "The god, of course, you silly brat."

She ignored Yagji. "Like caravan, Abajai? Obid rule slaves, Abajai rule Obid?"

Abajai smiled. "Clever Hekat. Exactly like that."

Pleased with his praise she smiled back and thought, *So this is the world. Slaves, and rulers. Anyone not a ruler is a slave. I will remember that.* She said, "Abajai. Godpromised means the god wants Et-Nogolor she-brat for Raklion warlord?"

He pursed his lips. "That is one way of putting it."

"Then how can Nogolor warlord give she-brat to Bajadek warlord? The god cannot want Et-Nogolor she-brat for Raklion *and* Bajadek. Which warlord the god want for Et-Nogolor she-brat?"

"That depends on which warlord's high godspeaker you ask," said Yagji, under his breath.

Abajai gave Yagji a dark look, then shook his head at her. "Hush, Hekat. It is the god's business. Do not question its workings in the world, that way lies madness."

Yes. Madness. If high godspeakers spoke the god's want, then how could they speak different words? Was the *god* mad, not knowing which want it truly wanted?

Petrified, not breathing, she waited for the god to strike her dead for asking such a question. The god did not, so she asked another question, inside her head where only it could hear her.

If the god did know its want, then did Et-Nogolor high godspeaker *lie* when he said the she-brat should go to Raklion warlord? Or was the lie it should go to Bajadek?

Why would the god let a godspeaker lie?

She did not know, the god did not answer. Abajai would know but she didn't dare ask him. She would wait, and in time perhaps the god would tell her. When it wanted to. If it knew.

Yagji chewed his lip, glancing ahead at the walking godspeakers. "I wonder if Raklion warlord knows Bajadek's warriors ride freely in the lands of Et-Nogolor?" he asked, softly so they might not hear him. "I wonder—"

Abajai kicked him. "You wonder too much, Yagji! Hold your prattling tongue!"

Chastened to silence Yagji stared and stared, his eyes slowly filling with water. "I am sorry, Aba," he whispered at last. "I am weary, I am homesick. I long for our villa in dear Et-Raklion."

With a deep sigh, Abajai patted his cheek. "I know, Yagji. I am homesick too. I will be well pleased when this caravan is over. Do not weep, friend. We will be home soon."

It took the godspeaker caravan thirty-seven highsuns to reach the lands of Raklion warlord. In that time they saw warriors of Et-Bajadek five more times. Abajai and Yagji said nothing about them, they closed their eyes and pretended not to see.

Hekat knew better than to speak on that.

When at last she saw Et-Raklion she knew then what a fat land truly looked like. So much water! Streams and lakes and rivers and bubbling springs, so much green grass, countless fruit-laden branches and fields of grain, fat grazing cattle and sheep, singing birds and well-fed wildlife. She understood that Abajai and Yagji were right, the rest of Mijak was turning brown.

She did not want to think what might happen when all the green was gone from the other warlords' lands.

As they slowly journeyed, caged in their uncomfortable wagon, Abajai continued to teach her. He gave her all the words in his possession, so many words she thought they must fall from her mouth every time she opened it or blow out through her nose whenever she sneezed. He bade her use them to talk of her life in the savage north, the caravan they traveled with, each newsun sacrifice, the road, the sky, the clouds, the trees, the flowers, the fruit, the crops and the herds of beasts in their open pastures. The villages they passed by and the harmless travelers they encountered. Everything she could see and remember she could talk about, said Abajai, so she did, because that was his want.

It was her want too, she would be more than a village goat bleating and shitting and waiting for the knife.

Twenty-three highsuns after crossing the border into Et-Raklion she was asleep on the wagon's hard jolting floor and dreaming again of the man's bone-crunching dogs when Yagji's finger poked her ribs and his voice said, crossly, "Lazy monkey! Open your eyes and look upon perfection! We have reached Et-Raklion city!"

The dogs' slavering growls fading, she opened her eyes. The sky was dimming, only a finger remained till lowsun. She sat up, ignoring the creaks and moans in her muscles. Abajai walked beside the wagon, he never tired. Even though his face was quiet it seemed to her that it was shouting. His strong dark face and its scarlet scorpion, shouting with happiness to see the city.

She looked ahead, where he was looking. Where Yagji was looking, stupid wasted water rolling down his fat cheeks.

"Oh," she said, and felt a silly pricky burning in her

own eyes. Her heart heaved and twisted and split wide open, all the blood in her turning red hot.

Raklion warlord's city was beautiful.

Unlike Et-Nogolor, squatting like half a melon on a plate and skulking in man-made shadows, the city Et-Raklion spread around the base of a towering hill, which rose resplendent from the green and growing plain as though the god's own fist had punched upwards from beneath the earth's skin. The road they traveled led straight to the city gatehouse, then into the city itself. Bright lamps and torches burned in myriad dwellings, their warm flames lighting pale cream rock, and blood-red rock, and rock as green as the fields of growing wheat. So many roofs in the city Et-Raklion, Hekat could not count them all. Trees, too, heavy-laden with blossoms. On the perfumed breeze a trilling of songbirds, and silver godbells calling down the night.

Seeing Et-Raklion city once, Hekat knew this wondrous place owned her. And she was content to be its possession, until the god closed her eyes and gave her bones to the hungry dark.

"Ah, Et-Raklion," sighed Yagji, his voice quivering. "The god is good, that I see you again."

Abajai's stern face was gentle with smiling. "See Raklion's Pinnacle, Hekat, gift of the god. There is the godhouse on its peak, and its godpost reaching for the world's ceiling, its godmoon and its stars. It is the greatest godhouse in all of Mijak." He pointed. "There below it, the warlord's palace. And below the palace at the Pinnacle's base, within strong walls, the barracks where his warriors live, guarding the warlord. Keeping everyone safe."

She looked where he pointed, and marveled how the

palace grew out of the hillside. Felt awe at the height and spread of the godhouse. Et-Raklion's godhouse made the godhouse Et-Nogolor look small. Look *nothing*.

Truly the god loved the lands of Et-Raklion.

"The god, the warlord, his mighty warriors, like eagles they keep watch over the city." Abajai crooked a finger. "Take off your sandals and walk with me, Hekat. Feel the rich cool soil of Et-Raklion beneath your feet."

Willingly she walked with him, and so did Yagji, still sniveling. They walked right up to the gates of Et-Raklion, and as they walked Hekat felt herself smile.

Home, home, her heart sang softly. *Here I am, god. I am home.*

CHAPTER SIX

The caravan's senior godspeaker joined them at the gates to Et-Raklion. Hekat felt her skin crawl but she did not give him ground. Showing fear was foolish.

The city Gatekeeper was a tall woman with muscles like a man and godbraids reaching below her knees. She had a blue lizard tattooed over her face; its eyes were her eyes, lazily blinking. She looked at the carved birds pinned to the senior godspeaker's robes and nodded.

"Godspeaker of Et-Nogolor," she said, hands lightly fisted on her leather-clad hips. Her earlobes stretched low with the dangling weight of many amulets. Her nose was pierced six times. The lizard's tail caressed her chin, and the single pink jewel studded in it. "State your business in Raklion's city."

The senior godspeaker looked down his nose at the city Gatekeeper. "Our business is the god's business, and the business of Et-Raklion's high godspeaker Nagarak."

The Gatekeeper snapped her fingers, and a small he-brat leapt out of the gatehouse's shadows. "Make haste to the godhouse," she told it. "Tell the first godspeaker you see that there are visitors from godhouse Et-Nogolor, craving Nagarak high godspeaker's permission to enter."

The brat pressed a fist to its brown woollen chest and darted up the roadway leading from the gatehouse into the city proper.

The Gatekeeper nodded at the godspeaker caravan. "Nagarak high godspeaker will see you in his time. Until then, godspeakers, you must wait."

The godspeaker's eyes narrowed. "It is not our custom to be kept waiting."

"Alas," said the Gatekeeper. "It is my custom to obey my warlord, and the decrees of Nagarak high god-speaker."

Displeased but thwarted, the senior godspeaker of Et-Nogolor returned to his caravan, and the Gatekeeper turned her attention to Abajai. "Trader Abajai," she said, her voice all warmth and smiling now. "Trader Yagji. Long has been your absence from us."

"And many tales to tell," replied Abajai. "We will sit over sadsa and I will tell them that you may laugh and wonder. We may pass in your good graces, Baruve Gatekeeper?"

Hekat stared, unflinching, as the Gatekeeper's curious lizard eyes considered her. "In my good graces always,

Trader Abajai," the Gatekeeper said. "Do you require a litter? I can send a brat for one, if you like."

"Thanks, but no litter," said Abajai, before Yagji could speak. "To walk the streets of Et-Raklion after so long an absence is the god's great gift."

The Gatekeeper snapped her fingers a second time, and another brown-wool boy appeared. "Take this brat, Trader. It will light your way home." There were many torches burning in the wall of the gatehouse. She tugged one free and thrust it at the he-brat. "Send it back when you are done with its service."

As Yagji withdrew to fetch Obid, the other slave and their cart, Abajai took a purse from his robe pocket and gave it to the Gatekeeper. "A Trader's thanks."

She pocketed the purse, her tattooed blue lizard leaping as she smiled. "The god sees you, Trader. It likes to see a generous man."

Yagji returned, their possessions at his heels. Abajai nodded at the Gatekeeper, put his fingers to Hekat's elbow, and they followed the he-brat with its flaming torch through the wide gateway into the city.

"What does this mean, Aba?" Yagji whispered, as they stopped before the gateway godpost and its offering bowl, to gift the god with exquisite amulets and four fat purses of coin. "It is not like Nagarak to keep Et-Nogolor godspeakers waiting at the city gates. Do you think he knows—"

"*Tcha!*" said Abajai, his voice a warning. "Not here, not now. Let us keep walking. You there, gate-brat—to the Traders district."

The sun was gone now, the godmoon and his wife striding the night sky together. Obid and the other slave's harsh breathing was loud in the hush as Hekat walked in silence between Abajai and Yagji. Flowering trees lined both edges of the smooth pavestones beneath their feet. Floating on the stirring night air, faint strains of music, of voices, and still the ringing of silver godbells. A teasing aroma of spicy meat.

"The Dining district dances," said Yagji, sounding mournful. "We could stop and eat, Aba. Roast lamb, sweet wine. I pine for something other than godcakes and ale."

"No," said Abajai. "I want a private night within our own walls before venturing to visit with Trader friends, Yagji. There will be questions we have not decided how to answer."

"But what if the villa has no food for us?" Yagji fretted. "That Retoth and the rest, the worthless slaves, they have likely eaten us out of all provisions."

Abajai laughed. "Retoth knows better. He knows your belly when it returns from caravan. *And* he knows well to keep the villa in readiness for our sudden arrival."

Hekat plucked at Abajai's sleeve. "Who is Retoth?"

"Our villa's chief slave. You will mind him, Hekat, for his word is my word," said Abajai, looking down at her. "If you disobey him Yagji will have his wish to see you beaten."

Yagji tchut-tchutted under his panting breath. "I should have had my wish many highsuns before now."

"Save your air for walking," said Abajai, kindly enough. "The Traders district is a distance yet."

Yagji groaned. "You should have called for a litter, Aba. A fine thing if I fall to the ground with a spasm at my own doorstep after so many godmoons on the road!"

"After traveling so far on a camel and in wagons, a little walking will do you good!" said Abajai, lightly scolding. "And think how it will spice your appetite!"

"My appetite needs no spicing, Aba. The godcakes of Et-Nogolor are the worst I've ever tasted!"

For the first time since she and the fat Trader had met, Hekat thought that he was right.

"What amuses, Hekat?" said Abajai.

She would have liked to hold his hand, but that wasn't a gesture for her to make. He must touch first, always. She smiled at him instead. "I am pleased to be here, Abajai. Et-Raklion is the city of cities."

"Tchut!" said Yagji. "Can it be possible? For once the monkey speaks words worth hearing."

Abajai just nodded, and kept on walking.

It took a long time to reach Abajai's villa. Once they reached the city proper they saw other people in the streets, on foot or traveling in litters carried by strong tall slaves. Abajai and Yagji were recognized over and over; many times they were stopped and welcomed home with smiles and invitations to share food and wine and all the gossip.

"Let us take the discreet way home," said Yagji at last. "Or we won't see our bed before newsun, and I'm tired!"

So Abajai dismissed the gatehouse he-brat, because now the roads were lit with torches, and they walked along narrow side-streets into the heart of the Traders district, a section of the city almost halfway between its gatehouse and the base of Raklion's Pinnacle.

The Traders district was peaceful, sweet-smelling. Every street was lined with dwellings, some with grass and trees and flowers between their closed doors and the cobbles, others hidden behind stone walls with doors built into them. Some of the houses had beautiful slaves by the doors. When they thought Hekat and Abajai and Yagji approached them they stood very tall, only to slump when she and Abajai and Yagji walked by, Obid and the other slave puffing behind them with the cart.

She wished she knew what they were for.

Abajai said, "Where there is a slave, Hekat, either the master is out and the slave will say so, or he is willing to see a visitor and the slave will give that visitor entrance."

Aieee, he was like the god to read her mind so easily. "And if there is no slave, the master wishes to be alone?"

"Exactly so," said Abajai. "No civilized person will argue with a slave, or attempt an unattended door. Such an arrangement prevents unpleasantness."

She nodded, sighing. "Aieee, Abajai. Hekat has so much to learn."

He tugged her godbraids. "And Hekat is learning. You speak beautifully now. I am pleased with you."

She gifted him with her widest smile. Pleasing Abajai was all she asked for.

At last they came to a blue wooden door set into a high wall of pale cream stone. The most beautiful slave stood guard before it. He was tall and muscled, clad in black silk pantaloons, with a fistful of amulets round his neck and his bare chest tattooed with snakes and lizards. His scarlet slave's godbraid was heavy with godbells. He saw them and dropped hard to his knees, his face lighting up in a radiant smile.

"Master Abajai! Master Yagji! The god sees you, masters! It sees you in its eye!"

"Stand, stand, Nim," said Abajai, laughing. "And open

the door. Your caravanning masters are finally come home."

The slave Nim leapt to his feet and flung open the blue wooden door so they might enter the villa's grounds. "Retoth will weep to see you, masters! Everything is beautiful, as you left it!"

"And what of Hooli?" Yagji demanded. "Does Hooli thrive?"

The slave bowed low. "Master Yagji, he thrives."

As Yagji made silly happy sounds, Abajai gestured at Obid and the other slave. "Take these ones and the cart to the villa's rear entrance, Nim. Help them unload the coin boxes into the strong room, then see them to the slaves' quarters for food and a mattress. We will receive no visitors tonight."

"Yes, Master Abajai!" said the slave Nim. Hekat could see him wondering about her, his gaze kept slipping sideways to stare, but he didn't say a word. He just stood back so she and Abajai and Yagji could pass by.

"Hmm," said Yagji, grudging, as they walked up a paved torchlit pathway to the villa. "It would appear my gardens haven't *died*."

Hekat marveled at Yagji's gardens, stretching as far as the largest goat pasture in the village. Flowers rioted in perfumed profusion, pink and yellow and pale blue and mauve. There were fountains, bubbling, their deep bowls filled with flitting green-and-silver striped fish. Delicate trees with silver branches and whiskery seed pods drooped towards the dark green grass. More torches flamed from tall poles. There was a crimson godpost, topped with a black scorpion. A vivid carved snake sinuously embraced it; the fat drop of poison at the tip of each exposed fang was a green gemstone larger than her own clenched fist. Hekat clutched her snake-eye amulet, amazed.

"The godsnake of Et-Raklion," said Abajai. "It is our symbol, given by the god itself. Proof that Et-Raklion is its most blessed city."

Ahead, the villa. Built of that same pale cream stone, perhaps one hundred tall man-paces wide, its roof was tiled in black and gold. The enormous double front doors were painted black and bound with bronze. Hekat stared. Aieee, it was beautiful!

The paved path ended at four wide stone steps. As Abajai put his foot on the first one the doors were thrown open.

"Master Abajai! Master Yagji!"

Another slave, wrapped head to toe in blue and golden fabric. His head bristled with godbraids like a spiny zikzik, shy sly predator of the desert. Over his robes he wore a green silk shawl, edged around with tinkling amulets. He wasn't a young man, Hekat realized. He was just well fed, and that made him look younger.

"Yes, Retoth," said Abajai. "Your masters are home."

"And we're starving," announced Yagji. "Get out of the doorway, you stupid man, and find us some food at once!"

Retoth bowed low, then retreated into the villa. "Of course, of course, master. Baths are being prepared for you now. I have roused the kitchen and your chambers are being scented as we speak."

Hekat followed Abajai and Yagji inside, and Retoth closed the double doors behind them. Stranded, struck dumb, she looked around her, at the shiny blue-green stone floor, at the green walls with images of people and places bound inside golden borders and hung from hooks, at the gold and silver tables covered in carved-stone people and animals, at the bowls and bowls of freshly cut flowers. Inside the villa was light as day, there were so many lamps and candles burning.

"This is Hekat," said Abajai to Retoth. "You and I will talk of her in due course. For now she goes below, but not with the others."

"Yes, master," said Retoth, smiling as though he knew a secret. He clapped his hands, and moments later a short woman slave with greying godbraids and lines on her face appeared. Her robes were wool, and dyed a soft yellow. "Nada! Take this Hekat below the stairs. See to her comfort and settle her in the single chamber."

"Abajai?" said Hekat, uncertain.

"Go," said Abajai. "Keep your counsel and obey Retoth and this slave Nada, or you will displease me."

Displease Abajai? She would rather throw herself from the top of Raklion's Pinnacle. The slave Nada turned and walked away. Following, Hekat was proud her eyes did not waste water.

The slave Nada led her along a wide lamplit passageway to the back of the villa, then down a long steep flight of twisting stairs to more lamplit passageways and many rooms. Hekat stared, astonished. Rooms below the ground? She had never heard of such a thing. She would ask Abajai what that meant when she saw him at newsun; there was no point asking the woman Nada. She was a slave. What would she know?

The slave Nada took her to a bath chamber, where the water flowed from bronze fish-heads stuck on the wall.

Amazing! While the bath filled, the slave Nada undid Hekat's godbraids. Then she pointed to a cupboard against the wall. "There is soap and a sponge. I will fetch you a clean robe."

Not afraid this time, Hekat stripped off her filthy clothes and slid into the bath. She washed her body, she washed her hair, all crinkly from the godbraids. The soap foam stung her eyes but she didn't care. She was clean, she was clean, she would never be dirty again. She lived in Abajai's villa. It was beautiful, and so was she.

The slave Nada returned with towels and a brush and a dark blue robe. Hekat climbed out of the bath, water streaming down her lovely clean skin. As the slave Nada waited, she dried herself, pulled on the robe, then dragged the brush through her hair over and over until it was smooth and barely damp.

The slave Nada led her to a lamplit kitchen, where she sat at a table with four slaves who stared at her and would have spoken, but the slave Nada frowned them to silence. Not caring she was stared at, Hekat ate hot meat and drank cool sadsa. When her belly was filled to bursting she followed the slave Nada out of the kitchen, past other rooms and two more staring slaves until they reached a small chamber with a bed in it, but no windows.

"Sleep," said the slave Nada, holding the door wide so light from the passageway beyond spilled inside. "I will fetch you one finger after newsun. There is a pishpot under the bed, if you need it."

As the chamber door closed, Hekat climbed under the blankets. Her head touched the soft pillows, her body sighed, and within a heartbeat she was sucked from the waking world and into sleep, where for once the dream dogs did not find her.

Hekat woke before the slave Nada came for her. Someone had put a lit candle beside the bed. By its small light she used the pishpot and soon after that the slave woman arrived, with a tunic, leggings and shoes for her to wear. Hekat dressed, and walked with her to the kitchen where the slave Retoth was waiting.

"Where is Abajai?" she asked him. "Abajai and Hekat eat breakfast together."

The eight slaves eating at the kitchen table made little noises of surprise and stared at her with stupid faces. Nada stared, and the big kitchen slave in charge of cooking. He stopped stirring a pot hanging from a hook above the firecoals, wiped his arm across his face and looked at her as though she was demonstruck. It seemed the whole room held its breath.

The slave Retoth smiled. "Poor child. The master has told me you come from the savage north. Forget that place now. Forget the caravan upon the road. This is Et-Raklion, we are civilized here. We are civilized in this house, where the master's lightest breath is law. It is his want that you attend me. Do I go to him now and say you will not?"

An arrogant man, this slave Retoth. She would speak to Abajai of him when next they sat together. Until then, she could play his stupid game. She shook her head. "No, Retoth. Hekat attends you."

He smiled again, his eyes were watchful. "Good. Eat now, then Nada will show you the places in this house where you might put your feet. Put your feet in these places only, not in the places she does not show you. Then you will be properly godbraided. Afterwards I will come for you, the master has tasked me with tasks for you."

Hekat looked at him. "All of this is Abajai's want?"

"Every word I speak reflects the master's want," said Retoth. "Of that you can be certain."

"I am certain of Abajai," she told Retoth.

More shocked noises from the watching slaves. She looked at them sideways, feeling contempt. Goat people. Bleating like goats, huddling like goats.

They would make me small, the slaves in this house. I am not small. I wear no slave-braid. I named myself. I call him Abajai, he is not my master. Abajai is my friend.

Retoth departed, she ate hot cornmush, she frightened the stupid slaves with her eyes. The slave Nada took her back to her chamber, four more women slaves joined them. They brought a tall stool, six burning lamps, combs, brushes, and a wooden box full of beads and amulets and tiny silver godbells. Hekat sat on the stool and the slave women stood round her, godbraiding her hair.

When they were finished it was after highsun. She slid off the tall stool and shook her head. The godbraids reached just past her shoulder blades, the beads and amulets rattled and clattered, the tiny silver godbells sang; she would make a pretty noise wherever she walked, people would hear her before they saw her, they would say to each other, *Who is this girl-child with singing silver godbells in her godbraided hair?*

She would tell them: *I am Hekat, precious and beautiful.*

After the highsun meal, Retoth said to her, "Come."

He did not own her, she was not his dog. She stayed at the table. "Where do we go?"

"To the Merchants district. To the bazaar."

"What do we buy there?"

"You will see. *Come.*"

It was Abajai's want she play Retoth's stupid game, so she followed him up the stairs and along the passageways towards the villa's front doors. Within one closed room she heard sharp raised voices. She felt her heart leap.

"That is Abajai," she said, and stopped. "I will see him."

Retoth slowed, turning. "Not before he sends for you. The master meets important men this day. He has no time for bratty children. Come."

She folded her arms. "I am not a bratty child. I am Hekat."

He halted, and pointed his finger. "I am chief slave of this house! I can beat you if you do not obey."

She speared him with a look. "No, Retoth. You cannot touch me."

Retoth's hands became fists. Ugly feelings struggled in his eyes. She knew he wanted to unfold his fingers and slap her beautiful face but he did not dare. He said he could beat her, she knew he could not. If Yagji could not beat her, or make Abajai beat her, no slave born in the world could raise a hand to her.

"Tcha!" said Retoth, and stalked away. "You waste my time. You will see Abajai when we return. He has said so."

Hekat smiled, and followed him.

Retoth did not speak to her on the long walk from Abajai's villa to the Merchants district. She didn't care. Being in the fresh air was better than sitting below the villa's stairs. She could see the city in sunshine now. She would have so much to tell Abajai when she saw him again.

There was a special place for people to walk, so the many slave-carried litters in the streets were not slowed down. Some of them traveled quite swiftly, their muscular slaves running in a flat-footed shuffle. The litters were beautiful, carved from exotic polished wood inlaid with bronze. Some were curtained in heavy silks, others were open so the world might admire the masters and mistresses they bore, wearing rich fabrics and jeweled amulets, bright as songbirds in rainbow colors.

At the end of some streets stood a godpost with a godbowl at its base. She saw a godspeaker dressed in brown linen and snakeskin empty the offerings from one of the godbowls into a leather satchel slung over his shoulder. He was very young, his brow bound with the tiniest scorpion. Retoth bowed his head as they passed him. So did she, after Retoth poked her with his elbow.

There were images of the hooded godsnake wherever she looked, not just on the godposts at the end of the streets. It was painted on the walls enclosing some of the houses, or sat as a bronze statue on top. It was picked out in green and blue and red stones where they walked, and in the middle of the road.

The godsnake of Et-Raklion was everywhere.

Twisting her neck, she looked up at Raklion's Pinnacle, rising from the center of the city. In the bright sunshine she could see a wide road winding round and round, leading past the barracks and the palace to the godhouse at its peak. If she squinted she could see many moving figures on that road, traveling up, traveling down. The scorpion on top of the godhouse's godpost blazed black and crimson in the light. The god's great eye, watching them all.

The roads and walkways grew steadily busier the closer she and Retoth got to the Merchants district. Now there were open slave-drawn carriages, hung with bells and amulets, seating one or two people and rolling swiftly on polished wooden wheels. The slaves wore a harness over their shoulders, their godbraids bounced and rattled as they ran with the carriages jingling behind them.

Hekat stared. One day she would ride in a carriage like that. Proudly, with Abajai, so all Et-Raklion would know she was precious. She thought of the man in that savage north village, and was sorry he would never know that sending her away with the Traders was the only good thing he had ever done.

She and Retoth reached the bazaar at last, an enormous covered place crammed end to end and side to side with stalls and booths and foodsellers with trays on leather straps around their shoulders, hawking sweet jellies and spiced nuts and pastries dripping with honey. The air was almost too thick to breathe, so many smells, sweet and sour and sharp and soft. They filled her lungs and made her gasp. There were more people beneath this one high roof, shouting and laughing and singing and arguing, than lived in that village in the north.

Retoth took her by the arm and pulled her close. "Stay with me!" he bawled into her ear. A few steps away a woman and two men played drums and cymbals and a wailing wooden recorder. It was hard to hear Retoth above their noise. "My shadow, brat, or Abajai will be displeased!"

She pulled a face. Retoth used Abajai's name the way the man had used his goat-stick, what a stupid slave. Abajai would never hurt her. But she'd be Retoth's shadow, all the same. It would be easy to get lost in this shouting, stinking, crowded bazaar.

He took her to a booth filled with racks and racks of clothing. Two fat women pounced, like sandcats on rock mice. She was pulled behind a saggy curtain, poked and prodded, made to undress, then try on tunic after tunic, pantaloons, robes, so many clothes, till she wanted to scream. The only reason she did not scratch out their eyes was because they had a mirror that showed all of her body, from her godbraided head to her bare brown toes.

She had never seen her whole body before.

Entranced, she let the stupid fat women coo and chatter and smother her in fabrics. She only snarled when they tried to take off the snake-eye amulet Abajai had given her. Then they squealed and groveled and Retoth demanded from the other side of the curtain to know what was going on! The women rushed to tell him that all was in order, but Hekat said nothing. She looked at her body, and was amazed.

Her arms were long. Her legs were long. Her head with all its heavy godbraids sat neatly on her long neck. In the village there'd been dull dry skin lying thinly over skinny hips and ribs and jutting shoulders. Now . . . she was not fat, but there was flesh on her bones. She'd felt her body changing as she traveled the road with Abajai and Yagji but now she could see it: smooth and sleek, her shape so pleasing to the eye. Her skin, not dull but rich warm brown, glowing in the booth's mellow lamplight.

Last of all she studied her face. Not as thin as when

last she'd seen it, shown to her by the woman Bisla in Todorok. Her eyes weren't frightened anymore, they were open and fearless. Proud. Defiant. Words she had learned from Abajai, that Yagji said described her, and should be beaten out of her. Abajai paid no attention to stupid Yagji. For herself, she loved those words. She loved herself, shining in the mirror.

I am proud. I am defiant. I am Hekat, precious and beautiful. All of me is beautiful. The god sees me. I am seen by the god.

CHAPTER SEVEN

After the longest time the fat women finished drowning her in clothes. They left her alone to dress and took armfuls of the tunics and pantaloons she'd worn for them out to the front of their booth. When she joined them they ignored her, they were busy squabbling over coin with Retoth. He ignored her too, he cared more for Abajai's money than for her.

Bored. Hekat wandered a small way from Retoth and the women, threading her way through the jostling crowd. Her interest was caught by a booth full of amulets. She wandered closer. The amulet-seller was busy with a customer. Hekat stood to one side and looked at the merchandise laid out on wooden tables and dangling from ropes stretched over her head.

Some of the amulets were as large as her fist, others

smaller than her smallest fingernail. Some were carved out of bone, or fashioned from lizard skulls and snake-skulls and even fleshless human fingers. The bones and skulls were banded in bronze, in silver, in gold. There were tiny stone snake-fangs as blue as the sky. Larger snake-fangs in rock striped cream and crimson. Snake-eyes of pale green crystal, of richest yellow and hot fire-flame. Tiny clenched fists carved out of ivory, and ivory feet with a snake carved into the sole to guard against fangstrike. There were lots and lots and lots of scorpions, in every kind of stone and crystal. One in particular caught her eye, snared her attention like a fly drawn to honey. She picked it up to look more closely.

It was the size of a living scorpion. Shiny black, with deep flecks of scarlet and gold that caught the bazaar's torchlight and shimmered, like breathing. It felt warm on her palm, almost alive. She almost expected to feel its feet move against her skin.

"What is this? What is this?" the amulet-seller demanded. Her other customer had gone away, they were alone in the amulet booth. "Whose child are you?"

Reluctantly, Hekat put down the carved black scorpion. "I belong to Trader Abajai."

The amulet-seller was a wrinkled woman, so old her skin was fading to a light and ugly brown. All her grey-ing godbraids were limp. Her eyes were filmed over with whitish scum, she was missing most of her teeth.

"Trader Abajai?" the old woman said. "Returned from the road? The god sees me. Abajai is Et-Raklion's son, beloved of the god. What is your name, and where are you from?"

"I am Hekat from the savage north."

"Aieee!" The old woman hitched up her shawl; it was sewn with so many amulets it kept trying to slide off her bony shoulders and rattle to the booth's threadbare floor. "The savage north. That is why the child is fearless, and stands before me with its head held high." She picked up the amulet, caressed it, smiling. "Does Hekat like my scorpion? I made it, you know. I made all these amulets. The god speaks to me in the night, in the wind, in the water. I make these amulets and the god sees me in its eye."

Hekat looked again at the beautiful scorpion. "I like it."

"Then you may have it," said the old woman. "A gift for Hekat from the savage north." She leaned forward. "But keep it secret, child," she whispered. "This amulet is special. I have never made another like it. The god thundered in my heart as it guided my blade. It thunders now. It wants you to have this."

Hekat nodded. If she told Retoth he would take this gift for himself. "I will keep it secret." She reached for the black stone scorpion, and her hand touched the hand of the old amulet-seller.

The woman gasped, she dropped the scorpion onto the table, not caring if it chipped or smashed, and seized her in a grasp too strong for such brittle, claw-like fingers.

"Savage Hekat!" the old woman breathed. Her scummy eyes lost their focus, rolled upwards in her head like a godspeaker's in the middle of sacred ritual. "The god sees you, it burns you in its eye! Great lady, mother of the god's desire, mother of the son! Rivers of blood, rivers of greatness! Wastelands of despair!"

As Hekat wrenched free, Retoth appeared at her shoulder. "Hekat, I told you to stay with me! Abajai will beat you when I tell him of your wickedness. He will not abide disobedience beneath his roof!"

She was so shaken by the old woman's rantings she said, without sneering, "I am sorry, Retoth."

Retoth's anger melted. "Oh. Very well. But you must come, it is wicked to dawdle."

"My new clothes?"

"They are sent to the villa. Now *come*!"

The amulet-seller was muttering and moaning, rocking on her seat. "Burning! Blood! Aieee, the god thunders!"

Stupid old woman, she was demonstruck and ripe for stoning. Hekat snatched up the scorpion amulet and thrust it into her pocket, then ran after Retoth just as the bazaar's milling crowds swallowed him entirely.

They left the noisy, smelly bazaar and walked even further to the School district, where Retoth paraded her before a variety of tutors until one agreed to teach her reading and writing and dance in the villa.

"I do not need a tutor," she told Retoth, as they headed back to the Traders district. "Abajai is my teacher."

"Tcha!" said Retoth, shaking his head. "The master is too busy to bother with you. Hold your tongue now, you give me a headache."

On the long silent walk back to Abajai's villa Retoth dropped silver coins into four of the godbowls they passed on the way. He even gave a copper coin to her, so she could please the god once. She thought, briefly, of giving the god the black carved scorpion. In the end, though, she just gave it the copper coin. The scorpion was so beautiful, and the god already had so many amulets in its godbowls throughout the city. Besides, it meant the amulet for her.

The first thing she heard when they returned to the villa was Abajai's voice, coming from a room near the entrance hall. Forgetting Retoth, she dashed through its open door to find him.

"Abajai! Abajai! Here I am!"

He was stretched out on a long low couch, nibbling dried grapes from a glazed green bowl. Yagji sprawled on a couch beside him, feeding ripe plum pieces to an odd-looking animal perched on his fat belly. It was brown and white and hairy, it had a little face that looked almost human and tiny hands with four fingers and a thumb and a long curled tail. It saw her and let out a screech.

"Hooli! Hooli, don't be frightened!" said Yagji, and clutched the hairy thing to his breast. "Stupid brat! Don't you know it is *rude* to enter unannounced? Look what you've done, you've frightened Hooli!"

Hooli? Then this was a *monkey*. What a creature! Safe in Yagji's suffocating arms it chattered and gibbered and hid its face behind its hands.

She pointed. "Yagji called Hekat a monkey on the road. Hekat is *nothing* like that Hooli!"

"No, she is not," said Yagji, scowling. "My Hooli is worth a thousand times more in pure solid gold!"

"Only to you, Yagji, I promise," said Abajai, chuckling.

Hovering in the doorway, Retoth said, "Forgive me, master, I could not stop her in—"

"It is no matter," said Abajai. "Leave us, Retoth. I will have private words with Hekat."

Retoth bowed and withdrew, closing the lavish room's

door. Abajai looked her up and down. "Your godbraids are pleasing," he said. "They honor the god. You have visited the bazaar? You have new clothes?"

Hekat dropped onto the nearest couch and sat with her spine very straight. Her godbells chimed softly, singing his praises. "Yes, Abajai. Thank you."

"What of a tutor?"

She pulled a face. "It would be better if Abajai taught me."

Yagji snorted. Abajai said, "No. This is best. There are many things to learn from a tutor, he can teach you what I cannot."

She felt pricky tears, she blinked them away. "I have a tutor. He comes from next highsun."

Abajai leaned forward and flicked his finger on her knee. "I am pleased. Do you like Et-Raklion city?"

She sighed. "Et-Raklion city is beautiful. Will Abajai show me all of it, soon?"

"Not soon," said Abajai. "Yagji and I have been on the road many godmoons. My time is for business now. The things you saw upon the road, Hekat—warbands and dead men, blood on the brown grass—have you sharpened your tongue on them to Retoth or any slaves below the stairs?"

He had no time to show her Et-Raklion? Disappointment was a snake-fang, piercing her heart. "No, Abajai. Hekat does not talk with slaves."

"Good," he said. "Those things we saw upon the road are our secret, they are things for the Traders and the warlord to know. No-one else."

Our secret. Aieee, to know how much he trusted her. "Yes, Abajai."

He nodded, serious. "I tell you this also. We are no longer on the road. This is the city, we must live city lives. Unless you are sent for, you will stay beneath the villa, you will learn your lessons and obey Retoth. That is your world now, below the stairs. Retoth will give me reports of you daily, I will know how you go on. You wish to please me?"

"Only to please you, Abajai," she whispered. From the corner of her eye she could see Yagji, feeding the monkey Hooli more ripe red plum-pieces. He was smiling. He had never liked her. He was jealous.

Now Abajai smiled, his eyes were kind. "Do not despair, Hekat. From time to time you will see me and I will see you and all the time the god will see us both. If pleasing Abajai is your true want let that be enough for now."

She was Hekat, beautiful and precious, come from Mijak's savage north. She was strong and proud and fearless. She plucked the snake-fang from her disappointed heart and flung it away.

"Yes, Abajai," she said, and left him to sit with Yagji and the stupid monkey. She went downstairs, to the slaves' world below the villa, and shut herself privately into her chamber, where she sat on her soft bed and bit her lip until her pricky eyes stopped their stupid burning.

The scorpion amulet was still in her tunic pocket. She had meant to show it to Abajai, but his stern words had stolen her thoughts. She took it out and held it tightly, feeling its sharp edges against her skin, recalling the words of the amulet-seller.

Great lady, mother of the god's desire, mother of the son! Rivers of blood, rivers of greatness! Wastelands of despair!

Stupid scummy-eyed old woman, gabbling nonsense. Demons lived in her babbling tongue, the godspeakers would come for her and cut them out. Hekat thrust the amulet under the pillow, rolled herself into her blankets, and fell asleep.

Days passed, drifting one into the next into the next. A little rain fell, mostly the sky was blue and cloudless. Abajai never went beneath the villa. His feet never touched the stairs leading down to the kitchen and the laundry and the workrooms and the store-rooms and the slaves' sleeping quarters, and out to the slaves' garden where fresh fruits and vegetables were grown. The slaves went upstairs, every day they went up to clean the villa or serve Abajai and Yagji and their Trader guests or do the things that Abajai and Yagji needed them to do.

But Abajai never once came down.

Hekat sulked. She was used to seeing Abajai every day. She'd seen him and talked with him every day from newsun to lowsun since leaving the village. Even when they'd traveled in silence, when he pinched her shoulder or tugged on her godbraids to still her tongue, he'd been there with her, a constant reassuring presence at her back. She missed that. She missed him. She was lonely.

The feeling offended her. Loneliness belonged to that nameless she-brat in the village, who'd slept under tables and chained to walls. That ignorant, naked, skin-and-bone creature destined for the dogs, or an end even worse, it had lived in loneliness the way fish lived in water. But she wasn't that sad she-brat anymore. She had a name now, she wore fine clothes, her godbraids sang with silver godbells. She had a tutor, bought and paid for. How could Hekat, precious and beautiful, be *lonely*?

Abajai's stupid slaves did not talk to her, they talked to each other but not to her. Even when she had to work with them, because the slave Retoth said she must *earn her keep*, even then they would not talk to her. She thought that might be Obid's doing, he lived at the villa, the slaves spoke to Obid and he spoke to them about her, she was certain. So they knew where she came from, the savage north, they knew what she used to be, a dirty nameless she-brat. They did not understand what she had become, and they let Obid's maggot questions writhe in their hearts and only when Retoth said they had to, would they ever speak to her.

Not that she cared. They were jealous because Abajai was *Abajai* and not *the master*. They were jealous because he dressed her in silk and cotton and paid a stupid tutor silver coins to teach her reading and writing and how to dance, tra-la. Reading and writing were tedious, but she liked to dance.

Twenty-eight highsuns came and went without her once sitting with Abajai to talk, and laugh, and poke silly fun at pouting Yagji. Twenty-eight highsuns and she never climbed the stairs into the villa at all. One time the slave Nada caught her looking up those stairs, the slave shook a fist at her and said, *Enter the villa without Retoth's word, Hekat, and you will be beaten.*

The way the slave Nada said that, Hekat knew she hoped there *would* be a beating.

There would not. Staying below stairs was Abajai's want, she would obey him. But oh, his want chafed like the slave chains chafed the merchandise on the road. It

poked her like Obid's spear poked those slaves to sit, to
stand, to eat, to pish. She stayed beneath the villa, she
learned her lessons and her dancing, she scrubbed pots in
the kitchen and sheets in the laundry, she toiled among
the vegetables and sat in the kitchen with the villa's stupid slaves and listened to them laugh and tease and joke
and tell tales of Et-Raklion city, which they could visit
sometimes but she could not.

She was not *free* here. On the road with Abajai she had
been free. But he would send for her soon, he *must* send
for her soon. Then she would walk in the world, with
him. She understood why he had not sent for her yet, he
was busy, he had Trader business. She knew from the
slaves' gossip how many Traders came and went upstairs—Abajai was respected, so many sought his counsel. Once he even went to the warlord's palace, the
warlord spoke to him in private conference. Aieee, he
was an important man!

Even so. He would send for her soon. She was precious, he must miss her as she missed him.

While she waited she learned her Mijaki picture-
letters and word-symbols, practiced writing them with
her stylus on the damp clay tablets the tutor brought
with him each day, and read aloud from the baked clay
tablets he left behind for her to study. And when she was
outside in the slaves' garden, pulling weeds and raking
leaves and spreading chicken dung on the vegetables,
she would hear in her head the chiming of his tambourine, and lightly dance the steps he taught her.

When Abajai sent for her at last he would be so proud
of his clever, beautiful Hekat.

*   *   *

He summoned her a finger before lowsun on the twenty-ninth day.

She was in her chamber, practicing her writing, when the slave Retoth entered unannounced. Such a rude man, she did not like him. "Get up," he said. "The master wants you."

She liked best to write lying flat on the floor, with the soft pink woven carpet tickling her skin. She leapt up. "Abajai sends to see me now? Aieee, I must dress for him!"

Retoth folded his arms. "You are dressed already."

"Tcha!" she said scornfully, and rummaged in the wooden trunk that contained her fine bazaar clothes. "I must be beautiful for Abajai! He will wait for me."

"Arrogant wretch," said Retoth, under his breath, but that was all. He knew she was right.

She selected a tunic striped in emerald and lapis blue, and pantaloons the color of flame. She pulled off her yellow shift, it didn't matter that Retoth could see her skin. He was a gelding, not a man. Except for Obid, all the villa's male slaves were geldings. Gelding made men docile, Nada said. Otherwise they got themselves in trouble.

Beautifully dressed for Abajai, with her snake-eye amulet dangling for him to see, she followed Retoth upstairs into the villa. Abajai sat in the same lavish room as before. Yagji was there too, reclining on his favorite couch with his stupid monkey Hooli leaping and capering and spitting date stones on the carpets.

She was so pleased to see Abajai, she wanted to run to him, to dance for him, to show him he could trust her above the stairs, in the villa, in the city of Et-Raklion.

But she didn't run, or dance. His face told her he wanted her to walk, to be silent, to hold inside all her shouting pleasure. She obeyed, because she loved him.

"Retoth," said Abajai, relaxed on his own couch. "You give a good report of Hekat below the stairs?"

Retoth's face was sour but he could not lie. "A good report, master."

"And what does the tutor tell you?"

"The tutor tells me Hekat learns swiftly, master."

Abajai turned to Yagji, who had captured the monkey Hooli and was holding it in his arms. "Was I not right, Yagji?"

Yagji shrugged. "Half right, so far." He began brushing his stupid pet's brown and white coat with an ivory-backed brush. "As for the rest, Aba, it remains to be seen."

Abajai took a large clay tablet from the table beside him and held it out. "Read this to me, Hekat."

The tablet was heavy. If she dropped and broke it Abajai would be angry. She would keep hold of it no matter how cruelly her fingers ached. She studied the tablet's writing closely, then took a deep breath.

" 'For obedience pleases the god,' " she read slowly, sounding out each symbol with teeth and tongue. " 'Sacrifice pleases it. Offerings—offerings—' "

"Swell," said Abajai. "That symbol means 'swell.' Do you know the word 'swell,' Hekat?"

Mute, she shook her head. She could not read Abajai the tablet. She had failed him. Pricky tears burned her eyes.

"It means to increase," said Abajai. "To make larger. It is an old-fashioned word. Keep reading."

Blinking, she looked again at the clay tablet. " 'Offerings swell the—the—' " Aieee, *another* word-symbol she did not know. She knew the word-sounds, weren't they enough? She stared at it, heart pounding. What did the stupid tutor say? The stupid tutor said to look at the word-symbols around the word-symbol she did not know and see if they could help her guess its meaning. She looked again at the other word-symbols. Offerings swell the *something*. But what?

That symbol there, it was almost the sign for the god. Almost, but not quite. Memory stirred, showed her the time she and Retoth walked through the streets to the bazaar. Godposts on street corners. Young godspeakers tipping coins into their leather bags . . .

" '*Godbowl*!' " she shouted, triumphant. "Abajai, Hekat knows this word-symbol now, it means godbowl!"

Abajai clapped his hands. "Well done, Hekat. Keep reading."

" 'Offerings swell the godbowl. The scorpion stings the man with—with—' " It was no good. She had not been reading so very many highsuns. She could not guess the rest.

" 'With a heart like stone,' " said Abajai. "These words are given us by Et-Raklion's high godspeaker, Hekat. Can you see his name writ on the tablet?"

She looked, hard. Yes. There was a name there. The stupid tutor had taught her to write her own name, and Abajai's, and even Yagji's. She frowned at it, sounding it out in the silence of her head.

"Nagarak," she said at last. "The name is Nagarak."

"Yes, it is," said Abajai. "You have been listening to your tutor, Hekat. Abajai is pleased with you."

Abajai is pleased. The words sang in her heart, she could not keep her laughter secret. Abajai retrieved the clay tablet, then from a wooden box by the chamber window took a painted tambourine. He gave it to Retoth.

"Make music, Retoth, so Hekat can dance."

Dancing, said the stupid tutor, was a way of honoring the god. Dancing made the body lithe and supple, it stretched the muscles and strengthened the heart. When she danced her silver godbells sang without ceasing, as the music sang within her blood. She felt alive, she felt connected to the ground and the sky and the air all around her. It seemed she knew how to dance before the stupid tutor showed her one thing about it, as though the dance was already inside her, waiting to come out.

She danced for Abajai, honoring him.

When she was finished, her body warm and glowing, the last tambourine chime died away, even Yagji praised her.

"Very pretty," he said, with the stupid monkey still in his arms. "That was a pretty dance."

"Hekat is graceful," said Abajai. "Graceful and beautiful."

"Abajai . . ." She stepped forward. "Abajai, I have been good. I work in the garden, I clean in the kitchen, I study with the tutor five fingers every day. I am not savage now, I read and dance, I have sweet breath and clean skin. When can I join you in the villa?"

"In the villa?" said Yagji, and tittered. "So, Aba, not so intelligent after all."

Abajai frowned. "You live beneath the villa. Hekat, with the other slaves. That is your place here."

He did not understand. She clasped her hands behind

her back. "Abajai, Hekat is thinking. Hekat wants to be a Trader."

Retoth dropped the tambourine, bang jangle jangle. Hooli shrieked and leapt out of Yagji's arms. Abajai sat up very slowly, his lips pinched, his eyes cool.

"I am not stupid, Abajai," she said, eager to explain. "I can learn Trader business. You have no son, I can be a son to you. I can help you in your Trading."

"*Aieee!*" said Yagji, and fanned his face. "It says it's not stupid, then asks to be one of *us?* Aba, Aba, did I not *tell* you? Did I not *warn* you? Did I not—"

"Silence, Yagji!" said Abajai, standing. "Hekat, are you demonstruck?"

Demonstruck? Dry-mouthed she stared up at him, so tall, so looming. "Abajai?"

He shook his head, as though he were pained with disappointment. "You are a *slave*, Hekat. I bought you with my silver coin. You were there, you saw your father sell you to me. You are not like a child of my bloodline, you are *property*."

Property? No. No. That could not be right. Hekat was precious, she was not a *slave*. "But, Abajai, how can that be true?" she whispered. "I rode on the white camel, I slept in your tent. I did not eat the slave food with the slaves. I never wore slave chains. I have no slave-braid."

"*There!*" said Yagji, pouty and cross. "Perhaps now you will grant me my wisdom, Aba. Buy it a slave-braid, I told you in Todorok. Don't make a pet of it, I said from the start. Would you heed me? No, you would not. And see what has happened? It is grown proud and ignorant, this precious slave of yours, it does not know its place in the world."

"Yes, I *am* precious!" she said, ignoring Yagji. "I am Hekat, precious and beautiful. I read, I write, I dance. I wear silk and linen, I am taught by a paid tutor, your *slaves* are not taught."

Abajai sighed, and dropped to one knee before her. His warm hands rested on her shoulders. "Hekat. Listen to me. It is true I have treated you differently. I bought you fine clothes, and pay a tutor to teach you. This does not mean you are not a slave. I have done these things to increase your value."

Increase her *value?* It was a good thing Abajai's hands held her shoulders, she would float away if they did not, her body felt so light, her head was a cloud.

"Abajai will *sell* me?" she asked him, faintly.

He could not sell her. How could he sell her? He loved her, she was certain. She knew she loved him. She knew what love was now, the tutor read her stories about men and women loving.

Stupid Yagji rolled his eyes. "*Tell* her, Aba. Tell her now what you should have told her from the first. Put her straight and end this nonsense!"

CHAPTER EIGHT

Heart pounding, Hekat glared her hate at stupid Yagji. She was hot, she was burning, if she touched the fat man he would burst into flame.

"Aieee!" he cried, and clutched his amulet. "See her

eyes, Aba! She wants to hurt me, she is *wicked*! I will not
have her here anymore! You say Hekat is an investment?
Investments become liabilities if they are not realized in
time. She reads, she writes, I grant she dances with the
god's grace. And yes, she is beautiful. But Aba, she is a
blight upon this household. The other slaves dislike her,
she sows discord below the stairs with her arrogant ways!
Ask Retoth. He will tell you."

Abajai stood, his face a frown. "Am I to care for what
slaves like or dislike? Am I not master of this villa?"

"You are to care if their disliking creates unrest," said
Yagji crossly. "Twelve other slaves we have here, all unhappy because of a thirteenth that daily costs us hard-
earned coin. Is this good practice? You know it is not.
The slaves obey because that is what slaves are for but
they are not brute beasts, Aba, you have always said so.
Our household is never plagued with slave mischief because you know that is true. But now you have forgot,
you are so besotted with this wretched creature you cannot think past the gold coin you think she will fetch! You
say the god guided you to that village? *I* say you listened
to a demon!"

"*Tcha!*" said Abajai, his hands turned to fists and the
scarlet scorpion in his cheek writhing. "Speak blasphemy
and the god will smite you. I am not *besotted*, Yagji.
Hekat is blooming, true, ripe enough now to make a man
look twice, but her full blossoming is yet to come. Are
you deaf to me, Yagji? Have I not said to you, over and
over, since we left the desolate village that spawned her:
of Hekat I will create a concubine worthy of a warlord.
Why else do I spend our good coin upon her? She is no
common, ordinary slave, to be bought and broken and put

into harness. She is a godgift, so we might be wealthy beyond our lifetimes. I *will not* sell her before she is ripe. I will sell every other slave here and change bed linens myself before I do such a foolish thing. Would you settle for a trickle of silver when soon enough she will give us a river of *gold*?"

If Yagji said something in return, Hekat did not hear his words. Her body was breathless, and in her ears a terrible roaring, raging flames to blacken the world.

It was true. He meant to sell her. Gold mattered to Abajai, she did not. She was a thing to him, not a person, not his precious and beautiful Hekat. She was walking, talking, dancing gold. She had no words. There were no words. There was only pain like the devouring of dogs.

I loved you. I loved you. I thought you loved me.

Abajai said, "It is a pity you misread your purpose, Hekat. I hope you understand it now?"

She nodded. "I understand," she whispered. Her throat was tight, it hurt to talk. "I am Abajai's slave."

"Yes. My slave. Still precious, still beautiful. But no more than a slave. It was foolish of you to think anything else." He turned to Retoth. "Take her beneath the villa, Retoth. I think she will give you no more trouble."

Retoth's face was solemn but his eyes were laughing, he was laughing at her, he was pleased to see her brought so low. "Yes, master," he said. "I think she knows her proper place."

Hekat flinched. Retoth snapped his fingers at her in passing. She did not scold him, but followed him to the door. Five paces from it she slowed, and turned.

"Trader Abajai? You never loved me?"

"*Loved* you?" said Yagji, and flapped his hands. "I was right all along, it is stupid, *stupid*!"

"Masters do not love their slaves," said Abajai, impatient. "I am fond of you, Hekat, I wish you no ill. But *love* you? Aieee! Perhaps Yagji is right. Perhaps you are stupid."

She ran at him screeching, reaching to claw out his eyes, his tongue, to tear his long godbraids out of his scalp. His swinging fist caught her, clubbed her sideways, she fell onto a low table and smashed it flat. The monkey Hooli screamed from the curtains and Yagji threw himself backwards, squealing.

Dazed, half unconscious, Hekat felt Abajai drag her onto her feet. His flat hand struck her, hard stinging blows. At first she fought him but it made no difference, he was strong, she was weak. In the end she stood there just like the woman, and let him hit her.

He was no different from the man.

"There," he said, when he was finished beating her. "You are punished, Hekat. Now go with Retoth, you will sit in your chamber until he gives you permission to leave, you will eat no dinner. Tomorrow you will get your slave-braid in the godhouse, I will have no more of this nonsense. If your defiance continues the god will smite you. Do you understand?"

Her eyes were full of pricky tears. She would die before she let them fall. "I understand, Abajai."

"I understand, *master*," said Abajai, sharply.

She nodded, even though that hurt her head. "I understand, *master*."

"Good. Now go."

She followed Retoth down the stairs, to the slaves'

place. He banged her chamber door shut behind her. She vomited the remains of her highsun meal into the pishpot, chicken and cornmush and spicy fried greens, then curled into a ball on the beautiful carpet, paid for by the sale of girls like herself. She felt small and cold yet still burning hot.

Yagji is right. I am stupid. Stupid.

In her dreams the man's dogs chased her, howling and growling and running behind Abajai's camel. Blood and spittle dripped from their open jaws, their claws like stone scythes scrabbled in the dirt. Abajai wasn't riding his camel, he wasn't warm and solid and comforting at her back, he was riding Yagji's camel. There was Yagji, there was Abajai, and there was the stupid monkey Hooli, they rode the white camel all happy together, laughing and pointing at Hekat alone, and the man's starving dogs were coming . . . they were coming . . .

"*Abajai!*" screamed Hekat, and sat up on the floor.

In the chamber's darkness her breathing sounded loud and frightened. Her skin was sweaty, her tunic and pantaloons damp and twisted about her body. She wiped her sleeve across her face and stood, silver godbells tinkling, feeling her heart hang hard on her ribs.

Retoth would not give her flint and striker to light her chamber lamp, she counted eight paces to the door and pulled it open, one finger wide. The passage beyond was lit with three candles, and she could hear no sounds of slaves walking or talking. It was late, then. The quiet time. She opened the door a little wider, some faint light creeping in, she counted six paces to her bed and sat. Her head felt sore, her mouth tasted mucky.

If I stay in this place, Abajai will sell me. In this place I am a goat fattening in the slaughter-pen, waiting for the knife. Waiting for a rich man's coin to buy me. If I stay in this place I am truly a slave.

It did not matter that Abajai had given the man coin for her. She was not a slave, a weak nothing person like Retoth or Obid or Nada. Not in her heart, where she was her true self. But if she stayed here past this night Abajai would have her marked with a slave-braid and then she *would* be a slave, in Mijak's eyes she would be property forever. Even if she cut off that slave-braid with the sharpest knife her hair would grow back again red as blood. A slave-braid was given by the god for life.

I have to run.

Shuddering, she remembered that runaway slave in Et-Nogolor city, the sound of his babbling agony, the flies in the slashed-open cavern of his belly. If she ran and was caught, that would be her. She would die as that slave died. Running was only the start, she had to run to somewhere, find a place where she could safely hide and make a new life.

But where? In Et-Raklion she knew Abajai, she knew Yagji, she knew the stupid tutor. They were the only free men she knew in all of Mijak, except for the man, and she couldn't go back to the savage north. Even if she knew how to get there, even if she could journey so far on her own . . . she never would. That life in the village was slavery too. The man was poor, and Abajai was rich. Otherwise, they were the same.

Where can I go? Where will I be safe, and free?

Gossip in the kitchen, slaves laughing over sadsa. Talking of other slaves in the bazaar, in the Slaughter district, with tales of Raklion warlord and his beautiful palace, his mighty warriors, the city within a city that was their warrior barracks.

Home to ten thousand fierce fighters and their horses, was Raklion's barracks. Home to the blacksmiths who shod those horses, the artisans who forged the warriors' weapons, crafted those leather chest-pieces to keep their godsparks safe inside, who built sleek swift chariots and the wheels they rode on. The cooks who fed the warriors and the workers, the laundries that kept their tunics clean. The stables to house the horses, the pens to house the animals whose carcasses fed the hungry ten thousand. Some were slaves who worked there, others were poor folk, eking out a living. That's what the slaves said, gossiping in the kitchen, the laundry, in the villa's gardens.

The barracks of Et-Raklion. A city within a city . . .

Surely one she-brat could find a home in such an anthill, unnoticed. Surely Abajai would not think to look for her in Raklion warlord's warrior barracks.

He would not, she knew it. In the barracks she would be safe. All she had to do was reach them. Except she'd learned other things from slaves' gossip in the kitchen: godspeakers walked the streets of Et-Raklion in the quiet time and to be found by a godspeaker then was to be punished by the god. If a godspeaker found her running away . . .

Hekat dropped to her knees on the beautiful carpet, she clenched her fingers into fists and pressed them to her pounding heart.

Let me leave here, god. Guide me to the warlord's barracks. If you do this—if you do this for me—I will be yours forever. I will serve you with my last breath. My blood and bones will belong to you. I will be Hekat, slave of the god.

How long she knelt there, she did not know. The god did not speak to her, or if it did she could not hear it. Did that mean the god was not listening? Or had the god turned its back to her, was she unworthy to serve? Was Yagji right, did the god not see her heart at all?

The god sees me. It sees me. It saw me in the savage north, it will see me in Raklion's barracks. It will. It must. I am Hekat, beautiful and precious. I was chosen by Aba-jai. I was chosen by the god.

Her heart still pounding, she got off the floor. If she was truly leaving it had to be now. Her godbells sang with every step she took and Retoth slept light as sadsa froth. She took a towel from the shelf by her bed and wrapped it round her singing godbraids so he would not wake. Then she slipped from her chamber, slid the nearest burning candle from its holder and crept down the passage to the kitchen, where she took one of the cook-slave's thin sharp knives. She took five small bread loaves from their basket, five small bricks of cheese from their stone bin and an empty leather flask from the pile left ready for the villa's outside workers. All the time she listened for Retoth, or Nada, or any slave stirring so late at night.

No-one stirred. No-one heard her.

Safe again in her chamber, she fixed the candle to her bed chest with drips of wax, searched through her clothes trunk and chose the plain dark blue tunic and pantaloons Retoth had thought she should have in case a godspeaker came calling to the villa. She tugged off her bright clothing and pulled them on, and her sturdiest shoes without the curly toes.

Then she cut one leg from the pantaloons she'd discarded and tied a knot at the bottom. That would be her food-sack. Into it she dropped the loaves and cheeses and put the leather flask on top. Last of all she sawed off her godbraids one by one and laid them like an offering on the bed. She looked at them sadly, silent silver godbells gleaming in the yellow candlelight. Now her hair was short and spiky, hacked-off godbraids unraveling, disrespectful to the god.

I am sorry. I had to do it.

The knife she slid into her pocket. On impulse, she snatched back two of the godbraids and buried them in her pocket too. And that was it. Unless . . . should she write something on one of her practice clay tablets? Her writing was not perfect yet but she knew enough word-symbols to cause some trouble . . .

Working as quickly as her trembling fingers would let her, she pressed her stylus into the damp clay. *Retoth say Hekat bad slave, Abajai angry, sell Hekat Trader visiting. Hekat sad. Go Et-Raklion.* Despite her pain, the knife in her heart, she laughed a little in her throat. She hoped Abajai would beat that slave Retoth until he cried.

Or died.

Touching the lapis snake-eye round her neck, Abajai's gift, she felt her face twist with hate. She wanted no gift from him: cruel, lying Abajai. She dragged the amulet over her head, unpicked the knot in its leather thong and unthreaded the carved blue stone. It fell from her fingers like a piece of camel dung. Ignoring it, she took her carved scorpion amulet out of hiding. It had a hole bored through its head, she threaded it onto the leather thong, retied the knot and put it on, letting it drop beneath her tunic. The scorpion was heavy, warm against her skin, promise of the god's protection. She left the practice tablet with her message on the bed beside the severed godbraids, then crept from the chamber with her food-sack, silent like the smallest breeze. Still no slave was stirring, they slept as though a demonspell had turned them to rock.

Unnoticed, she slipped out of the villa. Into the garden. Climbed the jaga tree by the villa's back wall, wriggled hand-over-hand along the branch that stuck out into the side-street beyond. Dropped soundless to the cobbles far below . . .

. . . and was free.

Barely four streets distant from Abajai's villa, flitting from shadow to shadow in the quiet time with her food-sack bumping bruises against her leg and her heartbeat so loud she wondered the godmoon and his wife did not hear it, she saw a godspeaker, striding in the moonlight, grim and vigilant for the god.

She stilled herself, like a lizard beneath the eagle's fleeting shadow. Her severed godbraids were silent in her pocket, he could not hear the godbells singing. But he did hear something, he stopped beneath a street torchlight and his bony face was listening. The scorpion bound with leather to his forehead was listening. The tall staff in his hand, carved and painted like a godpost, was listening.

Then she heard what the godspeaker heard: the sounds of stumbling feet, of voices raised in raucous whisper. Two men, traveling late. They fell out of shadow into light, from the mouth of the narrow alleyway between two Trader villas. Their faces were stupid with sadsa or some other rowdy drink, and shiny with grease around their sloppy lips. Their robes were fastened uneasily to their bodies, their arms wrapped tight around each other's shoulders. They saw the godspeaker and staggered to a halt.

"You Traders," said the godspeaker. His voice was soft, yet it sounded loud. "The god sees you. It sees you, Trader Voltek, it sees you, Trader Lopa. It sees you in the street, in the quiet time."

The Traders stared at the godspeaker, their eyes alive with fear. "Not by choice, godspeaker," said the Trader with his godbraids tied in a tail. "We got lost."

"Lost?" said the godspeaker. "In your own district?"

The other Trader nodded. His godbraids clacked together, he wore no silver godbells, only beads and amulets. "First we got drunk, godspeaker," he explained. His voice was high and squeaky. "Then we got lost."

"Drunkenness offends the god," said the godspeaker. "It blurs the mind and weakens the wits."

"We didn't mean to drink so much," said the first Trader. "It was an accident, godspeaker. So was getting lost."

The godspeaker did not answer, he just swung his godstaff hard and sharp. It caught the Traders behind their knees, it sent them crashing to the street so they cried out in surprise and pain. They wriggled on their backs, staring up at the godspeaker.

The godspeaker knelt between them and laid his godstaff on the ground at his side. Hekat saw no anger in his face, no sorrow, no pleasure. His face was smooth like sand before the wind rises, and his eyes were quiet, and calm, and terrible.

" 'And the god spoke to the people, it said: between

the time of working and the time of quiet there shall be the time of revelry, where men will sing and dance. But after revelry, then will *be* the quiet time, the streets will sleep and so will men beneath their roofs.' "

The Traders said nothing, they wriggled on their backs and made little gasping noises like dying she-babies on The Anvil.

"You breach the time of quiet, Traders," said the god-speaker. "Your sin offends the god."

His hands came up, fingers stretched wide. His palms glowed, like white fire they burned, but his face was calm. He touched the Traders with his hands, he pressed his burning palms against their faces. The Traders screamed, they shrieked like goats torn to pieces by sandcats, they writhed and flailed and thrashed upon the ground.

"The god smites you, Trader Voltek, it smites you, Trader Lopa. It leaves its mark upon you for one fat godmoon, in your folly," the godspeaker told them. "For one fat godmoon the god's smiting is upon you and for one fat godmoon no man shall speak with you or Trade with you, no woman shall spread her legs for you, you will kneel before every godpost in the city and when you kneel you will weep tears of blood in your pain and your sorrow as the godsmite in your faces cleanses you of sin. You will eat bread, you will drink water. All other food and drink will drop you dead. Traders, you are smitten."

Hekat swallowed a cry as the scorpion bound to the godspeaker's forehead flared bright crimson. The godsmitten Traders did cry out, their bodies bowed as though plucked up at the navel by invisible rope. The godspeaker removed his smiting hand. His scorpion faded to black. He picked up his godstaff and stood with graceful ease.

The Traders sprawled at his feet. On their faces, burned into one cheek each, the white-hot imprint of his smiting hand, pulsing in time with their frantic gasps for air.

"Get up," said the godspeaker. "Go home. Begin your godpost pilgrimage at newsun . . . and remember this. The god will know if even one godpost remains untouched by your penitent tears. If even one godpost remains untouched at the end of a fat godmoon, the god will know. It will kill you in its eye. You will fall down dead in the street where you stand."

Moaning, the Traders found their feet. From her hiding shadows on the other side of the road Hekat watched them stagger off in shame, sobbing their pain for the world to hear. Her mouth was dry. The godspeaker in the village had never punished wickedness so. His punishment for things was stone, stones, always stones. He did not have a hand of power.

This godspeaker of Et-Raklion . . . the god saw him in its eye.

Shaking his head, the godspeaker turned to continue his walking. As he turned, his terrible gaze swept over the street and through the shadows. He stopped. On his brow, the bound black scorpion waited.

Hekat's breath ended. He had seen her. He had seen her. He would beat her to the ground, he would lay his hand of power on her and his godsmite would burn her to cinders and ash . . .

For ever and ever, he seemed to look at her. For ever and ever, she held him in her eye.

The godspeaker walked away.

Aieee! thought Hekat. *The god sees me! It hides me! It grants me my want*!

Exultant, giddy with triumph, she left the shadows and danced through the night, precious and beautiful in the god's great eye.

She saw four more godspeakers roaming the Traders district in the quiet time, but they did not see her. The god kept her hidden. They were the only other waking people she saw. The rest of Et-Raklion city's people obeyed the god, they slept beneath their quiet roofs and did not tempt its fury. They were wise. They were not Hekat, hidden in the god's great eye.

When she reached the edge of the Traders district she paused in a shadow, to get her bearings. While learning from the stupid tutor she had coaxed him to tell her of the warlord's city. He had shown her with words and pictures how each district was laid out around the Pinnacle's base. To reach the barracks of Raklion warlord's warriors she must walk through six more districts, to the start of the Pinnacle Road. She must pass between the guarding godposts at its mouth, and make her way up the side of the mount, past the warriors' training grounds to the main gates in the barracks wall.

After that she must get inside.

The god will show me what I must know. I am its slave, I am Hekat, its chosen. When it wants to, it will tell me what to do.

She looked at the night sky, where the godmoon walked with his obedient wife. Four fingers until newsun. That was time enough to reach the warrior barracks.

Chilly in the quiet time, under the god's severe protection, she headed for the Pinnacle.

One wide street led from Et-Raklion city's gatekeep, through the city and its districts, around Raklion's Pinnacle to the Pinnacle Road. The street guided Hekat but, being cautious, she did not walk it. Instead she darted along the smaller side-streets, twisting and turning through the city's alleyways. With every swift soft footfall she left the Traders district behind her, left Abajai and Yagji and the stupid monkey Hooli behind her. She traveled through districts she knew only by name, *Artisan, Musician, Leatherworker, Seamstress, Jeweler, Potsmith*, past darkened villas that did not want her, past roaming godspeakers who did not see her, always keeping her fierce gaze pinned upon the Pinnacle, and the barracks, where the god told her she would find a home.

She passed a fountain, bubbling water from one of the rivers running beneath the land of Mijak. She took the leather flask from her food-sack and filled it, then drank a little from her hand, alert for godspeakers. None approached.

The city districts ended at last. At the place where the wide Pinnacle Road began its winding way up to Et-Raklion's godhouse, the two tall godposts the tutor had spoken of stood their grim watch. They looked like the godpost in Yagji's garden, sinuous snakes of Et-Raklion with a stinging scorpion upon each hooded head. The godbowls at their bases were the largest she had ever seen, their scorpion bellies half-filled with offerings.

She knelt before each one and buried a godbraid beneath the gold, the silver, the bronze, the amulets and the figurines.

This is for the god, she told each godpost. *This is for Hekat in the god's eye, for her protection, so she might serve the god.*

The godsnake of Et-Raklion smiled at her, twice.

The godmoon and his wife had walked almost to the far horizon. When newsun came she must be at the barracks, away from the road and eyes that had no business seeing her. She picked up her food-sack and kept on walking. The barracks of Et-Raklion's warriors were some distance ahead, they hid themselves behind a high stone wall. Torches burned along its top, throwing long dancing shadows onto the ground.

At first the Pinnacle Road remained flat, cutting through the warriors' training fields, but then she left them behind and the road tilted upwards. Her breathing deepened, her legs began to burn. Ignoring the discomfort she kept on walking, she did not take her eyes from the barracks wall.

When she got closer she saw a godpost standing at each end, and set in the middle of its red and black stone blocks two impossibly tall wide wooden gates.

There was no way to enter the barracks city. The gates were closed, the walls without footholds, and no trees grew close for her to climb. Where could she hide? Her searching gaze fell upon a tangled stand of stunted scrubby saplings that looked to form a kind of living, leafy cavern. They grew further up the hillside, a distance from the barracks wall. Close enough that she could see the barracks doings, far enough that those she watched would not notice her watching.

Those trees are the god's doing. Thank you, god. Your chosen slave gives you thanks.

The stunted saplings resisted her. Their spindly trunks and branches were thorny, they scratched her arms, her face, they tore her clothes and poked sharp points in her ribs and throat. She bit her lip to swallow the pain and kept on pushing. She was Hekat from the savage north, she could not be defeated by trees.

She wasn't. She found the small clear space at their thorny tangled heart and curled up in it like a lizard, like a snake, resting her head on the lumpy food-sack. The ragged thorn scratches in her flesh smarted, they burned. As her spilled blood lost its wetness she listened to her breathing, harsh and dry like the land she came from. She listened to her heart, beating like a drum inside her ribs. She listened for the god, but could not hear it. The god was not speaking now. The god was busy elsewhere. When she needed it, the god would speak.

She slept.

CHAPTER NINE

When Hekat woke it was three fingers past newsun. She could hear sounds coming from the barracks behind its red and black walls; men shouting, hammers striking metal, striking rock. Horses neighing. Goats bleating. Chickens cackling. The lowing of oxen. Many feet, striking the ground. The barracks city was awake.

She smelled smoke, it was laced with the scent of roasting animal flesh. Beneath the smoke were other smells, the stink of many men living together with animals inside closed walls.

She uncoiled herself like a snake and crawled to the edge of the tangled trees. Peering through the spaces between their vicious thorny branches she saw the barracks city gates stood open. Slaves pulling carts went in, came out, leaving and joining the stream of travelers toiling up and down the Pinnacle Road.

A group of warriors, their god braids heavy with solid gold beads, their bodies protected with leather vests blazed bright and bold with the godsnake of Et-Raklion, long spears in one hand, rode their lean striped and spotted horses onto the road, then swung them onto a smaller track that looked to lead around the hillside. The warriors were laughing, there was no scent of danger about them. Perhaps they were just exercising those horses, or exercising themselves.

The smoke from the roast-fires smelled so good. Her belly rumbled, demanding food. She crawled back into her secret space and emptied her food-sack. Five small loaves, five small bricks of cheese. One flask of water. Since leaving the village her body had been spoilt, it had grown used to lots of food and drink. In the village she had survived on less meat in two days than Abajai gave her in one highsun meal. She could make her bread and cheese last many, many meals if she became again, for a little time, that starving she-brat from the village.

She took the cook's knife and one loaf of bread and sliced it into six pieces. She did the same with a brick of cheese. One piece of bread, one piece of cheese at newsun, one piece of bread, one piece of cheese at lowsun. This food would last her fourteen highsuns, and one newsun. She had flesh on her bones now. It would be enough. Between now and when her food was gone the god would guide her into the barracks. She did not doubt that. She would never doubt the god.

Her supply of water would not last as long as the food. Men died fast without water, she had seen it in the savage north. She would not die like that. She would leave her safe place sometime between lowsun and newsun, she would find water and refill her leather flask. It would be safe to do that, the god would keep her hidden.

Hekat ate her piece of bread and her piece of cheese, and stored the rest safely in her food-sack. She sipped some water from her leather flask and carefully replaced its stopper. Then she crawled back to the edge of her secret space, to watch the gates into the barracks city.

By now, Retoth would know she was gone from Abajai's villa. Abajai would know, and stupid Yagji. Would they look for her? She didn't know. But if they did they would never find her. They would never look here, on Raklion's Pinnacle. She was dead to them. They were dead to her. Abajai, who had called her precious, he was dead to her forever.

He'd called her precious, he'd called her beautiful. She *was* beautiful. The mirror had shown her that. It was the only time Abajai hadn't lied. She was beautiful in her face, she was beautiful in her body. There was nothing she could do about her body . . . but her face?

Frowning, Hekat thought of her treacherous face. Its beauty had sold her to Abajai. In time that beauty would have given him gold, when he in turn sold her to someone else. She did not want a beautiful face. Not if that meant she was precious to Abajai, and Yagji, to all the men who sold beautiful girls for gold. In the barracks city, among the warriors, her beautiful face would be a curse. No warrior would let her stay there, a she-brat with a beautiful face. Some man would claim her, he would sell her for gold. To be safe in the barracks she must not be beautiful. To get into the barracks at all, she must not be beautiful.

She took her scorpion amulet from around her neck and held it on her palm.

Help me, god. Show me how to take away my beautiful face. Tell me how to get into the barracks.

The village godspeaker said no mortal could talk direct with the god. Only a godspeaker could hear it, only a godspeaker knew its will. Once she had believed him. Now she thought he spoke a lie, as all men spoke lies to ignorant she-brats. She heard the god. She knew its will. It had blinded its godspeaker to her in the street. She had offered herself to it, and it had accepted.

Quietly she sat with her legs crossed and her spine straight, the carved black scorpion crouching on her skin.

Tell me . . . tell me . . . tell me . . .

From the depths of her waiting mind, the god plucked free a memory. She remembered the beautiful slave-boy Vortka, gone with the godspeaker of Et-Nogolor. "*I was sold because the god took my father and gave my mother to another man. He had his own sons. He did not want my mother's son.*"

This was a story that could serve her now. She wasn't born a slave, the man had sold her and made her a slave but he was free and she was born free too, in Mijak's savage north. She could twist that slave-boy Vortka's story. Make it a story about her instead. The warriors would believe it.

But Vortka's story could not make her ugly.

She opened her eyes and looked at the scorpion amulet on her palm. The sleeve of her tunic was pushed up her arm, she saw the scratches the thorns had made as she forced her way into this secret space. She touched her face, felt the dried blood and scratches on her cheeks, across her nose, on her brow. Scratches were not beautiful. Scratches, if they were deep enough, could leave a scar. She had seen it, on the man's sons who cut and scratched themselves as they snake-danced on the edge of The Anvil.

Hekat looked at the cook's sharp knife.

It hurt so much she nearly cursed the god. The cook's knife sliced her cleanly, it sliced her flesh like it was fresh ripe peach. She cut her cheeks, her chin, her forehead, her nose. She cut her beauty till none of it was left. Her blood flowed like a river, it washed away that beauty, it washed away the gold Abajai saw in her face.

When she was cut enough, when even without a mirror to look in she knew she was ugly, she sat in painful silence until the weeping blood dried. Then she curled up in her secret space, the scorpion amulet in her fist, and went to sleep. A fever rose in her, sleep became a torment, she tossed and shivered, she dreamed the god's voice.

You are Hekat, precious and beautiful. You are the god's slave, you live for its purpose. The god is in you, you are in the god's eye.

*   *   *

A long time passed before she woke. When once more she opened her eyes, the world was in darkness, the god-moon and his wife boldly walked the sky. Her belly was hollow, her cut face puffed and swollen. It hurt when she touched it, dried blood flaking from her skin. The cuts in her face were cobbling together, lumps and ridges and soft wet wounds.

She had no idea how many highsuns she had slept through.

Her body felt trembly, she ate a piece of bread and a piece of cheese, even though eating hurt her face. She drank all the water in her leather flask, then took it with her as she fought her way out to the open hillside. Alone beneath the night sky she crept her way around the barracks wall and counted five closed narrow doors that might give her entrance. She found a water trough for the warriors' horses along the track leading away from the barracks. She drank from it, then filled her leather flask to the top.

No-one saw her. No-one heard her. The world thought she was dead, a spirit walking, and looked straight through her to the stars.

When all her bread and cheese was eaten, and the cuts in her face were healed and dry, she crawled out of the thorny trees' protection for the last time and walked in the newsun light to the barracks wall. Her skin was dirty, her body stank, her tunic and pantaloons were filthy, ripped and stained to stiffness with old dried blood. She looked like a she-brat who'd been running forever. She knew she was anything but *beautiful*.

It was exactly how she wanted to look. She thought

even Abajai would not know her now. Yagji would walk past her in the street, his fat face wrinkled, moaning his complaints.

The barracks' large gates weren't yet open, they didn't open till two fingers past newsun. But the other doors in the barracks walls opened earlier than that, she had seen it in the days she'd sat and waited. She walked around the wall till she found the first open door and looked through it into the barracks city.

She saw pens of goats and sheep, she saw crates of chickens, she saw slaughtered calves hanging on hooks and tubs of gizzards, overflowing. A row of tents, plain brown, not striped and pretty like Abajai's Trader tent, marched up and down, she could see nothing past them. The ground was bare in places, beaten hard and flat by many feet. Coarse grey-green grass grew in patches. The air was thick with animal smells, with blood stink, with shouted voices from beyond the row of tents. The goats and sheep bleated, the chickens cackled, from somewhere else came the lowing of cattle, the bawling of calves. Scrawny dogs quarreled and hunted for scraps to eat.

A young boy stood beside the caged chickens. His god-braids were stubby and he wore no silver godbells. One braid was scarlet, so he was a slave. He wore nothing but a loincloth and a chipped dog-tooth amulet round his neck. He held a cleaver in one hand and a chicken in the other, he was trying to lay the chicken on a chopping block and cut off its head. The chicken was squawking and flapping its wings, the boy was afraid of it. He struck it with a clumsy blow and cut off a finger instead of its head. The chicken cackled and ran away.

A huge man came out of a tent to see what all the

shrieking was for. He saw the boy with his blood-spurting finger and smacked him hard across his ear.

"Idiot fool!" the big man shouted. "Can't even cut off a chicken's head? What use are you when I'm short-handed already?"

The boy was clutching his bleeding stump, he wasted a river of water down his face. Hekat stepped from outside to inside, she crossed the threshold into the barracks. She picked up the cleaver the fool slave-boy had dropped, she snatched a chicken from the nearest crate and cut off its head with a single blow.

The boy stopped crying and the big man stared. "Who are you, you ugly brat?" he demanded. "What do you do here, killing my chicken?"

She held out the chicken's twitching corpse. "You wanted a chicken killed. I killed one for you. I am Hekat of Et-Nogolor."

The big man laughed as he took the dead twitching chicken. "Are you now, brat? What happened to your face? Looks like a hunting cat wanted you for dinner."

She had to look a long way up to his eyes. He was the biggest man she had ever seen. "My father married a woman who hated me for my beauty. My father died soon after. The woman who hated me cut off my godbraids, she cut up my face, she said she would sell me and see me die a wretched slave. I ran away from that woman. I ran away to Et-Raklion, Mijak's city of cities. I can read, and I can write, and I can kill chickens with a single blow. I will serve the city Et-Raklion. I will serve Raklion, its glorious warlord. I will serve you, if you will let me. If I can stay here, in these barracks."

The big man looked down at her. Blood dripped from

the chicken's neck, puddling by his feet. "Ran away from a miserable bitch, did you?" he said. He had a meaty face, his lips were thick, his nose was flat and his teeth were crooked. He wore seven amulets in his ears. "What's to say you won't run away from this place, too? Et-Raklion can he a miserable bitch and I was born and bred here, Hekat of Et-Nogolor."

She met his suspicious glare unflinching. "The god sees my heart. My heart is in its eye. It knows Hekat will stay, it knows Hekat will serve." She shrugged. "Hekat has nowhere else to go."

The big man looked at the chicken she had killed. He looked at the boy with two thumbs, seven fingers and a bleeding stump. "Get to a barracks healer, idiot, he can dip that in hot pitch." The slave-boy ran off, still sobbing with his stupid pain. "Hekat of Et-Nogolor," the big man said, looking at her again. His eyes were narrow, wondering. "Can I trust you?"

"Hekat of Et-Raklion," she told him. "I do not know Et-Nogolor."

The big man's eyes went wide, and then he laughed. "Hekat of Et-Raklion. Kill me all these chickens. Pluck them and gut them and spit them for roasting. Then we will talk about you serving me and the god in Mijak's city of cities."

She looked around. There was the tub for chicken heads and gizzards. There was the big sack for all their plucked feathers. There was the spit, threaded already. The chickens sat in their fastened cages, shitting and clucking and waiting to die.

"My name is Nadik. Fetch me when you're done," said the big man, and gave her back the chicken she'd killed.

As he walked away towards his tent, Hekat lifted her head and looked to the godpost at the distant top of Raklion's Pinnacle.

You have chosen me, she told the god. *You have brought me to your city Et-Raklion. Now you must show me why I am brought . . . and what it is I will do for you here.*

PART TWO

CHAPTER TEN

Raklion, son of Ragilik, beleaguered warlord of Et-Raklion, closed his eyes and released a silent sigh as his high godspeaker's rage scorched his skin like the god's wrathful breath.

"Nogolor warlord's insult must not go on breathing, Raklion," Nagarak thundered. "Et-Nogolor's Daughter was godpromised to you, not Bajadek. Why do you stand here in your palace, in the sunshine? Why do you not lead your ten thousand warriors to the gates of Et-Nogolor and demand the city's Daughter as was promised in the god's eye?"

Raklion swallowed annoyance. Keeping his back turned and his voice calm, because shouting would only inflame the man further, he said, "If I am the one insulted, Nagarak, am I not the one who decides if the insult breathes, or must be smothered by ten thousand warriors?"

Nagarak stood behind him, in the shadowed doorway to the balcony of his private palace apartments. "You think my godspeaker pride is slighted." The high godspeaker's displeasure filled the measured space between them. "You think my tongue is dipped in spite."

Raklion shrugged. "Et-Nogolor's Daughter is still un-blooded, her body cannot yet ripen with child. She has not left her father's palace, she is not taken by Bajadek warlord. I hear rumors, I am told certain things, but no godpromised oaths are broken, Nagarak. I do not know Nogolor intends to give his girl-child to Bajadek. If I treat rumor as fact and ride with my warriors to Et-Nogolor, to take the Daughter *before* she is blooded, then *I* am the oathbreaker. *I* am the one who shatters the treaty with Nogolor. Surely that is Bajadek's desire, he desires to provoke me into unwise action. He schemes to make of me a dishonorable man. Should I give him satisfaction? I think I should not."

Nagarak stepped closer. "What you should do, Raklion, is listen to your high godspeaker. While you stand on your honor Bajadek drips poison into Nogolor's ear. Nogolor listens, he is a weak warlord."

Raklion glanced over his shoulder. "Weak or not he is a warlord with his own high godspeaker, who talks to him as you talk to me. My past is no secret, Nagarak. Perhaps his high godspeaker says I am not fit for Et-Nogolor's Daughter."

"Not fit?" echoed Nagarak. He sounded baffled. "Warlord, are you ailing? I made the sacrifices. I read the omens. Et-Nogolor's Daughter is meant for *you*. Here is mischief brewed by a godspeaker of Et-Nogolor who has lost his way in the god's piercing eye. He listens to the whispers of earthbound men . . . or demons."

Moving to the edge of his palace balcony, Raklion looked down at the city sprawled about the Pinnacle's base. His sunsoaked city, Et-Raklion the glorious, his concubine and his curse. Master of every creature who lived here, in truth he was their slave and slave to the savage demands of his god with no name. The great Raklion warlord: born a fruit of the city's vine, steeped and pulped in his vinegar history.

Aieee, the god see me. Fingers gripping the balcony's red stone balustrade till they were bloodless, Raklion bowed his aching head. He was forty-nine and had no son. His past was a shadow, stitched to his heels, it followed him into every corner and was visible in the darkest night.

Three warlords' daughters have I killed in trying to bring forth a living son. I have sired seven and the god has inhaled them all as smoke. Is it to be wondered the warlords give their women to anyone but me?

He turned, resting his knotted spine against the stone railing, and looked into Nagarak's cold, hard face. "It is possible you misread the omens."

Nagarak was young to be a high godspeaker. Barely past forty. He was bones and skin and godbraids, his burning eyes were fixed upon the god. The black scorpion pectoral strapped to his naked chest glowed with flecks of gold and crimson, with the fiery passion of his devotion. Three seasons before he had walked unaided from the godhouse scorpion pit, the god's choice for its next high godspeaker in Et-Raklion. Eight of his fellow godspeakers had died in that choosing, deluded by demons and lost to hell.

He said, "Raklion warlord, I did not misread the omens. The god intends Et-Nogolor's Daughter for you. To permit Bajadek to entice her away is defiance of the god's will. Do not defy it. All warlords are men unto the god. Men are stones, to be blasted to powder with its lightest breath."

Raklion nodded. He often felt like breath-blasted

stone. Long since he'd ceased to ask why the god took his women, took his sons, reduced his future to a crucible of blackened infant bones. All his prayers in the godhouse, the sacrifices he paid for, the tasking of his penitent flesh, none of that had made a difference. The god still refused him, he did not know why. Unless a man was a god-speaker chosen, the god was unknowable. And even then he sometimes wondered . . .

He also wondered if Nagarak understood what it was to be a warlord. Nagarak was wedded to a black stone scorpion, he had no use for fleshly things. "Do you tell me the god desires I should go to war?" he demanded. "Do you tell me I should smite the brother-city treaty with my hammered fist, smash it to shards like a clay pot and send the pieces to Nogolor in a leather pouch? If I do that, Nagarak, he will run to Bajadek like a man runs to his lover. They will kiss and they will fondle, I will have driven him into Bajadek's eager embrace. Et-Nogolor's Daughter will slip through my fingers as though the god-promise was never made."

Nagarak banged his fist on his pectoral. "And if you do *nothing*, Raklion, Nogolor will take it as a sign of weakness, he will turn to Bajadek warlord's strength. He and Bajadek do not hide their flirting, they flirt at highsun so you will *see*."

"Nagarak, I have said already this is rumor unproven, I *cannot*—"

"No, not rumor. Truth from Trader Abajai. Do you *distrust* this Trader now, when for godmoons uncounted you have swallowed his words like wine?"

Raklion turned away, frowning. Trader Abajai was a useful man who dropped information like kernels of corn.

Not all had sprouted over the seasons but a wise warlord picked up each one and inspected it, to be safe.

"I do not distrust the Trader," he said at last. Particularly as, in the four fat godmoons since speaking with Abajai in the palace, others with business in Et-Nogolor had let him know they too had seen Bajadek's warriors freely riding.

"Abajai has also told you of Mijak's wide browning," Nagarak continued, relentless. "Of which we have already spoken, and have many eyewitness reports to confirm. Now I say to *you*, warlord, the god tells me in the godpool, your brother warlords in their browning lands look on Et-Raklion with hungry eyes and hungrier bellies. If you do not fight for Et-Nogolor's Daughter *they* will say you are weak. They will think to feed their bellies on the fat of Et-Raklion, they will call secret treaty in the Heart of Mijak and plot war against you." Again his fist struck the black scorpion pectoral. His godbraids trembled, so many godbells and amulets it was hard to see the hair. "I tell you this, Raklion. A warning from the god."

"And what does the god say of Mijak's browning?" Raklion said. "Anything? Does it tell you why the underground waters slowly recede from my brother warlords' lands, leaving only *my* lands green and fertile?"

Nagarak's eyes narrowed to slits. "Not even a high godspeaker demands answers from the god. When you are meant to know its reasons it will tell me, and I will tell you."

It was not enough. "I must know the god's purpose, Nagarak. It seems to me I am punished with a lack of sons, yet favored with green and growing lands. Have I displeased the god or have I not? *Tell* me! How can I be warlord if I do not know?"

"You undergo a test of faith," said Nagarak, after a moment. "To be endured without question. To question is to displease the god. A man who questions is food for demons, his godspark will be eaten, his flesh torn apart in the god's eye."

Throttling fear, Raklion pressed fingers to his throbbing eyes. *I am faithful, I do not question.* The browning of Mijak was a problem he must put aside, he had more immediate concerns. "And in the matter of Et-Nogolor's Daughter. If I ride against Nogolor, spill the blood of a brother warlord without a sin committed against me, if I spill my warriors' blood in that same spilling, do I not also displease the god? Nagarak high godspeaker, hear my heart. I am a true warlord of Et-Raklion. The scars of my body attest to this. But unless you say to me there is an omen that I *must* go to war with Nogolor warlord, and you show me that omen, I will not take ten thousand warriors to Et-Nogolor. I will not take so few as ten."

Nagarak stiffened. "Warlord—"

"How can I, Nagarak?" he persisted. "How can I risk death in a sinful war when no son of mine lives to give his name to this city? Surely the god would strike me down if I flouted its law so openly. If I die with no son, Nagarak, I abandon Et-Raklion and all its rich farmlands, its vineyards, its villages, its rivers, its springs, its cool lakes, its herds of horses and cattle, its wild birds flying, its people, *my* people, I abandon them to an unknown future. You say the warlords are hungry for Et-Raklion? If I am not alive to protect it, Et-Raklion will be devoured! *Is* there an omen?"

"There is no omen," said Nagarak sourly, after a long sunfilled silence. "Yet."

Raklion felt his clutched belly loosen. "Here is what I will call an omen, Nagarak. Let the god tell you when the Daughter is blooded. If Nogolor warlord does not send her to me, if after her blooding Bajadek's warriors ride free in his lands or ride with Bajadek warlord to Nogolor's city, *then* will I say the god sends me to war. *Then* will Raklion and his warhost ride to Et-Nogolor and take what was promised, spilling blood if he must."

Nagarak frowned. "That is an omen from the god." He nodded sharply. "The god see you, Raklion warlord. The god see you in its eye."

"The god see you in its eye, Nagarak high godspeaker," Raklion replied, dismissing him with all formality.

Alone, he paced his balcony for a small time, then struck the hammer to his chamber's bronze summoning gong. "Send at once to Hanochek warleader," he commanded the answering slave. "I would see him in my eye."

When Hanochek came at last into his warlord's presence he was filthy with dust and sweat. Custom decreed no man might stand before a warlord rank with toil, but Hanochek was rash and sometimes careless of custom.

"Warlord!" he said, his knuckled fist pressed to his leather breast. The godsnake blazoned there winked and leered. "I was thinking you had forgotten my name."

Raklion smiled. He and Hanochek shared no blood-tie yet so alike were they in thought and feeling they might have slithered from a single womb. Twelve seasons the younger, the difference never noticed, Hanochek was his trusted warleader, they led the warhost side by side. Hanochek was brother to him as his own dead blood brother had never been.

"No," he said. "But did you forget the purpose of water?"

Hanochek considered his unkempt body, short and muscular and dangerous as a knife. "I did. When the palace slave presented your summons I forgot everything, including how to ride a horse. I ran here till my legs begged for mercy. My stallion waits yet with an empty saddle." He was grinning, so sure he was in no danger of rebuke. "I thought making you wait was the greater offense."

"You were training?"

Hanochek nodded. "I was training."

"How is my warhost?"

"Longing for the sound of your voice, your face in its eye." Hanochek's gaze dimmed with shadows. "You have been many highsuns in your palace."

Raklion gestured at the balcony's chairs. "Come sit with me in the sunshine, Hano. My old bones need the warmth and it seems an age since we have spoken."

"Old bones," scoffed Hanochek. "If your bones are old, then so must mine be, and mine are the bones of a stripling youth!"

"You contradict your warlord?" Raklion teased, dropping onto spotted horsehide cushions. "Brave warrior indeed." Beside him stood a potted fig tree, drooping with ripe fruit. He plucked four soft sweet figs and held them out to his friend. Hano took them and settled into the balcony's other chair.

"My thanks," he said, around a moist mouthful. "Training works up a hearty appetite."

Raklion plucked four plump figs for himself and let his head fall back, content to hold them for the moment. "I am not *that* old, Hano. I remember."

Hanochek ate swiftly, like a greedy boy. When his last fig was swallowed he belched and wiped sticky fingers on his linen training tunic, adding to its stains. "So, Raklion warlord. When do we ride for Et-Nogolor's Daughter?"

Now it was time to eat a fig. Raklion chewed slowly, letting his hooded gaze rest on the city. The view from his palace was like a woman's stroking fingers, it never failed to smooth his brow. Et-Raklion city may well be his concubine and his curse but still he loved it, to the very last pebble and drop of spilled ale. He loved its roofs and windows, its alleys and wide streets, its districts and its slaves. It was the city of cities, it deserved his devotion.

"Why should I ride for Et-Nogolor's Daughter?" he asked, showing no temper. "She will ride to me soon enough, when she is blooded."

Hano's gaze sharpened. He had keen eyes, deeply set in his flat, broad face. "Did you summon me to play games, Raklion? You are the warlord, you hear whispers in the dark. I hear them. Your warhost hears them. Even the slaves in the barracks hear them. Your warhost is angry, it feels insulted."

That word again. "Nagarak high godspeaker reads omens in a lamb's tongue," he countered. "Do these whispers of yours shout louder than that?"

"Has the high godspeaker given you an omen?"

He ate a second fig. "No. Like you, Nagarak gives me warlike advice."

"I am a warrior," said Hano, shrugging. "I have no other advice to give."

"I know." Raklion slid his gaze sideways. "You think we should lead the warhost to Et-Nogolor?"

"I do." Hano stared. "You disagree?"

Raklion did not answer, brooding. Hano waited, brooding with him. At length he stirred, his troubled gaze lingering on the rich green carpet of grapevines growing beyond the city. "Nogolor is a godpromised husband tempted by a whore. He thinks to fuck the whore and escape his promised wife's anger." He looked at Hano. "But thinking is not fucking. A man may think of many things, but until he acts he has committed no sin."

"True," admitted Hano. "But if the promised wife knows he thinks of fucking the whore and says nothing to him of her knowing, does she not give that godpromised husband her blessing to dally outside their oath?"

A sharp question. "A man may suspect another man's thoughts, Hano, but only the god can know his heart. Only its godspeakers can point and say, this man is for stoning, he breaks the god's law. Smiting is of the god, not man."

"You could discourage the whore, Raklion. No-one can question Bajadek's intent."

Raklion shook his head. "Bajadek has committed no sin. It is not sinful to ride invited through the lands of another warlord. He has made me no godpromise, Nogolor's word to me is nothing to him. He cares only for his own portion, all warlords are alike in this."

"Raklion . . ." Hano's frustration knotted his voice.

"Bajadek warlord tempts Nogolor to oathbreaking. He must not go unpunished for that. You must—"

"I must do what is best for Et-Raklion! Is bloodshed best? A broken treaty? Abandoned trade, unsettled borders, disrupted days like a string of beads, are these things best for my city's people, for the people of my Et-Raklion lands?"

Hano looked at him. "A healthy son is best for Et-Raklion. And for that you must fuck a wife of warlord bloodlines."

Words like a spear-point, piercing him to death. Raklion pushed away from his horsehide cushions, out of his chair to the length of the balcony.

"I know that, Hano," he said, and looked at his clenched fist. Ripe fig dripped between his fingers, the clean Pinnacle air was sweetened with fig juice. He made a face and smeared his hand along the stone balustrade. "And I know it is likely we will soon be at war, if Nogolor warlord stops thinking and acts, if he breaks his god-promise to me and gives the Daughter to Bajadek instead. That is why I summoned you, warleader. Nagarak in the godhouse awaits the god's omen. Should it come, the warhost must be ready to ride."

"It is ready," said Hano. He sounded pleased. Relieved. "Come see for yourself. Leave your palace, come to the barracks and mingle with your warriors. Dance some time on the training field with them. You have god-speakers to manage Et-Raklion, they can manage it without you for a time. But only you can manage the warhost. How long is it since you set foot in the barracks?"

He had to think. "Two godmoons, twelve highsuns. You are right, warleader. Nagarak's godspeakers do not need my help in counting taxes and smiting sinners. My place is in the barracks, not this palace." He released a soft and sorrowful sigh. "It will hurt my heart to see my warriors, Hano. Knowing an omen will send them to war."

"Warriors fight, warlord," said Hano, brusquely. "Warriors live and die with the spear, the arrow, the sword, the knife. The god gives them fierceness, it drinks their blood. War is their purpose, it is their pleasure. Can you love them and deny them that?"

Raklion turned. "I do not shrink from bloodshed, Hano. I shrink from waste. From death without purpose."

"Which is why your warriors love you," said Hano. "And why they are eager to ride against Bajadek, the usurping sinner, and against Nogolor too if he proves a false friend. Now enough talking. *Come*. Ease your tired mind with sweat. Rest yourself in honest striving."

Raklion smiled, he could not help it. "Very well, Hano. *If* you promise to cease your nagging."

Hano stood and pressed a fist to his breast, his unspoken word. "Dress yourself in your finest training tunic, warlord, as I send a slave to summon your chariot. Your warriors are waiting, they will shout to see you."

Hanochek was the finest charioteer in all Et-Raklion, he knew the horses' minds as though they were his own, his touch on the reins was light and sure. The chariot horses loved him. Sheathed in thinly beaten gold, the warlord's chariot was the most beautiful in the warhost, it made a man beautiful to ride within it. Two snake-bound godposts topped with crimson scorpions guarded the chariot's occupants. Sunlight glittered on rubies and emeralds, on lapis lazuli and flaming firestone. Silver godbells sang and rang on the black horses' crimson harness, from the lip and rim of the golden chariot. Sunlight sparked on their myriad amulets.

Raklion felt the fresh breeze in his face and laughed aloud. "This is good, Hano. Do not let me stay so long in my palace again."

"I won't, I promise," said Hano, grinning. "A man cannot breathe within stone walls. Beneath the sky a man can breathe. He can breathe and he can see. Beneath the sky a man can think. He can run and throw a spear, he can sweat, he can sing."

"All that is true," said Raklion. "But alas, there is more to a warlord than sweating and singing."

Hano glanced at him. "Yes. There is worry. There are treaties. Godspeakers with questions and tally-tablets and city problems you must solve." He pulled a face. "There is Nagarak high godspeaker, who wills you to war. I confess that is curious, Raklion. War is the warlord's business, Nagarak should feed his scorpions and leave it to you."

They were alone on the road between the palace and the warriors' barracks, but Raklion thumped Hano's shoulder anyway. "Say that in company and he *will* feed his scorpions—with your stoned dead flesh."

"You do not think his warlike advice strange?"

Raklion shrugged. "Where Nagarak is concerned I do not think at all." Which was a lie, but he would not talk of high godspeakers to Hano. On some matters did a warlord hide his thoughts from all save the god. Hano was a good man but he had a warrior's heart. Straight and true like an arrow in flight, it was not made for twisting shadows.

The chariot traveled swiftly, as they drew close to the warriors' barracks. The main gates stood open, the warrior on gatekeep duty heard the chariot's wheels upon the road, heard the horses' drumming hooves and their godbells loudly singing, and came out to see who approached. She saw her warlord and waved her snakeblade in the air.

"Behold the god's chosen!" she shouted, her voice carrying clearly from the gatekeep. She rang the gate's godbell, still shouting. "Behold our warlord, Raklion warlord! The god see you, warlord, the god see you in its smiting eye!"

"Minka," said Hano softly, as he eased the chariot horses back to a walk, that they might pass the barracks godpost sedately. "Daughter of Yolen. He lost a leg in—"

"I remember Yolen," said Raklion. "When did he give a daughter to the barracks?"

"Last thin godmoon."

"Do you know her? Does Yolen breed true?"

Hano grinned. "True enough. She's sent four warriors to the healer's tent since she started her training. I have seen far worse in my time."

"Your warlord sees you, Minka," Raklion said as they passed between the barracks' open gates. "Does service in his warhost please you?"

Minka's nose had been broken already. It skewed sideways on her narrow face, left her snuffling for air. With her snakeblade safely sheathed she punched her fist against her breast. Her eyes glowed, to be noticed by her warlord was an honor. "I like it well, Raklion warlord. I will serve you to my last red drop of blood."

"A warrior's oath," he said, and nodded his pleasure as the chariot passed her by. The weight of her smile between his shoulder-blades was heavy as godsmite.

At the barracks godpost he pulled his solid gold snake-eye amulet from around his neck and dropped it in the godbowl, where it outshone the iron, the bronze, the clumsily carved carnelian. But the warriors liked to see his gold there, and so did the godspeakers sent to retrieve the warriors' offerings. The godhouse always liked to see gifts of gold.

Hano nudged him with an elbow. "Did I not tell you the warlord is missed?" he murmured.

Raklion looked up. Gathering on either side of the main road through the barracks, his beautiful warriors in their tunics and godbraids. Some had emptied their shields from leather shield-bags, they held them high and tapped their spear-butts and knife-hilts hard against them, a joyful fierce tattoo of welcome. Every mouth shouted, over and over:

"*Raklion! Raklion! Raklion!*"

Bare feet drummed against the ground, pipes whistled, while behind them Minka, daughter of Yolen, loudly sounded the barrack's godbell.

"*Raklion! Raklion! Raklion!*"

In the palace there was a brideroom, empty. A child's cot, empty. In the palace were slaves and servants and empty rooms.

"*Raklion! Raklion! Raklion!*"

Hano stopped the chariot and Raklion climbed down, he put his bare feet on the soil and walked with laughter among his warriors. His burdened heart lightened. Sunshine and shouting chased away the shadows. His warriors crowded round him, they reached out their hands, they touched his godbraids and the hem of his tunic, they welcomed him home like a long-lost brother.

"Raklion! Raklion! Raklion!"

CHAPTER ELEVEN

First of all he sparred with his spear-carriers, then watched his archers and slingshot throwers hone their skills among a herd of meat-goats. A good strike with a shot-stone would drop a goat dead with its skull crushed. No differently a man. And an arrow to the heart killed any living thing. It took much meat to feed his warhost, they practiced often in the slaughter pit and cook-slaves dragged the carcasses away.

Next he cheered a chariot race. His warhost boasted five hundred chariots, too many for racing. His charioteers drew lots, the disappointed losers gathered with him and Hano in the stands around the chariot arena and watched the chosen twenty drivers race each other with pride as the prize.

He gave the victorious charioteer Saraket a gold and onyx ring from his finger and paid fulsome compliment to Bodrik Chariot-leader, then lastly went to watch his knife-dancers. Often in battle the last desperate moments were reduced to this, to another warrior's killing eyes, the knife-blade glinting in his hand. Dirt churned to bloody mud, slippery and treacherous. Who was fastest, strongest, most determined to survive. A knife-dancer who forgot the steps was a dead man dancing on a grain of sand.

Raklion smiled to see his warriors weave and glide and leap through the set knife-dance patterns, the *hotas*, passed down from warrior to warrior from the world's first newsun. He sat on a stuffed calf-hide with Hano on another beside him and lost himself in the measured thumping of the knife-dance drum, the slow-motion sweeping of the sinuous snakeblades. Ten shells of warriors danced before him, thirty in each. The trod ground hummed beneath their feet, silver godbells sang in their swaying godbraids, they danced as one warrior beneath the sun.

Hano chuckled and nudged him, pointing through a gap in the crowd of watching warriors. "Look there, warlord. See?"

He looked. A skinny stripling child dressed in a ragged dirty tunic watched alone at the edge of the knife-dance field. Its godbraids were short and stubby, each end glued together with pitch. It stared at the knife-dancers and mirrored their sure movements through each complicated *hota*, showing promise, though its form was crude and riddled with error. It held a stick instead of a blade, but with the same amount of reverence as the warriors it echoed. The child's thin back was to him, he couldn't see its face.

Amused, Raklion watched the brat dance its way through the *hotas*. Obviously it knew them well, it did not hesitate when one shifted to another, then another, cycling through the ordered routine. After a time he stood, motioning Hano to stay seated, lifting a finger to Zapotar

Knife-dance leader as he saw the mimicking ragtag child and took a scowling step towards it.

Zapotar lowered his head and stepped back, perfectly obedient. Hano looked up at him, still smiling. "You think you have found another warrior?"

"I think to satisfy my curiosity," Raklion replied.

He threaded his way through the crowd of warriors and stopped three paces from the child. It ignored him, or was oblivious to his presence. As he watched, it attempted the supremely difficult falcon-dancing-over-the-meadow *hota*. One bare foot brushed against the other as it spun, the rhythm was ruined, the child fumbled the stick-knife and dropped it on the ground.

"*Tchut tchut tchut!*" it scolded, and bent to retrieve its pretend snakeblade. As he laughed at its crossness, the child straightened and turned.

Raklion felt the world stand still.

The child was female, a ruined beauty. Her brows were delicate, arching over deep-set eyes of clearest blue. Her lashes were long enough to cast a shadow, and extravagantly curved. Her nose was straight, thin nostrils flaring, her lips were full and blushed pale pink. Her small ears lay flat against her head, her cheekbones jutted high and haughty. Her rich dark skin shone with sweat from dancing. Laid upon that fine-boned face, a spiderweb of livid knotted scars.

His heart broke in his breast to see them.

"You like my knife-dancers, little girl?" he asked her, though she was not so little or such a girl, there were breasts beneath her dirty tunic, and hips, and long shapely legs. His loins were hot and heavy before her.

She looked him up and down. All her hair was black,

no scarlet slave-braid. She was freeborn, a citizen of Mijak. "Yours?"

He laughed. "Yes. Mine." He flicked one hand, to take in the warriors and their training fields and the distant barracks wall. "All of this is mine. I am Raklion warlord."

Her glorious eyes widened in her spoiled face. "You are the warlord of Et-Raklion?"

"I have said so. And who are you?"

"I am Hekat of Et-Raklion."

"Which means you also belong to me."

Her scarred chin lifted. "Hekat belongs to the god with no name. She is its creature, born to its will."

"All the creatures beneath the sun belongs to the god," he said, amused by her vehemence and her quaint turn of phrase. She had an unusual accent, not one he'd heard before. "And all creatures in Et-Raklion belong to me after the god. You wish to be a knife-dancer, Hekat of Et-Raklion?"

Her blue gaze shifted to his knife-dancers and their *hota*. "I wish to be a knife-dancer," she answered him. "I wish to be a charioteer. I wish to shoot an arrow, sling a shot-stone, bury my spear-point in an enemy's throat. I wish to be a warrior, warlord."

The calm declaration moved him. "And what are you now, Hekat of Et-Raklion?"

Her lips pursed in disgust. "I am a killer of chickens, I slaughter sheep."

He looked at her ragged tunic and saw the old blood-stains there. "What happened to your face?"

"My face?" She raised a hand, traced a fingertip along its raw red lines, the ridges of imperfectly healed flesh.

"My face was a curse, Raklion warlord. My beauty was a burden. It was cut away, by the will of the god."

"The god sees you in its eye, Hekat, that you could be so cut upon and yet not die."

"The god sees me in its eye always, warlord," she said. Her frank gaze glittered strangely. "And my scars see the god."

"Who cut you, Hekat?"

She shrugged. "Some woman, she is not important. I forget her name, I cannot say it."

Was that a lie? He could not tell. It did not matter. She was scarred, her beauty destroyed. That did not matter either, though he mourned its loss. Warriors had no need for beauty in the face, a warrior's beauty was speed and strength, a lust for blood, the knack of survival.

"Why should I grant your bold request, Hekat? Why should I make you a warrior of Et-Raklion?"

She looked at him with those clear blue eyes, in their depths burned a fervent flame. "Because it is the will of the god, warlord. Hear it whisper in your heart. It whispers to you: *make Hekat a warrior.*"

So much certainty in so small a body. Did the god whisper, or was that heat his stirred blood calling? Better to err on the side of caution. Any warlord who ignored the god invited disaster, triple-fold.

He looked where Zapotar Knife-dance leader waited with Hanochek, pretending not to be puzzled by his warlord talking to a bratty child. Zapotar answered his beckoning call, like a falcon to the wrist.

"Warlord?"

"This is Hekat of Et-Raklion. She wishes to be my warrior."

Zapotar frowned. "Many wish to be your warrior, warlord."

"I wish her to be my warrior also, Zapotar. I wish for her to train first with you. Seek out a godspeaker, pay for sacrifice and the proper omen-reading."

Zapotar wore battle scars the way other men wore amulets. Unlike Hekat, he'd had no beauty to ruin. His scars twitched in his cheeks as he nodded. "Warlord."

"I cannot be a knife-dancer now?" the child Hekat demanded. She sounded displeased. Bold child. Fearless child. What a warrior she would make!

"No. Not now. The timing is a matter of omen," said Raklion. "Kill me more chickens, Hekat. Slaughter me some sheep. That is service to your warlord. Zapotar will send to the cook-tents when your Knife-dance days can begin."

After a moment's thinking, she nodded. "Hekat obeys you, warlord. When I have learned the knife-dance *hotas* will you make me a charioteer? Will you give me a bow, a slingshot, a spear to thrust into your enemies' throats?"

"You have a fierce thirst for blood, child," he said, almost laughing.

There was no laughter in her face, her eyes were not the eyes of a child. "I thirst for the glory of Et-Raklion, warlord. I thirst for the glory of Mijak and the god."

He could see that. He left her watching the last of the *hotas* and returned to Hano.

"Is your curiosity satisfied, warlord?"

Raklion smiled, briefly. "My warhost stands at ten thousand and one."

"You take her as a warrior, Raklion?" said Hano, eyes

narrowing. "What are her bloodlines? Who is her sire? What woman birthed her? Where is she from?"

Hano was displeased, as warleader it was his right, his duty, to approve new warriors admitted to the warhost. "Tcha," said Raklion, gently reproving. "Do you doubt my instincts, Hanochek warleader? Am I an old man now, blind and infirm?"

"You were the one complaining about old bones," Hano muttered. "Warlord—"

"Enough," he said. "She is chosen. I am the warlord, do you presume to chide?"

"No," said Hano, and lowered his hot gaze. "Forgive me, warlord. I was surprised."

Not as surprised as I am, Hano.

But he did not say that. For all they were best friends and as close as brothers, there was a distance between them. There was a distance between the warlord and every man, woman and child he protected. More and more frequently, he found it oppressive.

If only my blood brother had not died. If only I were a plain, simple man.

The *hotas* ended. Hanochek stood. "Will you join us in feasting, Raklion warlord?" he said, strictly formal. "Your warhost would be honored."

Raklion frowned. "I should go to the godhouse."

"The godhouse isn't going anywhere," said Hano, his formality softened, his moment of displeasure passing. "Stay. We have missed you. I have missed you. Feast with your warriors, who will soon ride to war."

Nagarak would send word if the god spoke in omens tonight. He could eat here, or in the palace. Alone, or with good company, among his beloved warriors.

"I will stay," he decided, and was warmed by Hano's smothered delight. As he walked from the knife-dance field at Hano's side he flicked a last glance over his shoulder but the child Hekat was gone now, returned to her cook-tent and the animal killing that awaited her there. He felt a twinge of disappointment and scoffed at himself. *Foolish old man, she is just a brat like countless others. She will be swallowed by your warhost, you will forget her between now and the next fat godmoon.*

His loins, remembering, told him he lied.

Hano said something, and he abandoned uncomfortable thought to pay attention.

Highsuns passed, with no word of war omens from the godhouse. The godmoon waned thin, waxed fat, waned thin again. Raklion waited, he resisted the urge to send word to Nogolor, to sweetly inquire how the Daughter prospered, if there came any sign that her blood-time was on her. He ceased his haunting of the palace, he trained with his warriors, conducted city business, attended sacrifice, he winnowed more kernels of passed-on information, he bided and bided and bided his time.

Five godmoons and eight highsuns after receiving report from Trader Abajai, Nagarak summoned him to his presence.

Only a high godspeaker might send for a warlord as though he were an ordinary man. Raklion obeyed the summons, they met in private, in Nagarak's austere audience chamber at the top of the four-storey godhouse.

"The Daughter is blooded," said Nagarak abruptly. He was never one for easing into conversation. "The god has told me in the godpool. Take your warriors, warlord, and ride to claim her."

Only a warlord did not kneel in audience with the high godspeaker. Not unless it was a tasking. Raklion looked at the chamber's bare stone walls, its bare stone floor, the altar at the window, the stone desk piled high with tablets. At Nagarak on his stone chair, bathed in warm light. A bleak room. A stark room. A room with no comfort, no concession to flesh. So many times had he been here, yet each visit came as an unpleasant shock.

Here is Nagarak's godspark, revealed. No need for anything but the god.

"I will not ride yet," he said, content to stand. Which was convenient, since Nagarak provided no other seat. "Let Nogolor have his chance to inform me. Let him honor his godpromise, and send the Daughter here. That was the oath we made. He knows it is my expectation."

"And we know he has no intention of meeting it."

Raklion shrugged. "Do we? I know nothing, Nagarak. I have only suspicion. I will give him twenty highsuns. That is enough time for godhouse rites, and for the Daughter to be escorted to my palace."

Nagarak was unhappy, but this was warlord business. "Twenty highsuns," he said, his expression grudging. "But not one finger longer, Raklion. After twenty highsuns this becomes a godhouse matter. If the Daughter does not come I will ride with you to Et-Nogolor, that the god might show Nogolor and his high godspeaker the error of their ways."

Suppressing a shudder, Raklion nodded. "We are agreed then, Nagarak high godspeaker. We wait twenty highsuns before we ride."

Twenty highsuns passed, Et-Nogolor's Daughter did not come. At newsun on the twenty-first day, after sacrifice and solemn anointing, Raklion led a warhost of one thousand warriors to Et-Nogolor, to claim from its warlord his godpromised wife.

Hekat traveled with Nadik and ten other cook-brats in the cook's wagon at the rear of the warhost. At its head, Raklion warlord rode a splendid blue spotted stallion. He was not a young man, threads of silver glittered in his godbraids. His body was strong, though, his spine sat straight above his hips, he walked with the loose gait of a fighting man.

At his right hand rode the warleader Hanochek, at his left Et-Raklion's high godspeaker Nagarak. She'd only caught a glimpse of Nagarak, she knew he wore a giant stone scorpion strapped to his scrawny chest, and had heard enough among the chattering warriors to know he was feared above all men. Above all godspeakers, more than any high godspeaker in living memory.

She wondered if Nagarak knew of her. If the god had told him of its plans for her. She sometimes wanted to know them so badly her head ached and her belly twisted.

The god will tell you, chosen Hekat. It will tell you in its time.

She traveled in the cook's wagon because she wasn't yet a knife-dancer, no word of omens had come from Zapotar. She was losing patience, she suspected Zapotar of interference, of dawdling in the hope she would be forgotten.

I will not be forgotten. I am here for the god.

She would wait until they returned to Et-Raklion, then

she would go to the godhouse herself. She would pay a bronze coin to the godspeakers and the god would tell *her* it was time. So much for Zapotar, *he* would be beaten or worse for daring to thwart the god's desire.

At lowsun, after the march towards Et-Nogolor stopped and the warhost made its camp and attended sacrifice, she ran up and down the lines with bowls of salted goat and cornmush. She loved the warriors, they were tall and proud, they oiled their muscles and sharpened their snakeblades, they smiled at her when she handed them dinner, they knew who she was. Word had spread swiftly of the barracks brat who'd caught the warlord's eye, who was soon to be a knife-dancer. She was young, she was ugly, her face was full of scars. They were not threatened, they found her amusing.

They would not always, but that could wait.

Raklion warlord was one she did not serve. He had his own body slaves to attend him, he sat with Hanochek warleader and together they made warlord plans. She did not serve the high godspeaker, either, but she was not sorry. He made her skin crawl. He ate with the godspeakers riding with them, they kept to themselves, just like the godspeakers in the caravan from Et-Nogolor.

She finished running bowls of food up and down the lines of warriors and returned to the cooks' camp where it was her duty now to clean the pots and pans and make everything ready for breakfast at newsun. This was just like being on the road with Abajai and Yagji, except for the complaining.

She wondered about the Traders, sometimes. Had they ever tried to look for her? Had they given her up as dead? Had they beaten that stupid slave Retoth, as he deserved?

It didn't matter. That was her dead life, like the village in the north. She would be a warrior soon. That was her next life. She was eager for it like the barracks dogs slavered for blood and chicken gizzards.

When her camp work was done she took a lit torch and the sharpened stick she'd brought with her from Et-Raklion; she crouched on a patch of smoothed dirt and practiced her letters. Reading and writing were important, if they weren't Abajai would never have spent coin on them. She would not lose her reading and writing. They made her different, they made her special.

I will serve the god better if I read and write.

Serving the god was her purpose in the world.

At the border godpost between Et-Raklion and Et-Nogolor, Nagarak made sacrifice for the journey's good outcome. Raklion warlord drank the hot bull-calf blood, he cut his breast with the sacrificial knife and let his own blood drip into the sacrifice bowl. Hekat was impressed. That was a true sacrifice, to give the god his own blood. Raklion was strong, he was proud, he was a man who loved the god. She would serve him as his warrior and what must come, would come.

They reached Et-Nogolor city ten highsuns after crossing the border. In that traveling time they saw no other warriors, from Et-Nogolor or Et-Bajadek. They saw workers in the fields of wheat and corn, cattle and horses grazing the dry plain, they saw carts in the distance rolling to and from the villages of Nogolor warlord. That was all. Even when they rode past Et-Nogolor's barracks, squatting so close to the city, no warriors spilled out to offer them war.

Raklion warlord was clever, he timed their arrival for two fingers past newsun, when Et-Nogolor city was stirring at first light. The warlord and his thousand chosen warriors did not try to pass through the city gates. To enter uninvited would be an act of war, Hekat had learned that much from listening to Raklion's warriors. Raklion warlord's purpose was not war, not yet. Not unless he was refused his godpromised wife, the Daughter of Et-Nogolor.

As the warhost halted outside the gates, Hekat looked at the city with contempt. After Et-Raklion, Et-Nogolor was nothing, a hillock. She remembered herself as she was the last time she'd been here, small and slaved and owned by Abajai. Ignorant of her place in the god's eye.

She does not matter. That child is dead.

Raklion warlord and Nagarak high godspeaker rode to meet Et-Nogolor's Gatekeeper. Behind them the warhost sat on their striped and spotted and solid brown and red horses, they held their spears at rest beside them and told rude jokes. A rising breeze tossed the horses' manes and tails, tossed the warriors' godbraids and shivered the air with the songs of silver godbells. Hekat sat in the cook's wagon with Nadik and longed to be one of the thousand, with a horse and a spear to fill Et-Nogolor's warriors with fear.

The Gatekeeper who left Et-Nogolor's gate to meet with Raklion and Nagarak was the same one who'd let Abajai and Yagji and the slave train enter his city. He met with Raklion and Nagarak halfway between the gate and the warriors, too far away for their talking to be heard. After a little time the Gatekeeper bowed and walked back to Et-Nogolor's gate as Raklion warlord and his high godspeaker returned to the warhost.

"Warriors of Et-Raklion!" the warlord said, bold and mighty on his spotted blue stallion. "Word is sent to Nogolor warlord, here is his treaty-brother Raklion come to claim his godpromised wife. Let us play awhile as we wait for her."

The warhost shouted raucous approval. Beside her in the cook's wagon, Nadik laughed. "Ah, he's a wily one, that Raklion warlord. Warriors dancing on his doorstep will give Nogolor warlord fat to chew."

"Will the warriors of Et-Raklion and Et-Nogolor do battle, Nadik?" she asked him.

He glanced at her. He wasn't happy she would soon be a warrior, she was the best chicken-killer he had. But he was only a cook, his want did not matter.

"You'd like that, wouldn't you? Bloodthirsty brat." He shrugged. "The god will decide. It is not my business, it is not yours yet. Pots and seasoning, that is our business."

"Yes, Nadik," she said, and asked no more questions. He was like Retoth, a small nothing person who left no footprints on the world.

Not like Raklion.

Not like me.

Horses bred in the lands of Et-Raklion were wiry and tough, they could dance without rest from newsun to newsun. Hekat sat in the cook-wagon with Nadik and the other cook-brats, smiling she watched Hanochek warleader and Raklion's warriors as they danced upon the plain with their tough wiry horses. Running, leaping, vaulting in and out of their saddles, flipping from horse to horse and back again, riding in pairs, in fours, in eights, in tens, weaving patterns on the dry grass, tossing knives and spears to each other as they passed knee to knee at a pounding gallop.

Raklion warlord watched them in silence, on his spotted stallion beside his high godspeaker whose clasping stone scorpion flashed black fire in the light.

One finger past highsun the bell in Et-Nogolor's godhouse sounded. It pealed over the city, over the brown plain, over Raklion warlord's dancing warriors.

Raklion warlord held up his fist. As one horse, one rider, his warleader and his warhost wheeled to a stop. All eyes looked to the gates of Et-Nogolor.

The godhouse bell rang out again. Et-Nogolor's Gatekeeper stepped from the shadows, he sounded a booming ram's horn banded with gold. Raklion warlord with Nagarak beside him rode halfway towards the gatekeep and stopped.

Through the gates of Et-Nogolor rode two tall men, on horses pale as desert sand. Behind them in a snake-spine two horses wide, warriors of Et-Nogolor.

Nadik let out his breath in a hissing stream. "Nogolor warlord!" he whispered, pointing to the man with a headdress full of feathers. His fingers curled round his snakefang amulet. "The other is his high godspeaker, he wears the scorpion pectoral, see?"

Hekat leaned forward, smiling and fierce, as Et-Nogolor's warlord and his high godspeaker led his warriors out of the city.

Show me, god. Show me which warlord you favor in your eye.

It would be Raklion, she was sure already. And she

also knew that what happened here, what was done in this place, would shape her life for seasons to come.

Show me, god. Hekat is waiting.

CHAPTER TWELVE

Raklion watched Nogolor warlord ride to greet him, trailing warriors like a snake shedding its skin. First of those were Nogolor's sons Tebek and Kilik. At Nogolor's left hand rode his high godspeaker.

Nagarak made a disapproving sound deep in his throat. "Grakilon." He spat on the grass.

Raklion hid his surprise. What business there was between high godspeakers was no business of his, or any man in the world outside the godhouse. The faces godspeakers showed in public were not the faces they showed each other and the god.

"You do not trust him, Nagarak?"

"We studied the god together as novices. He has an arrogant mind. You will not deal with him, warlord. Grakilon is mine to chastise here."

Raklion hid his wry smile. A godspeaker was not a godspeaker without an arrogant mind. High godspeakers were the most arrogant of all. He had outlived two with Nagarak his third, they were all the same. "The god's business here is your business," he agreed. "You are high godspeaker, it is the god's desire. Warlords' business belongs to me. That is *my* desire."

Nagarak grunted. His fingers were loose upon the reins, he sat softly in his saddle, but tension rose from his skin like heat from a sunbaked rock. Raklion considered him from the corner of his eye. Was this personal, then, between Nagarak and Grakilon? If it was personal Nagarak should have said so before they left Et-Raklion. Nagarak had no business keeping secrets from his warlord. Not secrets that did not belong to the god. He had trouble enough without the godspeakers of Mijak raising spears to each other.

"Nagarak," he said sharply. "This is not a battle for the god."

Again, a grunt from Nagarak. "All battles are for the god, warlord."

Aieee. There was no arguing with a godspeaker. "Nogolor warlord is upon us. Use silence as a weapon."

As Nogolor approached, Raklion stared intently at his brother-warlord's face. He had always been a good reader of men, he read them better than he read any clay tablet handed to him by a scribe.

Nogolor's face told of fear and uncertainty, of advice followed that he now regretted. Nogolor was ageing for a warlord, fifty-seven seasons on his head. The treaty between their two cities had been signed by their fathers, in those great men's green days. Were Nogolor's wits shriveling under the sun, that he would risk their long and profitable alliance? Who whispered the advice he now regretted? Grakilon, mistrusted by Nagarak? Or Bajadek warlord, with ambitions of his own?

It does not matter. All whispers of treachery betray me. I must whisper louder. I must shout down the voice who would break our treaty.

Grakilon high godspeaker was seasons older than Nagarak. His godbraids were bleached as bone, the weight of his blue scorpion pectoral looked enough to kill him. Their burning eyes were the same, though, eyes that feasted on the god and devoured men like mice. He rode beside Nogolor as a vulture shadows a dying beast.

Nogolor's warriors were young and proud, as his own were young and proud. They looked eager, as his own were eager, to test their mettle in a dancing of knives. Nogolor's sons looked the keenest of all. Raklion hoped it would not come to that, he knew too well the pain of dead sons. He had no desire to spill their blood for a broken treaty.

If it is broken. In this moment the god gives me a chance to save it. For the sake of my warriors and my unborn son, I must succeed.

Nogolor rode a silver-sheened horse of Et-Raklion breeding. He halted it three paces distant and said, "Brother Raklion. You come upon us unannounced."

Raklion smiled. "I did not know a brother needed to announce his visit."

"It is held polite to do so," said Nogolor. He did not smile in return, his eyes were shadowed pits of fear. "And polite to come alone."

"A warlord without escort is a warlord without honor."

"Your *escort* dances on my doorstep, Raklion. It taunts and it teases, it flaunts and flirts with knives," retorted Nogolor. "*Is* it an escort? Or do you challenge me before my people?"

"Challenge?" said Raklion. "What challenge can there be between brothers, Nogolor? We are bloodbound by treaty. I am godpromised the Daughter to wife. These are sour words, warlord. Who perches on your shoulder dripping poison in your ear?"

Nogolor's fading brown eyes flicked sideways, once. "You are not polite to ask that question."

"Again you call me impolite," said Raklion, and let a little of his displeasure show. "How have I offended, Nogolor? I am told the Daughter is blooded. Do you tell me this is untrue?"

Nogolor looked shaken. Uncertain. "Who told you this?"

"Nagarak high godspeaker. The god told him, in the godhouse godpool."

"Nagarak speaks truly," said Nogolor, after a moment. The muscles round his mouth were tight. "She is blooded. She is ripe for a son."

Raklion nodded. "I am pleased to hear it. I will take her home, as was agreed between us in Et-Raklion's godhouse, in the god's seeing eye and witnessed by Nagarak, who you surely remember. Your giving of her was an invitation, here is my answer, I answer politely. Thank you for your girl-child, Nogolor. Bring her to me, I will take her now."

"It is not for Raklion warlord to say who takes Et-Nogolor's Daughter," said Grakilon high godspeaker. His godbraids were threaded with blue and green feathers, they shivered in the breeze. "She is given by the god to such as the god desires."

"Given to me," said Raklion, as Nagarak drew scorching breath. "Before the altar in my own godhouse. What mischief is this, Nogolor? Do you seek to overturn the god's desire?"

Nogolor's lips thinned. "I sit beneath the god's desire,

Raklion, the god sees me sit beneath it in its eye. My high godspeaker tells me the god's want and I obey, the god is god and it speaks to me with its high godspeaker's tongue."

So Grakilon was the one whispering poison. Raklion looked deep in the old man's burning eyes. *Beware the high godspeakers*, his father told him on his deathbed. *They are not like other men. They eat and sleep and breathe the god, but they are not immune to human corruption. High godspeakers can be demonstruck. They can be seduced by promises of power.*

Raklion had believed him. All words spoken at the portal of death were true. To lie at the portal was to freeze in hell until the sun burned to ash. Looking at Grakilon he saw a man seduced. By demons, or Bajadek, it made no difference. He had set himself against the god's desire.

He looked again at Nogolor. "To sit in the god's eye is to heed the words of your high godspeaker. It is a sin not to listen when he speaks."

Nogolor nodded, his eyes were relieved. "So we are taught. Raklion."

"It is a greater sin to speak with your own tongue and claim your words belong to the god!" said Nagarak. He was rigid with rage, his knuckles white upon his brown horse's reins. "The god does not accept sacrifice on its altar or witness the giving and taking of oaths, then claim those oaths were not given and taken and no sacrifice was made! You sinning Grakilon, you false speaker for the god!"

Nogolor's warriors heard Nagarak's angry words. Nogolor held up his fisted hand and their muttering silenced.

He said, "If this is the god's business, no warlord may interfere. Is this the god's business, Raklion?"

Raklion stared at his stallion's striped and spiky mane. Bajadek's name had not been mentioned. Until it was spoken, that meddling warlord had no place in this. To name him now would be to muddy waters already swirled with silt.

Nogolor will not live so many more seasons. Then his son Tebek will be warlord, with troubles like crows upon a carcass. If I speak of Bajadek when Nogolor seeks to put right what is wrong I risk the treaty, I will lose the Daughter. I cannot lose her, I must sire a son.

He lifted his gaze to Nogolor's strained face. "Et-Nogolor's Daughter is in my eye, she sits in my heart, my loins burn to possess her. Nagarak tells me the god desires that she bleed in my bed and give me a son. I am a man, I cannot know the god but through the words of my high godspeaker. I am bound by the god to heed his words."

The shadows in Nogolor's eyes shifted. "So you are bound, and I am bound, we both are bound to obey the god and its high godspeakers. This is the god's business, Raklion warlord. It is for the god to deliver the Daughter where it desires."

"And if that place is in my bed?" he asked. "If the oaths we swore in Et-Raklion's godhouse are proven?"

"Then you will leave here with my girl-child. She will bleed in your bed and give you a son."

Raklion nodded. "And if that is not the god's desire, I will take my warriors and return to Et-Raklion, our treaty unbroken, our brotherhood intact."

They nudged their horses forward until they stood beside each other, knee brushing knee, then withdrew their sharp knives from their belts and held out their palms. Raklion sliced his blade through Nogolor's flesh as Nogolor did the same to him. The pain was clean, and cruel. Blood welled and dripped, spattering the horses' glossy hides. Their curved ears flattened, they tossed their heads. Raklion twined his fingers with Nogolor's, mingling their blood to seal their swearing. When the blood was fully mingled they untwined their fingers and backed away.

Nagarak said, "I have brought with me three hundred scorpions from Et-Raklion's godhouse. Grakilon, you will fetch three hundred of your own. We will dig a pit for them before Et-Nogolor's gates. Naked in the god's eye we will swim with the scorpions and the god will choose who speaks the truth."

Grakilon hissed. "Who are you, godspeaker of Et-Raklion, to demand this or that from me? I am high godspeaker of Et-Nogolor, I do not bow down before your demands. I am the servant of Nogolor warlord, I answer to him, not you or Raklion!"

Nogolor swung his horse about to look at him. "My servant, Grakilon? The god's servant only, you are its high godspeaker. I am nothing, a puny man. You stood before me in the godhouse, Grakilon, you swore you spoke the god's true words, that I must break my god-promise to Raklion and give my girl-child to Bajadek warlord. That, you said, was the god's desire. Is it so, or did you lie?"

Grakilon's eyes widened with shock. "Warlord, you can ask me that?"

"I can ask you, Grakilon. If you speak the truth there

is nothing to fear. The god will smite Nagarak and see you in its eye."

Nagarak's burning gaze was fixed to Grakilon's hollowed face. "Send for your godspeakers and your scorpions, Grakilon. This matter must be proved by the god with no more delay."

"Nogolor warlord!" Grakilon kicked his horse forward. "Why do you support this? How do you stay silent? Did I come to you and say the god's desire was changed? You know I did not. You came to me, you were troubled in your heart, you wondered aloud before the altar: did the god truly intend Et-Nogolor's Daughter for Raklion warlord's blunted spear? Bajadek warlord sent you messengers, you came to me in the godhouse *after* they departed."

And Grakilon told Nogolor the words he desired to hear. Grakilon obeyed the wants of his warlord, not the desires of his god. His twisted plan was Nogolor's twisted plan, and Bajadek's, they were tangled in lies together. Raklion kept his face still, he showed no outward thought or feeling, but in his breast the fury raged.

You sinning man, Nogolor. This web of lies, this snare of deceit. The god will smite you in its eye for this.

Nogolor wore jet and silver amulets in long loops from his ears. They trembled, as he trembled, Grakilon's harsh words striking him like stones. Here was the break between them, here the ground gaped wide at their feet. Would Nogolor extend a hand to his high godspeaker, or push doomed Grakilon into the chasm?

Nogolor said, "A man may stand before the altar and ask a question. There is no sin in that. You told me the god's desire, how could I think you spoke false? Men must obey the god's godspeakers. Raklion warlord himself has said it: we must listen and obey. If you had told me the god's desire remained unchanged, Grakilon, Et-Nogolor's Daughter even now would be impaled upon Raklion's sharp spear."

Grakilon said nothing. He was thrust into the chasm, his bones were broken kindling. Raklion felt a rough pity. It would be far kinder to thrust a knife through the high godspeaker's heart than put him into the scorpion pit. The god would see him for a liar, it would sting him to a screaming death. But it was too late for mercy, his lies must be proven before the warriors of Et-Nogolor, who believed their warlord was in the right to overthrow his godpromised word.

"You and your godspeakers dig the pit, Nagarak," said Raklion. "Side by side with the godspeakers of Et-Nogolor and their high godspeaker Grakilon. I will wait with my warriors. Nogolor warlord will wait with his. The god's true words will be shown to all, and that will be an end to this matter."

He wheeled his horse and rode towards his waiting warriors. Nagarak rode beside him. When they halted, Nagarak said, "Warlord. Your hand."

Raklion held out his knife-cut hand, and Nagarak healed it with a godstone he took from the pouch on his belt.

"This is the god's business now," said Nagarak, putting the godstone away. "It will smite Grakilon. It might in some time smite Nogolor too, he was a fool to be corrupted."

"And Bajadek?" said Raklion softly, so none of his warriors could hear. "Will the god smite Bajadek also?"

Nagarak smoothed his godbraids with fingers as calm as the sky. "That is warlord business."

He withdrew to gather his godspeakers around him. Raklion motioned to Hanochek, silently waiting, and they rode a small distance from the godspeakers and the warriors, that they might talk in private.

"Warlord?" said Hanochek. "Is it war?"

He shook his head. "Not between Et-Raklion and Et-Nogolor. Not this highsun. Bajadek tried to beguile Nogolor into taking the Daughter away from me, and giving her to him. Nogolor was tempted, or afraid to refuse, he went to Grakilon to ask if the god still intended the Daughter for me. Grakilon is no fool, he heard the question that was not asked. He told Nogolor what he wanted to hear, for reasons I do not know, that do not matter. Now Nogolor puts distance between them and says he acted on the word of his high godspeaker. He has no intention of being blamed for Grakilon's sin."

Hano pulled a face. "You will let this stand?"

"I must," he said, shrugging. "I must have Et-Nogolor's Daughter. There are shadows in the warlord's eyes, I smell his fear like rank perfume. Bajadek is a vital man, his warriors are not known for mercy. Bajadek may have threatened him."

"And risked smiting by the god?"

"The god does not always smite, Hano. Warlords have broken their word before now and the god has left them unsmitten. Why that must be I do not know. The god is a mystery, I do not seek to understand it. I am not a high godspeaker."

"Bajadek warlord is the cause of this trouble," said Hano, taut with anger. "He wants a woman of warlord bloodlines and thinks there is gain for him in discord between Et-Raklion and Et-Nogolor."

"I know this," said Raklion, watching Nagarak and Grakilon, stiffly silent, seek the exact site for the scorpion pit. "At least, he is part the cause." *And I am the rest. This is my doing, I must somehow undo it.*

Hano punched his thigh, he read his warlord too easily. "Raklion, you are wrong. *None* of this is your doing. The god sees you in its eye, it knows you are not a sinful man. You are dogged by demons jealous of your greatness. They kill your women, they kill your sons, you are the battlefield between the god and the dark ones. Would they choose a man unseen by the god in its eye for such a battle? No. To wound you *is* to wound the god."

Raklion stared at him, surprised. "I thought you were my warleader, Hano, not my godspeaker."

"I am your warleader and your friend," said Hano fiercely. "You are father and brother and warlord to me. This time the demons will not win, Raklion. If I must with my own hands sacrifice one thousand bull-calves and throw my last gold coin in the barracks godbowl, Et-Nogolor's Daughter will bear you a son. Then will *I* sire sons, so they may serve him as I serve you."

Raklion was not a man of tears, but for a moment his tongue could find no words. "Brother Hano," he said at last, "that is an oath I will hold you to. My son could not be better served if the god itself became a man and pledged its body to him."

"When this is over," said Hano, his voice rough with feeling, "do we punish this faithless warlord of Et-Nogolor?"

Raklion shook his head. "Let the god smite him if

smiting is required. I do not wish our treaty broken, Hano. It is useful, it serves us well."

"Then do we ride upon Et-Bajadek with ten thousand angry warriors? Do we smite its scheming warlord for daring to trespass on the treaty between Et-Raklion and Et-Nogolor? For trying to steal Et-Nogolor's Daughter, promised to Raklion warlord before the god?"

Do we ride? Raklion frowned at his fingers, clasped upon the reins. It could rightly be said that stealing another warlord's godpromised wife was an act of war. Seducing another warlord into betraying his godsworn treaty was an act of war also. Bajadek had done these things. In secret, yes, but now the secret was discovered. These acts of war, could he close his eyes, turn his shoulder to them?"

No. I cannot. Bajadek is defeated here, he will try again when he thinks himself safe. Mijak's browning will be his excuse. He will rouse the other warlords to envy, he will promise them a share of Et-Raklion's spoils. If I do not smite him . . .

Hano said, "A wise man might see this thwarting of his desires as a fortunate escape, he might see it as a warning from the god. Bajadek is not wise. What he wants, he takes. Raklion, if you do not smite him . . ."

He smiled at Hano. "As ever we share a single thought. When the Daughter is planted with my son I will teach unwise Bajadek his lesson."

"And if he rides against us before she is planted?"

"Then we will meet him in battle," he said. "But I think he will not. Bajadek is a coward at heart, he skulks in the shadows and seeks to gain his desires with stealth. When he learns the Daughter is in my bed he will lie low, he will hide his teeth. Let him skulk, and think I have no heart for fighting. I will smite him, in my time."

Once the scorpion pit was dug, Nagarak and Grakilon each sacrificed a white lamb and drank the steaming scarlet blood. Then they stripped themselves naked and climbed into the pit. The witnessing godspeakers tipped the scorpions over them, three hundred from Et-Raklion godhouse, three hundred from the godhouse of Et-Nogolor. Larger than a man's hand, they were bred for venom and for spite.

Raklion felt his throat scald with bile. He feared little in the world, he was a warlord, but he feared the godhouse scorpions. He stared into the pit where the scorpions scuttled and swarmed and seethed around and over the seated bodies of the two high godspeakers. The men's eyes were closed, they breathed unflinching as the scorpions crawled up their godbraids, crawled over their faces, dropped from their shoulders into their laps and sought out the softness of their unguarded genitals.

The scorpions raised their barbed tails and stung the god's high godspeakers, stung them everywhere upon their flesh. Great scarlet welts bloomed in the wake of those stings, like tended gardens the godspeakers' naked bodies grew blossoms of venom.

Grakilon began foaming at the mouth.

Watching on either side of Nogolor warlord, the godspeakers of Et-Nogolor cried out in terror and despair. Still foaming, Grakilon began to convulse, he thrashed and flailed, unseen in the god's eye, smitten for his lies. He vomited blood, he vomited his entrails, he emptied himself from the inside out.

Nagarak sat in cool still silence, he did not watch as Grakilon died.

When it was finished, the scorpions stopped stinging. Nagarak opened his swollen eyes and stood. His god-speakers helped him from the pit, they fastened his pectoral over his chest, they dressed him in his loincloth and robes.

"The god has seen me in its eye," said Raklion to No-golor. "Its desires are known beneath the sun. Bring to me Et-Nogolor's Daughter. She will go to Et-Raklion and a son will follow upon our mating. Our treaty holds. We are still brothers."

Nogolor stared down into the pit, at the god's scorpions, slowly dying, and Grakilon's swollen, distorted body. He nodded, barely, as though movement pained him. "The god sees you in its eye, Raklion warlord. Its desires are known beneath the sun." He turned to his eldest son, the warrior Tebek. "Go into my city. Ride up to my palace. Bring to this place Et-Nogolor's Daughter."

Tebek obeyed, and Nogolor returned to his staring.

Nagarak said, "Your godhouse must choose its new high godspeaker, warlord."

"Yes," said Nogolor. He sounded lost. Dazed. He wrenched his gaze away from dead Grakilon and looked to the nearest godspeaker. "You. You will see to the choosing. But first take Grakilon from the pit, he—"

"No," said Nagarak. "Grakilon is unseen in the god's eye, he cannot be carried up to your godhouse. He will stay in the pit, a nameless man, the dirt will cover him and—"

The godspeakers of Et-Nogolor cried out in protest, some surged towards Nagarak as though they would touch him with their angry hands. Nagarak's godspeakers moved to stop them, and four were flung into the pit by Grakilon's defenders. The dying scorpions stung them, and they died.

Nagarak cursed the sinning Et-Nogolor godspeakers with his godstone, he seared them with its blinding light. They fell to the grass and wept out their suffering at his feet.

"Nogolor warlord, I will take four of your godspeakers for my own," he said. "See this pit filled in and the grass laid upon it. Horses will ride over it, carts and wagons will roll across it. Grakilon is dead to memory. Before newsun next you must have a new high godspeaker. I will know if it is not so, the god will tell me, I sit in its eye."

Nogolor nodded, subdued. "Yes, Nagarak. This will be done, it is the god's desire."

Nagarak climbed back into the pit and handed up the bodies of his four slain godspeakers. Those scorpions still living scuttled away from him, they did not raise their stinging tails.

Raklion returned to his warriors to wait while Nagarak made his choices from the chastened group of Et-Nogolor godspeakers, and for Tebek to bring him Et-Nogolor's Daughter, mother of his unborn son. He waited in silence and solitude, ignoring Nogolor who looked so old and defeated.

A voice beside him said, "The god sees you in its eye, warlord. That Nogolor is a stupid man. His high godspeaker was stupid also, to defy the god."

Startled, he looked down. It was the ruined beauty from the knife-dancing field. "*You*?"

She looked at him through her spiderweb of scars.

"That Zapotar, he says there is no omen for me to stop my chicken-killing and learn to dance for you with a snake-blade. I came here in the cook's wagon, I feed your war-riors salted goat and cornmush." She nodded at the scorpion pit. "Shall I dance with the scorpions, Raklion warlord? The god sees me in its eye, it has a use for me. I must be a warrior, Raklion. I will dance with the scorpi-ons and show you an omen."

She would do it, he could see it in her eyes. He caught her by the shoulder just in time. "No, Hekat! Return to your cook-wagon. When we are safe in Et-Raklion you will cease your chicken-killing, you will train to be a war-rior in my warhost."

Her blue eyes narrowed. "That is your word?"

"My word as the warlord."

Satisfied, she nodded. "I will trust it. In Et-Raklion, warlord."

Bemused, amused, he watched her run lightly to the cook-wagon where she belonged. The four godspeakers chosen, Nagarak returned to his side. He seemed un-affected by his ordeal in the pit. Raklion knew he should not be surprised, he had never seen Nagarak affected by anything.

"So," he said, as they waited for Et-Nogolor's Daugh-ter. "The god was with us. Nogolor is chastened."

"Bajadek must also be chastened," said Nagarak.

"He will be," said Raklion. "In my time. War is war-lord business, Nagarak. I will come to you for omens, when I am ready."

Nagarak nodded. "When you are ready, warlord. I will be waiting."

Soon after that, Raklion was given Et-Nogolor's

Daughter. She was shrouded in veils and linens, he had never seen her face. It did not matter what she looked like, only that she was the child of a warlord and fertile. Nagarak assured him she was both, it was all he needed to know of her.

"My thanks to you, warlord," he told silent Nogolor. Then he pulled the weeping Daughter behind him on his blue spotted stallion, and rode away from Et-Nogolor without looking back.

CHAPTER THIRTEEN

Three highsuns after the god killed Grakilon high god-speaker, rare clouds jostled the sky, then rained on the warhost returning to Et-Raklion. Not for long, but heavily, so that Vortka's novice robes were soaked to his skin. Even after the rain stopped the clouds remained to smother the sun, the temperature dropped, the world turned grey.

Cold, chafed and miserable, he plodded with the other godspeakers of Et-Nogolor chosen by Nagarak to take the place of his godspeakers killed in the scorpion pit.

Nagarak. He shivered, but not because he was wet. Grakilon had been a nothing man, feared and revered because he was high godspeaker, not because he was Grakilon. His eyes had not burned like Nagarak's eyes. His scorpion pectoral had not seemed to breathe. He could not smite with the lifting of a finger.

Why me, god? he wondered. *I never asked to be a god-speaker, but you chose me so I serve. Why did Nagarak choose me? The godspeakers who died weren't Et-Raklion novices. I cannot do the work lost because they are dead. Novices are menials, little better than slaves. Why would Nagarak choose me? I do not understand.*

The god did not answer. Vortka sighed, and ceased his wondering. Doubtless he would learn Nagarak's purpose if and when the god desired it. Until then he would do his best as a novice of Et-Raklion. His best was all he could do.

I hope it is good enough.

He had no ties to Et-Nogolor godhouse, no novices there it hurt him to leave. Godspeaker friendships were sternly discouraged, godspeakers needed no friend but the god.

Even so, godspeakers talked, they were not mute. Nagarak presided over a disciplined godhouse, that much he had learned in Et-Nogolor. Of all Mijak's people, god-speakers moved the most freely, even more than Traders. The godhouses had a loose alliance, their first allegiance was to the god, not any warlord. Warlords died, new warlords succeeded them, in time they died and were replaced in turn. Only the god went on forever. In Et-Nogolor's godhouse he had spoken with godspeakers born in Et-Zyden and Et-Takona and from far away Et-Jokriel. Every one of them said the same: *Nagarak high godspeaker is a fearsome man.*

Head down, heart heavy, Vortka prayed to the god.

He has seen me once. Please, I beg you. Do not let him see me twice.

Eventually the hot sun appeared again and the air

stank of wet wool and horseflesh steaming dry. Vortka walked among the godspeakers, Nagarak did not see him. He stopped counting the highsuns. Counting was pointless, it did not make the journey go faster. They walked and they walked, they reached Et-Raklion city at last. Once through its gates, Raklion's warhost continued through the streets to be greeted by the people with cheering and thrown amulets. Nagarak did not ride with the warlord, he led his godspeakers up the long, winding road to Et-Raklion's godhouse on the Pinnacle's peak.

Vortka's feet faltered when he saw how tall and wide and grim Et-Raklion's godhouse was, how its black stone walls seemed to drink in the sunlight and spew it out again as shadows. Compared to this place Et-Nogolor's godhouse was small and cheerful. Scores of godspeakers bustled in and out of the scorpion-guarded main entrance, they were silent and industrious, they stopped and lowered their heads as Nagarak passed by. So did the citizens of Et-Raklion who had walked the long road here for their own reasons, some even fell to their knees as the high godspeaker approached.

Nagarak led his godspeakers into the godhouse and left them standing in the enormous, echoing entrance hall. Vortka watched him climb winding stone stairs out of sight to some room high above. His fellow Et-Nogolor godspeakers were hustled away by the other Et-Raklion godspeakers. The only novice, he was left standing alone on the uneven black stone floor, surrounded by air and the distant sounds of godhouse business: prayers, sacrifice, chiming godbells, harsh wails of the godsmitten.

He had no idea what to do next. He was too afraid to ask.

A few moments later he was collected by a god-speaker, taken to the novice-room below the godhouse's ground floor and shown the straw pallet he must sleep on, one of many in the large stone chamber. It looked just like the novice-room he'd left behind in Et-Nogolor. Then he followed the godspeaker to the duty chamber on the first floor.

"So. Vortka," said Salakij the novice-master, seated at his small stone desk. He was an old man but his eyes were sharp. Vortka could tell he would brook no mischief. "What were your tasks in Et-Nogolor godhouse?"

"I cleaned the godhouse, master, I tended the sacrifices. I was about to start work in the godhouse library when—"

"Yes, yes," said Salakij. "Are you called as a vessel?"

Vessels were those godspeakers chosen to lie with the warlord's warriors. The god made godspeaker vessels sterile. Warriors needed to fuck, they did not need children. Not unless the warlord desired them to breed. A warrior discovered fucking anybody but a sterile god-speaker was delivered to an unspeakable death. In the godhouse it was counted an honor to be chosen as a vessel, mainly because only the vessels were allowed to fuck. All other godspeakers lived celibate, their bodies and their devotion reserved for the god.

Vortka shook his head. "No, master. In Et-Nogolor I was not—"

"You are in Et-Raklion now," snapped Salakij. "Let me not hear those words again."

"Forgive me," said Vortka, and received the testing stone handed to him. It was dark yellow, like the one in—

like the one that had tested him before. This stone did not waken either.

"You are not called as a vessel," said the novice-master, taking back the stone. "You were to start work in the library, you say? That means you read and write?"

"I do, master. I also have a good grasp of numbers. Before the god chose me I—"

"You did not exist before the god chose you," said Salakij, impatient. "You are a novice and do not know that? How long has it been since your last tasking?"

Vortka swallowed. "Master, it is forty-three highsuns since my last tasking."

Salakij was affronted. "Forty-three highsuns? *Tcha*! You overflow with sin. From newsun next you will toil in the library, Vortka novice, under the eye of Firuk god-speaker. Between now and lowsun sacrifice you will kneel before a taskmaster, that your sins might be beaten from your flesh. Tell the taskmaster not to spare you. Tell the taskmaster I will know if you are spared. *Forty-three highsuns*." Salakij leaned across his stone desk. "You will find, Vortka novice, life is very different in Et-Raklion godhouse. In Et-Raklion godhouse we serve the god." He waved his hand in curt dismissal. "Ask a godspeaker to show you to the taskmasters. I have stomached enough of you for one day."

Vortka wanted to say, *That is unfair, it is not my fault. I traveled with the warhost, there was no tasking then*. He held his tongue. A novice who questioned was a novice who walked with demons. Such a novice did not live long.

As he followed a helpful godspeaker down the stairs and through the godhouse's maze of passageways Vortka tried, and failed, to discipline his fear. Another sin he must confess to the taskmaster.

I must not mind. I must endure. My life could be worse, I could still be a slave.

Sadly, knowing soon he would weep beneath the taskmaster's cane, the thought was not as comforting as he would have liked.

Upon their return to Et-Raklion the warlord kept his word to Hekat. She left behind her chicken-killing days, she was given to Zapotar for training as a warrior. After she learned how to ride a horse—such stupid creatures—he assigned her to a knife-dance shell. She slept in the shell-barracks with twenty-nine other warriors who told her their names but did not make friends with her. She did not care, their friendship did not matter. Her bright new snakeblade mattered, her clean fresh linen training tunic mattered, and her stiff leather sandals she must soften with sheep-fat. Her knife-dancing mattered. That was all.

When they were not training, Raklion's warriors were free to sleep or game or fuck a vessel in the vessel-house. Hekat knife-danced. In the beginning Zapotar ridiculed her knife-dancing, but he did not laugh long. She learned fast, she learned well, soon he watched in silence as she danced the *hotas* with her snakeblade. His eyes were frightened.

His fear was food, his fear was drink. She ate and drank him as she danced for the god.

After two godmoons he summoned her to dance with him, he tested her as cruelly as he could. She pricked him four times, he pricked her once. He nodded, and said, *You are a warrior.* Before the knife-dancers and Hanochek warleader he heated his snakeblade and pressed it burning into her naked flank. She stared in his face, she did not scream. Now she bore her first warrior's mark. She could ride to battle with Raklion's warhost.

After Zapotar she trained with Antokoi and his archers and slingshotters. The armorer made her a special bow, she was strong for her size but a full bow was beyond her. The god sat in her eye and in her fingers, she struck her targets over and over with arrows and with stones, she killed as many sheep and goats for their dinner as any of the seasoned warriors.

After one godmoon Antokoi told her, *You are a warrior*. He shot her with an arrow, then. A godspeaker healer dug it from her thigh and sealed the bloody hole in her leg. The arrow's scar was her second mark, it was tattooed with crimson ink to make it different from the arrow scars she would later earn in battle. The armorer pierced the arrowhead for her, then passed a heated wire through her ear. She dangled the arrowhead like an amulet, its weight made her smile when she turned her head.

She was given to the chariots next, and her training continued with Bodrik Chariot-leader. He had seen her knife-dance and kill with slingshot and bow, he knew better than to sneer because she was young and ugly. She was too light to manage a chariot and its mad warhorses, she stood with the driver and loosed her arrows and her shot-stones, first at standing targets and later at godforsaken criminals let loose in the chariot field. No matter how fast the horses galloped, how desperately the criminals twisted and turned, she almost always hit her target.

She did not grieve for the ones she killed, they were sinners and deserved to die.

Bodrik said, one godmoon later, *You are a warrior.* She was tied to a chariot wheel and beaten with a chariot-whip, eight cuts to mimic the spokes of a wheel. The whip scars were her third warrior's mark.

She was not yet ready to learn the spear with Dokoy so she returned to Zapotar and her shell of knife-dancers. Through her other warrior-skill training she never once forgot her *hotas*, every day she had practiced them on the knife-dance field no matter how tired she was. Knife-dancing was her gift to the god and to Raklion, its chosen warlord. Of all her war skills, it was her best.

She danced with her shell-mates and wished the warlord could see her. But Raklion stayed within his palace, plowing the Daughter, planting a son. Hanochek warleader trained with the warhost, he told them each newsun: *You are Mijak's greatest warriors, you make me proud.*

Tcha. What did she care for Hanochek's praise? He had no power, he answered to the warlord. She wanted Raklion to see her, Raklion to smile and nod and say, *You are a warrior.* How long must it take him to plant his son? How long before they rode to smite that Bajadek, insolent warlord, sinning man?

She did not know. She would have to wait. And dance while she waited, and dream of the god.

Alone in the center of the knife-dancers' field, as low-sun's last light drained below the edge of the horizon, Hekat danced the steps of the *sandcat striking.* It was one of her favorite *hotas*, she felt like a cat as she flowed from pose to pose, leaping, twisting, flipping through the air to land lightly on her unshod feet. She could leap higher than any other knife-dancer in Raklion's warhost, she could somersault over Zapotar's head.

I leap for the god, I leap in its eye.

Someone called her. "Hekat? Hekat! Is that you?"

She twisted in mid-air to see who dared call her name while she danced for the god. After a moment's hard staring, she knew who it was.

"Vortka?"

He stood three paces distant, his beautiful face alive with surprise. He was tall now, he had grown many handspans since last she saw him in Et-Nogolor, in the slave pen.

"Hekat! It *is* you," he said. He was smiling. "How can that be? I did not think a sla—"

In a single striking leap the tip of her snakeblade pricked his throat. "You cannot be here! Only a warrior may tread this ground!"

"I am a godspeaker," he said, and touched the scorpion shell bound to his brow. "I tread where the god sends me."

It was a very small scorpion shell. Leaving her blade against his throat she said, "You are a *novice* godspeaker."

He was still smiling, he did not seem to notice her knife. "True. But a godspeaker, even so."

"You were taken by the godspeaker in Et-Nogolor," she said, baffled. "How are you here?"

"By the god's desire. And you? You are a *warrior*?"

He was beautiful, but she should kill him. He knew her from her dead life, he knew her with Abajai and Yagji.

She pressed her snakeblade closer and felt it slide beneath his skin.

He gasped. No smiling now. "What are you doing?"

"I am not a slave," she hissed. "I am Hekat, chosen by the god. I dance in the god's eye for Raklion warlord. Why do you come here? Are you demon-sent, to cause me trouble?"

His shining eyes were wide but not frightened. He should be frightened, she had killed many men. "Demon-sent?" he said. "*No*! I came down from the godhouse library with tablets for Hanochek warleader. I thought to walk my slow way back, I spend my days within four walls, it is good to see the open sky, feel cool fresh air against my face. I saw you knife-dancing, I thought you were beautiful. And then, as I watched, I thought I knew you." Despite the knife at his throat, the thread of blood trickling down his chest, he traced one daring fingertip across her scarred cheek. "What happened, Hekat? Your face was a glory to the god."

"The god took my face. It does not matter."

"The god would never take your glory," he protested. "Was it Trader Abajai? Did he—"

"That name is *dead* to me!" she said, and pressed his throat harder with her knife. "My life outside these barracks is dead to me! Remember that if you wish to live."

Still his eyes were unafraid. "You look and sound so different, Hekat," he said, his voice gentle. "Won't you tell me how you came here?"

"It is my business. Mine, and the god's."

"I will keep your words secret. The god smite me if that is not so."

She could smell no stink of treachery on him. The god

did not smite him. His word was his word. Slowly she lowered her blade from his throat. "Why do you care?"

He smiled again. "You gave me food when I was hungry."

From her own bowl, after his was stolen. She remembered. "Tcha!" she said, and looked away. "Stale dry bread, I did not want it."

"I watched you after the Traders bought me in Todorok village," he said. "Every day as I walked in my chains, I watched you riding Abajai's white camel. You thought you were not one of us, you wore no chains, you ate and slept and talked with the Traders. I knew different. I was sorry for you."

Sorry? Stung, she raised a fist to him. "Hekat needs no godspeaker pity!"

He covered her fist with his fingers, and held her. "Not now. But I was sorry then, Hekat. If the god took you from them and put you in this place and if you are happy here, then I am happy for you."

She should pull free of his fingers, she should strike him for touching her. She said, "You are truly a godspeaker? The godspeaker in Et-Nogolor did not lie?"

"Godspeakers cannot lie, Hekat."

"Tcha," she said, and did pull free. "You are stupid, Vortka. Grakilon lied. He said the god wanted the Daughter for Bajadek but that was not true. He was high godspeaker and he told lies."

"Grakilon was a man, corrupted by demons. He turned his shoulder to the god, that is not the same thing."

His beautiful face was calm, his voice was calm, the god was in him, she could feel it. "So you are a godspeaker."

He nodded. "I will be. One day. When I'm done with training and have suffered the testing."

Across the shadowed knife-dance field floated sounds of laughter, of music, as Raklion's warriors amused themselves around their nightly bonfires. The flickering light warmed the gathering darkness. Sometimes she sat with the knife-dancers before the flames and listened to the laughter, the stories, the songs that told of battles past. She was a warrior, and that was how warriors sometimes spent their nights. When she was not dancing or practicing her reading and writing, that was how she spent her nights.

"What is the testing?"

"A godspeaker secret."

She bared her teeth at him. "Now I see you, Vortka novice. You know *my* secret but keep *yours* in your heart. You are a man, like men you cheat, you lie, you would put chains on me if I was stupid, if I let you fool me." She turned her shoulder to him and walked away.

He followed. "Hekat! Wait!"

Aieee, she should kill him, if she did not slit his throat he would name her a runaway slave, see her nailed to a godpost with her entrails at her feet. Her fingers on the snakeblade tightened, her drumming heart drummed hard and loud, she tensed her body to leap upon him, sandcat striking. She spun on one foot, snakeblade rising . . .

Vortka was on the ground before her, on his knees before her, his throat was bare, like a lamb for sacrifice it was soft and waiting.

She pulled back her blade and stumbled to stillness.

"The god sees you, Hekat, it sees you in its eye," he said, without fear. "I see you. Your secret is my secret, it sits in my heart. The testing is for novice godspeakers, they go alone into a desolate place. The god stings them with tribulations, it beats them low, and if they are true they lift themselves into its eye."

"And if they are false? What does the god do if they are false?"

"It breathes upon them and they die."

She pressed her blade-tip into the softness under his jaw. "If you are false, Vortka, I will breathe on you and you will die."

His fingers closed around her wrist. He laid the snake-blade against his lips and kissed it. "I know."

She dropped to the dirt before him. "What else do you know, Vortka?"

Now his warm palm cupped her cheek. "I am a novice, I know hardly anything. Except I think we are meant to be friends. And I think you have a purpose."

His touch burned her, gentle against her scars. "What purpose? Does the god tell you?"

He shook his head. "No. Does it tell you?"

She did not want to answer that, but if she said nothing he would guess anyway. "No," she told him, grudging. "Not yet. Vortka, why are you *here*?"

He knelt in silence, his gaze turned inwards. "To find you, Hekat," he said at last, looking outwards. "We know each other for a reason. I think I am meant to help you in your purpose for the god, whatever it is."

"*Tcha!*" She gathered her muscles and sprang to her feet. Her scars were cold without his hand upon them. She melted her body into a *hota*, flowing like water, *lizard waiting on a rock*. "I am Hekat, warrior of Et-Raklion. I read, I write, I dance with my snakeblade. Do I need help from a godspeaker novice?"

"I think the god thinks you do," said Vortka, and stood. "Would you have me defy it, earn its smiting wrath? What have I done to you that you would do that to me?"

Aieee, he was a twisty one. "Nothing," she said, and kept on dancing. "Let the god show me I need you, and perhaps I will not send you away. Let it show me—"

She missed her timing in a complicated cartwheel, her foot slipped, she fell hard to the ground. All the hot air *whooshed* out of her lungs. Shocked, offended, she lay gasping on her back and watched Vortka bend low to help her onto her feet.

"Was that the god?" he said, his dark eyes laughing. "I think it was. I think you do need me, Hekat, though you wish you did not."

She shook his hand free of her and tossed her head. "Tcha. I think you think too much, Vortka novice. Go away, your silly face distracts me."

He retreated three paces, he did not leave. Ignoring him, she began dancing again. After watching for a while, he did go away. She let him go, she did not stop him. He was a novice, he was no-one. She was knife-dancing with the god.

She saw him again six highsuns later.

Every tenth highsun Raklion's warriors were given a day of freedom from training. Hekat spent that time mending torn training tunics and reading. With their copper coin warrior's portion her shell-mates bought sweetmeats and godbones, amulets and fancy leatherwork from the city pedlars selling their wares in the barracks. She did not care for those things. She cared for stories, and bought them when she could.

This free-day, she sat alone in the sunshine on the far side of the empty knife-dance field, mending a tunic, duty before pleasure, when a shadow fell across her face. She looked up, annoyed. It was Vortka again.

"Tcha! I am stitching, are you blind not to see that?"

He smiled, so beautiful, and sat beside her. "I see you stitching. You can stitch and talk, I think."

Mending tunics was a tedious business, she longed for a slave. "Of course I can. But do I want to? I do not think so."

He pulled his knees against his chest. "I have kept your secret, Hekat knife-dancer. Can you not give me a little of your time?"

He had kept her secret, did that mean he owned her? "Why?"

"I am freed from duties in the godhouse until highsun. I thought to sit a while with a friend."

"*Friend*?" She busied herself with the needle so he would not see her face. "What is *friend*? It is a word. What is a word? A puff of air, it weighs nothing, it means less."

"Not to me, Hekat," said Vortka, sighing. "Before Abajai bought me I had many friends in my village. I have none in the godhouse, friends distract from the god. I am not supposed to miss them but I do. I suppose you do not need another friend, you are a warrior now. You have your shell-mates."

Her hand jerked, the needle stabbed. Bright red blood-drops stained her mended tunic.

"You've hurt your finger," said Vortka. "I have my godstone. Shall I heal it for you?"

"There is nothing wrong with my finger," she snapped, and sucked the blood-drop from its tip.

Vortka laughed. "You are a funny one. Hekat. You make me smile."

She did not make her shell-mates smile, or Hanochek warleader when he watched her dance. She was one of them, but also apart. She made them uneasy, they knew she was different.

I am Hekat, godtouched and precious. What do I care for the friendship of men?

"Why are you here, Vortka? If you are found being friendly won't you be punished? Godspeakers are strict, even warriors know that much."

Vortka shrugged. "I am a novice, I sin daily. I am punished daily whether I sit with you or not."

Curious, she looked at him. "How do they punish you?"

"That is godspeaker business, I am forbidden to say." Then he sighed. "There are taskmasters. Pain in the flesh is our contrition."

She wasn't certain what that meant, but his eyes were sad. She felt a stir of pity. "It does not please you, to serve the god?"

"Serving the god is my greatest joy!" he said, stung to anger. But it swiftly faded and he was sad again. "It is the whipping I could live without."

"Then do not sin and they will not whip you."

"Tcha!" he said, pulling a face. "I have come to believe that to breathe is to sin. At least that's what Salakij novice-master believes." He sighed again. "There was not so much whipping in Et-Nogolor."

"You cannot go back there?"

"Not unless Nagarak sends me. He won't. The god desires me here, I am here for you."

Did that mean it was *her* fault the taskmasters whipped him? She threw down the tunic and leapt to her feet. "I did not ask the god for you, Vortka! You could go back to Et-Nogolor, *I* would not care!"

Now he smiled, it melted his sorrow. "I would. Aieee, it is not so bad, Hekat. Pay no attention. This is what friends do, they complain to each other, they pout and pull faces. I will not be a novice forever. I will survive this. I serve the god."

Did he mean that? She stared at him sitting on the ground. She thought he meant it, but before she could ask him a godbell's tolling broke the warm silence. On the other side of the knife-dance field she saw warriors stirring, heard excited voices raised in clamor.

Vortka stood. "There is the other reason I came to find you," he said, as the godbell continued to toll. "I heard the news as I left the godhouse. Et-Nogolor's Daughter is planted with a son and Nagarak high godspeaker has read omens of war. That means the warhost will ride upon Bajadek, doesn't it? I thought it was something you would want to know."

Yes, it was something. She gave him a wide smile, snatched up her half-mended tunic and ran across the knife-dance field to rejoin her shell-mates as though ravenous dogs snapped at her heels.

CHAPTER FOURTEEN

On the eve of battle a warlord bathed his body in blood.

Naked and alone, for this was a private ritual, Raklion trod the stone steps into the godhouse godpool, to sink his face in scarlet and show the god he was ready for war. The air was heavy with the smell of death. The blood was warm, it covered his feet, his ankles, his calves. It rose up his thighs, it lapped at his genitals like a woman's tongue, it sighed across his belly and drowned his scarred chest. Rank warm blood flowed over his lips, his eyes, it stopped his breathing. He swam in blood.

Beneath the red surface he heard his heart pound, the lack of air in his lungs was a fist squeezing tight. He opened his eyes.

I am here, god. I bathe in the sacred sacrificed blood. My son is planted, I have seen your omens. Nagarak says I am bound to war. I will smite Bajadek, I will lay him low. Yet I fear that will bring no end to trouble. I fear my trouble is only beginning. Et-Raklion stays fat as the rest of Mijak grows thin. I know my brother warlords, god, it will turn them against me. They will try to destroy me. How can I stop them? What must I do?

He waited and waited but the god did not answer. Disappointed, disturbed, pricked with his own answer, one too terrible to contemplate, he walked from the godpool to the cleansing room to be renewed in milk and water.

"Warlord, you are burdened with unquiet thoughts," said Nagarak softly, his strict hands bathing him, washing him clean. "Unburden yourself, my purpose is to listen."

Nagarak was high godspeaker, he always knew. "Yes, I am burdened," Raklion admitted. How could he not be? He was the warlord, every life in Et-Raklion lived in his hand. But he could not tell Nagarak what churned in his mind. Nagarak would smite him to his knees if he did that.

Should the browning of Mijak continue the nation will be torn to pieces, seven warlords at each other's throats, ripping and shredding till nothing remains. But if Mijak had a single warlord . . .

Aieee, what a sinning thought that was! A single warlord was against the god's law, written in blood at the dawn of their age. He suffocated temptation in his heart and asked Nagarak a question that would not wake his wrath.

"I am tasked to chastise Bajadek. Does the god desire his death?"

Nagarak anointed him with fragrant snake oil, his eyes, his lips, his heart, his hips. "The god desires Bajadek to acknowledge his sinning. It desires that he stay in his city and not stir trouble between the warlords."

Raklion looked at his hands. Blunt, square, and trained to kill. "And if he does not?"

"It is a mistake to defy the god."

Nagarak put aside the glass bottle of oil, he unstopped a clay jar of sacred ointment. Raklion sucked air through his clenched teeth, the ointment stung, it burned his skin.

"Nagarak, I ride to war. Will I ride home again? Will I survive?"

Astonished, Nagarak took a step backwards. "What is this, warlord? Where do these fears spring from? The god sends you to war, to chastise sinning Bajadek. You go with its omen, anointed with its desire. Why do you think you will die in this battle?"

Because I am filled with sinful thoughts, I am no better than Bajadek warlord. I think of Raklion, warlord of Mijak.

"I am a man, Nagarak," he said, in anguish. "Like Bajadek warlord, I have sinned. If I were perfect I would have a son."

"Raklion, you have a son, he ripens in the Daughter's belly. You will live to see him grow to be a man."

Nagarak's words loosened some tight knot within him. "I have lost so many sons," he whispered. "I am afraid to lose another."

Nagarak touched him, over his heart. "You are the warlord, the god cloaks you in strength. Go now, Raklion. Kneel your time before your palace godpost and leave your offerings in its bowl. Then lead your warhost to the lands of Et-Bajadek and show the world how the god is obeyed."

Raklion led six thousand warriors to the lands of Bajadek warlord. They did not travel by the Traders Road, the traditional path from Et-Raklion to Et-Bajadek. That was the peaceful way of entering the lands of Bajadek warlord.

Raklion's warhost did not ride in peace.

He led his warriors the quiet way, the purposeful way,

through Et-Raklion's pastures and crops, past its god-farms and villages whose inhabitants waved and cheered and exhorted the god to see him in its eye. He waved back and thanked them for their godspeed. His people loved him, and he loved his people.

They were nearing the end of Mijak's long hot season, they traveled for all the time there was light, as the burning sun climbed the vaulting sky and slid down again to the distant horizon. The cultivated country gave way to wilder terrain, to marshes crowded with frog and heron and watersnake, and from there to a harsh dry landscape cluttered with rocks and pocked with caves and crevices. Strange echoes woke, unsettling the horses. The chariots' wheels boomed hollow on the bare ground.

With steady traveling they left that strange place and came to Et-Raklion's open grasslands. The warriors sang their songs of war, Hanochek sang, and Raklion sang too, though his voice was cracked and lost the tune more often than found it.

Twenty-seven highsuns after leaving his city, Raklion and his warhost reached the border with Et-Bajadek. There was no godpost, just a boulder-sized chunk of pale grey crystal, a borderstone set by Bajadek's high god-speaker so he would know who entered the warlord's lands. If a traveler's intentions were not declared to the borderstone the god would smite him. He would wither and die.

Declarations of war were the warlord's business. God-speakers rode with Raklion's warhost, but this was not a task for them. They gave him a black lamb and a sacred godhouse blade and returned to their wagon. With the blade Raklion sacrificed the lamb and bathed the borderstone in its blood. The lamb's limp body melted as the last drop left it, vanished into sulphur smoke. The borderstone drank the sacred blood, turned blood red and glowed under the sun. Raklion took a deep breath and pressed his hand into it. As warlord he must break the crystal, force his will upon the lands of Et-Bajadek.

Resistance poured against him like a waterfall of air. Bajadek's borderstone was set against him, there was no treaty, he was not welcome here. His bones cried out against the power, he shouted at the blazing pain. He heard his warhost shouting with him. Hanochek shouted loudest of all. When Bajadek's borderstone was emptied of power Raklion turned to his warhost and raised the godhouse blade above his head.

"Behold Bajadek's borderstone, broken by my hand and the god's desire! Now our warhost rides into Et-Bajadek, to sweep like fire through the unrepentant grass!".

As his warriors hailed him, as they drummed their knife-hilts and sword-hilts and spears to show him the fury of their love, he returned to Hanochek who was holding his stallion.

"We must ride hard, Hano," he said, his voice low. "Knowing we ride on him Bajadek will lead his warhost to meet us. He is a foolish, proud man, he is deaf to the god."

"His deafness will be his undoing, warlord," said Hano, handing him the reins. "The god itself sends us to Et-Bajadek. We ride at its will, we smite at its desiring."

Raklion wiped the godhouse blade on the dry grass, returned it to a waiting godspeaker, then swung himself into his saddle. Heavy with purpose, he led his warhost into Et-Bajadek.

*   *   *

They traveled two highsuns and saw no sign of Bajadek warlord. A finger before lowsun on the third day past the borderstone they made camp beside a network of sluggish waterholes. As soon as they were halted, Raklion sent his four best Eyes running ahead to locate Bajadek's warhost. It must be close now, the open country was nearing its end. The other warriors washed the sweat from their skins, their cheerful laughter easing his heart. Body slaves fetched water for him, he bathed in cold and solitary splendor. After sacrifice was made, and rations were eaten, his warhost settled to watchful rest and Raklion walked among them. This was the time he loved the best. He did not love the bloody battles, the pain and the loss and the waste of death.

I am a warlord, bred from a long line of fearsome warlords. Death and knives are in my blood, yet I do not love them.

He wondered sometimes if it was this failing which summoned to him so much disappointment. A weakness in his seed that weakened his sons in their mothers' wombs, weakened them in the world beyond that if they were born at all they died so young and sickly.

With a grunt he strangled that line of thought. Whatever his failings in the past, they were in the past. The Daughter ripened with his son, the god was appeased, it was pleased, it saw him in its eye. Soon now he would ride into battle, the god would ride with him, this bloodshed was righteous and he would prevail. His son would cut teeth on tales of this victory over proud and godless Bajadek.

The sounds and smells of his war camp swirled around him. Murmured voices, random shouts and laughter, the squeals of warhorses squabbling, sharp acid urine from man and beast, the stinging sulphur smoke of sacrifice that would drift about them all night long, a pungency of grease as chariot wheels were oiled by dour loving charioteers and horsemen cleaned their charm-heavy bridles.

Six thousand numbered his warriors only, it did not count the godspeakers and slaves who traveled with the warhost. All his people, sworn to live and die for him. They were why he walked the camp site, why he delayed the respite of sleep. Why should they die for him if he did not walk among them, to show them his confidence and call them by name?

One by one he visited their separate encampments, for within their barracks and without, his warriors lived like families with each skill-leader as father or mother. It fostered bonds of blood between them and a healthy rivalry between the disciplines.

Warmed by their welcomes he spoke with his archers, his slingshotters, his spear-carriers, his charioteers and his knife-dancers. Every warrior promised him their life; he promised them victory from the god.

As he left the knife-dancers' camp, eager for bed, he saw at its edge a warrior, dancing. He knew who it was without seeing a face or asking for a name. *Hekat*. She danced beneath the night's black ceiling, the godmoon's light glittering the length of her blade. All knife-dancers were beautiful, it was the nature of their gift, but Hekat was glorious. In the starshine her scars were hidden, she was slender bones and uncoiling muscle, she was small breasts and long limbs and a promise of death in a breath, in a heartbeat. Aieee, god, she made him burn.

"Warlord," she said, her blue gaze sliding sideways as she flowed through her *hotas* like water over rocks.

"Hekat," he replied. "Why are you dancing?"

Her teeth gleamed, she was smiling. He had never seen her smile. He was enchanted. "Why does the sun rise, warlord?" she said. "Why do birds fly and dogs stand on three legs to pish? It is the nature of things."

"You should be in your camp and sleeping. There will be dancing enough come the newsun. Blood and screaming and dying men's entrails spread on the ground, a banquet for the crows."

He knew she was young, and yet she seemed ancient. "That is for the newsun," she told him, serene. Her once-short godbraids were longer, heavy with beads they caressed her shoulders. "Now is the time I dance for the god."

Silence cloaked them as she danced with her snake-blade, folding the darkness around its sharp edge. The desire to join her stabbed his heart but he could not dance with her, he was the warlord. He danced with all his knife-dancers or none of them, the night before war.

"Where are your friends, Hekat?" he whispered. "The other knife-dancers sit quietly together, they talk, they remember, they dream of the newsun after battle. Why do you not dream with them?"

For the longest time she did not answer. She wore a scorpion round her slender neck, truly she knife-danced with the god.

"Warlord," she said, as her last *hota* sighed to stillness. "I have the god. I need no friends. I am Hekat, I dance alone."

So cold, so proud. He could warm her, he could make

her beg. "I am Raklion. I dance alone also. Perhaps one day we could dance alone together."

Her head tipped to one side. "Alone. You are the warlord, at your back ride six thousand warriors."

He ached, he was throbbing. "And yet, Hekat knife-dancer, I am alone."

"Then you are in the darkness talking to yourself, and that is not a good thing, warlord," said Hanochek's voice, approaching.

Raklion turned. Hanochek's shadow resolved, became flesh. "You come hunting me, warleader? Are you Bajadek or his Eyes now, creeping silently in the night?"

Hanochek's hand clasped him briefly. "Your body slaves grew anxious when you did not return. They wouldn't settle unless I came to find you."

"And here I am found," said Raklion. "And in no danger. I was talking to—" He turned, but the girl was gone, slipped away in the dark.

"To Hekat?" said Hano, and sighed. "Raklion, she is a strange one. All the leaders tell me of her, they shake their heads. Even Zapotar, though he says she is the finest knife-dancer he ever trained. There is something inhuman about her, they say. I have watched her. I think they are right."

"She wears a scorpion round her neck," said Raklion. "When I saw it I thought of Nagarak's pectoral. Its shadow covered her, Hanochek. Like an omen. I think she is god-touched. So young, so brilliant. How can she otherwise be explained?"

Hano snorted. "You should find out where she comes from, Raklion. She tells a story, yes, but who is there to say that story's true? She could be anyone. She could be from anywhere."

"She is from the god, Hano," he said, and smiled at his warleader's loyal suspicion. "The rest of her story is unimportant."

"So you say," said Hano. Even in moonlight his disgruntled expression was clear to read. "You watch her closely, Raklion. I see her in your eye. You should beware. Not only the godtouched are young and brilliant."

"You think her *demonstruck*?"

Hano shrugged. "I think her strange. If she survives Bajadek's smiting I think Nagarak should bleed this Hekat and sniff her blood for omens. If she is demonstruck he will smell her out."

The thought of Hekat's death stopped his breathing. "She will survive, Hano," he said roughly. "I tell you she is godtouched and sent to me by the god."

"For what purpose, Raklion? She is an urchin, a ragged child. She is pretty with a snakeblade, that I won't deny. But—"

Raklion raised his hand. "Peace, Hano. It is Bajadek I wish to battle, not my warleader. I say Hekat is no danger. I am the warlord, my word is my word."

Defeated, Hano dipped his head. "Warlord."

There could be no coolness between them, not before a day of bloodshed. Raklion slung an arm round Hano's shoulders and they walked together to his private camp. "I need your counsel, Hano. What thoughts do you have on matters of tactics?"

Seated cross-legged before his camp fire they talked of strikes and counter-strikes against Bajadek's warhost, how best they could use the open plain to their advantage.

As they talked, two of the Eyes returned sweat-slicked and triumphant. Bajadek's warhost was found, some four thousand strong and camped five fingers' distance. Three of Bajadek's Eyes were discovered sneaking up to Raklion's warhost. They were dead now, staring blindly at the sky. Raklion praised his Eyes and released them to leisure.

"We will ride for Bajadek after newsun sacrifice," he told Hanochek. "Leave me now. I would sit in silence with the god."

Hanochek nodded and withdrew. Raklion pulled out his snakeblade, he cut his forearm and gave the god his blood.

By lowsun tomorrow Bajadek will be smitten, your wrath shall lay him on the ground. I am your knife, god. I am your arrow and your spear. Use me. Let the warlords of Mijak know that Raklion warlord sits in your eye.

Newsun came swiftly, staining the sky scarlet. With sober anticipation the warriors gathered to witness sacrifice. The white lamb died with grace, in silence. Wyngra godspeaker, appointed to the warhost by Nagarak himself, captured its blood in a golden chalice and gave it to Raklion to drink. Then he scooped out the lamb's eyes and burned them to ash with a purple godstone. The ash he sifted through his fingers, drifted it onto the silver omen-plate. Naked and squatting, amulets the size of fists dangling from thongs around his neck, his wrists, his waist, he lowered his eyelids and read the ashes' drifted patterns.

"*Here is the sign of the scorpion,*" said Wyngra, rasping. His gnarled fingers traced the omens in the air. "*Here*

*is its raised tail, here are its pincers. Here lie the bodies
of the vanquished, woe to the misguided and the tricked.
Ride triumphant to battle, Raklion warlord. The god sees
you in its eye, it hungers for the blood of the disobedient
and the greedy."*

Raklion raised his snakeblade high, it flashed in the
first light, red as blood. His belly churned with fresh hot
lamb's blood. Blood stained his lips and smeared the
snake on his leather breastplate.

"The omens favor us! We ride for the god!"

"We ride for the god!" his warriors shouted. "We ride
for Raklion, warlord of Et-Raklion, city of cities in the
god's land of Mijak!"

As Wyngra wrapped the lamb's body for later eating,
Raklion turned to Hanochek. "Gather the skill-leaders. I
will speak to them before we ride."

They stood before him grim and glorious, the skill-
leaders of his warhost: Zapotar, Antokoi, Bodrik and
Dokoy. He praised them for their training and their lead-
ership, he thanked them for their service and the blood
they would spill. He promised to honor their bodies if
they should fall.

"The god sees you," he told them, fist pressed against
his heart. "The god sees you in its eye, and I see you
also."

They departed to rally their warriors, and in private he
took his leave of Hanochek. They would fight together in
the battle but that was no time for thanks or farewell.

Hano embraced him. "You are my warlord, you are my
brother and my friend," he whispered. "If I fall today, believe I fall willingly for you and the god."

"No warlord was served as I am served by you, Hano,"

he replied, and held him so hard he heard ribs creak. His voice was soft, and almost lost in the rabbling noise of the warhost gathering itself for war. Tears pricked his eyes, he let them fall. "The god see you in its eye, my friend, my brother. I will see you when the war is won."

After that the talking was over. Raklion mounted his stallion, he rode it to the head of his warhost and led them to war.

The warhosts of Et-Raklion and Et-Bajadek faced each other on the Plain of Drokar. Raklion rode out alone, to meet with Bajadek in solitary council halfway between their gathered warriors. It was an honored custom, no danger attached to such a meeting. A warlord who killed in solitary council was demonstruck and sent to hell, his sons put to death by his own people, his bloodline washed from history in blood.

"Kneel to me, Bajadek warlord," said Raklion curtly. "Confess your wickedness and accept the god's smiting of your flesh alone. Your obedient warriors should not die for their warlord's sin."

Bajadek sneered. He had only one eye, the other lost in a skirmish with Takona warlord when he inherited his father's lands. He was squat and brutal, he wielded his two unloved sons like a double-bladed knife, to cut and wound and maim the warlord who sired no living sons to follow him.

"What sin? What wickedness? I am a warlord, what I want, I take. That is the way of things, do you deny it?"

"Not even a warlord can take what the god has given to another. Nogolor warlord received my mercy. You can receive it also, for your warriors' sakes."

"Nogolor warlord is old," replied Bajadek, scornful. "Old men are like wheat, they bend in the wind. I am stone, I am timber, my bones grow in the ground. You cannot bend me, Raklion warlord. I will kill you before highsun and take your lands and your people. Your water seed has sired no offspring, your spear is blunt. Your day is done."

Raklion kept his face cold. In Et-Raklion his son was ripening. "The god turned away from Grakilon high godspeaker, the scorpions killed him for defying its desire. Nogolor warlord was spared, he gave to me his godpromised Daughter. Even now my son grows in her belly, the god sees me, Bajadek. I live in its eye. Repent, warlord. We will make a treaty. I would not spill your blood for the pleasure of watching you bleed."

"Then you are a fool, Raklion," Bajadek whispered. "Bleeding you is a pleasure long longed for. Look not for mercy from Bajadek warlord. It is a word he never was taught."

Raklion sat for a moment, watching Bajadek gallop back to his warhost. If the warlord had bowed his head, had kneeled on the ground, had admitted his mischief, he would have asked the god to let battle end before it began.

Clearly, god, that is not your desire. Blood you desire, and blood you shall have.

CHAPTER FIFTEEN

Bajadek sent out his chariots first, a foolish move of arrogant bravado. He hoped to terrify his enemy's warhost, to break their ranks and send them fleeing. His hope was wasted. Not even Bajadek's thundering chariots could break the will of Raklion's warhost. Raklion countered with mounted archers and slingshotters on foot, and with running spearmen who could strike a charioteer and his horses before they reached their enemy's front line. Not all were struck down, some of Bajadek's chariots breached his defenses. He heard his warriors and their horses screaming, he heard the crunch of bone and the tearing of flesh, smelled the first rank flooding of their blood.

He closed his ears and hardened his heart, he was fighting for the god and his own smirched honor. They died for him willingly, they died for the god.

I will honor your bodies, I will burn them to ash, I will sing your names in the godhouse of Et-Raklion.

His own chariots, Raklion held back at each flank. Hanochek led them, he would know the right time to set them free and drive Bajadek's warriors into disarray and death.

With Bajadek's charioteers destroyed or driven off, the battle began in savage earnest. Raklion led his warriors

forward at a gallop, leaping Bajadek's smashed chariots
and the bodies of the slain. With a short spear in one hand
and his snakeblade in the other he slashed, he stabbed, he
punched holes in throats and bellies, severed heads and
arms and sliced bodies wide open to spill their stinking
entrails on the ground. The Plain of Drokar churned to
bloody mud, his eyes were full of blood, his ears were
full of screaming, the sky was red, the earth was red, his
arms were red up to his shoulders.

A spear thrust took his stallion through its throat, it
plunged to the sloppy ground and sent him flying. He
struck, he rolled, and found his feet. The dead and dying
clogged the plain beneath him, he had no choice but to
tread upon them as he fought for his life. A glancing knife
slash opened his cheek, he felt the blow but not its pain.
An arrow struck him in the thigh; he snapped it off and
kept on fighting. He knew the faces of the warriors beside
him, but he couldn't remember their names. They lived,
they died, they fell or they fought on. Names no longer
mattered. All that mattered was victory for Et-Raklion.

Thrust—slash—stab—scream—over and over and
over again. Breath seared and tearing, lungs in flames,
muscles over-reached and burning, blood from his
breached body slicking flesh, pumping hot. *Kill. Kill.
Kill.*

He caught a glimpse of Bajadek through the madness,
painted in blood and wielding a broad axe. The warlord
looked demonstruck, he was weeping, laughing. Four arrows jutted from his leather breastplate and two from his
arm; if he felt them his pain did not show.

Raklion shouted as a Bajadek warrior rose before him.
Half her face was cut away, peeled from the skull like the

skin of a peach. As he lifted his spear to skewer her like goat-meat her head was shattered by an Et-Raklion sling-shotter's stone. He leapt her body and stabbed a warrior striking for Dokoy Spear-leader's back.

"Praise you, warlord!" Dokoy wheezed.

"Praise you, Dokoy," he wheezed in reply, and then they were separated, forced apart by a fresh wave of Et-Bajadek warriors, fighting to their gruesome deaths.

A ragged cry went up behind him.

"The chariots! The chariots come! God see the war-leader! God see him in its eye!"

With a roar like a landslide Hanochek and his chariots galloped into the battle. Raklion saw Hano flashing by, godbraids flying in the wind of his passing, his face alight with the promise of death.

Does that mean we are winning? Does that mean we have won?

He did not know, he could not tell, he could see no further than the next enemy warrior, his next savage kill. Sobbing for air he raised his stone-heavy arm and sliced through a bared throat, then sundered a heart in an unprotected breast. Blood spurted, he tasted iron on his lips, heard a shrill scream, a grunt of pain. Wet thuds as two bodies hit the ground.

More screaming in front of him. Hanochek and his glorious chariots smiting Bajadek's warriors, herding them and crushing them and slaughtering them like sheep.

A second glimpse of Bajadek showed the warlord howling, showed him cleaving bodies with sword and axe. Blood sprayed, arms flung high in surrender, in defeat, godsparks fleeing to the sunbright sky.

Raklion sucked air into his starving lungs, forced his mind to ignore his body's agony, and willed himself through the press of flailing slashing dying bodies towards Bajadek, his enemy, god's enemy, who was killing his precious warriors. A desperate Et-Bajadek warrior's knife caught him across the back; without looking he spun, swung, and was pressing forward again before her body hit the tumbled corpses around them. On the edges of his scarlet vision he could still see Hano's chariots, chivvying and killing Et-Raklion's enemies. He laughed aloud, a breathless gasp, and kept on pushing.

A second knife-thrust opened his arm; he severed the wrist of the man who attacked him and tasted more hot blood in his gaping mouth. Bajadek was just four paces away, his back was turned, he did not see god's wrath approaching . . .

A wild swinging sword cut across Raklion's right hamstring. He stumbled, shouting, and as his tired feet tangled in a dead horse's entrails he fell forward, down across the spotted horse's slit-apart belly. The stinking air was driven from his lungs, his blurring vision showed him horsehide and arrow shafts and three severed fingers abandoned in the mud.

Bajadek turned. "Raklion warlord!" he shouted, joyful. "On his knees before me, among his dead. The god has delivered you, Bajadek is in its eye! *Hold!*" he commanded his war-lusty warrior. "This is a warlord, his short life is *mine!*"

Gleeful and bloodsoaked, the sinning warlord approached. Raklion grunted and tried to stand but his body was spent, his strength all gone. His slashed leg would not hold him, he had no choice but to sprawl on the hulk of dead horse and repent his sins. Not one of his warriors was close by to aid him, Hano was not here, he tried to shout but he was speechless, like a rock.

Aieee, Et-Raklion! I have failed you, I have failed the god. Will it desert me? Will my godspark go to hell?

Death came towards him, and he was afraid.

Why did you say I was godblessed, Nagarak? Why did you tell me I was safe in the god's eye? Are you not my high godspeaker, do you not know the god's true will? You said I would live, how can you be wrong?

Above the faltering sounds of battle, a lilting, laughing, challenging cry.

"Bajadek warlord! Bajadek warlord!"

Raklion lifted his dizzy pounding head to look where Bajadek looked. He saw puzzled disbelief in his enemy's face, felt his weary heart leap as he recognized who it was calling Bajadek's name.

"Bajadek warlord, it is time for you to die!"

The challenging warrior danced across the charnel plain, danced towards Bajadek, a scarlet snakeblade in her scarlet hand. She was lithe, she was beautiful, bathed in blood like sacrificial milk.

Hekat.

Beneath his blood, Bajadek warlord was an ugly man. Hekat danced towards him, repulsed by his ugliness. He was all brute force, no grace, no lightness. His one good eye was wide and blue like the sky, his crimsoned skin as dark as night. He wore many godbells in his braided hair, but they were clogged with gore and could not sing.

She took this as an omen.

The air she danced through was soaked in death. The

ground she danced over was littered with warriors and horses, their emptied bowels and bladders sludging the earth and the soaked, crushed brown grasses. Their eyes were dead, they stared at nothing.

Bajadek warlord's living eye saw her. He held an axe in one hand and a sword in the other, they were smeared crimson from blade-point to hilt. He was wounded, his own blood mingled with the blood he had spilled from Raklion's warhost. He stood up straight and laughed to see her.

She challenged him again, dancing like sunlight across the crowded plain. So many warriors she had killed already, she could not count them. He would be one more.

"*Bajadek warlord! You must face me!*"

"Face *you*? A *child*?" jeered Bajadek. He hefted his axe and brandished his sword. He stood there waiting, he was unafraid. An ugly man, and stupid, also.

Hekat smiled and opened herself to the god. The god's power filled her, it set her on fire, if Bajadek cut her she would bleed out its fury. Every one of his warriors she had danced with was left weeping scarlet tears as they died. A few of them had kissed her, she was cut in this place, bruised in that. Pain was a sacrifice to the god, she gloried in it, how else could she worship but with her blood?

She danced with Bajadek, whose godbells were silenced.

The warlord was a mighty man, and with his sword and axe was mightier still. He swung at her, he slashed at her, he roared his rage and screamed his hate. He could not touch her, she was in the god's eye, and its grim power was her blood, her heart, it was her solace and her strength.

Where Bajadek reached for her she was gone, twisting sideways or upwards or around him like smoke. Where he was, her snakeblade kissed him, it bled him like a black lamb on the god's altar. She danced on sand, on a clean-swept street, he stumbled through entrails and staggered over splintered bones. Her *hotas* flowed like honey, sweet in her fingers, sweet in her toes. She was the sandcat, the lizard, the falcon dancing over the meadow. Her snakeblade was keen as mercy from the god. Inside her was stillness, death whispered in her ear.

Lost in the knife-dance, feeling Raklion's hot gaze on her, she smote Bajadek for him and for the god, a terrible ecstasy welling inside.

I am Hekat, I know what I am. I am the god's snakeblade, dancing in its eye.

Bajadek warlord was ugly, and dying. His axe was fallen from his hand and Hekat had severed his wrist's taut tendons so his fingers could no longer make a fist. His own great sword was shattered, his stolen sword not long enough to reach her. She had cut off his breastplate with two swift knife-strokes and laid him open to the bone. His arms were slashed like lamb for roasting, his legs were shredded scarlet ribbons. His heart's blood pumped with each shuddering beat, there was more outside him than within. He breathed like a camel at the end of endurance.

She stood before him on the balls of her feet, looking up into his blood-slicked face. "Bajadek warlord, it is over. You displeased the god, the god has punished you."

Pain and fear dulled his bright blue eye. "Who are you? *What* are you?"

"She is Hekat," said Raklion's pale, satisfied voice. "She is a warrior, godtouched and mine."

Bajadek's fading gaze shifted to look past her. His slack face twisted with hate. "Raklion warlord. With seed like water, and a blunted spear."

Hekat killed him. Drew her snakeblade across his throat and watched without comment as the last of his red blood spurted from the wound. Bajadek stayed standing one moment, two moments. Then his dead knees buckled and he crashed to the ground.

"Hekat," said Raklion, and put his hand on her shoulder.

She turned to him slowly, emptied of the god, emptied of power. Raklion, standing now, was hurt and bloody, he favored one leg and breathed as though the air was poisoned.

She smiled at him, though she was hurting. "You watched me, warlord. You saw me dance."

"I watched you, Hekat." He smiled back at her, a grimacing effort. "I saw you dance. You have slain my enemy. I am pleased with you."

Her hollowed heart lifted. The warlord of Et-Raklion had seen her, and was pleased. *She is Hekat. Godtouched and mine*. She was precious to him now, she had slain his enemy, she had saved his life. Her home was the barracks, for ever and ever. "I danced for you, warlord. I danced for the god."

"I know," he whispered, and bent to kiss her brow. "The god thanks you, Hekat, and so do I."

"The battle is over?"

His gaze swept across the almost silent plain. "It is over. We have won."

"No, warlord," she told him, even as the sun was blotted from the sky and a dark veil fell before her face. "The god has won. It gives us the victory. Kill a bull-calf and drink in its honor."

"Hekat!" he shouted.

She barely heard him. The last thing she felt was his strong hand, reaching for her, as she crumpled witless at his feet.

Standing in the midst of carnage Raklion grunted as Wyngra godspeaker healed his sluggishly bleeding wounds. He had resisted godspeaker attentions as long as he could, his hurts were not mortal. Other warriors needed Wyngra's godstone far more urgently than he.

But he was the warlord and Wyngra had at last insisted, using the might of his office as leverage. He capitulated. To shout at Wyngra was to invite censure from Nagarak, once they were returned to Et-Raklion.

It was two fingers past highsun, and Bajadek's death. An unsteady hush mantled the bloody Plain of Drokar. The last of the dying had been sent to hell or to the god, a sharp knife in the throat their final gift. Bajadek's warriors who'd survived their warlord's folly sat defeated on the reddened ground, watched over by warriors of victorious Et-Raklion. Each warhost's dead had been separated and laid in rows, awaiting the godspeakers' attentions. The horses too badly injured to save were killed and skinned, their hides bundled for curing, their harnesses saved for living horses. Crows argued over their naked carcasses even now, quick to feast on such generous bounty. The sky was rotten with black wings, wheeling.

"You are certain Hekat has taken no serious hurt?" he said to Wyngra, clutching at the wheel of an upturned chariot. The godspeaker's godstone burned against his severed hamstring, his flesh crawled and stretched, healing with enough pain to make him grunt and bite his lip.

"The god protected her," said Wyngra, unperturbed. He was a godspeaker of many seasons, he knew his business and the god's. "She was exhausted and wounded a little. Her hurts are healed. She will sleep now until she wakes."

Raklion nodded with sharp relief. *She is Hekat. Godtouched and mine.* What a glory was in that child. Death and beauty, gifted to him by the god. She would be his warrior forever, fighting for him and for the god. "Good. Hanochek!"

Six paces distant, Hanochek dismissed the warrior he spoke to in lowered tones, and approached. The god had seen him in its eye, he was whole and unharmed save for a little split skin and some drops of spilled blood, hardly enough to moisten dry bread. He stood beside the chariot wheel and pressed his fist against his unhurt heart.

"Warlord?"

"Tell me again how stands the tally?"

"Of our number, four hundred dead, three hundred sorely wounded," said Hano patiently. "One thousand hurt but able to ride. Almost a quarter of our horses slaughtered. We'll make them up from Bajadek's horses, if there are enough left living."

Raklion winced. Twice already Hano had given him the tally but his tired mind was reluctant to grasp it. Four hundred dead. Aieee, how his heart wept. "What else, Hano? What bad tidings do you not give me?"

Hano hesitated, then sighed. "Warlord, among the fallen there are Dokoy Spear-leader and Bodrik Chariot-leader."

"Aieee!" The news was pain greater than any sword-cut or knife-stab. His fingers tightened on the chariot wheel, and splinters bit him. Dokoy and Bodrik, great warriors. He'd chosen them himself to stand as leaders. "They died for the god, Hano. They are not gone to hell."

Hano wept without shame, tears diluting the blood on his face. He and Bodrik had been particular friends. "I know, warlord."

Raklion gripped Hano's arm, lending him a little of his meager strength. He could not weep openly, he was the warlord. "You said nearly two thousand of Bajadek's warriors are slain?"

"Yes, warlord."

"No word yet on Bajadek's second son?"

Hano shook his head. "The godspeakers are searching Et-Bajadek's death piles. If Banotaj is there with his father and brother, they'll find him."

Wyngra straightened and slipped his godstone into its pouch. "Warlord, stand on your leg now. Show me you are whole again."

Raklion released his grip on Hanochek's arm. Tentatively at first, then with more confidence, he let his injured thigh take his weight. No pain, a little stiffness. He walked five paces, then nodded and walked back. "That is good, Wyngra. Join your fellow godspeakers in the search for Bajadek's second son among the slain."

Wyngra bowed. "Warlord."

As Wyngra departed, Raklion frowned at Hanochek. They were alone now beside the upturned chariot. For a short time unobserved. He could show his tiredness and grief to Hano, there was no loss of strength in that. He leaned his hip against the chariot's splintered pole-staff and let it take his burdensome weight. Wyngra had plucked the arrowhead from his thigh, but the wound was still sore.

"Perhaps Banotaj is fled back to his father's city," he mused.

"Leaving his father and brother dead on the battle-field?" said Hano, sounding doubtful. "Naked to the crow-filled sky, without the proper rites? Let us hope not, warlord. If he lives he's the warlord now. Such cowardice does not bode well."

Raklion agreed. Bajadek warlord had tried to steal another warlord's godpromised wife. Such godless trickery could be a disease, passed from father to son like plague, with kissing. Cowardice could be its symptom.

"Has our godspeaker returned from Et-Bajadek city?"

"Not yet, warlord."

"Send him to me the moment he returns, Hano, and also when this Banotaj is found. I will walk among my warriors now. I will shed silent tears for my fallen before they burn on the pyre."

"Yes, warlord," said Hano, and bowed his head. Then he looked up. "I will make special sacrifice when we are home again, Raklion. When I saw you bloody I feared the worst."

Raklion smiled, and held him close. "The god sees me, Hano. It sees me in its eye. It sent me Hekat knife-dancer, a child with the godspeark of a mighty warrior. Aieee, if you had seen her. Bajadek warlord fell like wheat before her scythe. There is no need for Nagarak to test her blood, I have seen what she is. The god has shown me. She is Bajadek's doom, my gift from the god."

Hano stepped back. His eyes were wary. "If you say so, warlord."

"I say so, warleader," he said, displeased by Hano's displeasure. "She is the god's gift, her teeth are made of gold. Now obey my want. There is much to be done before we can ride home in triumph."

"Warlord," said Hano, and departed to his duties.

Weary, heavy-hearted for his losses, Raklion thrust aside Hano's resentment of godgiven Hekat, put on his warlord's face and went to mourn the fallen with his warriors.

The funeral pyres were lit at lowsun, for the victors and the vanquished. Bajadek's only living son had been found senseless among the wounded. Revived, he torched his father's cold remains, and his brother's. Then he torched the warrior pyres, built from the bodies of his father's fallen and timber brought by Et-Bajadek's sullen godspeakers. Soaked in pitch the pyres burned and burned, sparks like godsparks flying into the starlit sky.

Banotaj was a young man, twenty seasons had he seen. Raklion, regarding him, his own pyres already burning, his silent tears shed, his warriors praised and comforted, wondered how he would fare as warlord.

It would be no bad thing if he faltered, I think. A neighboring warlord embroiled in domestic bickering is one kept safely inside his borders.

When the last pyre was set alight and Banotaj had returned to stand with Raklion and the godspeakers from both sides of the conflict, sacrifice was made by Wyngra and one of Bajadek's godspeakers. The bull-calf blood was caught in two gold cups and presented to the warlords. The warlords unsheathed their knives and slashed their arms, they dripped their blood into their cups, then swapped them, in silence. In silence they drank, in sight of the god and its godspeakers and the gathered warriors, to signify an end to war.

"Banotaj warlord," said Raklion, as his wounded arm was bound with linen. No godspeaker healing for this hurt, there must be a scar to record the peace. "The days of Et-Bajadek are done with and dead. That name now passes into history. You are Banotaj warlord of Et-Banotaj."

Bajadek's son had a sulky mouth. His eyes were small, and too far apart. His teeth were bad, with empty pits no longer jeweled. Healed of his battle wounds, the scars still livid, he said, begrudging, "Raklion warlord. I will take my warriors and return to my city, now that proper honors are done."

Raklion nodded. "My warhost will camp one more night on this Plain of Drokar. At newsun I will take funerary ashes from my pyres and depart. My quarrel was with Bajadek, defier of the god's want. He is dead. The god desires peace between us. My son ripens in Et-Nogolor's Daughter. Sire your own son, Banotaj. Teach him the lessons learned here this day and in doing so you will appease the god."

Banotaj's small, wide eyes slitted with impotent rage. "You are not my father, to give me advice."

Raklion leaned close. "That is true. I killed your father. Let his death be his last lesson to you."

"I was told a girl-child killed Bajadek," said Banotaj, his whole face a sneer. "*You* were crawling in the mud."

They had drunk the peace blood; striking the boy would be a sin. Raklion bared his teeth, though, to hint at possibilities. "I am the warlord, Banotaj. All your dead warriors died by my hand."

Banotaj smiled. "The warrior who killed my father is loved by me for slitting his throat. Which one is she, Raklion? Take me to her. I would give thanks for her clever knife. She has saved me from a tedious task."

Raklion stared. Banotaj would plot his own father's death? No wonder Bajadek had sought Et-Nogolor's Daughter if this was a sample of his get. Disgusted, he folded his arms.

"Our business is finished. Take your misguided godspeakers and your defeated warriors and go. Think not to disturb the peace of Mijak, unless you are eager for the god to smite you as today it smote your father."

Banotaj spat on the Plain of Drokar and walked away.

The night air was heavy with the stench of burned flesh. No kind breeze dispersed the smoke or the stink. With Hano beside him, Raklion watched Banotaj and his people depart the silent battlefield.

"You should rest now, Raklion," said Hano, solicitous. His temper was sweet again, their friendship returned. "All is done that can and should be done. Come newsun we will gather our fallen's ashes to take home to the godhouse, then sing songs of their courage all the way to Et-Raklion."

Raklion nodded. "Will you rest with me? My heart is

heavy with our losses, Hano. This is one night I would not be alone."

"Of course," said Hano. His eyes were gentle, and pleased. "You are my warlord and my friend."

What Raklion wanted was to rest with Hekat, but no warlord could lie with a common warrior. A chance child of their coupling would be abomination. Warlords fucked concubines and sired children on women bred from warlord blood. He could not—must not—lie with Hekat.

His body ached for need of her.

"Come, friend," he said, and draped an arm about Hano's muscled shoulders. "Lighten my heart and make me smile. Tomorrow we return victorious to Et-Raklion. Show me how to celebrate tonight."

CHAPTER SIXTEEN

They returned triumphant to Et-Raklion, and Et-Raklion greeted them with song and sacrifice. The warhost paraded the streets of every district so the people might see Raklion warlord and his mighty warriors, smiters of Bajadek, fist of the god. Even the slaves were allowed to dance. Raklion laughed as his people threw flowers, and coins, and amulets. His warriors kept the wilting flowers, Nagarak's godspeakers took the rest.

Riding beside him, Hano laughed. "You should show your face to the city more often, warlord. See how they love you? Like your warriors, they love you."

Raklion smiled, it was not his answer.

They would love me better if I gave them a son. Six godmoons from now I will have one to give them. Then will I show my face more often. Then will they have good reason to love me. Triumph is fleeting. A son is forever.

The ashes of Et-Raklion's fallen were interred in the godhouse, where Nagarak and his godspeakers prayed for them three highsuns without ceasing. Raklion prayed with them for one highsun, then for two high-suns witnessed his warriors' funeral games for the fallen. Hekat danced before him, one warrior among thousands. Raklion pretended not to see her, he did not smile. Hano sat with him, he would not approve were she singled out.

Five highsuns after the funeral games were ended, as the night cooled towards the quiet time, he was disturbed in his private chamber by a body slave.

"Trader Abajai is in the palace, warlord," the slave said softly. "He requests an urgent audience."

Abajai? Intrigued, concerned, Raklion put aside the tablet he was reading, dressed in his finest blue linen robe and crimson wool cloak and received the Trader in his public chamber. Abajai had not come alone, his partner Yagji attended with him.

"Warlord," said Abajai, prostrated beside Yagji on the marble floor.

Straight-backed in his warlord's chair, Raklion gestured for them to rise. "Traders. Why do you disturb my peace? Do you bring me further word of trouble on the road?"

Abajai bowed. "No, warlord. We bring you word of trouble in your warhost."

In his warhost? Raklion frowned, and put a bite in his voice. "What do Traders know of my warhost? It is warlord business, and none of yours."

Yagji whimpered. "Warlord, please hear us. We have had word something precious of ours is in your possession."

Something of *theirs*? Raklion drummed his fingers on the arm of his chair. "I cannot see how this is so. A warlord has no need of Trader baubles."

With a sharp glance at Yagji, Abajai stepped forward. A bold move, he was clearly distressed. "Warlord, may I explain?"

"You may. Swiftly. Or be swiftly punished for your temerity."

The Traders had worn their costliest robes, which was only proper. Abajai slid his hands into his green silk sleeves and said, "Warlord, you know Traders oft trade in whispers."

"I do."

"You also know whispers whispered to us, then to you, have served you honestly in the past."

He let them see his growing impatience. "We do not whisper now, Abajai. Now we speak plainly."

Yagji flinched, and Abajai nodded. "Warlord. It is whispered to us that Bajadek warlord was slain by a knife-dancer in your warhost. It is whispered she is a mere child, who appeared in your barracks from nowhere, alone, a handful of godmoons ago. Is that a true whisper, warlord, or must we smite the whisperer as a sinning liar?"

Raklion felt his heart thud, once. *Hekat.* What mischief was this? "Bajadek warlord was slain by a knife-dancer. That is true."

Yagji yelped and scuttled closer. "Warlord, warlord, is her name Hekat? Aiece! Your face tells me it is! Warlord, you are wickedly sinned against, you are her victim! *We* are her victims, Aba and me! Warlord, this Hekat is a runaway *slave*, bought by us in the savage north! She cost us a fortune in food, in clothing, in hiring a tutor to—"

Raklion lowered his upraised hand. "Trader Abajai. This is true?"

Abajai nodded, and the godbells braided into his hair chimed in sorrowful agreement. "Warlord, it is. If the knife-dancer Hekat is the girl I paid coin for beyond the lands of Et-Jokriel."

"This knife-dancer claims to come from Et-Nogolor."

"We passed through Et-Nogolor on our way to Et-Raklion," said Abajai. "But she did not come from there."

Raklion hid his pain behind his face, his heart beat hard with cruel foreboding. "The knife-dancer we speak of bears no slave-braid."

"She ran away before it was given her," said Yagji, his glance at Abajai an accusation. "Warlord, truly, she is our slave."

"What does she look like, this runaway Hekat?"

"She is beautiful, warlord," said Abajai. "I could have sold her for five thousand gold pieces, that is the limit of her beauty."

It *was* the limit. Traders could not sell a ruined face full of scars. But to him Hekat's scars were nothing. To him she was beyond a price. Hekat his warrior, his knife, his dancer. But if she were a runaway slave . . .

Hekat . . . Hekat . . . what have you done?

"Who knows of this?" he said. "Who have you told, that my warrior is your missing property?"

"No-one, warlord," said Abajai. "It hurts our reputation to be known as Traders who cannot control a single girl-child. And the whispers might be wrong. Until we see her, nothing is certain."

Raklion struck the bronze summoning bell. "Send to the barracks for the warrior Hekat," he told its answering slave. "Bring her before me, with discretion."

He waited in silence, without looking at the Traders. They stood together and stared at their feet, they knew better than to tempt his temper with uninvited talk.

Hekat . . . Hekat . . . what have you done?

She came to him softly, her bare feet kissing the cold marble floor. Her hurts from the battle were completely healed. Even her spiderweb scars were fading, turning to silver with the passage of time. She wore a linen training tunic, badly sewn around the hem. Her snakeblade was belted at her waist. In her left ear, her arrowhead dangled.

She saw Abajai and Yagji, and stood quite still.

"Hekat," said Raklion, his belly twisting, his loins on fire. "The Traders Abajai and Yagji disturb my rest with a tale of you. They claim your ownership. They say you are property, their runaway slave. Is this falsehood or is this truth?"

Before she could answer, Yagji turned on her. "You wicked brat, you ungrateful wretch, you horrible horrible little liar!" His eyes were bulging, spittle flecked his lips. "Retoth was *flogged* because of you, I couldn't keep a meal down for three full highsuns, he wept and pleaded for mercy so! How *dare* you run away from us? We saved you from that godforsaken village, we offered you life in the civilized south!"

She stood her ground in the face of his anger, like a

knife-dancer on the field of war. "A life as a slave. I did not want that."

Yagji gobbled. "Who are we to care what *you* want? You were bought and paid for, there is the end of it!"

"Hekat," said Abajai. His face was disdainful. "You lied to yourself, you cannot lie here. You knew you were purchased. You were ignorant but you knew that much. What foolish tales you told yourself after, because I was wise and protected my investment, they are no concern of mine. You were my slave then. You are my slave now."

Raklion watched and listened. His heart tolled like a godbell in his chest.

They cannot have her. And I will not give her to Nagarak for nailing. She is Hekat. Godtouched and mine.

Her blue eyes glittered. "The coin you parted with makes no difference, Abajai. I am no man's slave, I belong to the god."

Ignoring that, Abajai stepped close and touched her scars. "You did that to your face?"

She smiled unflinching until he stepped back. "No. The god did it."

Abajai sighed, and shook his head. "Foolish Hekat. When you were beautiful, you were precious to me. Now you are nothing, you are meat with maggots, you are a horse with a broken leg. Worthless. Useless. A waste of the air."

Hekat's scars tightened as she frowned. "I am Hekat. I dance with my snakeblade. I killed a warlord for the god." Her straight finger pointed. "You are a Trader. You peddle in flesh. Your purpose was to find me in the savage north so I could serve the god by serving Raklion, its warlord. Your purpose is done. You may go now, Aba."

As Abajai hissed and Yagji squealed his outrage, Raklion swallowed laughter. So bold, so proud.

Hekat . . . I love you.

Abajai turned. "Warlord, do you see we tell the truth?"

Raklion nodded, hiding reluctance. "I see my warrior is Abajai's slave. Does Abajai suggest I stole her from him?"

"*No*, warlord!" cried Yagji. "We suggest no such thing! How were you to know what she was? You were *grossly* deceived, and so were we!"

"You wish to take her?"

Abajai snorted. "Take home meat with maggots in it? Bridle a horse with a broken leg? She is a runaway, warlord. She spits on the god. Let the god take her. Let her perish in its eye, let her be nailed to the runaway's godpost and left to die in pish and pain. That is the fate of runaway slaves."

Hekat's head lifted, her fingers rested on her blade. Her eyes found Raklion's, wide and questioning. He drummed his fingers, and she relaxed.

"You are certain of this, Trader Abajai? You renounce your ownership, you give her to Nagarak high godspeaker for smiting?"

"Warlord, I am certain. She is Nagarak's now."

He nodded. "So be it. I will send her to the godhouse that she might be punished."

Yagji's fat face was bloated with spite. "When will the high godspeaker kill her, warlord? I want to be there. I want to see this vicious bitch die. We are owed that much, for what she has stolen."

"It is your right, Trader. A message will be sent. Return home now, and speak of this business to no-one."

The Traders bowed and withdrew from the chamber, not a single look for the girl-child they condemned.

Hekat said, "You will not give me to Nagarak for killing."

"No?" said Raklion, and looked at her with narrowed eyes. "But Hekat, you are a runaway slave. The law is the law, I must not flout it."

She shrugged. "The law is nothing beside the god. It sent those Traders to buy me for its purpose. It guided me to your barracks so I might serve."

"What if your service was to slay Bajadek warlord? You have slain him. Perhaps your death must serve it now."

"Tcha," she said, like a scornful nursemaid. "The god is not yet finished with me."

For the first time. Raklion felt a roil of unease. "The god? Or a demon? Hekat, you are no ordinary girl-child. I fear you have snared me in a demon's trap."

She reached beneath her tunic and pulled out her amulet, the black stone scorpion that drank the light. "Here is the god's symbol, warlord. Could I wear it un-smitten if I served a demon?"

Godspeaker wisdom said she could not. "How *old* are you?" he demanded.

She shrugged again. "Old enough to slay Bajadek in battle."

Old enough to stir his loins. She was his heart, standing outside him. "Are you truly from the savage north? I have never been there, I am told it is harsh."

"I am from the god, warlord," she said, impatient. "The rest is nothing, it is foam on sadsa."

"And what of Trader Abajai?" he asked her. "What of

his petulant partner, Yagji? They think I *do* send you to
Nagarak for killing."

She did not answer. The silence deepened, it filled
with blood.

He said, after some time, "If you are discovered I must
deny you."

She smiled, it was a fearsome sight. "I will not be discovered, warlord. I am in the god's blinding eye, no-one
sees me when I hide there."

Raklion sat back in his warlord's chair and fingered his
godbraids. Their godbells chimed, praising the god.

*The world is full of Traders, peddling flesh and useful
whispers. I could throw a stone from the palace and strike
another Abajai, another Yagji, without taking careful aim.
The Traders district is overrun with them, like rats.*

He sat in his chair, and watched Hekat leave.

It was the quiet time in Et-Raklion as Hekat walked
through the streets to the Traders district. The prowling
godspeakers looked past and through her, she expected it,
she was not amazed. The god was guiding her, she could
feel its presence. Its mystery cloaked her, closing every
eye to her silent passing.

The cream stone wall of Abajai and Yagji's expensive
villa was no barrier to her. She was a trained knife-dancer
now, she needed no convenient tree. She leapt from the
street to the wall's wide top, then lightly into the garden
below. Yagji's bubbling fountains sounded loud in the silence, but otherwise not even a nightbird broke the bush.
No lamplight showed behind the villa's shuttered windows, Abajai and Yagji were not entertaining, they were
safe in their beds certain she would soon die.

They mocked the god. She would prove them wrong.

She slipped through the darkness to the rear of the villa, to the door that led in and out of the slaves' vegetable garden. Easing it open, stepping inside the villa's slave quarters, she stood for a moment to see if any slave stirred. She heard nothing. Retoth slept, and the other slaves with him. Her unshod feet trod the passage to the staircase, they took her up into the villa where Abajai and Yagji dreamed, unawares.

The nightlamps in the corridors were burning, that was the only thin light in the villa. Every lavish room was sunk in shadow, shadows cloaked her as she breathed her soft way to the villa's sleeping chambers.

She would deal with Yagji first.

He was a mound beneath his blankets, all his god-braids tied up in a scarf. The flickering bedlamp on the table, lit against demons, burning incense, showed her his slack mouth drooping, drooling. His shifting eyes beneath their eyelids. His overfed flesh and the pettiness he carried with him like coin, that wafted from him like spoiled perfume.

Around her neck the scorpion amulet trembled. It was a carved stone thing, and yet it felt alive. She eased the amulet over her head and unthreaded it from its leather thong with steady, unhurried fingers. When it was free she held it before her eyes, feasting her gaze on it, seeking to know the god's desire.

I am a knife-dancer, I have my blade. Shall I slit Yagji's throat, god? Shall I kill him like a goat?

An answer came, not in words but as a feeling.

No. What happened here was sacred business, not the bloody slaughter of the battlefield. Guided by impulse, by the god's silent voice, she tugged back Yagji's covering blankets and set the stone amulet on his bare chest. The god was in her stone scorpion, let her stone scorpion be its instrument.

Die, Yagji. Die a sinning man.

She waited, barely breathing. Was it the lamplight or did the scorpion ripple? She could hear her heart beating, drumming for the god.

Yagji woke. His eyes flew open. He saw her standing there and tried to scream, but no sound left his open mouth. He looked at the scorpion on his skin, dark eyes wide with rising terror and pain.

Hekat leaned over him. "You stupid Yagji. I belong to the god. You cannot touch me. You belong to demons."

A whimper escaped him. He tried to throw the scorpion from him, he could not grasp it, it would not move. He tried to sit up, the scorpion pinned him. He was pinned to the mattress, weighed down by the god. Water filled his eyes, it slid down his cheeks. "*No . . . no . . .*" His voice was a whisper, his bones were chalk.

Slowly, so slowly, the god extinguished his godspark. Unmoved, Hekat watched the life drain from his bulging eyes. They dimmed, they faded, they died completely. Yagji was dead, and gone to hell. She lifted the scorpion from his unmoving chest and carried it along the passageway to Abajai's room.

Serene and sleeping, he did not stir. For a small time she stood by his bed and watched him, breathing deep of the incense he burned against demons. She stared at the scarlet scorpion on his cheek. She had never liked Yagji, but Abajai she had loved and trusted.

Only the god deserves love and trust.

She placed the stone scorpion on Abajai's chest.

Like Yagji before him the Trader woke startled, his body filled with pain and fear. He clawed at the amulet but could not remove it, its carved stone pincers were sunk in his flesh.

There was sorrow in her this time, for the Hekat who had loved him, for the man she'd thought he was. She banished it, coldly. Sorrow was weak.

"You go to hell now, Abajai," she told him. "Go to Yagji, he waits for you. The god wants no godspark of a wicked man. *You* are the meat with maggots in it. *You* are the horse with a broken leg. I am not your slave, I belong to the god. If you had seen this I would not be here. You would not be dying a sinner's death."

His ribcage labored as he struggled for air. His taloned fingers reached for her but she was beyond him. She was always beyond him, she knew that now. He should have known but he would not listen.

Stupid Abajai, deaf to the god.

When the scorpion was finished, and Abajai was dead, she left the villa as she had entered. Unheard, unseen, except by the god.

Sighing, Vortka shifted the offering-satchel from his left shoulder to his right. It wasn't as heavy as it could be, public offerings had dwindled since the celebrations of Raklion warlord's victory over Bajadek, but still it was heavy enough. With the satchel resettled and aching his spine, he took his small godknife from his robe pocket and nicked the side of his left hand's little finger. Crimson blood welled reluctantly, as tired of flowing as he was of cutting himself. Ignoring the small, familiar pain he smeared the snake-eye carved into the godpost at the end of Eluissa Way. Power swelled and surged and he felt a warm pleasure.

I am a godspeaker. I serve the god.

Leaving the newly sanctified and protected Eluissa godbowl behind him he trudged the city's cobblestones to the next. Its godpost guarded the end of Dog-tooth Alley, which marked the beginning of the Traders district. He'd started collection duty just after newsun, and still the city's streets were nearly deserted. A few slaves scurried about their masters' business, some early risers reclined on curtained litters or sat upright in slave-drawn carriages. He did not speak to them, they did not speak to him. Godspeakers were revered and feared, even the novices, something he had never looked for in his life.

Before his father's death, before his mother became wife to that other man, he'd always thought he'd be a potsmith. That like a good son he'd follow the path trod by his father and his father's father and his father's father's father, all the way back to the world's beginning. Potsmithing with clay and bronze and reed and carved stone was honest work seen in the god's eye. He had not asked for more than that.

He had not asked to be a *godspeaker*.

Like everyone in his village of Todorok, in all of Mijak, he prayed the god saw him in its eye. He attended sacrifice, he obeyed the god's law, he wore his amulets and made sure the godspeaker never saw him in *his* eye, for being seen by a godspeaker almost never boded well. He lived his life believing the god *did* see him, he worked hard as a potboy for his father, knowing he would soon be old enough for proper potsmithing tasks.

But then his potsmith father died and he disappeared entirely from the god's all-seeing eye. After that came pain and grief, then Trader Abajai with his chains. He saw himself a slave until the day he died. He did not dream the god had another purpose for him.

The instant his fingers closed about the godstone in Et-Nogolor city's slave pen he knew he was no slave but a chosen servant of the god. The god's power poured into him, scouring away the old Vortka, polishing the new. The path before him became unknown and unknowable, the god did not share its secrets with mortals. Not until a mortal was needed. That was its way, he would never question it.

True, life as a novice wasn't easy or painless, but what did that matter? Nothing mattered but the god. It had saved him from slavery, brought him to Et-Raklion, it had crossed his path with the knife-dancer Hekat, that strange fierce warrior-child he had never forgotten.

She is chosen, as I am. In its time the god will tell me why.

Until then he would serve in the godhouse, he would be the god's slave. Godhouse chains were not so hard to bear.

The godbowl at the end of Dog-tooth Alley was scarcely one-third full. Vortka frowned. Traders were rich men, they could do better than this. He emptied their miserly offerings into his satchel, sealed the godpost and its bowl and walked deeper into the Traders district. If its other godbowls were not more generously filled he would have to tell Salakij novice-master, who would tell Nagarak, and Nagarak would punish the Traders for disrespecting the god.

He shuddered. Foolish Traders, if that was their fate.

The sun was higher in the sky by two fingers now, and more people hurried about their business. If there was one good thing in tramping the streets, emptying godbowls, it was the chance to leave the godhouse for a time, see faces that did not surround him in the godhouse. Many tested godspeakers served in the city, they were the weft and warp of Et-Raklion, of every warlord city in Mijak, but never novices. They could not be trusted with important administrative tasks. If Salakij were to be believed, novices could barely be trusted with a broom.

As he walked the streets he tested his godsense, a godspeaker's ability to taste emotions and scent a man's sin, to sense the past and sometimes the future. To know things unknown by any man not touched by the god. It was whispered among the novices that Nagarak had the power to read men's minds as though they were common tablets of clay, but who could say if that were true? The high godspeaker spawned more rumors than a fly laid maggots. He could not read minds himself, that was all he knew. But ever since he'd woken the godstone in Et-Nogolor he'd been able to sense moods, and sometimes hidden meanings in the world.

That was impressive for a novice godspeaker.

Even as he opened himself to the mosaic emotions of hurrying slaves and bustling Traders he looked around him at the district's expensive villas. Life was odd, filled with the god's mystery. If the Trader caravan had not stopped in Et-Nogolor he might have ended up here, a humble slave with a scarlet godbraid.

Abajai and Yagji lived on one of these streets. He would know them at once, but doubted they would recognize him. He had never been a person to them, he was walking coin, gold in chains. Would they recognize Hekat if they saw her? He hoped not, for she was their runaway. Bad things happened to runaway slaves.

He pinched himself, to stop wrong thinking. *Worry for Hekat is a sin. She belongs to the god, it will protect her. If you doubt that, you must kneel for the cane.*

He did not want to kneel for the cane. Besides, how would Abajai and Yagji see her? Traders had no business with warriors. And Hekat was different now, not just because of the scars. She was taller, stronger, her bones were tightly roped with muscle. Her face beneath its spiderweb had changed, she was a warrior with blood in her eyes. It would be best for those Traders if they did *not* see her or show they knew her if they did.

With a deep breath in and out Vortka loosened his painful grip on the satchel straps and bent his thoughts towards his duty.

The godpost godbowl on Travas Street was half-filled with offerings, a more satisfactory result even if it did mean the weight of his offering-satchel almost bent him double. He could manage one more bowl's offerings but that was all, if he filled the satchel to the brim it would pull his spine to pieces, he was certain. To save himself from that calamity he would have to return to the godhouse after his next collection, deliver his satchel's contents into the godhouse treasury, then return to the city to complete his task.

Tcha. And the godhouse kitcheners wondered at the appetites of novice godspeakers . . .

Swallowing a sigh lest the god think he was complaining, Vortka trudged past villa after villa towards Rokbrot

Way, where the next godbowl waited. Just as he reached a long cream stone wall his novice godsense hummed a warning. A heartbeat later he heard a fearful screeching, the sound of panicked running feet. Then the villa wall's blue-painted door flew open and he looked in surprise upon a panting slave.

"Godspeaker! Godspeaker! My masters are dead! Both of them stone-dead in their beds!"

"What do you mean, slave? How are they dead? What has killed them?"

The distraught slave wrung his plump well-kept hands. "Demons, godspeaker! It must be demons! Please, I beg you, come see for yourself!"

Vortka hesitated. He was only a novice, demons were dealt with by those older and wiser than he. But if he sent for a superior and demons were not present, if he wasted that superior's time . . .

"Show me, slave."

The slave's tear-streaked face quivered with relief. "Yes, godspeaker. Hurry, hurry, follow me!"

Once inside the lavish villa, where more distressed slaves wept and milled, Vortka let his heavy satchel slide from his shoulder to the polished tile floor.

"Someone must stand with these godhouse offerings," he said. Seeing the slaves start with fright, he took off his amulet and held it out. "Here is my demoncharm, blessed by Nagarak himself. If demons abide here they will not dare strike the wearer of this amulet."

"You there!" said the slave who'd fetched him, pointing to a young strong man. "Take the godspeaker's demoncharm and guard his satchel with your life!"

"Yes, Retoth," the young slave murmured, and did as he was told.

"You are called Retoth?" Vortka asked. The slave nodded. "Then, Retoth, take me to your dead masters."

CHAPTER SEVENTEEN

The slave Retoth was reluctant to enter the cold, still sleeping chamber. Hanging back, he pointed through the open doorway and said, his voice unsteady, "There lies my master Abajai."

Vortka faltered. *Abajai?* Was there more than one Abajai in the Traders district? He took a deep breath and entered the room. One glance at the bed's occupant told him there was not. "You found him like this?"

"Yes, godspeaker. I have not touched him."

Abajai's eyes were wide and staring, a fearful glare of agony and despair. Raised and blistered, the flesh of his naked chest echoed the image of a scorpion. The tattooed scorpion in his cheek was faded. Shriveled.

This was godsmite, unmistakable.

"Show me the other one," he told the slave.

Yagji's face was a mirror of Abajai's, a dreadful rictus of terror and pain. Burned in his chest, the same angry scorpion.

"This was no demon," Vortka told the slave Retoth. "This was the god. Send a slave to the godhouse, tell them Vortka calls for aid. *Now*, Retoth."

But Retoth was transfixed. "The *god* has taken my masters from me?" he whispered. "But *why*, godspeaker? What was their sin? They were *good* men, they—"

Vortka struck him across the face. "You dare to question in a room still filled with the god's dread presence? Do you wish to join your masters in hell?"

Retoth gobbled in his throat, like a chicken. "*No*, god-speaker!"

"Then do as I bid you! And put the other slaves away where they will not be troublesome underfoot."

The slave Retoth stumbled from Yagji's chamber. A moment later Vortka heard him shouting, and the hurried shuffling of many feet. Ignoring that, he looked again at the body on the bed.

Why are you dead, Yagji, you and Abajai? Why did the god smite you? How did you sin, to be so struck doun?

Burdened with dread, with unanswered questions, he returned to the villa's entrance hall and waited for the senior godspeakers to arrive.

When they came at last, a breath before highsun, they dismissed him to the godhouse. Relieved, Vortka escaped the villa with his heavy offering-satchel and struggled with it up the Pinnacle Road. After attending sacrifice he witnessed the collected coins and amulets counted into the treasury, then was freed until lowsun to pursue private dedications.

It meant he could hide himself in the library and study the law and godhouse history. He could kneel before a godpost in the shrine garden and open his heart and mind to the god. He could train his body in the disciplines of godspeaker *hotas*, rigorous exercises designed to tone the body and keep it supple for the god. He could present himself to the taskmasters and offer his flesh for mortification, in remorse for all his novice shortcomings.

He did none of these permitted things. Instead he slipped from the godhouse and went to find Hekat.

She sat on a camp-bed in her shell-barracks, mending a pile of blade-slashed tunics. She was alone. When she wasn't training or eating she was always alone. Alone with her snakeblade, dancing her *hotas* again and again. That was how she worshipped the god.

He wondered if she ever got lonely, but so far hadn't asked her. Something in her face discouraged those kinds of questions. "Hekat," he said, and closed the door behind him.

She stared in surprise. "Vortka? You should not be here. What do you want?"

"To talk." He looked at the pile of mending on the floor at her feet. Many of the tunics were stained brownish-red about the fraying slices in the fabric. "These are all yours?"

"Tcha!" she said, and poked the tunics with a bare toe. "Not one of them is mine, stupid Vortka. You think a snakeblade touches me when I knife-dance with my shell?"

"Then who do they belong to?"

"Beginner knife-dancers come to join Raklion's warhost." She raised her arms above her head and stretched, like a cat. He tried not to notice the lift of her small breasts beneath the linen covering her body. She was a warrior and he was not a vessel, there could be no meeting of their flesh. To hope otherwise was to condemn himself to the most severe tasking in the godhouse.

"More knife-dancers is a good thing, isn't it?" he said, distracting himself.

Her scars tangled themselves with contempt. "They dream of glory because we defeated Bajadek warlord, they think every day is a day of war. They think it is easy, to be a warrior." She smiled, unkindly. "They are learning different. They make me laugh."

He looked again at the pile of tunics. "If they are not yours, Hekat, why do you mend them?"

"*Tcha!*" she spat, and leapt off her camp-bed to dance lightly down the shell-barracks center aisle and back again. "Stupid Zapotar, he punishes Hekat. I did not show myself to him when I came back to barracks last night. He says I sinned. He does not dare beat me, Raklion warlord sees me in his eye, so he says I must not dance my *hotas*, I must sit in this place and stab myself with needles." She made a face. "That is not really why he is angry. He is angry because I killed Bajadek warlord, I saved Raklion's life. He is jealous, I am the best knife-dancer and the warhost knows it."

Vortka felt his heart squeeze tight. He had heard about Bajadek's slaying, who had not? But the warlord's death was not important now. *Abajai and Yagji, slain in their beds.* "You were out of the barracks last night?"

With exquisite control she turned slow and steady cartwheels between the long rows of camp-beds. The scorpion amulet round her neck swung to and fro, fracturing shadows. As the stone caught the light something about it tugged at his memory, he could not think why and pushed the thought aside for later. She was beautiful, turning cartwheels.

When she was finished she stood before him, fierce

and fearless. "The warlord sent to see me. I went to him. We spoke. I returned."

"When did you return?"

She shrugged. "The godmoon and his wife were in the sky. I paid no closer attention than that."

"Hekat . . ." Aiece, how his heart was pounding. "Abajai and Yagji were killed last night."

Behind its scars her face was indifferent. But in her eyes he saw cold flames flickering. "You say so?"

"I saw their bodies. They are dead." She said nothing. She was not surprised. Seeing that, his skin went cold. "You did not need me to tell you. You knew already."

"And if I did?" she retorted. "Is that your business? I think it is not."

She had killed a warlord, slain him with her sharp snakeblade. That was warrior business . . . but the Traders were not. "Hekat, please. Are you bound in this? Is their blood on your hands? Did you kill them?"

"Tcha," she said, and bent herself backwards until her hands touched the floor behind her. "The god killed them, Vortka. If you saw them you know that is true."

"But you were there, weren't you? You are somehow involved." Curved like a horseshoe, she did not deny it. Staring at her, he felt sick and uncertain, his head felt light. "Tell me what happened."

With astonishing agility she flipped around and over and onto her feet. "You know what happened," she said, flicking him a dark look. "The Traders died."

"*Why?*"

"Because they were stupid, they defied the god. They stopped their ears and refused to heed its wanting. They are no loss."

He could have smacked her. "*Tell me properly*. Tell me everything."

Frowning, Hekat drifted her fingers to the snakeblade on her belt. Then she sighed. "They learned where I was, Vortka. They told the warlord I belonged to them. They told the warlord they wanted me dead. The god does not want me dead, the god sees me in its eye and wants me to live. I returned to their villa. I watched them die. I came back to the barracks and now I mend tunics. That is what happened. You can go away now."

He had no intention of going anywhere, not until she told him everything. "Hekat, they died by *godsmite*!"

She smiled, and touched the amulet around her neck. "I know. I put my scorpion on them and the god's power in me stopped their wicked hearts. They died in terrible fear and pain." The smile twisted. "Stupid Traders."

The god's power in her? How could that be? She was a warrior, only a godspeaker contained the god's power. Determined to prove her wrong he opened his godsense and looked at her with his inner eyes.

Touching her godspark was like breathing fire. He gasped, muscles spasming, and wrenched himself free of the cauldron that was Hekat before she burned him to ash and crumbling bone.

"You see?" she said. "The god is in me. I live in its eye."

"I see," he croaked, his throat scorched. "What you have shown me—it is dangerous to know. If Nagarak finds out . . . will you kill *me* now, Hekat? Will you put your scorpion on my flesh and watch it send *my* godspark to hell?"

She dropped to the nearest camp-bed, flames still

flickering in her eyes. He felt their echo in his blood. "Why would the god want your death, Vortka? You are godtouched as I am godtouched. You will not betray me. The god knows this and so do I."

He wet his dry lips. "Abajai and Yagji . . ."

"Are dead because they wished to deny the god's desire. You love the god, you serve the god, it chose you in that Et-Nogolor slave pen. Do not fear me, Vortka. I am not your death."

She was so young, yet she had killed a warlord. The god burned in her, its shadows darkening her face. Vortka shivered. "I am frightened, Hekat. You frighten me," he whispered. "I am a potsmith made slave turned godspeaker. What is my place here? What is yours?"

She laughed at him. "When you found me in the darkness, dancing, then you knew your place in this. As for mine, I will tell you in my time. The god is in us, Vortka. Let it guide you, let it fill you with its desires. Go back to your godhouse. Forget Abajai and Yagji, they are gone to hell. They are devoured by demons for their sins."

And she was devoured by the god.

She is far beyond me already, he realized, standing. *What will become of us as she grows in her power? Why has the god chosen her? What is her purpose? What is mine, that I know this about her?*

He had no answers. He returned to the godhouse, to ask the god. The god did not tell him.

He must wait, and see.

Raklion let nothing show on his face when Nagarak came down from the godhouse after highsun sacrifice to tell him of the two dead Traders. He said, "You are certain it was godsmite? It could be plague, returned to plague us. Pestilence sleeps in the sand and soil of Mijak, not long ago these Traders traveled the length and breadth of the land. Who knows what contagion they brought home with them on the soles of their shoes?"

Nagarak would never sit when in his warlord's private chamber, he paced within its confines, he was a restless man. "I am high godspeaker, yet you ask if I am certain?"

Raklion raised one hand in brief apology. In his chest his heart beat hard. They died of godsmite? *Hekat . . . Hekat . . . what have you done*? "Explain this, Nagarak. Why would the god smite these Traders, do you know? Has it told you?"

The merest hesitation in Nagarak's stamping stride, the slightest flicker of his eyes. "Some godspeaker business is not for discussion outside the godhouse. If these deaths have meaning beyond the sinful lives of the dead I will tell you, warlord. More than that you need not know."

He knew Nagarak, now. *He cannot answer. The god has not told him why the Traders died.* Relief and pleasure mingled hotly. It was a clear sign the god wanted Hekat safe. *She is a knife-dancer yet the Traders died by godsmite. How could that be, god? Hekat, who are you?*

Nagarak stamped to a standstill. "I am here in your palace, I will see Et-Nogolor's Daughter. Your son ripens in her, I would lay hands on her belly and feel his strength. Take me to her, warlord. I would—"

Knuckles rapped on the door, then his personal slave entered. "Warlord, forgive me. Hanochek warleader would speak with you on urgent warhost business."

Raklion nodded. "I will see him. Escort Nagarak high

godspeaker to the Women's Chambers, he would see the
Daughter and her growing belly. Nagarak, you honor me
with your presence and word of that other matter. You
will see me in the godhouse at lowsun, for sacrifice."

"Lowsun," said Nagarak, and departed with the slave.
Hanochek entered on the heels of their leaving, he looked
harried and tense.

"Raklion, I wish you would listen to me with your
head and not your heart," he said, throwing himself into
the nearest empty chair. "I tell you something must be
done, no matter how you feel for the girl, no matter her
skill on the Plain of Drokar."

Hekat, again. Raklion sighed and leaned his elbows on
his wooden desk. "Tell me, Hano. What must be done,
and why?"

Hano chewed the end of one godbraid, a boy's bad
habit he had never outgrown. "She slew Bajadek warlord,
I do not quarrel with that. But there are fools in the
warhost who would make eyes at her for doing her duty,
for wielding her snakeblade no better or worse than any
warrior of Et-Raklion. It bodes badly for discipline, warlord. She is one of ten thousand, not one alone."

He frowned. "She flaunts Bajadek's slaying? I have
not seen it."

"No," said Hano, irritably shifting. "She does not
flaunt it, it is flaunted by others. They see her, they flaunt
it, they praise her, I tell you it means trouble."

It was a fair observation. One thing for his warriors to
revere an older, seasoned fighter. But a girl barely out of
childhood who, according to Hano, kept herself apart and
mysterious? As his warleader said, such adoration could
only mean trouble, and trouble in the barracks would be

told to Nagarak by his godspeakers. He would pay attention to Hekat as the cause of that trouble, he would notice her. Ask questions.

He did not want Nagarak noticing Hekat.

"You are right, Hano," he said. "The Plain of Drokar was one battle, it is over. Send Hekat's shell into the wilderness for training. Send Arakun shell-leader's shell with them so they can skirmish together." He tapped a finger against his chin, warming to the idea even as it chilled him. Training in the wilderness was no easy business, warriors died in training. *God, keep her safe.* "Send them to train along the border with Et-Banotaj. Bajadek's whelp has been silent since Drokar but that might change with the changing wind. And even if he does not think to bark, knowing my warriors dance on his doorstep he will think twice before clearing his throat."

Pleased, Hanochek stood and pressed a fist to his heart. "Warlord, it will be done. How long should the shells remain in the wilderness?"

Raklion took a deep breath, and let it out slowly. "Send them out for three godmoons, Hano. That should be long enough for Drokar to fade. In that time let the knife-dancers live off the land, let them toughen their sinews and harden their bones. Three godmoons. No longer."

Hano nodded. "It is the right decision, Raklion."

"Yes. It is right."

Right, but not easy. He smiled at Hano and watched him leave. His heart was heavy, it was a cruel thing to be a warlord.

God, keep her safe.

*   *   *

Hekat laughed when she learned she was to train in the wilderness. She was tired of the barracks and being stared at, of pretending to fight tamely on the knife-dance field. Warriors were born for battle, *she* was born for battle, she knew that now as she knew her own name. In battle she felt herself close to the god, its fury boiled within her, she burned with its power. Skirmishing along the Et-Banotaj border was as close to battle as they could get for the moment . . . and if the god was pleased with her, it might send her enemies to slay.

Send me enemies, god. I would worship you with my knife.

The night before her shell and Arakun's were to leave for the wilderness they attended a great sacrifice on the warhost field. Vortka was one of the godspeakers present, when it was over they spoke swiftly, in shadows.

"Nobody in the godhouse knows about you and the Traders," he whispered. "Not even Nagarak. Your secret is safe."

"Of course it is safe," she whispered back. "Nothing is known if the god wishes it unknown."

He sighed at her sharply, he did not like it when she spoke for the god. "They say skirmishing is dangerous, Hekat. You should be careful in the wilderness."

"I will be Hekat," she retorted. "I am in the god's eye, no harm can come to me."

"So bold, so proud," he said. "If I spoke like that I would be caned for two fingers without stopping!"

She shrugged. "You are a godspeaker, that is your life. I am a warrior, chosen by the god. No man dares cane me, any man who tried I would kiss him with my snake-blade."

"Or smite him with your scorpion?" said Vortka, then looked sorry he'd mentioned it.

"No," she said, fingers brushing her amulet. "That is not my business, that is for the god to say. You should not talk of my scorpion, Vortka. It would be better if you forgot it."

"I wish I could!" he said. The whites of his eyes shone in the faint, distant firelight. "Hekat, did you know your scorpion and Nagarak's are carved from the same stone? Black, with gold and crimson flecks. That is special stone, meant only for high godspeakers. How is your amulet made from it? Where did it come from?"

She did not want to tell him, that could make trouble she did not need. "I do not know. It was a gift." A kind of truth, not quite a lie.

"Ah," said Vortka. "Then perhaps the god smote the Traders for dealing in the sacred stone."

There was no harm in letting him believe that. "Perhaps."

"Well, never let Nagarak see it closely. He will recognize that stone, he will not be pleased."

She did not care about Nagarak, she was in the god's eye. "I must go, Vortka," she said, as the rest of her shell-mates started drifting from the warhost field. "We are gone three godmoons. I will see you after that."

She left him in the shadows, standing alone.

After next newsun's sacrifice she rode out of the barracks with a godspeaker, her shell-leader Tajria and her shell-mates, and the other knife-dance shell led by Arakun. They rode away from the city and into Et-Raklion's hungry wild wilderness. Hanochek warleader wished them well as they departed. Raklion warlord did not come down from his palace, Hanochek spoke for him.

It was not the same.

When at last they reached the wilderness along the border with Et-Banotaj they wasted no time, they skirmished every moment between newsun and lowsun sacrifices, in darkness and in light. They lived off the land, hunting game and wild birds. Barracks life became a memory, a dream half-forgotten.

Hekat danced joyfully with her snakeblade, listening to the god whisper in her heart. She never thought of Vortka, and paid scant attention to the other warriors. Her life was the god and knife-dancing. Nothing else mattered. They saw no sign of Et-Banotaj warriors, slain Bajadek's son kept his teeth behind his lips. The days passed swiftly, Hekat did not count them. The godspeaker counted them, that was her task. One godmoon. Two godmoons. Three godmoons worth of days.

Then it was time to return to the city.

The godspeaker was a scrawny thing and would never make a knife-dancer, but she had a neat way with a sacrifice blade. As newsun's pale light filtered through high and insubstantial cloud she cut out the last godhouse dove's beating heart and pulped it between her fingers. Blood splattered on the black slate altar brought with her from Et-Raklion's distant godhouse.

When the heart was wrung dry she pushed it into her mouth, then tossed the dead bird into the air. It caught fire and vanished in smoke; she chewed and chewed and chewed and swallowed, then hunkered down to read the god in the scattered dots of dove's blood on the altar.

Kneeling silent with her fellow warriors, Hekat closed her eyes and let the growing light warm her face. She had come to love the wilderness, she would miss its open sky when they were once more in the barracks. Six warriors had fallen in their time of skirmishing here. They did not dance fast enough and the god blew out their godsparks. Their flesh was ash now, it was sealed into clay jars for the journey home. Two of those warriors had fallen to her snakeblade, she was not sorry. They had failed the god, they paid the price.

The godspeaker finished her divination and rose from her crouch. "The god says you have trained well, warriors. You may return with honor to Et-Raklion city."

A ripple of released tension sighed through the other gathered warriors. Three godmoons in the wilderness was a long time. No bathing house, no comfortable camp-beds, no rich fat goat and lamb to eat, no wine or ale or sadsa for drinking, no godhouse vessels for the easing of lust. Blood and dirt and sore, pulled muscles, cracked bones, split flesh, hot days, cold nights and hard ground to sleep on, plain water and dry, stringy meat, that was training in the wilderness.

Hekat knew the other knife-dancers were glad their wilderness time was over. Even Tajria and Arakun shell-leaders were glad. She despised them for it. Soft pampered warriors could not serve the god. They should give it thanks for these three hard godmoons.

If I were in charge of them, I would make them give thanks. In your time, god, put me in charge of them. I will teach them what true service is.

Her divining completed, the godspeaker said, "The god desires we ride the border with Et-Banotaj for three fingers, then turn inwards and travel home through the Teeth."

Tajria shell-leader stood and bowed. "We hear the god and obey its desires." She clapped her hands. "On your feet, knife-dancers. We eat and break camp, no time to waste!"

Less than a finger later they left their desolate training ground, bound at last for Et-Raklion city.

The open country along the border had little use beyond being a space that was not Et-Banotaj. The feral goats and stunted cattle they hunted for food roamed there, descendants of beasts escaped from holdings further inland where the grass grew green. Shy, elusive, they haunted the sparse waterholes and hid themselves in the spindly undergrowth as the knife-dancers and the godspeaker's mule-cart clattered by.

The god's desire that they ride the border a distance before turning towards Et-Raklion on its surface made no sense, but of course they did not question. It wasn't until they were half a finger from turning inland again to traverse the Teeth that Hekat felt a sudden stirring, a tickle in the back of her mind she had come to recognize was a prompting from the god.

Moments later they crested a rise and met with a band of raiding warriors, crossed over the border to steal Raklion warlord's goats and cattle. Some were warriors of Et-Banotaj, others wore the lizard-mark of Et-Takona and the horse-head badge of Et-Zyden. Hekat guessed there were perhaps fifty of them. Now became clear the godspeaker's divining. Now the god's purpose was revealed.

"Aieee-aieee-aieee!" she howled, and plunged with the others into attack. The raided goats and cattle fled, the warriors from Et-Banotaj and Et-Takona and Et-Zyden spun their horses and tried to escape.

After three godmoons training, fighting in earnest was a potent release. Hekat, laughing, hamstrung Et-Banotaj horses and their riders, slit Et-Takona and Et-Zyden throats. It was close-quarters fighting, no arrows or slingshots, just bright flashing snakeblades drinking enemy blood. Demonspawn that they were for daring to cross the border into Et-Raklion and take what did not belong to them, the raiding warriors did not die meekly, they hacked and slashed Raklion warlord's knife-dancers. Their sharp knives cut her, she did not feel the wounds. She was fighting for the god and Raklion warlord.

The hot air was shrill with shrieks and shouting, soaked in blood and smells of death. The godspeaker stood on the seat of her mule-cart, exhorting Raklion's warriors at the top of her voice. They answered her with their sharp snakeblades, slaughtering the enemy and screaming Raklion's name, they shook their godbraids even though in the wilderness they wore no godbells. It did not matter, godbells sang in their hearts.

When the last raiding warriors were dead and dying on the ground, Tajria slid from her horse and walked with Arakun shell-leader and the godspeaker among the fallen. She and Arakun slit the throats of their still-living enemies and, weeping, sent to the god five Et-Raklion warriors the godspeaker said could not be healed. Then they put down the horses too wounded for travel, all save one. No Et-Raklion horses had died in the battle, Hekat saw

Tajria smile at that. Fajik horse-master would be pleased, and Hanochek warleader who doted on the beasts.

On Arakun's signal ten knife-dancers skinned the dead horses, their hides would be cured for breeches and the barracks victory wall. Last of all Tajria stripped the leather breastplates from three dead enemy warriors so she might show Raklion warlord who had ridden against them. Her eyes were narrowed as she stared at those breastplates, the woodcat, the lizard, the fiery horse-head.

Hekat, watching, feeling at last the hot pain of her knife-wounds, did not blame Tajria shell-leader for that unhappy frown. In her heart she heard the god whisper, she saw dark shadows crawling beneath the sun.

This raid is a warning. Trouble stirs in Mijak, for Raklion warlord and for us all.

CHAPTER EIGHTEEN

The thieving demonspawn warriors of Et-Banotaj, Et-Takona and Et-Zyden deserved no sanctified pyres, they did not fall in honorable battle. They were left for the crows with their skinned dead horses. Et-Raklion's five dead were piled with the rolled hides into the god-speaker's mule-cart for proper burning in the godhouse. They would reach the city late that night, the corpses would not rot before then.

Eight knife-dancers were wounded more than cuts and bruises. The godspeaker healed them enough for riding and they were tied to their horses, the reins handed over to another warrior so they could safely be led. Hekat bound her slashed arm and thigh with strips of linen torn from her spare tunic, she needed no healing. She dedicated her pain to the god, kissing the scorpion round her neck. Its power trembled, she breathed its glory.

Those knife-dancers closest to Et-Raklion's fallen wept and cut their own flesh with their snakeblades. Hekat watched them grieve, unmoved. If they were dead it was their time, what use weeping and gnashing of teeth? Tajria and Arakun knelt with the godspeaker to thank the god for their victory. The godspeaker sacrificed the last injured horse, kept alive for that purpose. Then it was time to ride for the Teeth, and after that Et-Raklion city.

The Teeth were a series of craggy rises and sharp ravines separating Et-Raklion's rich farming lands from its scarce-watered wilderness. Enormous care was required riding through them, a shouted voice could start rocks lethally sliding, a careless horse could break its leg. The knife-dancers and the godspeaker in her burdened mule-cart minded their manners as they trod lightly through them, they held their tongues, they barely breathed. The Teeth were dangerous, but it was their fastest way back to the city.

Highsun passed. Lowsun approached. The Teeth did not bite them, they climbed at last over their sharp dry lip into the fat green pasturelands of Et-Raklion, where the underground rivers showed themselves to the sky and the grain grew plump and comely in the fields.

It was not so far to the city now.

Hekat rolled her head upon her shoulders to ease the aching in her neck. Horses were tiresome, she would much prefer to run but warriors must ride, it was the word of the warlord, tchut tchut, complain aloud and earn a striping.

Safely past the danger of rockslides, the warriors around her began to talk once more, to relive the battle so neatly survived, to reminisce with stories of those who had fallen, to tell jokes and announce, crudely, which vessel would service them on return to the barracks. Some arguments grew out of those claimings, but only with words. No blades were drawn. Mindful of Tajria and Arakun they satisfied themselves with insults and promises.

Not one of the knife-dancers spoke to Hekat, nor she to any one of them. They hardly ever spoke to her, she was not lonely. Who could be lonely when filled with the god?

The sun sank below the horizon. Dusk deepened into night. The godmoon was in the waning phase, his wife hid demurely in his shadow. Tajria ordered the torches lit, they traveled home in a flickering of light.

Three fingers after the godmoon's thin rising, they reached the city. The barracks' main gates were thrown wide for them, and they rode to the stables. Amid the jostle and bustle of stable-slaves attending the horses, and the busyness of other warriors coming to greet them and make a noise, the skinned horsehides and those three bloodied enemy breastplates were taken from the mule-cart. Then the godspeaker drove it to the barracks godspeakers, so they might prepare for the ritual cremations of Et-Raklion's fallen.

"Hekat," said Tajria, raising her voice. "Attend me."

Hekat threw her reins to a slave and attended her. "Yes, shell-leader?"

"Find Hanochek warleader. Tell him Arakun and I would like to have private words."

Of course. Hanochek must be told of the raid and the breastplates that warned of trouble. Hekat pressed her fist to her heart, acknowledging Tajria's command, and made her way out of the crowded stables, through the woken barracks, dancing around more curious warriors, goggling slaves and scuttling, sniffing barracks dogs. She hated those dogs. She hated all dogs, she would gladly see every last one dead.

Hanochek warleader lived in the barracks, he had private quarters beside the warhost field. "Hanochek warleader is not here," his servant told her. "He dines with the warlord in his palace."

Aieee, the god see her. Such a long way to run for a tired knife-dancer. Hekat sighed and jogged back to the stables, she took a fresh horse and rode it bareback in its halter, out of the barracks and up the road to Raklion's palace.

It was a beautiful building, terraced balconied chambers hugging the side of Raklion's Pinnacle. The walls were sandstone, great blocks of ochre and salt-white and cream like new butter, each section of sloping roof a dazzle of glazed tiles in red and green and blue and gold. It was pocked with gardens, riddled with tall hedges, lit like highsun with countless flaming torches. Splendidly dressed slaves stood at every entering pathway, no-one could visit here without drawing attention. Not unless the god hid them deep in its eye.

The slave at attention beside the main palace gates saw she was a warrior and did not challenge her entry. In the palace's paved forecourt an outdoors slave took the horse from her, an indoors slave admitted her to Raklion's empty audience chamber. It was a cool and glossy place, as the rest of the palace she had walked through was cool and glossy, not fussy like Abajai's villa, larded with trinkets to boast of wealth. Raklion's palace was plain, austere. Hekat approved. The only decoration a warrior needed was a snakeblade.

The warlord came to her soon after she arrived, with Hanochek warleader by his side. She thought he had aged since last she saw him, the night Abajai and Yagji came to kill her. His eyes were sunk deeper now, his godbraids were heavily silvered. Deeper lines were carved in his face.

"Hekat!" he said. He was startled. "You are wounded. What has happened?"

Wounded? She glanced at the linen strips binding arm and thigh, she had forgotten the knife-cuts earned in the border skirmish. She pressed her fist against her heart, to him, to Hanochek. "Warlord, I am sent by Tajria shell-leader to speak with Hanochek warleader. We are returned from the wilderness with a tale to tell."

"So it seems," said Hanochek. "What has happened that could not wait until newsun for its telling?"

As she hesitated, Raklion said, "Speak, Hekat. You are here, not Tajria. I wish you to answer."

Hekat nodded. "As we returned from the wilderness, warlord, we skirmished with raiding warriors from Et-Banotaj, Et-Zyden and Et-Takona. They rode together but are dead in the dirt now, the god sent them to hell." She smiled. "With our help."

Cold silence. Torchlight, dancing. Words unspoken, weighing on the air, as the warlord and his warleader stared at each other. Raklion said, "What did they raid for?"

"Meat, warlord. They were stealing our wild beasts."

Another look between the two men. "The warlords grow reckless," Raklion murmured. "Hekat, what of my warriors?"

"Five fell in the skirmish, warlord. Six more died in training." She straightened her aching body. "Warlord?"

"Return to the barracks. Tell Tajria shell-leader her message is given. Tell her also the warleader and I will hear the full story of Banotaj's raid after newsun sacrifice and the rites for our dead."

"Yes, warlord."

His stern face softened. "And be certain to have your hurts in my service healed."

"Yes, warlord."

His nod dismissed her. As she left the palace to ride tired and bareback to the barracks, she felt her stone scorpion hot against her skin.

It is a warning. I think the god will have need of me, soon.

Raklion paced his audience chamber, his warm pleasure in good food and sweet wine and Hano's company turned sour and restless in his gut. Not even a brief moment with glorious Hekat could ease the foreboding in his heart.

"I do not like this, Hano. I fear this one raid is but the beginning. With Mijak growing browner by the godmoon, with Et-Raklion remaining fat and green, we tempt the other warlords to make alliances based on blood and stealing. I think if the browning does not stop our ten thousand warriors will not be enough."

Hano leaned his shoulder against the stone wall. "I fear your warleader must disagree, Raklion. We are in no danger. Banotaj is the one who should worry, he is a fool to think he can keep Zyden and Takona appeased with a few stolen Et-Raklion goats. They ride with him not to raid us in earnest but to test *his* strength, they wish to see *his* warriors fight and taste their mettle. When they are satisfied he is not the equal of his father they will swallow him whole and spit out his bones. They will ride *against* him, not beside him. They will be too busy to dare threaten us."

"Perhaps so, Hano, for now," Raklion said, unconvinced. "But they will not be busy against Banotaj forever. You know what the Traders and godspeakers tell me. Beyond Et-Raklion's borders scarce rain grows scarcer. Crops are thinner in the fields. Waterholes shrink, rivers dwindle. Jokriel surrenders more land to the savage north, he fights with Mamiklia while Mamiklia raids Takona. Takona raided Zyden before joining him to raid with Banotaj. I tell you, Mijak becomes a bloodied carcass."

"Not all of Mijak," Hano insisted. "It is not a desert yet. And while the other warlords tear at each other we can strengthen our borders. Increase our warhost. We will survive until Mijak turns green again."

"Aieee, Hano. *Think*!" Raklion retorted, and fisted his hands. "We are facing a time of change. With Nogolor beside us, with his warhost and ours, we could withstand the other five warlords. But Nogolor is old, he is failing, his son Tebek will be warlord soon. Tebek looks at Et-Raklion's fat horses, he counts the ribs of the stallion he rides. When his father dies I fear our alliance will die with him. Then what will happen? Will Tebek risk his warriors against us alone, or instead make his peace with Banotaj or Mamiklia or one of the others so they together can turn on us?" He stopped pacing and glared at his friend. "Hano, you have seen starving dogs fight for a single bone, you *know* what could happen. Do not seek to soothe me with platitudes and lies!"

Hano pushed away from the wall, his eyes were hurt. "I have never lied to you, Raklion. I do not lie now. I agree we must keep close watch on the other warlords. That is why we have Eyes, we will send them to look hard at Et-Raklion's borders. But you must not give yourself over to bleakness. Et-Raklion is great, it is blessed by the god, and Mijak cannot stay brown forever. Trouble will pass, like a cloud across the sun."

"How do you know Mijak cannot stay brown?" Raklion demanded. "*I* do not know that. For all I know, Hano, it will stay brown forever."

It was a fearsome thought. Hano said, faltering, "I cannot believe that. Does *Nagarak* say Mijak will stay brown?"

Raklion turned away. "If Nagarak knows, he does not tell me."

"*If* he knows?" said Hano, in the taut silence. "What is this, Raklion? Do you say he doesn't?"

Aieee, his fears rode his tongue, he should not have said that. He turned back. "No. I mis-spoke myself. Pay no attention."

"Tcha!" said Hanochek. "And you chide *me* for platitudes and lies."

"*Hanochek!*"

Hano flinched but did not retreat. "Raklion, I am your warleader and your friend, but how can I help you if you hide your heart? Is there more to your misgivings than you've told? Do you know something of Nagarak you haven't shared?"

Aieee, there was more, but not to do with Nagarak. What terrified him was that voice in his heart whispering louder, ever louder: *the only way to save Et-Raklion from the other warlords is to smite them before they ride against me, to tame them utterly into the dust, to make myself Mijak's only warlord.* How else could he save Et-Raklion from death? Beg his brother warlords to leave him alone? Was that the strength of a warlord? Was that how he protected his people, kept his promise to the god?

"Raklion, what is it?" said Hano softly. "You stand there as if a demon turned you to stone. Let me help you, what else am I for?"

Shaking his head, Raklion sat in his warlord's chair. He could not burden Hano with his heart's sinful secret. Hano would risk the god's wrath to see it come true. *Raklion warlord, warlord of Mijak.* With an effort, he smiled. "You were right, my friend. I let myself become bleak, it is not helpful."

Hano knew him too well. "Tcha, you do not blind me. *Is* it Nagarak, Raklion? Does he—"

The chamber door burst open then, and a slave rushed in shouting. "Warlord! Warlord! You must come at once!"

It was the gelding Sabat from the Women's Chambers.

His yellow-brown skin was sickly with horror, his staring eyes awash with tears.

As Hanochek took an angry step towards the slave, Raklion pushed slowly to his feet. All the world was still and silent, the only sound his beating heart.

The gelding Sabat fell face down on the floor, his flabby, half-naked body shuddering like a man filled with fever.

"Speak," said Raklion, though he knew already what the slave would say.

"Forgive me, warlord," the gelding choked out. "It is Et-Nogolor's Daughter."

Hano had moved to stand again at Raklion's shoulder, war-calloused palm and fingers gripping tight. It was hard to feel him. Hard to feel anything beyond hell's cold wind.

"Show me," he said to the gelding Sabat. The slave heaved to his feet and bowed out backwards, hands pressed in entreaty to his womanish breast.

"Warlord?" said Hano, releasing his grip.

Raklion turned, looked over his shoulder. "Come with me, Hano. I cannot bear this alone."

"Of course," said Hano. "Warlord, lead the way."

The Daughter was dead, and her baby with her. Their blood soaked the bedsheets and pooled on the tiled floor. A snakeblade's hilt jutted between her ribs. The dead child's throat was cut to the bone, its lifeless body still yoked to its mother by the flaccid umbilical cord.

It was a boy. It had no eyes.

"*Why?*" said Hano beside him, his whisper incredulous. "How could this happen? Did she fuck with a demon when your back was turned?"

Raklion came close to striking Hano, then. Hano knew it, and retreated.

The gelding Sabat bowed his head. "Warlord, we did not know she was in labor. After her supper she dismissed her slaves and retired. She gave no sign that anything was wrong."

The chamber reeked of blood and death. Raklion nodded, hearing the slave's words as though they traveled from beyond Mijak's distant borders. "Fetch her slaves without delay."

The gelding bowed and withdrew.

As he waited for the Daughter's attendants, Raklion gazed upon his son. A delicate skull capped in drying black curls. Long limbs. Slender fingers. Beneath the smearing mucus, light skin hinting at a glossy darkness to come. If he'd had eyes, he would have been beautiful.

"Warlord, I grieve with you," said Hano, weeping.

He nodded, but could not speak. He had no tears, his heart was a desert.

The gelding returned with the Daughter's slaves. Ten in all, the youngest a girl of six or seven. Raklion ordered them to kneel. He pulled the snakeblade from the Daughter's flesh and killed them, one by one he watered his heart's desert with the blood of the sinners who had failed his son. He killed the gelding Sabat last of all, and not as swiftly as he'd killed the others.

Done with that, leaving Hanochek to stand guard over the corpses, he walked alone, daubed with scarlet, up Raklion's Pinnacle to the godhouse, to Nagarak, who must answer for this terrible thing. The bloodied snake-blade was still in his fist.

It was late but Nagarak was waking, seated cross-legged before the altar in his most private sanctum, whose scented air only he and the warlord were permitted to breathe. Carved jet scorpions climbed the walls, emerald and crimson snakes decorated each flat surface.

"Are you high godspeaker," Raklion demanded, framed in the doorway of that sacred room, "or some hell-escaped demon tasked to plague me?"

Nagarak wore a loincloth and his scorpion pectoral. Its black highlights gleamed as his thin chest rose and fell. "You bring a knife into this place? You tempt the god to a great smiting, Raklion."

He threw the blood-clotted blade to the floor. "My son is *dead*, Nagarak! Slain by the Daughter. He was abominate, he was born without *eyes*. What else could she do but slit his throat? She is dead too, she killed herself after." He took one step towards the silent high godspeaker, then collapsed disjointed as his muscles and sinews undid themselves. "How has this happened? If you are high godspeaker you must know! Or are you deaf to the god, Nagarak? Is your power drained into the dirt? Have your eyes been blinded to the omens in the entrails, the clouds, the tracks of scorpions in the dust? How could you let a demon deform him? *You said I would have a living son!*"

Like a striking snake Nagarak rose to his bare feet. His polished face was raw with anger, he loomed like the god's wrath with his fist raised high.

"You chastise *me*, warlord? The god desired you sire a

son. If that son is thwarted, look to yourself! What seed of sin is rooted in your heart, that has led to this grim flowering? What have you done, that the god would smite you so?"

Bruised and aching, Raklion stared up at him. "You tell me the *god* took my son's eyes?"

"I tell you Et-Nogolor's Daughter was surrounded by every amulet, every charm, every chanting this godhouse could devise!" said Nagarak. "Every day five pure white lambs given to the altar, their blood drained and fed to her by sanctified hands! No demon insinuated itself in the Women's Chambers, warlord. You are smitten by the god for an evil in your heart."

"There is no evil in my heart," he whispered. "Every day I make offerings to the god, I attend a sacrifice, I open my heart to the god's desires."

"Yet Et-Nogolor's Daughter lies cold and stiffening and your blind son is carrion for the crows." Leaning down, Nagarak thrust his furious face close. His breath was hot with blood and cloves. "There must be a secret sin. What demon writhes beneath your skin that you can hide such a truth from me?"

Sickened with sudden fear Raklion retreated from Nagarak's burning glare. "You call your warlord *demonstruck*? The god should kill me here and now if this is a true thing!" He tipped back his head to stare at the ceiling's mosaiced frieze of spitting snakes and stinging scorpions. "Kill me now, god, strike me dead if I nurse a demon!"

The god spared him.

"You see?" he demanded. "I nurse no demon! Raklion warlord is *not* demonstruck!"

Nagarak straightened. "Not demonstruck," he admitted, grudging. "So it is a sin. Name it, warlord."

Raklion smoothed his face with trembling hands. His fingers tangled in his godbraids, his godbells chimed like weeping doves. He knew his sin, he could not speak it.

Raklion warlord, warlord of Mijak.

"I see the shifting in your face, warlord," said Nagarak harshly. "You sift your thoughts and deeds like a miller sifts his flour, searching for unwanted husks and stones. Open your mouth. Let the words fall from your tongue. I am your miller, warlord, *I* will sift you."

Raklion looked dully at the tiled floor. *I must tell him, I must tell him. Only he can save me from myself.* "Nagarak . . ." He touched a fingertip to the high godspeaker's foot. "I dream of a Mijak made whole beneath the sky. Not seven warlords but one alone, obedient to the god and warlord to all men. When the stars were young, when the godmoon's aged wife was a girlish bride, Mijak was a whole land ruled by one warlord, fat and green and known to the world. Mijak—"

"*Silence!*" hissed Nagarak. His scorpion pectoral shivered with shadows, it came to life in the chamber's dim lighting. "You sinning man, you defier of the god! Those days are *dead*, Raklion. The god killed them in its eye and has forbade the men of Mijak crossing over its borders or kneeling to a single warlord upon a golden throne. Woe to he who would see the sun rise again upon those dark times. *This* is the secret sin in your heart? That you would be the warlord of Mijak? Aieee, it is a black sin, a sin to smite the god itself!"

From somewhere unknown, in the face of his high godspeaker's fury, Raklion found the courage to speak.

"Nagarak, Nagarak, what else can I do but dream of this? The ravenous warlords stare at my green lands and their high godspeakers urge them to raiding. If I do not stop them they will overrun us and strip the meat from our bleeding bones. Et-Raklion will die if I do not stop them, and I fear Mijak will die not long after that. I cannot sit idle and watch that happen, I must prevent it. *Not* to prevent it would be the black sin."

"You are the warlord, you are not the god," said Nagarak, his voice a smiting. "The god will prevent it in its time, a time of its choosing with an instrument of its desire."

Beyond Nagarak's chamber, the tolling of a godhouse bell. On a shuddering breath, Raklion sat up. The Daughter was dead, his son was dead with her. What more in the world did he have to lose? "Nagarak . . . high godspeaker . . . what if *I* am that instrument?"

CHAPTER NINETEEN

Y ou?" The high godspeaker's hooded eyes stared with disdain. "Raklion, you are nothing if the god does not tell me otherwise. It has not named you an instrument to me. It has killed the field and the seeds you planted there, that is your message from the god."

Unbidden tears rose in Raklion's eyes. "Then why am I still warlord, Nagarak? Why did the god not allow Ba-

jadek to kill me? How can I have these thoughts and live
if the god does not desire them of me?"

Nagarak said nothing, his fingers caressed his scorpion
pectoral and his eyes communed with shadows.

"Perhaps in thinking them I *do* obey the god," Raklion
whispered. "Perhaps these thoughts are its voice in my
heart. Perhaps I am punished because I do not act. Mijak
bleeds but I do not staunch its wounds!"

Nagarak stared down at him, his caressing fingers
turned to fists. "I am high godspeaker," he said at last.
"Such desires of the god would first be revealed to me."

"You are high godspeaker but I am warlord. Warriors'
business is my business, Nagarak. In matters of war the
god speaks to me in my heart."

Joint by joint, Nagarak's fingers unfisted themselves.
"It . . . is an explanation."

"Nagarak, I am not wrong about Et-Raklion's fate if
the other warlords are left unchecked."

"No," said Nagarak. "You are not wrong."

"They will steal my lands if the browning continues.
Will it?"

In Nagarak's face, a riot of thoughts. Then he nodded.
"I think it will."

"You *think*?"

"The omens are conflicting!" said Nagarak, goaded.
"The truth hides in shadows."

It was the closest Nagarak had ever come to admitting
ignorance. Raklion sat up, slowly. "I cannot stand
against six raiding warhosts. And where Et-Raklion falls
all of Mijak *will* follow, I *know* this, Nagarak. The god
tells me so."

Nagarak frowned fiercely. "It is . . . *possible* . . . these thoughts come from the god. They could also have been sent by a demon, nourished in your ambitious heart."

"I am *not* ambitious. These thoughts frighten me, Nagarak."

"As well they should!" said Nagarak, and turned to pace his private chamber. "One thing is clear, Raklion: you are a flagrant sinner. You have sinned in thinking these thoughts of one warlord, or you have sinned in not acting upon them as the god desires."

Raklion nodded, slumping. "And I am punished for it. I have no son, and no warlord bloodline on which to breed one. No warlord will give a daughter to me now. They want to take Et-Raklion for themselves, not help me breed its next fighting warlord."

"*You will have a son,*" said Nagarak. "I have said so, it will come to pass. But only when your sin is revealed and repented."

Eagerly Raklion regained his feet. "I do repent it, Nagarak. I will stand on the godhouse roof and shout to the sky, I am Raklion warlord, a sinning sinner! I have sinned, I have said so, I weep tears in my remorse."

Nagarak looked at him, cold and stern. "The tears you weep are tears of water. For the god's absolution you must weep tears of blood."

Shuddering, Raklion bowed his head. Nagarak spoke truly. Without weeping blood his penitence was air, was nothing. Aieee, it was a fearful thought. "You are right, high godspeaker. Water remorse is not sufficient. I am the warlord, a man of deeds."

"Through me, Raklion, the god will write on your flesh with a heavy hand," said Nagarak. His tone was a warning. "I will not spare you, though you are the warlord."

Raklion met his high godspeaker's obdurate glare. "You must not spare me, Nagarak. The god must know the length and breadth and depth of my sorrow."

Nagarak nodded. "Warlord, it must."

"And after I am punished, and the god knows my true regret, you will sink beneath the surface of the godpool and seek an answer to this mystery. Am I to become the warlord of Mijak?"

"That is the question I must ask," said Nagarak, slowly. "But not in the godpool. In the scorpion pit."

The *scorpion* pit? "Nagarak, men die in the scorpion pit."

Nagarak smiled. "Warlord, if you strive to make yourself warlord of Mijak you will fail without me by your side. Therefore in your striving so do I strive, to be Mijak's high godspeaker, its voice for the god. That too was forbidden in the dark past. If I support you I support myself. Therefore I must ask the god in the scorpion pit, baring myself to its killing eye."

Raklion shook his head. "No. I forbid it. This sin is mine, you will not pay the price."

"It is not for you to forbid a high godspeaker! This is the god's business, it falls upon me! There can be no gain without risk."

Gain? "You *wish* to be Mijak's one high godspeaker?" he asked, shocked.

Nagarak turned away. "I wish the god's true voice to be heard in Mijak. I wish for an end to untrue godspeakers."

"You think you are true and your brothers are false?"

Still Nagarak would not look at him. "I think there is a

reason why Et-Raklion stays green and fat, while the rest of Mijak turns dirt brown and thin."

He is ambitious. I never knew it. "Nagarak, if you must face the god's scorpions, then so be it. As I weep for my sin against the god I will pray that it knows you are its true godspeaker." He swallowed. "When will that be, Nagarak? When do I weep?"

Nagarak turned back to him, a hint of warmth in his merciless face. "Raklion warlord, it is known there is nothing gained by delaying a thing that must come to pass. You have sinned and must be punished. Come with me now, and weep your sorrow to the god."

Raklion nodded. On the slopes of the Pinnacle, in the heart of his warlord palace, his son's small body spoiled before its time. If ever he was to see the birth of a living son he had no choice but to follow Nagarak.

"You speak the truth. Take me, high godspeaker, and learn how much I love the god."

In silence Nagarak pulled on a robe, then led him from the quiet room, down stairs and more stairs, past closed chambers echoing with chanted prayer, past novices sweeping the godhouse's public places, past city suppli- cants praying before its altars, through open gardens and along cold corridors of stone. Not a witness to his pass- ing spoke a single word but all eyes followed and there was dread in their gaze, as though the truth were a trail of smoke that could be seen by anyone in the god's eye.

A clutch of chambers apart from the main godhouse was given over to the god's severe taskmasters. Follow- ing Nagarak through the night, across an open courtyard to that terrible place, Raklion heard the stinging slap of leather against bared flesh, the harder crack of birch, the sobbing sighs of men and women in supplication to the god. Through half-open doors he glimpsed private penitence, devout despairing, wholehearted misery in the pursuit of purity. Mijak's god demanded contrition, and in this place contrition ruled with whip and cane, it hungered for tears, it drank them like nectar. The godmoon and his wife still walked the starred sky, yet nearly every tasking room was full. The godspeakers of Et-Raklion were perfect in their bloodsoaked piety.

Raklion pitied them as he loved them, as he witnessed their suffering while passing them by. He was here to join them, to become their lowly brother, to weep out his own sins as they wept out theirs.

One dark room waited for him. Nagarak led him within it, and closed the door.

No words were needed in this place. Raklion was silent as he shed his fine linen tunic and his sandals trimmed with gold, as his high godspeaker lit a single lamp, as his wrists and ankles were bound with leather to the cold iron scorpion wheel.

I am here, god. I am penitent. Drink my tears and swallow my cries. Do what you will, for as long as you must, write on my flesh all the way to the bone. Know I am sorry, answer my prayer. Help me save Mijak.

Grant me a son.

In the last gasp of darkness before newsun, Hekat stood on the warhost field with Et-Raklion's warriors and watched the pyres of the fallen burn to ash. Raklion did not watch with them, neither did his warleader Hanochek. The pyres were lit by Tajria and Arakun shell-leaders, they had waited and waited for Raklion and Hanochek until they could wait no more. The bodies must be burned by the first newsun after death. A godspeaker gave permission for the pyres' lighting, death was the god's business. Ritual must be observed.

In the darkness around her, Hekat heard whispers. *Why was the warlord not with them for this burning? Why did the warleader not appear?* Like wind through a wheat field the questions rippled, unease mingling with grief in the smoke from the pyres. After the burning, Tajria took her aside.

"You said the warlord said he and Hanochek would come to the barracks. Why did they not come, Hekat? What have you not told me?"

Tajria should know better than to talk in a shrill voice, she should know better than to show her fear. "He told me they would come, shell-leader. That is all he told me, that is all I can say."

Tajria dismissed her. She did not report to a godspeaker healer as Raklion wanted, she went to the bathhouse and sat in hot water until it turned cold. Then she crawled into her barracks bed to sleep for a finger. After three godmoons in the wilderness her mattress felt like a cloud. It was strange, the warlord and the warleader not coming to the barracks. The scorpion amulet round her neck stayed sleeping, she did not permit herself to worry.

The god will tell me if I must fear.

Hanochek warleader appeared at highsun sacrifice, he expressed regret that he was not at the burning. "Raklion warlord was taken with a gripe," he told the warhost. "He weeps for our lost ones, he sees them in the god's eye."

Hekat thought he was lying, there were shadows in his

eyes. Raklion warlord was not sick when she had seen him.

After sacrifice Hanochek met with Tajria and Arakun and their knife-dance shells in the meal-barracks, where they talked of Banotaj's bold, wicked raid. On a bench beside him sat the three bloodied breastplates. As they talked, Hanochek's face grew grim, his shadowed eyes darkened, his fingers tapped upon his thigh.

"You are proud warriors," he told them. "I am proud of you, and so is the warlord. You have served him, you have served Et-Raklion. For three highsuns you may take your ease. Guard your tongues on this matter of Et-Banotaj, this is not gossip for the barracks' camp fires."

Laughing they left him, ready to play. Obedient to Hanochek they held their tongues, it made no difference. Those three bloodied breastplates had been seen in the stables by slaves, by others, the gossip ran wild. Before lowsun sacrifice every warrior in the barracks knew Banotaj was stirring, knew other warlords stirred trouble with him. Like a simmering cook-pot, the barracks seethed.

Not interested in playing, kept from reading for three godmoons in the wilderness, Hekat looked to amuse herself with stories. Tired of her small tablet collection, she thought to ask Vortka if he could bring her more from the godhouse. But the godspeaker healer she went to as an excuse to find him did not know where he was. She sighed and let the godspeaker heal her knife wounds then bought two clay tablets from her least favorite pedlar. The stories were stupid but they were something to read. She washed and mended her wilderness tunics, trained a little with the slingshot and bow. She ate round the camp fire after lowsun sacrifice, char-roasted sheep she had killed

with one arrow, and rolled her eyes at her shell-mates'
boastings and the eager believing of the newest recruits.
They were stupid, she was weary, she went to bed. That
was her first highsun at ease in the barracks, she thought
two more would drive her mad.

She survived them, they were not so bad. She helped
Zapotar with some of the new warriors, knife-dancers accepted into the barracks while she trained in the wilderness. She watched their *hotas*, she shouted at them when
they made mistakes. They knew who she was, someone
had told them, *She is the warrior who slew Bajadek*. They
strove to please her, they laughed when she praised them,
after their training they dawdled to talk.

"How did you kill that Bajadek warlord? Tell us of the
battle, Hekat. Tell us what that killing was like!"

She did not want to talk about it. "Knife-dancing is for
doing, not for gossip."

"Please, Hekat," they begged her. "We want to dance
with our snakeblades like you, beautiful and deadly in the
god's eye."

They were older than she was, every one of them, but
they made her feel as old as the god. "I will tell you this
much," she said to them sternly. "If you think to knife-
dance for *your* glory the enemy you dance with will slit
your throat. I did not kill Bajadek warlord. The god killed
that sinning man, I was its snakeblade. Dance for the god,
warriors. Dance in its eye."

That was not the story they wanted to hear, but she did
not care. She was tired of them. Lowsun approached, the
warhost attended sacrifice. The warleader stood with
them, still Raklion did not come. After sacrifice and the

night's roast goat and chicken, while the others gathered to drink sadsa or sing and dance or disappeared to rut with a vessel, Hekat went to the bath-house to wallow in warm water.

Vortka found her there a long time later, prodding at the bath's hotbricks. "Hekat! I thought you would be here. I am pleased to see you safe home from the wilderness. How went your training?"

"Training is training." She shrugged. "Have you heard of our skirmish?"

"Skirmish?" He dropped to the stool beside her tub. His face was still beautiful but now it was haggard, his eyes sunk in hollows. They made him work hard, those godspeakers in the godhouse. "No. I am not long returned from service beyond the city. For two godmoons I traveled Et-Raklion's villages with the godspeaker treasurers, counting taxes. I am no longer an initiate novice, I have more responsibilities now." He nodded at her forearm, where it rested on the side of the tub. "I see you were wounded. Are you in pain?"

She looked at the healed knife-cut. "No. It is nothing."

"It has left a scar." Vortka smiled, a quick twist of his lips. "Warriors like scars, so the healers tell me."

The other warriors certainly did, they boasted with their scars as they boasted with their tongues. Scars were unimportant, they did not impress the god. "It is nothing, I told you. Vortka, has something happened?"

He did not answer. The new scorpion shell bound to his brow was brown, and larger than the black one it replaced. There were blue beads in his godbraids, they were not there before, and tiny stone scorpions dangled from his ears. His novice robe looked too large for his bowed shoulders. Something was troubling him.

She said, "Have you heard how Raklion is faring? We were told his belly had a gripe, I do not believe that. He was well when I saw him."

The look Vortka gave her was almost unfriendly. "The god has not told you? Aieee, perhaps you are not so special after all."

His fingers held tightly to his knees. He was frightened, he was worried, she could read him like the simplest clay tablet. She sat up straighter, so her breasts came out of the water. That did not matter, she was not a woman to him. "Why would you say that? How have I hurt you, that you would use your tongue as a knife? Do you think I need another scar?"

"I should not have come here," he said, shaking his head. "I am not supposed to know these things. This is not my business."

She felt a shiver run through her blood. Her scorpion amulet glowed against her skin. "Vortka? Tell me. What is it you are not supposed to know?"

He rocked a little on the bath-stool. His eyes were bright with unshed tears. "Why did I come here? If it is known I heard words not spoken for my hearing I—"

"*Vortka*!" She wrapped her fingers round his wrist. "The god has sent you, that is why you came. You are its messenger. *What has happened*?"

They were alone but still he looked in the bath-house's four empty corners. "Et-Nogolor's Daughter is dead and the warlord's son with her. She cut the baby's throat at birth, then stabbed herself in the heart."

"Why would she do that? Was she demonstruck?"

"I do not know, Hekat. I do not *want* to know."

Beyond the bath-house walls the sounds of warrior carousing filled the ageing night. Hekat felt the air around her turn to syrup. All the muscles on the inside of her body softened, lengthened, a flush of heat rushed across her wet skin. A chiming sounded in her head, it was the god, the god was speaking, telling her Mijak's future. Her future.

Precious, beautiful, your time is come.

Languid, thrumming, she released Vortka's wrist. "When did this happen?"

"Three lowsuns ago."

The night she and the others returned from the wilderness. The night she spoke with Raklion in his palace. "And what of the warlord? Has this made him sick, is the gripe in his godspark instead of his belly?"

Vortka shivered. "Raklion warlord is in the godhouse, Hekat. He prays to the god on the scorpion wheel."

"*Prays?*" she echoed, and leapt out of her tub. "No-one prays on the scorpion wheel, Vortka." She snatched a towel and scrubbed away the soap and water. "It is an instrument of punishment, it is for the vilest sinners in the god's eye! The lowest slave in these barracks knows of the godhouse scorpion wheel! How is Raklion bound upon it? He is the warlord, chosen by the god!"

"I am only a novice, Hekat, I do not know the nature of Raklion's sin. I am not meant to know *this* much!" Vortka's voice was broken, he was nearly undone. "I am wicked to be telling you what I know. But I am afraid. Raklion is tasked by Nagarak himself, I fear for his life."

Roughly Hekat pulled on her clean loincloth and tunic, and belted her snakeblade round her waist. "Nagarak will not destroy the warlord. I will save him, it is the god's want."

Vortka stood and plucked at her arm. "Hekat, you cannot enter the godhouse. You cannot meddle in Nagarak's business. If you are discovered . . ."

Her godbraids were soaked, and heavy with purpose. "I am the god's shadow, I dwell in its eye. I glide through the air, hidden from the world. I am safe from your godspeakers, Vortka. Even that Nagarak."

She left distressed Vortka in the bath-house and ran lightly through the darkness, unseen and obedient to the god. Its truth was in her, it had told her its desires.

I am coming, Raklion warlord. Precious and beautiful, this is my time.

Raklion wept. The god had written so deep in his flesh its words would never vanish. It had written on his bones as though they were clay tablets, and breathed on them like a baking fire. It had read his heart, it knew his remorse.

All I want now is to know your desire. Give me your answer, god, show me the path I must tread with my feet. Am I to be the warlord of Mijak?

"Raklion!" a sweet voice whispered. "No more weeping. You have soaked the god with your tears of blood, you have wept enough. The god needs your strength, warlord, not your tears."

He forced apart his swollen eyelids. A single torch guttered in the stinking chamber, throwing just enough light to show him who spoke. "Hekat?" he said, his voice a rasp. "Are you here? Or is this a dream born of fever and pain?"

Her scars were golden in the torchlight. "No dream, Raklion. I am sent by the god."

He sighed then, almost moaning, as her fingertips pressed against his brow. There was healing in her, his pain retreated. Or was that only his fevered mind, brought by Nagarak to the brink of breaking? He longed to touch her but he was bound to the wheel. He smiled instead, though it hurt his bitten, swollen lip. "Thank you, knife-dancer. Now you must go. If Nagarak returns . . ."

She shrugged. "If he returns he will not see me. Warlord, why are you bound to this scorpion wheel? Why are you beaten like a common slave?"

"To the god all men are slaves, little Hekat. I am here to weep for my sins." Cold air rattled in and out of his chest. "How long has it been, Hekat? How long have I been bound here? Do you know?"

"I am told three highsuns."

Three highsuns of weeping in this windowless chamber. No food, scant water. Three highsuns of screaming his sorrow to the god. No wonder his throat was raw. No wonder his wrists and ankles felt cut to the bone.

Three highsuns since his son had died.

Something in her words disturbed him. After a moment, he knew what it was. "Told? Who told you?"

"The god told me, Raklion." Her tone said he should have known that without asking. "It tells me many things. It tells me things it keeps from Nagarak. He is high godspeaker, he is not the god."

She spoke in riddles, he could not unriddle them. "Please. You must leave me. I do not want you punished for seeking me out."

When Hekat smiled, her scars were forgotten. "Foolish Raklion. How can I be punished? I live for the god."

"I live for it too, yet you see me bound here. I have no son . . ." His voice cracked, and though he thought he had wept himself empty his eyes stung with fresh tears. After three days in this terrible place it was easy to believe his sonless state would never change. "Et-Nogolor's Daughter is dead, she will never bear me one."

Hekat shrugged. "She was never meant to, warlord."

If he had been free he would have struck her, beautiful Hekat with her wicked tongue. "What would you know of this, it is warlord's business! You are nothing, a runaway slave. The Daughter was my future, she was the future of Et-Raklion. Her blood was pure, she was the child of warlords. What do you know, a runaway slave from the savage north?"

Hekat smiled again. His words had not hurt her. "I know all the things the god has told me."

"The god does not speak to runaway slaves!"

She stood before him, lithe and strong and clothed in pride. "I am not a runaway slave. I am Hekat, knifedancer of Et-Raklion, slayer of Bajadek, precious to the god."

"How are you precious?" he demanded, the pain in his heart burning hotter than in his flesh. "Why are you precious? You have a wicked tongue, you do not seem precious to me!"

She leaned so close her breath caressed his skin. Her blue eyes were depthless, he fell into them unresisting. "I will be precious to you, as I am to the god," she whispered. "The god desires I bear you a son."

CHAPTER TWENTY

R aklion stared at Hekat dumbly, struck beyond words.
"I am meant for you. I will be yours. It is my purpose, warlord," she added, frowning at his disbelief. "It is
why I came to Et-Raklion, why you saw me, why the god
saved me from Abajai and Yagji. You must know this.
The god has told you, if only in dreams. It is why you desire me. Why your eyes eat me whenever we meet. I will
be a great warlord's mother. The god had told me this, so
it will be."

He rolled his head on the iron scorpion wheel. "No,
Hekat. You are mistaken. Only a woman of warlord
bloodlines is fit to birth a warlord's son."

"Tcha!" she said, and bared her teeth. "If that was true
your son plowed in the Daughter's field would be living,
and all the sons you plowed before that. *I* am meant to
birth the next warlord. Would you desire me if this was
not so?"

She was a temptress, he must not listen. "I never said
I desired you."

She laughed at him. "Do I have eyes? Has the god
struck me blind? You desire me, Raklion. It is the god's
want. That is why I am precious and beautiful."

Snared in the extremities of physical distress, still he

felt a throb in his blood. He wanted her naked, he wanted her lush. He wanted her long legs wrapped around him.

"And what of your wants, Hekat knife-dancer?" His voice was thickened, and slurred with many things. "Do you desire me?"

"I desire the god's desire," she said, her face a shadow among the shadows. "Whatever the god wants, I want it also."

His eyelids were heavy, he could not stop them closing. In the fresh darkness he breathed in and breathed out and tried to fathom the god's true purpose. Tried to imagine what Nagarak would say, the warlord taking a warrior to wife.

His eyes flew open. "The god talks to men with the tongues of its godspeakers. No godspeaker has talked to me of you. How can this be the god's true desire?"

"Godspeakers are also men," said Hekat. Her eyes in the torchlight were flat with contempt. "Men are imperfect. Men are swayed from the god's desires by petty wantings of their own. *This* is known too, Raklion warlord. We saw the god strike down a lying godspeaker, you and I. Do not doubt what the god does in this place. Could I stand with you in the heart of its godhouse if I was not precious in its eye?"

Could she? He would not have said so. Et-Raklion's godhouse was teeming with godspeakers, they were everywhere underfoot. How could she stand here with him if not by the god's want?

The god desires I bear you a son.

She rested her hand on his naked shoulder. If there was pity in her for his sufferings he could not see it in her face. She was still, remote, some sacred thing housed in flawed human flesh.

"Raklion warlord, you are bound to the scorpion wheel. For three hard highsuns you have wept to the god and bled your sins from your heart and bones. You are cleansed now, it is time to rise. Et-Raklion needs you for the dark days ahead."

Dark days. She sounded so certain. "What do you know of Et-Raklion's future?" he demanded. "What has the god told you, Hekat?"

Her eyes drifted closed. "It tells me Mijak will be reborn in blood and fire. It will rise to greatness in the world. You must not fear, you are Raklion warlord, seen and chosen by the god. You will be Mijak's warlord, the god has told me."

Her words struck him so hard he felt his heart stop beating. Before he could speak again the tasking chamber door pushed open and Nagarak entered. He did not see Hekat or sense her presence. She was blind to him in the god's hiding eye. She pressed a finger to her lips, desiring silence. Raklion said nothing, he was obedient.

She knows the secret of my heart. How could she know this and not be from the god?

"Warlord," said Nagarak, halting before the scorpion wheel. "The god has heard you weeping, it has seen you in its smiting eye. Your sins are purged. Return to your life outside this godhouse and serve the god in its desires."

Raklion swallowed hot, relieved tears. As Nagarak released him from the scorpion wheel, as he cut the blood-slicked leather thongs at ankle and wrist, Raklion said, "Do you go now to the scorpion pit?"

Nagarak nodded. "Yes. I go to ask the god's desire. I

go to ask if you must rule all Mijak as its warlord. If I am to be its one true godspeaker."

Raklion's gaze slipped sideways to rest on Hekat's secret, watchful face. He could see her smiling, he could hear her breathing, but Nagarak was deaf and blind. To Nagarak, they were alone.

The god has sent her. She is sent by the god. She has already answered Nagarak's question.

"The god will not smite you in the scorpion pit, Nagarak," Raklion said. "It will tell you I am to be warlord of Mijak."

Nagarak frowned. "You cannot say so, warlord. I am high godspeaker, I cannot say it. No man can know the god's desire before the god tells a godspeaker in its time."

So Nagarak said. But there in the shadows stood the knife-dancer Hekat, and she had said a different thing. She stood in the shadows and Nagarak did not see her.

Who do I believe now? Who knows the god best, Hekat or Nagarak?

"Come with me, Raklion," said Nagarak. "I will heal you before I go to the pit."

It was a terrible thing, to slide free of the scorpion wheel. Raklion heard his pained breath sobbing, he felt his head swim and his knees buckle after so long spent suffering for his sins. Nagarak's smiting arm slipped round his shoulders, Nagarak's strength kept him from falling.

"When I beat you," said Nagarak, "I was obeying the god. I took no pleasure from your weeping."

Nagarak, expressing regret? For a moment Raklion thought he must be fever-dreaming, that Hekat did not stand close by and unseen in the shadows, that he remained bound to the scorpion wheel awaiting further sorrow.

Nagarak said, "If I must die in the scorpion pit I would not have any misunderstandings left behind me."

Raklion shifted a little, and took more weight upon his feet. He was desperate to lie down. "The smiting hand was not yours, Nagarak, it was the god's. You were its instrument, I understand. And you will *not* die in the scorpion pit."

This time Nagarak did not chide him. "That is my desire, I confess it freely." He cleared his throat. "But a man's desires are nothing to the god. Its desires are not the desires of men."

Raklion looked at watching Hekat. "I believe the god desires peace in Mijak. I believe it desires an end to strife, to squabbling warlords, to untrue godspeakers. I believe it will tell you this in its scorpions' whispers. Now, heal me I beg you, Nagarak high godspeaker, and let that be an end to my sorrow."

As Nagarak helped him from the chamber he resisted the urge to turn back to Hekat. The god had seen her into this place, it would see her safely out again.

If it did not, her words were lies and she would be justly punished.

But if she does not lie . . . if Nagarak is spared in the scorpion pit and tells me in his own words what Hekat has told me, these terrible three highsuns will be as labor. I will birth a Mijak made new.

Hekat left the godhouse as she had entered it, deep in the god's eye, invisible to mortal men. Vortka waited for her on the Pinnacle Road, chilled in the deep cold that came before newsun.

"Tchut tchut, Vortka! What do you *do* here?" she whispered, as he took her hands in his. Voices carried on the cool night air. "This is the quiet time, the godmoon should not see you!"

His fingers released her, and folded into his sleeves. His teeth were chattering. "I wanted to be sure you were unseen and unharmed."

"I am both, Vortka. The god hides me in its eye," she said, impatient. "It does not hide you, you will be seen. You will be smitten. I have witnessed what the godspeakers do to men who break the quiet time. You are *stupid*, go away!"

His solemn face broke into a smile. "You are worried for me."

It was one thing to call him friend in the silence of her mind. That did not mean she meant to shout it from her tongue, or wished to see him smile like that or say out loud things best left unspoken.

"Tcha! Who wastes worry on stupid rocks?"

His smile faded. "Did you see the warlord?"

"Yes, I saw him. I told him what the god wants, he will do it. He has no choice, and neither do I. What the god desires the god must receive."

Vortka nodded. "It desires you to lie with the warlord. It desires you to bear him a son. Raklion will become the warlord of Mijak and the son you bear will follow him to glory."

Astonished, Hekat felt her mouth fall open. Then she stepped close to Vortka, her snakeblade in hand, and pricked its sharp tip into his throat. "*How do you know this*?"

He did not push her hand away. "Aieee, Hekat. How do you think? I asked the god for answers, the god revealed its plan to me."

"The god, or a demon seeking mischief in the world?"

"A demon cannot know the god's secret heart."

Still she kept her snakeblade to his throat. "A *man* cannot know its secret heart, Vortka!"

"A godtouched man knows whatever the god desires it to know," said Vortka. "I too am godtouched, Hekat, do you seek to deny it? Do you seek to thwart the god from jealousy or spite?"

Jealousy? Spite? How dare he say so! She snatched back her snakeblade and slapped his face. "I think *you* are jealous," she hissed. "I can stand before Nagarak, he does not see me. Nagarak will always see you. You must *ask* the god to tell you its desires, the god comes to me unbidden, I *never* ask and still I know what it wants."

"You think that matters to the god?" said Vortka, scornful. "The god cares only that we serve. I am its instrument, Hekat, no less than you. Accept it, or the god will smite you."

That was true. She sheathed her snakeblade. "You are its instrument, Vortka, I accept it, but I must be careful. No man is perfect. All men are weak."

"I am not a man," said Vortka, touching his face where her hand had struck him. "I am a godspeaker."

"Tcha!" she scoffed. "You were a man *before* you were a godspeaker. Little more than a boy. Sold to slavery for being unwanted."

"And you were a girl sold for the same reason," he

said, glaring. "That is the past, it does not matter. *Now* I breathe for the god, Hekat. I will not betray you, I will never hurt you. You need not guard yourself from *me*. Why do you attack me? I thought we were friends. I thought you trusted me."

"I can trust no-one," she told him coldly. "I am precious and godtouched, I can have no friends."

His face twisted with anger. "You ungrateful brat! I have kept your bloodsoaked secrets and told lies for your sake in the godhouse. I come to you when the god's will moves me and I tell you things it wants you to know. Things it does *not* whisper unasked in your heart. Even though I am put in danger, even though I would be tasked to mindless screaming if any godspeaker was to learn what I did. You are a stunted woman, Hekat. You have a mean spirit. That is your sorrow, it is not mine. Deny our friendship, I cannot stop you. But I am equal to you in the god's eye and you *will* respect that."

She felt a pricking, a sting of discomfort. There was water standing in Vortka's eyes. Scuffing her sandaled toe in the dirt she muttered, "I said I accepted you are the god's instrument. Did I not say I accepted that? There is no need to sharpen your tongue on me. You are not so precious you can sharpen your tongue on me."

"Is that so?" he said, and turned away.

She let him walk five paces, then called, "Wait! Vortka, wait!"

He stopped, but did not turn back. "What?"

Mindful of their voices carrying, she took four paces to be near him again. "Nagarak prepares for the scorpion pit. He will ask the god if it wants Raklion as Mijak's warlord. You must be there to witness the god's answer.

Whoever witnesses Nagarak's testing, those godspeakers will be seen by him as special. Soon enough Nagarak will be my enemy. He will work against me. You must work *for* me, in the godhouse. You must trust me in this, I speak the truth."

It showed in his face that he did not want to trust her, his feelings were hurt. He was stupid, *stupid*. What were his feelings, compared to the god?

"*Vortka*," she said, and took his robe in her fist. "This is what the god wants. You cannot refuse."

He plucked her fingers free, turned on his heel and stalked away up the Pinnacle Road. She watched until the darkness swallowed him, until he was a memory in her eye. Around her neck the scorpion dangled, and it was hot with the god's displeasure.

He is my instrument, you handled him roughly.

So said the god to her, deep in her heart.

Bathed in the godmoon's thin light she dropped to her knees, bruising them on stones scattered in the road. Her snakeblade glinted, it thirsted for her blood. If she refused its spilling, demons would take her. The power in her scorpion amulet would drain away, leaving her empty.

I did not mean to disrespect you, god. I did not mean to disrespect your instrument.

She pulled down her linen tunic, exposing her left breast to the night. Her snakeblade bit keenly. Dark blood welled. Pain rose like a hot wind from The Anvil, scouring away sin.

Three times her blade bit, and after that the god was slaked. The fresh wounds healed, no need for a godstone. It was the god who healed her, who sealed her flesh.

I am Hekat, beautiful and precious. Chosen. God-touched. Filled with the god.

How could Nagarak stand against her? How could any man stand against her?

Though her wounds were healed, wet blood still stained her skin. She dragged her fingers through it and touched them to the scorpion amulet. The stone pulsed and flared into life. She laughed to feel it, the god throbbing in her bones. Its presence soothed her, eased the prickly hurt of harsh words with Vortka.

I am Hekat, precious and beautiful. The god loves me, I will give it the world.

Et-Raklion godhouse's scorpion chamber had four bare walls, a bare ceiling, and a pit in the center of its stone floor. It had an altar at one end, but that was all. No lavish decoration was needed here, no godposts, no friezes, no mosaics, no elaborately wrought torch-holders. The god was here, and that was enough.

Kneeling naked before the altar, even his scorpion pectoral discarded, Nagarak felt the god's presence slide across his skin. Cool, caressing, but with a hint of heat and venom in it. Promise of the testing to come. He spilled no blood upon the altar. No sacrifice was needed for this ritual. He was the sacrifice, the sacred offering.

In the pit behind him, fat godhouse scorpions skittered and hissed. It was full of them, more scorpions than any high godspeaker had faced in the godhouse's ancient history. How could it be otherwise, when such a question trembled on his tongue?

Must Raklion be Mijak's one warlord? Must I be its one true high godspeaker?

There was a chance he would die in this sacred place. That the god, offended, would sting him to a screaming death. Raklion warlord had outlived two high godspeakers already. Would today's testing see a third outlived? He did not know. He could not tell. His godsense failed him, he saw no further into the future than the taking of his next breath. That had never happened before. Was it an ill omen?

It was something else he could not tell.

He waited with an empty mind for the witnesses to come. He knew not which three godspeakers the god would send, to be seen in its eye recording the question and the answer. That was the god's business, no part of him.

A godbell tolled, its sweet tones muffled by stone walls and distance. Outside the godhouse the sun was rising, chasing the godmoon and his wife below the horizon. The scorpion room contained no windows, he could not see the sunlight kiss the top of Raklion's Pinnacle, strike fire from the godpost as though the god's scorpion eyes were open. He felt a small regret for that.

This was his favorite time of day.

Sandals shuffled in the corridor outside. Three pairs, slow and steady. Unhurried, with the grace and dignity expected of a high godspeaker, he rose to his feet and turned to greet the god's chosen witnesses.

"The god sees you in its eye, my sister, my brothers."

It had selected Saskira, a healer, the taskmaster Bendik and one of the novices. Vortka, yes, that was his name. A pious youth, this Vortka, oft found in the tasking house repenting his sins. A godspeaker of uncommon powers and quiet devotion, so the novice-master said.

"The god sees you also, Nagarak," they murmured.

At all other times, in all other places, every godspeaker in the godhouse was subordinate to him. Only here, in the scorpion chamber, was he the supplicant and they his masters.

"Kneel to the god, Nagarak," said Saskira healer. "Be anointed, bare your godspark to its all-seeing eye. The scorpions await you, they are hungry to test your heart."

Vortka novice was first to paint his high godspeaker's body with the blood and oil, carried with him in a sacred stone jar. His dripping fingers were cool and confident, he knew precisely where and how to mark his high godspeaker's skin. When the anointing was done he smeared his own face, from brow to chin and eye to eye.

"Here is a sacred place, a silent place, a place of communing with the god," he said. "I will see the god here. It will whisper in my heart. Its mysteries will be revealed to my eye. May the god grind my flesh to dust and feed my godspark to demons if I reveal by thought, word or deed what is shown to me in this place."

"The god sees, the god hears, the god will grind you into dust," murmured the others.

Twice more the ritual was performed, with bloodied oil upon the face and fervent words falling from the tongue. Nagarak waited, silent, patient, as the witnesses swore their oaths of discretion.

When they were done, it was his turn.

"Here is a sacred place, a silent place, a place of communing with the god," he said. The oil and blood burned his naked flesh. "I have a question, the question is this. What does the god demand of Raklion warlord and his high godspeaker Nagarak?"

"*A question is asked, the god will answer,*" intoned the witnesses. "*Surrender flesh, abandon hope. The god sees you, seeker. It sees you in its eye.*"

The scorpions rattled and scraped in the pit. They hissed, tails raised, as Nagarak slid into their midst. Their heaving bodies closed over his head, he was swimming in scorpions, drowning in scorpions. He was a scorpion, inhaled by the god.

Time ended, suspended. Stung and stung, he screamed in torment. His blood turned to venom. His heart pumped pain. In his mind, the god's voice thundered.

One warlord for Mijak. One high godspeaker to guide him.

There was its answer and its desire. Raklion warlord had heard the god right. Seven warlords no longer. No Mijak divided. One Mijak. One warlord. One godspeaker, to lead him.

The god had answered. He would live.

On a shout of triumph Nagarak surged to his feet. Scorpions fell from his flesh like scales from a snake. The pit was filled with dead and dying scorpions but he breathed, he lived, the god had answered him and spared his life.

"*Tell us,*" the witnesses demanded.

"The god desires a united Mijak," he said, his voice ringing. "One nation, one warlord, one sacred altar beneath the sun."

He could not say why but it was the novice, Vortka, he looked to first. As Bendik and Saskira stared, eyes wide, pulses beating fast in their throats, the novice incompletely hid a smile. He was not surprised. He showed no alarm. No sweat beaded upon his brow.

Before Nagarak could wonder at that he began to shake like a man with fever. Saskira healer leapt forward and seized his arms. He was swiftly drawn from the scorpion pit and laid upon the cold stone floor. His body heaved and thrashed, he voided venom from bowel and bladder, from mouth and eyes and even his ears. Empty of poison, filled with the god, he let the godhouse healer mend him.

One warlord for Mijak. One high godspeaker to guide him.

When Saskira was done and he could stand unaided, he thanked the witnesses for their service, swore them to solemn secrecy, and departed from them for his private bath. There he cleansed his body, soaping and scrubbing until all traces of filth were removed.

His skin was welted with fresh scorpion scars. He counted hundreds, he was lumped like a lizard, like some survivor of a terrible plague, the kind that had in the distant past ravaged the nation, plundered its populace, reduced the fat empire of Mijak to bones.

The welts did not worry him. They were gifts from the god. Thumbprints of favor. He thought no other godspeaker living or dead had ever borne so many sting-marks. It was fitting.

I am to be godspeaker of a nation.

Cleansed, he strapped himself into his scorpion pectoral and draped his limbs in linen and wool. He alerted Peklia, godspeaker in charge of the sacrifices, and at the godhouse's largest altar he gave a black bull-calf, twelve black lambs and one hundred golden cockerels to the god. Blood ran like a river. The novice holding the basin of water, afterwards, was the same Vortka who'd witnessed in the scorpion room.

Sluicing the sacred blood from his hands, Nagarak said, "You desire something from me, novice?"

The novice shook his head. Beads rattled. Godbells chimed. "No, high godspeaker. I desire only to serve."

"I see that you do serve. I see the god calls you to important matters."

The novice Vortka stared at the floor. "I am the god's instrument. It uses me as it desires."

On the surface, it was a humble answer. On the surface, Vortka novice was a humble man. And yet . . . in the scorpion chamber . . . Vortka novice had smiled.

"See to the disposal of the sacrificed beasts," he said, abruptly unsettled. Angry, because of it. "And clean the altar by yourself. A novice called to witness in the scorpion chamber is still a novice. Until you are seen by the god in the time of testing you are not more than flesh, you are yet unproven. Give me your sleeve, I would dry my hands."

Obedient, the novice presented his sleeve. Nagarak used him, turned his back to him, and called for another novice to be sent to the palace, that the warlord might be summoned to his high godspeaker's presence.

Raklion must hear of the god's desire.

CHAPTER TWENTY-ONE

A warlord who neglected his warriors had no business calling himself a warlord. No matter his trials, no matter his private pains, a warlord must always place his warhost first.

Raklion thought this as he stood alone on the warhost field and watched his beautiful warriors dancing around him. Weary from his ordeal on the scorpion wheel, the loss of another son a bleeding wound in his heart, still he smiled to see his knife-dancers' grace and oiled muscles, the sunlight glinting on their snakeblades. Trained to perfection they flowed like water, like blood spilled in sacrifice for the god.

He watched Hekat dancing, and let his loins burn.

I am meant for you. I will be yours.

So she had told him, and so he believed. How could he not? She had come to him in the godhouse, unseen in Nagarak's eye.

As she danced with her knife-brothers and sisters, Hanochek joined him unbidden on the short grass. "A slave has come from the palace, warlord. Nagarak would see you in the godhouse, at once."

Nagarak. So the high godspeaker had emerged unscathed from the scorpion pit. The god had spared him, and given him an answer.

I know already what it is. Hekat has told me. I am to be warlord of Mijak. The god does not only speak through Nagarak.

It changed everything.

With his gaze still resting on dancing Hekat he said to Hano, "Send that slave to the godhouse with this message: Raklion warlord is about the god's business. Nagarak high godspeaker is welcome to join him in the barracks, where he will see how warriors worship."

Hano gasped. "Warlord?"

Now he turned his head. "You heard me, warleader. That is my message. See it is sent."

"Warlord . . ." Hano swallowed. "Raklion. Are you certain? I don't want you condemned to three more days on the scorpion wheel."

Aieee, his good friend Hano worried over him like a hen with one chick.

"More than certain," he said, smiling. "Do not fret or fear the high godspeaker's wrath. He is only a man. He serves the god, as we serve the god. We all have power, Hano. The god sees every man in its eye."

Hano nodded reluctantly, unconvinced but obedient. "Warlord."

The slave was sent up to the godhouse. By the time Nagarak arrived at the barracks the knife-dancers had given way to archers on horseback. Raklion sighed with pleasure to see them weaving so neatly past and around each other, the horses' hides gleaming, his warriors' godbraids singing under the sun. Their godbells shouted praises to the god, and so did he in his heart.

I survived the scorpion wheel. I will be Raklion, war-

lord of Mijak. My son will follow me, as beautiful as Hekat. The god is great, it will see me great also.

Hano joined him again, eyes wide with trepidation. "Warlord, Nagarak high godspeaker approaches the barracks gates."

"Go to him," he said. "Bring him to me with all gratitude and respect."

Hano shook his head. "Raklion, I am lost for words. We speak of *Nagarak*. The god sits on his shoulder, it whispers daily in his ear. Why would you anger him? Why tempt him to smite you?"

"He will not smite me, Hano. Never again."

"He is the high godspeaker!" said Hano, disbelieving. "He was born for smiting!"

Raklion rested his hand on Hanochek's shoulder. "And I am the warlord. I am in the god's eye. I tell you truly, he will not smite me."

Hano sighed, conflicted and anxious. "You are different, Raklion. You have returned from the godhouse a changed man."

Was he so fearful before? So unsure of his power? *Perhaps I was. Perhaps the deaths of all those sons shrank me, diminished me, made me small. But I am brave now. I will be Mijak's warlord, with Hekat in my bed.*

"I am not different. I am myself," he told Hano. "Go now and fetch Nagarak."

"Yes, warlord," said Hano, helpless, and obeyed.

In keeping with the god's decree that even the most revered godspeaker must walk whenever possible, Nagarak came to the warhost field on foot. He wore fine linen and wool over his scorpion pectoral, but the fabrics were splashed and stained with sacrificial blood.

It was strange, watching him approach, knowing that this man knew him to the bone. Knew him weeping, knew him screaming, knew him abject in his pain.

And yet I no longer fear him. He does not shame me, I feel no need to cringe. I look on him and feel nothing beyond what I should feel for any man who serves the god.

Truly god, I am changed. You have changed me.

As Nagarak came closer it was clear he was changed, too. The skin of his face was welted beyond any godspeaker's ever seen. All his flesh not covered with fabric was blotched with the mark of scorpion stings.

Raklion marveled. It was a thing of wonder, that his high godspeaker had survived the pit.

"Warlord," said Nagarak. The word vibrated with his displeasure.

"Nagarak. The god sees you in its eye. You have an answer?"

For a moment Nagarak did not reply. Clearly he expected some abasement, some recognition of this breach in their accustomed roles. Nagarak summoned, Raklion appeared, that was the way of things. Beneath the anger he seemed almost bewildered, that he was standing on the warhost field and not in his godhouse.

"I have an answer," he said at last. "But I will not give it here or now. This is no fit place to talk of the god's secret purpose."

Raklion shifted his gaze to his still-weaving archers. So trained were they, so attuned to his orders, not even the appearance of Nagarak before them could interrupt their *hotas*.

"The god is everywhere," he said mildly. "So everywhere must be a fit place to speak. Shall you tell me its answer? Or shall I tell you? I am to be the warlord of Mijak. I am to tame this nation to my fist."

Nagarak's face spasmed in a scowl. "Beware, warlord. I drank deep of the scorpions' venom, the scorpions died and yet I live. This is known as a sign."

"I see it, Nagarak. You are my high godspeaker, I deny you nothing."

"You deny me the courtesy of answering my summons!"

"I wished you to witness my obedience to the god. I wished you to see me do my duty as warlord of Et-Raklion, soon to be warlord of Mijak." He turned. "*Hanochek*! To me!"

Hanochek came running. "Warlord?"

"Stand down my archers. Command all my warriors here to me, assemble them on this warhost field. Go now. Quickly."

Hano pressed his fist to his heart. "Warlord."

"What are you doing?" Nagarak demanded as they were surrounded by the racket and dust of the warhost gathering. "Is your mind disordered by the death of another son? Or did you break on the scorpion wheel after all?"

"I am not broken," he replied. "I am whole, and strong. To be warlord of Mijak I must have a son. There is no woman of warlord bloodlines for me to sow with my seed. Nogolor has no more daughters to give me. To get one from another warlord I would have to treaty with him, and in these brown days a treaty with a starving warlord would be like baring my own throat for his knife. Besides." He smiled, wryly. "There are no more daughters of beddable age and I do not have the luxury of waiting. So I must look to a wider horizon."

"What wider horizon?" said Nagarak, still scowling. "Warlords couple with the daughters of warlords. Or those daughters' daughters, or their sisters, or some other female flesh traced through the warlord line."

Raklion nodded. "Once that was true, Nagarak. It is true no longer. Now *I* decide where I sow my seed. This is given me by the god. Do you doubt me? Ask it, Nagarak. I promise you I have its answer."

Nagarak was staring as though they'd never met before. In a strange way, they had not. "The god see you, warlord. I think you are demonstruck."

He laughed. "I am no such thing and you know it, Nagarak. I am chosen, the god's warlord, it desires what I do. If that is not so let it strike me dead at your feet."

The god did not strike him. He knew it would not.

Nagarak stood still beneath the sun. "And have you chosen the field where you will sow your seed?"

"No, Nagarak," he said, as the last of his summoned warhost gathered before him. "The god has chosen for me. I am obedient, I will sow where it desires."

Nagarak said nothing to that. Moments later Hano appeared, sounding a gilded ram's horn. Two slaves followed him across the grass, carrying a wooden dais. They set it down and withdrew. Hano stood beside it, still sounding the ram's horn. The warhost's muttering voices fell silent.

Raklion walked to the dais, Nagarak grim beside him. He climbed its steps and swept his gaze across his people's faces. He looked for Hekat, he could not see her. It did not matter, he knew she was there.

"Warriors of Et-Raklion, you see me, your warlord!"

"*We see you, warlord!*" they answered him, shouting.

"Warriors, I see you. The god sees you. It sees you in its smiting eye."

"*The god sees you in its smiting eye, warlord.*"

His heart was so full of them he had to pause and re-press his tears. "Warriors, I have sorrowful news. The god has taken Et-Nogolor's Daughter. It has taken my son in his moment of birth."

A moment of silence, then loud cries of dismay, shouts of grief. His warriors wept, they wept for him. He let them weep, he did not chastise them. They were his brothers and sisters, the children of his heart. He glanced at Hano, who wept silently with them. Their eyes met, and he smiled. He had no need for tears, the god had dried them.

Nagarak did not weep, his face was stone like his scorpion pectoral. He stood in his stained robes and communed with the god.

After some time, Raklion raised his hands. "Warriors, grieve no longer. It was the god's will, we do not question. It has happened, it is behind us. I have other news. You must hear it now."

One by one his warriors stopped weeping. The warhost field was hushed as they waited for him to speak.

"Warriors of Et-Raklion, the god has spoken. I *will* have a son," he told them, triumphant. "I will have a son like no son born in Mijak since the god breathed and there was light. He will not be born of a woman from diluted bloodlines, from the leached seed of a warlord who has no love for Et-Raklion, for me, or for you. He will not be born of a woman who has never killed in war. My son's mother will be a *warrior*! A warrior of Et-Raklion, chosen by the god itself!"

As the warhost shouted its amazement, Nagarak climbed the dais steps behind him. Reaching its top he demanded in a hissing whisper, "Raklion warlord, what is this?"

He turned and smiled. "The will of the god."

"*Raklion!*"

Raklion turned away. Nagarak had no power here, he was a witness, no more than that. As he turned he caught sight of Hano's face, stricken with astonishment and something less benign.

Be pleased for me, Hano. If you are not pleased, how can you say you are my friend?

Pushing Hanochek's displeasure aside he looked at his warhost. "Hekat!" he shouted. "Hekat. Knife-dancer. Bajadek's doom. Seen by the god in its blood-filled eye. You are chosen. Step forward and come to me. *Come to me now!*"

It was the god calling her, clothing itself in Raklion's voice. Hekat felt her scorpion amulet, warm and heavy against her skin, and the god in her heart giving her strength. As surprise shivered through the warriors pressed close around her, as their heads turned and their voices lifted, she answered the god and the warlord together.

"Hekat comes to you, Raklion," she said, pushing through the warhost. "Knife-dancer. Bajadek's doom. Chosen by the god, seen by the god in its blood-filled eye."

On the dais beside the warlord, Nagarak high godspeaker choked with rage, his nostrils flared wide like a horse that could not breathe. His eyes were molten fury, he would have killed her with a look, but the god did not listen to his hating heart. Hekat ignored him. She ignored Hanochek warleader, shocked and staring as she emerged from the ranks. She walked towards Raklion, the warlord, the god's chosen man for the making of her son.

He came down from his dais and waited for her, tall and strong, his spine unbowed, his shoulders wide and carrying the weight of Mijak upon them. His godbraids were silver, his face was lined. He was a man, there was hunger in his eyes. Lust for her body, boiling his blood.

He will make me a strong son, the only thing that matters. The rest of him I will tolerate, as is the god's desire. He is not a bad man, I can endure much worse.

"Hekat," he said when she reached him, and wrapped her godbraids round his fingers. "The god's knife-dancer, and Bajadek's doom. Chosen for me by the god."

Nagarak said from the top of the dais, "Raklion warlord, there is no custom. She is common. She has no heritage."

"She is beautiful and precious," said Raklion, with a flickering glance.

"She is *blemished*! See her face!"

"Her face does not matter," said Raklion. "I see her heart. She lives in the god's eye, it has decreed her for me."

"*I have not said so!*" Nagarak thundered. "The god has not told me!"

Raklion looked up at him, his smile was a knife. "But it has told me, Nagarak. I am the warlord, the god speaks to me. The god has spoken, I must obey. I must seed this woman with my son."

Nagarak bared his teeth. "She is a warrior, she lives in the barracks. Warriors rut like dogs in a ditch. Warlords bed virgins. That is the law."

"She is chosen for me by the god, Nagarak. Do you say the god has chosen a rutting bitch?"

"Tread lightly, warlord!" said Nagarak, eyes slitting. "I am high godspeaker, I will have you on the wheel."

"My scorpion-wheel days are behind me, Nagarak," said Raklion, calmly. "I know Hekat is virgin, but come down to her and satisfy yourself. The god will tell you she is untouched."

Hekat tensed. If Nagarak put his fingers in her as once dead Abajai had done, she would plunge her snakeblade into his throat and that would be the end of him. Her fingers strayed towards her knife's hilt.

Suspicious, unfriendly, Nagarak came down from the dais. He withdrew a godstone from his robe pocket and closed it tight within his fist, and his fist he pressed against her belly. She felt heat, saw light behind her closed eyelids. The light shone into the empty spaces inside her. Nagarak grunted.

"She is virgin," he admitted, grudging, and slipped the godstone out of sight.

"As I told you," said Raklion, serene. "She is virgin, and she is mine. You will witness her breaching in the palace, as custom decrees. This is the god's desire, Nagarak. I think you know it."

"No," said Hekat, before Nagarak could answer, and laid her hand on Raklion's heart. She swept her gaze across the silent warhost, then rested it upon his face.

"Claim me now, warlord, before your warriors. Beneath the sky in the god's open eye. Let the warhost witness I am taken by you. Let it witness this is the god's desire. If the god does not want this it will smite us together and the warhost will see. Nagarak high godspeaker will also see. I am the god's chosen. This is its desire."

Raklion frowned. "You are certain, Hekat?"

Her heart was pounding, it pounded her ribs. If Nagarak alone was their bedding witness he could lie to thwart her, claim the bedding had never happened; he was a man and not to be trusted. "I am certain, warlord."

Raklion turned to Nagarak. "You will witness, Nagarak, as is proper, and so will my warhost. In years to come, when their godbraids are silver and they sleep in the sun, they will boast of the day they saw Raklion's seed planted, Mijak's new dawning, the birth of an age." He stepped close to his high godspeaker, making them private. "Try to thwart me, Nagarak." His voice was a whisper. "Try, and the god will strike *you* down."

Nagarak's palm flattened against his scorpion pectoral. His eyes rolled upwards, became crescents of white. Hekat waited, her scalp burning as Raklion's clenched fist on her godbraids tightened, tightened. The god was speaking, she could feel its power in her scorpion amulet, hot against the skin beneath her linen training tunic.

The warlord's watching warhost was silent. Hanochek warleader, standing nearby, kept one hand lightly upon his blade. Nagarak released a shuddering sigh. His palm fell from his pectoral, the dark of his eyes reappeared. "Your snakeblade, warlord," he demanded, his voice clipped and cold.

Raklion held out his other hand so the high godspeaker might cut him. The blade bit deep, he did not flinch. Blood welled and swiftly covered his palm.

Hekat held out her own palm next. Nagarak slashed it, almost to the bone. Bright pain rushed through her but she made no sound, she would not give him even that much of her. She knew what to do next, the god whispered in her heart. She laid her wounded hand in Raklion's and gasped as the heat of his blood burst through her body. She reached for his godbraids, tangled her fingers in them as his tangled in hers. They were joined, they were one, their hot blood was mingled.

Dimly she heard a roar from the warhost. Her knees were folding, he was forcing her downwards, onto the short grass of the warhost field. Their wounded hands were clasping still but now his other hand had released her godbraids, his fingers fumbled beneath her linen training tunic. His body was on hers, covering hers, smothering hers. She knew what this was, this was fucking. She had seen it, oh, over and over in that village, in the kitchen, so long ago in the savage north.

In her head she heard the man's dogs howling.

The god wants it. The god wants it. Close your eyes, Hekat, you obey the god.

When her body was breached she scarcely felt it. The god was in her, filling her with fire. The scorpion amulet was burning through her, her bones were melting, Raklion was nothing. All that mattered was the god.

The howling dogs weren't dogs at all, they were Et-Raklion's warriors. But they howled like dogs, they howled to see the warlord plow her, fuck her, make her the son the god had promised.

The pain in her cut hand vanished, then was reborn. She felt it in her belly, in that untouched place between her legs. Her legs were spread, she was split in two pieces, Raklion labored and panted above her, inside her. His blade was not puny and her field was fertile. He plowed without mercy, she thought of the god.

The god sees me. It sees me. I do this for the god.

With a shout of triumph Raklion spilled himself into her. Dazed, head spinning, she felt herself free of him, felt him pull her upwards to her feet. Her loincloth was discarded, her tunic torn, her bruised breasts kissed by sunlight but not by him.

He traced a finger over her scars. "Beautiful Hekat, mother of my warlord son. Mine, all mine, until death defeats us."

She was Hekat, chosen by the god. She belonged to no man. But if Raklion wished to think otherwise, he could. He could think and think and never change the truth.

Nagarak took their cut hands and inspected them closely. The wounds were gone, their palms smooth and unscarred. Her blood was in Raklion, his was in her. She was no longer virgin. His seed was planted in her belly.

Let it grow, god. Let it grow. Let it grow into my son.

The watching warriors had not stopped howling. They waved their swords and snakeblades in the air, they drummed their spear-butts into the ground, they leapt and shook so their godbells rang out. Hekat thought the sleeping godmoon and his wife would wake and hear them, in their bed below the horizon.

"What now, warlord?" she asked Raklion as he laughed and punched his fists in the air, drinking down his warhost's acclaim.

"Now?" he echoed, smiling at her. "Now we retire to the palace."

The palace. "I will live there, warlord?"

"Where else would you live?" he asked, puzzled. "You are chosen for me, to bear my son. Do you think I should live with you here in the barracks?"

As Nagarak muttered something beneath his breath, she shook her head. "No, warlord."

Raklion's hand cupped her scarred cheek, briefly. "You will miss the barracks? You have shell-mates in your heart?"

Only the god was in her heart. "No, warlord."

"Yet you do not wish to leave them. Why?"

Was he angry, or only confused? She blotted out the rest of the world, glaring Nagarak and staring Hanochek and all the shouting, celebrating warriors. "Warlord, Hekat is a knife-dancer. Hekat knife-dances for the god. For the god, and for the warlord. Can Hekat knife-dance in the palace?"

He smiled. "Hekat will always knife-dance for the god and for her warlord. She will knife-dance where she pleases. Hekat is beautiful when she dances with her snakeblade. Of course you can knife-dance in the palace."

She nodded, relieved. Without her knife-dancing she would not be Hekat. "Then I will go with you and live in that place."

Raklion laughed, and called for a horse. The warleader Hanochek brought one with his own hands, his own horse, a blue-striped stallion with a long mane full of godbells. He brought a light linen wrap also, and gave it to Hekat.

Raklion thanked him and vaulted into the saddle. Her

nakedness covered in the linen wrap, Hekat vaulted behind him, clasped her arms around his waist and pressed
her face into his muscled, linen-covered back. He smelled
of sweat and dirt and of her as well. His long, fine godbraids tickled her nose.

The warriors cheered and howled so loudly the striped
stallion reared and lashed out its hooves. She and Raklion
sat it easily. They were warriors of Et-Raklion and did not
flinch from horseflesh.

Raklion's head turned over his shoulder. "It was a
rough taking, Hekat. I am sorry for it."

She shrugged. "It was nothing, warlord. Hekat is a
warrior."

A small sigh escaped him. "Hekat is much more than
that."

As the warhost shouted, they galloped away.

She knife-danced for him in his private palace chamber,
all her *hotas* for him and the god, and after that he fucked
her again. It meant no more the second time than it had
the first. He sweated and grunted, he stroked her and
pressed her, seeming eager that she find pleasure in the
act. She had not thought there was pleasure in fucking,
the woman in the village never spoke of pleasure, just rutting men and the pain they caused. Not even the man had
enjoyed it, or so it had seemed to that nameless child she
had been. Despite Raklion's strivings she felt no pleasure,
fucking was a thing to be lived through, not enjoyed.

Raklion enjoyed it. He kissed her fingers, he kissed her
toes, he praised her breasts and called her the empress of
his heart.

He was a strange man.

In a damp, sweaty knotting of limbs they lay upon his chamber bed, caressed by a breeze from the open doors. Slaves waited outside, she did not care for them. Playing with her godbraids Raklion said, "Truly the god has favored me."

She stared at the ceiling, painted with pictures of warlords in battle. Knives. Blood. Vanquished enemies. "Did Et-Nogolor's Daughter sleep here with you, warlord?"

"No," he said curtly. "She is dead, Hekat. Never speak of her again."

"Wherever she slept, I will not sleep," she said, and rolled over on her elbow to look into his face. "I will sleep here. Your bed is my bed. I am no soft womanthing. I am a warrior, Bajadek's doom."

His fingertips traced her silver scars. "You are the doom of more men than Bajadek. Tell me what happened, the night you killed the Traders for me."

"I did not kill them," she said. A finger strayed across her lips. She took it in her teeth and bit until she felt the bone, then spat it out and smiled at his wincing. "They did not die for you. The god sent them to hell for thwarting its desires."

His gaze shifted to the scorpion round her neck. "I have never seen you without that amulet. Is it so precious? Where did you get it?"

He was jealous. Afraid some man, some boy, had given her a gift. "It came to me by the god's design. I must always wear it, that is the god's desire."

"Who were you before you came here?" he asked, cupping his hand beneath her breast. "Tell me of your life beyond my lands of Et-Raklion."

"I was nothing. I was no-one. I was a seed waiting for the god to give me life."

The smile in his eyes faded, his look was intent. "I think you frighten me a little, Hekat. I have never known a woman like you."

"There has never been a woman like me, warlord." She covered his cupping hand with her own. "Fuck me again, if that is your wanting. Then we will bathe and dress and talk of Mijak."

"Fuck again?" he said, and laughed. "Later, Hekat. I am no young bull to rut and rut without rest."

"Then talk to me, warlord. Tell me of the warlords Banotaj and Jokriel, of Zyden, Takona, Mamiklia and Nogolor. Tell me all you know of them, that we may decide how best to tame them."

"*We*?" Raklion sat up. "Not *we*. Wars and warlords are the warlord's business. He talks of these things with his warleader and his high godspeaker, not—"

She rested her palm on his back and let the god's heat fill her hand. "Nagarak resists the god in me. I knew before he did what it desired. I told you on the scorpion wheel. Did Nagarak know? Did he see me there? Did he sense my presence in the godhouse?"

Troubled, Raklion shook his head, and shifted so her hand fell from his back. "No. He did not."

"Then do not think so much of him."

"Three times has the god kept Nagarak safe in the scorpion pit. You cannot dismiss him like a slave, Hekat."

"I do not dismiss him. He is in the god's eye. *I* am in the god's eye also, warlord. Nagarak would see that if he was not blind. You say I am no usual woman and you are right. I am godtouched and godchosen, I am the warrior whose son will follow you as the warlord of Mijak. What is Nagarak, next to that?"

Raklion looked at her. "A man of power, Hekat."

"*Tcha*!" she said, and slapped him lightly. "You are the warlord. *You* have the power. You are in the god's eye so deep there is no room for Nagarak there. I am Hekat. I do not lie."

He turned and lowered his mouth to hers. "You are Hekat," he murmured against her lips. "Precious and beautiful, the god's gift to me. I will gift it with bull-calves, I will drown it in lambs' blood, I will soak the stones of the godhouse with proof of my love."

She clutched at his buttocks. "Fuck me first, warlord. There must be a son, or the blood will mean nothing."

CHAPTER TWENTY-TWO

Within a godmoon of her first taking, Hekat was planted with the warlord's seed. There were wild celebrations in the streets of Et-Raklion, the godspeakers sacrificed for twelve highsuns unceasing. With her belly protesting the sight and scent of blood she knelt with Raklion before the godhouse's largest altar as Nagarak gave beast after beast to the god. She did not see Vortka, she did not seek him out.

He is still angry with me. I do not care. Do I need him? I think I do not.

Five godmoons after Nagarak pronounced her pregnant she miscarried of a female child.

Raklion was away from the palace when it happened, training with Hanochek and twenty-five shells of warriors along the border with Et-Nogolor. Nogolor watlord was ageing swiftly, failing. Word came he was deeply grieved by the Daughter's death, and the slaughter of her child. Word also said his son Tebek was enraged by it. Raklion wished to remind Tebek of the might that would ride against him if he was so foolish as to discard the treaty with Et-Raklion.

Hekat had wanted to ride out with the warhost, she wanted the warriors to see her by Raklion's side and know she was Hekat knife-dancer, precious and beautiful. Raklion forbade it.

"You carry my son," he said, impatient. "Are you brain-fevered to think you might skirmish on the border?"

Aieee, the child. How unsettling not to be alone inside her own skin. To be sharing blood and bone with some growing faceless creature, planted in her by a rutting man. She wondered if she would love the baby, she could not imagine it. She thought she hated it already, for keeping her from battle.

She tried to argue. "But Raklion, I am your fiercest warrior. If you wish to strike fear in Tehek's heart I should—"

"*No!*" he shouted, and banged his fist on the table between them, making the wine in their goblets splash. "While I am gone you will not set foot beyond the palace, Hekat. That is my word, it will be obeyed."

She could not dissuade him. He rode away with

Hanochek and his warriors and left her behind, fretting and prisoned, no better than the Hekat kept below stairs in Abajai's villa or that nameless she-brat cowering in a mud-hut kitchen.

I am Hekat knife-dancer, she told herself in her palace mirror. *With an empty belly or with a full one I will knife-dance for the god. Who is Raklion, to say I will not?*

The first newsun after Raklion's riding out and every newsun after that she sent to the barracks for a handful of warriors, she met with them in her private palace garden and they danced their *hotas* side by side. Different warriors each time, she wanted them to see her dancing, to take tales of her power and unchanged prowess back to their shells, to the warhost's skill-leaders, that they might remember her as Hekat the warrior, Bajadek's doom. They must forget her powerless and fucked on the warhost field.

Because Raklion will not live forever. And if he dies before my son is a man . . .

Then must she be seen first as a warrior. The warhost must know her with a snakeblade in her hand. When Raklion died her son would be the warlord. And if Mijak's other warlords still had not been tamed . . .

Then I will tame them, they will kneel at my feet. Mijak will know Hekat as godtouched and chosen, beloved of the god. The warhost will follow me, Hanochek forgotten. Am I not Bajadek's doom? I will be the doom of any man who thwarts me.

And so she knife-danced, though her growing belly was a hindrance.

At every highsun while Raklion was away, a god-speaker sacrificed in the palace godroom. She was sick to vomiting of sacred blood but she had no choice, she must drink so the godspeaker would tell Nagarak she was chaste, she was obedient, she bowed her head before the god. She would give Raklion's high godspeaker no chance to find fault with her.

He did not. She had no need to see him to know of his disappointment, she could feel it in the breeze, taste it on the wind. Thinking of it made her laugh. Nagarak would never defeat her, she was chosen by the god.

Or so she thought.

The first pain struck her two fingers past newsun, in her private garden, soon after Raklion's warriors had returned to the barracks. She danced for herself and the god alone. Sweat slicked her warm skin, her heart drummed in her chest, this was how she honored the god. Any slave could drink a cup of blood but only she could cut the sunlight with her blade.

It was like a sandcat's ripping claws, that first pain, tearing through her belly and up her spine, leaving her mouth in an agonized scream. Her snakeblade dropped from her slackened fingers, she dropped beside it onto the grass.

Slaves came running. They kept out of her sight, she beat them if they hovered, but still they were never far away. That was Raklion's want, and he would not beat them, he would kill them if they disobeyed. Her displeasure was nothing beside his wrath.

A second pain raked through her, snapping her knees against her round belly. She could barely breathe, her arms tightly clutching, her mind a windstorm of disbelief. She had seen babies birthed before their time, she knew what this was, but it could not be happening. Not to her.

How have I failed you, god? Am I not Hekat, precious and chosen? Why do you do this? How have I failed?

She heard Vortka's voice, felt his hands on her shoulders. "Be still, Hekat. Do not struggle."

"The sin is not mine, it is not mine," she whispered, forcing open her eyes, looking into his face. He was not angry, there were tears in his eyes. "Do not tell Nagarak I have sinned."

"Hush, Hekat," he told her. "A healer is coming."

But the child was born before the healer reached her. Stripped naked by slaves upon the grass, she felt her body spit it out, felt herself empty in a groaning spasm as a giant fist closed itself around her womb and squeezed her like a fig.

"Don't look, Hekat, close your eyes," said Vortka, but she was no coward, she sat up and looked at the twisted, misshapen lump of bloody flesh on the ground between her bent legs.

"Aieee, the god see us, she's birthed a demon!" cried one of the slaves. Her snakeblade took him through the throat, he was dead before his next breath, before she realized she had found and thrown the knife.

"It is no demon!" cried Vortka, glaring at the wide-eyed slaves. "Anyone who says so will be struck down by the god!"

Cowed to silence they huddled together as Hekat stared at the thing on the grass. No, not a demon, but almost as bad. A stunted she-brat that had no hope of life. A worthless lump of woman-meat. Not a son. Not the son she had promised Raklion.

Not the son the god had promised her.

Why? Why? How has this happened?

"Do not weep, Hekat," whispered Vortka. "There is a reason, the god will tell us in its time."

Two of the slaves fetched a litter from the palace, they carried her inside and the healer came. He purged her and dosed her with elixirs and potions, he burned her blood free of poisons with his godstone.

"She can breed again," she heard him tell Vortka. "Once her strength returns. Come with me now, we must see the high godspeaker."

No, no, she wanted to shout. *Nagarak will blame me, he will say to Raklion I fuck with demons, Vortka, no, do not leave me, please. Do not let Nagarak tell his lies.*

But the frantic words stayed inside her head, the healer's elixirs had sewn shut her lips and deadened her tongue. Vortka left her surrounded by slaves, she was alone, abandoned, she had no son.

Darkness took her, and the god was not there.

Raklion was honing his snakeblade when Hanochek brought him the news. It was dusk, lowsun sacrifice had been made, and the settling warhost camp was hazed with cook-fire smoke, its rustic pungency overlaid with the sweetness of fresh meat roasting over hot coals. He was weary, but not exhausted. Proud of his warriors, who danced so splendidly along Et-Nogolor's border. Et-Nogolor Eyes watched them from a stretch of nearby Et-Nogolor woodland. They had watched for six highsuns now, it would not be long before Nogolor, or Tebek, arrived at the border to admire his warhost and swear protestations of friendship.

I will nod at that swearing, I will tell Nogolor, or Tebek, that their friendship is all. I will not let them see

*the god in my eyes, or read its purpose for me in the lines
on my face. That time will come, but it is not yet.*

Nagarak had cautioned him against rising too soon
against the other warlords. For himself, he did not disagree. Let them fight each other first, let them plunder
each other and winnow their warhosts. As they fought
and plundered he would increase his own warhost until it
was immense.

Ten thousand warriors? Tcha. He would have twenty.
Thirty. *Fifty* thousand at his back. Every child of Et-
Raklion would carry a knife. Then who would dare stand
against him?

Not the warlords of Mijak, seared in their brown lands,
forsaken by the god.

He looked up, smiling, as his warleader pushed the
tent-flap aside and entered. "Aieee, Hano," he said, cheerful. "Does the warhost not please you? It pleases me, I
think—" What he thought, he did not say. Hano's face
was stricken, there were tears in his eyes.

"A godspeaker has ridden hard from Et-Raklion, warlord," he said, his voice choked. "He has told me a message from Nagarak, I must give it to you. Forgive me,
Raklion. I would rather die."

A terrible silence. The sharpstone slipped from his fingers to the ground. He knew already what Hano would
say, he did not need to hear the words.

My son . . . my son . . . and his beautiful mother . . .

"Hekat is miscarried of a daughter, warlord. The child
was not usual. You must return to the godhouse. So says
Nagarak, high godspeaker of Et-Raklion."

With an anguished cry Raklion plunged his snakeblade
into his thigh.

"*Raklion!*" Hano reached him as he slid from his campstool to the ground. Cradling him in desperate, loving arms his warleader shouted, "Godspeaker! Godspeaker! I need a godspeaker in the warlord's tent!"

The pain in his leg was nothing to the agony in his heart. He wept unrestrainedly, he wept like a child. Hano held him, Hano's tears fell on his face. A godspeaker came and pulled the snakeblade from his flesh. His hot blood pumped freely, the godspeaker cursed and then she healed him.

"Hano," he whispered, when they were alone again and he lay still on his camp-bed. "I will ride to Nagarak at newsun. You will stay with the warhost, you will dance with them for Nogolor's Eyes. You will do this for me, Hano. I am the warlord, it is my want."

Hano nodded, and smoothed the covering horsehair blanket. "Yes, Raklion."

He shifted a little. His leg was healed and still his body roared with pain. "This is not Hekat's doing. She is godchosen, the light in my eyes. I am demonplagued, Hano. Demons know what the god intends for me, they seek to thwart its will."

Hano frowned. "I don't understand."

He beckoned his friend closer, pressed cold lips against Hano's ear. "The god desires me warlord of Mijak, Hano, and my son the warlord after me."

"*Warlord of Mijak?*" Hano jerked back, his eyes wide and fearful. "Raklion—"

He closed his fingers round Hanochek's wrist. "Breathe nothing of it beyond this tent. I would have to kill you, it would break my heart."

"I will say nothing," Hano promised.

Nodding, trusting, Raklion released his harsh grip. "As Mijak's warlord I will make war on all demons and the men who worship them with dark deeds. The demons know this, they know my intent. So Hekat is struck down and my son with her, he is malformed in her belly, made female and dead. But they will not defeat me! The god will triumph, and so will I."

Hano looked down, his face was troubled. "Raklion, you cannot be certain Hekat is innocent."

"*I am certain*! If you love me, Hano, never question her again." His brief rage guttered out, leaving him empty. "I must rest now, I must ride hard tomorrow." His eyelids drifted closed. "Do not leave me, Hano. I would not be alone."

"I will not leave you, Raklion," Hano's voice said softly. "I am yours to command, and always will be."

After newsun sacrifice he rode for Et-Raklion. Highsun after highsun Raklion spared neither himself nor his stallion, the horse dropped dead within sight of its stable. Only his knife-dancer training saved him, even so he was bruised and scraped from the fall. Ignoring his horrified slaves he ran into the palace, to find Hekat. Another slave told him she was kept close in the godhouse, suspected by Nagarak of being a demon.

He smashed that slave to the floor with his fist and ran up the Pinnacle Road as though he were demonstruck, deaf and blind to all other travelers, half-mad with fear and a trembling fury. In the godhouse the godspeakers stared. He ignored their inquiries and shoved them aside.

"*She is not a demon!*" he shouted at Nagarak in the high godspeaker's private chamber. "You sexless man who has never known a woman, do you think I would not know if I fucked a *demon*?"

Nagarak's face tightened. "I do not say she is a demon. I say she has deceived you *with* demons. With a demon's help she tainted your seed so the child she carried was not only female but deformed."

"*No*! You are *wrong*!"

"You mated with a barracks bitch," said Nagarak, remorseless. "Warlord, I told you it was unwise."

"You told me the god would give me a *son*! You said if I purged my sins on the scorpion wheel the past would be the past, I would be the future of Mijak. I would at last sire a living son!" Goaded beyond sense he took Nagarak's shoulders in his hands and shook him. "I was purged, Nagarak! I gave myself into your smiting hands, three highsuns I begged for mercy while you wrote the god's wrath in my suffering flesh! *Where then is my promised son? How can it be that you let this happen*?"

Nagarak struck himself free. "Do not blame *me* for this thwarting of the god!"

"You are the high godspeaker, who else can I blame? The god has turned its face from you, why would that be? Is there a secret sin in *your* heart, Nagarak? Shall I bind *you* to the scorpion wheel and beat *you* until you scream for mercy?"

Nagarak hissed like a snake, with fury. "No mere man may touch a godspeaker's flesh! Only the god through the hand of its godspeakers may chastise one of its own!"

"But you are *high* godspeaker, who chastises you?" demanded Raklion, nauseous with his terrible grief. "Who names your sin and metes out tasking? Power lies in your hands, you have no master save the god, yet only you can hear the god, you say, and what does that mean? It means I have your word to take and no-one else's! I must trust you or be accused of sin and here am I, Et-Raklion's warlord, chosen to be the warlord of Mijak, there are more seasons behind me than before and *I have no living son!*"

He could not bear it. His heart was beaten to a pulp, he was a warrior and he was defeated, bludgeoned to his knees by this new disaster. His fists pounded the stone floor, skin tore, blood smeared.

Nagarak stood over him. "You know I am sinless, Raklion. You know where the sin lies. Lust stopped your ears, you were blinded by flesh. You took this Hekat when I told you not to, how then can this be my fault?"

Raklion pressed bloodied hands to his face. Was Nagarak right, had Hekat betrayed him? Had he been seduced by demons? He could not bring himself to believe it.

"I love her, Nagarak," he whispered, broken. "I loved her since I saw her, I had no choice. She danced for the god, she danced into my heart, I did not touch her, I turned my face from her, I obeyed the god and touched only Et-Nogolor's Daughter. Yet that bitch is dead, the son I planted in her is dead, now Hekat spawns demon-flesh, *how can this be?* She was with me always till I rode to the border, you and your godspeakers were with her after. How did this happen? How did she deceive me, deceive you, to sport with demons?"

"Warlord, you wrong me," said Hekat from the doorway. "Your high godspeaker wrongs me. I consort with no demons. I am sinned against, not sinning."

Hekat. Raklion staggered to his feet and confronted

her. Little more than two godmoons since last he'd seen her, and there was less flesh on her bones, her eyes were sunk in hollows, her belly was flat between her hips. Grief in her face, grief in her voice, the faintest tremor in her hands. She did not kneel, she stood before him, grief had not diminished her pride.

Even though he loved her, he felt his anger stir. If she wept, if she begged, if she asked his forgiveness . . . "You are not summoned here, Hekat. You are not sent for."

"I had to come," she said, not looking at Nagarak, looking only at him. She wore no fine wools, just an old linen training tunic and weathered sandals on her feet. "Nagarak condemns me, he curses me in his mouth. He tells you I consort with demons. He lies. My heart is filled with the god, there is no room in me for sin."

"So protest all demons," said Nagarak, sneering.

Now she looked at Nagarak, with pride and temper in her eyes. "Perhaps it is you who consorts with hell's children."

Raklion struck her. "You will not say so, he is my high godspeaker! On your knees, you will kneel to me!"

A thread of blood trickled from the corner of her mouth. She knelt, obedient, but did not take her eyes from his. "He did not want me in your bed, he thinks I am not godchosen. He does not know what we know, warlord, he has not seen what you have seen."

No, but what was it he had seen? Who had hidden her from Nagarak's sight in the tasking house? The god? Or a demon she served in its place? Who told him the truth here, Hekat or Nagarak?

"What does she speak of?" Nagarak demanded.

Hekat said, "I do not deceive you, Raklion. I suckle no

demons. The child I miscarried was blighted in my womb but I did not blight it. The god strike me dead if that is not true."

The god did not strike her. Confused and wretched he examined her face for long heartbeats, searched over and over to discover the truth.

"I do not lie," she told him proudly. "I am the god's servant. I spit on demons, they are enemies to me."

He could see no guile in her, he could hear no lies. She grieved as he grieved, how could he disbelieve her? He reached for her hands, and helped her to stand. "Then who?" he whispered. "Who stole from me another son? Who cursed your womb, who fouled my seed?"

She laid her cool palm against his cheek. "Warlord, how can I tell you what the god has not revealed to me? Ask this instead: who in Et-Raklion hates and fears me? Who has the power to defy the god?"

His reluctant gaze dragged slowly sideways, to fall upon his high godspeaker's face.

"You will not heed this barracks bitch!" Nagarak cried. "I am high godspeaker, I live in the god's eye. I am tested by scorpions, I breathe and I breathe, they cannot kill me!"

"Let them try to kill me," said Hekat softly. "Put me in the pit, warlord. I will lie down with scorpions and get up with the god."

Put Hekat in the scorpion pit? Raklion struggled for air. In his mind's eye he saw her like Et-Nogolor's high godspeaker, like the godspeakers who had challenged with Nagarak so long ago, he saw her distorted in agony, bloated with venom, stung to a lingering, hideous death.

"It is the god's desire," said Nagarak, nodding. "It will be done."

Raklion stared at him. "The god's desire, Nagarak, or your own?"

"You question my service to the god?"

He could see in Nagarak's slitted eyes how much the high godspeaker wanted scorpions to sting Hekat. "No. Not to the god."

"You think I seek to thwart you, warlord? Foolish man, you know that is not true. Those words are *her* words, her tongue drips poison."

Raklion shuddered, he looked from Nagarak to Hekat and back again. Never had Nagarak counseled him wrongly, he was a true servant of the god. Yet Hekat was also in the god's eye. He had seen that, how could he doubt her?

"Raklion," said Nagarak, his voice less bladed. "This is the god's business. Let the god decide it. Hekat must come with me, she must be prepared for the scorpion pit. Go into the shrine garden, pray there till lowsun. Then the scorpions will test her, and the god will show us the truth of her heart."

Raklion nodded, and watched Nagarak push Hekat from the chamber. She did not fight the high godspeaker, she did not look back. Her spine was straight, her head was high, she walked like a woman with nothing to fear.

My endurance is ending. If she is false, god, my heart will break. Show me her heart, show me she is your chosen. Let me not be disappointed again.

Nagarak gave Hekat to four silent godspeakers, who took her to a cold stone chamber far below the godhouse.

Silently they stripped her naked and cleansed her in blood, they anointed her with sacred oils and clothed her in a plain wool robe.

"Kneel," they told her, pointing to the chamber's scarlet godpost. "Pray until you are taken to the pit for testing. Prepare your sinning godspark for hell."

They left her and she was pleased to see them go. Nagarak's slaves, though they wore no scarlet godbraid. Chained to each other by blind obedience.

Fools. They see a lump of burning wood and think it is the sun.

Flickered with candlelight, the godpost's red scorpions looked alive. She stroked them with her fingers, caressed them with her lips. She missed the touch of her scorpion amulet, but when Nagarak came for her in the palace the god had told her to leave it behind.

She wished Vortka was with her. She had not seen him since the miscarriage. Banishing regret, she turned her mind to the god.

I am here, god, where you desire. Show me what I am to see. Tell me what I am to know. I was afraid, I was lost, you were lost to me. Now you are found, and I am found, and I am ready for what must come.

Vortka was among the witnesses at the scorpion pit. Nagarak was there, and Raklion, and five other godspeakers she did not know. Nagarak stripped her of the plain godhouse robe, baring her skin to the chamber's cool air.

She did not look at Vortka, she did not need to look to feel his concern for her. Foolish Vortka, there was no need to worry. No need either for Nagarak to tell her what she must do. She walked to the pit's edge and stared at the heaving, writhing mass of scorpions within. Black. Red. White. Green. Sliding and hissing, pincers slashing, jointed legs scuttling. Venom seeped from their upcurled tails.

I am here, god. Show me your heart.

Almost eagerly, she slid into the pit. The mass of scorpions parted for her, they closed over her head and sucked her down, like a fish in water she swam in scorpions. The moment she joined them they began to sting her, she tasted their venom on her tongue.

There was no pain.

Instead her body was drowned in pleasure, in waves of heat and searing light. She remembered honey on Yagji's corncakes, her blood was honey, she wept with joy. The god was in her, the god was honey, sweet sweet venom, flowing through her veins. The god's desire was pouring through her, she shuddered in ecstasy, she moaned with delight. There were no words but she heard the god. She knew its desires, she laughed to hear them.

Yes, god. I will do that. Yes, god, I obey.

And then she was rising, the scorpions raised her out of the pit. Sprawled on the stone floor of the chamber she stared into the witnesses' looming faces, into Nagarak's shock and Vortka's relief. She stared at Raklion. He was smiling.

"It is unheard of," said one godspeaker, hushed. "Her skin is unmarked. Yet we saw the scorpions sting her, we saw the god testing her heart. What can this mean?"

The five godspeakers and Vortka turned to Nagarak. He said nothing. Did he even realize his fingers plucked the welts on his face, where the god had tested him and left its marks?

Raklion said, "It means she is untouched by demons. She is chosen by the god. She is Hekat, mother of my unborn son." He sounded triumphant. There were tears on his cheeks.

Still Nagarak said nothing.

Raklion helped her to her feet. Smoothed his fingers over her scarred face, then clothed her nakedness in the godhouse robe.

"It is done, and decided," he said, his warm gaze resting on her face. "She will come with me. She will come into the palace and give me a son."

Yes. Yes. She would have a son. But the boy-child she birthed would not be his.

He will be mine, he will belong to the god. He will serve the god's purpose in this world.

Nagarak said, "The god has spoken. It sees Hekat in its eye. She will go to the palace with the warlord, she will give him a son, for the god and for Mijak."

He sounded breathless. Subdued. His eyes were empty. His godbells were silent.

"Come, Hekat," said Raklion, and they left Nagarak behind.

CHAPTER TWENTY-THREE

Much, much later, in the coldest darkness of the night, Hekat woke in the palace, curled up beside Raklion in his bed. Hidden in the god's eye she dressed in her tunic and left him sleeping, gliding out of the palace to make her way back to the godhouse, and Vortka.

He slept in the novice-quarters, where she had never been. The god guided her footsteps, she knew where to walk. Godspeakers were waking, the godhouse never slept, but they did not see her, they did not hear her or see her passing. She was air, she was shadow, she wore the night like a second skin.

There were no locks on godspeaker doors. She entered the novices' sleeping chamber and crouched beside Vortka's mat. Twenty other novices slept on, unaware. Candles burned along the walls, their dim light showed her Vortka's face sunk far in dreams. Swiftly, silently, she peeled back his blanket. He was naked beneath it, his skin cruelly welted from his latest tasking. She took his blade in her warm hand and encouraged its attention. His breathing deepened, harshened, he responded eagerly to her touch. The other novices remained oblivious, their senses smothered by the god.

When Vortka's eyes flew open she pressed her other hand across his mouth and straddled him, holding him tight between her thighs. Then she leaned close to him until her breasts touched his chest.

"When I was in the scorpion pit, the god poured its desires into my heart," she whispered. "It told me things I did not know. Raklion warlord's seed is salted, Vortka, the taint is in *him*. It is not in me. It was not in Et-Nogolor's Daughter or any other woman he fucked to make a son. Raklion cannot sire a living child. But he is the warlord, a son must be born."

Vortka plucked at her pressing fingers. She eased her grip slightly, that he might speak. "Hekat, what are you *doing?* I am not a vessel, I cannot fuck you! The other novices, they will *see* us!"

"They will see nothing, and you can fuck me if it is the god's want," she told him fiercely. "Do you doubt me, Vortka? Do you think I lie? Do you think you *dreamed* me in the scorpion pit, tested and untouched by the god itself?"

She could feel him hard and ready beneath her. His eyes were clouded as Raklion's clouded when he feasted his mouth on her nipples. She knew enough of fucking now to know Vortka desired her. It was all she needed of him, the rest of the business she could do herself.

Vortka swallowed a tiny moan. "Hekat, you are sunstruck, we can't, this is *madness . . .*"

"What we do, we do for the god," she said, and shifted upon him until he groaned. "It is not madness, we will not be found out. The god wants this, Vortka. We must obey."

His fingers closed upon her tunic-covered breasts. She raised her hips, wrapped her hand around him, and guided him deep between her legs. At first she rode him but then instinct took over and his hips were plunging, he thrust hard into her, like Raklion fucking he mewled and sobbed. He was a man, he could not help it. She covered his mouth again to keep him quiet.

When he was finished and panting, his seed spilled inside her, she eased herself off him and lay down for a moment. Her body was sore, Raklion had fucked like a mad thing in his desperation for a son.

"Hekat," said Vortka, and took her hand. "You are certain that was for the god?"

She nodded, and let his fingers enclose hers. "I am certain."

"I think I liked it," he said, sounding wistful. "How many times will it take us to make Raklion his son?"

Her other hand drifted to her belly. She pressed her palm flat there and felt something shift. "It will happen quickly. The god has said so."

"Oh," said Vortka, disappointed. "Then you will not come to me again?"

"I will come if the god desires it," she said, and rolled to her feet. "Go back to sleep, Vortka. Do not think on what has happened. Nagarak will watch me, he hates that the god whispers in my heart. If he sees you seeing me he will read your thoughts, he will see in your face you have feelings for me." She gave him a brief smile. "You think you hide them but you do not. You are stupid, Vortka."

He returned her smile, sadly. "Yes. I think I am."

At least he admitted it now, that was something. She left him in the godhouse and returned to ignorant sleeping Raklion.

Four times more, in the deepest part of night, the god woke her so she might fuck with Vortka. Quick couplings in ragged silence, they spoke no more before or after. What use were words? Words would change nothing.

Nagarak conducted his business in the godhouse, except for sacrifice she did not see him. She was not sorry, let him stay there and rot. Raklion remained in Et-Raklion, he left Hanochek and the warhost on the border to frighten Nogolor warlord and his belligerent son. He kept her with him in their chamber, fucked her with vigor and told himself he was making a son. He would not let her knife-dance in the garden, he said she was too beau-

tiful and precious to risk herself dancing with an unsheathed blade.

She wanted to stab him, but the god would not let her.

Twelve highsuns later she was pronounced pregnant
for the second time. She knew it already, the god had told
her, but it was safer to let Nagarak say so. It was stated,
with certainty, this child was a boy.

She knew that, too. The god withheld her nothing.

Raklion kissed her, and then he wept. Five hundred
black bull-calves were slain upon the godhouse's great
altar, five hundred black lambs lost their small lives. Et-
Raklion's godbowls were filled to overflowing, godbells
rang until their tongues wore away. She was exiled to the
godhouse soon after. She raged, she fought, Raklion
would not listen.

"This son will be born safe," he told her. "In the godhouse no evil can reach you. No demon can strike you or
my son. If it is as Nagarak has said, if all my ills come
from the ill-will of the other warlords and their high godspeakers, only in the godhouse will you be protected.
Hekat, be silent. I will beat you if you cross me on this."

He could beat her and not hurt the baby, so she held
her tongue and did as she was told. She and her slaves
were settled in the godhouse where she prayed five times
daily, drank too much sacrificial blood, walked sedately
in the shrine garden and tried not to go mad. If the warlords knew she was pregnant, no-one told her. If they continued their squabbling, rode to war against each other,
made and broke treaties, continued their sinful dances
with demons, no-one told her that either. She never saw
Vortka, ten highsuns after she was banished to the godhouse he was sent far away to serve on a godhouse breed-

ing farm, where the perfect sacrifice animals were born and raised. She hardly saw Raklion, he trained with his warhost beyond the city, riding the Et-Nogolor and Et-Banotaj borders with Hanochek, cowing the warlords with Et-Raklion's might.

She begged to be let into the godhouse library, where she could read and forget the forbidden world beyond its walls. Nagarak resisted, whenever he saw a chance to thwart her, he took it. She prayed, then sent word to Raklion so her want might prevail. The god and Raklion defeated Nagarak, she was permitted to spend her time in the library, where she was largely ignored by godspeakers and novices alike. She did not care about that, all she cared for was learning.

To guide my son I must be wise, I must know the things a warlord should know.

The godhouse library's vast collection of clay tablets saved her from madness, when she wasn't praying or taking air in the shrine garden she read and read, gorging herself on all the things she never knew. Caravanning through Mijak with Abajai and Yagji, then her journey to knowledge was begun. In Nagarak's godhouse it was completed, for nearly eight godmoons she put aside Hekat knife-dancer and became Hekat scholar, warrior for learning. She unsheathed her mind, it became her snakeblade.

Nagarak's godhouse library did not only hold accounts of Et-Raklion's history, in its cool, dim-lit tablet rooms she learned of all the warlords who ever ruled in Mijak, their treaties and battles, their victories and defeats. She read of high godspeakers who communed with the god, of the demons who tempted them and how those demons were destroyed. Demons were mysterious creatures, no-one ever saw them with their eyes, their presence was marked by the chaos that surrounded them and the sins men committed when fallen victim to their hellish wiles.

Hekat read from newsun to lowsun and far into the night. She would never much like godspeakers, except for Vortka, but it was a good thing the god created them. They wrote excellent histories, they kept meticulous records.

The days passed swiftly enough, her belly grew rounder. Her son grew within it, she talked to him as he slept.

You will be a great warlord, you will fight for the god. You will vanquish demons, you will smite the world.

Her pregnant body felt different, this time, she knew this growing life was not demon-blighted. Whatever sins had tainted Raklion's seed, she did not know nor did she care. He would never again sire a godforsaken baby. The god would protect her from Raklion's poisoned seed, her son would have no rivals, no deformed brothers or sisters to raise questions of his fitness to rule.

You will never know whose planted seed sired you. You are my son, that is all you must know. When old age claims Raklion you will be Mijak's warlord. I will still be your mother, my hand will guide you, my voice will counsel you, you will see the world through my godchosen eyes.

At long last Raklion and his warhost returned from skirmishing on the borders. He did not clean the dirt of travel from his body but came straight to the godhouse weary and stinking.

"Aieee, Hekat, you are ripe enough to burst!" he marveled, pawing at her enormous belly in the godhouse shrine garden, where she sat in the shade feeling grossly misused.

She struck his hand away, irritable. "Do you think I don't know that, warlord? I waddle like a camel, I pish ten times a finger."

"I know, I know," he told her, kindly. "You are near your time, it is expected."

"*Tcha*! You are a man, what do you know of such things? Talk to me of what you *do* know. Raklion. Tell me of the warlords and their skirmishing ways."

He sat beside her on the carved stone bench, took her hand with its swollen fingers gently in his, and kissed her tenderly on the brow. "My fierce Hekat. You have not changed."

"You desire me to birth a fierce warlord for Mijak, it would be a sad thing if I turned soft like milk!" she retorted. She wanted to pull away from his touch but that would offend him. She must not do that. "The *skirmishing*, Raklion. How fared the warhost? Did you meet in battle with Nogolor or Banotaj, or any other warlord daring to challenge Et-Raklion's might?"

He shook his head. "No. Nogolor still breathes in his palace, Tebek dares not disobey him and send warriors to break our treaty. We did see riders from Et-Banotaj, we glimpsed warriors from Et-Zyden and Et-Takona riding with them. It seems their fragile alliance still holds. I think they desire to raid again in our lands, if we did not show them our snakeblades they would have crossed our border. It was good we were there, Hekat."

Aieee, I wish I had been there. She pressed a fist into

her aching back. "The god will break that alliance, war-lord. When it says the time is come for you to rule over Mijak they will be at each other's throats, not standing shoulder to shoulder against you."

"I wish it would say so soon, Hekat," he whispered. "I am not a young man, I grow old in my bones."

It will say so soon enough. First my son must be grown out of his cot, and I must know more of what it means to be a warlord.

"Et-Raklion's warhost is not big enough yet," she said, resting her head against his shoulder. He liked such gestures from her, they soothed his mood. "The other warlords are still too strong. Let the god further diminish them, Raklion. Let them sin, and grow weak. The god will tell us when to strike."

"How will it tell us? What sign will it send?"

She did not know, she would never say so. He must never suspect she could not summon the god. She groaned, and flattened her palms to her belly. "Aieee, Raklion. I am so tired, I must lie down."

Raklion was distracted, she knew he would be. Tenderly he helped her onto her feet, and walked with her into the shadowed godhouse, to the chamber where for so long she had slept alone.

He sat beside her till she drifted to sleep.

Six highsuns after his return, as newsun made the Pinnacle's godpost shine, she felt the first birth pains, faint griping spasms that promised more to come. Her godspeaker attendant sent for Nagarak, Raklion and the godhouse's senior healer. Nagarak came, with the healer he helped her to a different chamber, one with an altar in it and waiting godspeakers with sharp sacrifice knives.

Raklion came soon after, he brought Hanochek with him. In between the deepening contractions she swore at him for doing so. She did not want the warleader there.

"He is my best friend, he leads the warhost after me," said Raklion. "He and I will make my son a warrior, I desire him here. Hanochek will stay."

Sweat poured down her straining body, it soaked her godbraids and stung her eyes. "*I* will make my son a warrior, I am Hekat knife-dancer, I am Bajadek's doom!"

"He is a witness, approved by the god," said Nagarak, standing with the healer beside her bed. "Hanochek will stay to see the warlord's son born."

He only said so to thwart her, she could see the mean pleasure in his face. She was defeated, at least for the moment. She said nothing more against Hanochek's presence, or the warlord's claim of his part in her life. Let Raklion and his dear friend think they would guide her son. She and the god had a different plan.

Soon enough she did not care Hanochek was present, soon enough she forgot he was there. All she could think of was the tearing pain, her body was being pulled apart, torn open, ripped wide. As the godspeakers sacrificed an endless stream of lambs and doves upon the altar, as they burned the sacred blood to stinking smoke, a deterrent for demons, she clung to the birthing stool and pushed and pushed her son from her body. She kept her teeth gritted, she did not scream. She was a warrior, she had her pride. Time lost its meaning, she hardly knew where she was.

Then she heard the healer shout, "I see the head, warlord! Nagarak high godspeaker, the child is coming!"

With one last strangled groan she felt her son slide into the world. Nagarak caught him, he used his sacrifice knife to cut the pulsing cord still binding them together. As the healer moved in to do things with his godstone, she heard an indignant, wailing cry.

"He is perfect! He is beautiful!" cried Raklion, weeping. "See my son, Hanochek! See my glorious, godgiven son!"

Hanochek was weeping too, they both wept like babies. "I see him, Raklion. You are right, he is perfect." He had his arm around Raklion, to keep him strong on his feet.

"Give him to me, Nagarak," Raklion demanded. "I will hold my perfect son."

"Not until he is bathed in the god's blood, warlord," said Nagarak. "Not until he is judged free of taint."

Exhausted, nearly fainting, Hekat tried to speak. *He is not tainted, you fool, he is my son. Give him to me. Did you birth him? I think you did not!*

The words would not leave her, she had no breath to speak. She grunted as another pain rippled through her, as her body expelled the unwanted afterbirth. She struggled to see past the busy healer, she wanted to know what Nagarak was doing. There was a large golden bowl on the altar now, the godspeakers were filling it with fresh hot blood.

Her son wailed again, she heard Raklion shout. She saw Nagarak lower her child into the bowl, hold him there for a moment, then lift him out, high over his head. He said, "I am Nagarak high godspeaker, the god's voice in Et-Raklion. I say this boy is demon-free. Take him, warlord. He is your untainted son in the god's judging eye."

Raklion held out his arms, taking her son from Nagarak. He turned around and at last looked at her. "See him, Hekat. See his perfection!"

The baby was dripping with sacrificial scarlet, he howled in protest, he had strong healthy lungs. The healer was finished between her legs, she pushed herself upright and shoved him away.

"I see him, warlord. Give him to me!"

Raklion came to her, the wailing infant held close to his chest. Tears washed his face in a waterfall of joy.

"*Zandakar*," he whispered. "That is my son's name. The world will know him as *Zandakar*."

"It is a good name, Raklion!" said Hanochek, too close beside him. Too eager to be part of this, it was not his business. He should go away, now.

But it was a good name, she could not say it wasn't. Raklion placed her son in her outstretched, eager arms.

"Zandakar," she agreed, her throat so sore and tired from groaning. He was small, he was warm, his small legs kicked, his small arms pumped, the thickening blood on him smeared her skin. She did not care, she was holding her son.

Zandakar opened his eyes and stared into her face. She stared back at him . . . and fell headlong into love.

PART THREE

PART THREE

CHAPTER TWENTY-FOUR

*A*ieeeee!" screamed Raklion, and plunged his snake-blade through the throat of a faltering enemy warrior. Fighting at his back, Hanochek killed two more warriors of Et-Banotaj, then turned and caught him by the elbow as he slipped in the muddy stew of blood and entrails underfoot.

"The god see you, warlord!" Hanochek gasped. "I think they are finished here. Does that mean it is over?"

Raklion coughed, his throat was raw with screaming, with urging his warriors to slaughter and death. He bent double, bloodied arms braced against his thighs, and sucked in drafts of stinking air. His head was swimming, he could hardly see for the blood in his eyes.

"I think it must be," said Hanochek, answering himself. His voice was tight with pain, and strain. "We have killed the last of them."

That was true. Antobar's Ravine was choked with corpses, most of them warriors of Et-Banotaj and Et-Tebek. Some were dead warriors of Et-Raklion, he would weep for them later. Raklion straightened, groaning. There was not a muscle in his body that did not protest, not a sinew that did not cry for mercy.

I am growing too old for bloody mayhem. If I do not break these warlords' hearts soon they will break mine and that will be that.

Around them, Et-Raklion's surviving warriors stood and waited, dazed and exhausted as he was dazed and exhausted. The ravine's hot close air thrummed with that strange after-battle silence made up of panting warriors, sliding stones, faint moans of the dying and an absence of blade clashing blade, knife slicing flesh, screaming as godsparks fled to hell, or the god.

A thudding of hoofbeats staggered him about, snake-blade lifted, a new scream rising in his throat. *Kill them kill them kill them kill them*! He choked it down, seeing it was Iriklia Spear-leader on his horse, his wide face split wider in a smile. His godbraids were bloodsoaked, his dull brown horse turned a wet bright red.

"Warlord, they are routed! The warriors of Et-Banotaj and Et-Tebek fly from Et-Raklion! We have the victory, victory is ours!"

"The god sees us," Raklion murmured, as the last of his strength drained from his limbs. He felt his snake-blade drop from his weak grasp as Hano's arm slid round his shoulders, keeping him from the ground. "Iriklia, fetch the godspeakers here," he commanded. Iriklia cantered away.

"Hano . . ."

"Warlord," said Hano, still holding him.

"Gather our living warhost beyond this ravine, up on the flatland where the battle began. Praise them in my name, I will go to them soon. I desire a moment's solitude with the god."

"Raklion—"

"Obey me, warleader! Our enemy is dead or running, I am in no danger. I am in the god's eye."

Hanochek did not want to leave him, behind the blood

his face was anxious. But he was the warleader, the warlord's word was his word. "Raklion," he said, unhappily.

Raklion nodded at a nearby boulder. "I will sit there."

Hanochek helped him to the boulder, then retrieved his dropped snakeblade and handed it to him. "Do not keep your warhost waiting, warlord," he said softly. "They need you in this time of strife."

Raklion nodded, and waved the knife. It was too bloody to glint in the sunshine. "Go, Hanochek. I have said I will follow, and I will follow in my time."

Hanochek and those warriors able to walk departed the bloodsoaked ravine. As they passed him sitting on his boulder, most wounded, some limping, they pressed their fists against their hearts and grinned at him through their masks of blood, grime and sweat. He tried to grin back, though feared it was more a grimace.

The god see you always, my beautiful, brave warriors. The god see you dancing in its eye.

Alone at last, he braced his elbows on his knees and let his head drop into his hands. His godbraids swung round his face in a curtain, shielding the world from the sight of his tears. As he wept he heard the first crows gather for their feasting, eager cawings and the flapping of black wings.

You test me, god. How you test me. I am naked before you, see me naked in your eye. When will you tell Nagarak I must unite this nation? The warlords have stolen all they can from each other, they dare now to challenge me. My warhost has grown from ten thousand to twenty but still they challenge. Their fear makes them desperate. My fat green lands taunt them, they cannot help but attack. With Nogolor dead I am truly alone. Tebek and

Banotaj eat their meat at one table, I cannot hold my borders against them forever. I cannot be sure to defeat two treatied warlords, I will never defeat six if they stand shoulder to shoulder.

If I am to be the warlord of Mijak, god, it must be soon. Am I a young man, with a long road before me? I think I am not. I think you forget that.

He held his breath then, expecting the god to smite him for his thoughts. He was not smitten, all he heard was the crows, stripping flesh. All he felt was the sun on his skin.

Aieee, he missed Hekat. He wished she was with him, dancing with her snakeblade beside him in battle. Holding him in the night-time, easing his body, soothing his mind. When doubt assailed him she was always there, her strength had no limits, she was strong in the god.

I am Hekat knife-dancer, Bajadek's doom, mother of Zandakar, seen by the god. You will be the warlord. The god has said it.

So said Hekat, whenever he fretted. It would ease his heart to hear her say so now but she was far away, she led three thousand warriors in a dance along the furthest end of the Et-Tebek border. His warriors loved her, she led them bravely with blood in her eye. He longed to see her, and Zandakar his perfect son.

Let me go home now, god. Let me ride to Et-Raklion. The warlords are chastened, let me go home.

Smudging the tears across his face he stood and stretched his aching back. The bold crows did not cease their gobbling, he bent again and picked up stones to chase them from the corpses of his own people. He threw the stones, the crows swore at him and would not leave.

They are bold, as warlords are bold. They seize what they want and do not let go.

Like the crows and the warlords he must seize his own heart's desire or see it slip through his fingers. If the godspeaker's omen said he could take his warhost home he would ride to the doors of Nagarak's godhouse and demand the high godspeaker make sacrifice for war. The god had told him after the scorpion wheel that he would be Mijak's warlord. Let that be his omen. He would not seek another.

Resolute and sorrowful he moved among his fallen warriors, kissing those who could not be saved and killing them with his gentle snakeblade. Then he climbed out of the ravine as his warhost's godspeakers appeared at its lip, ready to give aid to the living and gather the dead for their last dance on the pyre.

I have waited long enough, god. I will be Mijak's one true warlord. I will make of Mijak a gift for my son.

"Yuma! Yuma! See me, Yuma!"

The sound of that beloved voice, shrill with excitement, turned Hekat's head as she led her warhost through the wide open gates and into Et-Raklion's vastly expanded barracks. All her weariness fell away, her body's aches deserted her. She forgot her knife-cuts and her strained muscles. Here was Zandakar, her heart in the world, trotting towards her on his blue-striped pony. Warriors and slaves stepped hastily aside, smiling, laughing, calling his name. Head high, shoulders wide, he rode between the smithies and the armorers' booths and the leatherworkers' tents and past the pedlars' stands as though they were his, as though he owned them.

And so he does, my son, my little warlord.

"Take the warhost to the stables, Arakun," she ordered the warrior who once had ordered her. "I will join you on the warhost field for sacrifice in a small time." She tossed him a coin-purse. "This is for the godbowl."

Arakun caught the purse and pressed his fist to his breast. Unlike Tajria, who was dead now for disobeying Hekat's want, Arakun never complained that she was above him. He led the warhost on to the stables, she slid from her saddle and waited for Zandakar to reach her.

"Yuma!" he shouted, and threw himself into her outstretched arms. "The god told me you were coming, it told me you were safe."

His godbraids printed patterns in her cheek, she held him so hard his godbells were silenced. "Did it, my son?" she murmured. Aieee, how she loved him. He owned her heart, let him eat it like cornmush. "The god sees us both, we are safe in its eye." Releasing him, she stepped back. "Let me look at you!"

Past four seasons old, he was growing so tall. His godbraids brushed his shoulders, his horsehide leggings were almost too tight. She'd been gone to the border one godmoon, twelve highsuns, not long. Yet he seemed changed in her eyes, he looked more like a man. His eyes were blue, like hers, his cheekbones high, his nose narrow and straight. His lips were beautiful, curved always in a smile. He was a child still but his body had muscles, he would be strong as a sandcat when he was truly a man.

"Yuma, Yuma, did you smite the wicked warriors?" he

asked, then giggled as his pony lipped at his neck. He loved the stupid creature, he did not get that from her.

She pulled a fierce face at him, to make him giggle louder. "Yes, I smote them! Am I not Hekat, the god's knife-dancer? Did I not slay Bajadek, who dared defy the god? Were you my good son while I was away, Zandakar? Did you study your *hotas*, did you practice with your bow?"

He nodded vigorously, now his godbells sang. "I did, I did, Yuma. I am your good son."

"And did you do your duty to the god?"

He lowered his eyelids, his lashes brushed his cheeks. "Yes, Yuma," he murmured. "I prayed with Nagarak."

He did not like Nagarak, she could not blame him, but he also disliked sacrifice and that she would not excuse. His heart was too soft when it was a question of creatures, he was sorry to see the lambs' throats cut. He did not like to drink their sacrificed blood but she had only needed to punish him once for betraying that. He drank the blood now, he knew better than to cry.

"Then you are my good son," she praised him. "Ride with me to the warhost field, I must attend sacrifice for our successful smiting. You can show the god what a good boy you are."

He leapt on his pony, she mounted her horse, side by side they rode through the barracks to the warhost field. Every busy warrior and slave stopped to watch them, called out a greeting, asked the god to see them always. They loved her son, they loved her because of him, for herself alone she frightened them. She did not care. They were obedient, they died at her word. That was important, the rest was nothing.

As she rode she gazed upon her son. He chuckled and waved, called to warriors by name. Aieee, she was his mother. It still amazed her. If she closed her eyes she could see him a baby, gnawing on his snake-rattle, plump and naked on the grass in her private palace garden, playing with his wooden chariot and horse, reaching for her snakeblade, laughing in the sun. The time had flown swiftly, blink twice more he would be a man grown, the warlord of Mijak, with Raklion dead, a memory in the sand.

When she looked at Zandakar she could see Vortka in him, the angle of his jaw, the tilt of his eyes. It was a good thing, then, that Vortka served beyond the city. So long since she had seen him, perhaps in making Zandakar his service to the god was done. Perhaps once he was tested and proven a godspeaker in the bone Nagarak would send him away forever, to serve in some village and never come back. She would not see him again, then, and neither would Zandakar come to know him.

That would not be a bad thing. Raklion did not question Zandakar was his, he was besotted, he was good to the boy. That suited her purpose. Vortka and Zandakar together in the world's eye, that did *not* suit her purpose. It must be avoided.

"Zandakar," she said, as the warhost field came in sight, overlaid with shadows as the sun slid down the sky. "Is the warlord returned to Et-Raklion?"

"No, Yuma," he said, jogging neatly on his pony. "Nagarak says he will return soon, he says the omens say it."

Aieee, but did the omens also say he must be warlord of Mijak? It was time they said it, she had waited long enough. For Zandakar to be Mijak's warlord first Raklion must lay claim to that name. He was an old man, growing older. Every battle might be his last. All very well to pray to the god to protect him, demons sought to thwart the god. If they could kill Raklion before Mijak was made obedient her son would be threatened. It had come time to act.

Around her neck the scorpion amulet throbbed with power. The god agreed with her. It would see she got her way.

She rode with Zandakar onto the warhost field where her three thousand warriors and the godspeakers waited, ready for sacrifice.

"*Hekat*!" the warhost shouted as they saw her riding. "*Hekat the knife-dancer, Bajadek's doom*!"

In their border skirmishing they had killed eight hundred of Tebek's inferior knives. It was a good slaughter, the new warriors she trained had not disgraced her or the god. She laid her fist above her heart, acknowledging their greeting.

"*Zandakar, the warlord's son*!" they shouted next. There was love in their faces, he was their own son, their little brother, the child of their hearts.

"See the warhost, Zandakar," she told him. "It is your warhost, you will lead it one day."

It was the same thing she always told him, from his days in the cradle she made sure he knew who he was.

Zandakar's fist against his heart was small, but steady. It would be a big fist when he was a man. He would grasp the whole warhost in it, Et-Raklion's warriors would sleep in his palm.

Hekat smiled and smiled as she rode with her son.

* * *

One finger before newsun Vortka woke in his small, solitary chamber to the tolling of the godhouse bell and a hand on his shoulder.

"It is time, novice," said Brikin novice-master. Salakij was two seasons dead, Brikin had been chosen his successor. Vortka hardly knew him, the last two seasons of his novitiate had been spent away from Et-Raklion and the godhouse. It was strange to be back within its stark stone walls after so long worshipping under the sun. Strange to think that not far away, his son was sleeping.

Don't think of Zandakar. He is not your son, Vortka. Best to think of him as dead.

Except that was impossible. The previous highsun, toiling up the Pinnacle Road to the godhouse, threading his way between the other travelers, as he passed the palace he felt his heart tug him sideways, urge him to leave the road, abandon duty and obedience, make up a reason to visit Hekat and their child. He had resisted. He was a novice at the testing time, what hope for him if he could not resist this temptation?

Then, in the godhouse, he had seen his small son Zandakar, giggling, chattering, lit up with excitement because Hekat would soon be home from war. His wayward heart had nearly stopped altogether, seeing that small boy, hearing Nagarak speak his name. Aieee, how tall and strong he was, how much he looked like his mother. A handful of times had he seen the child since his birth, each greedy glance pain and pleasure combined. And with every glance a vivid memory, how Zandakar was made, that plunging ecstasy, that exquisite throbbing of the flesh. Hekat hot upon him, her eyes filled with the god. He missed her too, though he tried hard to forget.

In the end it was a relief to be sent away for service.

"Vortka!" said Brikin, and shook him less gently. "Are you listening? You must go at once to the godpool. Would you keep the high godspeaker waiting?"

No! No, he would not. He sat up, wincing, his flesh smarting, sore from the previous day's severe tasking. It was the custom, he had known what he faced when the summons came from the godhouse. His testing was upon him, he must face the god and show it his heart, first in the godhouse and then in the wilderness. But before that he must kneel on the floor of the cold tasking chamber and shout his contrition with every blow of the cane. It was the same for all novices about to be tested. He could not complain.

"The god see you, novice," said Brikin, and stepped back. He had younger novices to chivvy, his task here was done. "If it pleases, we will meet again."

"If it pleases," Vortka echoed, as the door closed behind the novice-master. Moving cautiously, he eased himself off his sleep-mat, pulled on his robe, then left the chamber. At the first privy alcove he emptied his bladder. Like every godspeaker in the godhouse he'd long ago learned to discipline his body, make it wait to pish till after newsun sacrifice. He did not wait now, bad enough he would soon be swimming in blood, no need to swim in blood and urine.

After relieving himself he padded through the unsleeping godhouse to the godpool chamber, where Nagarak was waiting.

"Enter novice, and disrobe," said the high godspeaker. "Here is the beginning of your beginning, or the beginning of your end."

The godpool chamber was small and silent, its cold air laced with the iron tang of fresh blood. No other novices were present, it must mean his was the only testing. Was that significant? He did not know. He stepped over the threshold, removed his robe and all his amulets.

Nagarak looked him up and down. "I remember you, novice. Vortka, chosen by the god to witness my testing. I have a question."

Surprised, wary, Vortka bowed his head. "I am yours to examine, high godspeaker."

"Why did you smile in the scorpion chamber, when you heard the god declare its desire: one warlord for Mijak, one high godspeaker at his side."

I smiled? thought Vortka. *I don't remember. How stupid of me if I did.* He looked up. "Forgive me, high godspeaker. It was long ago, I cannot recall."

Nagarak's eyes were narrow. "I saw your face yesterday, when you saw the warlord's son. What is that child to you, for you to smile again?"

Aieee, god, his stupid face, betraying him! Nagarak could not know the truth, he *could not* know. "High godspeaker . . ." He looked at the floor, it was the safest place. His heart was beating at a painful speed. "The warlord's son is a beautiful child. It was a joy to see him, that is why I smiled."

"You are a novice, your eyes should see the god and nothing else."

"Yes, high godspeaker. I do see the god."

"Tcha!" spat Nagarak, he was not appeased. "What matters here is if the god sees you." He stepped close. "I think you are not as humble as you seem, Vortka novice. I think you hide secrets in your heart. If I plucked it out I could read them, Vortka. Return from the wilderness and I will. Beneath the sun there is the god, and there is me. Get into the godpool. Your testing time is come."

Torchlight played on the pool's still, red surface, lending it warmth and an echo of life. Here was the first obstacle a novice must face in the quest to become a godspeaker in the god's eye. Bathed in blood, novices bared their godsparks for inspection by the high godspeaker and if they possessed even the slightest flaw it would be revealed in the sacred godpool. Denied the last rite of the wilderness they would be cast out from Et-Raklion's godhouse and into the sprawling city below, where they would live the remainder of their lives as lowly citizens, forever cut off from close communion with the god. The merest thought of such a disaster could make a novice weep.

Vortka stared at the godpool, abruptly aware of sweat and fear. *What if Nagarak can read my mind? A man's mind is opened in the godpool. Zandakar floats there like froth on sadsa, he fills my eyes, he is my heart's greatest secret, if Nagarak sees him . . .*

Such a thing was beyond his control. He must not worry. He was given by the god to create that child. The god would not abandon him now.

As Nagarak began to circle the godpool, his scorpion pectoral glowing with reflected red, Vortka trod the descending stone steps one by one until the waiting blood closed over his head. Blood swiftly soaked its way through his godbraids, his head was heavy, his godbells clogged. He felt his body dragged down to the bottom, felt the god heavy in his flesh and bones. On his hands and knees he started crawling, as the cold blood grew warm, then warmer, then hot. In the red darkness he thought he felt Nagarak, the power in him questing and cruel.

No. Not cruel. He is the high godspeaker, he serves the god even if it keeps secrets from him.

Nagarak pushed harder, seeking to read him. The god would not allow that, it pushed Nagarak aside. Still crawling, on fire with the god's power, Vortka bumped into the stone wall of the godpool, turned, kept on crawling, bumped again. Blood sloshed against his naked skin, slapped against the godpool walls, rushed into his open nostrils. He tried not to sneeze, his lungs were bursting, he had to breathe or die untested in a scarlet drowning. His head broke the surface of the godpool and he gasped for air in a heaving rush.

"Come out now," said Nagarak, curtly. If he was disappointed he did not show it. "The god sees you, Vortka. You are sent into the wilderness."

On trembling legs Vortka climbed from the godpool, sank to his knees on the chamber floor, dazed and shivering and sticky with blood. Nagarak ignored him, he pulled a godstone from his robe pocket and passed it across a blue crystal set in the wall. There came the sound of stone grinding against stone, followed by sloshing as the godpool drained of its sacred blood. When it was empty he passed the godstone over the same place and Vortka heard stone grinding to its accustomed place. Next Nagarak passed the godstone over a black crystal, and water began gushing into the godpool.

As it filled, Nagarak passed the godstone over a green crystal in the wall. A stone block shifted, and he withdrew from the space behind it a pair of shears and a plain linen bag. With the shears he cut the bloodsoaked god-braids from Vortka's head, he clipped him like a sheep. The severed godbells rang in mourning. Nagarak put the sundered godbraids into the linen bag and held it out. Vortka took the bag numbly, he felt unnatural, too light, he felt like weeping, his godbraids with their singing god-bells were gone, they were gone.

"You will take your godbraids into the wilderness," Nagarak told him. "You will burn them for the god, you will breathe deep of that sacrificial smoke, and the god shall work its will on you."

The godpool was almost full of water. Nagarak turned off the flow with his godstone and pointed. "Cleanse yourself, Vortka. Your novice robes and amulets are for-ever discarded, other clothing will be brought to you here. If it is the god's desire, you and I will meet again in this godhouse after your testing in the wilderness."

He left the chamber. Vortka eased himself into the water, it was bitterly cold, it stole his breath and pained him to the bone. As he sloshed the cold water over his skin, sluicing away the tacky blood, exploring the strange shape of his stubbled skull, a godspeaker entered with a pile of clothing and a folded rough towel.

"Dry and dress yourself," he said. "Brikin novice-master awaits you in the novices' sacrifice chamber."

Clothing and towel were dropped on the floor. Without a backwards glance the godspeaker picked up Vortka's discarded belongings and left the chamber.

My amulets, thought Vortka, but he did not protest. Dripping, he trod the stone steps out of the godpool.

His testing time had come at last.

*   *   *

"Kneel, Vortka," said Brikin, standing before the plain black novices' altar. His face was stern and self-contained, sacrifice was a solemn business.

Vortka knelt and bowed his head. After so long in god-speaker robes, to be kneeling barefoot in leggings and tunic felt strange, almost as strange as the lack of god-braids down his back. His shoulders felt cold without them, his ears were bereft of their amulet piercings, his chest naked without its snake-eye charm. He held his godbraids in the linen bag, clinging to the past like a child to its mother's hand.

Three doves waited in a wicker cage. One by one Brikin gave them to the god, he plucked out their small hearts and read the blood patterns on the altar. On the floor beside him was a pile of goatskin satchels. After the third divination Brikin hesitated, frowning, then selected a satchel from the pile and held it out.

"Here is food and here is water. Enough to last you till you reach the wilderness. A strikestone, that you might make a fire. Here too is a godstone decided for you by the god, that will guide you to where it desires you to go. Place the godstone round your neck. While it is warm you tread the proper path. If the godstone cools, you face the wrong direction. If it grows completely cold you are lost, and the god no longer sees you in its eye. When the god-stone drops to the ground of its own accord, there you must wait for the god to instruct you."

Vortka took the offered satchel and rummaged within. Hard cheese, dried goat meat, four flat rounds of bread and a stoppered flask. Greed would see him hollow with hunger long before he reached the wilderness. The sliver of strikestone was sharp, it cut him. The lump of godstone, small as a peach pit and threaded on a leather thong, felt warm in his hand. He tugged it over his head, then stuffed his blood-damp linen bag of godbraids into the satchel.

Brikin looked at him, unsmiling. "Go now, Vortka. Be guided by the god, may it see you in its eye."

On the steps outside Et-Raklion's godhouse Vortka took a moment to breathe deeply of the unbloodied air. Standing so high he could see into the distant barracks, where the warriors seethed and teemed. A rising breeze carried the faint sounds of voices shouting, of horses calling, of bleating goats and bellowing cattle. Smoke flavored the air, and the ripe scents of many animals gathered close. He could see into the palace gardens, too, but no-one stirred there. He could not see Hekat, or their son.

Godhouse business roiled around him. He was not part of it. He had to go.

Tightening his grasp on the satchel he struck out on the road down the Pinnacle. As he passed the entrance to the warlord's palace he prayed.

See them in your eye, god. While I am gone and learning your secrets, see Hekat and my small son in your omniscient eye.

He kept on walking, marched past the barracks, where the din was much louder and the mixed smells much stronger. At the place where the Pinnacle Road ended and the city began, between the two towering godposts, he stopped, hesitant. There were many directions he could take from here, many streets that would lead him out of the city. It was not a decision that he could make.

From here, the godstone must guide his feet.

There was some shuffling then, false steps taken and taken back, as he sought the path the god wanted him to follow. In the end he discovered the godstone warmed him if he faced to the west, along the street leading to and through Et-Raklion's Livestock district. Beyond that district lay the city's boundary . . . and beyond the god-posted city gate, a narrow track leading through farmland to Et-Raklion's wilderness.

Slinging the satchel over his shoulder, Vortka went to meet the god.

CHAPTER TWENTY-FIVE

A godspeaker was waiting at the barracks gates when Raklion led his warriors home, Hanochek dirty and tired by his side. It was a finger past highsun, the sky was blue and bright. Hanochek saw her first.

"Warlord, it seems we are expected."

"I see that," said Raklion, and held his stallion to its slow jog. In his breast, his heart was beating.

Is it Hekat? Has she fallen on the border? Let it not be Hekat, god, I am lost without her.

When they reached the gates he drew rein and stared down from his horse at the patient godspeaker. "You wait for me?"

"Warlord," she said, wrapped throat to ankle in a soft wool robe. "Nagarak high godspeaker sends for you to join him."

"Sends for me?" he echoed. These past seasons, as Zandakar grew tall and beautiful, the high godspeaker had chosen his summoning words more carefully, he had no whip of failure for beating his warlord now. "How sends for me?"

The godspeaker bent her head, so all her godbells chimed in contrition. "Warlord, his purpose is not for me to know."

"My son thrives? His mother?"

"Warlord, your son sits in the god's eye. His mother is returned triumphant from war."

Relief was a pain, sharp in his side. "Returned when?"

"Eight highsuns ago," said the godspeaker. "She was cleansed in the godhouse, sacrifice was made and accepted. Warlord, Nagarak high godspeaker waits."

Raklion sighed and slid from his saddle. His bones creaked, his muscles groaned in chorus. Twenty-two suns hard riding from Et-Raklion's far border took its toll on a man, even if he was a warlord. Tossing his reins to Hano he said, "See my warriors praised on the warhost field, warleader. Tell the barracks godspeakers I wish two hundred bull-calves sacrificed to the god in thanks for our victory, then have the meat roasted for a feast. Ale and sadsa for all, without measure."

"It shall be done, warlord," said Hano, tactfully sympathetic for the groaning muscles and the summons, and led the warhost into the barracks proper.

No mere man might approach the godhouse on horseback, his feet must tread upon the ground. Bruised and aching, longing keenly for a bath, Raklion trudged up the winding Pinnacle Road to meet with Nagarak, the messenger godspeaker toiling in his wake. He passed a handful of city suppliants walking up, walking down, they stopped and bowed their heads to see him, he noticed them with a swift "the god see you' but said nothing further, Nagarak was waiting and he wanted this done. After three godmoons away, patrolling, fighting, he yearned to see Zandakar, his loins burned for Hekat, but they would have to wait. Hiding his reluctance, he kept on walking.

He and the godspeaker reached the godhouse. "I will tell the high godspeaker you are come," she said, hands meekly hidden inside her wool sleeves. "Please wait for me, warlord."

She disappeared into the godhouse, he remained outside. The godhouse stank of old, cold blood. Releasing a sigh, Raklion clasped his hands behind his back and let the stirring air caress his face and coax his godbells to whispered song. The business of the godhouse continued around and behind him, godspeakers and novices flitting by, never paying him attention, he was merely a warlord, they served the god. He saw no more suppliants, warlords did not enter the godhouse by the suppliants' door.

So high above his city Et-Raklion he felt a little like the god, the roofs of homes and businesses winking in the sunlight, fields and pastures and crops and grapevines covering the fertile lands beyond the city's boundary. Horses grazing, and fine fat cattle. The godhouse pastures full of breathing sacrifice. His fertile lands, while the rest of Mijak still was failing . . .

From up here he could see over the walls of his barracks, he could see his returned warriors and their brethren rejoice. Warriors of the god, every last one of them, no warlord could be better served by snakeblade and spear and arrow and slingshot. They were his people, in a way Et-Raklion's citizens would never be. It was not something he often considered, of course every man, woman and child of Et-Raklion was his . . . but oh, his warriors. Every last one the son and daughter of his heart.

"Warlord," said the godspeaker, returning. "Nagarak desires to see you now."

Did he, indeed. And there would be a separate conversation. *I am no longer cursed Raklion without a son. Nagarak must be reminded of that.*

She led him through the shadowed halls of the godhouse, past all the rooms with their secret doors and godspeaker mysteries, more rooms around him, below him, and above him than he had ever seen, would ever see before he died, until they reached a room with which he was uneasily familiar. The Divination chamber, which reeked of blood and death even after novices had worn their knees raw scrubbing it.

Naked but for his scorpion pectoral, Nagarak was up to his elbows in gore, knee-deep in entrails and slaughtered beasts. The severed heads of black goats stared blindly, yellow and orange eyes clouded in death. Flocks of doves littered the stone floor. Gutted white lambs slumped in scarlet piles. A mound of bulls' hearts glistened in the torchlight.

"Strip," said Nagarak, not turning from the altar as his godspeaker sealed the chamber door behind her. "The god requires your hand in this."

The air was rank with blood, shit and pish. The last living animal, a young white goatkid, lay panting and terrified beneath the high godspeaker's hand, a knife across its pulsing throat. Raklion tried not to breathe deeply, the chamber's stench was offensive. He had seen less bloody battlefields.

"*Strip*," said Nagarak, and the god was in his thundering voice. "But keep your snakeblade, you will need it."

Raklion pulled off his boots, peeled off his leggings, slid out of his tunic. There was nowhere to put them where they would not get ruined.

He did not think it wise to mention that.

With his knife held in his freshly calloused fingers he joined his high godspeaker at the altar. Picking his way across the chamber floor was a test in itself, the stone flags were slickly dangerous underfoot.

"Is it permitted to ask what purpose this divination serves?"

The scorpion-marks from Nagarak's last testing in the pit had never faded. Every part of the high godspeaker's flesh remained blotched, painted with blood the god's fingerprints gleamed and glowed. Not answering the question, Nagarak stabbed the white goatkid to the heart with his sacrificial blade, then thrust its body at his warlord.

Warlords took no part in divinations, Raklion had only ever entered this place to hear the god's desires, not coax them from the blood and guts of sacrifices. Clumsy and uncertain he clutched the goatkid's small warm carcass and struggled to remember what he'd seen other godspeakers do.

Nagarak waved his knife at him. "*Tcha*! Hold it high, warlord! Let the blood fall where it will upon the sacred altar!"

Raklion swung the sacrifice above the white marble carved in the shape of a sleeping scorpion.

"While you fought on the border, warlord, the god sent me difficult dreams," said Nagarak, eyes slitted as blood dripped and splotched and dribbled, a message from the god to those who could read such things. "Mijak is stirring, war is in the air."

"I know it is stirring, Nagarak, I have been fighting warlords and their warriors for godmoons now!" he retorted, as the hot blood splashed and sprayed. "You keep me from my son and woman to tell me things I already know?"

Nagarak bared his teeth, he thrust his face close. "Do not sharpen your tongue on *me*, warlord. This is the god's house, *I* am warlord in this place. You are here to learn the god's desires, you are here, a man of bloodshed, to see what the blood says in the god's name!"

Raklion felt his heart constrict and his mouth suck dry. The god was raging in Nagarak's eyes. "High godspeaker."

"You prayed in the wilderness, you thought to come home and tell *me*, the high godspeaker, what the god desires of you! Foolish sinning warlord, did you think I would not *know*? I hear all prayers to the god, it whispers to me all men's petty wantings. It whispers to *me* what it desires of you, that I might tell you. I am telling you now. War is stirring, your time is come."

Dumbfounded, Raklion stared at him. Aieee, god. What a terrible man. "High godspeaker."

Nagarak stepped back. "That is enough blood. I will divine the god's message now."

Raklion tossed the dead goatkid aside and retreated, that he might not interfere in Nagarak's sacred work.

Round and round the altar his godspeaker trod, stepping nimbly over discarded entrails, hearts and heads, his dark eyes rolled to crescents of white, his fingers outstretched above the mysterious blood spatters on the white marble. A low keening moan built in his throat, his breath rasped and rattled like a man dying from war wounds, his godbells sang in discordant counterpoint.

Chilled, still aching, Raklion stood in the midst of sacred death and waited.

At last Nagarak stopped walking and his labored moaning ceased. Intent as a falcon striking its prey he leapt to the pile of bull's hearts, seized one in each hand and threw them onto the only clear space remaining in the chamber, the sacred sand circle at its center. Four more bulls' hearts joined the first two. Then two goats' heads. Next, slippery piles of animal entrails, there and there and there. The pure white sand stained swiftly scarlet. Nagarak snatched up armfuls of slaughtered doves, and threw them into the air. They fluttered to the ground, a sad parody of flight, to thud without grace on the wet red sand. Last of all he flung the dead goatkid into the circle, where it lay so quietly, as though it were asleep.

"Your snakeblade," said Nagarak, and held out his hand.

Raklion gave it to him. "What does the god say?"

Nagarak's answer was to cut him with his own knife, more swiftly than a striking snake, a stinging scorpion, the wrath of the god. Before he had cried out even once his flesh was opened in eight separate places, his blood was flowing like a woman's tears. Nagarak thrust him into the circle, and he fell to the floor among goat's heads and bulls' hearts, his hands tangled in entrails, his blood weeping on dead doves.

Blue flames leapt to life around him. He felt their heat but his skin stayed cool. He did not catch fire, though he breathed fire in and breathed it out, he was made of fire, his blood was light. In his mind he heard the god singing.

The bulls' hearts were beating, throbbing with life.

The sound was in his ears, his bones, thrumming through him like the voice of the god. The eyes in the goats' heads watched him, blinking. The ropes of entrails were burned away, burned to black glass, burned to diamond. The doves' wings fluttered, they fanned the blue flames.

Raklion fumbled to his knees, his wounds in cheek and breast and thighs and arms gaping open, healing to silver even as they burned. Outside the circle Nagarak was dancing, his godbells rang louder than the birth of the world. Pain was pleasure and pleasure was pain, he watched the dead goatkid return to life and gambol round the circle of sand, bleating his name as it hopped and skipped.

Raklion! Raklion! Warlord of Mijak! Raklion, Raklion, praise his name!

He tried to touch it, the goatkid crumbled to ash.

Raklion warlord! the fluttering doves cooed. Then sighing, weeping: *Zandakar . . . Zandakar . . . Zandakar . . .*

He slumped to the stained sand, his mind a maelstrom. *What does this mean, god? Give me an answer! Is my son threatened? Will he not follow me? Is this a divining or a curse? Tell me, I beg you! What does this mean?*

The god told him nothing, its singing sank to silence. The blue flames died, the bulls' hearts stopped beating, the goats' heads went blind. Of the doves there was nothing left but beaks and clawed feet, a drifting of feathers.

"Warlord," said Nagarak, kneeling beside him. "Raklion. Open your eyes."

Reluctantly, Raklion obeyed him.

Nagarak was smiling, his blotched face fierce. "The god has spoken. Your time is come. Mijak's suffering is at an end."

Raklion felt his eyes fill with tears. "If I were a novice

you would beat me, Nagarak. I doubted on the battlefield, I railed at the god for its long harsh silence."

Nagarak struck him twice across the face, brutal blows. "You sinned, you are smitten. Look forward now, not back. Raklion, we are tasked by the god to bring peace to Mijak. You the warlord, I the high godspeaker. We will journey to Mijak's Heart, we will stand at the center of the god's seeing eye. The lesser warlords will kneel before you, their high godspeakers will kneel to me. If they defy us demons will claim them, the snake will devour them, the scorpion sting them until their bodies burst. Hell will refuse them, they will die in the dark."

Raklion lowered his hand from his aching face. "This is certain?"

"It is certain."

"In my vision, in the sacred circle . . ." He closed his eyes, remembering. As with all dreams it was fading, vanishing like smoke. "My name was called, and then was called Zandakar. What of my son, Nagarak? What does the god say? I could not understand its meaning."

"You are not high godspeaker," said Nagarak, complacent. "It is not your purpose to know, it is mine, and mine to tell you. You are Raklion, you are great in the god's eye. It has chosen you the warlord of Mijak, first of your kind since the long dark age. But your son, warlord? Aieee, your son is the future. Where you are great, he will be greater. The whole world will know him. His name will be legend. Zandakar dwells deeply in the god's eye."

The relief was so great it threatened to shatter him. He was not a young man, every season saw him older. If he could only stay strong until Zandakar was grown . . . "Help me stand, Nagarak," he said.

Nagarak helped him stand and dress, too, in his spoiled leggings and stained tunic and bloodsoaked boots, and handed him his snakeblade without comment or hint of apology. He was exhausted and exhilarated, emboldened and terrified, his heart shrank and sang.

The god has spoken. It is time.

He wanted to go home. He wanted his son's smile and Hekat's embraces. He wanted solitude, to absorb what he'd seen and heard and learned in this chamber.

Nagarak said, "At the next fat godmoon we must ride to meet with the warlords at Mijak's Heart. You must prepare your warriors, Raklion. I will send word to Mijak's other godhouses, that their small high godspeakers might instruct the lesser warlords of where and when we must meet for the god."

"You are high godspeaker," said Raklion, humbled. "You are the god's voice and I am its fist. Between us we will see Mijak reborn."

He walked alone and slowly to the palace, surprised to see the sun close to the horizon. Had he been so long within the godhouse? He must have, but it did not matter. Time meant nothing to the god.

Slaves hurried to greet him as he entered his warm halls, he waved them away, they could wait and so could his bath. He found Hekat and Zandakar in her private garden, they were knife-dancing together, slicing the lowsun to ribbons with their blades. He stood in the shadowed doorway and watched them, joy washing away his dirt and weariness.

She loved his son, he loved her for that. He loved her for many reasons, but that most of all. He wished he could breed another son on her—he tried and he tried, his seed would not take root. It made him weep, sometimes, although Hekat told him to be patient.

When the god desires a brother for Zandakar, the god will give him one. Till then, warlord, be content.

So Hekat told him, it was wise advice.

Watching her and Zandakar knife-dance together, it was like watching the god and its shadow. Her form was perfect, his echoed hers completely.

Aieee, what a warrior his son would make. What a warrior was his beloved Hekat, she led warhosts for him as fiercely as Hano, she was without mercy on the battle-field. The warriors gladly died for her, the god had blessed him, he would never forget it.

The final *hota* glided into stillness. Hekat and Zandakar stood perfectly poised, immaculately balanced, their snakeblades flashing in the sun's dying light. He could wait no longer, he stepped out of the shadows and onto the grass.

"Aieee, you are beautiful, you honor the god!"

"Warlord!" cried Zandakar. "Did you see me dancing? I danced with Yuma, soon I will dance with a *proper* snakeblade!"

His knife was child-sized, crafted to fit a small fist. Since he could talk he'd asked, *Where is my proper snakeblade?* He was born a warrior in his bones.

Hekat tugged his godbraids. "Sheathe your blade and embrace the warlord, Zandakar, then go to your bath. We will eat together when you are clean."

Raklion folded his arms about the boy, marveling as always at the sweetness of him against his chest.

I never thought to hold my living son. I am blessed, god, you see I am blessed.

Zandakar wriggled free and ran into the palace. Hekat sheathed her snakeblade and came to him for kissing, he drank deeply of her sweet-tasting mouth.

"You were victorious on the border?" he asked her, his fingers fisted in her godbraids.

"Tcha!" she said, and pulled a face. "I am always victorious, that is my purpose. A slave told me you did not ride into the barracks, you ran to the godhouse."

Of course a slave told her. She knew everything that happened in the barracks, she was his eyes and his ears and his swift smiting fist, even more than Hano, sometimes. He released her godbraids and kissed the tip of her nose. "That is so."

She stared into his face, her eyes were blue flames. "Shall I tell you what Nagarak wanted? He wanted you to know the god has spoken. Your time is come, warlord. You will be warlord of Mijak."

For the longest moment he could not speak. How did she know these things? How did she hear the god so clearly, no need for sacrifice and omens, no searching for answers in a circle of sacred sand?

"Yes, Hekat," he said at last. "That is what Nagarak wanted to say."

Her shrug was careless, she turned away. "You should ask me, warlord. I will tell you, I will not make you beg. Nagarak likes your begging, it makes him feel big."

Aieee, the god see her. So certain, so proud, she would never change. He leapt to catch her as she left the garden. "You should not speak of Nagarak like that," he chided as they walked the corridors together to join their son in the bath. "He is in the god's eye."

"Not as deeply as I am, warlord," she said. "Remember that."

He would never forget it. She was Hekat, godtouched and precious, mother of his beautiful son.

Much later, in the cool night, after bathing and eating and fucking with Hekat, he sprawled on the bed beside her, flickered by lamplight, his appetites sated, comfortably tired. She had wanted to talk more of warlord business, he did not want to think of it. He preferred to think of other things.

I am happy. I was never happy before. There is little pleasure in being a warlord, there is only pain and pressure and sleepless nights. Here is a better reason to be sleepless.

"Are you happy, Hekat?" he asked her. It was suddenly important, that she be happy. That she find pleasure in him, as he did in her. She was not talkative, she rarely opened her heart. She was carefree only in Zandakar's company, then he saw her face unguarded, then she laughed, then she looked young. He was old enough to have sired her, to have sired the man who did sire her, yet so often, so often, she made him feel young.

"I am happy if you are happy," she said, sounding drowsy. He could not see her face.

"That is no answer," he said, and tugged her godbraids till she was looking at him. "Hekat, tell me truly. Are you happy?"

Her eyes were half-lidded, they gleamed like a cat's. "I am Zandakar's mother."

He smiled. "You are a good mother. You are the mother he deserves. Is that all you need to make you happy?"

Her eyelids lowered even further, her lashes cast shadows upon her cheeks. "Why does it matter if I am happy? I am here by the god's will, I do its bidding. The god does not care if I am happy, it cares only if I do its will."

He rolled towards her and nuzzled her breast. "I am a man, I am not the god. Men care if the women they love are happy."

She did not believe him, he could see that in her face. She said, "Did you care if the Daughter was happy?"

Et-Nogolor's Daughter, dead on her bed. The old image stabbed him, he pushed it away. "Do not speak to me of her," he said harshly, rolling over. "She was a mistake, I should have given her to Bajadek with my blessing."

"Tcha," said Hekat, and poked him with her elbow. "There are no mistakes, warlord. There is only the god and its desirings. She served a purpose, she unmasked Bajadek that I might kill him in the god's eye. I am known in Et-Raklion as Bajadek's doom, the god desires I am known by that name. Bajadek's doom birthed Zandakar warlord. That is his bloodline, it is pleasing to the god. You raised me above the other warriors, they would dislike that if not for Bajadek."

Aieee, she had such power to surprise him . . . "How are you so wise, and still so young?"

She sat up, and set her godbells singing. "When I was a she-brat, then I was young. I am Zandakar's mother now, old as Mijak."

She would never tell him truly if she was happy. She would leave him wondering, he would have to hope. He pressed his lips against her spine, her flesh was sweetness on his tongue. He starved for her body, every day on the borders he pined, and pined.

"I love you, Hekat," he said against her warm, moist skin. *Say you love me. Say it. Say it.*

She lay herself down on his sheets of blue silk. "Fuck me, warlord. Raklion, fuck me."

It was not the same thing . . . it was better than silence.

He took her, groaning, and prayed to the god.

When Hekat woke two fingers past newsun she was alone in the bed she shared with Raklion. Her body was mildly sore, he always fucked hard when he came back from fighting. One day he might not come back, and she would be spared his breathless gruntings.

Still he hopes for another son, it will not happen. The god has sealed my womb, it will not quicken for him. What need have I for any other child? I have Zandakar, he is all I need.

She rose from the bed, bathed in warm water, dressed in her training tunic, frayed at the hem. Her snakeblade she belted round her waist. She went to Zandakar in his chamber and there found Raklion also, playing trap-warrior with her son.

Zandakar was winning.

With a look and a nod she dismissed his attending slaves. "My son, have you eaten breakfast?"

"Yes, Yuma."

"Then leave your game, you may finish it later. I will have words with the warlord, go to the stable and saddle your pony. When I come we will ride out hunting."

"We will all ride out hunting," said Raklion, and kissed her son. "It is a good day to go riding together."

Zandakar slid off his chair, bowed to the warlord and rushed past her, out the door. Raklion laughed, then ruefully considered the trap-warrior board and the many pieces he had lost in the game.

"He plays like a grown man. He is a constant amazement."

"Yes," she said. "Raklion, we must speak more of this warlord business. Do you think to lead the warhost against the warhosts of those other, godforsaken warlords, so they might fall before you on the field of war?"

Raklion shook his head. "No. We will meet in peace at the Heart of Mijak. Nagarak is sending to the other godhouses, the warlords cannot refuse the call."

She was not pleased. "No, not the call. But they can refuse to see you warlord of Mijak. You can take no warhost to that sacred place, you must go there almost undefended. If you tell them the god's desire, that you will be their warlord, and they refuse to hear the god's words, then are they forewarned of your intentions. They are godless, they might raise a knife to you there or hurry back to their lands and send their warhosts against you."

Raklion smiled. "Precious Hekat, you think of me always. Do not be afraid. Warlords are forbidden knives in Mijak's Heart and Nagarak will be with me. In the god's eye, he will keep me safe."

Tcha. Nagarak. "Raklion, hear me. I must ride with you to Mijak's Heart."

"You do not need to," said Raklion, rising. "Hanochek is my warleader, he will ride with me, you will watch over my warhost here, you—"

"Yes, I need to!" she shouted. He was stupid. Around her neck, the scorpion amulet burned. "I am Zandakar's mother, I am Bajadek's doom. The warlords *must* know I am with you, they must see I am the snakeblade belted at your hip. If you should die before Zandakar is a man I must ride at the head of your warhost. The warlords must see me, they must learn to fear."

Astonished, he stared. "I will not die before Zandakar is a man. I am in the god's eye, Hekat. It sees me, I am blessed. It will make me warlord of Mijak, and I will rule Mijak for seasons to come. That is the omen, do you say it is not?"

She stepped towards him. "Will you listen if I say what I say? You are a man dogged by demons all his life. Raklion, you dwell in their envious eyes. You would have *died* on the Plain of Drokar, warlord. You would be *dead* now, if not for me. I slew wicked Bajadek, I killed him and you live. I tell you truly: *I must ride to Mijak's Heart.*"

He stood before her in silence, he breathed in and out. "You are Hekat, godtouched and precious," he murmured. "You are Zandakar's mother and Bajadek's doom. You are in the god's eye, I cannot deny it. The god whispers to you, is this the god's whisper?"

Of course it was. Her amulet burned, her heart burned with it. The god's want was in her, using her tongue. "Yes."

He sighed, and nodded. "Then you will ride with me to the Heart of Mijak."

CHAPTER TWENTY-SIX

The stench of bloodsoaked burning godbraids poisoned the unstirring air. Choking, Vortka fought the urge to smother his nose and mouth, he must breathe the smoke, the smoke would guide him to the god and its desiring.

Naked, he sat cross-legged before the fire, deep within Et-Raklion's harshest wilderness, the cruellest crucible for testing, where no godspark could hide itself from the god. The landscape here was twisted, tortured, barren rock and stone-turned tree. Only the god's creatures thrived in this place, lizards, snakes, centipedes and scorpions. Nothing green here, nothing scented, nothing soft. The rocks were red and yellow and orange, striped with black, spattered with brown. Whipped by the wind, scoured into fevered nightmarish shapes, into looming spindle spires and giant godbones scattered by a madman's hand, they cast irregular shadows, promising shelter they could not provide.

The god withheld its water here, the underground rivers did not flow. This was a hot place, a parched place, the air panted, the blue sky rarely wept rain. His food was eaten, his water drunk. His clothes he'd had to use as tinder so his godbraids could be burned. He had nothing.

I am nothing. Only what the god makes me. If Zan-

*dakar was my single purpose, then I will die here alone
and unnoticed. The god will not see me. My bones will be
lost.*

The fire was melting his silver godbells. He felt a
small grief for that, he'd loved his godbells, always
singing to the god. His godbraids burned with a steady
flame, years of his life reducing to ash. He breathed in, he
breathed out, his tongue was coated with the stink. His
mind was melting with his godbells, the world was dimming, he was floating away . . .

Dreamlike, suspended, he felt his legs unfold themselves, he felt himself stand beneath the burning sun. The
god's voice was calling, it whispered, it beckoned. He
followed it stumbling, shrouded in smoke. His bare feet
clung to the sun-scorched rocks, if he was not careful he
would drift from their surface, he would spiral like smoke
into the sky.

Deeper and deeper he walked into the wilderness. His
eyes were open but he was blind to the world, deaf to all
sound save the voice of the god. He left the fire fat behind
him but its smoke was in him, it guided his steps. The
smoke was the god's breath, breathing for him. He grew
tired, muscles aching, he kept on walking. Sweat slicked
his skin, stones like snakeblades sliced his feet, a sandcat
could track him by the scent of his blood. Hunger plagued
him, thirst shriveled his mouth, he kept on walking, following the god.

Without any warning the ground gaped wide beneath
him. With a cry he fell, and knew no more.

When consciousness returned it was the deep of night. At
first he thought the fall had blinded him, but after long

panicked moments he looked up and saw a brief scatter of stars. He frowned, relief surrendering to confusion. What had happened to the rest? Nights in Et-Raklion meant a ceiling of stars watching the godmoon and his wife stride through the sky. He could see hardly any, it was as though some malicious demon had extinguished all save a small child's handful.

Then fresh air stirred against his skin and he realized he had fallen into a cave where the fat godmoon's light could not reach him. He was looking at stars through a ragged hole in its roof.

Not dead, not blind. Trapped.

It was cold. He hurt. Tentative exploration told him no bones were broken, the god had spared him that much, but his shorn head was battered, his flesh was split, he was bruised and bloody. His groping fingers felt rough walls, a rough floor, loose rocks. He sat up, slowly, but encountered no obstacle, there was empty space between himself and the cave's rock ceiling.

He looked again at the hole through which he had fallen. Through which the god had led him to fall.

Why am I here, god? What is your desiring?

The god did not answer, its voice was silent and its smoke disappeared. He breathed alone now, his wits were his own.

The cave's darkness was oppressive. It swaddled him like a baby's blanket, crushed him to the floor. He lay down again, skinned knees tucked against his bare chest, forehead resting on them. He was bewildered, he tasted sour fear. When the sun rose again, letting light into this place, what would he learn? That he was trapped here forever, rejected, discarded by the god, his purpose achieved, destined to die starving and maddened by thirst?

God, god, is that your desiring? Am I now punished for my doubts?

He steadied his breathing, imagined himself still, like stone, so he might hear the god's answer.

For a second time it did not come.

Fear overwhelmed him. Seasons of study in the godhouse meant nothing, all the times he'd given his body to the taskmaster, trusting that pain would drive out his sinful doubts, but he'd suffered for nothing, doubt was in him, it raged within him like the god's wrath, unstoppable.

I think I wish I had stayed a slave.

Control deserted him, then, along with his faith in the god. Shouting, cursing, he waved his arms in the air, drummed his heels on the ground even though they were bloody. Blind in the cave's dark, pale starlight, with no comfort, he groped for little rocks to throw, found them and snatched them and laughed wildly as they smashed to pieces against the walls.

His fingers closed on a rock that felt different. Heat flared in his loins and the pitch-black cave blossomed with light. His mind came alive with godsense unleashed.

"*Aieee!*" He dropped the rock. His loins cooled. The light vanished, extinguished like a pinched-out candle.

Heart frantic, breath strangled in his throat, he sat in the dark and wondered if he dreamed. If he was fevered and raving on the brink of ugly death.

If I am dying, god, let me die in peace I beg you. Do

not torment me with such terror. Do not take my mind from me.

The god was everywhere but in this cave. Unanswered a third time, Vortka felt his fingers reaching, as his heart pounded he felt them grope in the darkness for that strange rock. If light came again, if his godsense stirred, it might prove he was not raving. That this was real and not a dream. He could see where he had fallen. Perhaps even find a way out before he starved.

A pebble—nothing. A shard of stoneglass that cut his fingers—blood, but no light. A gritty, grainy chunk of sandrock—more darkness.

Something smooth and cold and briefly familiar—

"*Aieee!*" he cried out, in the new light, in the roaring of his power. In the heat that was like fucking Hekat.

He clutched a crystal in his hand. It was dark red, but the light it emitted was purest white. Power pulsed within it and it pulsed in him, his eyes were burning, his flesh was on fire. He looked around him, saw another red crystal, this one as large as a man's head. He had never seen crystal like it before. Never heard it mentioned, or found reference to it in the godhouse library.

Is this why I am brought here, god?

Despite the light and power, the dark red crystal was cool against his skin. The heat was in him, pouring out of him and through its rough-hewn facets. He remembered his testing in the slave pens of Et-Nogolor, how it felt when he took hold of the godstone and power woke within him for the first time in his life.

That was water. This was blood.

More time passed and he felt himself grow dizzy. He uncrooked his clutching fingers, let the crystal tumble to the gritty ground. This time the heat and light faded slowly, as though the crystal were a goblet with a hole punched in it and his godsense was rich wine trickling out.

Darkness returned, not as an enemy but as a friend, a refuge. Somewhere to hide while he struggled to make sense of the crystal, the light, the stirred power within him.

Not one godspeaker in Et-Raklion's godhouse, not even Nagarak high godspeaker himself, had sensed this potential in their novice.

I am godchosen, like Hekat I hide in the god's secret eye.

If only he understood what that meant. Understood what he was meant for, besides the siring of a child.

This dark red crystal that seemed to channel his god-sense, did Nagarak know of its existence? Was it kept a terrible high godspeaker secret? If so, what might happen if Nagarak learned a newly tested novice had held it in his hand? Or was Nagarak ignorant, kept unknowing by the god? If that was so, then did he have a duty to tell the high godspeaker of his discovery? Surely not. If the god wanted Nagarak to know, he would know. If he told Nagarak when the god wished it secret, what dread retribution might he invite?

Questions scuttled round the bowl of his skull like rats in a dry well, he could not catch them, they would drive him mad. The god sent him no answers. It had brought him here, the smoke from his godbraids had led him to this place. There was a purpose to this discovery, he was sure of that much. As for the rest . . .

Hekat will know how to learn what this means. The god speaks to her when it will not speak to me. I must re-

*turn to Et-Raklion. Hekat will know what to make of this
mystery.*

There was a measure of comfort in that, at least.

Exhaustion overcame him, then. He was so weary the
cold meant nothing, his scrapes and bruises meant nothing, his clamoring belly and sand-dry throat, they also
meant nothing. His bones were chalk, his muscles turned
to sadsa dregs.

He stretched out on the ground, and slept.

When he woke again, filtering sunlight lifted the cave out
of deep shadow. For a moment he thought again of
dreams, of fevered ravings, but the dark red crystals were
no dream. With the newsun's help he searched the cave to
see if there were more. He could not find any. One large
crystal and one much smaller, that was all.

Squatting on his battered haunches, he looked at the
large lump of dark red rock. He was afraid to touch it.
Holding the small crystal had woken such power, what
might happen if he roused the larger crystal to life?

He did not know. Turning aside from that thorny
problem, he distracted himself with another no less
uncomfortable.

How to get himself out of the cave.

But there, the god saw him, it answered his pleas. Exploration showed him the cave was a kind of bubble
blown into solid rock. The hole in the roof, too high for
him to reach, no rocks to help him upwards, was one
breach; a narrow passageway behind some tumbled boulders was another. Whether it led all the way to the outside
world he could not see, or even guess. The only way to
learn that was to traverse it. He had no hope of walking

upright in the passage, he had to lie on his back and shuffle his way along the ground like some crippled snake, like a lizard with no legs. It was a harsh tasking, he could feel his naked skin tearing, the solid rock pressed upon him, there was air but he could not breathe.

He thought of Zandakar, and throttled his fear.

The passageway ended just as he imagined, despairingly, he would never see the sky again. With a grunt he wriggled free of the oppressive crawlspace and regained his feet with great effort, shaking and mucky with dirt, blood and sweat. Aieee, had any novice before him endured such a testing?

He stood in the shadow of a crumbling rock cliff. As his harsh breathing eased and the thundering blood in his ears slowed to silence, he heard another, welcome sound. Running water, near at hand.

Vortka staggered towards that godsent flowing, to the fringe of green lining a rocky depression off to the right. It was an oasis, a grudging trickle of water from deep underground that fed into a shallow basin. Laughing weakly he thrust his face into it and drank, drank till his belly distended and threatened to burst. Then he wept, in fear and gratitude. The night's doubts shamed him now, safe in sunlight, he knew the god would not abandon him but even so, he'd felt abandoned. He saw a brown lizard, torpid and sluggish, and killed it with a loose rock before it could escape. Ravenous, he devoured it raw.

After that he bathed his body as best he could, inspecting himself for wounds less than superficial. He had lost much skin, scored grooves, punched holes, but in truth the damage was no more dangerous than any brute strapping he'd received in the godhouse.

He would survive.

Letting unshaded sunshine dry him, he wondered what he must do about the crystals. Where he stood was a featureless plain, he saw no tree or outcropping he could recognize. He realized then he had no recollection of how he found this place. His last clear memory was setting fire to his godbraids. After that, it was smoke and wonder.

God, you must guide me. If this is my testing and I have passed, show me how to get home to Et-Raklion, to Hekat and our Zandakar. Tell me what you desire I do next.

His godsense stirred then, and he turned from the oasis to tread further across the stony plain. He walked until the god told him to stop, then dropped to the hard ground and lay on his back beneath the sun. The rock was burning, it woke all his small hurts and made them larger. The light dazzled his eyes, he closed them and was lost in blood-red shadows. His skull was vulnerable, pillowed on rock.

Here I am, god, at your mercy. Write your desires in my naked flesh.

The surrounding silence was vast and deep. But then something broke it, a skittering sound, faint at first but growing louder. He opened his eyes and turned his head.

Scorpions were coming.

Called by the god, whispered to its service, they covered the rocks in a carapace carpet, black and brown and red and ochre. Not the lovingly bred monsters from the godhouse, larger than a large man's hand spread full wide, these were creatures of the wilderness, small and agile, bred to survive all of nature's casual cruelties.

Vortka's heart faltered, he felt it stop. Every muscle, every sinew, screamed at him to leap up and run. Run before the scorpions reached him, run before that first kiss of venom, run before it was too late.

If I run now, it has all been for nothing.

When his father died, he'd thought he knew fear. When his mother re-married, then he thought he understood it. When the slave chains closed about his wrists, his ankles, he was certain at last he grasped its meaning.

Now he knew those times were but seedlings, shy suggestions of what was to come.

Oh, Hekat. Oh, Hekat. I wish you were with me.

She had braved the scorpion pit, she had swum with godhouse scorpions and drowned in their venom. She had embraced that destiny, urged it upon herself. How could he do less when the god had chosen him to give her a son?

Swallowing a whimper, he watched as the rock plain disappeared beneath an onslaught of scorpions. Who knew so many lived in the world?

The god knows. The god made them. They serve its mysteries, and its purpose.

The scorpions reached him, covered him, stung him. They made of him a scorpion man. He forgot his name, he felt his flesh welt, his blood curdle, the god roared through him, leaving him weak. Hissing, scratching, the creatures scrambled upon him, he heard words in their voices, they whispered in his ears.

Vortka . . . precious . . . chosen . . .

Was he dying? He did not know. Consciousness left him. He sank into shadow. When he woke, he was alone. No sign of scorpions. No marks on his flesh.

He knew exactly what he must do.

*   *   *

Raklion waited until it was almost time to ride to Mijak's Heart before telling Hanochek he would not be riding there with his warlord. He knew Hano would be hurt, so hurt, to have his rightful place taken by Hekat. He was the warleader, he stood tall in the world. Wherever the warlord rode, so rode his warleader.

But not this time. This time I must be guided by the god. The god tells Hekat she must ride beside me, who am I to say she will not?

After meeting with Nagarak for the taking of omens and private sacrifice on his knees, he walked down to the barracks. There he found Hano at warplay with Zandakar, they were the best of friends, his friend and his son. A ring of warriors surrounded them, cheering and shouting as Hano and Zandakar sparred on the warhost field. Zandakar was blindfolded, in his hand a blunt wooden snakeblade. He was learning to fight with senses not fed by his eyes, he was nimble on his feet, swift to feel Hano's approach and retreat.

Raklion slid between two laughing warriors, held his finger to his lips so they would not betray his presence. He did not wish to distract his son.

Zandakar danced like his beautiful mother, he was light on the green grass, he leapt without weight. Hano was strict with him, he did not make exceptions for Zandakar's age or his father. Twice Zandakar misjudged Hano's movements, once he went sprawling hard on the ground when Hano caught him a sharp blow on the rump. Below his blinded eyes Zandakar's face twisted with anger, he spat out a curse and bounced to his feet.

"Again, warleader! Come at me again!"

Aieee, he was a brave boy, he was a warrior bred in the

bone. Raklion held his breath as his small son flew at Hanochek, tapping him smartly with his blunted blade, he did not make a single mistake. He caught Hano in all his vulnerable places, his belly, his hamstring, the soft inner elbow. Hano dropped to his knees, crying surrender.

"You defeat me, I am beaten, see me cowed before you!" he declared.

Zandakar tore off his blindfold, laughing. "I have beaten the warleader! I am Zandakar the mighty!"

Hano snatched him into a crushing embrace, saluting his grimy cheek with a kiss. "Yes, you are mighty! I am defeated by a mighty warrior!" Standing easily, sweeping Zandakar up and over and onto his feet, his head turned. "Warlord!"

Raklion came forward. "Hanochek warleader, I see you train a mighty warrior."

Zandakar pulled himself to attention, he bowed his head and pressed his fist to his heart. "Warlord."

He returned the salute with a small ache in his heart. He was always the warlord. Hekat was *Yuma*, he was never *Adda*. Hekat knew it bothered him, she called him stupid. *He will be the warlord, he shows you respect. You fret because he respects you? How foolish are men.* She was right, of course. She was always right.

Reading him as he always did, Hanochek dismissed the watching warriors with a gesture and stood with his hand on Zandakar's shoulder. "You need me?"

"Where is Hekat?"

"She trains with the new recruits on the horse-field, warlord. Shall I send a—"

He shook his head. "No. It is you I need." But it was better that Hekat was safely somewhere else. Her voice added to his would not make this easier. "Zandakar, low-sun approaches. Return to the palace, bathe and don clean clothes. We attend special sacrifice in the godhouse this night."

"Special sacrifice?" said Hano, as Zandakar departed. "What do you pray for, Raklion?" Then his face changed. "Aieee . . . it is time, warlord? It is time to take Mijak in your fist?"

Raklion cast a swift look around them, they were alone but even so. "Not here," he said sharply. "Walk with me, Hano."

On the far side of the warhost field grew an expanse of woodland, where warriors practiced stealth among the trees. It was quiet, private, they could talk in that place undisturbed. Raklion led Hanochek there, and when they were swallowed by leaves and shadows he stopped.

His warleader eyed him warily. "You are making me nervous. Whatever you must say, I wish you would say it."

Hano was not the only man with sweaty palms. "You are right, my friend. The god's time is come. Five high-suns from now, at the next fat godmoon, it sends me to Mijak's Heart to change the face of Mijak forever. The warlords are called to meet me there with their high god-speakers in attendance, so they might learn their fate: to kneel before me in submission, to lose their autonomy, to be cast down."

"Tcha!" said Hano. "They will not be pleased to hear that news." He frowned. "Are you certain you must tell them at Mijak's Heart? If you tell them elsewhere, if you summon them to Et-Raklion and meet them with every warrior in your warhost—"

Raklion shook his head, his godbells sang. "This is not warlord's business, Hano. This is the god's will, it is given through Nagarak, the god's voice in the world. They can be told nowhere but in the Heart of Mijak."

Hano did not like to hear it, but he swallowed his protest. "You are permitted to take ten warriors, that is true?"

"Yes. It is true."

"Have you chosen who will ride with us, or do we meet now to—"

"Hano." He lowered his hand, it hurt to breathe. "We meet so I might tell you of the god's desire, and also that you will not ride with me to Mijak's Heart."

"*Not* ride . . ." Hano was puzzled. "Raklion, you cannot ride to tell the warlords such a thing without a sharp blade at your side, you—"

"I will have a sharp blade, Hano. I will have Hekat."

Hano's face stilled, like a lake unstirred by any breeze. In the woodland's hush his breathing was loud, almost labored. "Hekat is not your warleader, warlord. I am your warleader, the snakeblade at your side."

Aieee, god, the pain in him. He and Hekat were not easy together. It was a grief to him, he could not change their hearts. "She is more important than my warleader," he said gently. "She is Zandakar's mother. After me he will be the warlord of Mijak, greater than any warlord in our history. The god has said so, and I know it in my heart. Hekat is a part of this, she must be witnessed by the other warlords, they must see her beside me and know she is chosen by the god as the mother of my living son who will be warlord after I am dead. The god desires I heal bleeding Mijak and lead it kindly into peace, to make of it a gift for Zandakar. I will do that, you will help me. In truth, I will not do it without you. But for the throwing down of the warlords, there I must have Hekat. I am sorry, Hano. This is not my will, but the will of the god."

"She tells you that?" Hano demanded, vicious. "Is this *her* doing?"

"Hano, Hano . . ." He took his warleader's shoulders in a biting grip. "Would you have me choose between my knife-brother and my son's godchosen mother? Are you so cruel? Is your heart so small?"

Hano tensed, he did not pull away. "This is not about my heart, Raklion. I think only of you, and keeping you safe. The warlords will not greet your message with a smile, they will foam at the mouth, they will spit on you in fury. The warlords know me, seasons of fighting have burned my name into their flesh. When they see me beside you they will know better than to challenge your might."

"They will know not to challenge when they see Nagarak," he said. "And when they see Hekat, Bajadek's doom."

Now Hano did pull away, he thudded his fist into a tree. "*Raklion*—"

"I will be safe in the Heart of Mijak, Hano," he said. "That place is sacred, there can be no bloodshed there. Not even a warlord as hungry as Banotaj, as angry as Tebek, would dare thwart the god's will in that place."

"I think the warlords would dare anything if they think their days of power are come to an end!"

Raklion stepped back, he stiffened his spine. "Hanochek, you risk the god's wrath. It has chosen me, I am in its eye. No harm can come to me in the Heart of Mijak. Nagarak will be with me, he too is the god's chosen. He will be high godspeaker of Mijak."

Hano's eyes were bright. "I am sorry, Raklion. I do not mean to doubt the god, or you." He heaved a sigh. "Aieee, my warlord, the warlord of Mijak. What a thing that is. How deep are you in the god's great eye."

"So deep I think I cannot see," he confessed. "If I tell you I am afraid, Hano, will I seem less than a man to you?"

"You are the greatest man I have ever known!" said Hano, swiftly. "And while you are with the god in the Heart of Mijak I will be here in Et-Raklion, warlord, I will guard your city and your warhost. I will guard your son, he will live in *my* eye."

Raklion embraced him. "I trust Zandakar with you as I trust him to no other, not Nagarak himself. Hano, if I were free to choose you would ride with me. You know that. You must."

"I know it," Hano whispered.

Raklion swallowed. "If you love me, Hano, never tell Nagarak what I said about not trusting him with Zandakar."

Hano eased free, and took a step back to look at him. "I keep your secrets, Raklion. You know how well I keep them."

"Yes," he said solemnly. "I do."

"Have you chosen the other warriors you wish to ride with you to Mijak's Heart?"

"Not yet. I thought perhaps we could choose them now."

Hano nodded. "As the warlord desires."

"Then let us go to the warlodge, we can take our ease

with mugs of ale and choose who is most worthy of the honor."

"Tcha!" said Hano, and fell into step beside him. "Worthiness is a thing for godspeakers to decide. *You* should be concerned for the speed of their kills!"

It was the kind of bold thing Hekat might say. Raklion laughed, and nodded, and let his hand fall on Hano's shoulder.

My friend, my friend. I would be lost without you.

CHAPTER TWENTY-SEVEN

So, Vortka," said Brikin novice-master. "You are returned from the wilderness, a tested godspeaker."

Exhausted, filthy, scoured hollow with hunger, Vortka nodded. "Yes. What should I do now? Should I clean myself and attend a sacrifice or go to the high godspeaker as I am?"

It was a finger after highsun. They stood in the godhouse vegetable garden, where Brikin supervised a new crop of novices, most of whom hardly knew one end of a hoe from the other. As he waited for Brikin to advise him, despite his weariness and discomfort Vortka released a rueful smile. He was tested in the wilderness, transformed by the god and its infinite mysteries, yet part of him still felt like a novice, felt he could easily join the young men and women on their bare knees in the dirt as they grubbed up weeds and wondered why the god had called them for this.

Brikin said, "Nagarak high godspeaker is not free to see you. At newsun he rides with the warlord to Mijak's Heart. He is secluded till then, seeking guidance in the godpool."

Vortka felt his heart thump, hard. "Novice-master?"

"The god has chosen us for great things, Vortka," said Brikin, smiling fiercely. "In time you will be told what you must know of them. Until then, go about your business. Bathe, godspeaker. Attend sacrifice, and eat. The god is not served if you fall stinking and starved on the godhouse floor. Nagarak will see you upon his return."

Bathe, godspeaker. Vortka felt a surge of warmth. He was tested, he was returned, he had earned the right to be called *godspeaker*. He did not show his pleasure to the novice-master, such feelings of pride were strictly frowned upon. Instead he looked down at his unfortunate attire, leggings too short for him, a threadbare sleeveless vest. "Brikin, I have no clothing but what I was given by villagers upon the road."

Brikin snorted. "See Oolikai provisioner on your way to the bath-house, he will give you a godspeaker robe and what else you may require. Once you are presentable and not likely to collapse, report to Peklia in the Sacrifice chamber. You must receive your sacrifice blade and make your first sacrifice under her exacting eye."

And then what? What did the god expect of him then? He had asked, it had not answered.

"Brikin—"

But Brikin was no longer paying attention, he had noticed a sin in the vegetable garden. Leaping on the sinner he cuffed her smartly on the back of the head. "That is not a *weed*, fool, that is a *seedling*! Do you desire your fellow novices to starve to death? Ten stripes in the tasking house for not paying attention! Go now! Run! Come back when you are smitten and can tell the difference between *liver*-rot and *car*-rot!"

Fighting tears, the sinning novice ran. Brikin continued to rant at his charges, Vortka withdrew quietly and presented himself to the godhouse provisioner, who made no comment on his newly won status, just handed him a robe, new sandals and an untied loincloth.

The bath-house water was hot and welcome. He eased himself into the communal stone tub and let the dirt and dried blood soak free of his weathered skin. The several godspeakers bathing at the same time nodded politely, they did not address him. They did not know each other, and idle chatter was strictly discouraged.

Alone with his thoughts, he considered what it meant, that he was back in the godhouse possessed of strange knowledge and those stranger crystals. Well, possessed of one. He had not brought the large crystal back to the godhouse with him, he had buried it in woodland beyond the Pinnacle's base, where it would remain hidden until the god desired its unearthing. The small crystal was wrapped safe in the pocket of his gifted clothes, he would carry that with him, it seemed to him safest.

I must show it to Hekat, the god will tell her for what purpose it must be used.

It had not told him. That was the only thing about the crystal the god had not shared in the wilderness.

His aching body eased a little, Vortka found a brush

and scrubbed himself to respectability. Clean and refreshed, he climbed from the bath and dressed like a godspeaker. The small crystal he slid discreetly into his robe pocket, the gifted clothes he bundled for burning, they could not be salvaged even by Oolikai.

I will make a sacrifice for the family who gave me them, I could have walked naked all the way here but I am glad I did not have to. Even though it means I must suffer in the tasking house.

He had no choice in that. Godspeakers did not possess money, they could not purchase a godhouse sacrifice. All he possessed in this life was his body, the only thing he could give the god in thanks for that family's kindness was his pain.

So I will give the god my pain, and pray it gives them good fortune in return.

They had fed him, too, those traveling villagers who took pity on him, the poor naked godspeaker stumbling out of the wilderness. He had lost his strikestone and could not start a fire. After highsuns of raw meat and bird eggs and gnawed sour roots, their dry bread and old cheese had seemed a feast fit for a warlord.

Warlord.

Raklion and Nagarak rode to Mijak's Heart at newsun. Only the gravest of matters could prompt such an action. Was it chance that had him tested at this time, sent into the wilderness to find the red crystals, just as Nagarak and Raklion were bent upon some great and secret task?

I do not think so. I think I am part of the god's plan, as they are, and Hekat. I think change is upon us, I feel its winds blow.

His heart was racing. It was a fearsome thing, to be so deeply enmeshed in the god's great workings.

As he left the bath-house and made his way to Peklia in the Sacrifice chamber he heard a hushed, familiar voice. *Zandakar*. He turned, and saw his son walking at Hekat's side, barely six paces away, towards one of the four great entrances into the godhouse.

"I wish I was riding with you and the warlord. I wish I did not have to stay behind." Zandakar sounded disconsolate, his beautiful face set in lines of sorrow.

"Tcha," said Hekat. In the busy godhouse's dim lighting her scars shone muted silver. "Mijak's Heart is no place for you. We ride there on warlord's business, you are not the warlord yet."

Halted, Vortka stared. *Hekat* was riding to Mijak's Heart with Raklion and Nagarak? As though the thought were a shout her gaze slid sideways. Their eyes met, hers narrowed, her lips tightened and then relaxed. Was she pleased to see him? He could not tell.

Hekat, I must speak with you. Hekat, we must meet.

She heard his thought, or read it in his face. One eyebrow lifted in agreement. Vortka nodded, the smallest gesture. Walking slowly now she flicked a careless finger towards him, then tapped it casually over her breast. He could read her easily too, even though they had spent so little time together. She meant, *come to me*. He nodded again, then turned away before one of the other godspeakers or novices noticed their exchange.

Zandakar had not noticed him. It was better that way.

Banishing all thought of his son he hurried to Peklia.

* * *

Et-Raklion's godhouse was a place of constant sacrifice. From newsun to lowsun, sacrifices were made at all the godhouse altars for as many reasons as there were people with needs to be seen to, questions that sought an answer, sins that required a swift forgiveness. A fee was paid, a devotion offered, a godspeaker killed a cockerel or a lamb for the godspark of the supplicant. It was the main business of Et-Raklion's godhouse, and the meat not consumed by the rites of supplication and divination fed the godspeakers and the novices.

Novice godspeakers prepared the chosen animals, they cleaned the altars, washed blood from the floors, fetched fresh robes for the sacrificing godspeakers and sharpened their knives, loaded the unconsumed carcasses into wooden barrows and wheeled them to the godhouse kitchens where more novices toiled alongside slaves in heat and fatty smoke. All the menial tasks, the novices did. Vortka had done them himself, for more godmoons than he cared to remember, as he studied in the godhouse.

Novices did not make the sacrifice themselves. That task was reserved for tested, godseen godspeakers.

The Sacrifice chamber was not the same as the altar alcoves that littered the godhouse, where city supplicants washed away their sins with purchased blood. In this place were the great sacrifices offered, for the warlord and his offspring, to bring victory in war, success in treaties, the approval of the god that life might continue safe and prosperous in the warlord's lands. It was a large stone room, it stank of blood, it echoed with death. Its walls were blank, there were no windows. Fat candles in iron holders were fastened to the walls, they shed thin light on the floor, and the blood. The animals for sacrifice were penned and tied and caged along one wall. Dominating the chamber's center, the altar of black stone was carved with snakes, lizards and scorpions, and banded by centipedes. The god's presence was strong, it silenced the sacrifices and the novices alike. The god's work was done here, in profound awareness of its might.

Peklia godspeaker ruled the chamber. Next to Nagarak she was the most senior, most revered godspeaker in the godhouse. She was also the largest, strongest woman Vortka had ever seen, she could sacrifice a bull-calf on her own. She glanced at Vortka once as he entered her domain but did not pause as she plunged her long knife into a black goatkid's throat, expertly slicing through the large vessels under its jaws. Blood flowed, a novice caught the hot gush in a bronze basin. As the sacrifice died Peklia held a snake-eye amulet over the goatkid's warm body, guiding its godspark to the god. Emptied, the goatkid's carcass shrank, it shriveled, it fell to dust.

All sacrifice here was consumed by the god.

Peklia wiped her blade on her red-soaked robe and turned. "You are Vortka, returned from the wilderness. Tested by the god and seen in its eye. I remember you from your novice time."

He bowed to her, still missing the musical swing of his burned godbraids. After so many highsuns his head still felt too light. "Peklia godspeaker, I am Vortka. I remember you, of course, I learned much here in your service."

She snorted. "In the god's service. I am its instrument, we are all of us its instruments. You are sent to me to learn the way of proper sacrifice?"

"Peklia, I am."

"You will learn quickly, Vortka, we sacrifice as fast as animals are brought in from the farms. Do you know why?"

"For Raklion warlord and Nagarak high godspeaker," he said, without thinking. "At newsun they travel to the Heart of Mijak."

Peklia godspeaker's thick eyebrows rose. "This is true. You know of their journey?"

He shook his head. "Peklia, I do not, beyond that they go."

To his disappointment she did not enlighten him. "So, Vortka godspeaker. You are pleased to learn my business? Not all godspeakers have the knack of sacrifice. They serve better in other ways."

He bowed again. "I am pleased if it pleases you."

"Pleasing the god is what matters, Vortka," she replied. "Come."

As two of the attending novices began the arduous task of cleaning the altar he followed Peklia through a narrow door into a smaller chamber, where fresh robes and sharpstones and cleaning tools and the blood basins were kept. She went to a cupboard at the rear of the chamber and withdrew from it a long wooden box. Jutting from its top were the hilts of thirty knives, each one fashioned with a different grip and patterning. She put the box on the bench in the middle of the chamber and stood back.

"One of those knives is the sacrificial blade the god desires you to take as your own," she said. "Open your heart, Vortka, let the god guide your choice."

Vortka stepped close and held out his hand, fingers spread, above the jutting knife-hilts. Not one of them called to him. Instead he was tugged to the chamber's cupboard, to a shelf within it, to a leather-bound case wrapped in a square of red wool. He withdrew it, and looked at Peklia.

Her face was set in a puzzled frown. "This is unusual," she said, her eyebrows pulled low. "This knife is one of two that were offered to Nagarak after the god chose him as the next high godspeaker. He did not take it, the knife did not call to him."

Vortka dropped the case onto the bench. "Forgive me, Peklia, I did not know. I will choose again, I—"

"No," said Peklia, and held up her hand. "The god is here, you found the knife it wants you to have." She picked up the case, unwrapped its red wool covering, unlaced its fastening and raised its lid.

Shivering with uncertainty, Vortka stepped close so he might look inside. "This knife is beautiful," he whispered. "Too beautiful for me."

"Tcha!" said Peklia, and thrust the case at him. "The god does not think so, do you tell the god no?"

Not if he wished to stay in its eye. He took the knife. As his fingers closed round its hilt, bone carved into a scorpion and black with age, its blue-sheened blade the shape of a snake's flickering tongue, a jolt of power shuddered through him, reminiscent of the power he'd felt in the strange red crystal.

Peklia must have caught its echo. She dropped the case, gasping. "This is strange, the god stirs in that knife!"

Vortka looked at her. "Peklia, what do you know of it, what can you tell me?"

"It is old," she murmured. "As old as Mijak. It was forged in the dead past, it belonged to the first high godspeaker chosen in the land."

"And you keep it in a *cupboard*?"

"Things are things, Vortka, we dress in plain robes, we keep knives in boxes, those boxes in cupboards. This knife is offered to high godspeakers, and then put away."

He felt his heart beat against his ribs. "Offered *only* to high godspeakers?"

"So I was told."

And yet the god had guided *him* to it. The hilt fit his hand like skin, like the flesh that clasped his bones. He loved this knife. It belonged to him.

If Nagarak discovers this knife has chosen me I will be in danger. No-one can tell him . . . he must never know it is mine. No-one can know. Not even Hekat.

"Who was the last person to use it?" he asked, as the knife's power caressed his bones.

"I do not recall," said Peklia, shaking her head. "A godspeaker long dead, that much I can tell you. Vortka godspeaker, I will open my heart. This choosing disturbs me. I think it an omen. A portent. But of what, I cannot say."

"Peklia, are you sworn to tell of this choosing? Must others know what has happened here?"

She stared, surprised. "Other godspeakers? No. But—"

"Then please, I beg you. Let it be our secret. When the god is ready it will reveal its purpose in giving me this knife. Until that time I do not wish this choosing to be known. I am newly tested, I was not born in Et-Raklion. I have no desire for others to hear of this and treat me differently."

"I understand that," said Peklia, nodding. "But you must understand, Vortka, I cannot keep secrets from Nagarak high godspeaker."

Nagarak. Nagarak. "Yes, he must be told," said Vortka,

slowly. "But will you let me tell him, Peklia, when he returns with the warlord from the Heart of Mijak?"

Her broad, plain face settled into stubborn lines. "That is not proper. I am godspeaker of the Sacrifice chamber, responsible for the sacrificial knives. It is my duty to record which knife is claimed by which godspeaker."

Vortka took a deep breath and let it out, subduing frustration. "Peklia, I feel I am guided by the god. I *must* be the one to tell Nagarak high godspeaker of this strange choosing."

It was no small thing, to invoke the god like that. No godspeaker did so lightly, if the claim was false the god would smite without mercy. Peklia's eyes widened, her lips pressed tight. "You say so?" she said, after a long moment. "You are certain?"

"I am. I hear the god's voice in my heart." And that was no lie. The god was a burning coal, waking and sleeping he felt it, he heard it. "Please. Let me tell him."

Peklia sighed. "Very well, godspeaker. You have my silence."

He touched his fingertips to her arm. "Thank you. And if I might ask for one more thing?"

"*Tcha!* You are bold for one so newly tested!"

"Forgive me," said Vortka, truly contrite. "Before lowsun I swear I will kneel in the tasking house, that I might be chastised for my sin."

"And in the meantime?" she said. Her lips twitched a little, she was not a sour woman. "What is this other thing you desire?"

He looked at the ancient knife in his hand. "This blade will draw attention whenever I wield it. Until I have spoken to Nagarak, until he gives me leave to use it, I think

I am better served with something plainer. Can I choose another, to learn the art of sacrifice with you?"

She shoved the knife-box across the table. "It would be wiser. Choose quickly, Vortka. You take much of my time."

"Thank you, Peklia. The god see you for your understanding."

She snorted. "And may it see you for your speed, godspeaker!"

He chose a knife at random from the box. The god did not care which one he took, he felt no surge of power as his fingers closed about its hilt, it was a plain tool that would help him serve the god.

Peklia gave him the sheath that fitted that blade. As she returned the knife-box to the cupboard he attached his working knife to his belt, then wrapped his true knife in the square of red wool and slid it into his robe pocket to keep company with the small red crystal.

"Come," she said, and glanced at him. Shadows lurked within her eyes, he could see she was not comfortable with her decision. "The novices will be finished their preparations by now, sacrifice must continue."

"Yes, godspeaker," he said, and followed her out of the knife-room, the ancient snakeblade heavy in his pocket.

In the main chamber the novices stood ready against the wall. The altar was clean, the sacrificial blood taken away. Peklia chose the next sacrifice, a white lamb. "A single stroke must kill it," she told him. "An unclean death displeases the god."

Vortka nodded, his time as a novice here had shown him that much. He stood at the altar and sacrificed the white lamb, his plain knife took its life with one sure stroke. Peklia gave him the snake-eye amulet and he passed it over the dead lamb's body, the god ate its essence. It was pleased in his heart.

"A proper first sacrifice," said Peklia, not smiling. "You are adept already. Continue, Vortka. I will watch with the god."

More lambs he sacrificed, and golden cockerels and twelve black goatkids. There was no end to the god's great appetite, the more he fed it the hungrier it grew. The candles burned down to their holders, the sacrifice pens were stripped bare and refilled. Peklia stood in a corner and watched him, unspeaking. The blade in his pocket weighed heavy, then heavier, it began to pull him down. He resisted, his spine straight, he would not fail the god, not in this place. Not before the chamber's strict guardian.

"Enough," said Peklia, as he gave the last goatkid's godspark to the god. "You have served the god well today, Vortka."

"Yes, Peklia godspeaker," he answered, and put his knife down on the bloodied altar, beside the snake-eye amulet. Relief was a hammer, pounding his head. he was hungry, he was thirsty, all he could see with his eyes was blood.

Peklia said, "When you have paid for your sins in the tasking house, Vortka, Brikin will assign you a god-speaker sleeping cell of your own."

Aieee, the tasking house! He had forgotten. He was sworn to go there, he could not break his word.

"The god see you, Peklia," he said to her, bowing. "The god see you, novices."

"The god see you, Vortka. Return here at newsun," said Peklia, briskly. "There is still much I have to teach you."

He cleaned his working blade and safely sheathed it, washed himself in a bucket supplied by one novice, dried himself with a towel supplied by another. Then he walked to the tasking house. He walked slowly, but in the end he reached it, as he must. He told the taskmaster chosen for his tasking of his debt to that village family, and his impudence to Peklia. The taskmaster listened, frowned, pointed. So Vortka removed his robe and folded it carefully, then knelt on the floor to receive the god's judgement.

The god treated him kindly, he was tasked with just twenty strokes of the strap. He had in the past been tasked far more severely, this time the strap did not draw his blood. Smarting, humbled, he thanked the taskmaster, wincingly pulled on his robe, and made his way to the shrine garden for a moment of solitude.

It was late, no light in the sky, the godmoon and his wife strode among the stars. Somewhere behind him, in the godhouse, Nagarak swam in the godpool and communed with the god. Or perhaps that was done now, and he made private sacrifice for the great journey to Mijak's Heart.

Hekat will tell me why they ride to that sacred place. If she rides with Nagarak, surely she will know why. I will have to meet her before newsun, I cannot let her ride away without first telling her of the wilderness and the crystal. It might have meaning at Mijak's Heart.

His pocket weighed heavy with that other, mysterious sacrifice knife. He should not take that with him when he went to meet with Hekat at the palace. He should find out where he was meant to sleep while he remained in the godhouse, and leave it there, safe.

Leaving the garden, he returned to the godhouse and made his way to the kitchens. After so much sacrifice his belly was empty again. Sitting by himself with a bowl of soup and a round of flat bread he let the soft conversations of the other godspeakers wash over him, he thought of Hekat in the godhouse. She looked well, she looked lethal, life with the warlord had honed her to a sharpness. Truly she was born to be the god's warrior.

It would be a relief to share his experience in the wilderness with her, and learn at last what the god meant by it.

He had only eaten half his bowl of soup and three mouthfuls of bread when Brikin came to the kitchen. "Vortka!"

He shoved his bowl aside and bowed almost to the bench-top. "Novice-master."

Brikin rapped his knuckles on the wood. "I have seen Peklia, she speaks well of you. Nagarak will be pleased to hear it when he returns from Mijak's Heart."

Would he? *I think he would be pleased if he never heard my name again.* He could not say so to Brikin. "Yes, novice-master."

"Are you finished eating? You must come with me. My last task as your novice-master is to assign you a sleep-cell. I have done it, I will show you, I must be about my novicing business."

Brikin waited while he disposed of his half-emptied bowl, his bread and his spoon, then led him up staircases and along corridors to the godhouse sleep-cell wing.

"A pallet, a candle, a pishpot and a blanket," said Brikin, opening one cell's door and standing aside. The room was grey, stone-built and small, three paces by three, a thin slit in the stonework its excuse for a window. "For as long as you remain in the godhouse this is your place."

Vortka nodded. "Do you know how long that will be, novice-master?"

"No," said Brikin. "Nagarak will decide your fate after his return. While he is away you will serve in the library. Go there after newsun sacrifice."

"Yes, novice-master." He hesitated. "Must I stay in my cell now, or am I permitted some time for contemplation in the shrine garden?"

Brikin looked at him, something approaching affection in his eyes. "You were always a dutiful novice, I know you love the god. If you feel the need to pray in the shrine garden, I say you may do it. If you are questioned there, tell that godspeaker to see me."

Vortka lowered his face, he felt a twinge of discomfort, telling lies to Brikin. *But I lie for the god, so there is no sin.* "Yes, novice-master."

Brikin departed. Vortka took the sacrifice knife from his pocket and slid it for safety under his pallet. It would be safe there, till the god told him the best place to keep it.

Then he left the godhouse, unseen, and made his way down the Pinnacle Road to the palace, and Hekat.

CHAPTER TWENTY-EIGHT

Hekat sat beside her sleeping son's bed and watched the dreams swirl behind his closed eyes. She was alone in the palace, as Raklion spent this night in the barracks with Hanochek. The warleader was not happy he did not ride to Mijak's Heart. On the surface Hanochek pretended to accept the god's will but she knew better. She saw with the god's eyes, she knew he was jealous and filled with spite. Raklion tried to ease Hano's hurt. She thought he was stupid, but did not say so.

Who are you, Hanochek? You are no-one, nothing. If you are not dead by the time Zandakar is warlord you will not be his warleader. When Zandakar is warlord if you are not dead you will be banished to the savage north. He will have no need of you. I will be with him, I am all that he needs.

Beneath his light covers Zandakar stirred and sighed. She smoothed his godbraids, she stroked his cheek. "*Yuma,*" he murmured, and was lulled to rest.

Aieee, how she loved him. How her heart beat for him, how he melted her bones with a single look. She wished she could take him with her at newsun but she did not dare show him to the warlords when he was still a child. The warlords were wicked, they listened to demons. A demon might strike Zandakar, he was too precious to risk.

The god would abandon her were she careless with its greatest gift.

Time passed, she sat with her son. When at last she felt her scorpion amulet stir, when she felt a throb of heat against her skin, she left his bedside and sent in his nurse-slave to watch over him. Then, hidden in the god's eye, she slipped from the palace onto the Pinnacle Road, and waited there for Vortka to arrive.

"Come," she whispered when he reached her, and led him in the god's protection past the slaves at the palace gates to her private garden where they could speak undisturbed and she was nearby to Zandakar.

Vortka's face was still beautiful, his godbraids were gone. His skull was covered in black fuzz, his eyes were enormous. How young he looked, and so vulnerable. "You are certain we're safe here?" he said, glancing at the shadowed palace.

"Tcha! Vortka, you are stupid. We are hidden in the god's eye, surrounded by godspeakers we would be alone."

He shook his head, faintly smiling. "I have missed you, Hekat, and your sharp tongue."

It did no good to say she had missed him. He was a godspeaker, she was a warrior. Their lives were their lives, they walked different paths. They were almost strangers now, so much time had passed since their last secret meeting. "So you are tested, Vortka. The god sees you in its eye. I knew it would, I knew it would reward you for your service. That is your purpose, to be a godspeaker. Why do you seek me out now?"

"Why do you ride to the Heart of Mijak?"

She frowned. "Does that concern you? I think it does not."

Her words hurt him, she saw the sharp pain in his eyes. He said, "And I think it does. Hekat, in the wilderness the god did more than see me. It spoke to me. It gave me visions. It led me to a secret place, it gave me something I do not fully understand. I think you are meant to know of it, also. I think you are wrong to think our journey together is finished. Tell me, Hekat. Why do you ride to the Heart of Mijak?"

It did not matter if she told him. All of Mijak would know why, soon enough. "So Raklion might throw down the godforsaken warlords. His time is come. Mijak must be united in the shadow of his snakeblade."

"Ah," said Vortka. Hesitantly he reached into his robe pocket and withdrew something she could not see, it was hidden in his hand. "I burned my godbraids in the wilderness, it is part of the test," he said slowly. "The smoke consumed me, I wandered witless till I fell into a cave. In the cave I found this." He opened his fingers, and showed her a lump of something wrapped in cloth. "Watch."

He shook the cloth free to reveal a piece of dull red crystal. Closing his eyes, he tightened his fingers, he gasped and shivered. The crystal glowed, it burned bright white, it did not hurt him, though she could feel its great heat. She felt her scorpion amulet tremble, it shivered with reflected power.

"*Aieee*!" she whispered. "What else does it do?"

Vortka opened his eyes and loosened his fingers. The crystal faded back to dull red. "I dare not show you. Not here. Not now. But I will tell you what I did in the wilderness with this crystal. I destroyed solid rock. I melted stone. With this crystal I shattered the cave, it is ruined forever. As I returned to Et-Raklion I blasted trees into splinters. I killed a stray cow, its blood boiled in its veins. Hekat, this red stone is a mighty weapon."

"How did you know what to do?" she demanded. "The crystal is a mystery, Vortka, I have read every tablet in the godhouse library, there is no mention of such a thing."

"The god told me, Hekat," he said simply. "I lay down on a rocky plain, it sent scorpions to sting me, when I was myself again I knew how to use the god's gift."

She frowned at the small stone in his hand. "Is that piece all you found?"

"No. I found one other, larger and heavier."

"How much power was in it?"

He shook his head. "I did not dare touch it. The god sent me a wild goat to eat, I killed it and skinned it with a shard of rock. I wrapped the large crystal in its hide and carried it with me out of the wilderness. It is buried safely beyond the city."

Her scorpion amulet continued to burn. "It cannot stay there. The world is full of demons, Vortka, they seek every way to thwart the god. You must bring that large crystal to me. We must bury it in my private garden, it will not be found here."

"Bring it to you?" He looked at her, uncertain. "Hekat, I think it is meant as a weapon for the warlord to wield."

Aieee, there was a singing in her heart. "No, Vortka. Not the warlord. This weapon is meant for me. *I* am the god's warrior, *I* am its knife-dancer in the world. If the god intended this crystal weapon for Raklion it would have guided Nagarak to find it. It did not, it guided you. You are godchosen for me, Vortka. Have we not seen this? Do we not know?"

Still the stupid man looked uncertain. "The god did not say—"

"Tcha!" she spat. "Does the god tell you everything? I think it does not." She held out her hand. "Give me the crystal."

Vortka hesitated. "Hekat . . ."

"Give me it, Vortka! You know who I am, you have seen me in the god's eye! I am meant for this weapon, *give it to me*!"

Unhappily he gave her the crystal. She held the red stone before her eyes, waited for the flaring light, the god's power rising. Nothing happened. It was rock in her fingers, it contained no power. She felt nothing in it, or herself. Even her scorpion amulet was silent. She glared at him.

"What is this? Is there a summoning word to be spoken? I warn you, Vortka, do not thwart the god. Tell me how you wake the crystal."

Vortka spread his hands wide, helpless. "Hekat, there is no summoning word. I hold the crystal and it comes to life."

"Then why does it not come to life for *me*?" She reached for her snakeblade, pricked him with it in a heartbeat. "Are you my enemy now, Vortka godspeaker? Have you tasted power and hunger for more? I will gut you, I will spread your entrails on the grass, the god will spit your godspark into hell."

He looked at her, not at the knife-point in his belly. His eyes were sad, his expression untroubled. "Hekat. Believe me. We are not enemies, I cannot tell you why the crystal sleeps. It is not my fault if it wakes for me and not you. Perhaps you are wrong. Perhaps the god does not intend it for you."

She stared, struck silent. Was it possible? Was the crystal *not* meant for her? It was a bitter thought. *I am the god's knife-dancer, I throw down its enemies! I dance with my snakeblade for the god!* What was her purpose then, if not to wield the god's mightiest weapon?

Vortka was frowning. How wrong his face looked, unframed by godbraids. "Hekat. I sired Zandakar, he sprang from my seed. If I can wake the crystal . . ."

Tcha. Was *that* it? "Come," she said, and turned on her heel.

Vortka followed her unquestioning into the palace, along the silent corridors, past waking slaves who did not see them, to her son's chamber where he slept, lost in dreams.

Zandakar's nurse-slave slumped by his bed. Hekat saw her snoring and could have beaten her. The bitch would be beaten at newsun, before the journey to Mijak's Heart. Bending over her son in his bed she pulled back his blanket and nestled the crystal in his hand.

Bright white light bloomed in the candlelit chamber. Zandakar stirred, but did not wake. Nor did the nurse-slave, that was lucky for her.

"Hekat!" said Vortka, his voice a hushed exhalation. "The god sees him. Zandakar stirs the crystal to life."

"Yes," she said. Her eyes drifted closed, the god's voice rose like thunder within her. "This was the god's plan. I was stupid before, I know the truth now. You cannot be warlord, you can wake the crystal. Your seed sired Zandakar, there is the link. With this weapon he will be more than a warlord. He will be the god's hammer. He will smite its enemies, and they will all be destroyed. I am to guide him into manhood. Train him as a warrior. Advise him how to rule. That is my purpose, he is my son. Yours is to teach him the secrets of the crystal."

"Aieee," whispered Vortka. "The god is in your voice, Hekat. Can you hear it? Can you feel it? Zandakar, our beautiful son, the hammer of the god!"

My son, Vortka. Zandakar is mine. "Of course I can feel it," she said, and opened her eyes. "Am I not Hekat, godtouched and precious?"

He sighed. "Yes. You are Hekat." He sounded resigned.

She watched him take the crystal from Zandakar before the light woke him, and wrap it in its protective cloth. As she watched him her heart pounded, once.

Yes. I am Hekat. And you are Vortka. You can wake the crystal's fury. You are godtouched, you are also a man. Men are not perfect, they fall prey to demons. Your seed could sire another son. Another son could rival Zandakar . . .

At the thought, her amulet shivered.

Vortka, serious, touched her son's soft cheek. "When the god desires it, Hekat, I will teach him what it taught me in the wilderness. I hope it is some time from now. The crystal's power is brutal and he is still so young to wake such fury."

"He will not wake it till he is a man," she said. "He has much to learn of warfare before I can trust him with the crystal. He must master the knife-dance and the slingshot, learn to throw a long spear, drive a chariot, send an arrow straight into an enemy's heart. When he knows what it is to be a warlord, *then* will he become the god's hammer."

Vortka frowned at her. "Do not forget he must first be a child."

"A child?" She snorted. "You are stupid, Vortka. Sons of potsmiths are children, they play mud games, they laugh with stupid friends. This is Zandakar, son of Hekat knife-dancer. He plays with snakeblades, he swims in blood." She held out her hand. "Give me the crystal. I will keep it safe."

"Zandakar's power must be left alone for now," he said, dropping the cloth-wrapped stone into her palm. "Do not be tempted to let him play with it. Do not reveal its existence, not even to Raklion. Until I found it this crystal was the god's secret. It must *stay* a secret. *No-one* must know."

Stupid Vortka, did he think *she* was stupid, to risk Zandakar's future by being reckless? She would never risk his precious future. She would do anything to keep him safe.

She slipped the crystal into her pocket, then closed her fingers about her scorpion amulet, feeling its heat and its promise of power. Feeling again the god within her, as she had felt it in Abajai's villa.

I have no choice. The god desires this. Zandakar is its hammer, he must be protected.

Vortka was staring. "Hekat? Is something wrong?"

She released the amulet. "No. I am humbled by the god's great purpose, Vortka, that is all. I will see you in the god's eye out of the palace, onto the Pinnacle Road. We leave for Mijak's Heart after newsun sacrifice, I must seek my bed."

He nodded. "Of course."

She led him from the palace, tugging the scorpion

amulet from her neck as she walked. Safely beyond the palace gates she stopped and faced him. "So now we part."

He smiled at her. "For a short while. I wish you a safe journey to the Heart of Mijak, though perhaps I do not need to. The god will see you, it sees you always."

Yes, it does. Vortka, forgive me. You do not need another son in this world. Zandakar is enough son for any man.

She pressed the scorpion amulet to his cheek.

Vortka gasped, wide eyes staring, and slowly sank to his knees. His arms fell helplessly by his side, his fingers were lax, he could not stop her. The scorpion rippled, it shivered to life. Its clawed feet clutched him, its tail stung him once, twice, and two more times. It shivered again, and returned to stone.

She took back the amulet and watched Vortka closely. He swayed in the road, his chest laboring with each harsh breath. Sweat stippled his forehead, his cheeks, his throat. In the godmoon's pale light it shone like silver. Sweat burst from his body like an underground river, soaking his new godspeaker robe.

The marks of the scorpion were bright on his skin, as she watched they faded away. A moment later his breathing returned to normal, the sweat dried on his face and the rest of his body. He pushed to his feet, he turned away from her and began to walk up the road, towards the godhouse. She did not fear his discovery, the god walked with him in his bones.

She watched him until he was swallowed by the night, then returned to the palace and her bed, empty of Raklion.

It is done, now. It is the god's will. Let the god's sun

*rise and set, let the seasons come and let them go. Zan-
dakar is safe. Let him grow to glory, the god's smiting
hammer, Mijak's warlord for the god.*

After solemn newsun sacrifice on the warhost field, with
the warhost as witness, Hekat prepared to ride with Raklion, Nagarak and the ten chosen warriors out of Et-
Raklion to Mijak's sacred heart. Zandakar stood beside
Hanochek, who was tasked by Raklion with her son's
safekeeping. She could see from his face Zandakar
wanted to weep, she warned him with her eyes that he
would sin if he did.

He obeyed her warning, he did not weep.

Raklion embraced Hanochek first, he held him hard
and close. "The god see you, warleader. Keep my warhost
in the palm of your hand until I return, the warlord of
Mijak."

"Warlord, I will," said Hanochek thickly. "I will keep
your son, also. His heart beats within me. His life is safe
in my hands."

Next Raklion dropped to his knees and rested his
hands on Zandakar's shoulders. "You will heed the warleader. He speaks with my voice. You will be my proud
son, we will rejoice upon my return."

Zandakar nodded. "Yes, warlord."

As Raklion stood, Hekat smiled at her son who would
be warlord of Mijak. "You know what you must do while
I am gone, Zandakar. Tell me."

He straightened his spine. "Yuma, I must study my
reading and writing three fingers every day. I must dance
with my snakeblade four fingers every day. I must obey
Hanochek warleader when he gives me other training

tasks. I must kneel before the altar in Et-Raklion's god-house every newsun, so Peklia godspeaker might sacrifice for the god and the warlord in the Heart of Mijak."

Nagarak said, "Your duty to the god should have been spoken of first."

"He is to be warlord, not a godspeaker," Hekat replied, as Zandakar blinked, trying so hard not to show his fright. She had no fear of Nagarak, he was only a man, *he* did not dance in the god's eye.

Nagarak's lips pinched tight, aieee, how much he hated her, he had no power over her. It made her smile, that he had no power. Raklion said, "My son knows his duty to the god, I am sure. It is time to leave Et-Raklion, high godspeaker."

Nagarak nodded curtly and turned away. Raklion bent low and embraced Zandakar. Hekat looked at Hanochek. "Keep him safe, warleader." Her voice was a threat, she made sure he heard it.

Raklion heard it, he released Zandakar. "He will be safe in my knife-brother's eye. Come, Hekat. The god's purpose awaits."

They mounted their horses, they rode with the chosen warriors from the warhost field. The gathered warhost cheered them loudly, Zandakar cheered but there were tears in his eyes. Hekat frowned.

Silly boy. What have you to weep for? When Raklion is Mijak's warlord, how much closer are you to your glory?

She rode away from her solemn-faced son, she looked to their future, she did not look back.

Mijak's Heart was neutral ground, owned not by one single warlord but by all. It was a place where the seven warlords might thrash out their differences without bloodshed. It was rarely visited, warlords liked their skirmishing ways. What use were warriors who never drew blood? They were like trained sandcats, easily distracted into mischief and strife if not regularly sated with a hunt, a kill.

Hekat rode a red mare, gifted by Raklion, who rode a blue-striped stallion by her side. At his left hand Nagarak rode a black stallion, grimly determined on the god's business. Behind them rode the ten chosen warriors, proud men and women with death in their hands. They rode swiftly through the lands of Et-Raklion, highsun after highsun, living off their fat green bounty, easily finding abundant water and well-fed game. Before this day's lowsun they would cross the border into Et-Tebek, and twelve highsuns after that into Et-Banotaj. Then their living would grow much harsher, the other lands of Mijak struggled mightily in the god's displeasure.

After fingers of silence, Raklion glanced at Nagarak and said, "You sent word to the warlords and their high godspeakers. Are you certain they all will come?"

Nagarak wore tanned leather leggings and his scorpion pectoral. His chiming godbraids, choked with amulets, dangled down his back and covered his shoulders. At Raklion's question his face closed tight. "No summoned warlord can refuse the call to Mijak's Heart without earning the god's unstinting wrath. I have read the omens, warlord, they will come. If you doubt me we stand in shadow."

"I do not doubt you, Nagarak. I doubt my sinning warlord brothers."

Nagarak's deep eyes blinked, like a snake before its striking. "No. You doubt the god."

"He does not," said Hekat, before Raklion could answer. "You should not say so."

Nagarak said nothing, since leaving Et-Raklion he had not spoken to her once. She shed no tears for his stubborn silence.

I am Hekat, godtouched and precious. What do I care if he speaks to me or not?

His expression uneasy, Raklion said, "Hekat—"

Ignoring Raklion, she stared at Nagarak. "Raklion knows the warlords are flesh and blood, he questions their obedience. High godspeakers are not perfect, they stray, they dissemble. They guide their warlords into waterless deserts. Why else has the god decided Raklion must rule them? *They* have offended the god, not him. Raklion warlord is seen in its eye."

She and Raklion rode so close together he could reach out and touch her knee. He touched her now, half-frowning, half-smiling, he was pleased that she had come. The first night of the journey, as they lay under the star-filled sky, he had told her. Then he had fucked her, he still hoped for a second son.

He said now, making peace, "I do not doubt the god, Nagarak, I do not doubt you. I am a foolish warlord, chattering like a child."

Nagarak snorted. "Then bite off your tongue. The god does not care for chattering and neither do I."

Hekat hid her own smile. *Raklion is pleased I ride with him, but Nagarak is sour grapes on the vine. Tcha. His feelings are hurt, I do not care.*

Silence returned. They rode until the light began to

dwindle, then made camp by one of Et-Tebek's mean, trickling streams. They had brought no godhouse doves or lambs for sacrifice, Nagarak shed his own blood for the god without flinching, and afterwards healed the deep cut with his godstone.

After sacrifice, six warriors departed to hunt what meat could be found for their dinner. Nagarak lost himself in prayer. Hekat took her other, dirtied tunic to the stream to clean. No slave rode with them, it was a task she must perform herself. She did not mind, it was something to do.

Raklion joined her at the stream's muddy edge and watched her work. Behind them the other four warriors played chance with their godbones, laughing at each poor toss and guess. Feeling Raklion's eyes on her, Hekat looked up. The sinking sunlight gilded his dark face, his eyes were shadowed, he did not smile. "You are so beautiful." He sounded sad. "I wish you would let me dress you in riches, you deserve every bright color and all Mijak's gold."

She pulled a face. "Tcha. I am a warrior, I need nothing but my training tunic and leggings when we ride. Raklion, you are troubled. Was Nagarak right? Do you doubt the god?"

He looked away. "No."

"Then what is it?" she demanded, straightening. "You cannot lie, you know I see you."

He tried to smile, as though afraid of frightening her. "Yes. You see me. And I see you, I see more than that. I am uneasy, Hekat. There is a worm within my gut, it feasts on fears, it is growing fat."

Her tunic was clean. She spread it to dry on the tangled

brown grass, then dried her fingers on her leggings. "Speak plainly, warlord. You are fearful of meeting with the others? Why?"

He did not wear a training tunic, his tall, broad frame was covered in light wool and leather, the snake of Et-Raklion coiled on his chest. His snakeblade sat quietly in its jeweled sheath. He was splendid, if she was not a woman consumed by the god, a woman who had no time for men, she might lose her breath at the sight of him.

He said, lightly frowning, "Since leaving Et-Raklion I have had dreams."

"All men dream, warlord," she told him. "If those dreams came true we would live in a strange world."

He reached for her, and pulled her close. "I dream of crows' wings blotting out the sun. I sink into shadows, I see, I hear, I cannot move."

His heart beat strongly beneath her cheek. "Have you told Nagarak of these dreams?"

He shook his head. "In Nagarak's mind this journey is the outward expression of an inner truth. The god has told him I am Mijak's warlord, and so I am. Sometimes I think he does not understand. We ride to turn the warlords' world upside down, to throw them in the dust, to press their necks beneath my heel. These are proud men, will they kneel meekly like lambs, will they accept the slaughter of their ambitions without protest? The god has said it must be, so Nagarak thinks they will. I think he might be wrong."

"He is not wrong," she said. "They will submit to the god or they will die. This is the god's desiring. Nagarak is right. They must accept you as their warlord or be cast into hell and devoured by demons."

Raklion tipped her face to look into his. "You are as bad as Nagarak. Can you not see how this might end in bloodshed?"

"Tcha! What I see is a warlord uncertain of his worthiness," said Hekat, impatient. "You fear for no reason, Raklion, you have been tested and tested, you spent three highsuns on the scorpion wheel, you did not break, you bared your body for smiting and your godspark to the god. It ate your cries, it drank your tears. Whatever imperfections led you to that humbling, they are burned away now. You insult the god if you insist you are not worthy."

He kissed her. "No. I question my good fortune."

"Then question it no further!" she snapped, and yanked hard on his silvered godbraids. "The warlords *will* submit."

He would have said something else then, found more words for the feeding of his doubts, but the hunting party returned and it was time to eat, and sleep.

After the newsun sacrifice their journey continued through brown Et-Tebek. Game grew scarce, they ate more dried corn from their saddle-bags than fresh-caught meat. They rode beneath the hot sun along the border between Et-Tebek and Et-Banotaj, crossing over it not far from the place where it met with the border of Et-Mamiklia. In those highsuns of riding they saw no enemy warriors, they did not meet with the other warlords.

Forty-six highsuns after leaving Et-Raklion they reached the sacred Heart of Mijak, where the godforsaken warlords of Mijak were waiting.

CHAPTER TWENTY-NINE

Mijak's Heart was an enormous crater in the middle of a barren red plain where the borders of Et-Mamiklia, Et-Takona and Et-Banotaj converged. The crater's rim was bound by seven black stone godposts evenly spaced, each çarved in the shape of a scorpion and topped with a warlord's traditional sigil; though a warlord's territory changed name to echo his own, the land's symbol remained unchanging. A steep pathway descended from the base of each godpost to the floor of the crater. Waves of heat rose from the bare red rock, shiny like glass from its creation: it was a cauldron, an anvil, where potential futures were mixed and measured and beaten into history. Raklion led his ten warriors to the godpost marked with a striking snake and halted.

"How did you ensure we would be last to arrive?" Hekat murmured.

"The god told Nagarak how we should travel at last lowsun's divining," Raklion replied, just as softly. "He told me at newsun which path we should ride."

She had not been told this, she felt her teeth clench. Nagarak was attempting to exclude her, that was something she could not allow.

One by one she stared at the other godposts, at the warlords and warriors gathered in their proper places.

They could not go down into Mijak's Heart until the summoning warlord had bared his godspark to the god in their witnessing presence. If the god did not smite him for a wicked summoning, then could their meeting proceed.

The silence in this place was oppressive, immense. There was the sky, there was the sun, there was the crater where the god's hammered fist had punched into the earth. The warlords and their warriors sat their horses and did not speak, even their godbells were muted, muffled.

Raklion swung down from his stallion. Nagarak followed and untied the robe strapped to his horse. Hekat slid from her saddle. Her joints jarred sharply as she struck the bare ground, the heat striking fiercely through her sandaled feet.

When they looked at her, surprised, she lifted her chin. "I come with you into Mijak's Heart. I am Zandakar's mother, the warlords must know me."

"No. You stay behind with the other warriors," said Nagarak, pulling on his high godspeaker robe. "When the god's will is made known they will be told who you are. Know your place, woman. You are not the warlord."

She had never shown him her scorpion amulet. She showed him now, and smiled to see the arrogance drain from his face. He could feel its power without even touching it, he saw her for the first time, chosen by the god.

"I am Hekat, who swam with scorpions. I am the mother of Mijak's future. I am here by the god's desiring, born to its purpose as is my son. You are high godspeaker, Nagarak, you have your place here. Do not think to unseat me from mine."

Nagarak's robe was plain, and dirty. Dust stained it,

and horse-sweat, and traces of blood, he looked like some poor village godspeaker forgotten by the god. He stared at her with eyes full of angry questions and pointed at her scorpion amulet.

"That is carved from sacred stone, it is not for a common warrior to possess!"

"Try and take it from me," she invited. "Touch it and see your hand shrivel to dust. The god gave me this amulet, Nagarak. You may not have it."

Nagarak glared at Raklion. "You knew she had this?"

Raklion nodded. "I did."

"Tcha!" spat Nagarak. "You sinful man! Why did you not tell me this was in her possession? She is not bound to the god, she is untested, she cannot—"

"She survived your scorpions and bore me a son, that is test enough," said Raklion, removing his sheathed snakeblade from his belt and tucking it for safekeeping beneath his saddle's sheepskin cover. "Why do we bicker about an amulet when the warlords have gathered to hear the god's desire? Let us go down into the Heart of Mijak, the god has waited long enough."

Hekat saw in Nagarak's eyes how he wanted to argue, his arrogance was returned as strong as ever. He was a man grown complacent in the god's eye. *Tcha*. She had no time for him.

With a glance at Raklion she started down the stone path leading to the floor of the crater. Raklion followed her, and then came Nagarak. He was not happy, she could feel his rage. On the crater's rim above them Et-Raklion's warriors drummed their knife-hilts on their pommels, to show their loyalty and their love. Raklion smiled up at them, he punched his fist in the air, pressed it hard against his heart. A warlord's salute.

Safely at last on the crater's bare floor, its scorching air searing, sucking them dry, Nagarak drew Hekat sharply aside. Raklion walked to the crater's center, raised his arms to shoulder height, dropped to his knees and tipped his face to the sun.

"I am here, god, Raklion of Et-Raklion! I call warlord council at Mijak's Heart! Before my brother warlords I kneel before you, my godspark bared to your seeing eye! Smite me to ashes if my cause is not just!"

His words thrummed and bounced and shivered round the crater, doubled and redoubled into thundering echoes.

The god did not smite him, Hekat knew it would not. Nagarak cried out to the watching warlords. *"Aieee! You are witness! Raklion of Et-Raklion is in the god's seeing eye, it does not smite him, his cause is just!"*

As Raklion stood, the other warlords and their high godspeakers began their own descents to the crater's hot floor. Hekat stood with Raklion and Nagarak, watching them come. She had never seen Mijak's other warlords face to face, their sigils told her who they were.

Mamiklia, heavyset but still in his prime, his skin was lighter than the others', his eyes pale blue and narrow with suspicion. For the moment treatied with Takona and Zyden, they would be fools to turn their backs on him.

Takona, a younger man and virile, he walked lightly on the ground. As he descended he glared at his brother warlords, his fingers curled as though he held a knife.

Zyden, even older than Raklion. He had a son to follow him but showed no sign of dying. Nor, so Raklion said, did his son seem eager to put him on a pyre. That was a rare thing among the warlords.

Jokriel, the warlord who might have ruled her village in the savage north if his long-dead forebear had not abandoned it. He was near to Raklion's age, worn thin and dry by his profitless lands.

Tebek, sullen in his recent defeats by Raklion, stung and eager to prove himself. A stupid boy, he should have followed his father's wisdom and kept the treaty with Et-Raklion.

Banotaj, most dangerous of all. Poisoned by his father Bajadek into belligerence and blood. Greedy, vicious, treacherous as a demon.

Hekat smiled at the warlords walking down to the crater's red floor. *They could die soon, I would not weep.* She glanced disinterested at the high godspeakers walking with them. They were the god's business, it would deal with them. If they truly lived in its eye they would hear Nagarak's words and know he spoke for the god. If they were false the god would smite them.

Around her neck, the stone scorpion shivered.

At last the warlords and their high godspeakers reached the crater's red floor. Stiff with dignity and with pride they spread out beyond arm's reach of each other; even unarmed and some of them treatied, still they were wary.

"The god see you, my brothers," Raklion greeted them calmly. "May it see you in its judging eye."

Banotaj ignored the greeting. "What is that ugly bitch doing here? You insult us before we begin!"

"She is no bitch, she is Hekat," said Raklion. His face and voice were cold with temper. "Mother of Zandakar, my son, born the hope of Mijak. She is my finest knife-dancer, you should beware."

Banotaj laughed, a harsh crude bark. "You coupled with a common barracks slut? *That* is the bloodline of your precious son?"

"Common?" said Hekat, before Raklion could answer. "I slew your sinning father, Banotaj. I am Hekat, I am not common. Your tongue is common, if you are not careful the god will pluck it out."

"*Tcha.*" Banotaj stabbed his brother warlords with a look. "He was never fit to be a warlord, here is more proof. A barracks bitch. Ha!"

The other warlords said nothing. Hekat watched them carefully, saw the ones with daughters frown, considering. Could they find a way into Raklion's good temper, tempt him with female flesh for his son?

No. You could not. Zandakar is destined for greater things than rutting with the offspring of weak, godblinded fools.

Banotaj threw back his shoulders. "What do you want, Raklion? Why are we brought here? Speak quickly, we are not slaves to be sent for at a whim."

"Of course you are slaves," said Nagarak. "Slaves to the god. You are here to learn how you will serve it in its new age."

Takona's high godspeaker spat on the red glassy ground. "Be careful you do not choke on your arrogance, Nagarak. The god does not love a conceited man."

"Nor does it love a man deaf to its desires," Nagarak retorted. "Open your heart, Vijik, or see it eaten by the god."

Vijik high godspeaker's fleshy face grew ugly. "The

god be blind to you, Nagarak, I am not some novice in your godhouse to be spoken to like a clod of earth! *I* have a godhouse, I—"

"*Peace*!" said Raklion, and raised his hands. "We are not here to bicker, we gather at the god's will so you might learn its desire."

"That is godspeaker talk," said Zyden, his eyes suspicious. "And you are no godspeaker. I will tell you *my* desire! I desire to know why *my* lands are dying when Et-Raklion is green and fat!"

"That is my desire also," said Takona, broad hands fisted at his sides.

"And mine!"

"And mine!"

"And mine!"

"And mine!"

"Do not look to me for an answer, brothers!" cried Raklion to the hostile warlords. "Look to yourselves and to your high godspeakers! If the god smites you how am I to blame?"

"You are to blame if the god does *not* smite us!" said Tebek. "*Demons* might smite us, with *you* their master!"

"You accuse *me* of consorting with demons?" Raklion's face twisted with fury. "When one of *you* called on demons to blight my seed, murder every son born to me before Zandakar? I am *not* touched by demons! If I were it would have killed me when I knelt before it in this crater. You were all witness, I was judged pure. You proud warlords, you haughty high godspeakers, if you love the god you will listen to Nagarak. If you do not there will be a harsh reckoning."

The warlords and their high godspeakers drew apart

and huddled, they whispered and poked fingers, they threw hot glances over their shoulders. Smiling, Hekat touched her fingertips to her scorpion amulet.

They are blind, stupid men, their ruling lives are over and they cannot see it.

Raklion turned to Nagarak. "Is the god in even *one* of them?" he asked amazed.

Nagarak shrugged. "The god is in me, warlord. It speaks to me, I hear its voice. That is what matters. These other mere men are dust on the wind."

The huddling warlords and their godspeakers broke apart. "Say it is true," said Jokriel. His voice was reedy, thin as his godbraids. "Say Et-Raklion is not protected by demons. What do you know of the god's desire that has not been revealed to any of us?"

Raklion said, "Brother, it is not for me to speak of the god. Nagarak will tell you of sacred things, but know this: I have been shown wonders and omens, the god has whispered in my heart. What Nagarak will tell you is its truth."

"Speak then, Nagarak," said Mamiklia, his raised fist a threat silencing Banotaj and Tebek. He had an odd voice for such a large, square man, high-pitched and fluting. "We will listen."

"You please the god," said Raklion, and glanced at his high godspeaker. "Tell them, Nagarak."

Nagarak tipped back his head, rolling his eyes to crescent slivers. His arms stretched wide, his robe fell open, revealing his scorpion pectoral.

"I am Nagarak, the god's high godspeaker!"

His voice rolled round and round the glassy crater, full of echoes and strange harmonies.

"I am the god's vessel, I speak its words, I dress its words in my voice that they might fall like honey from my truthful tongue!"

As Raklion stared at his high godspeaker, Hekat watched the faces of his brother warlords and their high godspeakers. Anger, suspicion, fear, hatred: she saw all these things and felt herself tense.

"Hear the god's words, you warlords and you high godspeakers!" Nagarak commanded. *"You sinning men who are tasked to protect Mijak, you who have failed so your lands have turned brown, you warlords who have displeased the god!"*

The warlords muttered and looked at each other, they looked at their high godspeakers with their eyebrows raised.

"The god desires that you are cast down, it throws you from your mighty heights, it bends your knees and lays you in the dirt before Mijak's one warlord, its true warlord, the warlord desired by the god," cried Nagarak. *"You will kneel to Raklion, he will be your warlord, you will breathe beneath his godchosen fist!"*

"What demontalk is this?" demanded Zyden. "Mijak is ruled by seven warlords, you speak not for the god but for Raklion alone!"

"You dare dispute me?" Nagarak demanded. His eyes were still white crescents but he stared straight at Zyden. He tore off his robe and tossed it aside. Sunshine struck his scorpion pectoral, the scorpion-marks on his shining skin glowed fiery red in the searing light. "I warn you, warlord, the god will not be denied!"

"Your words do not come from the god," said Tebek's high godspeaker. "It has long been suspected you are a demon clothed in human flesh. You are not normal, Nagarak. Your power is too great."

"My power is great because of the god!" shouted Nagarak. "Are you a high godspeaker, Trag? Is the god's voice in your heart? Listen, fool, before it smites you!"

"No, Nagarak," said Jokriel's high godspeaker, a wizened old man with godbraids white as sadsa, one hand a clutching, withered claw. His spine was bent, his chin sat level with his breastbone. "What you are saying is against the god's law. Would you destroy Mijak a second time? Curse it with one warlord, when one warlord brought us to ruin?"

"I destroy nothing, I inflict no curse, I say the words the god gives me to say," said Nagarak. "It is the god's desire that Raklion be your warlord, and after him his son Zandakar. Accept the god's desire, Goruk and you others, or be destroyed in your sinning pride."

Goruk high godspeaker waved one fist, incensed. "The pride is *yours*, Nagarak! We did not come to hear your demon-words spill like bile from your wicked tongue! We are also high godspeakers, the god speaks to us, it has said *nothing* of one warlord, your Raklion, his common son, this common slut he fucked to make him! You—"

"*Aieeeeeeee!*"

Nagarak's scream almost shattered the sky. A great shudder ran through him, he rose high on the balls of his sandaled feet. His arms flung wide, his head fell back, all the muscles and tendons on his body stood out.

His scorpion pectoral came alive.

Shocked to stillness, the warlords and their high godspeakers stared. Hekat stood her ground, she was not afraid of the god, but Raklion slid his arm around her. She tried to resist, he pulled her sideways.

"Tchut tchut, Hekat," he whispered in her ear. "Let Nagarak see nothing between him and the objects of the god's rage."

Hekat stopped resisting, she stood to one side with Raklion's hand on her arm and watched the god in its smiting fury.

The living, hissing scorpion on Nagarak's chest lashed its tail, snapped its pincers. It was still strapped to his body, it had not detached from the fastenings that wrapped his ribs. Nagarak's eyes were turned bright red, they glowed as though his godspark was burning. He opened his mouth and screamed again, the terrible sound rolled round the crater, shivering rock-falls from its rim to its floor.

Zyden's high godspeaker was the first to move. He stirred like a man waking from sleep and looked in the faces of his fellow godspeakers. "Tcha!" he said, pointing. "You see this trickery? This demon Nagarak? He thinks to frighten us, he thinks we are blind to his demon ways! We are brought here under false pretenses, he and Raklion seek to overturn our minds and steal the authority given us by the god!"

The other high godspeakers held their tongues, their gazes darted nervously from him to Nagarak, who stood still as a godpost while the living scorpion bound to his breast hissed and snapped and whipped the air with its tail.

Their own scorpion pectorals remained cold stone.

"Zyden, we are leaving!" declared the warlord's high godspeaker. "To stay longer is to insult the god." He turned on his heel with an arrogant flourish, he reached out one hand to catch his warlord by the elbow—and stopped in his tracks, like a man become rock.

Nagarak extended one finger. Zyden's high god-speaker spun about, gasping, his pale eyes wide with fear and disbelief. His feet began moving, step by panting, unwilling step he walked to Nagarak, who looked barely human he was so filled with the god.

Zyden's high godspeaker reached Nagarak and staggered to a halt, he tried to speak but the words would not leave him, he drooled, he dribbled, tears of blood wet his cheeks. Nagarak's fingers clenched into a fist and Zyden's high godspeaker lunged towards him, into his living pectoral's furious embrace.

It held him, it stung him, he screamed and screamed, then slid to the ground. Twisting, flailing, his body swelled, his skin split open, blood and venom sprayed into the air.

He died.

Before the warlords or their high godspeakers could beg for mercy, drop to their knees before their new warlord Raklion, Nagarak's smiting fist clenched again. This time the scorpion needed no contact, its tail lashed wildly and the remaining high godspeakers crashed to the crater's floor, jerking and thrashing, voiding their bodies of wastes, of life.

Nagarak staggered as the last high godspeaker died, Jokriel's Goruk, so thin and dry he spilled little blood. As though Nagarak's body was her own Hekat felt the god's power leave him. His eyes faded swiftly from scarlet to brown, the living scorpion returned to stone. Exhausted,

depleted, Nagarak dropped to the ground. Raklion leapt
to aid him even as Banotaj woke from his trance.

"Demon! Usurper!" Bajadek's son shouted, and suddenly there was a snakeblade in his hand, he was a man
without honor, his face distorted with madness and rage.
He leapt towards Raklion, sunlight flashing on his blade.

Raklion turned, unbalanced, one arm raised to shield
himself. Nagarak was almost senseless, he could not help
Raklion. Banotaj's knife slashed and plunged, opening
flesh, spraying blood. The other warlords shouted but
they did not step forward, they were cowardly men of
honor who brought no blades, who refused to defend
Raklion.

Hekat reached beneath her tunic, seizing the snakeblade secreted there. Her first strike caught Banotaj
across the back of his neck, severing his godbraids, scattering them like straw. He let out a roar of pain and surprise, he clamped his fingers to the wound in his flesh and
spun around, forgetting Raklion, seeing her.

Raklion's blood dripped down his face, slathered his
leather breastplate, soaked his linen tunic. Hekat leapt
upon Banotaj, her snakeblade raised. There was no mercy
in her, Banotaj had tried to thwart the god.

She cut him and cut him, he did not cut her. She severed his tendons and opened his veins. At any moment
she could have killed him, she did not want to, he must
suffer first. He suffered, screaming, his own blade abandoned, he fell to his knees first and then to the ground.

She dropped beside him, soaked in his blood, and
dragged him onto his back to face her.

"You Banotaj warlord, you defier of the god," she said,
and spat into his clouding eyes. "You broke the god's law,

you harmed a warlord in this sacred place. You spit on the god, you deny its desires. Raklion is its chosen warlord, you would change this? You seek to rule Mijak in his place? It will not happen. You will die here by *my* hand, like your father Bajadek. Demons will take your godspark to hell and my son Zandakar will rule your bones!"

Wheezing, bubbling, Banotaj gasped for air. The hot sun baked his wet blood dry, it boiled him in his leather breastplate. "Bitch," he whispered. "Demonspawn. Hellcat. Mijak's death is in your eyes, your evil corrupts it, your spawn son will—"

She plunged her snakeblade into his throat.

"Hekat . . . be with me . . ."

Ignoring the silent, staring warlords she danced to her feet and went to Raklion. He smiled through his pain, he struggled to touch her. "Be still," she scolded. "You are sorely hurt. Nagarak will heal you."

"Nagarak," said Raklion vaguely. His legs were splayed, they lolled without purpose. Banotaj had stabbed him over and over, his wounds bled slowly, his heartbeat was weak.

She looked at the high godspeaker. Nagarak stirred feebly, pinned to the ground by his scorpion pectoral. Still holding her snakeblade she retrieved his robe and rummaged in the pocket for his godstone, no godspeaker traveled without one. She thrust it into Nagarak's cold fingers and pressed the point of her snakeblade in his throat.

"Raklion needs you, *heal him*, godspeaker. Will you disappoint the god *now*, you stupid man?"

Blinking, Nagarak shoved her away from him, then staggered piecemeal to his feet. The watching warlords retreated, fearful, their mouths were open, they held their amulets in their fists. Their grossly dead godspeakers littered the glassy ground around them. They did not look at them, or at slain Banotaj. The god had eaten their pride and arrogance, they were men without bones. They could hardly stand.

"You warlords," said Nagarak. Though he was exhausted, power remained in his voice. "You have seen the god here, you have seen its fury. Banotaj is struck down in his sinning pride. Deaf to the god, your godspeakers are slaughtered. Learn from their smiting, do not repeat their mistake."

The warlords did not look at him, their eyes fed on his scorpion pectoral. It was asleep but could wake in a heartbeat. They nodded and pressed their fists to their chests.

"Nagarak!" Hekat said sharply. "The warlords are chastened, the god sees them in its judging eye. Help Raklion!"

Nagarak limped to Raklion and knelt, his godstone flashing weakly in his grasp. His power did not pour in its usual torrent but trickled reluctantly, as though from its dregs.

Hekat dropped to a crouch beside him. "Nagarak, why do you not heal him?"

"I have no power," said Nagarak, his voice low. "I am emptied by the god."

"No, you are not emptied!" she insisted. "We have not come to this place to fail in the god's eye! He is Raklion, warlord of Mijak! *Heal* him, high godspeaker. That is your purpose!"

"Hekat . . ." Raklion's voice was a thready whisper. "Show respect to the god's chosen speaker. Nagarak is mighty, he lives in the god's approving eye."

She did not love him, but it hurt to see him weakened. "Hush, warlord," she said, and wrapped her fingers around his cold hand. "Save your strength, you must stand so these craven warlords might kneel. Nagarak, *heal him*."

Groaning, Nagarak pressed his godstone against Raklion's breast. The godstone flared into stronger life. Raklion choked back an anguished cry, his face twisted, his harsh breath shuddered in difficult gasps. His body convulsed, his head struck the red glassy crater floor again and again.

"*Aieee!*" said Nagarak at last, collapsing onto his meatless haunches. "Warlord, forgive me. I can heal you no further, I have done my best."

Raklion nodded. "This is the god's business, Nagarak," his thin voice whispered. "We are in its eye, what must come will come. Help me to stand, I would speak to the warlords."

Help him to *stand*? Dismayed, Hekat stared at his limp body on the ground.

What is this, god? He is the warlord and he cannot stand? If he cannot stand how can he rule? This is madness, god, what have you done? Why did you not warn Nagarak that wicked Banotaj carried a knife?

It did not smite her for such bold questions, the scorpion amulet round her neck was still and silent.

He is the warlord and he cannot stand. I am Hekat knife-dancer, godtouched and precious. Zandakar's mother. Bajadek's doom and the doom of his son. I can stand. I will stand for him. I must stand for him, there is no-one else.

"Leave him, Nagarak," she said, and squeezed Raklion's lax hand. "You are weary, warlord. Rest. I will drive these warlords to their knees."

He smiled at her, a slow curve of his lips. "My own fierce Hekat, in the god's eye. Two warlords now you have killed for me. Twice my life is in your blade. Speak for me, Hekat. Dress my words in your sweet voice. Nagarak . . ."

"Warlord," said Nagarak. He sounded almost as weak as Raklion.

"Here is Hekat, my beloved. Her words are my words. She speaks with my tongue."

Nagarak's face twisted. Did he also wonder at the god's strange silence? "She brought a knife into Mijak's Heart, that is strictly forbidden. She—"

"Forbidden to warlords," Raklion whispered. "Banotaj broke that law, not Hekat. Without her knife I would lie here dead. Will you smite her, Nagarak, for saving me?"

"Her words are your words, warlord," said Nagarak, bitter. "She speaks with your tongue."

Hekat rose to her feet and stalked to the waiting warlords. She showed them her snakeblade, still stained with blood, and scorched them with her burning gaze.

"You are standing, you will kneel!"

Like whipped slaves the warlords dropped.

"I am Hekat knife-dancer, Zandakar's mother," she told them. "Bajadek's doom and the doom of his son. Your days are done, you are no longer warlords. Do you think to deny this?" She pointed her knife at dead Banotaj. "Think again. You have seen my snakeblade, you have seen me dance. Pray to the god I never dance for you." One by one, she glared into their eyes. "Who is the warlord of Mijak, united? Tell me *now* or face my wrath!"

One by one, the warlords answered. One by one, they said his name:

"Raklion."

"Raklion."

"Raklion."

"Raklion."

"Raklion."

She bared her teeth, it was not a smile. "Raklion is warlord in the land of Mijak. Never forget it, if you wish to live."

And never forget who stands as you kneel. Hekat stands, she stands as you kneel. I see the god's purpose. I understand now why Nagarak was not warned, My time is coming, Raklion's flies past. I am Hekat, the god's knife-dancer. Mijak will be mine, it will be my son's.

CHAPTER THIRTY

Vortka sighed, and shifted beneath his blanket in the godhouse sickroom. The worst of the fever was burned from his bones now, all that remained was a strength-sapping lassitude and a vague irritation of his spirits. Through the chamber's window a small square of blue sky, taunting him with a freedom he was still denied by ill-health.

I am tired of staring at four cold stone walls. I long for fresh air and a breeze in my face. Surely I am well enough now to leave this place and walk under the sun.

The fever had come upon him swiftly, two highsuns after Hekat rode with Raklion and Nagarak to the Heart of Mijak. A pain in his head as he served in the library, a racking shiver that saw a clay tablet slip from his fingers and smash on the floor. Then sweat and heat and countless highsuns of suffering as he moaned and thrashed and begged the god to ease his torment.

The god heard him eventually, he had feared it never would.

Have I displeased you, god, that you would mortify my flesh so hard for so long? Tell me, I beg you, what wrong thing have I done? I will go to the taskmaster as soon as I am able, I will prove on my knees and weeping I am still your true servant.

The god did not answer him, not exactly. But as he prayed he felt a warmth, a wash of calm acceptance. His disquiet eased and he drifted again into sleep.

When he woke it was night, and the sickroom was lit by flickering candles. A bowl of steaming soup sat on the stool nearby, scenting the air with strong garlic fumes, and Sidik healer stood beside his cot, her thin cool fingers pressed against his wrist pulse.

"You are much improved, Vortka," she said, releasing him. "I think you might leave us, after newsun."

"Truly?" he said, and felt his face split in a smile. "Aieee, Sidik. You make me a happy man."

She raised a warning hand. "But you must be careful, you are not at full strength yet. You are able to use your godstone again, but using it will tire you swiftly, Vortka. You must wait for my permission before you heal, or do anything more taxing than organize the archives. I have spoken with Peklia, she says you might serve in the library but for only three fingers between newsun and lowsun until I say otherwise. Other than that you must take gentle exercise to rebuild your lost vitality, and make sure to eat four nourishing meals daily in the godhouse kitchen. I will speak with Neelij cook-master, he will prepare special food for you. You will come to me before each lowsun sacrifice until I am satisfied your recovery is complete. You will be yourself again I promise, Vortka, provided you are sensible and do not run before you can walk."

He pressed his fist above his heart, the warrior's salute. "I will obey, healer. My solemn vow. You have been a blessing, the god see you in its eye."

She nodded. "It already sees you, Vortka. I know many strong men who would not have survived such a fever."

"I know," he said soberly, and repressed a shudder. Never to see Hekat again, or beautiful Zandakar. It was a terrible prospect. He knew his life belonged to the god, to keep or take as suited its purpose, but even so . . .

Is it sinful to want to live, god? To want to see my son grow into a strong, proud man? I cannot think so, you must tell me if I am wrong.

The god did not correct him. He smiled again, Sidik thought he smiled at her. She patted his rough-stubbled head and left him to rest and drink his invalid's broth.

If I am to take gentle exercise each highsun, perhaps I might wander through Raklion's barracks. That is not so far away. I will not overtire myself, surely. And perhaps I will be granted a glimpse of my son . . .

Broth finished, he slid again beneath his blankets and let that sweet thought lull him to sleep.

*   *   *

It must have been a sweet thought the god found pleasing for he did indeed see Zandakar in the barracks, on the fifth day he took his exercise there. No warrior or slave disturbed his tentative wanderings, he was a godspeaker and not their concern. The barracks godspeakers let him be also, once he met them and explained his presence.

His son trained with the warleader and a half-shell of warriors, they danced with their snakeblades on the warhost field. Vortka watched from beneath a shading tree, unnoticed, torn between pride and terror, as Zandakar challenged grown men and women who had killed with their snakeblades. It eased his fears, if only slightly, to know Hanochek warleader was there to guide and guard his boy. Hanochek's love for Zandakar shone in his face, he laughed as he taught him, laughed as he praised him, laughed for laughter's sake, and Zandakar laughed with him.

Zandakar leapt and cartwheeled, his godbraids flying, godbells singing his triumph to the sky. He slew a thousand unseen enemies, he looked like Hekat as he danced with his child's blade. Vortka knew almost nothing of fighting, he could not tell one *hota* from the next, all he knew was that Zandakar was beautiful, like Hekat his mother, even though she was scarred.

I see nothing of myself in him, we could stand together and no-one would know. This is a good thing, the god protects my secret, but I cannot deceive myself. It does hurt my heart.

The training finished, at last. Hanochek dismissed his sweating, panting warriors with smiling praise, then he and Zandakar stood alone on the warhost field. Zandakar was breathing fast and loud, he was not quite five seasons of age, it was hard work for a child so young.

"Hano, when will Yuma return from Mijak's Heart?" he asked, sweat trickling down his face.

"The warlord will return when he returns," said Hanochek. "That is the god's business, we must leave it alone."

Zandakar heaved a disconsolate sigh. "Hano, I have been thinking."

The warleader tugged one of Zandakar's godbraids, teasing. "Should I be frightened, my little warlord?"

"*Tcha*!" said Zandakar, with a grin. Aieee, so like Hekat, he had her voice entirely. "You know I love Didi-jik, but he is a pony. I am thinking I would like to show Yuma I could ride a proper horse. I am not such a small boy, I have grown a whole hand-span."

"Zandakar, Zandakar," said Hanochek, sighing. "You are many seasons from a proper horse."

Zandakar's face fell, his lower lip trembled. "But—"

"You listen to me," said the warleader, and dropped to one knee so he and Zandakar were closer in height. "The warlord will never let you ride a tall horse yet, Zandakar. But if you show him what a skilled warrior you are, perhaps he will let you choose a foal from the next dropping. Then it will be yours to train as it grows, and when you are old enough to ride a horse your colt will be old enough for you to ride it."

"Aieee!" breathed Zandakar. "Hano, the god see you. Can I really do that? Will you show me proper warrior tricks in the horse-field, so Yuma can see I am worthy of a foal?"

Vortka saw Hanochek's face tighten. Clearly, he did not like to hear of Hekat. And Zandakar seemed not to care for the warlord's opinion, his heart was full of *Yuma, Yuma*.

The warleader nodded. "I will show you a trick or two, Zandakar, so the warlord will be proud and give you a foal."

Zandakar kissed him soundly on the cheek. "The god see you, Hano! You are my good friend!"

Laughing, Hanochek kissed him back. Vortka felt a cruel pain pierce his heart. *My son will never kiss me, he will never know he is my son.* Some sound of hurt must have left his lips, Hanochek heard him, he leapt to his feet and lifted his knife.

"You there! In the shadow! Show yourself or die where you stand!"

Cursing, Vortka stepped into the sunlight. "Do not be alarmed, warleader. I merely stopped in the shade to catch my breath."

"Godspeaker!" Appalled, Hanochek lowered his snakeblade. "Forgive me, I did not realize. It is a grave sin to threaten a man of the god, I—"

Vortka stepped closer, his hands held out. "No, no. It was a simple misunderstanding. Please, do not distress yourself. I overheard a private moment, it is I who should beg forgiveness from you."

Hanochek blinked. "That . . . is not necessary."

"I am Vortka godspeaker." He looked down at his son. "And this is Zandakar, to be warlord of Et-Raklion in the god's time." He pressed his palm to his heart. "The god see you in its eye, Zandakar warlord."

Zandakar considered him critically. "The god see you, Vortka godspeaker. You are very thin, and you have no godbraids."

Vortka smothered a smile. "I have been ill, Zandakar. I am better now. As for my godbraids, I gave them to the god." He looked at Hanochek. "I am under healer instruction to walk daily for my health. I like to walk about the barracks, there is much to see and learn. I hope you do not find that unpleasing, warleader."

"Unpleasing? No," said Hanochek faintly. "You are a godspeaker, you walk where the god guides you, it is not for me to say."

"True," said Vortka. "And it is also true I must leave you, and return to the godhouse." Again, he pressed his palm to his heart. "I think you looked most impressive, Zandakar, dancing for the god with your snakeblade. Perhaps I will see you dance again."

"Thank you, godspeaker," said Zandakar, grinning, and punched his small fist against his breast. "The god see you in its eye. I hope you are well soon, and the god quickly gives you back your godbraids."

With a nod at Hanochek, Vortka walked away from them. It hurt like fever, but he left his son.

I have seen him dance, we have spoken together. I should not see him or speak with him again. It is too dangerous, and Hekat would be angry. Truly he is her son, he is not mine.

Or so he told himself, to ease the pain. But he did not believe it. And when it came time the next day to walk again for his health, his heart silenced his head and his feet guided him back to the barracks, to the horse-field, where Zandakar raced his blue-striped pony and laughed, and laughed. Again he stood concealed in shadows, he stood and watched, he was filled with joy.

See my son, god. See the son you gave me. He is your glory. He is a happy, carefree boy.

Hekat could easily have wasted water when Et-Raklion city finally came into sight. She would have, if not for Nagarak beside her and the five chastened, fallen warlords riding behind her. If they saw her weeping they would not remain chastened for long.

Raklion warlord was tied to his horse with strips of leather. He was a proud man, a strong man, he would not let them see him slump, but what it cost him etched deeper and deeper into his face with each passing newsun. He was in no danger of death, but his imperfect healing at Mijak's Heart had left him weakened. Not even Nagarak's later healings had restored his full strength.

Behind the fallen warlords rode their silenced warriors and dead Banotaj's men and women too. Raklion's warriors surrounded them, goatherds to ragged goats. Their days as warriors of those chastised sinners were ended, their allegiance was to Raklion now.

To Raklion, and me. This is the god's plan, who am I to question it? Raklion is weak, but I am strong. I am strong for a reason. The god sees me in its eye.

Banotaj and the smitten high godspeakers remained in the red rock crater of Mijak's Heart. Nagarak had decreed it, their impenitent bodies were too wicked for burning, he said. They must lie there forever, to shrivel and bleach, and remind all who came after, what price was paid by those who defied the god.

I would rather we brought back their heads, I would nail them to the gates of Et-Raklion and let their blind eyes shout the god's warning to the world.

They entered Et-Raklion city by the Warriors' Gate, it was the warhost roadway that led directly to the barracks. No man or woman from the city was permitted to walk that road, Raklion's infirmity would not become known.

Vortka waited at the end of the warhost road, between its two imposing godposts. He was some distance ahead, his face was indistinct but she would know him anywhere.

Nagarak straightened in his saddle. Squinting along the roadway he said, "What is this? I know that godspeaker, that is Vortka. He has no godbraids, he is returned from the wilderness. What is he doing, barring our path?"

It was clear from his tone he was deeply displeased, and had not realized Vortka was safely home. "He stands at the Warriors' Gate, this is warlord's business," said Hekat. "I will see what he wants, you stay with Raklion. Do not trot, stay in walk. Make sure the warlord does not fail so close to home."

Ignoring Nagarak's furious protest she dug her sandaled heels in her red mare's dirty flanks. The animal bounded forward, head tossing. Hekat galloped to the godposts and waiting Vortka.

"What has happened?" she demanded, hauling the red mare to a rearing halt. "Why do you stand there? Is it Zandakar? Is he—"

"No," he said swiftly. "He is not dead. But Hekat, he has been gravely injured."

Vortka's face was much thinner than when last she had seen him on the Pinnacle Road, the fever the god put in him had stripped him to the bone. She took deep hard breaths, subduing her terror, it did not help to see the fear in his eyes.

"How injured? *What happened?* Tell me, Vortka, or I swear by the *god* I will—"

"He fell from his pony. Split open his head, broke his leg, and his arm. The godhouse healers have mended his body." Vortka paused, his voice was shaking. With an effort he disciplined himself. "He is in no danger now, he has woken once, the healers are keeping him quiet. He is weak but his wits are intact."

Even walking slowly, Raklion and the warhost drew inconveniently closer. She pressed one hand hard to her eyes, feeling sick. "You say his wits are undamaged? He is right in his mind?"

"Yes. I promise."

"And his body? There will be no infirmity, he is not crippled or maimed?"

"No. He is as he was."

She took her hand from her face. "I do not believe he just *fell from his pony*. Zandakar rides as though he were born half-horse, this must have been demons, he—"

"No," said Vortka. "It was an accident, it was no demon mischief."

She stared. "How would you know?"

"Because I was there in the horse-field, Hekat. I saw it happen."

"*You* saw—" She gritted her teeth. "What were *you* doing in the barracks horse-field? What were you doing watching Zandakar ride?"

He cast a swift look past her, at approaching Nagarak. "Does that matter? I was there. I tell you Zandakar's falling was not caused by demons. I am a tested god-speaker and he is my son, I would sense if demons touched him in front of me. Zandakar wanted to impress you on your return, he is eager for a foal from one of the war-horses, that he can raise and train as his own to ride. Hanochek was teaching him a warrior trick, the pony mis-stepped itself and—"

"*Hanochek*?" she said. She could scarcely breathe, her heart was beating so hard. "*He* is responsible for nearly killing Zandakar?"

Vortka stepped back. "No. No, Hekat. Will you not hear me, *this was an accident*. You cannot blame Zandakar, you cannot blame Hanochek. You cannot blame the pony, or demons, or the god. And Zandakar is mended, he rests in a godhouse sickroom but I swear in the god's eye he is whole again. I have sat with him since it happened, I—"

"When was that?" she asked coldly. "When did Hanochek nearly kill my son?"

"It happened two days ago," said Vortka, resigned. "After highsun sacrifice."

"The pony *mis-stepped* itself?" She spat on the ground. "I want that pony dead, Vortka. When I have seen Zandakar unharmed I will slit its throat myself, I will—"

"You are too late, Hekat. It is already dead. It died when it fell, that is why Zandakar fell. The pony missed its footing, it broke its neck and died in the grass."

"A pity it did not fall on Hanochek and kill *him* when it died! Where *is* the warleader, Vortka? Skulking in the shadows, too much a coward to face his crime?"

Vortka stepped closer and put his hand on her knee. "Hekat, he is in the godhouse sickroom with Zandakar. He has not left our son's side since the accident. Word was sent that the warlord was coming, *I* told Hanochek to stay with Zandakar. I told him I would tell you what happened and that you would understand. I told him you would see he was not responsible."

She struck his hand from her leg, she almost kicked him in the face. "You had no business telling him anything! *I* am Zandakar's mother, *I* decide who is to blame!" She turned her head, Raklion was almost upon them. He was close enough for her to see his concern, and beside him Nagarak's simmering rage. "Stay here, Vortka," she commanded. "Tell the warlord and the high godspeaker that I go to Zandakar. We will speak again later. I will find you, do not fear."

He nodded and stepped back again, he did not try to stop her. That was a good thing, she would have ridden right over him.

She galloped all the way to the godhouse's main doors. Godspeakers leaving after the highsun sacrifice stared and protested, but she did not care. She threw her reins at one of them and flung her way inside, snared the first godspeaker she saw and demanded her son.

The godspeaker took her to him without saying a word. *That* was a good thing, she was in a killing mood.

When at last she saw Zandakar her eyes did waste water. Tall for a boy, so beautiful, so precious. He slept on a narrow bed in a small, private sickroom, protected by a light blanket. His breathing was deep and sweetly unlabored, his limbs beneath the covers straight and whole. His many godbraids were crowded with amulets, he wore golden godbells, he was Mijak's son. A narrow pink line marred his beautiful forehead, where his head had been cut open. She could see clots of dried blood in his godbraids. They would need unbraiding so his hair could be washed thoroughly. How he hated that: he moaned and complained, he sounded like dead Yagji.

Beside him sat Hanochek, hunched in a chair. He stood when he saw her standing in the doorway, his face was drawn, his eyes full of tears.

"Hekat . . ."

"Outside," she said curtly, and stepped aside to let him pass into the corridor. Then she closed the sickroom door gently, so Zandakar would not wake. Leading Hanochek to a safe distance, banishing two nearby godspeakers with a single burning look, she took out her snakeblade and pressed it to Hanochek's throat.

"Tell me why I should not kill you."

His eyes overflowed, water washed down his cheeks. "The god see me, Hekat, I am not to blame. The pony stumbled, it could have happened anywhere."

"The pony stumbled because you were teaching Zandakar *tricks*. Who gave you permission? Who said you could risk him? Who are you, Hanochek, to *endanger my son*?"

Water ran down his face, blood trickled from his throat. Her snakeblade was biting, it was hungry to drink. "I did not endanger him," said Hano, the wicked man. "I *love* him, you know that. I—"

"Aieee, yes, you love him. You love *yourself* more. Zandakar is above you, he will rule when Raklion is dead. If Zandakar dies you dream Raklion will name you his warlord heir, you dream of Et-Hanochek, of Hanochek warlord!"

"No! *No!*" he protested. "I never dreamed that, Raklion is my knife-brother, he will be warlord of Mijak and

Zandakar will succeed him! I am their warleader, it is *all* that I want!"

Warlord of Mijak? Hanochek knew? Raklion had *told* him? Aieee, the *fool*! "Do I care what you want? I think I do not! I care for my son, *you* nearly killed him. Do you think I will not *punish* you? Do you think I will *forgive*?"

Hanochek stared at her, his lips thinned in a snarl. "You do not have the power to punish me. *Raklion* is warlord. *You* are—"

"His voice." She smiled at Hano, and knew *she* was snarling. "Banotaj tried to kill him in the Heart of Mijak. I saved his life, I slew that wicked man like I slew his sinning father. Raklion is injured, he may never be himself again. I am Raklion's voice, I am Zandakar's mother. You *will* be punished." She turned her head. "*Godspeaker*!"

Within two heartbeats a godspeaker appeared. "Yes?"

She lowered her snakeblade and looked at the man, she had never seen him before. Et-Raklion was overrun with godspeakers. "Do you know who I am?"

The godspeaker nodded. "You are Hekat knife-dancer."

She jerked her head at Hanochek. "This man is a criminal. Take him to an empty chamber, he must be attended at all times. *Do not* let him leave or speak to *anyone*. I will sit with my son till the warlord arrives. *Do not* tell him of this criminal, Hanochek. That is my place, the god will smite you if you usurp it." She glanced at Hano. "You can take him away."

"*Wait*!" said Hanochek, as the godspeaker put a hand upon him. "What do you mean, Hekat, Raklion is injured? What do you mean he may never be the same? How is he injured? What are his wounds?"

Aieee, the pleasure it gave her to deny him. "Raklion warlord is no longer your business."

Hano's fists clenched, a strangled sound of rage escaped his throat. "Bitch! I want to see him! I will stay here till I have seen him, I will speak to him before you poison his heart against me, I will speak to him in my own defense! I am *Raklion's warleader, I will* be heard!"

She laughed in his face, laughed harder to see that wound him. *My son nearly died, are you really so stupid?* "Call yourself whatever you like, Hano. Words are empty, they are puffs of air. Take him, godspeaker. He is nothing and no-one. He talks and he talks, I do not hear him."

"Your arrogance will undo you, Hekat!" said Hanochek, as the godspeaker pushed him away from the wall. "Your blindness will bring you down, demons will devour you!"

She turned her back on him, she walked away. Zandakar waited in the sickroom, no-one else existed in the world.

She sat in silence beside her sleeping son, she did not know how long she sat there, watching him dream. One hand held his, the other clasped her scorpion amulet. It slept, like Zandakar, but it gave her comfort. It was her connection to the god.

You saved him, you saved him. How can I thank you? Ask me for anything, it will be yours.

At last the pattern of her son's breathing changed, grew shallow, his healed head shifted on his pillow, waking his godbells, waking him. His eyes flew open and he saw her beside him.

"*Yuma!*"

She bent low and kissed his scarred forehead. "Zandakar warlord. I have returned."

His gaze searched the room. "Where am I, Yuma?"

Her heart hitched sharply, she did not show it in her face. "You are in a godhouse sickroom. You hurt yourself, you do not remember?"

"Remember?" He frowned. "No, I do not—" Then he gasped, and sat up. "Yes! I *do* remember. Yuma! My pony!"

"Didijik is dead, Zandakar," she told him sternly, and pushed him flat to his pillows. "He broke his neck when he fell in the horse-field. He is dead for your wickedness, his blood is on your sinning hands. *Tcha!* No weeping!" she added, as his eyes filled with water. "Mijak has many ponies, it has but one Zandakar. What were you doing, riding tricks in the horse-field?"

His gaze slipped away from her, he knew he had done wrong. "I meant a surprise. To show you, and the warlord. I wanted to show you I can ride a horse. I knew that riding trick, I did it over and over for many highsuns before I fell." Now his face was mutinous. "I am not a baby, Yuma, I ride better than any other boy. Even warriors fall, Hanochek says so."

"Yes, you ride better," she snapped, unappeased. *Hanochek, you wicked man, I will see you thrown down.* "You do everything better, you are born a warlord, Zandakar warlord in the god's eye. To be better, Zandakar, is to tempt wicked demons. They seduce you with sweet songs, they entice you to sin! Have I not told you? When will you learn? If the god did not see you, you would be dead."

"I am sorry, Yuma," her small son whispered, chastened. "I am sorry for my pony."

"Tcha! You are sorry for your pony, you must be sorry for Hanochek warleader. You sinned with him behind my back, is *he* your mother, that you would plot and plan secrets with *him*, that you would have *him* teach you warrior tricks that *I* would teach you, in my time? Aieee, you have hurt me, Zandakar. You have broken my heart. And Hanochek will be sent away, he will be sent from Et-Raklion, he will die far from his home."

"*Yuma*!" cried Zandakar, and wept like a slave. "No, Yuma! Please. I *love* Hano. He rides with me, he trains with me, Hanochek warleader is my *friend*!"

She stared at him unflinching, she turned her heart to stone. "You loved your pony and it is dead. It was your friend, your wickedness killed it. Give thanks to the god your friend Hanochek is not dead too. *Tcha*. Stop your weeping, it does not change what is. Does a warlord weep? I think he does not."

Choking, hiccuping, Zandakar defeated his tears. "Will I have another pony, Yuma?" he asked, staring at his tight-clenched fists. "I promise I will not kill another pony, I will never sin like that again."

"It is too soon to be talking of ponies," she told him. "You are barely mended, I—"

A soft knock on the door, and then it opened. "Your pardon," said another godspeaker she had never seen before. "The warlord is here. He speaks with the warleader in the chamber assigned him, I—"

"What?" Enraged, Hekat leapt to her feet. "You stupid godspeakers! Did I not *tell* you—"

"The warleader grew violent, he demanded to see Raklion warlord," said the godspeaker. "We could not deny him, it was his right when the warlord came."

With a bone-cracking effort, she subdued her fury. "Take me to Raklion, I will see him at once." She turned to the bed. "Zandakar, you will stay here. This sorry business is not yet finished. You must be punished for your wicked ways."

She watched him flinch, she saw his lips tremble. Satisfied for the moment she left him alone, and followed the godspeaker.

Raklion, you fool, you stupid man. Hanochek blinds you, I must open your eyes.

CHAPTER THIRTY-ONE

Raklion sat on a straight-backed wooden chair, his hand resting lightly on Hanochek's bowed head. Hanochek knelt before him, his body heaving with grief.

"*Tcha!*" said Hekat, slamming the chamber door behind her. "See how this wicked man twists your mind! Zandakar lies broken nearly to death and you comfort the criminal who tried to *murder* him?"

Raklion was beaten down with fatigue and pain. He lifted his slow hand from Hanochek's head and tried to appease her. "Hekat, beloved—"

"*I am not your beloved*! How am I your beloved when you would plunge your snakeblade into my heart?"

"Aieee, Hekat," said Raklion, there were tears in his

voice, his sunken cheeks were wet. "I knew you were with Zandakar, I knew he was not alone. I will see him, of course I will see him, but Hano begged for my presence, how could I refuse my—"

"How could you *not*?" she demanded, advancing towards him. "What is this wicked man, compared to my son?"

Raklion's face hardened. "He is *our* son, Hekat. I think you forget that. You also forget I am the warlord, I will not be spoken to like a slave! Not even by you, who are in the god's eye."

Releasing a shuddering breath she stopped, and closed her fingers round her scorpion amulet. *Give me your strength, god, you must give me your strength. You must help me rid Raklion of this inconvenient Hano.* "I never forget you are the warlord, Raklion. You are the warlord walking and sitting, you are the warlord in my dreams. This wicked Hanochek is *not* the warlord. He is only a warrior, like any warrior in your warhost."

"He is more than that! He is my warleader and my friend! He was my friend long before we met, am I a fickle man who will *forget* that?"

As though the words were a declaration of forgiveness, Hanochek rose from his knees and stood beside Raklion. In his red-rimmed eyes, malicious triumph. Hekat saw it, she longed to smite him. She did not unsheathe her snakeblade, this was a battle of words, not knives.

"Raklion, every warrior in the barracks knows how Zandakar was nearly killed. Every warrior knows this man, this *friend*, took Zandakar to the horse-field, which is dangerous, and let him gallop his pony there where he had no business to ride. Before we left for Mijak's Heart this man swore an oath to you, he said: *His life is safe in my hands*. Leave this man in his wickedness, Raklion. Go to Zandakar and you will see how safe he was in Hanochek's hands."

Hanochek said, "Zandakar's fall was an accident. Raklion knows how I am contrite. He knows how truly I love his son."

She laughed. "He knows what you tell him. *I* am Hekat, I know more than words. I know men's hearts, I see with the god's eye. *Raklion*." She walked forward until she was close enough to touch him. "If this Hanochek goes unpunished every warrior in your warhost, every citizen in your city, every warlord thrown down in the Heart of Mijak, all those people and every man, woman and child of Mijak, free or slave, it will make no difference, they will *all* know that a man may cause harm to Zandakar and *you* will not act. Is that a warlord? I think it is not."

Words *could* be weapons, she watched them puncture Raklion like arrows, watched him bleed behind his eyes.

But he must do more than bleed. He must surrender. I will have my way here or I am lost.

"If Hanochek warleader was truly your friend he would *beg* you to punish him. He would *beg* to be strapped to the scorpion wheel. He would *demand* his punishment on the streets of Et-Raklion, he would *insist* he be whipped from one side of the city to the other, so the people might see how a sinning man is corrected. So the world can see how a warlord is mighty and will not permit weakness to temper his wrath. He does not do that, he kneels at your feet and begs you to *excuse* him. Is that a warleader? Is that a *friend*? I think it is not. And I think that you know it."

Aieee, such torment in Raklion's face. With a stifled grunt of pain he pushed to his feet, he limped to the furthest reach of the godhouse chamber, weary almost to dying. He kept his back to Hanochek, and to her.

"Warlord," said Hanochek. "Do not listen to her. Her tongue drips poison, she seeks to kill your love for me. Why do you keep her, she has served her purpose, you have your son. What use is she now? If you keep her she will destroy you, she was never worthy, *send her away*."

"Send *me* away?" Hekat felt the god's fury rise. "When I saved your *life*, Raklion? When I saved you from Bajadek *and* his sinning son? Send *me* away, banish Zandakar's mother, banish Hekat, the god's knifedancer? Hekat the precious, Hekat the godchosen, send *me* away and let *him* remain?"

Raklion turned, he was like a sandcat cornered by dogs. "I desire to send no-one away."

"Raklion, you *must*!" said Hanochek, vicious. His eyes were desperate. "How long have I known you, served you, *loved* you? How long have I counseled you, how often have you profited from my advice? I advice you now, *discard this bitch*. You will live to regret it if you don't!"

"You hear him, Raklion?" said Hekat. "I am Zandakar's mother, he calls me a *bitch*. Does he call me that to Zandakar, I wonder? Is that what he tells him when your back is turned? *Zandakar, your mother is a bitch*."

Raklion's face hardened. He looked at Hanochek. "Is it, Hano? Is that what you tell my son when my back is turned? Do you tell him his mother is a *bitch*?"

Hanochek stared, he stepped back. "No. Raklion, *no*."

"If he does not say it, warlord, then he thinks it!" said Hekat, quickly. "He has *never* accepted me, he *hates* me for saving your life with my blade, if *he* cannot save you he wishes *nobody* could!"

Aieee, and there was truth in *that*. Raklion saw it, he saw the truth of her words in Hanochek's face. The wicked warleader faltered, his tongue stumbled to silence.

"Oh, Hano. *Hano*," Raklion whispered. Tears filled his eyes, they spilled down his cheeks. "I thought we were brothers."

The chamber door swung open then, to admit Nagarak. "Warlord," he said, entering the room. "I have seen your son with my own eyes, I have poured the god into him with my godstone. He is well, he may leave the god-house. You may not. You must remain here for healing, you must recover your strength. Mijak needs its warlord, Mijak will have him."

Raklion nodded, wiping the water from his face with the palm of his hand. "Yes."

"What is this?" said Nagarak, frowning. He looked at each of them in turn, his displeasure deepening. "What goes on here?"

"The warlord sends Hanochek from Et-Raklion," said Hekat. Raklion could not bring himself to speak. "He is no longer warleader, he is a sinning man with hate in his heart. He is no longer welcome, the warlord does not know his name."

Almost, Nagarak hid his surprise. "Warlord? This is true? You banish Hanochek?"

"Yes," said Raklion. His face twisted with grief, his fingers clenched to fists. "Hanochek has failed me, he has failed my son. He insults my son's mother, he insults his warlord and the god. He is not welcome here, I do not know his name."

"Who then will be warleader?" said Nagarak, his gaze resting on defeated Hanochek and his tears.

Hekat felt a surge of hot pleasure, she felt her scorpion amulet burn. "I will be warleader, Nagarak high godspeaker. I will lead Raklion's warhost against the god's enemies."

"*You?*" said Nagarak, disbelieving. "Tcha. You are a woman."

Aieee, god. How many times must she tell this stupid man who she was? "I am no woman, Nagarak. I am Hekat knife-dancer, Bajadek's doom and the doom of his son. I am the god's knife-dancer, I am Zandakar's mother. I swam with scorpions, at Mijak's Heart the god saw me with its eye. It did not smite me, it has raised me high."

"*Warlord?*" said Nagarak. He could not prevent this, it was warlord's business. He only protested because he was jealous, like defeated Hanochek he was jealous of her.

Beware, Nagarak. I have beaten Hanochek, I will beat you also. When will you learn I am in the god's eye?

"Hekat is my warleader," said Raklion, faintly. He swayed where he stood, threw his hand against the wall. "Did I not tell you, Nagarak, that she speaks with my voice?"

Aieee, the god see him. Here was Raklion's purpose, to see her with power, so she might make of Zandakar the greatest warlord in the world.

So long as demons do not claim him. Provided he grows to be a man.

The thought was knife-sharp, slicing through her unready heart. Where did it come from?

God . . . is that you?

The god did not answer. She pushed the pain away, and the cruel thought with it. Later she would pray in solitude; later she would examine that thought.

Nagarak said, "Hekat is warleader, you are the warlord, she speaks with your voice. What of this other man, whose name is unknown to you?"

Raklion could not remain standing. Unsteadily he returned to the straight-backed chair, he lowered himself into it. He looked an old and tired man. Hekat went to him, she touched her fingers to his wrist.

"I will do this, Raklion," she whispered. "Let me do this, you are burdened enough."

His pained eyes softened with a smile. "You are Hekat, godtouched and precious. You are Zandakar's mother, I owe you my life. Take this burden from me, I would count it a blessing."

"I will," she said, and gestured Nagarak aside. "This unknown man should be sent to a godhouse in a city far from here," she told him, her voice almost a whisper so Raklion would not hear. "Send him in secret to the godhouse of Et-Jokriel, high godspeaker. The lands of Et-Jokriel are dry and distant, let him sweat there for the god until he dies. Let him never see Et-Raklion again."

Not Et-Raklion, or Raklion warlord. Not Zandakar, my precious son. They are dead to you, wicked Hanochek. You are dead to me. I have killed you in my eye.

Nagarak looked at her, then glanced at Raklion, so still and quiet. "The warlord says you speak with his voice. So I take this as his decree. At newsun this unknown man shall be taken by godspeakers from the city. He will die in a strange place. He will never return."

"*Good*," she said, no need for more words.

Hanochek said nothing, he did not protest. His eyes would not meet hers, he knew she had won. He stood like a whipped slave, like a man made of water.

She wanted to laugh, it would not be wise. "Nagarak high godspeaker, you are the god's voice. If it is permitted I will withdraw to my son. You say he may leave his sickroom? I will take him away."

Raklion stirred and lifted his head. "No, do not take him. I desire to see him, I—"

"Raklion, see him later, when you are well and strong again," she said firmly. "You are weary now, you are not yourself. I fear you will frighten him. You cannot desire that."

Inside his warlord wool and leather Raklion was shrunken, his flesh had reduced. Losing Hanochek had weakened him further, his eyes were unfocused and sheened with tears. "No. No, I do not desire it. You go to him, Hekat. Tell him I will see him soon. Tell him he is forgiven, I know he repents."

She nodded. "I will tell him. Nagarak—"

"Hekat?" he said, his eyebrows lifted.

"What has become of the fallen warlords?"

Nagarak's smile was cold. "They pray on their knees in this godhouse, warleader. Surrounded by godspeakers, they pray for their sins. They beg the god not to smite them, they will pray a long, long time."

Good. Let them pray till their teeth fall out. "When I have finished with my son, high godspeaker," she said, "I must tell the warhost I am their warleader. When those tasks are completed, I would consult with you on what must happen next in Mijak. I do not think it wise to wait until Raklion is himself again, we must—"

"Insolent woman!" said Nagarak, offended. "He named you warleader, not warlord. Do not over-reach yourself, I—"

"She is right," said Raklion. His voice was only a thread of sound. "Nagarak, she is right. Mijak's Heart was the god's beginning, it is not the end. The warlords' cities must be dealt with. There is much to do. Hekat understands. You must take Mijak in your tight fist, you must close your fingers upon every godspark in the land."

Nagarak's palms flattened against his scorpion pectoral, he released a slow, hot sigh. "You are the warlord. Hekat, we will speak."

She nodded to Raklion, and to Nagarak. She did not look at Hanochek. She went to her son.

"Yuma!" He wriggled upright in his sickroom bed. "The high godspeaker came to see me, he said I was healed, I can ride again." His smile faded. "When I have a new pony."

She did not sit beside him, she stood at the door. "It will be some time before you are trusted with a pony, Zandakar. You say you are healed. Can you stand upon your feet?"

Zandakar nodded. "Yes, Yuma," he whispered. "I can stand."

"Show me."

He kicked the light blanket aside and slid off the low bed onto the stone floor. His tunic and leggings had been taken, he wore only his loincloth. She inspected his limbs for any sign of their wounds and was pleased to find none. His broken bones were knit clean again. Vortka had not lied, he was neither crippled nor maimed. He was beautiful, and perfect, and precious in her eye.

"Come," she told him, she was not smiling. "The god desires a conversation with you."

He followed her from the sickroom and through the busy godhouse. No godspeaker stared, but supplicants from the city did. She ignored them, they did not breathe. She led her son to the tasking chambers and stood outside them in silence, Zandakar mute by her side. From behind closed doors came sounds of suffering and regret. Zandakar's eyes widened, he shrank against the wall.

She did not comfort him, he was not here to be comforted.

Soon a tasking godspeaker approached. He was younger than Raklion, older than herself. His godbraids reached below his waist. He wore a plain robe, he carried a cane, his eyes were pale brown and serene. "Hekat knife-dancer."

"No," she told him. "I am Hekat warleader." She heard Zandakar gasp, she did not acknowledge it.

"Hekat warleader," said the taskmaster, and nodded, respectful. "The god sees you in the godhouse. How may I serve?"

"Taskmaster, here is Mijak's son, its future warlord, Zandakar. He has sinned and much displeased the god. He must be chastised, he must wash clean his sin with water from his eyes. He must do so on the scorpion wheel."

The taskmaster frowned. "You desire *me* to—"

"Yes."

"On the *scorpion wheel*?"

"Has the god struck you deaf? Yes, the scorpion wheel."

"Hekat warleader, you are in the god's eye," he said with care. "But this is Zandakar, the warlord's son. It is custom that Nagarak—"

She dismissed his objection with a flick of her fingers. "Nagarak high godspeaker has healing business with the warlord. As Zandakar's mother *and* the warlord's voice I bring him to you."

"And I receive him," said the godspeaker. "But warleader, forgive me. He will one day be warlord, today he is a child. The scorpion wheel—"

"You talk of custom? Is it not true that custom says a warlord's contrition is shown upon the scorpion wheel?"

Reluctantly, the taskmaster nodded. "Yes. It is true."

"It is also true he will be the warlord. He is not too young to learn what that means. Take us to the wheel, taskmaster, and help my son appease the god."

Zandakar swallowed, there were tears in his eyes. His bottom lip trembled, his fingers fisted at his sides. Hekat's heart broke for him, that could not matter. He was old enough to make decisions, he was old enough to pay their price.

She followed the taskmaster to the scorpion wheel tasking room, trembling Zandakar by her side. She heard his breath catch in his throat at the sight of the cruel iron scorpion wheel.

The taskmaster fetched leather bindings from a box, then looked at her. "How angry has he made the god?"

She looked at Zandakar's perfect body, so recently broken, so newly healed. "Five strokes should appease it, taskmaster. And do not be gentle. In the god's time my son will rule Mijak, he must know how to be obedient so others might obey him."

Zandakar whimpered softly as he was bound to the wheel. She forced herself to watch as the taskmaster took up his cane and raised five welts upon Zandakar's flesh, she made herself listen to her precious son's cries. His golden godbells cried out with him, he was a small and penitent boy.

When the tasking was over, she said, her voice hard, "Remember this moment, Zandakar. No man, however great, can thwart the god and remain unchastised. You will go into the godhouse shrine garden, now. You will kneel before a godpost unmoving until lowsun. A god-speaker will take you to the palace then, you will fast until newsun, you will speak no words unless you speak them to the god. At newsun a godspeaker will fetch you from the palace, you will pray alone in the shrine garden till lowsun, when the godspeaker will return you to the palace. You will do this every day for five days. By then your godspark should be purged of sin." She looked at the taskmaster. "You will arrange this, taskmaster. I have business to attend."

The taskmaster bowed. "Yes, Hekat warleader."

She did not smile at her son, or kiss him, or touch him. She turned on her heel and walked away.

She fetched her red mare from the godhouse stables and rode it to the barracks. The constant stream of supplicants and penitents, godspeakers and novices, trudging up and trudging down, crowded around her on the Pinnacle

Road. It was difficult not to trample them, she wished she could trample them, they were in her way.

They are stupid, they do not know who I am. But in the god's time they will know. They will know better than to crowd me.

Hiklia and Gret, the warriors on duty at the barracks' main gates, pressed their fists to their hearts when she rode in. She did not stop to talk to them, she kept her red mare walking. As she passed the godpost and godbowl she tossed in a single gold coin, it was a mean offering but it was all she could give.

I will give more, god. You know what I will give you.

She jog-trotted through the barracks, past curing fresh horsehides, their tails still attached, and three tall warriors arguing coin with an amulet-seller come to ply her wares, and another slave threading war-charms on the reins of a bridle. Neatly side-stepping a slave pushing a cart piled high with new-sewn tunics, she headed more deeply into her warrior city.

After so long away, returning to the barracks was a physical pleasure. Whenever she left it, to go border skirmishing or on missions like riding to the Heart of Mijak, she missed its rough and violent charm. She did not miss the palace, that place was rich and scented with flowers, soft floor rugs underfoot, honey-sweet pastries in a green glass dish. There she had only to raise one eyebrow, lift a finger, and slaves fell to their knees begging to serve her. They fanned her with feathers, they lulled her with lutes, they dulled her sharp edges with comfort and smiles. She found it distasteful. Knife-dancers needed regular whetting if they wished to stay alive.

Sometimes, wallowing in her palace bath, she thought

if she wasn't careful she might melt completely, turn into soap. Barracks life was robust, it was muscular. There were slaves in the barracks but their service served the warlord, they pampered no-one. Barracks slaves shouted, they argued, they laughed at the warriors, they knew their value and were not afraid. The air here stank of horse shit, of sheep pish, of smoky fires and heated iron, of butchered goats and roasting fowls. Music was made by hammers on anvils, by the chanting of warriors as they danced their *hotas*, the rattle of chariot wheels as the horses trotted by. This was a *real* place, the palace was a rancid dream, life in it rotted by not enough strife.

She felt herself smile. *There will be strife enough to please me now, even in that stupid palace. The god has made me its warleader. Every snakeblade in Mijak is mine.*

She rode to the stables and gave the red mare to one slave, sent another to find Arakun shell-leader. He came to her running and pressed his fist to his breast.

"Hekat knife-dancer. How is Raklion? He brought us the warriors of those fallen warlords, he did not stay for sacrifice. Nagarak led him away. He looked—" Arakun swallowed. "Weary."

The stables were bustling, they always bustled. She jerked her chin and led Arakun outside, to some empty shadows behind a blacksmith's forge.

"He is weary, Arakun, and more than that," she said, her voice soft. "Wicked Banotaj tried to slay him. I killed that sinning warlord, his flesh rots in the sun. Nagarak heals Raklion in the godhouse, he will be himself again. Until he rides among us I speak with his voice."

Arakun's slanted grey eyes widened. "Aieee! Hekat knife-dancer!"

"No longer, Arakun. I am Hekat warleader. Hanochek is banished, you will never see him again."

"*Banished?*" said Arakun. "Because of Zandakar?"

She frowned. "Because of many things. It is a lesson. No man is mightier than the god."

Still Arakun was staring. "You are the warleader . . ."

"And I speak with the warlord's voice. I say to you, shell-leader, summon every warrior to the warhost field. Have the warriors of those fallen warlords taken there under close guard."

His fist thumped his breast, he seemed almost overcome. "Warleader."

He turned to leave her, on impulse she stopped him. "Arakun!"

"Warleader?"

"Zandakar's dead pony. Was its hide stripped for tanning?"

Arakun looked puzzled. "I think so, warleader."

"I want that hide given to the barracks seamsters. I want it swiftly made into leggings for my son."

"Yes, warleader. I will take the hide to them myself."

She bared her teeth at him. "That was my meaning," she told him, still softly, and laughed in her heart at the fear in his eyes.

Ram-horns were sounded throughout the barracks, the warhost assembled on the warhost field. Hekat stood on the warlord's dais and waited for the last warrior to arrive. The sixty warriors serving those fallen warlords came last of all, chivvied before her by Arakun and some spear-throwers. They stood uncertain in their plain tunics and leggings, their sigiled breastplates were taken from them, they were slaves without masters. Men and women, they needed a leader.

Hekat considered them. *I am your leader. I am your master. From this moment forward you will serve me.*

Then she looked at her warhost. "Warriors, it is I! Hekat knife-dancer, mated to Raklion. Zandakar's mother and Bajadek's doom. Raklion was wounded by wicked Banotaj, he recovers in the godhouse, in the god's healing eye. Until he returns my voice is his voice. I speak with his tongue. His tongue says I am your warleader. Hanochek is gone. Banotaj is dead by my hand, the other warlords are thrown down. The god has spoken in the Heart of Mijak. Raklion is its chosen man. Raklion is now the warlord of Mijak. Where the sun shines in Mijak, he is Mijak's warlord. Where the rain falls on the ground, he rules over all."

In the humming silence, one fallen warlord's warrior broke free. "*Lies!*" he cried, waving his fists in fury. "I have a warlord, his name is Takona. Raklion is nothing, I spit on his name!"

Smiling fiercely, Hekat leapt from the dais. She killed the warrior, danced her snakeblade through his heart. He fell at her feet, his blood on the outside, his eyes were empty as they stared at the sky.

"Now you are nothing," she told his corpse. "You are in hell." She looked at the others. "Who wishes to join him?"

Not one of them answered. There was whispering in her gathered warhost. Some of her warriors even laughed. She did not chastise them, they were pure in her eyes.

She said to the fallen warlords' warriors, "The god has spoken. Mijak has one warhost, one warleader. *Hekat.* You will serve it, warriors. You will serve me. If you refuse I will give your godsparks to demons. You will join this stupid man in hell. *Arakun!*"

"Warleader!" said Arakun. He was not stupid.

"Take them away, keep them under guard. They will be assigned to their own shells, in the god's time."

Arakun nodded, he summoned the spear-throwers. They herded the chastened warriors away.

She turned her back on them, and looked at her warhost. The faces that were close enough to see belonged to warriors she knew, had trained, had fought with. She had no friends among them, but they were still familiar. She saw confusion, uncertainty, doubt and fear.

She raised her hands to them, the god was in her voice. It was in her scorpion amulet, heavy round her neck. "Do not be concerned, brave warriors of Et-Raklion. Warriors of Mijak. You are the god's chosen, it has chosen you. It sees you in its admiring eye, it knows there are no greater warriors under Mijak's burning sun. You will lead Mijak's warhost, the other warhosts will kneel at your feet. The god has blessed me, to make me your warleader. I would lead no other warhost, you are precious in my eye!"

Her carrying voice freed them from silence. If they thought of Hanochek, they did not say his name. They surged towards her with their arms outstretched.

"Hekat! Hekat! The god sees Hekat! Raklion's warleader, Zandakar's mother! Bajadek's doom and the doom of his son!"

She let them surround her, crowd her, touch her. She greeted them kindly, they were hers to kiss or kill.

Aieee, Zandakar, my son, my son. See the gift I have to give you. See how I love you, all these warriors are yours.

CHAPTER THIRTY-TWO

"So. Vortka. You are returned from the wilderness a tested godspeaker." Nagarak's fingers drummed his stone desk. "In a time of upheaval, the god sees you in its eye."

Vortka's hands were clasped behind him, he felt his knuckles crack. The high godspeaker had summoned him after lowsun sacrifice, he had stood waiting outside the high godspeaker's chamber for a finger, maybe more. The standing was a punishment, he knew that. He had expected it, and was resigned. Nagarak was not happy he had been waiting at the Warriors' Gate.

He nodded. "Yes, high godspeaker."

Nagarak sat back, his eyes were half-lidded. He blinked like a sandcat, slow and dangerous. "I am told you were present when the warlord's son was injured."

Of course someone had told him. He had not said so himself, there had been no time. Nagarak had dismissed him to the godhouse after the briefest of explanations on the road. "Yes, high godspeaker."

"What were you doing in the barracks, Vortka? You are not a barracks godspeaker. I am told you were assigned to the library until my return from the Heart of Mijak."

"I was ill, high godspeaker. I—"

"A fever," said Nagarak. "Yes. I am told. The healers say it was a *strange* fever. It came on you suddenly and no other godspeaker was afflicted. Can you explain that?"

No. He could not. Feverish maladies were common in Mijak, a legacy from the distant past, but they claimed many victims. Not just one. He had his suspicions, he would not voice them to Nagarak.

I can hardly bear to voice them to myself.

He said, "Forgive me, high godspeaker. I am at a loss to understand it."

"It is known, Vortka godspeaker, that a demon in the flesh brings with it strange fevers."

Vortka felt himself go cold. "You think I am *demon-struck*?"

Nagarak pretended he did not hear the question. "So. Vortka godspeaker. You were in the barracks because you had been ill."

"I was walking, high godspeaker," he croaked. "Regaining my strength. Sidik godspeaker said I should. It is peaceful in the barracks, where the warriors are not training. It is a pleasant place to walk with the god."

Nagarak's eyebrows lifted. "And you walked there when the warlord's son fell from his pony. When the animal lost its footing, I am told, and crashed to the ground."

He nodded, his mouth dry. "Yes, high godspeaker."

"Is it not a wonder the pony did not fall on Zandakar and crush him to death."

Aieee, a great wonder. When he closed his eyes to

sleep in the godhouse, that dreadful moment rose to torment him. Zandakar galloping, laughing, his godbraids flying with his joy. Hanochek watching, encouraging, shouting. A falter, a mis-step, and the pony was twisting, falling, its hindquarters flailing, its neck snapping like wood. And Zandakar, vulnerable Zandakar, tossed from his saddle and into the air, striking the hard ground and screaming his pain.

Repressing a shudder, he made himself meet Nagarak's piercing, lidded stare. "Yes, high godspeaker. The god sees Zandakar in its eye. It kept him safe."

Nagarak sat forward. "Your godchosen sacrifice knife, Vortka. Show it to me."

His true knife was hidden in the trunk of a half-dead tree in the godhouse shrine garden. It was the only safe place he'd been able to think of, no tree was cut down in the godhouse, not until it was fully dead. He gave Nagarak the other knife, the one he had chosen without the god's guidance, and waited as the high godspeaker held it before his eyes.

The god has kept my secret safe, Peklia has not told him of that other knife. If Nagarak knew of it I would be on the scorpion wheel, screaming. The god will protect me now, be still.

"Your hand," said Nagarak.

Vortka held out his hand. Nagarak seized it and sliced the knife's blade through his palm. Blood welled, pain blazed. Nagarak dropped the knife to his desk and dragged his fingers through the thick red blood. Then he raised them to his lips and sucked.

Vortka watched light-headed as Nagarak tested him. "Your blood is clean. I taste no demon-taint in you," the high godspeaker said at last. He sounded grudging. Disappointed.

Vortka released the air from his lungs and willed his knees not to give way. "High godspeaker."

Nagarak took out his godstone and healed the deep cut he had made. Then he handed back the sacrificial knife. "I do not like that you were there when the warlord's son fell from his pony. I do not like that you waited at the Warriors' Gate for the warlord to return from Mijak's Heart. I do not like that you are afflicted with strange fevers. Before you went into the wilderness I told you, Vortka: you are not humble, there are secrets in your heart. I told you I would pluck them out."

"Yes, high godspeaker," he whispered.

Nagarak sat back again, his expression disgruntled. "You are tested in the wilderness, the god has seen you in its eye. You are tested in this godhouse, I have tasted your blood and it is clean. It makes no difference, *I do not trust you.*"

He almost protested, he bit his tongue to blood. One ill-considered word and Nagarak would smite him to pieces. *Aieee, god. If I am sent away now . . . whisper in his heart, god. Do not let him send me away!*

Dropping to his knees before Nagarak's stone desk he said, "If that is true, high godspeaker, I have failed you. I beg your forgiveness. I swear to you I serve the god, the god dwells in my heart, I feel its presence. I believe the god guided my feet to the barracks horse-field. I waited with Zandakar as Hanochek warleader ran for help, I staunched Zandakar's bleeding wound, I kept him calm and quiet until the healers came."

In his dreams he still heard his son, weeping, heard

him call for his mother, heard his piteous moans of pain. The sounds woke him, sweating, as he woke he heard his own voice, saying again what he'd said then: *Hush, Zandakar. Hush, little warlord. Vortka is with you. Do not be afraid.*

Nagarak slammed his fist to his desk. "You are arrogant, Vortka! You do not presume to say what the god has done! That is *my* purpose, *I* am high godspeaker."

Vortka bowed his head. "Yes, high godspeaker."

"You are godseen and tested, you are here to serve the god." Nagarak stood, he loomed over his desk. "You will not serve it far from my sight. You will present yourself to Hadrik godspeaker, he is in charge of the godspeakers who walk Et-Raklion in the quiet time. Every night until I say the god desires your different service, you will walk the city's streets, you will smite any sinner who dares violate the god's peace. If you are not walking the streets you will remain in the godhouse. You will not set foot in the barracks again. You will not see Zandakar in your eye. You will not speak with the warleader, Hekat's voice is forbidden to you."

He felt a jolt of shock. *Hekat* was the warleader? What had happened to Hanochek? Had she killed him in her rage?

The fault was not his, Hekat. God, let her not have killed him.

"Lift your head, Vortka! Look into my face!" commanded Nagarak. "Do you hear my words? Do you hear them in your heart?"

Beneath his worry for Hanochek seethed a harsh relief. *I will stay, I will stay. He does not banish me. Thank you, god.* He looked up. "Yes, high godspeaker. I hear your words in my heart. In the god's eye I swear to you, I am its true and honest servant."

Nagarak smiled, it was a smile filled with rage. "Your mouth dribbles sweet words, do not think I am swayed. If you disobey even one of these commands, Vortka, the god will throw you down in the dirt. It will destroy you. *I* will destroy you. *I* am the god's smiting hand in the world."

Vortka nodded. "Yes, high godspeaker. I hear your commands, I will obey them. I serve the god."

"See that you do. I will be watching," said Nagarak. "Go now. You begin your service on Et-Raklion's streets after lowsun sacrifice."

Sweating beneath his godspeaker robe, Vortka escaped the high godspeaker's impotent fury. He presented himself to Hadrik godspeaker, who expected him. Hadrik gave him a godstaff, for the smiting of sinners abroad in the quiet time, and left him alone with tablets that explained all he must know of sins, and sinners, and how to smite them for the god. When the godbells rang he went to lowsun sacrifice, and after that ate soup and flat bread in the godhouse kitchen. It was three more fingers until the quiet time, he returned to Hadrik to be tested on his understanding. Hadrik pronounced him competent enough. He took his godstaff and walked the almost empty Pinnacle Road down to the city.

As he neared the barracks he saw a familiar figure walking towards him in the godmoon's half-light.

Aieee. Hekat. She said she would find me . . .

She saw him. She stopped. She said, "We must talk together, Vortka."

He cast an anguished look up and down the road but,

for the moment at least, they were alone. "Hekat, we cannot," he whispered, as though Nagarak might hear him. "The high godspeaker forbids me your company, I will be thrown down if I disobey."

"Nagarak forbids you?" she said, disgusted. "Tcha! What is Nagarak to us, the god sees us in its eye."

"Hekat. I cannot thwart the high godspeaker. I serve in his godhouse, I answer to him. He tested me for *demontaint*, he knows I hide something. I *must* take care, would you have me discovered?"

She folded her arms, she still wore her dusty linen tunic. "Nagarak knows nothing, he is a stupid man."

Aieee, she was stubborn, she thought no man could touch her. "You have seen Zandakar?"

"I have seen him."

He smiled, he could not help it. "I told you he was healed, and whole."

"Yes. You told me." In the half-strength moonlight her face was cold and hard. After a moment, it softened slightly. "You are very thin. Have you been ill?"

"A fever. I am better. Hekat," he said, though he was foolish to keep on talking, "what has happened to Hanochek?"

Her teeth shone, she was smiling. Vortka felt his flesh crawl. "Hanochek is an unknown man. Never speak his name again."

Unknown? What was that, some obscure warrior ritual? "Hanochek lives? You did not kill him?"

"You think I should have killed him?" She pulled a face. "Vortka, I wanted to."

"No! I am glad he lives! What happened to Zandakar was not Hanochek's—"

"*Do not defend him!*" She had her fingers on her snakeblade, her fury was so fierce he thought it might scorch him. "Or *I* will smite you, there will be no need for Nagarak!"

"I am sorry," he said, stepping back. "I will not speak of him again."

She took a deep breath and leashed her temper. "The large crystal, Vortka. The one you buried beyond the city. Did you fetch it while I was gone to Mijak's Heart? Is it hidden in my palace garden?"

"No," he said. "I—"

"*No?*" she echoed, and her rage again unleashed. "Did I not *tell* you—"

"It was not safe!" he protested. "I retrieved it from the woods but I did not dare risk the palace. Hekat, I do not walk in the god's eye as easily as you. Only with you do I trust myself fully hidden. The crystal is buried in the godhouse shrine garden, no demon can touch it there. And Nagarak says he desires me within his reach, only the god knows if or when he will send me from Et-Raklion. I will guard the crystal, Hekat. I will keep it safe for Zandakar."

She released a hard breath. "You are the god's chosen. If you say it is safe I must believe you." Her hand brushed her breast beneath its covering of linen, and some memory shifted behind her eyes. "But if Nagarak should decide to send you from his godhouse—"

"Yes. Then I will make sure it is left in your safekeeping. I promise, Hekat. I want that weapon for Zandakar as much as you do."

"*Zandakar . . .*" she whispered. "Aieee, Vortka. He nearly died."

There were tears in her voice, he would not say so. "I know," he said. "But he did not."

She nodded slowly, her face was so troubled. "No. He did not."

He longed to hold her. Comfort her. Kiss her. *I cannot touch her. She would not let me.* He said, "Tell me quickly, what happened at Mijak's Heart? What happened to the warlord, did the god smite him?"

"No, of course not. Stupid Vortka. The god has thrown down those sinning warlords, they knelt before me on the ground."

"But Raklion—"

"Was injured, he is not dead. He will see Mijak united, he will make of it a gift for my son. That is his purpose, he is not finished yet."

She had fed his curiosity, not sated it. There was no time to ask her more. No time to ask her about his strange fever. *Do I really want to? I did not die, do I need to know more? I do not think so. My fever is passed, let it stay behind me.*

He was being a coward, he knew it, he did not care. If the god wanted him to know more, the god would tell him. *I will leave that decision to the god.* He looked towards the distant godhouse, shadowy figures were approaching. "Hekat, I must go, I am expected in the city. I am tasked to keep the god's peace in the quiet time. I do not know when or how we will speak again. I have told you Nagarak's edict, I must obey him. To disobey the high godspeaker is unwise, and unsafe."

"Yes. Go," she said. She seemed distracted, her eyes were still troubled. "You are expected in the city, I must see Raklion and consult with Nagarak. If the god desires us to speak again it will make that possible. The god see you, Vortka."

"The god see you, Hekat."

They walked swiftly away from each other. Despite his misgivings, he tried not to care.

"Well, Nagarak?" said Raklion faintly. "Does the god say I will recover my strength?"

Nagarak looked up from the healing chamber's red-spattered altar, where he read the omens in a dead dove's blood. After his confrontation with sinful Hanochek, Raklion had all but collapsed. He had been so weak a healing had been too much for him, he was put to bed and allowed to sleep for a time. Woken now, with some vitality restored, he had tolerated his high godspeaker's godstone and the god's power pouring into his faltering flesh. Nagarak was relieved, he had never seen Raklion laid so low.

He said, "The knife struck you deeply, warlord, in many vital places. You will recover, but not completely. Your strength will never fully return. You are Mijak's warlord, that is your purpose, you must live carefully if you would live long."

Raklion sagged on the low couch, his scarred, naked body full of bones. "I see."

Nagarak watched him in silence, noting the carved lines of pain in his face, the empty places beneath his skin where his flesh had melted as they rode home to Et-Raklion. "Raklion," he said sternly, "you must not despair. If the god desired you dead, you would be dead. The god does not desire that."

Raklion smiled. "No. It gave me Hekat, to save my life not once but twice."

Hekat. Nagarak felt his mouth shrivel. "The god has many instruments, do not place more faith in this one than in that."

"She is beautiful, she is precious. She is the god's gift, Nagarak," said Raklion, frowning. "Do not seek to harm her, you will displease the god. She is the god's warrior, she dances in its eye. Until I am myself again her words are my words. I am Mijak's warlord, that is my want."

Nagarak said nothing, what could he say? Where Hekat was concerned the warlord was blinded, he thought with his male parts, his tongue was in his heart. He sluiced his hands clean of blood in a basin of water and dried them on a towel.

Raklion said, "Nagarak. Why did you not warn me that Banotaj had a weapon?"

Nagarak did not look at him, he cleaned his sacrifice knife instead. He could feel his heartbeat in his stone scorpion pectoral. "Like his father before him, Banotaj was a man who danced with demons. Demons live to thwart the god. That is their purpose, they sometimes succeed. The god has its vengeance, Banotaj is dead."

"Because of Hekat," said Raklion. He did not sound appeased. "If she had not insisted, if I had listened to you, Hekat would not have stood with us in Mijak's Heart. Banotaj would have killed me. Do you deny this? Do you still deny *her*?"

Aieee, the god see him. How much simpler his life without that knife-dancer in it. Nagarak dried his knife and sheathed it on his belt. "Be warned, warlord. You are a man, you cannot say what would or would not have happened. Hekat was there, the god made use of her. If she had stayed in her place it would have used another instrument."

"You say," said Raklion. "I tell you, Nagarak. I am not so sure."

Nagarak felt his fingers clench. Who was Raklion, a mere warlord, to question *him* in that tone? If the man were not so recently wounded he would make him dearly repent those words.

Am I not Nagarak high godspeaker, smiter of sinners, smiter of high godspeakers in the god's wrathful eye?

The memory of that moment, when his stone pectoral had turned to living scorpion, when the god's power had thundered through him with a fury never known, that memory lingered yet. In his cold blood, a hot thread of that power.

He let it echo in his voice. "Warlord, you do not need to be sure. I am high godspeaker, *I* am sure, I—"

The healing chamber's door swung open, it was a novice with suitably downcast eyes. "Forgive me, high godspeaker. Hekat warleader says she will see the warlord."

Curse the woman, god, send her godspark to hell. "The warlord is resting. She may return after newsun."

"No," said Raklion. "She has come, I will see her."

Nagarak turned. "Warlord—"

"You tell me I am not dead or dying? *I will see her*. Do not deny me, this is warlord business!"

Nagarak nodded to the novice, then looked at Raklion. "You are warlord of Mijak, with a warlord's authority. That is the god's will, I say nothing to that. But this is *my* godhouse, Raklion, I am its warlord. Do not raise your voice to me here, or think to command me like one of your warriors. No man sits above the scorpion wheel, I will see you on it and weeping for the god if once more you disrespect the god's warlord within these walls."

In Raklion's wasted face, a tumult of feeling. "Forgive me," he said, through teeth clenched tight. "As you say, I am warlord. My brain is filled with warlord thoughts, my journey has begun, it is not ended. It—"

"High godspeaker," said the novice from the doorway. "Here is Hekat warleader, to see the warlord."

Nagarak glared at her, she was a plague in his heart. She returned his stare calmly, she had no shame. "He is weary, warleader," he said. "You will not tire him. Stay a short time only, I will know if you linger. I must commune with the god now. After newsun sacrifice we will speak of other matters. Come to me then, I will not see you before."

That did not please her, anger flickered in her face. She was a proud, haughty woman too used to having her own way. Raklion had spoiled her, it was a great pity.

Reluctantly, she nodded. "High godspeaker."

Raklion was smiling, his eyes shone to see her. "Thank you for your care of me, Nagarak. I am grateful, I will remember your words."

Nagarak closed the chamber door behind him. He stalked through the godhouse, godspeakers scattering before him.

As the god is my witness I will bring that bitch down. She has given us Zandakar, she saved Raklion in the crater. Let that be her legacy. Let her now rot.

Raklion held out his thin hand, he did not rise from his bed. "Hekat. Beloved. Come, sit beside me."

Pushing aside her hatred of Nagarak, she crossed to the low stool placed near to Raklion's pillows and sat. He looked ancient and wasted, his silver godbraids had no life. "Warlord."

"Hekat . . ." Smiling, he stroked her scarred cheek. "Will you dress yourself in nothing but plain linen? What must I do, what can I say, that will convince you to dress in silk and wool and golden jewelry! You are Hekat, you are beautiful. You are beautiful and mine."

She shook her head. "I am Hekat, the god's knife-dancer. I have no need for silk and bangles. My snakeblade is my jewelry, my beauty is the dance."

"You are Hekat, slayer of two warlords," he said, easing himself beneath his blankets. "You will sit at my right hand as I reshape Mijak. The other warlords will quail before me, for you are the snakeblade in my fist."

"What other warlords?" she asked him, smiling. "Those sinning men, are they not thrown down in the dirt?"

He laughed, it was a sickly sound. "Yes. They are thrown down. Together you and I will see they stay down, or die." He sobered. "I see in your face how changed I appear. Do not fret, beloved. Nagarak promises I will be myself again in time."

Nagarak was lying, did he know it or was he blind? Raklion was ruined, he would never be the same. She would not say so, she had need of him yet. "It pleases me to hear it, warlord. And until then you will trust me as your voice? You will trust me to continue what the god began at the Heart of Mijak? The warlords are chastened now, Raklion, but if they are not beaten to the ground and their warhosts taken from them, their godhouses taken from them, everything that made them warlords, if it is not all taken from them soon they will rise to their knees and then to their feet. They will turn to demons and abandon the god."

The chamber was lit with a handful of candles. In the soft light she watched him smile again. "Aieee, my knifedancer. So savage for the god, so savage for me."

I am savage for Zandakar, he will not inherit chaos. "I am the god's servant, Raklion. I do not rest until its will is done."

"I know. You are fearless." His words were slurred, his gaze unfocused. "I trust you, Hekat. You speak with my voice. Together you and Nagarak will subdue the warlords. You will take from them what they must lose. You will continue what the god began at the Heart of Mijak. And when I am myself again, I will finish it."

"You honor me, warlord. I am humbled in your eye."

"Tcha," he said. "Will I forget how you saved me from Bajadek and his son? My life and Zandakar, you have gifted me with both. I do not forget it, you are Mijak's first woman. All other women are beneath you."

She touched his wrist. "Where I am, warlord, the god has placed me. If I have saved you, you also saved me. You did not return me to Abajai and Yagji, or give me to Nagarak for killing on a godpost."

"The god would not let me," said Raklion. "It meant you for my warlord bed."

That is the least thing I am meant for. "You are the warlord. You know the god's want."

He nodded, slowly. "When I am well again I will ride with my warhost through the streets of Et-Raklion. You will ride at my right hand, you and Zandakar. The people will see my son beside me, they will see you, his mother, the warhost's warleader with my heart in your hands."

She smiled to think of it. "Godspeakers will stand on every street corner. The word will ring out with godbells of the god's desire. One Mijak. One warlord."

Who soon will be Zandakar. I am his mother, I will be his voice.

Raklion heaved an unsteady sigh. "Hekat, beloved, I am so weary. I must sleep now. Stay. Hold my hand."

"Of course, warlord."

As he slid into dreams he whispered, sadly, "Aieee, sweet Hekat. I am sorry for Hanochek."

Tcha. I am not. She sat beside him, she held his hand. In the chamber's silence, as Raklion slept, fears and suspicions seeped once more into her heart.

Vortka is wrong, Zandakar's fall was no accident. Demons seduced him to wickedness in the hope he would die. In causing his death they seek to thwart the god. He is born to destroy them, he will be the god's hammer when he is a man. The god saved him this time . . . what of the next?

For there would be a next time, and a next, and a next. The demons had to destroy him if they were to survive. Demons were wily, the god did not always defeat them. Had she not read that in the godhouse library, as Zandakar grew inside her belly? Yes, she had read it, tale after tale of demons thwarting the god. If the god itself could be thwarted by demons, so could she. *I am not the god.* And if they succeeded in killing Zandakar, what would the god do? Would it abandon her, reject her, cast her down in the dirt? Would Hekat the godtouched become Hekat the godforsaken?

I am the god's knife-dancer, it is my purpose to lay its enemies low. If I fail to protect Zandakar, if the god's hammer is destroyed, the god will desert me. It will not see Hekat, she will be dead in its eye.

There was only one answer. She must create another son. One to be warlord and hammer if the demons triumphed and Zandakar died. The thought of him dying was a knife in her breast. She bit her knuckle to the bone.

I need a man to sire me a second son. A man with the power to wake the crystal. It cannot be Vortka, I must have faith. The god will send that man to me, I live in its eye, I am its willing slave. It will send me another man in its time.

CHAPTER THIRTY-THREE

A breath before newsun Hekat ate a brief breakfast with Zandakar on her private palace balcony. He was woeful, his five highsuns of penance in the godhouse shrine garden commenced after his honeyed cornmush and sadsa.

"You will be warlord, Zandakar," she told him, unrelenting. "You cannot be warlord with an unclean heart."

"No, Yuma," he murmured, he did not lift his gaze from his cornmush bowl.

"When the god knows you are penitent, when it has heard all your prayers, you will live again. You will rejoin the world. You will be my son, the warlord Zandakar."

He sighed. "Yes, Yuma."

A slave came to the doorway. "Warleader, there is a godspeaker."

Zandakar sighed again and slid from his chair. He wore his linen training tunic and plain brown leather leggings, as soon as the seamsters were finished he would wear blue-striped Didijik.

Not even five highsuns of prayer will teach him a better lesson.

"The god see you, my son," she told him. "Live in its eye."

He pressed his small fist to his breast, his godbells were mournful. "The god see you, Yuma. I will live in its eye."

She ate more quickly when he was gone, she must hurry to the barracks for newsun sacrifice. She was the warleader, it was her expected place. Besides, if she did not attend sacrifice there she must attend it in the godhouse and already she was tired of Nagarak's sour face.

I must meet him after sacrifice and discuss warlord business. That will be enough time spent in his shadow.

She cantered the red mare to the barracks and left it in the stables, she must walk to the godhouse after or invite Nagarak's wrath. She did not have Zandakar as an excuse today.

The warhost was assembled and ready for sacrifice, she knelt on the grass among them, one of them, Hanochek had never done that. She felt their cautious approval, it pleased her. When sacrifice was done she spent some little time showing them her unchanged face, letting them see that she was still Hekat, still a knife-dancer, she wore a plain linen tunic, she did not wear gold. No-one mentioned Hanochek, if they missed him she could not see it in their eyes. Their eyes were warm, they were pleased to see her.

You are Zandakar's warhost, I hold you in my hands.

She took Arakun aside. "How fare the warriors of those fallen warlords?"

Arakun's twisted face twisted further in a smile. "Warleader, they spent a wise night, they did not cause trouble. I think the memory of that sinner you slew rode them in their unquiet dreams."

She nodded. "Good. Collect the other shell-leaders, sit together in the warlodge. Distribute those warriors among yourselves, each according to their skills and temperaments. Let our warriors of Et-Raklion keep them busy, let them see how hopeless rebellion is. I go to meet Nagarak, we must soon move to subdue all of Mijak with our sharp knives."

"Yes, warleader," said Arakun, and shook his head. "It is a fierce blessing, Hekat, to be the warhost of Mijak."

"If we were not worthy the god would not raise us high," she told him. "After you have decided what to do with those warriors, Arakun, you and the shell-leaders must consider the expansion of our warhost. Soon the warhosts of those fallen warlords will join us, they must have somewhere to sleep at night and we must decide how best they will serve our purpose."

"Join us?" said Arakun. "Warleader, they will come to Et-Raklion?"

"Of course," she said, staring. *Was* the man stupid? "Mijak's warhost cannot be scattered, not until those other warriors are tamed. Until that time the warhost must dwell here, in our barracks. Those inferior warriors must be trained to our ways." •

Arakun's jaw dropped. "Forgive me, warleader. In *our* barracks? On the Pinnacle? I think that is impossible, I think the barracks is stretched to breaking already, in the past few seasons Raklion has recruited so many more warriors."

"Tcha! I know that." She cowed him with a scornful look. "Slaves will be brought from the other cities, they will toil until a new barracks is built. On the flatlands and far slopes of Raklion's Pinnacle, there is a great deal of open ground there."

"Yes," said Arakun, sounding cautious. "We skirmish over it with the new recruits . . ?"

"We will have all of Mijak for our skirmishing. That is where the new barracks will be built. When I return from meeting Nagarak I wish to hear your thoughts on its design and how best we will salt our shells with so many new warriors. We will need many more shells and shell-leaders, you will give me a list of those you think deserve that rank, I will discuss it with you shell-leaders and make my decision in my time."

Arakun pressed his fist to his breast. "Yes, warleader." He sounded daunted.

"Arakun," she said. "We have worked well together in the past. You have been a man who hears my voice. Should I now seek a man with *sharper* hearing?"

He shook his head, his godbells chimed his fervent alarm. "No, warleader. There is nothing the matter with my hearing."

She smiled. "Good."

He saluted her again. "Warleader, all will be done as you command."

She left him and walked leisurely to the godhouse,

through the barracks that were her home. She would not hurry for Nagarak, he must learn to wait for her. As she walked she inspected the forges where the snakeblades were born, she dallied with the fletchers making their arrows and the craftsmen who constructed the bows. She inhaled the rich scents of leatherworkers' row, where a warrior grown too old for fighting presented her with a bridle for Zandakar's new pony. It was small and perfect, inlaid with lapis lazuli and banded with silver.

"The god sees you, Hekat warleader," said the battered old man. He had lost an eye to war, he had lost two fingers and one of his feet. There was water on his cheeks. "I served Raklion's father, the warlord Ragilik. I served Raklion warlord, who is warlord of Mijak. If the god desires I will serve his son. Zandakar the beautiful, he is known by that name."

The bridle was as perfect as her son. "Warrior, you have served him already," said Hekat, touched. "Raklion will know of this gift, when his godhouse business is behind him he will come to thank you himself. What is your name, we have not met before."

The old man pounded his fist against his breast, almost too overcome to speak. "I am Tuglia. I was a knife-dancer."

"You are still a knife-dancer, Tuglia," she said, clasping his shoulder. "In your heart, you dance with your knife."

She left him weeping, and went to meet Nagarak.

"You bring an *animal harness* into my chamber?" he demanded. He did not rise as she entered. He was a man with no manners, too arrogant to live.

She looked at the silver and lapis pony bridle. "It is a

gift for Zandakar from a brave godseen warrior. You say I should drop it in the dirt?"

"I say you should sit so we might talk of things that matter. I am high godspeaker of Mijak, I have much to do."

She dropped to the other chair in the cold, spare chamber, the bridle she laid carefully across her lap. It was the only beautiful thing in the room. "Before we talk of Mijak, tell me: is Hanochek gone? Is he taken from Et-Raklion?"

"Yes. He is gone," Nagarak admitted. He hated to tell her even that small a thing.

I must not care for that, is Nagarak important? I think he is not. "To Et-Jokriel, in secret, as I suggested?"

"Yes. To Et-Jokriel, in secret."

She felt the fiercest joy well up inside her, she wanted to sing, to dance, to shout. *He is gone, he is gone, I am free of him forever!* She nodded. "That is good, Nagarak. It is good for the warlord, for Mijak and my son. You must never tell them where Hanochek is sent. Let it be our secret. Let it not burden their hearts. If they ask, say it is the god's want."

Nagarak nodded, grudging. "Agreed."

She swallowed a smile. "How fares the warlord this newsun, after his healing?"

"He is much improved."

"How long before he can ride to war? The warhost must chasten Et-Banotaj city. Those people must be taught how to kneel on the ground. Of all the cities they must be taught first, they were led by a warlord who consorted with demons."

Nagarak looked down his nose. "Raklion will teach them, in the god's time."

Tcha. He was not stupid, he was being difficult. She leaned forward. "Nagarak, we have the warlords, we do not have their warhosts. Before many highsuns their warhosts will ride on us, they will know, or suspect, their warlords are in Et-Raklion, they will come to claim them unless they are subdued. If Raklion is not well enough for war, then *I* will lead Et-Raklion's warhost, I will make war on the cities of those fallen warlords, I will smite them with my snakeblade, I will smite them for the god!"

Nagarak stood and crashed his fist on his stone desk. He looked like the man in the hovel of her childhood, spittled and angry and wanting to hurt. "You smite *nothing* and *no-one* for the god, Hekat. The god will smite *you* in your arrogant pride!"

She wanted to slap him, she kept her hands by her side. "Aieee, Nagarak! You are stupid. If I am arrogant does it mean I am *wrong*? Do you say the cities must not be subdued? Do you say Et-Banotaj is not demon-tainted?"

"I do not say that! I am Mijak's high godspeaker, I know where there are demons," sneered Nagarak. "The warlord and I have spoken already. We know what must be done in Mijak, woman."

They had spoken? Without her? Tcha, they were foolish. "Yes? Then you must also know it must be done *quickly*."

Breathing heavily, Nagarak sat back in his chair. "Of course it must."

Tcha, it was a wonder he did not drop dead from agreeing. "The warhost must ride within three highsuns, we can wait no longer," she said. "Will Raklion be recovered enough by then?"

Nagarak stared at his barren stone desk. "No," he said,

frowning. "It will take longer than that for him to regain his strength."

She felt her blood stir and her amulet quicken. "Then I will lead the warhost. Will those fallen warlords be chastened three highsuns from now?"

Nagarak smiled, if he had power over her she would grovel before him. "As we speak they are chastened. They will be chastened further."

"They must ride with me to wicked Et-Banotaj. They must see that sinning city thrown down."

"No," said Nagarak. "They will ride with *me*. I am high godspeaker in Mijak, Hekat. The god is wrathful, its wrath is mine. There are warriors in Et-Banotaj, there are also godspeakers. Godspeakers are *my* business, they are not yours to chide."

She looked at his sleeping stone scorpion pectoral and remembered it living and killing for the god. She remembered the warlords, smitten by the sight. "Agreed," she said. "The godspeakers are yours. The warriors are mine, if they will not surrender they will die by my hand."

A small silence, then, as they considered each other. Nagarak said, "Do not become comfortable speaking with Raklion's voice. He is feeble now, he will be strong enough soon. He is the warlord, that is the god's desire."

"I know."

He tapped the stone desk with a single finger. "Your amulet, Hekat. Where did you get it?"

Aieee, her amulet again. "I told you, Nagarak. It was a gift from the god. Do you question the god's gifts? I think you do not." She bared her teeth. "I do not question either. That would be a sin."

He breathed in, he breathed out. Sunlight from his

chamber's single window played over his pectoral, the shadows gave it an illusion of life. "I will tell Raklion he cannot ride to Et-Banotaj."

That suited her purpose, in this he would listen more readily to Nagarak than to her. "Tell him it is the god's desire he stay behind and become a strong man," she suggested. "There is much to think and pray on in the reshaping of Mijak. The god has given us great work to do."

Nagarak shook his head, his heavy godbraids clattered and chimed. "Be warned, woman. Dare to think you can speak for the god, and the god will smite you in a smiting never seen before in the history of the world."

Tcha. He was a stupid man, his godbells were so loud he was deaf to the god. She stood, the pony bridle in her hand. "After Et-Banotaj is thrown down, then must the rest of Mijak be swiftly brought to heel. That must largely be godhouse business, Nagarak. The warlord and I must eat, sleep and breathe Mijak's new warhost. Are you and your godspeakers ready, do you know yet how that task will be accomplished? Perhaps we should—"

Nagarak snorted. "Ignorant woman, it is already begun. I am the high godspeaker, do I need a *knife-dancer* teaching me how to impose the god's order in its own land? Godspeakers of this godhouse are even now being chosen, they will be sent to those other godhouses to ensure obedience to the god's will." Eyes narrowed, his finger again tapped upon his stone desk. "It is in my mind that one of those chosen will be Vortka godspeaker."

She stood very still, she did not let him see her thinking. *It is a test, he tests me. He wishes to see Vortka in my heart.* "Who?" she said, she made her voice puzzled, disinterested. "As you say, I am a knife-dancer. The names of godspeakers mean nothing to me."

"Are you so certain? This godspeaker was waiting for us at the Warriors' Gate. He seems to have an interest in the warlord's son."

Nagarak can see nothing the god does not show him. The god shows him little, he is seldom in its eye. "That one? His name is Vortka? He never said so. As for Zandakar, what heart in Et-Raklion does not beat for him? My son is precious, he is beautiful, he is the god's gift to Mijak. I would be worried, Nagarak, if this Vortka were *not* interested." She shrugged. "If you think he will serve the god best in some other city, in Et-Zyden, or Et-Takona, send him to the godhouse there. Why should I care where a godspeaker goes? I am the warleader. I care only for warriors."

Did he believe her? She thought he did not, his eyes were suspicious. It was no matter. Whatever he thought, he would never know the truth. The god would not let him. She and Vortka were precious in its eye. Nor would Nagarak send Vortka away, not if the god did not desire it.

As she left the godhouse, ignoring as always the avid stares of city supplicants, she put an offering in one of the godbowls at its main entrance. Reaching for the golden coin in her pocket, her fingers brushed against the cloth-wrapped red crystal she kept with her all the time.

Its touch made her shiver, it made her think of Zandakar . . . and the brother she must give him, in her service to the god.

How long must I wait, god? When will you send a man to me?

The god did not answer. She would have to be patient.

* * *

Nagarak permitted no dissent, Raklion accepted he could not ride to Et-Banotaj. After a full highsun of rest and healing he rose from his bed, closer to himself again, and walked slowly on his own feet from the godhouse to the barracks where his warhost greeted him with shouts of joy. Hekat walked with him, she was his warleader. The warhost shouted to see her as well.

After wandering through his busy barracks, making sure to thank Tuglia for Zandakar's bridle, he sat with her and the shell-leaders in the warlodge, a small stone building filled with plans and secrets, and they talked of many warhost things, the new shells, the new barracks. The remaking of Mijak, and the mighty warhost they would create.

He told them he was not riding with them upon Et-Banotaj. "The god has made its desire known to me. I must remain in the godhouse, I must spend much time in prayer. To be warlord of Mijak is a solemn, sacred thing." He took Hekat's hand, he raised it to his lips. "Here is my warleader, she will lead the warhost to that wicked place. Nagarak will ride beside her, he takes the god to a godless land. You are my godgifted warriors, you will bring Et-Banotaj to its sinning knees."

Arakun and the other shell-leaders pressed their fists to their breasts, they were pleased to hear Hekat would lead them into battle. They knew they could trust her to give them the victory.

Raklion said, "The warhost will number ten thousand warriors. Hekat, with them you will take those fallen warlords. They must see in blood and fire, for they might still have doubt in their secret hearts, that their old lives are finished. They serve Raklion now, no man serves them."

Hekat looked at him, he sounded weary. He should not appear weak before the shell-leaders, it was too soon for him to fail. She said, "The god speaks through you, warlord. Your commands will be obeyed. Ten thousand warriors in the warhost, I will ride with those of the fallen warlords myself. Do you have any other commands for your shell-leaders? They must prepare the warhost to leave in two highsuns."

Raklion pushed himself to his feet and looked at the shell-leaders in turn, round the table. "No. I am pleased with each of you. I am well served. I return now to the godhouse, to pray for the god's smiting of wicked Et-Banotaj. Hekat . . . walk with me to the barracks gates."

They made slow progress, Raklion was often stopped and blessed. Still he managed to say to her, in private, "I wish you had not given Zandakar such a penance, Hekat. Five highsuns on his knees in the godhouse shrine garden? I think he was already punished enough."

Aieee, he was stupid. If she left Zandakar's raising to him her son would grow into a soft, weak man. "I do not think so."

"How can you say that?" Raklion demanded. "He lost his pony . . . he lost Hanochek, his friend . . ." His thin, aged face tightened, it hurt him to say that sinning man's name.

Let it hurt him, I do not care. His blind trust of Hanochek nearly killed my son. "Warlord, Zandakar is no ordinary boy. Zandakar will be Mijak's warlord. He cannot sin and escape the god's wrath."

Raklion sighed. "I know. But Hekat, I remember what it was like, to grow up in a warlord's shadow, knowing my life would never be my own, knowing I was not an ordinary boy. I was Zandakar's age when my brother died, when I learned I would be Raklion warlord. Do you know, I wanted to be a winemaker? Even so young, I knew I wanted that. I never wanted to be a warrior. I never wanted to hold so many lives in my hand. The god decreed otherwise, I am obedient to its will. I have served Et-Raklion, I will serve all of Mijak. Zandakar will serve it after me. That is also the god's will. But there is time yet for him to be a boy. Let him be a boy, Hekat. He will be a man a long, long time."

Tcha, he was as bad as Vortka. "He will be a man, yes, but to be a *strong* man first he must be a strong *boy*."

Raklion laughed, he kissed her cheek and took her hand. "I sometimes think *you* should be warlord, Hekat. You are stronger than any man I know."

True, true, Raklion, that is true. And I would be the greatest warlord Mijak has ever known. She smiled. "You flatter me. I am the warleader and Zandakar's mother. I am content, do I need more? I think I do not."

They reached the barracks' gates, she stopped and slid her fingers from his grasp. "I will lead the warhost to victory in Et-Banotaj. The god is in me, I cannot fail."

Raklion kissed her again. "I believe you, Hekat. The god is deeply in you. So deeply I think my prayers are not urgent. Something else is urgent. I think it past time we gave Zandakar a brother. He needs a closer friend than the warriors' children he trains with in the barracks. He needs blood of his own to bond with, to play with. It is not good for a boy to grow up alone."

She looked at him. The marks of his suffering had not faded from his face, he was thin, no longer robust. His eyes were sunken, he was not a well man. Did he have the strength to fuck? She could not ask him, he would take offense. And even if he did, nothing would come of it. He was destined never to sire a son.

She did not want to fuck him. She did not want to fuck anyone, not even the man the god would send her in its time. She did not like fucking, she thought she never would. "And the warhost, warlord? There is much to do, with little time before we ride to Et-Banotaj."

He recaptured her hand. "There is time enough for you to lay with your warlord. My warhost is long-trained to ride out at short notice. And a good warleader trusts her shell-leaders, Hekat. They can manage without you. I cannot."

He would not be dissuaded. Resigned, resentful, she let him lead her away.

Later that night, after lowsun sacrifice, Nagarak brought the chastened warlords down to the palace. Raklion waited for them in his torchlit audience chamber, shadows flickered its cold stone walls. Hekat stood by his right hand, Zandakar at his left. The warlord was dressed in his finest wools, crimson and dark blue and rich Et-Raklion green. His breastplate was new-made, its snake picked out in rare diamonds. Emerald snake-eyes stared unblinking at the world. Zandakar's clothing echoed his, for this important moment he was excused his penitent linen and leggings.

Hekat wore her training tunic. Her only decoration was her well-blooded snakeblade, she held it naked in her fist.

The godforsaken warlords knelt before Raklion's great chair. Their godbraids were silent, no bells to lament. Except for their loincloths they were naked. They bowed their chastised heads at Raklion's feet, all their arrogance was sweated out of their skins. Nagarak stood close behind them, his scorpion pectoral fully revealed. Three lesser godspeakers stood behind him. Vortka was not one of them, Hekat felt no surprise.

Raklion said to his fallen brothers, "You must know I did not seek this. I did not know this would be my life. But the god has spoken, I must obey. Mijak is whole again, I am its warlord. Nagarak is its godspeaker, no voice but his now speaks for the god. Hekat is my snakeblade, the god dances in her. She is Zandakar's mother, Bajadek's doom and the doom of Banotaj, his son. Hekat is the warleader of Mijak's warhost, there is no-one more powerful after me. Here is Zandakar, my son in the god's eye. Your sons will obey him, as all men's sons will obey him, as all men breathing now obey me. Zandakar will be warlord in his time. Say his name. I would hear it on your lips."

"*Zandakar*," said the kneeling men in a ragged chorus.

"And who is he?"

"*Your son in the god's eye. He is the warlord after you.*"

"And who am I?"

One by one, the warlords looked up. Each face was a wasteland, their eyes were full of tears. Hekat examined them, she searched them for demons. Her amulet stayed silent, she could sense no sin. Nagarak had done what was needed, these proud men were indeed chastened.

"*You are Raklion*," they said, they sounded humble. "*Warlord of Mijak, in the god's eye.*"

Raklion nodded. He was tired after fucking, he did not show that in this room. "I am Raklion, warlord of Mijak. Banotaj is dead, he defied the god. You five are chastened men, the god has thrown you down. It has thrown down your high godspeakers, they will never rise again. If you once disobey me, you will join them in hell. I warn you, do not tempt me, do not tempt the god. The past is the past, *I* am your future."

"He is your future," said Nagarak, echoing. "And the god *will* be watching you. It knows all your hearts. If you are sinful my scorpion will wake."

The kneeling warlords shuddered, remembering, they moaned in their throats and rocked on their heels.

"Listen to me, you fallen warlords, as I tell you what your lives will be," said Raklion. "In this whole Mijak, ruled by Raklion warlord in the god's eye."

Hekat listened, but she had heard it already, as she lay in bed with Raklion after fucking. Mijak's future had been swiftly decided between Raklion and Nagarak in the godhouse healing chamber. She could find no fault in their plan for Mijak, the god had guided them. She must be content.

The fallen warlords' mastery of their territories was ended. No longer would their sons succeed them, their sons and their daughters would serve Raklion in Mijak's warhost. They would live in his city, far from their own blood, away from temptations. The warlords' cities would still be cities, they could keep their names and the fallen warlords could rule them as governors, for as long as they remained obedient to the god and Raklion warlord in its eye. The cities must lose their warlord prefix, no longer *Et*-Zyden, but Zyden plain, and the same with all the rest. Nor would their godhouses remain independent. Godspeakers from Et-Raklion would be sent to those godhouses. Each city's godspeakers would come to

Et-Raklion, to be examined in Nagarak's eye. If they harbored demons they would go to hell.

The fallen warlords' sad faces grew slowly more sorrowful, but they said nothing. What could they say? The god had spoken. Their time was done.

Raklion told them more of Mijak's warhost, that their warriors were his now and Zandakar's after. Hekat watched those words strike them, they were proud fighting warriors who would never again fight. She saw their eyes again fill with water, they grieved for their losses, they were wounded men. The god did not see them, they were blind in its eye.

Should I feel sorry? I think I should not.

At a signal from Nagarak one of the three godspeakers departed the chamber, returning with a gold basin full of sacred blood. Nagarak took his sacrifice knife, he cut Raklion's hand and bled it into the basin, he cut each kneeling warlord's hand and added their blood to Raklion's. Last of all he cut himself, his blood mixed in the basin, he took a cup, filled it, and the fallen warlords drank. That was their oath to Raklion, and the god. Then Nagarak whipped them with a scorpion flail, it was the god's promise of retribution should they break that oath. After the beating Nagarak healed them, that was the god's protection against demons.

The audience was over. Nagarak led the five silent men from the chamber, they were chastened, they were broken, they walked like slaves in heavy chains. Raklion turned to Zandakar.

"You see, my son, how a warlord deals with his people."

Zandakar nodded. "Yes, warlord. I see."

"Zandakar," said Hekat. "It is time for your bed, you

have not finished your penance in the godhouse shrine garden. A godspeaker comes for you at newsun, and you must be ready."

"Yes, Yuma," said Zandakar. He saluted her, he saluted Raklion, he left the chamber. He was a good boy.

"Aieee, Hekat," Raklion sighed when they were alone. "This task the god gives me, I fear for my strength."

"You are foolish, warlord. You are chosen, the god will not let you fail." *Not until it requires your failure.* "Now we must sleep, too," she added, and helped Raklion down from his warlord's chair. "I ride for Et-Banotaj with the warhost at newsun."

Aieee, how it pleased her to say so.

I am the god's knife-dancer, I hunger for war. Come the newsun I will worship with my blade.

CHAPTER THIRTY-FOUR

Vortka concealed himself in the godhouse shrine garden and watched the smiting warhost depart, Hekat and Nagarak side by side in the lead. He wondered which of them chafed most at that, and had to smile at the thought.

They are unlikely oxen, yoked by the god.

He stifled a yawn, after another night on the streets of Et-Raklion seeking out sinners he was so weary. He had attended sacrifice, he was free to sleep, but how could he shut himself away in his cell when Hekat was riding to smite Et-Banotaj?

The warhost was vast, thousands of warriors, slaves to see to their needs, five carts full of living sacrifices and *three hundred* godspeakers. So many had never ridden into battle before. They rode behind Nagarak, surrounding the fallen warlords who were being taken to see the fate of cities seduced by demons. They were already chastened, those warlords, he had heard snatches of gossip in the kitchens as he ate his quick meals. Nagarak had shown no pity, they were wicked sinners.

After Et-Banotaj they will not dare sin again.

He was not sorry to see Nagarak ride away, the warhost would be gone for more than a godmoon. A whole godmoon free of Nagarak and his suspicions, aieee, it was a blessing. More than ever, Nagarak terrified him. He knew now what had happened at the Heart of Mijak. The chosen warriors who rode there had spoken in the barracks of Nagarak's scorpion pectoral coming to life and killing the high godspeakers of those warlords. The barracks godspeakers had heard the stories and repeated them in the godhouse. It was gossip, it was forbidden, but it spread even so.

If ever I speak with Hekat again I will ask her if that gossip is true. I have never heard of a stone scorpion killing, I—

Aieee! Except he had. Once. Abajai and Yagji's deaths in their villa. The scorpion scarring on their chests. Hekat had told him her scorpion amulet had killed them, the god in her amulet had sent them to hell. He remembered that day, how could he forget? He had touched Hekat's godspark and nearly burst into flame.

The god in Nagarak's scorpion pectoral, the god in Hekat's scorpion amulet. Both made of the same stone, sacred and rare. Both wielded by people deep in the god's eye.

I think this is too much for me. I think I am a humble man. In my heart I remain a potsmith.

He did not like walking Et-Raklion's streets in the quiet time, seeking out sinners. The first time he found a man breaking the law, the first time he smote someone with his bare hand, he had fallen to his knees after and vomited in the road. He thought the god would strike him dead for that, how could he be a proper godspeaker and have no heart for the smiting of sinners?

The god had not struck him dead, it did not smite him at all. Perhaps it was busy and had not noticed his weakness.

He did not vomit again after that first time, but he still heard the smitten screams in his uneasy sleep. Hekat was right, people were stupid. They *knew* the godspeakers walked the streets in the quiet time, they *knew* if they were found sinning they would pay a heavy price. And yet they took that chance, they risked the god's wrath. With Raklion's elevation to warlord of Mijak it seemed many folk had lost their wits.

They think because Raklion is godchosen, then they are too. They think the god's laws can be broken because their warlord is special. When will they learn? No man can break the god's law and escape unpunished. Not even a warlord.

The warhost was leaving by the main city gates, as Vortka climbed up the Pinnacle Road to the godhouse that newsun he had left hundreds gathering in the streets to praise it and cheer. He thought Hekat would like that, hundreds of people, perhaps thousands by now, waving and cheering as she rode to war for the god.

And may the god help those foolish warriors in the city of Et-Banotaj. If they do not throw down their snake-blades at the sight of her eyes she will slay every one of them, she will drink all their blood. Then Nagarak will scorch their godsparks, together they will send those sinners to hell.

Vortka shuddered. At first he'd been sorry Nagarak had not chosen him among the three hundred godspeakers to ride with the warhost in the smiting of Et-Banotaj. Now he was relieved, not only because it gave him time free of the high godspeaker's merciless scrutiny, but also because he had no stomach for slaughter. Even the slaughter of sinners. It just made him sad.

Another yawn overcame him, weariness was in his bones. He would sleep for three fingers, then rise to serve in the library. Or kneel before a taskmaster, Nagarak would be certain to discover if he had done so and punish him personally if he had not.

Aieee, god. It is not easy, serving Nagarak. I know he has his purpose, I know he is in your eye. I just wish, sometimes, I was not in his.

It was so early the shrine garden should be empty. He turned away from the sight of Hekat's warhost, departing, and slipped between the high hedges that turned the open ground into many small, private sanctuaries. First he inspected the half-dead tree where his proper sacrifice knife slept. It was still there, safe and undiscovered. Then, acutely aware of every rustle in the trees, every stirring in the godhouse, he sought the place where he had buried the large crystal, that would one day, somehow, be a weapon for the god.

The ground in that sanctuary remained undisturbed. He had buried the crystal beside the shrine's godpost, certain the god would keep it safe. This was the third time he had risked coming to see its hiding place, he felt light-headed knowing he had not failed.

You see it, god, the crystal lives in your eye. Let it remain there, let your powers thwart demons who would pluck it from your sight.

His knife was safe, the crystal was safe. Now he could sleep, he was desperate for bed.

As he turned to leave the shrine garden he heard a sob, coming from the other side of its hedge. He stopped. A heartbeat's silence, then another sob, anguished and incompletely stifled. He frowned.

I know that voice, I know the sound of those tears . . .

"Zandakàr!" he said, standing in the hedge's narrow opening. "Zandakàr, what is it?"

His son knelt before the sanctuary shrine, it was a carved scarlet scorpion with a raised, stinging tail. At the sound of his name Zandakàr wrenched around and nearly fell. His expression was shamed, his face was wet. His beautiful eyes were full of woe. "Vortka godspeaker! I am sorry, I am sorry."

"No!" he said, and stepped further in. "Do not be sorry, tell me why you weep. Tell me why you are *here*, so early in the shrine garden. Does your mother know you pray here at this time?"

Zandakàr dragged his forearm over his face, the rough movement made his godbells shiver, a muted chime.

"Yuma sends me, it is my penance for sinning. I have prayed here four days with only flatbread and water, godspeaker. After today my penance is done."

"I see," said Vortka. He had not known. She had not told him, though there had been the chance. *She guards him so jealously. There is no need.* "And you weep because you sinned against the god?" Zandakar hesitated. "You can tell me, Zandakar. I am a godspeaker, what you tell me is private."

Zandakar looked down, he smoothed a hand over his blue-striped horsehide leggings as though they were warm living skin. "It is nothing, godspeaker," he whispered, brokenly. "I am sorry, I must pray to the god."

"*Zandakar . . .*" Vortka moved closer, he dropped to one knee. "You are too young to weep like a man. Let me help you." *Let me help you, my son.*

Zandakar's breath caught in his throat, he could not stop fresh tears from falling. "I lo—*loved* Didij—ik," he said, almost incoherent. "I did not mean—mean to hurt him, I did not think it was a—a *sin* to ride like a warrior. I wish Yuma had told the taskmaster to whi—whip me *ten* times. He could have whipped me till I *bled* on the scorpion wheel, I—I would not care." He sucked in a shuddering breath. "But she gave me these leggings and I have to *wear* them."

The leggings. Blue-striped horsehide. Newly tanned, they had lost none of their color. Vortka felt his belly lurch, saw a beautiful pony in his mind's eye. "*Didijik?*" he whispered, incredulous.

Zandakar nodded. "Yuma said now I will never forget."

Never forget? Their son would be scarred for life,

like her knife-slashed face this memory would sear him forever.

Hekat, how could you? You make him wear the hide of his beloved dead pony? You had him whipped on the scorpion wheel? He is only a child, how could you do that?

He remembered, aching, his own happy childhood, his ordinary life before the god intervened. He had loved his father and loved his mother, they expected obedience but he was never *whipped*. Never starved of food, never forced to pray. He remembered laughter, he remembered joy, he remembered games and tickling and praise and forgiveness. They were strict, they were never harsh, harshness had come only once his father was dead.

What do you remember, Hekat, that you could so punish our precious boy?

"Zandakar," he said, and though it was dangerous, forbidden, he pressed his palm to his small son's cheek. He had no choice, his child was suffering. He would have done it if smiting Nagarak were in the godhouse. "Hekat warleader is a fierce, proud woman. She burns in the god's eye, she is unique. She loves you as she loves the god, whatever she does is because she believes it is right. When you fell and hurt yourself, you frightened her badly. She is trying to make sure it never happens again. You must wear the horsehide leggings, do not wear them with pain. Didijik was always going to die before you, you lost him a little sooner but the loss was waiting. When you wear your blue-striped leggings, Zandakar, do not think of it as punishment. Wear them with love, remember your pony. Show the world his beauty, and do not weep."

Zandakar's eyes were wide, and surprised. After a

moment he nodded, slowly. "Yes, Vortka godspeaker. I did not think of it like that. I will do what you say. When I wear these leggings I will think of all the times we galloped together, me and Didijik. I will not weep. I will thank the god I had such a pony."

Vortka kissed him on the brow. "Good. That is good. Zandakar . . ."

Trusting, so trusting, Zandakar looked at him. "Godspeaker?"

He lowered his voice. "I must tell you, we are not supposed to speak together. I am a godspeaker, my duties are in the godhouse. You will be the warlord, your world is in the palace. If someone asks you, you must not lie. But if nobody asks, it would be better if you do not mention our meeting here."

"If nobody asks, I will not tell," said solemn Zandakar. Then he smiled, unexpectedly, he was so beautiful. "We have a secret, Vortka godspeaker. Secrets are what friends have. Does this mean we are friends?"

Aieee, god, thought Vortka. He could have wept. "Yes, Zandakar," he whispered. "We are friends. If you are ever in trouble, you can come to me. I want you to know that. You can come to me."

Zandakar nodded. "You are not so thin now," he said, considering. "But your hair is still fuzzy. When will the god give you back your godbraids?"

"I do not know," he said, his voice uneven.

"Perhaps the god likes them so much it keeps them for itself."

"Perhaps," he agreed, and for the second time—most likely the last—he kissed his son, and held him close. "I must go, I have duties. And you have prayers. Be in the god's eye, Zandakar. Be a good boy. Grow a strong man. You will not see me, I will be watching you."

The god saw him safely out of the shrine garden, safely into the godhouse and up to his cell. He closed the door, he lay down on his mattress. He covered his face and cried till he slept.

Hekat led her warhost to Et-Banotaj. Nagarak rode beside her, they rarely spoke. The chastened warlords rode behind her, she felt their gazes on her back, she never looked at them. Like Hanochek, they were unknown.

After each day's riding the warhost stopped for lowsun sacrifice. When it was done, as the slaves cooked the night's meal, she danced with her warriors under the sky. She danced to remind them she was their warleader, she danced to remind the fallen warlords that she was with them, and watching. If once the warlords forgot who she was, what she had done, if they forgot she had danced two warlords to death, they might also forget to be afraid.

Her warriors were beautiful, dancing with their snake-blades in the god's eye. The ground drummed with the sound of their disciplined feet, they trampled the grass and summoned the stars.

See your warriors, god, see them knife-dancing for you. See me dancing, I am your slave. Will you send me a man for fucking soon? If he does not come soon, does it mean you will not send him? Does it mean Zandakar is safe from demons until he dies an old man?

The god did not answer, it was silent in her heart, it slept in her amulet. She clutched the stone scorpion till her fingers hurt.

I wish you would answer, god. I grow weary of waiting.

The journey to Et-Banotaj continued. When the warhost reached the border godposts on the main road to the city Nagarak sacrificed two grown bulls, one black, one white. Their gushing blood dyed the brown soil red. Their heads were left at the base of the godposts, the god ate the bodies' flesh so the bloody bones could be piled as a warning.

Two fingers' riding from the city the warhost caught sight of Et-Banotaj warriors, galloping ahead as though demons snapped at their heels. Hekat let them go, she did not send warriors in pursuit. It was not possible to hide her warhost, and she did not want to.

Let them know we are coming. Let them tremble on their feet and in their sinning hearts.

Dead Banotaj's defiant warhost rode out from its barracks to meet the warriors of Et-Raklion on the open land before the city. Hekat met three of its shell-leaders in the middle ground with Arakun beside her, and one of Et-Banotaj's warriors taken at the Heart of Mijak.

"Surrender," she said, staring into the shell-leaders' faces. "Banotaj is dead, I killed him with my snakeblade. He was a sinning man, he burns in hell. Raklion warlord is your warlord now, he is warlord of Mijak. You will kneel to him. You will kneel to *me*, I speak with his voice. I am Hekat warleader, warleader of Mijak. Bajadek's doom and the doom of his son. I will smite you to death if you do not kneel."

One of the Et-Banotaj shell-leaders, a grizzled woman

missing an ear, spat on the brown grass and sneered. "You are a liar."

"No," said the taken Et-Banotaj warrior. "Hestria shell-leader, she tells the truth. Banotaj is dead, we saw him die. Hekat warleader killed him in Mijak's Heart. The other warlords are fallen, their high godspeakers are struck dead by the god. Raklion is the warlord of Mijak. It is the god's will, you must accept it."

Hestria shell-leader spat again. "She is a liar, and *you* are a traitor." Her snakeblade took him through the throat. He died with a gurgle, his body toppled to the ground.

Hekat did not look at him. She looked at Hestria, she bared her teeth. "You stupid woman. You will join that man soon."

She and Arakun spun their horses and galloped back to the warhost. The dead warrior's horse galloped beside them. "Well?" said Nagarak sourly, waiting with his three hundred godspeakers.

"They reject the god, they reject Raklion warlord," she told him. "They must die, Nagarak. I cannot let them live."

Nagarak nodded. "The god see you, warleader. Slaughter those sinners, send their demon-tainted god-sparks to hell."

She smiled, it was another rare moment when they both agreed. She raised her hand, Arakun summoned the shell-leaders. "Prepare yourselves," Hekat told them. "The warhost rides to war."

Nagarak and his godspeakers and the fallen warlords withdrew, to witness and pray. Hekat led her warhost against the warhost of Et-Banotaj. It was a mighty smiting, the god was in every Et-Raklion heart. The sinning warriors of Et-Banotaj had no hope of victory, they died in their thousands, they died in their blood. They died with their demons, every last warrior cast down. The god gave Hekat the greatest victory, not a single Et-Raklion warrior was lost.

When it was over the bodies of Et-Banotaj's warhost were not burned, they were left to rot. Nagarak cursed the ground they died on, every living thing of Et-Banotaj in that place died, the grass, the flowers, the trees, the insects, the burrowing creatures beneath the earth. Even the crows dropped dead from the sky. Nothing would live or grow there till the end of the world.

Hekat led her warhost on to the city, and its godhouse.

The godspeakers of Et-Banotaj shouted their defiance. They refused Nagarak's authority, they begged the god to strike him dead, to strike Raklion dead and Hekat with him. They begged the god to kill Zandakar.

Nagarak's stone pectoral again came to life. He smote all the godspeakers. All the godspeakers died. The godhouse tumbled to stone and dust. The ground opened beneath it and swallowed it whole.

The city of Et-Banotaj surrendered.

"You see the god here," Hekat told the fallen warlords, as they stared with wide, frightened eyes where the godhouse had stood. "Remember its wrath. When you return to your cities, when the people who live there ask what you have seen, tell them of Et-Banotaj. When demons crawl on your pillows at night, whispering their promises into your hearts, remember this city. Remember how its godspeakers died, and its warriors. Remember how its warlord died, and your high godspeakers, for that is how every wicked sinner will die. Slain by my snakeblade, thrown down by the god.

I am Hekat knife-dancer, warleader of Mijak. I speak for the warlord, I speak with his voice. Remember this place, or face its fate."

Subdued and godsmitten, Et-Banotaj city was handed over to one thousand warriors and Nagarak's godspeakers, that it might remain obedient and learn the new laws.

Hekat renamed it *Zandakar*.

Raklion wept when Hekat brought the warhost home. "You are the god's greatest warrior," he told her, astride his stallion at the barracks' main gates with jubilant Zandakar at his side. "You are Hekat knife-dancer, you dance for the god."

Zandakar had been given a new pony, it was plain black, not blue-striped. He wore the blue-striped leggings. The pony wore the silver and lapis bridle. "The god see you, Yuma!" he said, his fist on his heart. "I prayed for you, it heard my prayers!"

She smiled at her beautiful son, she nodded at the warlord. "The god was in me. What sinner could prevail?"

They rode together to the warhost field, at the head of her glorious warhost. There were prayers and sacrifice, there was praise and laughter. The warhost was exultant, it was the warhost of Mijak. It had witnessed the god's glory, it had thrown down many demons.

Et-Raklion city sacrificed and feasted six highsuns without ceasing, to celebrate the victory over Et-Banotaj. Before each highsun's bloody offering Raklion, Hekat and Zandakar rode through the streets, Mijak's warlord, its warleader, its beautiful son.

When he was not performing the important sacrifices at newsun, highsun and lowsun Nagarak remained in the godhouse, he worked without sleeping. With Et-Banotaj laid low it was time to subdue the rest of Mijak. He examined the names of Et-Raklion's godspeakers, he drew up lists of those who would be sent to serve the god in other cities.

The first name on the first list he wrote with a smile. *Vortka godspeaker.*

When he learned he was to be sent far away from Et-Raklion, to serve in the godhouse of Takona city, Vortka was not surprised. *Nagarak cannot prove anything against me, he gets rid of me the best way he can.* The face he showed to Farhja godspeaker, who gave him the news, was perfectly accepting. In his heart, he wept. *I must leave Zandakar. I must leave Hekat.*

He must also leave the great crystal in her keeping, it could not stay in the godhouse if he was not there to protect it. Somehow he must get it to Hekat before he was sent away, Farhja had said he would be leaving soon. To do that he must see her, speak with her, if only for a moment.

Aieee, god, I need your help. Nagarak watches me, he sets other godspeakers to watch me. Speaking with Hekat will be no easy feat.

The god answered his prayer, it always did. The following newsun, as he returned to the godhouse from walking the city streets in the quiet time, he recognized Hekat, slender and linen-clad, slipping like a knife's shadow towards the godhouse shrine garden. It was so early few godspeakers were about in the godhouse grounds, and not one had noticed him.

He looked around, he could not see Nagarak.

I think it is safe, god. Please, keep me safe.

He found Hekat kneeling before a greenstone snake-eye shrine in the sanctuary furthest from the godhouse. She held the small shard of red crystal in a bloodless grip, she was praying fervently, he had never heard her *desperate* before.

"I try to be patient, god, I do not hear your answer. I come to you here, in your godhouse. You *must* speak to me here. You must tell me, I must *know*. Is it your desire that I birth another son? I thought so before, when demons tried to kill Zandakar, but you *still* have not sent me a man to fuck who can wake this crystal! Does that man not live? Or is he not yet in Et-Raklion, must I wait and wait until he arrives? I—"

"No," said Vortka, puzzled, and joined her in the sanctuary. "I am the man who wakes the crystal, Hekat. If the god desires you to bear another son, why do you not come to me?"

She turned on a gasp, and leapt to her feet. "Vortka!"

He felt his heart beat harder, the air catch in his throat. *Aieee, the god see her. She is so beautiful.* The spiderweb scars on her face were pale now, a subtle whisper instead of a shout. She was thinner too, since last he had seen her. Riding with the warhost, smiting Et-Banotaj, she had stripped the last softness from her bones. She was lean and hard like an unsheathed snakeblade.

A snakeblade glitter was in her eyes.

"I speak to the god, Vortka. You should not be here."

He did not leave the sanctuary. The crystal could wait, this was more important. *A brother for Zandakar.* "Hekat. We can make another son together. Come to me hidden in the god's eye, like before. We will fuck, you will quicken, we will give the god its desire."

She shook her head. "No. Vortka, go away."

He did not like that glitter in her eyes. "Do not tell me to go away. I will go nowhere till you tell me why you will not—"

"Aieee, Vortka, do I owe you a reason?" she snapped. "I think I do not."

Baffled, he stared at her. "Yes, you do. I wake the crystal, Hekat, *I* have the power to give you a son. Why—"

"No you do *not*!" she said. "Not anymore. You have a blade but it is blunted, it will not plow. Your seed is dead. The fever killed it."

Her words were a snakeblade, sliding between his ribs. He could not breathe, it was hard to see. "The fever?" he whispered. *I knew it. Aieee, the god see me. I knew it in my heart. Hekat made me sick . . .* "I am gelded? Like a horse?"

"Do not stare at me with those eyes," Hekat told him, defiant. "It is not my doing, the god desired this."

"I do not believe you!" he retorted, anguished. "Why would the god desire such a thing? This is *your* doing, Hekat. Why? *Why*? Did you think I would spread my seed all over Mijak? Seek to make a new warlord, another child to be the god's hammer, fuck with some ungodchosen woman? How could you *think* that? I am *godtouched*, like you! But you do not accept that. I think you never have. You are Hekat, godtouched and *precious*. You see me as—as a *threat*. Now you say the god desires a brother for Zandakar, a brother who can also wake the crystal, and I cannot serve the god because I am *gelded*?"

She flinched, and held out her hand. "Vortka—"

He struck her hand away, tumbling the crystal to the grass. "Do *not* speak my name, on your tongue it is sour!" Bending, he snatched up the small red stone. "If you are *precious*, Hekat, then so am *I*. This crystal is the god's hammer, only *I* can wake its—"

He stared, not believing. He held the crystal, it was in his hand. He felt nothing within him. No presence. No power.

The god's smiting crystal did not wake.

"What is this, Hekat?" he whispered. "*What have you done?*"

CHAPTER THIRTY-FIVE

Hekat stared at the unwoken crystal.
I do not understand, god. How can this be?

Vortka held it so tightly its sharp edges cut his flesh. Blood dripped between his fingers, his face was full of desolation. "Did you know this would happen? Did you? *Did you?*"

She fumbled for her scorpion amulet, it was cold in her grasp, she could not feel the god. "No. Would I thwart the god like this? I think I would not! Vortka, perhaps it is not you, perhaps it is the crystal, its power may have leached away, or—or—"

He was not listening. He could not hear her. "Are you still precious, Hekat? Are you in the god's eye? I think you are blind to it. I think you are *deaf*." Desolation had turned to rage, she had never thought to see Vortka so angry. "When you fucked me to make Zandakar, *then* the god saw you. But your pride and arrogance, Hekat, they have brought you down. They have brought *me* down, I—"

"No," she said. "Vortka, no. There must be a reason, the god will tell us what it is. The god will—"

"*Vortka*," said a hated voice, at the shrine garden's entrance.

Hekat turned. Vortka turned beside her. She felt him shudder, felt her own guts twist.

Nagarak.

He walked to them smiling, it was a terrible sight. "So. Vortka," he whispered. "At last I learn the truth of you, I see your heart's secrets, I have plucked them out. No god-speaker, but a demonfucker. True father of the warlord's son. You wicked man. I will see you on the scorpion wheel. I will send your sinning godspark to hell. You will die screaming, with your entrails in bloody ropes about your throat."

"Nagarak," Vortka croaked. He looked ready to fall on the grass. "No. You do not understand. Hekat—"

"*Is a demon*! I have always known it. She stinks of sin, she reeks of hell. She blinded the warlord, she did not blind *me*."

"Tcha!" said Hekat, scornful. Her heart was drumming, she would not show fear. "You are a stupid, *stupid* man. You are the blind one, you are the demon spat from hell. If you were truly in the god's eye you would know the truth of Hekat knife-dancer, Hekat warleader, Hekat the god's snakeblade in the world. You do not know the truth, Nagarak. You know *nothing*."

"I know you are corruption incarnate, an evil bitch, the

spawn of hell! I know you have lied and lied and lied! I know you have tainted the warlord Raklion, his heart is rotted, his blood is turned *black*."

"No!" said Vortka. "Nagarak, you must listen. Hekat—"

Nagarak hissed at him. "Still your tongue, you godforsaken sinner! You consorter with demons. You *betrayer* of the *god*! You cannot defend her, she is putrid to the core!"

His fury was so scorching Vortka stepped back, he flung one hand before his face.

Nagarak pointed. "What is that crystal? Give it to me."

"No, Vortka," Hekat said quickly. "It is not for him. It is not his business. Give the crystal to me. The god will protect you, it knows Nagarak cannot be trusted."

Nagarak laughed, a shivering sound. He seized Vortka's wrist and closed his fingers around it, he held him so hard that Vortka cried out. The crystal slipped from his blood-slicked grasp, into Nagarak's greedy hand.

With a thrumming of power, it burst into life.

Hekat heard herself scream in her head. *No, god! Not Nagarak! He is repulsive! He hates me and fears me, his seed must be poison! Do not make me fuck him! Make Vortka whole!*

Nagarak stared at the blazing red stone. "What is this? More demon trickery? Where is this crystal from? What is its purpose? Does it summon demons, open a doorway to hell?"

Beneath her tunic, against her skin, Hekat felt her scorpion amulet shudder, she felt the god stir from its stubborn sleep. She heard at last its longed-for voice, it did not whisper, it thundered through her bones. *Here is*

Nagarak. He will make you a son. She wanted to vomit. She had to obey.

"I am Hekat, mother of Zandakar, Bajadek's doom and the doom of Banotaj," she said, staring at Raklion's high godspeaker. "I am the god's warrior, its sacred knife-dancer. Nagarak, I smite you blind in its eye. The god is deaf to you, you are deaf to the god."

With a roar of fury Nagarak dropped the crystal and lunged towards her with murder in his eyes. His stone scorpion pectoral came thrashing to life. She heard Vortka's cry, saw the horror in his face. Around her neck, her stone scorpion burned. She snatched it up and thrust it at Nagarak.

"The god see me, Hekat, the light of its eye!"

Nagarak's scorpion pectoral seized his body, it crushed him to stumbling, threw him onto the grass. He lay on his back, tongue protruding, nostrils flaring. The pectoral did not sting him, it only held him tight. He tried to speak, the god had taken his voice.

She looked at Vortka, he was sweating, gasping, he could hardly breathe. "You cannot be here," she told him softly. "Go into the godhouse. Speak to no-one. I will come to you when I can."

"Hekat—"

"Go," she said, and let her voice bite. "What I do now, I must do alone." Then she felt a sudden stab of guilt. "Vortka, I tell you, I am sorry for the fever. It *was* the god's desire, I am its true slave. I do not know why you cannot wake the crystal. The god will tell us, in its time."

He nodded, his eyes were still unforgiving. "Whatever you do here, Hekat, do it quickly. The godhouse is stirring. You do not have long."

She did not watch him leave, or look at Nagarak. She pulled her scorpion amulet over her head and pressed it throbbing against her belly. She felt the god's heat suffuse her, she felt its power, it reached into her center and woke her womb.

Nagarak was panting, his chest heaved within the pectoral's tight embrace. The scorpion did not sting him, its raised tail hovered above his face, promising swift punishment if he did not lie still.

Hekat stripped off her loincloth and knelt beside him, pulled his robes open and his loincloth down, then pressed her scorpion amulet into his groin. He moaned and twisted as the god poured its power into him. He was helpless before her, she was in the god's hands. When he was ready she straddled his hips and impaled herself on his blade.

"Do not think," she said, as she bitterly rode him, "I do this for anyone but the god. Do not think the son you sire will make me happy. This is the god's want, I am its slave."

With a silent scream Nagarak poured himself into her. She clamped her thighs on him, she ground herself against his hips. She felt his seed take root within her, the god had made her hot and fertile, nine godmoons from now she would spawn Nagarak's son.

She lifted herself from the high godspeaker's limp blade and sat on the grass, willing her racing heart to calm. Held down by his merciless scorpion pectoral, Nagarak stared at her. He seemed overcome. As he stared, the scorpion's barbed tail struck him hard between his eyes.

She thought he was dead then, but after a moment saw

he still breathed. The fresh red welt above the bridge of his nose faded as she watched it, became one more scorpion-mark among so many. She watched his eyes glaze, their horror fade. His taut muscles relaxed and his cramped limbs lost their tension.

His scorpion pectoral returned to stone.

She re-tied her loincloth before he roused fully, found the dropped crystal, slipped it into her pocket, and re-turned her scorpion amulet to its rightful place. Then she retreated to the sanctuary's snake-eye shrine. As she knelt beside it, fingers caressing its beauty, the godhouse god-bells began to toll.

Nagarak stirred. He stood. In silence he straightened his robes and his loincloth and, unspeaking, unseeing, he walked away.

He was the third dead man walking she had seen.

After consuming breakfast, boiled eggs he could not taste, and too disturbed to sleep, Vortka offered his labor to the godhouse library. With three hundred godspeakers gone to Et-Bano—no, Zandakar now—the library archivists were pleased to have him. They did not ask if Nagarak had sent him, he did not enlighten them. In the godhouse library he would hear any commotion, and while he worked sorting, cleaning and stacking the clay tablets he would have a chance to think.

His night's duty in the quiet time had left him ex-hausted. The revelations in the shrine garden had left him numb. Walking away from Nagarak had left him . . .

Aieee, god. God. Is this your purpose? Nagarak is your high godspeaker, you chose him in the scorpion pit.

I do not think he will survive Hekat in the sanctuary. I saw her eyes. Is she your chosen? Does she do your will?

Until this moment, he had never doubted. Hekat was godtouched, godchosen, precious. He had seen her work miracles in the god's eye. He knew she was arrogant, proud, impatient.

I never thought she was evil. Tell me, god, have I been wrong?

If Hekat was evil, what did that make Zandakar?

My son is not evil, god. He is pure. I can sense his godspark, there is no darkness in it. He desires to serve you, as do I.

He wished he knew what the god desired of him. To raise the alarm over Nagarak would be the same as putting a knife through Zandakar's heart. As killing Hekat. *As thwarting the god?* He saw again Nagarak's living scorpion pectoral, lashing and hissing and crushing him to the ground.

That was the god's power. That was the god. I am its servant, I must hold my tongue.

And it was not certain Nagarak would die. Hekat hated Nagarak but the god could stay her hand. It might take this newsun from Nagarak's mind. The high godspeaker would never know what Hekat had done to him, never remember what he'd heard. He might forget about the crystal, and what had happened when he held it.

Aieee, god. The crystal. It was not flawed, the flaw is in me. In burning my seed Hekat damaged my power. Yet I am still a godspeaker, that power remains. What is the difference? Will you not tell me? If I cannot wake the crystal can I still help my son?

A stupid question. Of course he could. He had helped

him already, by being his friend. How else he could help him, the god would reveal.

As he worked in the library his thoughts ground on, like oxen yoked to a grindstone they trod around and around.

What is it about me, about Nagarak, that makes us special? What is this power in us that can wake the crystal? We have nothing in common . . . except we are godspeakers. Although Nagarak is high godspeaker and I am only—

Vortka caught his breath. The clay tablet he was stacking nearly slipped from his fingers, he managed to snatch it before it fell.

If Nagarak dies . . . if the god does desire his death . . . then Mijak must have a new high godspeaker. God. God. Do you mean it to be me?

Vortka high godspeaker? He had never dreamed it. Never *imagined* . . . Was it possible? Was the godspeaker power within a *high* godspeaker the thing that made the crystal wake? And if his special power was burned out by the fever, would the god even choose him now? In siring Zandakar, was his purpose truly served?

Aieee, god. So many questions. I wish you would answer me, I am lost. Reveal your desires, I will bring them to pass.

The godhouse godbells tolled, startling him. He looked at the library candles, it was highsun. Time for sacrifice. Since he started working there had been no commotion. If Nagarak were dead in the godhouse shrine garden, surely someone would have noticed by now.

He went to the Sacrifice chamber for this highsun ritual, that was where Nagarak sacrificed in public for the god. He could have observed it anywhere in the godhouse but he needed to see the high godspeaker for himself. Nagarak did not appear, Peklia said he was occupied in his chamber, she performed his duty, she did not seem alarmed. Afterwards, Vortka ate a hurried bowl of mutton stew in the kitchens, then returned to his labors in the library.

The day dragged towards lowsun, there was still no commotion. Nagarak lived. Vortka sighed his relief. The high godspeaker did not appear for lowsun sacrifice, Peklia once more wielded the blade. No reason was given, Peklia still was not alarmed. After dinner, Vortka slept for a short while, then took up his godstaff and walked down the Pinnacle Road to the city, praying with every step that its people would respect the god and save him from the distress of smiting.

He kept his eyes on the road as he passed by the palace. If Hekat was in there he did not want to see her.

I am still angry, god. I still have questions. She said she was sorry. Can I trust her? She could have told me the fever was your will. I am your servant, I would have accepted it.

The god could have told him. The god did not, it was another question.

The streets assigned to his authority remained peaceful, he breathed a prayer of heartfelt thanks. Twice he heard distant sounds of smitings, wicked sinners found by other godspeakers. As he walked among the small, humble houses of the Weavers district he thought about the lives of the workers who dwelled within. The life he would have lived, had he remained a potsmith. Simple. Uncomplicated. He sighed, there was no point in regret.

As the sky lightened towards newsun he returned to the godhouse.

Its bells were tolling, louder and longer than the call to sacrifice. Nagarak high godspeaker was desperately ill.

"It is the same fever that recently afflicted one other godspeaker, warlord," the healer Sidik explained in a low voice. "That godspeaker recovered, we must pray Nagarak high godspeaker will recover also."

Hekat stood with Raklion in the healing room, beside fevered Nagarak in his bed. Raklion was deeply upset, he was stupid wasting water on a man like Nagarak. For herself, she pretended to care.

Raklion turned to her. "You are *certain* he seemed well when he rode with the warhost to smite Et-Banotaj?"

She met his eyes unflinching. "Warlord, he seemed very well. He threw down that city's wicked godspeakers, he was mighty in his wrath."

"Aieee," said Sidik. "Perhaps he was cursed by those sinning godspeakers, we know that Banotaj consorted with demons." She frowned. "But I can sense no demon-taint in him."

"This other godspeaker you say was afflicted," said Raklion. He could not shift his gaze from Nagarak's sweating, restless body, he flinched every time the dying man groaned. "Had he traveled to or from Et-Banotaj? Perhaps there is a sickness in their soil, perhaps he—"

"No-one else is fevered, warlord," said Sidik, regretful. "If that other godspeaker were the cause, *I* would be fevered. I was the healer who nursed him to health. Many would be ill, we live closely here."

"Aieee . . ." Raklion pressed a fist to his lips, so deeply moved he could not speak.

Hekat said, "Sidik healer. I wonder if I might ask some small favor. Since I am here, I mean no disrespect to Nagarak."

The healer bowed. "Of course not. Hekat warleader, you honor me."

She took a deep breath, let it out. "Would you lay your godstone on my belly? Would you tell me if you sense a new life?"

"Yes," said the healer, and pressed her godstone deep.

"*Hekat*?" said Raklion, his grief forgotten. "Do you think . . ."

Hekat smiled at him, she knew she had quickened, she knew Nagarak's spawn seed had taken root within. It was a good thing after all Raklion was strong enough to fuck. "I cannot be certain, warlord, but yes, I *hope . . .*"

"Your hope is answered," said the healer, removing her godstone. "Hekat warleader, you are with child. It is a boy, it has a vigorous godspark."

"*Hekat*!" said Raklion, he crushed her to his breast. "Hekat, beloved, you are in the god's eye! You are in my heart forever, you are the greatest of women!"

As Sidik smiled, and Raklion wept, Hekat rested her gaze on moaning Nagarak, sweating and tossing his way to death.

You stupid man, you did not have to die. Is Vortka dead? I think he is not. You provoked the god when you called me a demon. See how the god has answered you.

*   *   *

Nagarak died two fingers before lowsun. Vortka woke in his cell to the sound of solemn tolling godbells.

He stared blankly at the low stone ceiling. He had been expecting it, but still he was stunned. For some time he lay on his thin pallet and listened to the murmur of agitated voices, the swift shuffling of sandaled feet beyond his closed door. A curious lethargy weighed upon him. Nagarak's death was a momentous event, he should join the other godspeakers in observing sacrifice for Mijak's dead high godspeaker. Instead he pillowed his head on his folded arms and tried to calm his troubled mind.

Now there will be a high godspeaker choosing. God, god. Do you mean to choose me?

Someone's fist battered on the door. "Rise, Vortka, quickly! Have you not heard the news? The god has taken Nagarak from the world! Peklia calls us to sacrifice. Come!"

Vortka sighed, and rolled to his feet.

The god see you, Nagarak. You have served your purpose. The god has used you. It uses us all.

Sacrifice for the high godspeaker went on and on. Every godspeaker in the city had come to the godhouse, and now shed blood for Nagarak's godspark, their own and that of one sacred beast. Vortka killed a white lamb, he cut open his left arm, he joined the godspeakers who had sacrificed before him and waited for the ritual to end.

When at last the blood stopped flowing, Peklia godspeaker addressed the assembly. "Godspeakers," she said, her voice loud in every ear. There were thousands of godbraid godbells in this place, not one sounded, nobody moved. "At newsun the god will select Mijak's next high godspeaker. Et-Raklion godhouse is the god's godhouse in Mijak, no godspeaker not tested from this place may enter our scorpion pit. If you were tested from this god-house, and by the god's desire you are in this place at this solemn time and believe in your heart you are called to serve, present yourself in the Scorpion chamber when next the newsun godbells toll. Know that the god will smite you to death if your belief is proven false."

Now the thousand of godbells sounded, now a breeze of voices sighed.

"The god see you in its choosing eye, godspeakers. Go to a still place and listen to the god."

Vortka left the godhouse, quickly, and went to the shrine garden, to the sanctuary where grew the half-dead tree. He reached within its gnarled, knotted trunk and pulled out his godgiven sacrifice knife. When his fingers closed about its hilt it did not wake as it woke before in Peklia's chamber, proof it did have some strange connection to the red crystal he'd found. Still, in grasping the knife he felt the god's great presence.

Vortka knew, at last, why the blade had chosen him.

Are you certain, god? I will serve as I must. I do not look for this authority, I never thought it would come to me.

In his heart the god said, *Serve.*

He took the knife with him, back to the godhouse.

At newsun, naked, he stood in the cool, bare Scorpion chamber as the godhouse godbells tolled the new day. He was the first godspeaker to arrive for the choosing. Peklia's eyes widened when she saw him, but she did not comment on his youth, his inexperience or the short time that had passed since he was tested in the wilderness.

"Vortka godspeaker," she said. "You hear the god's voice in your heart?"

He nodded. "Peklia godspeaker, I do."

"And you are sure you desire to test the god's scorpions?"

"Peklia godspeaker, I am sure."

"Then take your place by the scorpion pit, Vortka. And may the god see you safely in its eye."

She was not the only other person in the chamber. Also present were Raklion warlord, and Hekat, and Zandakar.

Vortka took his place by the scorpion pit, his heart stuttering as he looked at his son. Zandakar was dressed in blue-striped horsehide and bright light wools, greens and golds and deep blood reds. His godbraids were newly strung with snake-eyes and lizard-feet and scorpion amulets. Golden godbells caught the light.

Aieee, beautiful. So beautiful. Zandakar, my beautiful boy.

He was very good, and except for one bored glance he did not look at Vortka, his secret friend. Raklion, beside him, stared into the air, he seemed overcome. Grief-struck. Together he and Nagarak had remade Mijak. Vortka had only ever felt fear for the high godspeaker, but it was good to know one man felt honest pain for his passing. How sad it would be if nobody mourned.

Hekat's eyes were downcast, her face showed nothing. Her hands rested gently against her belly. She flicked him a single look, he knew what that meant.

Nagarak will have a son in the world, breathing while he is a pile of ash.

He could not help wondering, was she surprised to see

him here? As though reading his thought she raised her eyes to his.

No, her face told him. *Stupid Vortka, I am not surprised*.

Aieee, god, Hekat. She would never change.

Before the godbells ceased their tolling four more naked godspeakers joined them, three men, one woman. Vortka thought the woman was foolish, in the history of Mijak there had never been a female high godspeaker. All four supplicants were much older than himself, he was seasons younger than Nagarak had been when he was chosen the god's high godspeaker. The other godspeakers stared, they were shocked to see him. Their eyes showed anger, their faces were calm. Peklia asked them the ritual questions, they replied with the ritual answers.

"May the god see you, godspeakers," she told them, gravely. "Take your places at the scorpion pit."

The pit was filled already with fat, venomous god-house scorpions. They rattled and hissed, they seethed for the god. Vortka felt no fear, he had worn live scorpions before, and he was here by the god's desire. He was chosen before setting one foot in the pit. At Peklia's signal he and the others trod the stone steps down to the scorpions.

One by one the others died, lied to by demons, enticed to their doom. Vortka heard them screaming, he heard their laments. He felt a passing sorrow, that godspeakers could be so blind to the god.

Not a single scorpion stung him. Instead he heard the god's voice in his heart.

You are Vortka, godchosen and precious. You have a purpose, it is not fulfilled. Mijak's high godspeaker,

Zandakar's savior, the doom of demons, the god's instrument in the world.

Humbled almost to weeping, he surged to his feet. The scorpions parted for him, he walked from the pit. Peklia stared, robbed of speech. It was a wonder her eyeballs stayed in her skull.

Raklion said, "The god see you, Vortka. My chosen high godspeaker." He frowned. "Vortka. Why do I know that name?"

"Warlord, he is the godspeaker who helped me when I fell in the horse-field," said Zandakar. His eyes were bright, and proudly shining.

"Yes," said Raklion. "I recall. I thank you for—"

"Warlord." Vortka pressed his fist to his heart. "Thank the god, I was its servant that day."

Hekat looked at him. "Vortka high godspeaker. The god sees you in its *excellent* eye."

She was its instrument, as he was its instrument, they were yoked together also, two oxen for the god.

I think I begin to understand the god's purpose in this. I think it desires me to keep Hekat steady and walking the path it has chosen for her. She can be proud, she must also be sensible.

Again, he pressed his fist to his heart. "Hekat warleader, in the god's watching eye. I will serve you, I will serve your son. The god has chosen me, it has its reasons."

With a shuddering breath, Peklia found her voice. "Vortka, the god's chosen. If you would come with me." She led the way from the Scorpion chamber, he followed her without a word, the warlord and his family followed him.

As they emerged from the Scorpion chamber the godhouse godbells sounded, the godspeakers waiting for the god's decision flowed like water into the large godspeaker hall. With them came the fallen warlords, to witness the god's choice of Mijak's high godspeaker.

Peklia led him to the altar, on which sat the stone scorpion pectoral of Et-Raklion's godhouse, and newly made brown high godspeaker robes. Raklion, Hekat and Zandakar stood to one side, their presence was important but they were not the purpose here. Vortka stood naked and unstung beside Peklia, letting his gaze sweep the assembly. Not one of the gathered godspeakers expected to see him, each of their faces was a riot of surprise.

"Godspeakers of Mijak, the god has chosen," Peklia said. "Here is Vortka, Mijak's high godspeaker."

"The god see Vortka," said the gathered godspeakers, with only a brief hesitation. *"High godspeaker of Mijak."*

Peklia turned to him. "Where is the knife? You know the one of which I speak."

"In my cell, Peklia. Under my pillow."

"Brikin, you arrange the sleeping assignments," she said, nodding at the novice-master. "Go to the cell that was Vortka godspeaker's. Bring me the knife you will find under his pillow."

Brikin departed, returning swiftly with the sacrifice knife, wrapped in its protecting square of woven red wool. Peklia let the cloth fall and held the knife high so all could see.

"This sacrifice knife is offered to all new high godspeakers! It is ancient, and touched by the god. It rejected Nagarak but chose Vortka when he was newly tested in the wilderness. I know this, I was present. I stand as witness. Truly, the god sees Vortka in its eye."

Peklia cut him with the knife, he let the blood flow, and then the god healed him. She strapped the scorpion pectoral onto his body. Vortka held his breath as she fastened its buckles, but stone remained stone, it did not come to life. Then she dressed him in the high godspeaker robes. When that was done, she took a step back.

Vortka looked at his gathered godspeakers. "The god sees you before me, godspeakers of Mijak."

"The god sees you, Vortka, Mijak's high godspeaker," they chanted. *"The god sees you in its choosing eye."*

The stone scorpion pectoral was heavy, he had to brace his ribs and spine against its solid, imposing weight. How much heavier would it grow as the seasons passed? *I cannot think of that. I am chosen, I must wear it.* "Godspeakers," he said to the men and women before him, whose lives he now commanded, who knelt at his whim. "The god has seen me, I am its servant. We are all the god's servants, we serve in our way." He turned to Peklia. "Where are those warlords cast down by the god?"

Peklia snapped her fingers and the five fallen warlords were chivvied before him by ten guarding godspeakers with godstaffs in their hands. He looked into the warlords' faces, he had never seen them before. He did not know which man was which, that did not matter.

They now knew him.

"You are men who fell prey to demons," he told them. "Now demons might say to you: *Nagarak is dead. Who is this Vortka, so young, with no godbraids? Mijak does not know him. Why should you fear?*" He smiled. "Here is your answer, warlords. *I am the god's chosen.* Its power is in me. Thwart me, and you will face the god's smiting wrath. Thwart me, warlords, and you will die."

He raised his arms, he reached for the god. He felt the god's power surge through the stone scorpion pectoral. Strapped to his body, it came to life.

God. God. How much honor you do me. I cannot wake the crystal, I can still be your voice.

The fallen warlords cried out, they threw themselves facedown on the floor. Every godspeaker gasped, even Peklia was shocked. Vortka breathed out slowly, he breathed out the god. The scorpion pectoral returned to stone. He slid his gaze sideways, he looked at Hekat. She looked back at him, there was laughter in her eyes. He shook his head, she was impossible.

Aieee, god, god. What a yoke-mate you have given me!

"Godspeakers," he said. "Nagarak's pyre awaits. Let us give him to the god, and do its will in the world."

CHAPTER THIRTY-SIX

Tcha!" said Hekat, and slapped her hand on her knee. "Stupid Raklion! Of course I will ride to Mijak's cities, I am *pregnant*. I am not *dying*."

Raklion frowned. "Hekat—"

She turned to Vortka, behind the desk that had belonged to Nagarak. "Vortka high godspeaker, what does the god say? Does it say I am too weak to do my duty? Does it say I cannot ride with Zandakar and the warlord as they show their faces to the world? I am Mijak's warleader, I am Zandakar's mother. Mijak must *see* me, it must know who I am!"

"Warlord," said Vortka, "if you fear the journey might harm Hekat's unborn son, you fear without reason. The god has decreed this child will be born, it will be born if Hekat rides with you or not."

"So I will ride with you, Raklion," she said, and smiled, triumphant. "Warlord, you are foolish to fear for me. I am Hekat, I am in the god's eye. You ride to Mijak's cities not only to assert your own authority but to show them Zandakar, who will be warlord after you. This journey will take six or seven godmoons. I am Zandakar's mother, we cannot be parted for so long. I *will* ride with you, Raklion. It is the god's desire."

"You are certain of this?" said Raklion, looking at Vortka. "The god desires Hekat to ride with the warhost? My unborn son will be unharmed, there is no danger from demons?"

Vortka nodded. "Warlord, I am certain. I will of course take omens before you depart, but I say again: the child will be born unharmed."

"If there is any worry, Raklion," she added, "it is for you. When Banotaj struck you with his blade, he—"

"*Did not kill me*, Hekat," said Raklion, coldly. "I am the warlord while I breathe. You need have no fear for me."

He said the words, did he truly believe them? When he looked in a mirror, was he blind to his own face? She thought he must be. Eyes and cheeks sunken, deep lines carved round his mouth. His body still fleshless, a tremor in his hands. His endurance was failing, would he survive six godmoons in the saddle?

Do I care? Do I want him to? I think I do not.

She said, "If we ride, Raklion, we must ride well within the godmoon, before the cities' warhosts are stirred to war. Before their warleaders declare themselves warlords and in their arrogant pride challenge the god's will."

"Agreed," said Raklion. "High godspeaker, how stands godhouse business in Mijak?"

Hekat looked at Vortka. Aieee, god, he wore the scorpion pectoral! He was high godspeaker, she could still feel surprise. The god had not told her that was Vortka's purpose. It had not told her he could wake the scorpion pectoral. She had been pleased to see it, pleased to know the fever had not killed him to the god.

I still do not know why you made me fuck Nagarak. His spawn squirms in my belly, in my sleep I can feel it. Is it a smiting, for killing Vortka's seed? If it is, you are unjust, god. You know I thought that was your desire.

"Warlord," said Vortka. "Before the god took him, Nagarak high godspeaker was working to see Et-Raklion's godhouse the godhouse of Mijak. He left notes, he left lists. In the god's eye, I continue his plan. When the warhost rides to discipline your cities my godspeakers will ride with you, they will see the godhouses disciplined, also."

"High godspeaker, perhaps you should ride with us," said Raklion. "The sight of your stone scorpion, hissing . . . it will make any sinner kneel."

Hekat looked at Vortka. *That must not happen. Zandakar and Vortka riding together? Demons could make mischief.* "Warlord—" she began, but Vortka raised his hand.

"That is not possible, warlord," he said, with regret. "Mijak's high godspeaker must remain in Et-Raklion. There is much work to do here, as the greatest city in Mijak Et-Raklion will soon grow fat. We will provide a temptation to demons. And the godspeakers from the other godhouses will need strict discipline, they might not readily accept the god's desire." He smiled. "The fury of your warhost will chasten any sinners. And I will send Peklia with you, she is a mighty godspeaker. The god's power is in her, warlord. You need not fear."

"That is true," said Hekat. "And the fallen warlords will ride with us, Raklion. They will bear witness to the fate of demonstruck men."

Nodding, Raklion stood. "High godspeaker, you have spoken. I am warlord, I must ride. As you say, there is much work to do. You will read the omens, tell me when the god desires us to leave?"

"I will read them at lowsun, warlord," said Vortka. "I will tell you after what the god says."

Raklion pressed his fist to his breast. "The god see you, high godspeaker. If you have need of me, I will be in the barracks. Hekat—"

"Warlord, I will join you there. I would have words with the high godspeaker, concerning . . ." She folded her hands across her belly. "A woman's fears. I seek guidance from the god."

His grave expression softened into a smile. Bending down, he kissed her lips. "I will be in the warlodge, consulting with our shell-leaders. Come to me there as soon as you can."

"Aieee," she said, after Raklion had left them. "Vortka high godspeaker, three highsuns after choosing. Has your life grown tedious yet?"

"Tedious?" said Vortka, and pressed his hands to his face. "Aieee, Hekat, I think the god has gone mad."

"*Vortka*!" She straightened. "You sinning man to say so!"

Vortka lowered his hands and looked round the chamber, cold and spare, no trace of Nagarak at all. Were it not for the squirming in her belly, how easy to think he had never lived. "You did not feel doubt when you were made warleader?" he said. "You did not wonder if you would fail?"

She looked at him, incredulous. "I think *you* are mad. Whatever we are, Vortka, the god has made us. Do you think the god makes *mistakes*?"

"No," he said, after a moment. "It is men who are fallible. The god is the god."

Tcha. He wanted her to admit she was wrong in giving him that fever. "Vortka, I have no power but what the god gives me. I am its slave, how often must you hear it? The god killed your seed, it has its reasons. It will tell us its purpose, in its time." She frowned. "Or do you still think a demon made me do it?"

He would not look at her, he turned in his stone seat to stare through the window. "No. Of course not."

He might not think it, but he was still angry. Stupid Vortka, his feelings were hurt. She said, "I will be gone a long time, riding through Mijak. While I am riding, there is something you must do."

With a frustrated snort he swung round to face her. "Hekat, while you are riding there are *many* things I must do! When I was a godspeaker I thought my days were full, I toiled for the god from newsun to lowsun, my idle moments were rare. I never wondered what Nagarak did, *how* he led this godhouse for the god." He pointed to a long, low cupboard. "That is *full* of tablets, godspeaker histories, meant for high godspeaker eyes alone. I must read them, I do not know when. As the high godspeaker I am responsible for every godspeaker and novice in Et-Raklion, soon in all Mijak. It is a large place! I condemn criminals, I assess taxes, I approve travel for Traders, I oversee the breeding programs on the godhouse sacrifice farms and work with the other godhouses to see the bloodlines do not become stale. I examine novices, I sacrifice thrice daily, I read the warlord's omens, I pray for the warlord's son." He stopped, his eyes suddenly smiling. "My son," he said softly. "I pray for Zandakar. That is no hardship, I pray for him in my sleep." He sighed. "Hekat, there is no end to the many things I must do, now the god has made me high godspeaker in Mijak."

"Tcha," she said, and waved her hand. "I do not ask for many things, Vortka, I ask for *one* thing. It is not so hard. While I ride with the warhost through Mijak, in the center of the city I wish there to be built a great open godtheater. Zandakar will be warlord of Mijak, there must be a place where he can be seen and admired, where the people can kneel to him and show him their obeisance. Where sacrifice can be made for him, before his people, and sinning criminals can be publicly chastised for thwarting his desires. The god has the godhouse. Zandakar must have this."

Vortka stared. "And where exactly do you think such a godtheater can be built, Hekat? Perhaps it is some time since you walked through the city. If you walked through the city you would see there is no open place large enough for your vision of this *godtheater*."

"Then make one, Vortka," she said, blankly. "What else are slaves and criminals for?"

He rubbed his chin. "And the buildings already standing where your godtheater would be?"

"Pull them down. Destroy them. This is for *Zandakar*." She stood. "I will send a slave, I have drawings on clay tablets. I do not expect you to oversee the godtheater's building yourself. You are the high godspeaker, Vortka. You will simply see it is done."

He sat back. "Yes, Hekat. I will . . . see it is done." His eyes narrowed. "Does the warlord know of this godtheater for Zandakar? Perhaps he might think it should be for Raklion."

She shrugged. "He can make use of it, he will not need it long. Have you not noticed? He is an old, failing man." She looked once more around the cheerless room and then at Vortka, in his robes and scorpion pectoral. "The god sees you, high godspeaker. It works its will upon the world."

She left him thoughtful in his godhouse and walked to the barracks, where preparations were under way for the mightiest warhost Mijak had ever seen.

He did not ask about Nagarak's ending. He did not ask about the spawn in my belly. That is good, I would not have answered. I will not speak of it. What is done, is done.

Twelve highsuns later, after sacrifices and omens and a public celebration for the warlord's unborn son, Raklion, Hekat, Zandakar, fifteen thousand warriors and one thousand Et-Raklion godspeakers rode out of Et-Raklion to tame sprawling Mijak to their fists. The fallen warlords rode with them in plain linen, they knew their duty, they knew better than to fail.

The memory of Et-Banotaj and Vortka's hissing stone scorpion pectoral rode with them in their eyes.

First the warhost reached the city Tebek. Confronted by Et-Raklion's fierce warhost, Tebek's vastly outnumbered warriors still wanted to fight. With Raklion and Zandakar silently watching, Hekat brought before them their fallen warlord. With tears in his eyes Tebek ordered them to kneel. Stunned at such a bloodless defeat, his weeping warhost knelt and surrendered.

In Vortka's name Peklia disciplined the city's unruly godhouse, placing one hundred Et-Raklion godspeakers in authority there. The Tebek godspeakers she thought most troublesome she sent back to Vortka. With them rode all of the fallen warlord's family, they would live in Et-Raklion where they might cause no dismay. Also returned to Et-Raklion was Tebek's capitulated warhost. Stripped of their sigiled breastplates they rode in plain linen to Et-Raklion's barracks, escorted by five shells of Raklion's blood-hungry warriors and godspeakers who would smite them if they rebelled.

Tebek city was tamed.

In Tebek's godhouse its fallen warlord swore obedience to Raklion and after him to Zandakar, on his knees he swore in the god's eye to keep the warlord's peace in Tebek and all its villages, or die smitten by the god. Raklion accepted his godsworn oath, Zandakar accepted it, Hekat smiled, and the warhost rode away to the sound of Tebek's walls falling down.

One by one, in the same fashion, Mijak's other cities were tamed. Mamiklia, Takona, Zyden and Jokriel, they had no choice, the god's will was its will. Their chastened warlords swore obedience to Raklion and Zandakar and promised to die if they broke their oaths. The cities were easy conquests, Mijak's browning had brought them to their knees. The promise of bounty from fat, green Et-Raklion came as the god's blessing. Some people wept openly, they were so relieved.

City by city, godmoon by godmoon, Hekat's belly swelled. She did not look at it, she looked only at Zandakar. He rode like a warlord, he heard the oaths like a man. As each highsun saw Raklion grow smaller, more weary, Zandakar excelled in the god's proud eye. He outgrew all his clothing, she had more made for him. He outgrew his pony, she gave him a horse.

Every day they knife-danced together, they galloped their horses, they gloried in the sun. Every night beside his campbed she whispered: *This is Mijak, Zandakar warlord. It is the god's great gift to you.*

And he would shift, and sigh, and smile in his sleep.

The warhost rode no further than dispirited Jokriel. "Beyond here, warlord, is the savage north," Hekat told Raklion, seated together in their warhost tent. "A rock place, a dry place, forgotten by everyone, even the god, full of lice-ridden goats and a few dry men. We could ride for five godmoons and never see one. There is nothing there, and no need for you to see it." No need for *her* to see it, she had left that place behind.

To her surprise, Raklion agreed, he put his hand on her distended belly. "I am tired, Hekat. I want to go home. I want to be with you when my second son is born."

She kissed him gently, it did not hurt her. Aieee, god. He had grown so old. When first she knew him he would have scorned her suggestion, he would have taken his warhost into the savage north and torn it to pieces like the wildest sandcat.

In that time, he was the warlord. Truly, he is not a warlord anymore.

"Then when Jokriel is tamed, Raklion, we will go home."

Before they left the city she spoke secretly in the godhouse with a Jokriel godspeaker. She asked after Hanochek, who had not been seen.

The godspeaker sighed, and looked at the floor. "Ah, warleader. A sad story. He was crushed to death when a dry wall collapsed."

Dead? Dead? Wicked Hanochek was dead? She swallowed her laughter, she kept her face still. "I see. Yes, that is sad. Make sure not to mention it to the warlord or my son. Hanochek's death is better unremarked."

After next newsun's sacrifice they left Jokriel. Hekat rode with her warhost until they reached Tebek city, then was forced to lay in a padded cart, her belly enormous, her feet swollen and sore. Raklion sat with her, he said to keep her company, but he was worn out, a man of skin with bones beneath it. Zandakar stayed in the saddle, he rode his red horse, he led the remaining warriors in the warhost. He made the seasoned knife-dancers laugh.

Hekat watched him as Nagarak's spawn tried to kick a hole in her stomach.

Aieee, Zandakar, my beautiful son. You are the warlord, you live in the god's eye. I was mad to think you needed a brother. No demon spawned could ever touch you. If the god is good Vortka's omens will be wrong. This brat will die in its birthing. It will never breathe.

Fourteen highsuns later they reached Et-Raklion. She

went straight to the palace, and waited for her unbearable pregnancy to end.

"*Aieeee!*" screamed Hekat, and dug her fingernails into the arms of the two slaves supporting her. Rancid sweat coursed down her naked body, splashed onto the stone floor of her palace chamber. Fresh blood splattered between her spread legs.

Curse this brat, this is Nagarak's revenge, it will tear me in two before it is born!

"Courage, Hekat!" Raklion urged. "The god sees you, beloved, do not despair!"

She would have raked her nails across his face if he had stood close enough, if she had not needed to hold on to the slaves for support. Another pain ripped through her, she flung back her head and howled like a dog.

"*Yuma!*" cried Zandakar.

Panting, she unslitted her eyes. "You will be warlord, you *do not* show fear!" she grunted, glaring. "Must the taskmaster explain that *again*?"

Zandakar shrank against Raklion and shook his head. Raklion rested a hand on his shoulder, stupid man, always coddling, and said, "There is pain in childbirth, Zandakar. It is no great matter."

Hekat grimaced. That was easy for *him* to say, he did not struggle to expel the brat from *his* exhausted body.

Sidik looked once more between Hekat's legs. "Warlord," she said, "the child comes feet first. It is caught inside her and cannot be turned."

Raklion frowned. "What do you tell me? I am not a healer, you must use plain words."

Sidik plunged her hands in a basin of water held by her

novice assistant. Sluicing away the muck she said, "In plain words, warlord, your son cannot be born in the usual way. More of this will kill Hekat warleader and the child."

"No!" shouted Raklion. He stepped forward, fists raised, suddenly his old warlord self again. "If Hekat dies, if my son draws no breath, I will see you burned alive on a pyre, I will tear down the godhouse stone by stone, I will pluck out the eyes of every godspeaker and stitch their flayed hides into sandals for my feet!"

Sidik met his fury unflinching. "Warlord, the god would not let you. I can save Hekat and her baby but I will need to cut her open."

Cut her open? "What butchery is this, am I a goat?" Hekat demanded, panting. "I am Hekat warleader, I slew two warlords, I gave birth to the next, I dance for the god! You will *not* cut me open, you will pull this brat *out* of me, you will—"

Raklion fell to his knees beside the birthing stool. "Hekat, be easy! You must—"

"Cut the brat from *your* body! I will not be *butchered*!"

He gripped her shoulder and pressed his lips to her ear. "Is that *fear* in your voice, Hekat? Do you show *fear* before our son? Perhaps the taskmaster should speak to *you*."

Hating him, hating Nagarak's spawn that tore her apart, she unclenched her teeth. "Demons eat your godspark, Raklion!"

He kissed her. "You are Hekat warleader, the god's knife-dancer, you slew two warlords, your son follows me. You can birth our new son, Hekat. I know you can."

Aieee, god! She did not *want* this child! But if she

fought Sidik she would die and they would cut her open anyway, the brat would live and she would be dead.

I will not give Nagarak his revenge.

Raklion turned to the godspeaker. "Send your novice for Vortka. I want him to wield the knife that cuts her open, he is the god's high godspeaker, he dwells in its eye."

"Yes, warlord," said Sidik, and the novice ran out.

"Be strong, Hekat," he said, and kissed her eyes. "Hold on to me, we will endure this together. Before you know it we will see our son."

Tcha, you stupid man. I do not want to see it.

She looked for Zandakar, she beckoned him closer and brushed the water from his cheeks. "My brave little warlord, do not fear. I promise the god will not take me from you."

"I am not afraid, Yuma," he said, his voice unsteady. "The god sees you, I trust in the god."

When Vortka came she was half-fainting from pain and exhaustion. Blindly she tangled her fingers in his robes and dragged his ear against her lips. "Get it out of me, Vortka. Get it out of me *now*."

Vortka looked at Raklion. "There will be blood and screaming, warlord. It might be best if Zandakar—"

"No!" she said. "He stays! A warlord cannot turn from blood and pain, Zandakar stays!"

Raklion hesitated. "Hekat—"

"I am not afraid, warlord," said Zandakar. His bottom lip trembled. "I want to stay."

"You hear him?" she whispered, she was shaking with pride. "That is my son. Zandakar stays."

Vortka ordered the slaves to lift her from the birthing stool, lay her on the cold stone floor and pin her legs and shoulders. Turning to Sidik he said, "Be ready to receive the child."

The godspeaker bowed. "High godspeaker." She knelt, her arms cradled ready, holding a soft cloth.

As Vortka straddled her spasm-wracked body and unsheathed his sacrificial knife, Hekat looked into his calm eyes and wrapped her fingers round her scorpion amulet. Her heart beat so hard she could scarcely breathe.

"Now, Vortka. Do it now."

He nodded. Glanced at the slaves bracing her back, holding her arms. Hekat turned her head until she could see Zandakar. She smiled for him, he smiled for her.

Vortka opened her with his knife.

She screamed until she vomited bile, she thrashed and twisted, throwing slaves aside. The baby was hauled wailing out of her body, she heard Raklion shouting, she wished it was dead. Vortka thrust his hands inside her, she felt his godstone burning, burning . . .

"Hekat!" cried Raklion. He sounded far away. "The god sees you, Hekat, it will not take you from me, I need my knife-dancer, Hekat, *stay!*"

She was floating above her body. She looked down, incurious, strangely detached. There was Zandakar, her brave little warlord, on his knees and praying to the god. There was Vortka with his hands inside her, arms bloody to the shoulders, his scorpion pectoral wet with blood.

My blood, she realized, and could feel no sorrow.

Raklion shouted and cursed the god, he waved his fists, he demanded she be saved. His thin grey godbraids flailed around his face, godbells ringing in alarm.

Something small and squalling squirmed in Sidik's

arms. It was Nagarak's brat, that would please the god. Would her death please it? She knew she was dying.

Vortka healed the damage inside her, she felt her body writhe and twist. He sealed the great gaping slit in her belly, his godstone was as bright as the god's red crystal. It looked like the red crystal, covered in her blood. She felt its heat sear her, she felt her flesh mold closed, her godspark was seized and sucked back in her body.

She opened her eyes just as Raklion shouted in agony, clutching his chest and sagging to the floor. She tried to sit up, she could not move. She was smothered with exhaustion, her bones were milk.

"Warlord!" cried Vortka. He dragged himself off her and leapt to Raklion. The warlord sprawled on his back, his dark skin was clammy, his lips pale blue.

"I am dying—I am dying—" His words were a thin protest. His godbells were silent.

"Vortka," she said weakly.

He shook his head. "I am sorry, Hekat."

The chamber filled with Raklion's harsh gasping. "The child, Vortka! Show me my son."

Sidik knelt beside him, showing him the bloodsmeared brat. "His name—is Dmitrak," said Raklion. His voice was faint. "I name him for my brother—who was to be—warlord. Zandakar—"

Hekat watched her son go to him. "I name you—warlord after me, I give you Mijak," groaned Raklion. "Here is—your brother. Love him. Protect him. The god—sees you in its—eye. I love you, my son. Do not forget me."

Zandakar was weeping, when would he be strong? "No, warlord."

Raklion's gaze was clouding, with an effort he raised

one shaking hand. "See this woman? She is—Hekat. She is the empress—of my heart. As warlord I name her— Empress of Mijak. She will rule until Zandakar is a man. Vortka—high godspeaker, do you hear my words?"

"I hear them, warlord," said Vortka, calmly. "The god hears them also and it agrees. Zandakar is warlord, Hekat is Empress, she will rule until he is a man."

"Aieee—aieee—I am so sinful," Raklion whispered. "The god is calling, I do not wish to go. Hekat—" He gasped again. "My beautiful knife-dancer . . ." He released a sigh. "I wish I had not banished Hano." His chest rose with an effort, dragging air into his failing body. He breathed the air out, he did not breathe again.

The chamber's slaves began wailing. Hekat half-rolled over and forced herself upright. She sat in her own blood, it was thickened and cool. "You slaves, be silent!"

The wailing stopped, cut dead with a knife.

"You slaves, you are blind here, your ears are stopped, your tongues are shriveled in your mouths. Mijak will learn of this when *I* say it must, it is not your place to speak of Raklion's death. Tell them, Vortka."

Vortka nodded. "Silence is the god's desire. You will die in torment if you disobey."

Her arms would not hold her, she had to lie down. "Tell your godspeakers to hold *their* tongues, Vortka. Tell the whole godhouse to hold its tongue."

Vortka frowned. "I am the high godspeaker, Hekat. I know what to do."

She relented. "Yes. I know."

"Yuma?" said Zandakar. He stood alone, hands tightly fisted.

Vortka closed Raklion's eyes and went to their son.

"Zandakar, this is the god's will. Go to your chamber and sit there quietly. I will come to you as soon as I can."

"Yes, Vortka." Zandakar's gaze slid sideways. "My mother . . . the Empress . . ."

"The god has healed your mother, Zandakar. Do not be afraid, she will not die." Vortka smiled, a solemn curve of his lips. "The god see you in its eye, warlord of Mijak."

Zandakar nodded, fighting tears. "The god see you also, Vortka high godspeaker."

As Hekat watched her son leave, Vortka knelt beside her and pressed his fingertips against her pulse.

"I do not want that brat to nurse," she told him, furious at her thready voice. "There is a slave in milk somewhere in the palace, give it to her. I must think of Zandakar."

"It is not Dmitrak's fault his birthing hurt you," he said sharply.

"*Tcha*! I am Empress, Vortka. My body is mine now, it belongs to no man. If I say the brat will not suck, *it will not*. I can say this. The god has seen me, it has raised me high."

"It will throw you down again just as swiftly," he warned her. "That child is desired by the god. Forget that, Hekat, and you will be sorry."

She was tired, she wanted to sleep. "Give it to that slave for nursing," she said, listening to her weak voice slip and slur. "I will not touch it, that is my word."

Vortka sighed. "Sidik, give the Empress's son to the slave in milk." To the remaining chamber slaves he said, "Show Sidik godspeaker to that slave, then come back with a litter for the Empress. She must be bathed and put to bed."

Alone with Vortka, struggling to stay awake, she said,

"I am Empress, Vortka. I am Empress of Mijak. It is the god's will. Raklion—"

"I will take care of him."

She closed her eyes. The slaves returned with a litter. As it carried her away from the chamber, away from Raklion, and her dead past, she closed her fingers round her scorpion amulet.

I am Empress, god. You have gifted me with power. I will use it to serve you. I am still your slave. Do not smite me for rejecting Dmitrak. You desired his creation and I obeyed. He is alive, do not ask me to love him. I love Zandakar. That is enough.

CHAPTER THIRTY-SEVEN

After three highsuns of ritual sacrifice and purification Raklion was burned on a pyre in the city's magnificent godtheater, which Vortka had seen finished eight highsuns before the warhost's return. Recovered enough from her grueling childbirth, Hekat rode behind him to his funeral in an open litter, carried on the shoulders of four perfect male slaves. Instead of her favored plain linen training tunic she wore yellow silk and red wool, and ropes of gold and bronze and carved green jasper. They tangled with her scorpion amulet. Of course she wore that, it was part of her skin. She thought of Raklion as the slaves carefully dressed her, he had not lived to see her attired as he thought she deserved. A passing sadness, she let it go. Zandakar rode his red stallion beside her, splendid in horsehide, leather, silk and jewels. Vortka led the funeral procession, his scorpion pectoral gleaming in the sun.

Nagarak's brat stayed with its nurse-slave in the palace. It could stay there and rot for all she cared.

Raklion's body was carried through Et-Raklion's district streets to the godtheater by the weeping shell-leaders of her warhost. The streets were crowded with mourning Mijakis, as Raklion passed by they threw coins and amulets and bloody scraps of sacrificed flesh. They called his name, they begged the god to see him in its eye. They called her name, called her *warleader, Empress*. They shouted to Zandakar and praised him to the god.

"Do not disgrace me," she had told him that newsun, helping him fasten his polished leather breastplate with its striking snake. "You are son to an empress, you must not weep. Weep in your heart, the god sees all secret tears."

"Is that where you weep, Yuma?" he asked her. "Do you weep for the warlord in your heart?"

She had to lie, how could she be truthful? How could she tell him, *Weep? I laugh. I dance in my heart, I am free at last. More than free. I am Empress of Mijak. I was sold as a slave, how can I not dance?*

The funeral procession made slow progress, it left the godhouse at highsun and did not reach the godtheater till two full fingers later. Hekat sighed when she saw it, more magnificent even than in her dreams.

The godtheater was large enough to admit many thousands, guarded by twenty-four towering godposts, twelve well spaced down each long side. Carved from the finest Mijaki obsidian, they were decorated with scorpions and snakes, wild falcons and centipedes. Each was banded and inlaid with gold and bronze and silver, with diamonds and emeralds and lapis lazuli, and topped with a coiled striking snake, the snake of Et-Raklion, the god's one true city.

At the far short side of the godtheater was erected a high stone platform, and on it stood a sacrifice altar and an enormous throne. The throne was carved from that same obsidian, a standing scorpion with its raised tail curved high overhead. A throne for a warlord, it was stark and imposing. Hekat smiled to see it.

A throne for an Empress. That throne is mine.

The open space of the godtheater was crowded with people, the chosen of Mijak, and godspeakers, and as many of the warhost as Vortka would permit. So many people, yet the silence was oppressive. Even when Vortka led Raklion's body into the godtheater not a word was spoken, just a sweeping sigh of grief.

Weeping still, her warhost shell-leaders placed Raklion on the pyre at the edge of the stone platform, then joined the other warhost witnesses to this solemn event.

At the altar Vortka sacrificed a pure white bull-calf, it was garlanded with flowers and painted with green snakes and crimson scorpions. Its blood was mixed with sacred oil and poured over Raklion on the pyre. Zandakar turned the pyre to flame, and lit it with a torch Vortka gave him, then stood beside Hekat as Raklion was burned to ash.

He did not weep, he was her true son.

When nothing remained of Raklion but cinders and charred bone, Vortka made another sacrifice, this time a bawling black bull-calf. He sacrificed for Hekat the Empress and for Zandakar her son, who would be Mijak's warlord when he was a man. She sat on her scorpion throne, never showing how the unyielding chair pained her. She did not flinch as Vortka poured the hot blood over her head and down her body.

Her silk robe was ruined. She did not care.

"*Hekat!*" the people shouted, and dropped to their knees. "*Hekat warleader! The Empress of Mijak! The god see our Empress in its powerful eye!*"

She feasted on their worship, she drank their acclaim. She sat on her scorpion throne and thought:

God, is there more?

Six fingers after lowsun, when tear-stained Zandakar was fast asleep and the godmoon slid down the night sky with his wife, Hekat went to the godhouse and disturbed Vortka high godspeaker.

"Hekat?" he said blearily, in the doorway of his sleeping chamber. "Is something the matter? Why have you come?"

Her bloodsoaked finery was discarded, she wore her linen training tunic again. Her scorpion amulet was alone round her neck. "I have come to swim in the godpool, Vortka."

"The *godpool*?" He took her wrist and tugged her into his chamber. In the corridor, his godspeakers stared at the floor. As he closed his door on them, he said, "Aieee, Hekat. What madness is this? Take a draft if you cannot sleep! Do not seek to swim in the *godpool*!"

"Why?" she asked him, looking around his room. It was as spare as his work chamber, no doubt exactly as

Nagarak had left it. "The godpool is where the warlord speaks to the god."

He shrugged on a brown robe over his loincloth. "You are not the warlord."

"Oh, but I am." She bared her teeth in a dangerous smile. "Until Zandakar is grown I am the warlord. I am also the Empress. You cannot say no."

"Aieee, Hekat!" Vortka tugged at his stubby godbraids, did he know how stupid he looked? "Why must you speak to the god in the godpool? You speak to the god wherever you please!"

"And I please to speak with it in the godpool," she snapped. Then she sighed. "Vortka. The godpool is a sacred place, Raklion would talk of it with such *awe*. And the question I must ask the god, it is—difficult. I must be certain to hear it clearly, it must answer me strictly, I cannot misunderstand its reply."

"Then perhaps you should ask your question in the scorpion pit," he grumbled. "The god can answer most strictly there."

Was he serious? She did not think so. She took his hands, she almost never touched him. His skin was warm, she could feel his pulse leaping. "Vortka, listen. You were born a potsmith, I was a goatman's unwanted slut. Then I was sold, and you were sold, Vortka, you and I were made into *slaves*. Now you are high godspeaker and I am the Empress. We are godchosen people, we are chosen by the *god*. Our lives are not small lives, the air we breathe is not petty. We have a purpose, Vortka, beyond a palace and a godhouse. We have a purpose in the *world*."

He slid his hands free of hers. "Our world is Mijak and

together we rule it. There is no other world or purpose, Hekat."

She looked at him steadily. "Foolish Vortka. You know that is not so. You know there are lands beyond Mijak's borders."

"*What*?" He stepped back. "Hekat, you *are* mad. To think of crossing beyond our borders? You are *mad*!"

"I do not think so. But if I am, then let the god tell me. Let me ask my question in the godpool, let the god answer it there."

"*Hekat . . .*"

"It is my right, Vortka. Raklion told me. A warlord can seek the god in the godpool and not even a high godspeaker can say he will not." Vortka opened his mouth, and she added quickly, "And if you say again I am *not* the warlord I will prick you with my snakeblade so you cannot sit down."

He shut his mouth with a snap of teeth, he went to the door and pulled it open. "Prepare the godpool," he said to his godspeakers. "The Empress desires to speak with the god."

In the black and red darkness, she swam with the god.

Here am I, Hekat, naked in blood. Here am I, Hekat, I have a great question. You have raised me high, I am precious and chosen. I am your Empress, I am also your slave. You are the god, the true ruler of Mijak.

Should you not also rule the world?

Vortka watched Hekat emerge from the godpool, her skin dripping scarlet, her eyes alight with the god. She was beautiful, naked. He could not think of that. He felt his heart slow, felt the air melt around him.

She has her answer . . . and I am afraid.

"Vortka," she said. She was smiling. Radiant. The scars on her face and her belly glowed. "I heard the god. The god has spoken. Mijak is not the end. It is only the beginning."

"The beginning of what?" he said, leading her to the cleansing room, with its milk, water and towels. "Hekat, it is late. I am tired. No riddles. What did the god say? What does it want?"

She laughed. "The god desires a godhouse in every city, godposts in every village beneath the sun. It desires to be taken beyond Mijak's borders, into every godless corner of the world. Where there are demons, it desires their destruction. I will be Hekat, Empress of the world. You will be Vortka, the world's high godspeaker."

The blood was drying on her, he should wash her clean. All he could do was stand and stare. "*And Zandakar?*" His voice was a whisper.

"Zandakar will be what he is: the god's smiting hammer, smiting the world. Vortka, I understand everything now. *This* is why you found the crystal. *This* is why my son was born. He is not needed to smite Mijak, Mijak is conquered. It is tamed to my knife-dancing fist. No. The hammer was born to tame the *world*."

Jerkily, he began to fill the cleansing pool, so he might free her of blood. "Hekat . . . I know you are precious. I know you are chosen. But so am I chosen and the god has told me *none* of this. Each newsun and lowsun I make private sacrifice, I read omens in the blood and the entrails, I pray to the god to show me its want. Not *once* has it spoken of conquest, of destruction. Of Empress Hekat, Empress of the world."

She stared at him, disdainful. "You did not ask in the godpool, Vortka. You have not clearly heard the god."

"I think I have," he said. "I think I have heard it more clearly than you."

"*Tcha!*" She began to wash herself, he did not try to stop her. "That is not possible. You know who I am and what I have done. Because you are high godspeaker will you believe a cockerel's gizzards before you believe *me*?"

Aieee, the god see her. So arrogant, so proud. "Hekat, it is not a question of *believing*. It is what I *know*, that you do not."

She reached for a towel and began drying herself. "And what do you *know*, Vortka, that the god did not tell me?"

There were no stools or benches, so he shifted to the wall and let himself sag. "Those tablets in the cupboard, remember, in the high godspeaker chamber? Sacred to high godspeakers, read by no-one else alive."

She shrugged, indifferent. "So?"

It was not her fault, she had not read them. He beat down his temper and kept his voice calm. "Long ago, Hekat, in a time lost to all men but me, as the last high godspeaker, Mijak was a mighty empire. Its borders extended far beyond the Sand River, into lands whose names are no longer remembered, or even thought of under the sun. In that time many conquered peoples were brought here as slaves or new citizens of the Mijaki Empire. Mijakis of this age are their descendants. That is why there are differences among us, varying shades of skin, eyes of many colors. Hekat, it was the Empire that brought Mijak to ruin."

He had her attention. She had always loved stories . . . "Ruin?"

"Yes. *Ruin.*" He straightened, and folded his arms. "The warlord then, he was called the Emperor, listened to demons, he abandoned the god. Deaf to the god's voice, Mijak grew greedy, it stretched too far, demanded too much. Plagues were brought here by a new conquered nation, they killed Mijak's people, killed horses and cattle and goats and sheep. Infants starved to death in their cradles. Starving men, desperate, gnawed on their bones. Corpses filled our cities to the rooftops, unharvested crops rotted in the fields. The Empire of Mijak stood on the brink of destruction. It was the god's judgement, its wrathful smiting. The few surviving godspeakers prayed to the god, they asked its forgiveness, they begged for mercy."

Hekat clutched her towel, her eyes wide, intent. "And the god? Did it answer?"

"Yes. It answered," he told her. "It promised to save those who were left, but only if they swore perfect obedience until the end of time. The godspeakers swore obedience, what else could they do? And *that* is why we live within Mijak's borders. *That* is why godposts are everywhere a man looks and godbowls are there for filling, we must be humble, *always*, lest we too are tempted by demons, lest we should, like our forebears, abandon the god. It is why godspeakers rule our streets, why sacrifice is constant, why *nothing* can happen beyond the god's eye. We are wicked people, Hekat. We betrayed the god's trust, we must live in its wrath. We must live on our knees, and hope to be forgiven."

After a moment, Hekat smiled. "No, Vortka. You are

mistaken. We *were* wicked people, we are wicked no more. Forgiveness is ours, we can stand, and not kneel. Our sins are behind us, the god wants us in the world! Nagarak told Raklion that when he was warlord of Mijak the underground rivers would flow again, the lands beyond Et-Raklion would grow green and lush. Nagarak was wrong. I have ridden through Mijak, it is not so. I tell you truly, until the god's will is worked on the world, the underground rivers *cannot* flow. I tell you Mijak's browning is the god's sign that we must turn *outwards*. If we do not, Mijak will die. The god will forsake us for not heeding its want."

Vortka stared at her. "You are certain? You have no doubt at all?"

"Tcha!" she said, and lightly slapped his cheek. "Vortka, Vortka, *this* is why you and I were given power, the potsmith, the goatslut. Abajai and Yagji, Raklion and Nagarak . . . they were the god's instruments, nothing more. It used them to help us. *We* are the precious ones, we are precious for this reason: to create Zandakar, the god's smiting hammer. To make the god a gift of the world."

After Hekat left him, unshakeable in her belief, Vortka discarded his robe and his loincloth and lowered himself into the godpool.

Are Hekat's words true, god? Are we forgiven, is our past the past? Is Zandakar your hammer? Did I create him so he could smite the world?

The blood was cold, and cloying. Sunk beneath the godpool's surface, he lost all understanding of time.

Then he heard the god, it whispered:

Watch.

Wait.

Speak.

Act.

Love.

Startled, he broke the cold red surface. Plunged to the pool's edge, gasping for air.

Love? Never before had the god said *love*. It did not matter, the god had spoken. It did not deny what Hekat believed. Hekat knife-dancer, Empress of the world. Vortka, the world's high godspeaker. Zandakar, their beautiful son, born the god's breathing, smiting hammer.

He felt sick. *Dizzy. Must this fall to me?*

It was the god's desire, he would obey. He would stand by Hekat, he would guide their son, he would see the god's will done in the world.

Humbled, he cleansed himself and returned to his chamber, where he sought in vain for elusive sleep.

Hekat slept easily, she slept smiling in the god's conquering eye. At newsun she waited on her balcony for Zandakar to join her, every newsun they ate honeyed cornmush and figs together. He did not come, she went to find him.

He was in Dmitrak's chamber, holding the drooling, cooing brat, the nurse-slave was giggling, encouraging, as Zandakar laughed to see Nagarak's spawn suck his finger. She wanted to shout at him, to scold him, to beat him, but his face was so beautiful, it was shining with love. He held the brat tenderly, as though it was breakable, one day he would hold his own son with such breathless care.

In the godhouse Vortka had asked her, *What is the*

god's purpose for Dmitrak, Hekat? Did you ask it? Do you know?

Nagarak's brat? Revulsion had shivered her. *He has no purpose. He sits in the shadows, burping and wailing and shitting his wraps.*

"Zandakar," she said. "Give him to the nurse-slave and come eat your cornmush. I have been waiting for you, that is not polite."

"I am sorry, Yuma," her son said quickly, and did as he was told. As they walked to her balcony he added, "The warlord said I must protect my brother. He is so small and helpless. Please, do not be angry."

She breathed hard, once. "I am not angry. I wondered where you were."

His glance was doubtful, he knew better than to question. They sat on the balcony, listening to the birds sing, watching the god's sky fade from pink and gold to blue. Slaves served them in silence, they ate their honeyed cornmush. When they were finished she dismissed the slaves.

"My son, our lives are very different now. The god has spoken, it has tasked me with a special purpose. It has tasked you too and we must speak of that. Our words must be secret, no-one else can know."

His eyes were large and limpid, so expressive. "I can keep a secret, Yuma."

"The god has made me Empress of Mijak. It desires to make me Empress of the world. It will make of you its smiting hammer, to destroy ungodly demons in its name."

She watched his beautiful lips shape her words in mimicry. *It will make of you its smiting hammer.* He said aloud, wondering, "What does that mean?"

"It means you are special, Zandakar. It means you are so deeply in the god's eye it cannot see any other boy."

Zandakar frowned. "It cannot see Dimmi?"

Dimmi? Ah, yes. His stupid pet name for Nagarak's brat, she let it pass, for now. "I told you, Zandakar. It can only see you. This task is an honor, it is a burden. From this newsun forward you cannot be a small boy. You are Zandakar, the god's hammer, the Empress's son. That is who you are, and will be, forever."

"I thought I was the warlord," he whispered.

"Tcha. You are more than a warlord. A warlord is *nothing*. The god throws down warlords, it smites them in the dirt."

Zandakar looked frightened, he sought refuge in silence. When he did speak again, his beautiful eyes were bright. "Why am *I* chosen, Yuma? Why *me*, and not some other boy?"

She left her chair and gathered him to her, she did not often show softness. He must be hard. "Because you are my son. That is why, Zandakar."

He hid his face against her shoulder. "Yuma . . . can you send for Hanochek to come home? He has been gone for a long time, he must be punished by now. And I miss him. He could lead the warhost since I am not the warlord anymore."

She opened her arms and let him fall. "*Stupid* boy! You nearly died because of Hanochek! He nearly thwarted the god's great plan! And I have no need of a man to lead the warhost. Before I was Empress I was Hekat warleader. I am *still* Hekat warleader. The warhost is *mine*. I would not bring him home even if I could, Zandakar, and I cannot. Hanochek is *dead*."

Crumpled on the ground, he stared up at her, shocked. "Hano is *dead*?" he whispered. "Yuma, *no*."

She leaned down, her shadow fell over him. "If you weep for him, Zandakar, I swear *I* will whip you on the scorpion wheel!"

He shook his head, she saw he was shivering. "No, Yuma. No weeping."

"*Good*," she said, and rewarded him with her smile. "Now, my son, up on your feet. It is time to attend the newsun sacrifice. Then we will go to the barracks. We must knife-dance for the god."

As soon as Vortka saw his son, kneeling before the altar in the Sacrifice chamber, he knew that something was troubling him. He did not comment, he sacrificed the ten white lambs and poured their blood in the sacred bowls, then prayed in silence as Zandakar, his mother and the attending godspeakers took their sip and were sanctified in the god's eye.

Hekat dismissed their son to the barracks and lingered to speak with him once sacrifice was done. When they were alone she considered him in silence, then said, "So, Vortka high godspeaker. You understand the god now?"

He nodded. "I understand you heard its will. I understand my purpose in its plan."

"Good." She smiled. "Vortka, that is good. We have walked in the god's eye together this far, I do not wish to walk on alone. The god is mighty. We are its mighty slaves."

He would never accustom himself to her utter conviction. He accepted she did not doubt the god, but that she would never doubt *herself*? Aieee, such confidence. He confessed it, he felt envy.

He said, "When, Hekat? When must we take the god into the world?"

"When Zandakar has become a man, and I have made of the large crystal a weapon. When the god has shown him how to use it. When my warhost numbers in the tens of thousands, each warrior in it sworn to die for the god." She touched his arm, a fleeting brush of calloused fingers. "Then will Zandakar and I smite the world. There is time yet. I have much to do. Mijak must grow green and fat again, it must be beautiful to honor the god."

Zandakar. He said, "What has upset our son, Hekat? Do you know?" *Do you even notice? Your eyes are so often fixed on the god.* "I thought he—"

She waved her hand. "I told him sinning Hanochek was dead. He fancies himself grieved, he will not grieve for long."

"Dead? What happened? How did you—"

"Tcha! Does it matter? I think it does not. I must go, Vortka. I am expected in the barracks."

He took a step after her. "*Hekat*—"

"No!" she said, turning. "You are too kind-hearted, you will make him soft. Zandakar is *my* son, he is born for the god. Is the god soft, Vortka? Does a smiting hammer weep? I think not, high godspeaker. Do not interfere."

She was Hekat the Empress, she was Zandakar's mother. He bowed his head. He did not interfere.

Eight godmoons after Raklion's pyre burned out, Hanochek warleader wept for his death. A small distance away, beneath the pitiless sun on a stony, makeshift warhost field, forty threadbare warriors danced with snakeblades made of charred sheep bones. More than half bore faded scarlet godbraids, or scarlet patches on their ragged shaven skulls.

Aieee, Raklion. Raklion. That bitch killed you, I know it. Hekat killed you, my beloved knife-brother. She turned you against me, and you sent me away. I would have saved you if I'd been there, Raklion. I would have killed that poisonous bitch first. Aieee, god, god. Why did you let him send me away . . .

He smudged his cheeks dry with a sunburned hand. It was hot and ugly in the savage north. Primitive. Uncivilized. Godforsaken, for the most part. More snakes and lizards than upright men.

But I am free, here. I am not known or watched. I am making a warhost. I will avenge you, Raklion. I will save Mijak from Hekat, I will save Zandakar. That is my oath to you, my warlord. My friend.

He shaded his eyes and looked at the knife-dancers. Aieee, god, what a sorry lot. But it was a beginning. He had to start somewhere. The savage north stretched a long, long way, a haven for runaways and criminals and escaped prisoners, like him. He had turned less promising recruits into lethal killers for his warlord, Raklion.

And here I am, a fugitive, doing it again.

When he had first reached Et-Jokriel's godhouse, the godspeakers had never let him from their sight. Nagarak was not their high godspeaker but they were no fools, they knew to fear him. They had fed Nagarak's prisoner stale bread and flyblown meat, offered him water that was three parts pish. At first his anger would not let him touch it, then his belly took over and he forced it down.

Then it forced it back up again, moments later. But he knew his hunger meant he wanted to live. To live and one day go home to Et-Raklion, forgiven, reinstated, returned to his life.

In those first few godmoons he truly believed Raklion would relent. That his friend would turn away from Hekat's poisoned whispers and remember the laughter, the blood on the battlefield, and the rare, precious moments of intimacy after, their life together before Hekat came.

But the highsuns kept passing, with no word of forgiveness from Raklion warlord, or his high godspeaker. Only a stubborn determination not to let Hekat win had kept him alive, when the pain of living threatened to throw him from Et-Jokriel's godhouse roof.

It was Hekat's doing, I will not blame him. He was her victim, like I was. Like Zandakar.

Aieee, god. The poor little boy. That bitch for a mother and his father dead. And now there was another son, he was told, another helpless child facing ruin.

News traveled slowly in the savage north, but it trickled in eventually. As it had trickled today, bringing word of Raklion's death.

He felt fresh tears, he did not hold them back. He shouted at his faltering knife-dancers, threw stones to make his point. They hopped, they yelped, the tears retreated.

It was hard to recall exactly when he had decided to take revenge. To reject his harsh exile, and reclaim his life. It did not matter. What mattered was he was able to plan an escape, right under the noses of a godhouse full of godspeakers. Aieee, god, he was a warrior. Of course, it helped that the godhouse was distracted, disheveled, that the warlord and high godspeaker's failure to return from the meeting with Raklion and Nagarak cut their legs out from under them as neatly as any snakeblade.

By then they had almost forgotten about him. He was quiet, obedient, he toiled in the stables, he cleaned the godspeakers' shitboxes, emptied their pishpots and never complained. Never once gave them cause to notice him, after his shine had rubbed away.

Was it a sin to steal one slave from that slave pen in the city? Break his neck, dress him in my clothing, collapse that old dry godhouse wall on his body and run away in the night? If it was, god, you must forgive me. What is one more death, after the hundreds of warriors I have killed? And I did it for you, as much as me. I did it to save Mijak from that murdering bitch Hekat. I did it to save Zandakar, who I love like a son. And the other one, whose name I do not know.

He had forty warriors, the seedling start of a warhost. He only needed a few thousand more . . .

It might take me five seasons. It might take ten. What does that matter? I'm a man rich in time. I will build my warhost. I will train it in the savage north, where no warlord rules but me, no warleader wields a snakeblade but me, where no warrior rides who does not answer to me. We may ride camels, we may throw spears made of bone, we may cut an enemy's throat with less style than I would like. But dead is dead, Raklion. You know that now. And before I join you . . . I will send Hekat to hell.

CHAPTER THIRTY-EIGHT

Five horses raced on the barracks horse-field, leaping ditches, logs, piles of stones, heaped goat carcasses, they slithered down steep slopes, plunged through water and blood and fire and smoke. A single mis-step meant a fall, or worse, a broken leg or snapped neck, death, for horse and straining rider alike.

Zandakar leaned low over his red-striped stallion's sweaty shoulders, he urged it with eager cries and kicking heels, but he could not reach his speed-maddened brother. Dimmi was only just past his twelfth season, but he rode like a man grown, and like the Empress, their mother, he knew no fear. The other three warriors had fallen far behind them, this race was between him and Dmitrak now, and Dimmi was winning.

He often won when they raced over obstacles in the horse-field. He did not care if a horse broke its leg, he did not care if he ran it to windless exhaustion, all that mattered to him was leaping the last obstacle first and snatching the goat's head from the pole, a victory.

Zandakar did not like to lose, but losing to Dimmi was a bearable sting. This race he had lost to him in front of Hekat. Perhaps, this time, she would see her younger son's skill. This time, she might reward him with a smile.

She did not often smile at Dimmi. Zandakar knew why

now, the whole warhost knew why. Dimmi's birth had ruined her; they had forgiven him, it seemed she never would.

The finish pole was on them, his brave stallion was clipping Dimmi's heels, too late, he'd lost. The goat's head was snatched by Dmitrak's quick hand, held high in the air, his prize, his trophy.

The watching shell-leaders and the other warriors selected for the day's training shouted and hooted and drummed their snakeblade-hilts on their saddles. Hekat sat her black mare stiffly, her eyes were disappointed. She did not smile.

Her displeasure was a knife in Zandakar's side, he tried not to feel it as he eased his stallion to a blowing halt. Dmitrak galloped in circles around him, laughing and brandishing the goat's severed head, adoring the warriors' wild acclaim. Zandakar watched their mother watch him, then turn for quiet words with her shell-leaders. It was as though, to her, Dimmi no longer existed. He saw his brother reef his pony to a rearing halt, saw him see her indifference, saw his brother's face go cold and still.

Aieee, Yuma. Is it so hard to praise him?

She turned her horse and rode away, not words for him either, he was in disgrace. She left the horse-field slowly, she could not gallop anymore. She did not look back, he did not ride after her.

As the other straggling warriors finished the contest he urged his stallion to join Dimmi's brown pony, a fiery thing with blood in its eyes. It snapped at his horse, he backed away. "Dimmi—"

Dimmi ignored him, he pitched the goat's head into

the crowd of warriors, flung himself from his saddle and stalked away, towards the horse-field's fringe of trees.

Zandakar turned. "Arakun!"

The grey-haired old shell-leader, retired now to training younger warriors, left his fellow trainers and came to his side. "Warlord," he said, fist pressed to his heart.

It was a courtesy title, he was not warlord yet, even though he had killed his share of godforsaken criminals in training, and led the warhost when it rode once each season through Mijak. He would not be warlord till the Empress decided.

She is so often angry, she might never decide.

"Take my stallion, Arakun, and my brother's pony," he said, sliding to the grassy ground. "Walk them till their breathing is eased. If you can keep them from killing each other, that would be good. My brother and I will not be long."

Arakun took both sets of reins. "You rode the course well, Zandakar," he offered, briefly smiling. "If Dmitrak did not take so many chances . . ."

It was the closest he would ever come to criticizing the Empress's younger son. Zandakar nodded. "I know," he said, rueful. "I will tell him."

Leaving Arakun with the horses, he went after his brother.

He found Dimmi in some miserly shade, kicking a tree trunk, beating it with a dead fallen branch. The boy spun around when he heard footsteps approaching, his cheeks were wet, his eyes stretched wide.

"I am not *weeping*!" he shouted. "This is *sweat*, I am *sweating*, I rode hard and I *beat* you, Zandakar!"

Zandakar sighed. Every time he saw Dimmi he saw a

small, swaddled baby with his finger in its mouth. He could not help that, he did not tell his brother. "You rode hard, you rode well, I could not catch you. The warriors saw you, they shouted your name."

Dimmi's face was rebellious. "Tcha! What are warriors, they are dogs to be trained. *She* did not see me. She has no eyes. I am less than the wind to her, if I blew she would not feel me."

"Dimmi . . ." Zandakar took a step forward, his hand outstretched.

His raging brother struck him with the dead branch. "Do not call me *Dimmi*!"

He hated that pet name, he said it made him small. *It is hard to remember. You are my little brother.* Zandakar glanced at the groove the branch had made in his forearm, swiftly filling with his blood. Dimmi gasped and dropped his makeshift weapon.

"I am sorry, Zandakar! Please, do not tell her! I did not mean to hurt you, it is not my fault!"

No, it was not. He was young, he was high-strung, his heart was bruised by the Empress. Zandakar pulled him into a tight embrace. Dimmi's head barely reached the middle of his chest. His thin body was shaking, he was nearly undone. "I know, I know, it was an accident. Dimmi—Dmitrak—please, do not mind so much. She does not mean to hurt you, riding is a pain to her, it shortens her temper, it hardens her heart."

"Her heart is always hard," muttered Dimmi, muffled against his linen training tunic. "At least towards me."

"She is the Empress, Dmitrak. She *cannot* be soft. It has been twelve seasons since the god threw down the warlords and their high godspeakers and gave her Mijak to rule in its name. *Twelve seasons*, little brother, and not one hint of rebellion, not a single disobedience, we have perfect peace in our land. Would that be true if she was soft? I tell you, Dmitrak, I think it would not."

Still muffled, Dimmi snorted. "She is soft with *you*, Zandakar. For *you* there are smiles and kisses, for you there are always words of praise. She does not praise *me*. I am never good enough."

He released his brother. "Dmitrak," he said, his voice a command. Sniffing, trembling, Dimmi stepped back and looked up. "Here is something I have never told you. Do not repeat it, these words are just for you."

Dimmi's face brightened. "Our secret? I promise."

"When I was small, seasons younger than you are now, I was wicked and foolish and galloped my pony in the old horse-field. Didijik fell, he died and I was injured. After I was healed, the Empress took me to the godhouse. A taskmaster tied me to the scorpion wheel and he whipped me for my sin. Four highsuns later I was given a new pair of horsehide leggings, made from the skin of my beautiful pony, that died because I was a wicked boy."

Even now, so many seasons later, he felt his eyes prick at the thought of dead Didijik. He did not care about the whipping, the whipping had been well deserved. It was the memory of what he'd done to his pony, and of Hanochek who was sent away, that hurt him. He did not speak to Dimmi of Hano. Hano lived in his deepest heart, a secret he could never share.

"She did that?" said Dimmi, an awestruck whisper.

He nodded. "She did that. I know she is hard on you, little brother. She is hard on me also, when we are alone."

"Maybe," said Dimmi. His expression was stubborn.

"But I still say she is hardest on me. It is not fair, is it *my* fault her body is broken? I could not help that, I did not ask to be born!"

Another memory, bloody and sharp. The Empress cut open on a chamber floor, Vortka's hands thrust deep inside her, the sight of her agony, the sound of her screams. Raklion warlord, dying of his old age. He'd been such a small boy, he had never forgotten. Not even Vortka's kind comfort, later, had softened the impact of that night.

He offered his brother his gentlest smile. "None of us ask it, Dmitrak, we are born by the god's will."

Dimmi kicked the dirt with the toe of his sandal. "I wish I knew why, Zandakar. Do you know why?"

He could not answer, that was another secret never to be shared. Its shadow lay between them, he prayed Dmitrak would never see it. "Am I a godspeaker, to know the god?" he said lightly, and tugged on Dimmi's dusty godbraids. Their godbells jangled, so often out of tune. "Go to the godhouse, ask it yourself."

"Tcha," said Dimmi, and pulled a face. "I do not like the godhouse, it stinks of old blood. I only like the stink of sweat."

"That is good, you must like yourself!" Zandakar said, teasing. "So now we should go back, I think. Tomorrow we attend sacrifice in the godtheater, before the people. You like that, Dmitrak. They always cheer to see you."

He slid his arm around Dimmi's shoulders, swinging his brother with him into movement. Dimmi groaned, and slipped himself free. "Yes. I like it. But first we must fast, and I get so hungry."

"Aieee, little brother!" said Zandakar, only half-joking. "Must you complain so much? The god does not like it, such a moaning man are you!" Then, to forestall any temper at the rebuke, he broke into a jog, grinned over his shoulder and added, gently taunting, "I say you cannot catch me twice, Dmitrak!"

Laughing, they ran and left the pain behind them, in the branch-beaten tree, in the air.

Later that night, long after lowsun sacrifice when his brother was safely asleep, he went to his mother in her private chamber. She took one look at his face and tossed aside the clay tablet she was reading.

"I warn you, Zandakar, *do not say it*! I am your mother, the Empress, am I to be chastised by *you*?"

He did not answer, just dropped to the floor beside her chair, where so often he sat when he was a boy, and let his head rest against her knee.

"Tcha!" she said, after a long silence. "*You* are the hammer, Zandakar, not him. What business does he have, trying to defeat you?"

He sighed. "Dimmi does not know I am the hammer, Yuma. I am his big brother, he walks tall when he wins."

"Tcha!" she said again, and touched her fingers to his godbraids. His godbells sang softly, they said she forgave him. "Does that matter, Zandakar? I think it does not. Soon you must smite the world for the god, you must ride with me and the warhost against the world's demons. Dmitrak cannot walk tall then, he must walk *behind* you. He must be content to live in your shade."

He twisted round so he could see her. In the chamber's lamplight her scars shone silver in her beautiful face. She would never tell him how she got them. Vortka would not tell him. Nobody else knew. It was a mystery, his mother was a mysterious woman. "When, Yuma?" he asked, his heart pounding. "When must I smite the world for the god?"

She smiled, he truly was forgiven. "In the god's time. I will tell you when I know."

"But you are certain it is soon?"

Her smile faded. "Yes, Zandakar. Very soon. Brown Mijak cries out for relief, Et-Raklion's water cannot water it forever. Our water is less bountiful than even three seasons ago. The god grows impatient."

"But it has not given you the sign."

"It will."

"Yuma . . ." He took a deep breath, she would not like this question. "Are you sure you are strong enough, to ride into the world?"

Her silver scars tightened, her lips pinched tight. "That is not your business. You have no right to ask me."

"I have every right. You are my mother, and I love you."

She leaned down and took his chin in her fingers. "Before I was your mother, I was the god's slave. Before I am *anything*, I am the god's slave. The god desires me to fight for it in the world, Zandakar. In the world I *will* fight for the god. It makes me strong, I am strong in its eye. *Never* ask me that again."

He loved her, she frightened him. When the god was in her, she was to be feared. "I am sorry," he whispered. "Yuma, forgive me."

She released his chin, caressed his cheek. "Of course, my precious boy. I always forgive you. That is my weakness, did you not know?"

Hekat? *Weak*? He almost laughed. He said, "Yuma.

About Dmitrak. All he wants from you is a word of praise. Will you not praise him? Once? For me?"

She sat back. "Perhaps. Now leave me, Zandakar. Tomorrow we sacrifice in the godtheater, my mind must be peaceful so I can hear the god."

He stood and kissed her, then retired to his chamber. In bed, his fasting belly rumbling, he stared at the ceiling, unable to sleep.

God, let her praise him. Warm her heart towards him. He is my brother, I weep when he weeps.

One finger before highsun Hekat rode in her slave-borne litter from the palace to the godtheater, with Vortka leading, walking in his glory, and Zandakar beside her, riding his stallion, and Dmitrak behind on his runty pony, out of her sight where he deserved to be. *Praise him? I must praise him? Aieee, sweet Zandakar. The things I do for you . . .*

Beneath her silk and wool and gold she wore her plain linen training tunic, her snakeblade was belted at her waist. She dreaded the knife-dancing expected of her as Empress, her body ached from the long ride to and from the horse-field. In truth, her body ached all the time, thanks to Nagarak's murderous brat.

Three godmoons after Dmitrak's violent birth she had known the claw-marks he'd left in her body would never fully heal. Riding was torment, knife-dancing a crueler tasking than any godspeaker could devise.

How could you allow this? she had railed at Vortka. *You said you healed me, you said I was whole!*

Vortka had frowned, and touched his scorpion pectoral. *You did not die, Hekat. Be grateful for that.*

Tcha, and tcha. *You did not die*. How did that help her? What a stupid man.

Et-Raklion's citizens and its visitors from elsewhere in Mijak, those not chosen by Vortka's godspeakers to witness in the godtheater, lined the streets leading to the great, sacred godtheater. The city was still called Et-Raklion, that was Zandakar's plea, how could she refuse?

As was customary, it rained offerings as they proceeded through the city's districts. Such devotion pleased her, but Vortka complained his novices took far too long to clear the pavestones of the amulets and coins thrown before her. Nor did he approve that she made certain each journey to public sacrifice took them through the Traders district, past that villa once owned by Abajai and Yagji. It had long since been sold, someone else owned it now, the door was repainted, not blue but red.

She hoped Yagji knew that, screaming in hell. Red was the color he disliked most.

They reached the godtheater, it was crowded and hushed. She sat on her scorpion throne and hid her pain in her throat. Zandakar and the other one stood behind her, one on each side. Vortka sacrificed a bull-calf, and a black lamb, and a cockerel, and a dove. She drank the steaming blood from a golden chalice, so did Vortka, so did Zandakar, and so did Dmitrak, the last.

"Behold your Empress, the Empress of Mijak!" cried Vortka. "Behold godtouched Hekat, precious in the god's eye!"

Twelve seasons a high godspeaker, and he had borrowed nothing from Nagarak. He ruled the godhouse not with terror, but with a smile. It was not her way, it was not her godhouse. That was Vortka, if the god disliked it the god would long ago have thrown him down.

He turned and nodded, his face not beautiful anymore, twelve seasons as high godspeaker had seasoned him out of beauty. Deep lines marred him, she was sorry for that. Once he had been a pleasure to behold.

His pronouncement was her signal. She stood and stripped down to her tunic, no longer the Empress but Hekat warleader, the god's knife-dancer, beautiful and precious, the doom of Bajadek and his son. She heard the crowd suck in its waiting breath, she felt its righteous passion as flames on her skin.

Vortka struck his godbell. It was time.

She exhaled sharply, willing her hurting body to obey her, willing the *hotas* to flow without reluctance. The godforsaken criminal selected to die by her hand was brought before the platform by two of Vortka's godspeakers. A man this time, but she had killed women and children too. Some were slaves, and some were not. All were wicked sinners, they deserved to die. She had started the practice of public execution four godmoons after Raklion's burning.

I am the Empress, with the god's power of life and death in my hand. At every godtheater sacrifice let the people see it. Let them be reminded. Let them know who I am.

The prisoner was weeping, he knew he was doomed. His godbraids were cut off, he did not need them. "The god is in me," she told him, coldly. "You are judged, I am your smiting."

She did not know his sin. She never knew, she never asked, that was the god's business, hers was death. She unsheathed her snakeblade and danced to him lightly, on the balls of her unshod feet. There was pain, she ignored it, she gave it to the god.

As her snakeblade plunged into the sinner's heart, as she looked in his pale eyes to watch his godspark blow out, she saw his face change, ripple and transform. The man she killed was the man from the village; the man who had sired her and sold her to the Traders.

He fell slain before her, he slid from her knife. She stood over his body, unable to move.

It is a sign. I knew a sign would be given. The god has spoken. The past is dead, with my snakeblade I killed it. The future is now, and the god wants the world.

"Hekat?" said Vortka, coming to her side as the crowd praised the Empress, and Zandakar, and Dmitrak, as it gave thanks to the god in its wrathful smiting. "Hekat, is something wrong?"

She turned to him, smiling. "No. Vortka, I must swim in the godpool, I must speak to the god. The time has come to make Zandakar its hammer. I must forge the crystal weapon, the god will tell me how."

He drew back from her as though her words were a snakeblade, pricking his skin. "Hekat! You are *certain*?"

She rolled her eyes. "Tcha, stupid Vortka. When was I not?"

When the godmoon and his wife stood on top of the sky, she swam in the godpool, the god whispered in her heart. Afterwards, Vortka unburied the large red crystal from the godhouse's shrine garden, where it had slept safely for so long. She carried it with her down to the palace, then summoned a slave.

"Go to the Artisan district. Tell the best goldworker in Et-Raklion to expect a visit from the Empress."

Palace slaves now wore gold-stitched tunics, their scarlet slave-braids were bound in gold wire. The whole city knew them, they were never disobeyed. Even god-speakers in the quiet time knew to leave them alone.

The god would have the artisan it required.

While she waited for the slave's return, she prepared the heavy red crystal, picked it free of rotted goathide, cleaned it of old blood and crusted dirt and set it on the floor before her. Then she took the scorpion amulet from round her neck, unthreaded it from its leather thong and balanced it upon the dull red stone.

The amulet rippled. The crystal glowed. It fractured into myriad pieces, chunks and shards no bigger than a large plum, no smaller than a peach stone.

"Tcha!" she said softly, pleased. She rethreaded the stone scorpion and looped it over her head, gathered up the chunks of crystal, placed them carefully in a leather satchel, and wrapped herself in a woollen cloak.

The slave returned, it led her on foot to the Artisan district and a goldworker so overcome he could barely speak. He asked no questions.

That was wise.

"Empress, exalted, there is some risk," he warned her once the slave was gone, as they stood alone in his workshop surrounded by lumps of gold and copper, crucibles, metal tools, a fierce hot fire. He was an old man, bent almost in half like a blighted sapling, scarred over and over with burns and cuts. "Working with gold is no simple business, you might be hurt. *I* could—"

"No," she said. The god had been clear, the gold wire

for the weapon must be made by its Empress, the god's weapon for Zandakar must spring from her hand. "Begin."

With the artisan guiding her she melted the gold and copper together in the exact amounts he told her, she rolled it and pulled it, sweating, cursing, she transformed it into strong wire for the god's smiting hammer. Newsun broke beyond the workshop windows, she ignored it, she toiled for the god and so did the artisan. She was burned, she was cut, she ignored her small pains and her large ones. The artisan's assistant brought ale and roast meat, she ate without tasting, the god was in her, whipping her on.

Time passed and passed, she did not heed it. When the wire at last was ready, coiled like a thin snake, she tipped the lumps of red crystal onto the workbench. "The crystals and the wire must fashion together." She smoothed burned fingers over her left hand and up her arm. "Into a glove that will fit a man's arm from fingertips to elbow: Do you understand me?"

The artisan frowned. "A glove made of gold wire and lumps of crystal?"

The god had shown her in the godpool but she was an ignorant slave-girl again, she did not have the words. She seized a lump of charcoal and scribbled on the bench, drew for him the picture the god had seared into her mind.

"There! That is what I must make, that is the god's desiring."

He gaped. "The *god*, Empress?"

"Are you deaf?" she demanded, and bared her teeth at him. "Yes, the god! Open your ears!"

"Forgive me, Empress," he croaked, cringing. "I think this is possible. Let us begin."

With his help, she created the weapon, a long woven glove crafted from gold wire and crystal, a gift for Zandakar from the god. Soft leather straps stitched there, and there, so it might be fastened securely to his arm. When the weapon was finished she slipped her hand inside it. Too large for her, it would be perfect for Zandakar, born the god's hammer in the world. The red crystals shone with a dull, sleepy light, waiting for her son to wake their fury.

Only as she slipped off the weapon did Hekat realize the depth of her exhaustion, feel once more her deep-seated pain. The artisan could hardly stand, he clutched at the workbench and groaned.

"You have pleased me," she told him. "You have pleased the god."

The artisan thudded hard to the floor, water dribbling from his eyes. "Empress! To serve you, to serve the god, I am a fortunate man!"

She nodded. "Yes. You are."

He gave her a soft bag for the gold-and-crystal weapon, she put that bag into her satchel and left him alive. Outside his workshop it was once again night, the quiet time. How many highsuns had passed since she came here? She was uncertain. It might be four. Slowly, painfully, she walked back to the palace, unseen by the godspeakers in the god's eye.

She went straight to Zandakar's chamber and slipped inside. Breathing softly she stood by his bedside and watched him sleep, as she had watched him sleep when he was a small boy, riding with the warhost throughout all of Mijak, taming its cities, accepting their oaths.

In those days you were a warlord, my son. Your life

would be simpler if that were still true. But you are the god's slave, as much as I. The god has its desires, and we must obey them. You were not born to be warlord, you were born the god's hammer . . . and the time has come to smite in its name.

Aieee, god. He was so beautiful, he made her heart ache. She could watch him forever, she would never grow tired. Now he was a man she could see Vortka in him, he was as old today as his father had been when a goatslut and a potsmith spoke together for the first time, in the slave pen of a city whose name had long since blown away like smoke.

You must see my son, god. You must see Zandakar in your eye. He will smite for you, I have raised him in that purpose. Do not abuse him. Do not shatter him in your wrath.

Zandakar sighed and shifted, he opened his eyes. "Yuma?" He sat up. "Aieee, Yuma. Where have you been?"

"About the god's business," she told him, and hid her aching heart. "Do not ask stupid questions." She tossed the weapon in its leather satchel onto his bed. "Dress, Zandakar, then take that to Vortka in the godhouse. Do not open it until he says you may. He will tell you what you need to know."

CHAPTER THIRTY-NINE

When Zandakar entered the godhouse, just before newsun, a godspeaker took him straight to the Sacrifice chamber.

"High godspeaker," he said, wary, as the door closed behind him. "I am come to you at the Empress's command."

Vortka nodded. He was dressed in nothing but a loincloth and his scorpion pectoral, lean and weathered by his service to the god. His sacrifice knife lay on the altar before him. To one side, in their pens, the waiting sacrifices panted. "And by the god's desire," he said calmly. "Come closer, Zandakar. We have much to discuss."

He closed the distance between them, the leather satchel heavy in his hand. "Yuma said you will explain everything. Was she right?"

Vortka snorted. "Is she ever wrong, warlord?"

They exchanged rueful, conspiratorial smiles, and Vortka was Vortka again, even without his comfortable robes. His secret friend, since Dmitrak's birth not a secret at all. After Yuma was made Empress his tutor was dismissed, and all the lessons that did not involve war he took with Vortka high godspeaker. They studied, they laughed, Vortka never chastised him, never froze him with cold, hard eyes, never whipped him on the scorpion

wheel. There was never a time when he thought Vortka
did not *see* him, see his true heart and know what he felt,
and what to say.

*The way he knew what to say the newsun I was given
Didijik's tanned and stitched hide to wear for my sin. The
way he knows, with no words being spoken, that I would
gladly spend my life riding across Mijak with my
warriors.*

And how being born the god's hammer fills me with fear.

Vortka said, sober now, "Since Dmitrak's birth you
have known what it is the god made you for, Zandakar.
You have known what you *are*, but not what that *means*.
Now it is time to learn its meaning. Now it is time to *become* the god's hammer."

Zandakar felt his mouth suck dry. *Not yet, not yet. I am
not ready.* "High godspeaker . . ."

"I know," said Vortka. His eyes were so kind. "Zandakar, I know. But this is your purpose, would you thwart
the god? Give your godspark to demons? Defy the
Empress?"

He shivered. "No. I love the Empress, I worship the
god. I have spent twelve seasons preparing for this moment, even though I did not know why, or what it meant.
I will do what I must, it is why I was born."

"Good boy," said Vortka. There were tears in his eyes.
"I am proud of you, Zandakar. Aieee, god. You make me
proud."

Hearing the words, his own eyes burned. He did not remember Raklion warlord clearly, the man had always
been distant and so often unwell. Even on the journey
through Mijak, all those dreamlike godmoons riding
under the sun, knife-dancing with the warhost, seeing the

god throw down the sinning cities, staring into the faces
of the fallen warlords as they knelt and gave him their
oaths, even though he had ridden all that time with Raklion, it was his mother the Empress he remembered best
from those days. Then Raklion had died as Dmitrak was
born, and after that there had been Vortka.

*Would I weep if Raklion warlord said he was proud? I
do not think so. We were never close.*

He said, "Tell me what to do, Vortka. I do not know
what I must do."

"Put down the satchel," said Vortka. "And hand me a
black goatkid from the pen. First we will sacrifice, then I
will tell you what the god desires you to know."

Vortka's sharp blade was merciful, he knew how to kill
without causing pain. Twelve times he slaked the god's
thirst with sacred blood, twelve times the blood was collected and drunk. Zandakar struggled to control his heaving belly, hot blood on an empty stomach was a recipe for
woe.

When the sacrifice was over, the last white lamb's carcass vanished in the air, Vortka put his knife aside and
washed his hands in a basin of water. His eyes were still
kind, they were also sad.

I think he is like me, thought Zandakar, surprised.
Vortka is sorry for the slain creatures.

He would never say so. It might anger his mother, and
the god.

Vortka said, "In that leather satchel, Zandakar, is a
powerful weapon. Your mother made it, the god told her
how. Your mother made you, another powerful weapon.
Now the god will tell you how you fit together, how to-

gether you and this weapon will be its hammer in the world."

The *god*? Not Vortka? Zandakar stared. "I—I thought *you* were going to—Vortka. *Vortka*. I cannot speak to the *god*. The god, it is—it is—"

"To be obeyed without question or complaint," said Vortka, frowning. "Or have you lied to me in this sacred place? Are you the god's willing instrument, Zandakar, or are you not?"

He went cold, he was nearly sick. "I am. I am. I was born for the god. I was born for this weapon, the god will tell me how."

Vortka reached beneath the altar and withdrew a small godstone on a leather thong. "Put this on," he said, handing it to him. "Your horse is waiting for you outside the godhouse. This godstone will tell you where to ride. When it is hot, you follow the god's desire. When it is cold, you have turned the wrong way. When it drops from your neck, you have reached your destination. Leave your horse safely tied at a distance, sit on the ground beneath the sky. Take the weapon from the satchel, put it on and close your eyes. That is when the god will speak to you, Zandakar. That is when you will learn what you must know."

Zandakar nodded. "The god told you this?"

"The god told your mother. Your mother told me."

Aieee, the Empress. Greater even than Vortka. He nodded again, and fumbled the godstone over his head. "I am ready." He was lying, but what else could he say?

Vortka smiled, again reading his heart. He came round the altar, he picked up the satchel. "Do not fear, Zandakar. You are the god's chosen."

Vortka took the satchel from his friend, the high god-speaker, and was startled when Vortka kissed both his eyes. "The god see you, hammer. When you are finished in the wilderness, do not return here. Ride straight to the godtheater. I will wait for you there."

Zandakar nodded, he could not speak. He left the god-house, found his horse, swung into the saddle and rode away, the godstone hot against his skin, the leather satchel heavy across his back.

He rode hot and hard for nearly four fingers, the god was in him, urging him on. He rode far from Et-Raklion, into the wilderness, until the godstone dropped from his neck. Sweating, aching, he slid from his saddle and tied his horse to a tree, staggered twenty paces, then dropped to the ground.

It was a wild place the god had brought him to, nothing living between him and the sky. He saw scattered boulders, a line of dead trees, heard the breathy chuckle of a nearby stream. No other sounds, the world was nearly silent. He opened the satchel and removed the god's weapon, his breath caught in his throat as he saw what his mother had made. Red and gold, a thing of mystery. Fashioned by the god for brutal smiting. He emptied his lungs, it was nearly a sob, and with his heart pounding to pieces he put on the glove.

And screamed, as the wilderness around him disappeared in a flash of white heat. Lost within that terrible maelstrom, Zandakar heard a distant voice. Thought he heard a voice. Thought he heard something.

Is that me, screaming? God, am I dying? God, have I failed you? God, tell me what to do.

Unimagined power flailed inside him, blinding, boiling, burning him away. There was pleasure and pain in a dreadful confusion. Almost he panicked and surrendered his reason. Then he heard Vortka, calm, his voice kind.

I am proud of you, Zandakar. Aieee, god. You make me proud.

He stopped fighting, then, he sat inside the chaos of his power and waited for the god to come. It came at last, it drowned him with its presence, in understanding without crude words. Poured knowledge into his empty mind, remade him in a blazing heartbeat, changed him in the blink of an eye.

Clasping his arm, the weapon yearned to be free.

Despite his godgiven knowledge he felt suddenly uncertain, clumsy, like a child again, learning *hotas* from his mother.

Tchut tchut! he heard her. *Are you stupid? I think you are not. You can do this, Zandakar!*

He imagined the power within his control. He imagined it fiery but obedient, wild but responsive to his will. Like his stallion Davilik, snapping teeth and striking hooves, aggression contained with his voice, his hands, his heels.

The power rippled, its mad outpouring slowed, slowed, slowed to a stop. He held his breath. Then, just as slowly, he felt the power pour back, pour strongly towards him, into his gold-and-crystal hand.

Pouring . . . pouring . . . pouring . . .

Complete.

He opened his eyes. There was his hammer hand, gold-and-crystal fingers outstretched, there was the god's power balanced on his palm.

It felt as though he held the sun.

He raised his arm. He clenched his fingers. He stared at a boulder thirty paces away. He breathed out slowly, and released the god's wrath. Hot white light streamed from his fist and struck the boulder. With a thundering boom the rock blew apart in dust and shards. Davilik whinnied, he danced and plunged. The horse was well trained, it did not run.

With the god's mighty weapon he destroyed six more boulders, he reduced four trees to splinters, he boiled the chuckling stream in its rocky bed. The power sustained him, it fed him with life. He released it like a fireball and punched a smoking crater in the ground. Laughing, exultant, he held his fist high, his body on fire with pleasure and power. His mind was spinning, he was drunk on sadsa squeezed from the sun.

After he laughed, he wept like a child. He knew now what the hammer was, he knew now what *he* was. He was Zandakar, he was a stranger.

I am the god's hammer, born to smite the world.

It was a difficult thing, to remove the god's weapon. It felt like his own flesh, solid blood and bones of gold. Carefully he returned the glove to the satchel, carefully he threaded his arms through the satchel's straps. He swung onto his stallion, his body still thrumming with the remnants of power. A liquid pleasure was in his loins, like the pleasure he felt when he fucked a godhouse vessel. *That* was not something he had looked for.

Ride to the godtheater, Vortka had told him.

Trusting the god to guide him through the wilderness, Zandakar turned his horse for the city.

*   *   *

He reached Et-Raklion city a bare finger before lowsun. Its streets were crowded, they were always crowded. The godspeakers saw him approaching, they cleared a path swiftly. He reached the godtheater while there was still light.

It was filled with people, warriors and citizens, and more godspeakers than were usually present. He rode in behind the huge stone platform, slid dirty and sweat-stained to the flagstoned ground. A slave took his stallion, he ran up the platform's steps to its top.

The Empress was waiting on her scorpion throne, and Dmitrak behind it. Vortka stood at the altar, in his finest high godspeaker robes. In the dirt at the steps of the platform, a godforsaken criminal on her knees.

"Zandakar, my precious son," said his mother. She was dressed in red silk, her wrists were laden with gold bangles, her godbells were shining and so were her eyes. "Tell me you have met the god. Tell me it has spoken to you, and you are returned from the wilderness a man reborn. Returned the god's hammer, to smite the world."

Dimmi was staring at him with a puzzled frown, dressed plainly, as usual. Zandakar spared his little brother the swiftest smiling glance. "Empress, I met the god. I return from the wilderness a man reborn, I am the god's hammer born to smite the world."

With a triumphant look at Vortka, she raised herself from the scorpion throne. Zandakar, so close to her, saw the violent pain in her eyes. She took his hand and guided him beside her, to stand and face the multitude.

"People of Mijak!" she called to the hushed, waiting crowd. "Here is Zandakar, my beautiful son. He is your warlord, he is much more than that! He is the god's hammer, born to smite the wicked world!"

An excited buzzing from those close enough to hear her, voices repeating her words into the crowd. She let them whisper, she let them gasp, she turned to him and said, "The god spoke to you?"

He nodded. "Yes, Yuma."

"The weapon is yours, you have made it your own?"

"Yes, Yuma."

She laughed. "Then put it on, my beautiful son. Become the god's hammer, your purpose in the world."

It was like rejoining himself, sliding his hand and arm into the gold-and-crystal glove. In the sinking sunlight the weapon caught fire. The crowd cried out to see it, they pointed and sighed. He closed his eyes and called on the god, he felt its power ignite inside him, he felt his blood burst into flame. He raised his hand above his head, pointed his fingers at the sky. Blue-white fire streamed from his body, he heard the crowd shouting, he heard some screams.

"Behold the god's hammer, he will smite the world!"

It seemed to Zandakar his mother's words reached him from far away, as though she stood in the godhouse and whispered on the wind. The cheering of the watching crowd seemed just as distant, not quite real.

"Zandakar warlord! Zandakar godhammer!"

He opened his eyes. The power still poured from him, like one of Mijak's underground rivers it flooded without ceasing into the sky, he thought it might even singe the sun.

Beside him his mother looked at him, proudly smiling.

"Now kill the prisoner. Smite it with the god's hammer, Zandakar."

Kill the—Startled, he pulled back the blue-white fire and spoke without thinking. "Yuma? Are you certain?"

Nothing angered her more swiftly than to have her word questioned. Her lips tightened, her eyes narrowed, he felt the echoing crack of the taskmaster's cane. As he stepped back she said, "When have you known me not to be certain?"

"Empress," he said, and bowed his head.

Vortka came forward, he trod the stone steps down to the dirt and cut the godforsaken criminal's bindings. She was a large, clumsy woman with small breasts and wide hips, her skin was not uniformly dark, but strangely patchy, pale and brown. She bore a scarlet godbraid, she was a slave.

Zandakar looked at the god's gold-and-crystal hammer, he felt his power simmer, like water on the fire. All he had to do was to take a deep breath and release it. He did not.

"Zandakar," said his mother, softly, the edge of a snake-blade in her voice.

I have killed before, why do I hesitate? She is condemned, godforsaken, yes she breathes but she is dead.

His gaze flicked sideways, his mother was waiting. He looked over his shoulder, at his staring brother. Dmitrak's gaze was eager, his fingers were fists. He had yet to make his first kill as a warrior, but not because he was not keen.

I am the god's hammer, its chosen, its weapon. What I do with my power, I do for the god.

"*Zandakar,*" the Empress commanded.

He raised his gold-and-crystal fist and killed the slave.

The blue-white stream struck her, it turned her to flame. She stood before him a burning pillar, she burned to nothing, to a sifting of ash. The power seared him, this time it was different, it was not the same as smashing rock. He felt it smite him, curdle his blood and melt his bones. He cried out as the crowd cried his name, he heard Dmitrak shouting, heard Vortka gasp.

He did not hear his mother's voice.

The power left him, he swayed on his feet, he felt weak and dizzy. He could have wept. It was Vortka who went to him, who helped him to steady. His mother ignored him, she turned to the crowd.

"See the god's might in him! See its proud fury! He is my son, he is Zandakar, the god's hammer!"

Trembling, he stripped the gold-and-crystal glove from his arm. His skin was unmarked, he had expected to see scars. He felt tentative fingers touch his tunic, he turned and looked down to see Dmitrak, staring.

"Zandakar—Zandakar—what happened to your hair?"

His *hair*? He snatched up a godbraid and held it before his eyes. It was blue. It was *blue*.

"Zandakar, tell me," Dmitrak whispered. "Tell me how it feels to kill like the god!"

He could not answer. All he could do was stare at his godbraid, blue as the blue fire, blue as its merciless killing flame.

"I cannot explain it," said Vortka, in a low voice. "Except to think it is the god's mark upon you, the god's mark of favor, that you smote a sinner in its name."

His hair did not change when he used his power to smite rock and earth. This had happened because he killed a human. He did not understand it, he likely never would.

"You are godtouched, Zandakar," said his mother, delighted. "I have always known it. Now the world will know, too."

The patch-skinned slave was not the last criminal he hammered before he rode from Et-Raklion at the head of the warhost. Every highsun, in the silent godtheater, he smote five more godforsaken sinners. He smote them in front of his witnessing warhost, he smote them in front of godspeakers and ordinary folk brought in from Et-Raklion's outlying villages, and from all the cities and villages in Mijak.

"*The word must spread*," his mother told him. "*Every godspark in Mijak must know who you are.*"

He did not question, he was serving the god.

When he wasn't smiting criminals in the godtheater, he was training with the warhost, preparing to ride. He knew now what the god's plan was for him, he knew he must lead the warhost into the world. Or, at least, his mother the Empress must lead it, with him by her side, smiting wherever and whatever the god told him to smite.

Dmitrak would not be riding with them.

"It's not *fair*," his brother wept, inconsolable. "I am old enough to be a blooded warrior, I have heard the stories, *she* joined the warhost when *she* was my age."

Sitting beside him on his small bed, Zandakar sighed, and patted his shoulder. "Dimmi, if it were only a question of joining the warhost, then—"

"*Do not call me Dimmi!*"

He withdrew his hand. "Forgive me. Dmitrak. If it

were only a question of joining the warhost, then there is no doubt. You would be assigned to a shell. But we are not remaining in Mijak, we will cross the Sand River into the unknown. Yuma is being careful, she does not want to risk you, she—"

"*Tcha!*" spat Dimmi, and flung himself against the wall. His dark brown eyes were bloodshot and furious. "She does not *care*, she does not *want* me. She *hates* me, I tell you. She wishes I was *dead*. She only wants *you*, her precious Zandakar!"

The words cut like a snakeblade. There was real hatred in his brother, Zandakar had never heard it before. "That is *not* true. Has she not praised your riding skills of late, Dmitrak? Did she not let you have a new horse?"

"No. It's a *pony*."

"Yes," he admitted. "But a better-bred pony than the one you had before. She does not *hate* you, Dmitrak, you must not say she does. She is busy. Distracted. What the god has commanded, it is a *frightening* task."

Dimmi fell silent. "Zandakar, are *you* frightened?" he asked, at last.

Aieee, god. Am I frightened? I am frightened to death. If I fail the Empress, if I fail the god . . .

He forced a smile. "How can I be frightened, little brother? I am the god's hammer, I live in its eye."

Tears and temper forgotten, for the moment, his little brother grinned. "You still have not told me how it feels to kill like the god."

No, Dmitrak. And I never will. He said, "This thing we do for the god, you must know it will take us a long, long time. The world is a big place. Who knows how big it is? You are not a warrior yet, Dmitrak, you will be one soon.

And then you will join me in the world. We will fight together, we will fight side by side, as brothers. We will throw down the world's demons as we fight for the god."

Dimmi frowned as he thought about that. "And the Empress will not live forever," he said, almost to himself. "One day she will die, and you will be *Emperor*. Then *I* will be warlord, *I* will lead the warhost to war."

Aieee, god, what a blessing we are alone! Zandakar slapped his hand over Dimmi's mouth. "You must *never* say that, it is a *smiting sin*. You wicked boy, I should tell Vortka. I should drag you to the godhouse and beat you on the scorpion wheel!"

Above his silencing hand, Dimmi's eyes were stark with horror. He shook his head, his fingers tugged. "No! No!" he begged, his desperate voice muffled. "Zandakar, no!"

He removed his hand. "Say you are sorry, Dimmi. Say you did not mean it."

Now there were fresh tears, now there was weeping. "I am sorry. I did not mean it. I want to *ride* with you, Zandakar! I do not want you to go *away*!"

Echoes of his own voice, begging for Hanochek. "I know," he said helplessly. "But what can I do? I am born the god's hammer, Dmitrak. That is what I am."

With a despairing wail, Dimmi threw thin arms around him, weeping as he had never wept in his life. All Zandakar could do was hold him until the worst of his grief had passed.

"Here is my promise, little brother," he said, when Dimmi was calmer. "Even though I ride far away, the Empress and Vortka are planning our war so we can always send and receive news to and from Mijak. You will write me a clay tablet every highsun, and I will write one to you. It may take some time for us to read each other's letters but we *will* read them, I promise. And as soon as you are old enough I will send for you, Dmitrak. You will join me in the warhost, you will ride in my shell."

Dimmi sniffed, suspicious. "Even if the Empress does not want me there?"

"Dimmi, she will want you. But not as much as *I* will."

Another sniff. "Very well. We will write letters. But when you address me *do not* call me *Dimmi*."

Four godmoons after Zandakar blooded the god's hammer in the godtheater, Hekat thought she was close, at last *close*, to taking the god into the world. She would be far happier if she knew even a little of what people lived beyond the Sand River, but she could learn nothing of them. Not a single tablet in Et-Raklion's godhouse library or in any other library in Mijak could tell her the name of *one* sinning, demonstruck land. She was certain of that, she had sent for them all. Not even Vortka's secret high god-speaker tablets made mention of who lived with demons beyond Mijak's borders.

They would only learn that by going there.

It does not matter. I will defeat them, whoever they are. They are not in the god's eye, they do not have its hammer.

She was so proud of Zandakar, so proud of his power. He was a fierce warlord, she had raised him well, he would never disappoint her. She was his Empress, he was her beautiful son.

Mijak's warhost numbered fifty thousand. It was a vast hungry horde, the plains around Et-Raklion groaned beneath its weight. Ten thousand warriors would remain in Mijak, she would choose the man to lead them closer to the time. The rest would follow her across the Sand River, they would ride with her and Zandakar into the world. A mighty warhost, they would cut down the sinners as a scythe cut wheat, she would pluck them from their lands as a thorn from her flesh. Those who survived her smiting would live to serve the god and Mijak, their lands would become Mijak, the god's people of Mijak would live in those places after. Five thousand godspeakers would ride with the warhost, Vortka was choosing them even now. They would ride to build godhouses in the conquered lands and cast down the demons who thwarted the god. One by one those unknown lands would fall.

Mijak would become the world, and she would give it to the god.

After every lowsun sacrifice she stayed in the godhouse to talk with Vortka in his private chamber. They talked of her plans, they talked of the god, they took omens together, they made many lists.

"I wish you would travel with us," she said, not for the first time. "The god dwells in you, Vortka. You live in its eye."

"Hekat, I cannot," he refused, not for the first time. "My place is in Mijak, working for the god. You will have Zandakar, he is all you will need."

Aieee, he was right. But the god see her, she would *miss* her high godspeaker, she was used to his company. He was a man, that was not his fault. He was a better man than any other, save her son. "You will come to the warhost *sometimes*," she commanded. "You must see the new lands we have cleansed of demons for the god."

He smiled, looking older, though in truth he was not old. "Yes. Sometimes. But not very often."

"Tcha!" she said, and looked down her nose. "I am the Empress, you will come when I call!"

Before he could chide her, there came a knock on his door. "The god see you, godspeaker," he called.

The godspeaker entered, crossed to Vortka. Bent low to his ear and whispered, whispered. She saw Vortka straighten, she saw his face. "What?" she demanded. "Vortka, what is it? Not Zandakar—not *Zandakar*—"

He shook his head, he could barely speak. "No. It is worse. Hekat—Empress—the god is thwarted. A warhost is raised against you in the north."

CHAPTER FORTY

Jokriel city slept sweetly in the sunshine, with no outward sign it was infested by demons. No outward sign, either, of the warhost raised against her. That warhost was a mystery, its demon warleader faceless, nameless.

Hekat sat her black mare on a rise a safe distance from the rebel stronghold, and stared at its roofs with hate in her heart. *Let that sinner remain faceless, do I care what his name is? I will smite him to pieces, he can die with no name.*

On either side of her sat Zandakar and Vortka. Her son wore his hammer, since they rode from Et-Raklion he had not taken it off. Vortka wore a sour frown, he did not think she should be here.

"This is godspeaker business, Hekat. Jokriel city's god-house is overthrown, some godspeakers are murdered, others have joined in this rebellion! I must smite these sinners, I must lay them in the dirt!"

So he had told her, after giving her the news. She had turned on him, her rage was incandescent.

"How did this happen, Vortka? Why did you not see it in an omen? You say your eyes are open to the god! You say you hear its whisper in your heart! When did you shut your eyes, when did you go deaf?"

He struck her face. "I am not blind, I am not deaf, you dishonor the god to say such things! This bloodshed is the omen, Hekat! You plan to lead a warhost into the world, and as you plan demons strike at home? Did I not say the god spoke against the empire, did I not tell you what the secret tablets said?"

"You told me you agreed with me, that the god desired its new empire!"

"I never agreed. I let you convince me, I must pay for that sin. I tell you, Hekat, Jokriel city's fall is a warning. Ignore the god and be cast into hell!"

She had almost snatched her snakeblade, then, almost shed his blood in her fury. "You are right this much, Vortka. It is a warning. It warns me demons grow stronger in the world, it tells me I have waited too long in the god's eye. I must give the god my empire now, I must kill every demon and every man who worships them, everywhere I find them under the sun. I will start with Jokriel, in defiance against me."

Nothing more he could say made a difference to her,

she was godtouched as he was, he did not know better
than she. He said he would ride with her, she did not forbid it. She wanted him to see her smite for the god. She
gathered a small warhost, five thousand strong warriors,
she did not wish to tire more than that before she crossed
the Sand River into the world. Five thousand of her warriors could deal with this rebel warhost, the one godspeaker escaped from Jokriel thought it only three
thousand strong.

Three thousand, *three thousand*. How had three thousand rebels gathered in secret against her? How had
Vortka and his godspeakers not seen this? How could her
high godspeaker have failed?

*As the seasons passed peacefully he grew soft in his
heart. I planned for conquest, he built schools for the
poor. He let slaves earn their freedom, if they were old
and could not breed. He said the god desired it, why
would I disbelieve him? We are both godtouched, we both
hear the god.*

She shifted uncomfortably in her saddle, the long hard
ride from Et-Raklion had tasked her severely. It was her
punishment, demons had risen and she did not see them,
her body's pain was her sorrow to the god.

*It is a small failure, I will soon make it right. When
these rebels are cast down, when their sinning blood waters the ground, when their heads are cut off and carried
home on our spears, the god will see me again in its eye.
Then will I lead my warhost from Mijak, then will the god
be seen in the world.*

"Yuma?" said Zandakar, and touched her arm.

He was worried for her, there was no need. "Lowsun
approaches, Zandakar, we will camp behind this rise and

smite Jokriel city after newsun sacrifice," she told him. "Walk among the warhost once it is settled. Show them your hammer, let them see the god in you. Drink their praises, eat their love. That will sustain you in any battle." She had learned that from Raklion, knowing him had not been a complete waste of her life.

Zandakar nodded. "Empress, I will."

They returned to the warhost, Zandakar saw to their camping and their comfort, Hekat withdrew with Vortka for a private sacrifice. As he cut their flesh and caught the blood in his gold cup, Vortka said quietly, "We are alone now, I will say it once more. You should not do this, Hekat. You have misread the god's desire."

She watched the blood drip from her sliced arm, watched it mingle with his. When the cup was a finger full she took off her scorpion amulet and poured that mingled blood upon the stone. Then she held the amulet high in the air and watched the drips fall on the bare ground, watched them splash and splatter. "There is an omen, Vortka, *I* will read it to *you*. I will give the god victory, Jokriel city will weep for its sin. This faceless warhost will weep out its blood, I will send those thwarting demons back to hell. Zandakar will stand beside me, I tell you *this* is his blooding. *This* will see him smite with his hammer, he will *be* the god's hammer, as the god decreed."

Vortka said nothing, he healed her with his godstone, he healed himself and stared at the bloody ground. After a moment, she realized he was weeping.

"I have failed you, Hekat. I have failed the god." Water trickled down his thin, lined cheeks. In the fading light she saw silver in his godbraids. "You always heard its voice more clearly, you always stood tallest in its hidden eye. I am at fault here, that I did not see these rebels rising. My sin has placed you in danger, placed Zandakar in danger. Aieee, sweet Hekat, if he should fall . . ."

"*Zandakar fall?*" she said, and slapped him lightly. "*Tcha*, stupid Vortka, what nonsense is this? Zandakar is the hammer, how can he fall? He is the god's child, he lives in its favor. Raklion knew this, the god told him in a vision. My son is the future. The whole world will know him. His name will be legend. So said the god, the god does not lie."

Vortka looked at her, such fear in his eyes. "You promise, Hekat? Zandakar will not fall?"

She was always the strong one. She cupped her palm to his cheek. "I promise, Vortka. It is my word."

The godmoon and his wife had walked almost to mid-sky by the time Zandakar finished wandering among his warriors. When the last words of praise were drunk, when his belly was full of his warhost's love, he joined his mother by her small, smokeless fire and dropped to the grass with a sigh of relief.

"Have you let Vortka heal you, Empress?" he asked, reaching for the pouch of dried corn left near the heat. "You say you are strong, I know you are, but I am not blind. Our pace was relentless. You are tired, you are hurting. Tomorrow will be battle. If I am to see the great Hekat knife-dance, if I am to have a story to tell *my* son, you must be rested, you must be well."

She threw a clod of dirt at him. "First you must *have* a son to tell. To have a son you must have a wife, do you have a wife, Zandakar? I think you do not."

Aieee, god. This again. "I will have a wife when the god

sends her to me," he said, brushing bits of soil from his linen tunic. "The god has not sent her, what can I do?"

"You can agree to see the girls *I* find for you," his mother retorted. "I have found you seven, you refused them all unseen."

He smiled at her frowning, he shook his head. "Within a godmoon we ride out of Mijak, Empress. Can I take a wife with me? I think I cannot. You say I am godchosen, I believe you. I say a wife will come in the god's time. I wish, precious Yuma, you would believe me."

"Tcha," she said. "Stupid boy."

For once she used those words without anger, her eyes were smiling, they were full of love. Though she was often harsh, he knew she loved him. She wanted his excellence, it made her strict.

He said, "Dimmi is sorry that he misses this battle."

Her lips thinned, and her eyes went cold. "He is a child, Zandakar, he has no place here."

Aieee, if only he knew why she would not love his little brother. It was more than her damaged body, instinct told him that, but he could not ask her, it would be his ruin. "He is growing fast, Yuma. He will be a mighty warrior. The other warriors admire him, they see his proud heart."

"You should sleep, my hammer," she said, gaze fixed on the fire's glowing coals. "Newsun will bring us a busy task for the god."

He looked down at his gold-and-crystal weapon, so comfortable against his skin. He had used the long journey here to let its presence seep through him, to ride in silence and commune with the god. Its power slept sweetly now, he controlled it like breathing. It did not wake unless he woke it, did not rise without his summons.

A day from now I will be blooded in battle, blooded for the god, a true warlord at last. A day from now I will be different. I will be a man, no longer a boy.

He kissed the Empress his mother on the hand, then he kissed the scars on her cheek. It did not make her godbells ring, for she wore no godbells and neither did he, or the warhost, or even Vortka high godspeaker. This would be a war without singing.

His mother smiled. "The god see you sleeping, Zandakar warlord. The god see you sleeping, and when you are awake."

"The god see you, Yuma," he replied, and left her to seek his rest beneath the stars.

Newsun broke, the godspeakers sacrificed, and the warhost rode upon Jokriel city. Vortka and his three high godspeakers stayed behind upon the rise, they sacrificed their last doves that the god might see them and their victory.

His mother rode grim-faced and silent beside him, her eyes were full of shadowed pain. She was angry at this smiting of her, as well as pain there was blood in her eyes. He was angry too, that she was subjected to this.

Give me the strength to avenge her, god. Give me the strength to smite her enemies.

As the warhost swept down on sinning Jokriel city, the rebel warhost rode out to meet them. It was a small band of warriors, he thought it less than three thousand, they rode skinny horses and camels, their tunics were torn.

Compared to his warhost they were pitiful, pathetic, they were defeated before the first blow was struck.

What are they thinking, god? Why would they do this? They must know we will slaughter them, they are demon-struck, they must be.

Then he saw the rebel's leader raise his clenched fist. The rebel warriors slowed towards halting, their leader rode forward without them. Zandakar was startled.

"Do you think he surrenders, Empress?" he shouted above the thunder of galloping hooves.

"He wishes council," she shouted back. "I am willing to talk. If this unknown demonfucker throws his knife at my feet I will kill him quickly, that much will I do for the sinning sinner. If he does not I will kill him slowly, the god will grow fat on his cries of woe." She held up her clenched fist, signaling their own warhost to slow. "Come," she added, glancing at him. "Let us meet this dead man, let us show him the god."

They kicked their horses, they galloped to meet him. The plain before Jokriel city was flat and dry, dust kicked up around them and stuck to their skin. Dust covered his hammer, that did not matter. The hammer would strike when he called on its power.

The riding rebel came closer, closer. He was old, he was work-shrunk, his godbraids were thin. Closer, closer, his face was revealed to them—

"Hanochek!" said the Empress. Her voice crawled with loathing, there was also surprise.

Hanochek warleader eased his rawboned brown horse to a halt. One eye was clouded, he had lost some teeth. Zandakar saw that because he was smiling, smiling, there was demonstruck laughter in the man's ravaged face.

"Aieee, Hekat. Dirty barracks-bitch. I knew if I waited, you would come to me."

Zandakar stared at the shriveled old man, he heard his heart beating, felt tears burn his eyes. *Hano*? This was *Hano*? The friend from his childhood that his sin sent away, whose death he'd wept for in secret for so long? *Hano* conspired with demons against them?

God, god, this is not fair. Living Hano fallen to demons? How much better if he were dead.

His mother pointed to Jokriel city, to the ragged warband behind him. "This is *your* doing, Hanochek? *You* have enticed these stupid slaves to sin, to their deaths? Aieee, a blessing that Raklion is ashes, you would kill him with your treachery, with your sin against his son!"

"*My* sin?" said Hano, his face full of hate. "*You* are the sinner, Raklion's death is in *your* eye, bitch! Hold your tongue or I will cut it out." He swung his horse sideways, he held out his hand. "Zandakar, Zandakar, have you no words for me? Your beloved father's beloved friend? Your friend, too, if you can remember."

He had never forgotten. "You call Raklion your friend yet you raise a warhost against his son?" Zandakar blinked hard, willed away the pain behind his eyes. "If you can do this, Hano, then I never knew you. I do not know you now. We were *never* friends."

The Empress his mother laughed softly beside him. Hanochek ignored her, he nudged his tattered horse closer and pressed a scarred, scabby fist to his heart. "Zandakar, listen. I am not your enemy, I tell you, believe it. What I have done is done for you and your brother, to save you from this demon-bitch who destroyed your father."

Pain turned to rage in a blink, in a heartbeat. He backed his stallion three paces, if Hanochek touched him he would vomit blood. "You corrupted a godhouse to save us? You slaughtered faithful godspeakers to save us? You consort with *demons*, Hano, to save us? May the god save us all from friends such as you!"

"I did not kill godspeakers, I killed demons in human flesh!" Hano shouted. "*Her* creatures, summoned from hell to do her bidding, and the bidding of her tame high godspeaker Vortka!"

Zandakar felt his fingers tighten, felt the power surging in his blood. On his arm the god's hammer heated. "Do not speak of the Empress like that. Do not speak of Vortka high godspeaker like that. They are godchosen and precious, they are in the god's eye."

"Aieee, Zandakar, *listen* to me!" Now there were tears on Hano's old cheeks. "I loved Raklion warlord more than my life. When I heard he was dead I swore I would save you *and* your brother. I gave my life to you both from that moment on. Every breath since that day has been for you. This warhost behind me, I created it for you. I harvested the savage north and made warriors for you."

"*Tcha!*" said Hekat, she spat upon him. "How well do I know the savage north! Goat men, lizard men, men who are blinded to the god. If those men fight for you, Hano, you are dead in my eye!"

Hanochek ignored her, to him she did not breathe. "Zanda, little Zanda, not only warriors from the savage north fight for me in Raklion's name. Others have joined me, from all over Mijak. Throughout this brown land there are men and women who do not worship your

Empress, they remember their dead or thrown-down warlords and their slain high godspeakers. They chafe for release from their cruel Et-Raklion chains. For season after season I have worked, I have waited, I have drawn these people to me, I have promised them relief. They want their freedom, I will give them *you*! In the god's nameless name I beg you, Zandakar, do not cross the Sand River. It will be your undoing. Stay here, in Mijak. Save your people from hell."

Shaking his head, Zandakar backed his stallion two more paces. "Your heart is eaten by demons, Hano. You are deaf to the god, you are blind in its eye."

"I know this is difficult, I know my words hurt you," said Hano, still weeping. "I am sorry for it, I hurt you for love. Turn your back on this Empress, Zanda, throw down your mother so Mijak might live. The god requires it, Mijak will die if you do not throw her down."

Who was this man, this demoncrazed jabberer who wore the face of a loved, dead friend? "I will never do that, I will never turn against the Empress. Hano, this is madness." Zandakar shook his head. "If you are truly a warleader do not spend your warriors' lives for *nothing*. You cannot defeat us. Your rebellion is finished."

Hano's wet eyes opened wide. "Not if you join me! If you join me, Zanda, the victory will be ours. Mijak's warhost will follow you, it will follow Raklion's son."

Helpless, Zandakar glanced at his mother. Her face was peaceful, Hano's death was in her eyes. "Stupid Hanochek," she said, her voice was a knife. "You think you can cajole Zandakar from my side? You think he will turn on me, his Empress, his mother? The savage north has rotted your brain. You knew Raklion all his life, he did not choose you over me. And now you think to steal my *son*?"

"Zandakar!" cried Hano, and kicked his horse close. "You *cannot* follow her, she did *not* love your father, she cursed him with demons, Zanda, she *ruined* Raklion. Jokriel's godspeakers tell me she fucked outside his bed, she—"

Before he could strike the man for his wicked lies, the Empress his mother screamed and threw herself on Hano. Her snakeblade was unsheathed, her godbraids were flying, she leapt from her mare's back as though she were a lithe girl of twelve. Her knife flashed in the red newsun, it plunged into Hanochek, her arms were around him, they crashed to the ground.

As though it were a signal, Hanochek's ragged warhost attacked. Howling, screaming, they galloped forward from a standstill, makeshift weapons above their heads. The god's warhost responded, five thousand warriors on Et-Raklion's best horses, surging on a roar of righteous fury towards Hano's rebels. Arrows whistled through the air overhead, some struck the hard earth and stuck there, quivering. Others found living targets, four enemy horses cartwheeled to the ground, crushing their riders to death beneath them.

On the plain at Zandakar's feet, demonstruck Hanochek and Mijak's Empress tangled together in a desperate embrace, grunting, shouting, rolling over and over on the blood-slicked dry grass. Both of them were panting, both of them flailing, both of them striking with their blades.

Aieee, god, protect my mother! She will kill me if I interfere!

He wrenched his fretting stallion round on its haunches, his galloping warhost was almost upon them, Hanochek's rebels were heartbeats away.

Forgive me, Yuma! I cannot see you killed!

He slid from his stallion, his gloved hammer hand holding fast to the reins, his other hand reaching—reaching—

As his fingers brushed his mother's bloody shoulder she gave a shout of wild triumph and sank her knife hard between Hano's ribs. Hanochek screamed, his eyes wide and staring. His mother rolled off him, she was covered in blood.

Zandakar hauled her barely conscious from the slick grass, he flung her facedown across his stallion, then vaulted behind her and looked down at Hanochek.

"You stupid man, you demonstruck sinner! The Empress has killed you. Hano, you are *dead*!"

"Zandakar—" Hano's voice was a moan, almost lost in the thunder of oncoming hooves. "She is evil . . . *evil* . . . you must *destroy* her . . ."

His mother's blood stained his stallion red. He wheeled away from Hanochek—*Hano, I loved you, how could you, how could you*—and galloped for Vortka as the opposing warhosts clashed in battle.

Behind him he heard Hano's despairing, choked scream, as the first of the god's warriors trampled him to pulp.

Hano . . . I loved you . . . I thought we were friends . . .

Blinded by tears he urged his stallion onwards, to the distant slow rise and the waiting, watching godspeakers. Vortka ran to meet him, helped Hekat from the horse. Her plain linen tunic glistened wet, bright red. Zandakar flung himself beside her, he caught up her hand.

"Yuma—*Yuma*—"

Her beautiful scarred face was masked with blood. She opened her eyes and frowned. "Wicked boy," she whispered, her voice was a thread. "You have abandoned your warhost. What warlord does that, you must lead them, you must fight."

On the plain below them shouts and knife-clashes, howls of men and horses, screaming. His beloved warriors were fighting, dying, his mother was right, he should be fighting beside them—

"*Go,*" said Vortka, looking up as he and his godspeakers worked furiously with their godstones to staunch her pumping blood. "The god sees the Empress, it will not let her die."

Zandakar nodded, he released his mother's hand. It fell to the grass like a dying bird. Fighting grief and weakness he stood and turned away from her, reaching for his stallion's reins.

"*Zandakar . . .*"

He turned back, she would scold him now for weeping. "Are you my son, Zandakar? I think that you are." Her eyes were shining, with love and rage. "I think you will *smite* that sinning Jokriel city. I think you will smite its people to *hell.*"

She did not scold him. "I will," he promised. "Empress, I will."

She did not reply. Her voice had faded to silence, he could not see her ribcage lift, her hands were still, she did not see him.

"Empress! *Yuma*!"

"You heard her, Zandakar!" Vortka's face was terrible. "You are the warlord, obey her command!"

He leapt on his stallion and galloped to the battle, unsheathing his snakeblade as he rode. He entered the bloodbath with his mouth wide, screaming. Hanochek's warhost was no match for his. Hano had been demonstruck to pit them against him.

How long he fought for he never knew, after. He knew he was wounded, he knew he was bloody, he knew every rebel he met died by his hand. In every direction there were warriors dying, some were his own men, most were not. When nearly all of Hano's warhost was defeated, slaughtered and sundered and strewn upon the ground, he signaled his warhost to fall back to safety. He confronted Hano's survivors with their deaths in his eye.

The god's hammer struck them, its power ignited them, beneath the high blue sky their flesh was consumed. When the last of Hanochek's rebels were dead, were nothing, he rode with his warhost to sinning Jokriel city. He rode in dreadful silence, his mother, his Yuma, so wounded behind him. He had failed to protect her, he would not fail her now.

The sinning people of Jokriel city saw him coming. Some hid in the shadows, others hid behind doors. He saw their faces in windows, he saw them cowering behind pillars, he saw wicked men and their women, he saw their sinful sons.

At the entrance to the city, where its gates had once stood, he halted his stallion, he halted his warhost, he bent his cold gaze upon doomed Jokriel. In his leatherclad breast his heart was a hammer, it tolled like a godbell, it echoed his grief.

Yuma . . . Yuma . . .

Grief became rage, tears turned to flame, the god's furious power built in his bones. His gold-and-crystal weapon shimmered into life. He raised his arm, he clenched his fist.

"Behold, you sinners of Jokriel! I am Zandakar warlord, son of the Empress! Warlord of Mijak in the god's eye! This city is judged and condemned, it is given to demons, it must not stand beneath the sun!"

In the early cool stillness, his voice carried cleanly, Jokriel city's people heard it, they cried out in alarm, they huddled together or else tried to flee. Zandakar watched them, he felt no pity. They had turned on the Empress. His mother, his Yuma. They had sinned with demons. They did not deserve to live. With his eyes wide open he summoned his power, he sent blue-white fire in streams against the city. As the god's wrath burst from his body, his warhost cried out.

"Zandakar! Zandakar! Zandakar warlord! Son of the Empress, in the god's eye!"

The nearest buildings blew apart. The empty sky rained stone splinters and ragged chunks of rock. The air filled with smoke, with the stench of death. Screams of the godforsaken rang in his ears. Controlling his stallion, riding forward, he called upon the power again. More buildings shattered, more sinners perished. More blood ran like water in the streets.

He laughed to see it. He wanted more.

As he laid Jokriel city low with his smiting hand, as he reduced it to rubble, to a charnel house, to memory, he shouted and shouted and shouted out loud:

"For the Empress! For Hekat! For the god in the world!"

CHAPTER FORTY-ONE

The god was appeased by Jokriel city's smiting. Hekat did not die of her many wounds, Vortka high godspeaker and his healers saved her. After Hanochek and his rebels' destruction, warriors were sent to the nearest village, they returned with a cart that might carry her home to Et-Raklion. Zandakar drove it himself, Vortka rode in the back with the wounded Empress.

Hanochek's demonstruck rebellion was thwarted, yet it was a slow and sorrowful journey home. Not one warrior among them had believed the Empress was *mortal*.

Et-Raklion city greeted them with sacrifice and amulets and coins of bronze and gold; by that time Hekat could sit on a horse. A warrior was sent ahead to warn Vortka's godspeakers, the godtheater was filled, Et-Raklion's people cheered their return. Hekat sat on her scorpion throne, only Zandakar beside her could see what that cost.

It broke his heart, he wept on the inside.

Afterwards Vortka took her to the godhouse, where she might receive more healing and regain her lost strength. Zandakar distracted himself with his warhost business, soon they would ride from Mijak across the Sand River. Into the unknown world, full of demons. It was a daunting thought, he tried not to think of it. He lived in the barracks, and hardly saw Dmitrak.

A godmoon after riding triumphant through the gates of Et-Raklion city, Vortka sent for him from the god-house. He answered the summons at once, running hard up the Pinnacle Road. Despite the whisper in his heart, he prayed and prayed with every stride.

Do not let it be Yuma, god. Let it not be bad news.

"There is no use in softening the blow, Zandakar," the high godspeaker said, standing before the altar in his private chamber. "The Empress is stricken. She lives, she will not die, but only if she remains in Et-Raklion. Hanochek's wounding of her, together with the hurts she suffered when birthing Dmitrak, they have stolen her strength, Zandakar. I cannot reclaim it. She cannot ride with the warhost. She must stay behind, it is the god's changed desire."

Zandakar nodded. Hadn't he known this? Hadn't he felt this shadow on his skin? He looked away. A moment later, Vortka's consoling hand came to rest on his shoulder.

"This *is* the god's want. I have lived three highsuns in the Divination chamber, I have read more omens in that short time than in my previous seasons as Mijak's high god-speaker. I am not mistaken, the god's voice shouts."

"I do not doubt you, Vortka," he said. "The god is the god, it will have its way. Does the Empress know?"

Vortka nodded. "Yes. I have told her."

A shiver of apprehension touched him. "How did she receive the news?"

"She attempted to smite me with it," said Vortka dryly. "Your mother is a fighting woman."

Despite his pain, Zandakar laughed. Vortka laughed with him, it was a kind moment. "The god knows she is." He could not keep smiling. "Aieee, it is a cruel thing. Did the god tell you, Vortka, why its desire changed?"

"No. The god does not share with us all of its mysteries. Zandakar, she wishes to see you."

"Then, high godspeaker, I must go."

"Zandakar—"

He looked back, half a step from the chamber door. "High godspeaker?"

Vortka's face was concerned, his dark eyes cautious. "We have not spoken of Jokriel city."

No. They had not. Hekat had consumed them on the hard ride home, and besides, he was not ready.

I am not ready now.

"That city's destruction was the god's desire, Zandakar," said Vortka firmly. "It could not have fallen were it not the god's will."

It could not have fallen without me, Vortka. Without me, the god's hammer, that city would still stand. He said, "Yes. I know that."

Vortka came a little closer. "And yet you grieve, I think."

Yes. With his rage burned away, and his mother still living, there was room for some grief in his heart. In his heart were the memories of all those dead people. Many charred to cinders, many more crushed beneath stone. Poor smitten city, reduced to rubble and ruin. He made himself look into Vortka's eyes. "Am I stupid, high godspeaker? I am the god's hammer. Hammers are bone and iron, they do not grieve."

He had never before told Vortka a lie.

Vortka smiled. He said, "The wicked in that city are gone to hell where they belong. The innocents who died there, if there were innocents, they are with the god. Let that be your comfort, Zandakar, when your dreams are dark."

Aieee, Vortka. How well you know me. "High godspeaker," he said, and pressed his fist to his heart.

He left the high godspeaker and went to his mother, in the healing chamber that had become her home. She laughed to see him, her face was so thin, beneath her laughter he could see anger, and anguish.

He sat beside her on the healing couch, he kissed her fingers and held her hands. "Vortka has told me. Yuma, I am sorry."

She was rarely moved to softness, she tossed her head and looked away. "Tcha! He is stupid, that Vortka, he fusses and fidgets. Much more of this nonsense I will ask the god for a new high godspeaker!"

"Yuma . . . you do not mean that."

"No," she sighed. "I do not." Her water-sheened eyes looked around the chamber. "Raklion rested here, after Banotaj's smiting of him in Mijak's Heart. He never truly recovered." Her face twisted. "But I am not Raklion, an old man of many seasons. *I* would not be here if I had been whole to begin with."

Of course. She blamed Dmitrak. She always blamed Dmitrak. "Yuma, I know the god's want disappoints you, but Dimmi—"

She pulled her hands away. "It is the truth, Zandakar, I will not hear you deny it! That brat spoiled my body, he has thwarted my plans!"

He took a deep breath, he let it out slowly. "Your plans, Empress, but not the god's."

She almost struck him, he felt her whole body tense. He was a man now, he did not flinch. After a moment, the urge to violence left her. She settled on her pillows and folded her arms. "I have decided you will take him with you."

Astonished, he stared at her. "Across the Sand River? Into the world and the godless lands? Yuma, how can I? You said it with your own tongue, Dimmi is a *child*."

She would not look at him. "Tcha! *You* said he is growing fast, you said he will be a mighty warrior. Where best to become that than with you and my warhost?"

"Yuma . . ." He shook his head, his godbells chimed dismay. "I do not think this a wise decision. If I should fall beyond the Sand River, Dmitrak must be warlord after me. If I should fall, he might be in danger. He—"

"*You will not fall!*" His mother's eyes blazed with fury. "It is a *sin* to say such a thing, you doubt the god with those words, do you think yourself too old for tasking? I will send for Vortka, he will bind you to the scorpion wheel, he will—" She broke off, coughing, wheezing for air.

Alarmed, he reached for her, she pushed him away. "Aieee, Zandakar, you disappoint me!"

Her words were a snakeblade, slid between his ribs. "*No*, Yuma, I—"

Her clenched fists beat against her laboring chest. "That demon Hanochek, from hell he thwarts me! From hell he conspires with Nagarak to thwart me. I *cannot* remain here, I am Hekat, the Empress, godtouched and precious, I must ride to the world!"

Nagarak? She was raving, overcome by her infirmity. This time, when he reached for her, she did not push him away. She fell against his shoulder, for the first time in his life he heard her weep. Appalled, he held her, like a child he rocked her, she wept like a baby.

His world was undone.

"Zandakar," said Vortka's soft voice beside him. He looked up, taken unawares, he could barely see the high godspeaker for his tears. "She is overwrought, let me soothe her. You are needed in the barracks, you and the warhost must ride soon."

He did not release her. "She wants me to take Dmitrak with me. Vortka, he—"

"I know," said Vortka. "And I think he should go. He will pine without you. Zandakar, you must know you are more than his brother, you are the father he never knew. He needs your guidance. He needs to be with you. And your mother . . ." Vortka sighed. "To see him and not you, it will cause her great pain. It will hurt him, too. You ride with your warhost, you ride in the god's eye. How can harm come to him, Zandakar, or to you?"

That was true, he could not deny it. He was the god's hammer, it would not let him fall.

But Yuma is the Empress, and now she weeps in my arms.

"Zandakar," said Vortka, so gently. "The god chooses its instruments, it uses them until it does not. We have no say in when we will be used, and when we will be put aside. We obey the god's want, we live our lives in obedience. That is our purpose, Zandakar. Content yourself with that. Hekat has served, it is your turn now."

Do I have a choice? I think I do not. "Yes, high godspeaker," he said, and eased himself free of his mother so Vortka might take his place beside her on the couch. "If she calls for me again, I will be in the barracks."

Vortka nodded, he did not reply. For a moment Zandakar watched them. The high godspeaker held his mother tenderly, he smoothed her silent godbraids, he pressed his palm to her scarred cheek. A new truth burst upon him, he felt it warm his bones.

Vortka loves her. He loves my mother. Why did I not see that, as I was growing up?

Softly he left them. As he reached the chamber door he heard his mother say, bewildered, "I am lost, Vortka. I am lost in the god's eye. Why does it smite me, how have I sinned?"

"Hush," Vortka told her, his voice was full of love. "You are not smitten, you have not sinned. This is the god's mysterious will, we must learn it together. We will have time."

Zandakar closed the door behind him.

He found Dimmi in the main barracks slaughter-pen, practicing with his slingshot on a huddle of sheep. The warhost consumed so much meat, so much ale and sadsa and fruit and grain, he lay awake at night worrying how he would feed them beyond Mijak's border. He worried now, surrounded by his thousands of warriors, their horses, their equipment, their eagerness for war.

Worry is sin, the god will protect us. Trust in the god, it sees you in its eye.

"Zandakar!" cried his blood-spattered brother. "Look, I have killed fifty, see how skilled a warrior I am!"

Aieee, killed fifty, and maimed twenty others. Dimmi

did not seem to notice that, or hear their pained bleats. Zandakar nodded to the watching slaughter-slaves, that they might leap into the pit and finish the job. Then he beckoned to his brother.

"Come with me. I have news."

Eagerly Dmitrak clambered from the slaughter-pen. "What news, Zanda? What has happened?"

He slung an arm round his brother's shoulders, they were closer to his now. He was growing fast. They walked through the blood-stinking air, through the noise and bustle of warrior business, towards the warlord's lodge where more decisions and preparations were waiting. "I am come from the godhouse, Dmitrak. I have spoken with the Empress. You are to ride with the warhost, it is her decree."

Dimmi stopped dead in the road, like a horse struck by an arrow. Incredulous, he stared up, hope and disbelief in his eyes. "The warhost, Zandakar? Beyond the Sand River? You are certain, she said so?"

He nodded. "She said so, and also Vortka high godspeaker. It is decided, little brother. You will ride with me."

"Aieee-aieee-*aieee*!" shouted Dimmi, ecstatic. Throwing down his slingshot he threw himself into a *hota*—the falcon striking. He twisted and leapt, passing slaves and warriors scattered, laughing. He was not a graceful knife-dancer, but he could kill.

"This is your doing, I know it!" he shouted. "I thank you, Zandakar, I will love you forever!"

Zandakar smiled, he did not contradict him. Let Dmitrak think that, how could it hurt? Better to believe a small lie than to learn the harsh truth: he rode with the warhost because his mother despised him.

The warhost preparations continued. Released from the godhouse, resigned to the god's will, Hekat slaved without mercy for Zandakar's great purpose. Vortka withdrew to the Divination chamber, to learn which godspeakers must ride with Zandakar, and discover when precisely the god desired the warhost to ride. He trusted Peklia and the other senior godspeakers to administer Mijak in his absence. He knew they could be trusted, the god had told him so. They had been shocked by Jokriel city's wicked betrayal, even now they worked to discover further demons in their midst. Every godspeaker in Mijak must be tested, every potential sinner rooted out. Only the godspeakers of Et-Raklion could be trusted until the last seducing demon was cast back to hell.

For himself, he felt Jokriel city's fall to demons like a deep knife-wound. As high godspeaker he could not be tasked by another's hand so he fasted relentlessly to punish his flesh, he deprived himself of sleep and small pleasures, he bent his heart upon the god.

If Jokriel city and Hanochek's sinning are because I have failed you, god, I bare my godspark to your wrath. Send it to hell, if that is your desire.

The god did not kill him. Either he was forgiven or, for reasons he could not begin to understand, Jokriel city's fall and Hekat's resulting diminishment were indeed a part of its plan. The god spoke to him in sacrifice, as it always did. After two days of seeking, his questions were answered. He summoned Hekat and Zandakar and Dmitrak to attend him in the Divination chamber.

"I am given an omen," he said, still bloody before the altar. "The warhost will ride five highsuns from now. Zandakar, you must be prepared for this sacred journey. Come to me at newsun. You will remain in the godhouse for three full days, you will be cleansed and tasked, you will swim in the godpool, you will hear the god."

As Zandakar nodded, Dmitrak scowled. "Zandakar already hears the god, why must he be cleansed, why should the taskmasters task him? He is the god's hammer, he lives in its eye. He needs no—"

"Hush, Dimmi," said Zandakar, and put an arm around Dmitrak's shoulders. "No man is perfect in the god's eye. Vortka high godspeaker must attend my godspark, lest I fall into sinning unaware. This is the god's desire, you must not question it."

"*Don't* call me Dimmi!" said the boy, and wriggled out of Zandakar's grasp. "I don't question the god, I question Vortka, he—"

Hekat seized his godbraids and threw him to the floor. "To question Vortka *is* to question the god!" She bent over her unwanted son, gleaming snakeblade in her hand. "Are you *stupid*? Every breath you take reflects upon Zandakar! Every word you speak is echoed in his eye. He *is* the warlord, he is the hammer, he is the god's will in the world. If you love him as you say, you will honor Vortka, he is the god's voice, he speaks with its tongue. *Tcha!*" She thrust her snakeblade back in its sheath. "Get to the tasking house. Find a taskmaster. Tell him you are sinful and must be corrected before the god."

"Yuma . . ." Zandakar murmured. "Dmitrak only—"

She speared him with a look. "Do you wish to join him? You are the warlord, *I* am the Empress. Do not try my patience. Return to the barracks, I will join you there."

Dismissed, Zandakar bowed and withdrew. Dmitrak went to find a taskmaster for his tasking. Vortka cleansed himself of the sacrificial blood and said, "We are the only ones here now, Hekat. You can admit you are afraid for him."

She stood by the chamber's godpost, her fingers tracing a carved and inlaid Et-Raklion snake. "I am Empress. I do not feel fear."

"Hekat," he sighed, and shook his head. "Before you were an Empress you were a knife-dancer, before you knew one *hota* you were a slave. To the world you are the Empress. To me you are Hekat. The god will not smite you for loving your son."

Resentful, scowling so she looked so much like Dmitrak he almost laughed, she said, "You do not fear for him?"

Of course he feared. He would never say so. "He lives in the god's eye. He is the warlord you created. Like you and I, he is godchosen and precious. The god will protect him, it will allow no harm to befall its hammer."

"He goes to war without a son. He will not marry, I have asked him and *asked* him! He is disobedient, I am pleased he will be tasked before he leaves."

She did not mean that. "He is a good man, Hekat. He has a good heart."

Risking the god's wrath she smacked the godpost. "I want to ride with him, Vortka! I want to ride out with my warhost! It *is* my warhost, as much as his. I want to see what lies beyond the Sand River, I want to smite sinners for the god!"

His hands were free of blood now, he went to her. "Hekat, my dear friend. Even if your body could bear the journey, you are the Empress. Mijak looks to you. You are its tongue, its voice in the world."

She turned. "You are high godspeaker, you could speak for me. Your godspeaker healers riding with the warhost, they could ease my body when the pain grows bad. Vortka—"

"*No*," he said, and grasped her shoulders. "It is not the god's desire, Hekat. You hear the god, you know what it wants."

"It wanted Dmitrak and look what that cost me," she muttered. "At least the brat rides with Zandakar, I will not have to look at him and see Nagarak."

"Do not speak so," he said, reproving. "I do not wish the god to smite you. Your duty here is as important as Zandakar's beyond the Sand River. Mijak must be ruled, it must see its Empress and see the god. There is also the matter of the savage north to consider. Godless lands within our own borders, they must be cleansed. That is your task, the god has told me."

She pulled a face, but her temper was calming. "I will cleanse them, Vortka, I promise you that. The savage north will be emptied of sinners, I will see that sinning place left to the goats." She smiled. "And after its cleansing, I will go on an imperial progress. Comfortably, in stages. The cities will not forget again who is their Empress. I must find Zandakar a proper woman, and send her after him so he can sire a son. He *must* sire a son or Dmitrak will succeed him." She shuddered. "I could not bear that. He is mud to Zandakar's gold."

If he is mud, you helped to make him, Vortka thought.

But he could not say so. He understood her hatred of the boy, a little, he tried to, but the god had created Dmitrak for a reason. In its time that purpose would be revealed. It was wrong to hate what the god desired.

He said, "I must withdraw myself, to prepare for Zandakar's cleansing. Be easy in your heart, the god sees him. It sees our son. He will be safe."

My son. He saw the thought leap into her eyes, as it always did when he said *our son.* He did not say it often, it hurt him when she rejected his part in Zandakar's creation. He knew why she did it, that did not ease his pain.

"Remember when you cleanse him, he is the warlord," she said, her eyebrows raised in warning. "Do not spare him, Vortka, to spare your own heart. I have *never* spared him, you can do no less."

He watched her leave the Divination chamber, he saw the pain that lived within her now, Dmitrak's fingerprints in her flesh, Hanochek's handiwork in her limp, and her eyes. He flattened his hands across his scorpion pectoral, sleeping still as it had for so long.

Keep her in your eye, god, I beg you. She will need you when Zandakar goes.

At lowsun before the god's time of his departing, after three days of fasting, sacrifice and tasking at Vortka's unflinching hand, Zandakar stripped off his godhouse robe and prepared to enter the god's sacred godpool.

He had never entered it before.

"Every warlord experiences it differently," Vortka told him. "Some receive guidance. Some an admonition. Some are praised, it happens rarely. Open your heart, and you will hear what you must hear."

The air in the candlelit chamber was cool, blood-scented. His belly roiled. A lifetime of discipline had hardened him to sacrifice and killing and the drinking of hot blood. To swim in it was another matter . . .

Naked and nearly shivering, he looked at Vortka. "What did my father hear?"

"Your father," said Vortka, after a moment. "I do not remember you calling Raklion that, before."

"In this place I feel closer to him. It has been so long since he died, even in dreams I cannot see his face." A small pain pierced him, adding its voice to the larger pains of his ruthlessly tasked flesh. "Does his godspark see me, wherever it is? Is my father proud, high godspeaker?"

Shadows shifted across Vortka's face. "Your father is proud, warlord. Your father knows you are in the god's eye."

It eased, a little, some of his tension. "And do you know what Raklion warlord heard, when he swam in the godpool?"

Vortka shrugged. "I cannot tell you, I was a novice in that time. Nagarak accompanied him."

Nagarak. "That is someone I do remember. He frightened me. He was fierce for the god."

Vortka smiled. "And I am not fierce?"

"You are fierce in your devotion," Zandakar said slowly. "You were fierce in your tasking of me, I understand why. But you do not need others to fear you. Nagarak needed that, he fed on terror."

Vortka frowned, and turned away. "Warlord, we are not here to talk. The god is waiting."

The blood was thick, it clung to his welted skin as he trod down the stone steps into the godpool. Vortka had told him he must immerse himself completely, he must keep his eyes open and search for the god. The blood soaked his godbraids, they pulled his head back and under the surface. He felt himself sinking, then he struck the stone floor.

I should be drowning. I do not breathe. Is the god with me? Does it know I am here?

A great warmth suffused him, as though loving hands held him close. He felt peace. Acceptance. Sorrow. Love.

Zandakar, my son, my son. I am with you, though the road is long and steep and strewn with stones. All that will come to pass must come to pass. Grieve, weep, endure, surrender. I will be with you, unto the end.

He burst from the thick blood, gasping and confused. "*Vortka!*"

The high godspeaker knelt at the edge of the godpool. "Zandakar, what happened? Did the god speak?"

Was that the god? He thought he had heard the god before in his heart, a cold voice, a hard voice, full of knives and spear-points and shooting arrows. It sounded nothing like the voice he'd heard in the blood.

My son, my son . . . It had sounded so mournful, so full of pain. Yet proud and loving, strong and brave.

I liked that voice.

"Yes," he said, and climbed from the godpool. "I heard the god. It sees me in its eye."

When Vortka smiled he looked seasons younger. "Bathe now, warlord. Eat, and rest. At newsun you ride for the god's great glory."

The following newsun, as light broke over the horizon, the god's conquering warhost, its godspeakers and its slaves assembled on the plain of Et-Raklion. Beyond the thousands of mounted warriors the remaining war-host and the chosen witnesses prayed with their heads bowed, for Zandakar warlord, the god's chosen, its mighty hammer.

Zandakar stood with his mother the Empress and his brother Dmitrak as Vortka high godspeaker sacrificed to the god. Five black bulls, five white lambs, five golden cockerels, five pure white doves. The god took all of them, it inhaled them completely, their blood soaked the earth, it watered the ground.

His gold-and-crystal hammer was strapped to his chest in a horsehide satchel made by the Empress's own hands.

"The god will tell you when to use this weapon," she told him, when sacrifice was finished. Her face was stern, her eyes unmoved. "Never let it from your sight. Never permit another hand to touch it. You are the hammer, it is your second skin."

"I will not. I promise."

Her gaze flicked sideways, it touched on Dmitrak. "*No* hand, Zandakar. I charge you, in the god's eye."

He would never risk his brother's life with the hammer. "You have my word, Empress. The hammer is safe."

She believed him, her eyes were full of tears. They did not fall, she did not falter. "Go with the god, Zandakar. Smite the world in its eye. Destroy every demon beyond the Sand River. Remember your mother, the Empress of Mijak. Know she rides with you, in your heart."

Aieee, Yuma. He wanted to hold her, kiss her, weep into her godbraids. If he did, she would never forgive him. He nodded. "I know it always. I will not forget her.

She will hear of our victories, she will laugh with the god."

She gave him a small smile. She said nothing to Dimmi.

The farewell was ended. It was time to ride.

Vortka turned to face the multitude, his strong, clear voice cried to the god. The people heard him, they chanted with him. *"Zandakar warlord, Zandakar god-hammer, Zandakar precious in the god's great eye!"*

Their voices beat on him, his skin was a drum. He turned to his mother, the Empress, Hekat, he saluted her with a fist to his heart. He saluted Vortka, Mijak's high godspeaker, then he mounted his stallion. Dmitrak, on his own horse, rode at his side.

Zandakar led his mighty warhost away from Et-Raklion, towards the Sand River and the unsuspecting world. He left his mother behind him.

He did not look back.

CHAPTER FORTY-TWO

Aieee!" said Dmitrak, and jabbed his elbow into Zandakar's ribs. "There is a woman ripe for fucking. Pity she is piebald. The godspeakers say piebald women will make your cock rot and drop off, do you think they are right? Or are they just jealous and itchy, they are not vessels, they cannot fuck."

Zandakar sighed, and looked at the hole his stylus had

torn through his damp clay message tablet. Swallowing annoyance, he handed it to his scribe-slave, snapped his fingers for a fresh one, and began again the laborious task of composing a letter to the Empress, their mother.

"Do not bother to send her my love," Dimmi added, watching. "She has never asked after me in six seasons of warring, why should I care if she lives or dies?"

Zandakar glanced up. "You talk like a barracks slave," he said curtly. "And watch your tongue. To disrespect the Empress is to disrespect the god."

"Tcha," said Dimmi, but nothing else. He held out his ale mug for a slave to refill.

They sat side by side in the open-fronted warlord's tent, protected from the highsun glare. Beyond it lay the Harjha village called *Yanowe*, the largest they had found since crossing a river into this land. The houses were built of saplings and mud, their roofs were thatched reeds. Harjha was poor, even though it was green.

Godspeakers glided among the awe-struck villagers, performing sacrifices, chastising sinners, selecting the animal stock that would form the basis of godhouse breeding farms which would, in time, supply sacrifices to the new godhouses in this land. The only woman he could think might catch his brother's attention sat beneath a tree, a stone's throw away, with three young men and two boys, also piebald. They received instruction from solemn-faced Valik godspeaker.

Dimmi said, staring into his mug, "Do I dream, Zanda, or have I seen piebald slaves at home?" He sat up sharply, liquid sloshed into his lap. "Aieee! I remember! That god-forsaken slave you killed in the godtheater, the first woman you smote with the hammer. It was piebald, I am certain. Or do I misremember? It was so long ago, and you have killed thousands since then."

Zandakar felt his heart constrict. *Yes, Dimmi. Thousands. Thousands of godsparks slaughtered in the god's eye. Scores of cities like Jokriel, smashed to the ground.* "You do not misremember," he said. He had never forgotten the day his hair turned blue. "What is your meaning?"

"I have none," said Dimmi, shrugging, and drained his mug. "Except to say that once, in the dark past, these people of Harjha belonged to Mijak. Now they are conquered, they belong to us again. As do the peoples of Drohne, of Targa, of Bryzin and of Zree. Aieee, the god see us! I did not think it could take so long to conquer so little. How big is the world, Zandakar? Will we be old men before we see it fall?"

He sighed. Dimmi was in a talking mood, there was no use trying to write a letter till his words had run out. His little brother was grown strong and tall, he had hundreds more fingerbones than he could wear round his neck, tokens from the wicked sinners he had killed for the god. With a sharp nod Zandakar dismissed the slaves. Dimmi with ale in him was not always discreet, his brother said unwise things, often about the Empress. He did not want a godspeaker to hear.

"*Look*, Zanda," said Dimmi, nudging and pointing to the girl beneath the tree. "Is she not a fuckable woman? Hellspawn demons, why does she have to be piebald?"

Zandakar put down his stylus, covered the clay tablet with a damp square of cloth and pushed his rough work table a little to one side. "I cannot say. Who knows the god's purpose?"

"Tcha," said Dimmi, and leaned forward appreciatively. "If I rolled her in mud she would not be piebald. Do you think my cock would drop off if I fucked her then?"

Sometimes it was hard to like his brother. The older he got, the cruder he became. "Dimmi . . ."

"Do not *call* me that," Dimmi growled, a warning. Once he could only wave his small fists, now he was a warrior with a snakeblade in his belt. "You play with fire, you know that you do."

What does it matter, if I can distract you from that woman? In the last three seasons, since his manhood came fully on him, Dimmi had been tasked over thirty times by the godspeakers, for lewd behavior that offended the god. Dimmi seemed not to care for their smitings, he laughed at their whipping, he told them *whip harder, do you wish to tickle me to death*?

"What do you think of this land, this Harjha?" Zandakar asked. "We have been here a godmoon, it seems a green place."

Dimmi snorted. "Greener than Drohne, at least, and Zree. Targa was green, but too full of demons. The same with Bryzin. I think this is the first place we have found where I will happily sit for a while."

"On that point I will not argue. It is green, it is peaceful, it seems there are no cities or large villages to be smitten with the hammer. Its people have welcomed us for saving them from the demonstruck men of Targa. They speak our tongue, in a fashion. They may be piebald, Dmitrak, and dangerous to cocks, but I can see no demons here. I can see no offense against the god."

The words earned him a sharp look. "Their *existence* is offensive, Zanda. There are no godhouses, no godposts, the sign of the scorpion is nowhere to be found. They are not Mijaki, *that* is their sin."

It was the answer their mother would have given, had she been there to hear them. In many ways Dimmi was very like her, though to say so would earn him a blow, or worse. Dimmi was a man now, tears were beneath him, but Zandakar knew the pain in his heart. How could he not know, he had grown to manhood watching it fester.

"Even so, they offer us no warfare, unlike those other nations. They are misguided only, not rotten with demons. As you say, Dmitrak. Harjha is a good place to rest."

And I am pleased, so pleased. I am weary of smiting, I dream of dead faces, I dream of blue-white fires and cities blown apart. I hear the dead thousands screaming in my sleep.

He held his breath—such thoughts, so sinful. A wonder the god did not strike him dead. The god did nothing, said nothing, it was silent.

It has been silent since we crossed the Sand River. Silent to me, at least. The godspeakers hear it. They say they hear it, I must believe them. Their godgiven smitings have not grown faint.

He turned on his leather camp-seat, aware of Dimmi, staring. "Are you all right, Zanda? Have you taken a sickness?"

"No."

"Are you certain? You are not yourself. You have been different, distant, for godmoons now. Even the warhost has noticed, Zandakar. They wonder if you weary of conquest."

Zandakar felt his face go still, heard his heart in his

chest thud against his ribs. "To weary of conquest is to weary of the god. I attend sacrifice. I am given the omens. Every fivesun the godspeakers task me, to ensure my godspark is pure for the god. If they whipped any harder they would break their canes. I tell you I am the warlord, Dmitrak. Or do you say I am not?"

Taken aback, Dimmi raised his hands. "Aieee! Do not bite me! I thought you looked sad. Are you sad, big brother? Perhaps I should roll that piebald in mud for *you*. Five virgins has the Empress attempted to send you, five times you have told her to leave them at home. Will you die unwedded, unbedded, alone?"

"I am not unbedded," he muttered. "I was fucking vessels before you knew what they were."

"But not since we left Et-Raklion." Dimmi grinned. "Unless of course there is something you have not told me."

"Tcha!" he said, and made a fist at his brother. "You are the one who takes conquered women in the shadows. Enough talk of fucking. It is not the god's business, it is not why we are here."

"I know," said Dimmi, and rolled his eyes. "Zanda, how many more godmoons do you plan to stay in this land?"

"As many as the god needs for it to be conquered. Besides," he added, and glanced sideways, "six seasons of fighting, the warhost is weary. There is plentiful game and water here. We would be wise to take our ease awhile. Send some warriors home to Mijak, replace them with younger, fresher knives."

"The Empress will not like that," said Dimmi, considering. "She will say the god has no need of rest."

"The god is not a man, Dmitrak. The Empress is not with us. Conquest has a price, she does not see it."

"And I for one am glad that is so," said Dimmi. "I am happy here, where I am valued. Do not tell her I said so, in that letter you write. If she thinks I am happy she will call me home."

Zandakar groaned. "Dmitrak . . ."

"You always defend her," his brother said, resentful. "Why do you not see that your truth is not the only truth?"

"I defend you, too!" he protested. "I will always defend you. You are my brother, you are half of my heart."

Dimmi ignored that, he could not be sensible where the Empress was concerned. "You have not properly answered my question. How long do we stay here? How many godmoons?"

"How can I tell you what the god has not told me?" he said. "The godspeakers say we have time yet, before we must move on. I will take that time, all the time that they give me. I am not sad, Dmitrak, but I admit I am weary. I have lost count of the cities I have killed, do you think it is *easy*, to wield the hammer?"

"I know it isn't," said Dimmi, quietly. "Don't I sit with you after, and look in your face? You never speak of it, though I wish you would. I am your brother, I could share the burden."

Their mother's words inscribed in clay, sent to him when the first supply line to Mijak was secured: *Remember the god's will, my son. The hammer is yours, let no-one else touch it. It is your purpose, to keep in your heart.* She meant, *exclude Dmitrak. Keep him at arm's length.*

And he did, but not for lack of trust. He did it to protect his brother, to save him from the hammer's fury.

The longer I wield it, the harder it becomes. Sometimes I fear it is killing me, slowly. I will not let that happen to him.

"One hundred and seventy four," said Dimmi, breaking the silence. "That is how many cities you have killed for the god. Before the world is conquered, I think it must become thousands."

Aieee, god. *Thousands.* Which meant tens of thousands of slaughtered godsparks, if the people of those sinning cities did not fall on their faces before the god. He had seen twenty-five seasons, he felt twice as old.

"There is only one hammer, Dmitrak, you cannot help me. But . . ." With an effort, he smiled. "Your company cheers me, and that is no small thing."

Dimmi brightened, it was important to him to know his big brother needed him. Even though he helped lead the warhost, even though he was feared and respected for himself, and not because his brother was the god's hammer . . .

None of that means anything, if he thinks I do not need him.

"Dmitrak," he said. "I would ask you a question. What do you hear, when you hear the god?"

Surprised, Dimmi stared at him. "I do not think of it. If I hear the god, it speaks to me in dreams and they vanish like mist when I open my eyes. Why? What do you hear?"

He had never spoken of that voice in the godpool. The feeling of warmth and love he had not felt since. He did not want to speak of it now, not openly. It was . . . private. Not even to be shared with his flesh and blood.

"If you do not hear words, do you at least sense its presence?"

Dimmi shrugged. "Of course. All warriors feel the god's presence, Zanda, the god fills us in battle, it guides our snakeblades."

"Tell me what it feels like," he persisted. "What you feel, when it is in you."

"I think I was right, Zanda, I think you are sickening!" said Dimmi, but then he sighed. "Heat. Hate. Cold. Rage. Those are the things I feel when I am filled with the god."

I think I did too, once. I can barely remember. Now I only feel sorrow. When I smite with the hammer, when I raze those sinning cities, sorrow and sorrow. All I want to do is weep.

He could never tell Dimmi that. Even to Dimmi, he would sound demonstruck. *Perhaps I am. Perhaps I am eaten by a demon from Targa, the godspeakers say we did not kill them all, there are steep hills in Targa, mountains filled with deep caves. Vortka could tell me. I wish he was here. I miss his kindness, and his wisdom.*

He said, "Yes. Yes, Dmitrak. That is what the god's warriors feel."

And if I no longer feel that, what have I become?

A slave came to the tent-front then, bowed its head and said, "Warlord, Akida shell-leader and her warband have returned."

Akida, Arakun's fearsome daughter. Better with a snakeblade than even her sire. Another woman Dimmi had eyes for, but not even Dimmi risked fucking a warrior on conquest. If he was caught between her legs, the godspeakers really *would* tickle him to death, or close enough as would make little difference.

Dimmi said, "You have letters to write, Zanda. I will deal with the warband. After two tensuns of scouting I hope they bring fighting news. My snakeblade is bored with sun and gentle smiles."

Mine is not, Dimmi. Mine sighs with relief. He nodded. "Give them my greetings and my praise. When you have heard their news, bring it to me. I will be here, as you say. Writing letters."

Dimmi grinned and departed, pushing the slave ahead of him with a careless shove. Zandakar tugged the work-table back into position, and reached for his mother's letter to read again before replying.

Looking at her stylus-work, nobody would guess she had not learned to write until she was thirteen. Her symbols were neat and confident, closely spaced, an echoing reflection of her impatient spoken voice. It brought her into the tent with him, if he closed his eyes he could hear her godbells.

It was the first letter he had received for nearly three godmoons. As soon as Drohne was smitten and obedient, the first land they encountered on the other side of the Sand River, he had sent warriors back to Et-Raklion with the news. They had returned to his warhost with more godspeakers, warriors, and citizens of Mijak selected to repopulate the conquered land. The desolate, dangerous Sand River was also tamed, it was as safe to traverse now as they could make it.

With every nation his warhost conquered, the same pattern was followed. It meant warrior-messengers could ride swiftly and securely back to Et-Raklion, and the

Empress. Of course, the further away from Mijak they pushed the longer it took for godspeakers, warriors and chosen settlers to arrive and impose the god upon the godless in these lands. That was another reason to wait here, in Harjha. He dreaded the idea they might ride too far, too soon, overstretch their resources, exhaust the warhost. Mijak was so far behind them now, they had the god, but the god did not feed them, clothe them, replace their injured horses, their ruined tunics and breastplates, their damaged weapons, their *lives*, when they were lost.

I am the warlord. That is my task.

His fingertips stroked the hard dry clay, stroked his mother's words as, when a child, he had stroked her scars. She told him of her Mijak warhost, growing to fill the barracks emptied at his leaving. She wrote of the chastened savage north and all the slaves it had brought her, of the chastised cities still weeping for smitten Jokriel, let them weep, let them tremble, let them not forget its fate. *Zandakar*, she admonished him, *do not think I have forgotten you need a wife. You must sire a son, a warlord to follow you. I have found another virgin, she is beautiful and obedient. If I do not hear you are willing to meet her I tell you in the god's eye, I will shut Vortka in a cupboard and ride across the Sand River to drag you home.*

Aieee, the god see her, she made him laugh. She would do it, he knew her, he must find a way to soothe and placate. He did not want her docile virgin. He did not want the burden of a son, not until his conquering days were done with. If that meant never, then so be it.

Let Dmitrak follow me, he is also a man, a warrior, the son of an Empress, he is in the god's eye.

She had not written one word about Dimmi.

The second new letter he had received was written by Vortka, a short note. As Mijak's high godspeaker, and with Mijak expanding, very little time was his own. Almost completely, he wrote of Hekat. *Your mother keeps busy, she is the god's Empress. Her health is not perfect, I do what I can. Mijak remains peaceful, I trust now every last sprouted seed of Hanochek's wicked rebellion is plucked out and poisoned, it will not grow again.* Of himself he said only, *I keep in the god's eye, as I know you do also. I see you in the omens, you do the god's work. The god see you in its conquering eye, warlord. I hope your brother Dmitrak is thriving.*

As he reached once more for his damp clay tablet, to report to his mother of the warhost's successes, a shadow fell across the table. He looked up, frowning.

"Warlord," said the piebald woman who had woken Dimmi's light-sleeping lust. "I disturb you. Forgive. May I speak?"

She was young, perhaps eighteen seasons, or nineteen. Her patched skin was odd, but not ugly. At least, not to him. Her blue eyes were beautiful, as beautiful as his mother's. Her thick black hair was unbraided, falling down to her hips. She wore typical Harjhan clothing, a linen shift dyed pale green, no shoes on her feet. Her demeanor was chaste, retiring, demure, but when he looked in those beautiful eyes he thought he saw mischief, and a swift dance of humor.

He nodded. "Yes. Speak. Start with your name."

"I am Lilit. I come from father, chieftain. He wishes you." She made a face. "To see you."

The chieftain's daughter? He had never seen her. Like her fellow Harjhans, her accent was odd, not unpleasant.

So many uncounted seasons had their peoples been apart, there was a drifting of language but they understood each other well enough.

"Lilit," he repeated, and felt himself smile. "The chieftain's daughter. I am Zandakar, son of the Empress."

"Yes," said Lilit. "Dmitrak's brother."

"You know my brother?"

She shrugged. "I see him look."

"Does his look upset you?" Suddenly, that was important. He did not want this woman upset.

"Many boys look Lilit." A delightful smile flashed, revealing white teeth. "No boys touch."

He laughed out loud. "I will tell my brother. He will not touch, or look."

"Looking not hurt. Eyes are eyes."

Aieee, she was wonderful. "Why have we not met before?"

"I was away in other village, warlord. I am here now."

"Where is your father? He does not come to speak?"

Sorrow touched her face. "Father sick. Begs you go to him. This is wrong? Forgive, if wrong."

It was very wrong, warlords held audience, they did not visit the conquered. He did not say so. "If it is important, I can go. How is he sick? What do my godspeakers say?"

The patches of pale skin on her face flushed pink. She looked at the bare ground inside his tent. "Godspeakers not see father. Father is conquered."

Of course. He thought of Vortka, and wondered what the high godspeaker would do. Then he remembered one of Dimmi's favorite sayings: *It is easier to seek forgive-*

ness than permission. "I will see your father, I will send him a godspeaker. I am the warlord, this is my word."

"Aieee!" she cried, and clapped her hands. They were small hands, and slender. He wondered if they would feel soft on his skin. "Thank you, warlord. When you come?"

"After lowsun sacrifice, I will visit your father. I have work to do now, I cannot leave. Wait for me until the god's business is tended. You can take me to your father then."

She tipped her head a little to one side, she considered him gravely. "Your god is a god that drinks much blood."

"My god is your god. It is the only god, it rules the world." He leaned forward. "The godspeakers tell me you accept the god. Are the godspeakers mistaken? Have you told them a lie?"

Stepping back, her eyes frightened, she seemed to shrink. "Lie to warlord? No, *no*! God is god, Harjha knows this. In Harjha god is green, it is gentle, it floats in clouds, it sits in flowers. God in Mijak lives in scorpions." She spread her hands, a helpless gesture. "No scorpions in Harjha, warlord. We have looked."

He stared beyond her, to the imposing godpost newly placed in the village center. "There are scorpions now, Lilit. Do not forget that."

She shivered, there was no more mischief in her eyes. "Yes, warlord. I go now. I wait for you after lowsun sacrifice."

He watched her leave, conflicted, unsettled. She was a piebald woman, the Empress would call her unclean, born of a slave-race, imperfect, impure. He could not agree with that. *She seems pure enough to me.* Something about her attracted him, but not the way Dimmi was attracted. He did not feel lust, he felt . . .

Curious. Protective. Aieee, perhaps there is a little lust. That does not matter. She is not for me.

Banishing her smile, he returned to his letters.

Empress, he wrote, his stylus stabbing swiftly, distractedly. *We are come to a green land, sparsely peopled, they call it Harjha. It is a small country, rich and fertile, I think no larger than the lands of Et-Raklion. Its people are grateful, they know the god. Not as we know it, the godspeakers correct them. We saved them from the demonstruck of Targa, those sinners would raid them and steal their children for food. The god does not ask me to smite the Harjhans, Yuma. My hammer sleeps and the warhost rests. We build godposts and godhouses, we serve the god. Vortka's godspeakers whisper of Targa's demons returning, we must not ride onwards until they say all are destroyed.*

He put down his stylus, and re-read the letter. Nowhere had he mentioned that the Harjhans were piebald. He did not wish to say it, his mother would despise them and order him to enslave every last one.

Empress, he continued, moving on to a second tablet, *here is a good place for the warhost to wait some small time, before pushing onward. I trust that you trust my judgement in this, I trust you trust me in the god. Send godspeakers to Harjha, send settlers, send slaves and sheep and cattle and horses and grain. But please, I beg you, do not send another virgin, or endanger your godspark by locking Vortka in a cupboard. The god will send me a wife when a wife is its desiring. Feel my lips,*

Yuma, they kiss your cheek. Dmitrak greets you, he sees you in the god's eye.

Satisfied with that, hoping she would be satisfied also, he put the tablets aside to dry, and reached for a new one that he might reply to Vortka high godspeaker.

"Zanda!" said Dimmi, striding back into the tent. "Enough of this scribe's business, it is why we have slaves. Come speak to Akida, she and her warband have thrown down three villages, they have word to tell you of other lands."

The world must be conquered, even though it felt endless. Even though he feared he would grow old as the hammer and never know peace, only war and slaughter. He stood, felt his muscles groan, complaining, and went with his brother to the warband camp. His warhost was so vast, the chieftain's village and its surrounding lands could not contain it. He had split his thousands into thirty warbands, some still scoured Targa to rid it of demons, some waited and rested, the remainder, like Akida's band, rode the length and breadth of Harjha, bringing the god to the godless places. His warbands knew where to find him, they would return in the god's time.

"Akida," he said, pleased to see her unhurt. He loved her father, and had played with her when they were children. "My brother says you have news for your warlord."

Akida pressed her fist to her heart. Not even her father could call her beautiful, her nose was skewed half-over her face, her jaw was jutting, her neck was thick. But aieee, she could knife-dance. He loved to see it. "Warlord," she greeted him, smiling. "I am told two things, you must know them both. First, at the far edge of Harjha there is a great desert, more vast than the Sand River,

more difficult to cross. The Harjhans who told us this believe there is no world beyond it, the godspeaker's omens
say this is a lie. Second, there is a rich land to the newsun
side of Harjha. They call it Na'ha'leima. That is all I am
told."

Zandakar and Dmitrak traded glances. "This is good
news, Akida. You have served the god well. Your warband is stood down, you have a day to rest. I meet with
the village chieftain after lowsun sacrifice. I will see what
he knows of this Na'ha'leima. When you are rested you
will ride with Dmitrak to its border, and see what must be
seen. As soon as Targa is demon-free, and the omens are
with us, it will be our next conquest."

With his warlord business done, and Dimmi pleased to
be scouting, he mingled with the warband, hearing their
stories, praising their feats. Some had fresh fingerbones
to show him, from the Harjhans who had not knelt
quickly enough.

The sight of them saddened him, but he did not show
his warriors how he felt. He did not show Dimmi, who
praised them and laughed.

*What is wrong with me, god? They were sinners, they
died. It was your desire, why do I hurt? I have killed so
many thousands, why care for twelve?*

The god did not answer. He would demand another
tasking, he must scream out his sin. It was his wickedness
that kept the god from speaking, sorrow for the smitten
was a terrible crime.

*If I scream loud and long enough, I know the god will
hear. It will hear, it will answer, I will not be alone.*

CHAPTER FORTY-THREE

"Tell me again, Zandakar," said Lilit, smiling, "how you saved your brother crossing the Sand River."

Zandakar laughed. "Again, Lilit? I have told you already, more than once!"

It was the soft time before lowsun, that Lilit called *dusk*. A little more than one godmoon had passed since the first time they spoke and yet his world had been made anew. They walked the banks of a lazy stream, picking their way through bluebells and starshine, as birds called *owls* soared through tree shadows overhead. The air was warm and moist, sweetly scented. *Frogs* croaked tunelessly in a nearby pond, they were ugly creatures. He must draw one on a clay tablet so his mother could see.

Lilit's fingers tightened around his, they walked hand-in-hand. When he walked with Lilit he was not alone, the screaming thousands were silenced. Now in his dreams he saw her face, not the rubble of hammered cities. When he walked with Lilit he was a man, not the warlord.

If that is a sin, then god, I am sinful. But could I walk with her if you had not sent her? I think I could not. I think this is meant.

She said, still smiling, "It is a good story, warlord. There can never be too many good stories in the world."

"Then I will tell it," he said. "If that will please you."

"Yes," she said, and raised his hand to kiss it. "It will please me very much."

So he told her again of that bad time when Dimmi, impatient, had galloped ahead of the warhost to see if the next rocky outcropping held hidden water fit to drink. He had blundered into a quicksand sinkhole, already three hundred and nine warriors had perished that way and they were barely halfway across the Sand River, so the god-bones said.

"I heard my brother screaming, my blood turned to fire. I galloped too, though it was madness. I was so afraid, and I was angry. With his dying breath Raklion warlord said I must protect my little brother but I had failed him, now Dmitrak was dying!"

By the time he reached Dimmi, his brother's horse was gone. Dmitrak was sinking fast, his head, his shoulders and one arm in the air, that was all, and not for much longer.

"That was when the god spoke to me, Lilit, it showed me in my heart how to save my brother. I used the hammer, the god's mighty weapon, I fused the sand that swallowed Dimmi's body so I might walk upon it, and pull him free."

Why he had not thought to do it for those other fallen warriors he could not explain. He had loved them also, but they were not his little brother. They were not angry Dimmi, brave Dimmi, laughing, fighting, infuriating Dimmi, begging Zanda to save him with tears in his eyes.

"Aieee," sighed Lilit, leaning against him. "How mighty is Zandakar warlord. If I were in danger, would you smite with your hammer to save me, too?"

He pushed her against the trunk of a moss-covered tree

and leaned his forehead against hers. "You know that I would, Lilit. I would smite anything, anyone, to save you from harm."

In the dusk-light the pale parts of her skin glowed, translucent. He smoothed the dark hair away from her face, kissed her eyes and her cheeks and last of all, lingering, her pliant lips. Kissing her was not like kissing a vessel. The vessels felt duty, what he felt was lust.

He lusted for Lilit, too, but in a pure way. The need rising in him was for more than flesh, the fleeting release of a hard, fast fuck.

What I feel for Lilit, I think it is love.

Drawing back, breathless, marveling at how she could move him, he said, "You never ask to hear of my other smitings. You do not ask for stories of Drohne, or Bryzin. Not even of Targa, when you say yourself the warhost saved you from those sinners."

She looked at his chest, played her fingers along the edge of his linen tunic. Her touch woke fires in his flesh. "I have heard those stories. Your godspeakers tell them. They are stories of death, Zandakar. I do not like death. The story of Dmitrak, that celebrates life. Here in Harjha, life is important. Life is a beautiful thing, we do not waste it."

Her words stung him. "Nor do I, Lilit. I do not smite for the sake of smiting, every city I have thrown down, first I have given them the chance to kneel. If a city does not resist me, I do not destroy it. Did I destroy your village? I think I did not. You did not resist me, I have left you in peace."

She smiled at him, and stroked his cheek. "I know. You do not like to destroy those cities, the dead sinners in them haunt you. I see it in your eyes, Zandakar. When you sleep you hear them screaming, I hear you weeping in your heart."

Stunned, he stared at her. "I do not speak of that. Only the god hears my weeping heart. How do you know this? *How do you know*?"

She stood on tip-toe, she kissed him gently. "I know because I love you. Your heart is my heart, what it feels I feel. When you weep in your dreams, beloved, Lilit weeps with you."

They had been lovers for seventeen highsuns. Though he'd wanted it badly, he had not meant to fuck her. She was conquered, she was piebald, the Empress would not approve. But the Empress was in Mijak, and he was in the world. For six seasons uncomplaining he had slaughtered for Hekat. Only the god knew how many more seasons he would fight. He did not want to live his whole life without softness, with nothing but blood to warm his skin.

He told himself: *the god sent Lilit to me. We do nothing wrong.*

He'd learned swiftly that with Lilit, it was not fucking. It was gentler than that, it was sweeter, kinder. He was her first man, she was his first love. They'd wept together, afterwards, as she held him close.

"*Zandakar*," she whispered. "The god wants us together, I know this. You know it."

He wanted to believe her. "The godspeakers have not told me so. They take omens daily, they did not tell me this."

"Tcha," she said, a word she had learned from him. "They are men of blood, they look for reasons to kill. They see the god in dead animals, you hear it in your heart. You do not need them to tell you things that matter. Those things you know yourself. Tell me I am lying."

He kissed her. "You are not lying."

She smiled, she laughed. She filled his aching, empty heart.

The god must want this. Lilit sees my godspark. She is my gift from the god.

That was their first time. Every time since, it grew sweeter and sweeter. With each passing highsun, his feelings deepened. Strengthened. Loving her, he began to change.

There is more to life than war and killing. She has shown me this and I hardly know her. What else will she show me, as time goes by?

Entwined together, they walked through the fading light back to the village. Before reaching his warcamp he let her go, reluctantly, so she might return to her dying father. The godspeakers had eased the chieftain, as far as they could. He was an old man, and failing. His life was almost done.

The warband camped outside the village was two thousand warriors strong, the rest of his warhost in Harjha still scouted, preparing the way for the godspeakers and settlers to come. As he approached his private warlord lodging, a mocking voice greeted him out of the dark.

"When I said she was a fuckable woman, brother, I did not think she was fuckable by *you*."

Aieee, Dimmi, returned from riding with Akida and her shell. He slowed, he turned, he joined his little brother at the opening to his tent. "Are you jealous?"

Dimmi shrugged. "I'll wait to see if your cock drops off. If it does, the jealousy will not be mine."

"And if it does not?" Zandakar said, grinning.

"Then I will have to find a piebald of my own." In the lamplight, Dimmi's face was wryly amused. "I confess, you surprise me." He sat on a camp stool, kicked another closer. "I was come to think you are not like other men, with their urges."

Zandakar lowered himself to the other stool, and rested his elbows on his knees. The business of nightcamp continued about them, without imminent battle snapping at the warhost's heels the camp felt almost restful.

"I have my urges," he said, after a moment. "But still, you are right. I am not like other men."

"I know," said Dimmi, and reached out with a comforting hand.

His brother's touch on his shoulder was almost his undoing. "I love her, Dimmi."

For once, Dimmi did not shout at the use of that name. Instead he sighed, and tightened his fingers. "I would not do that, if I were you. She is a prime piece of she-flesh, fuck her till she bores you. Do not give her your heart, Zanda. That will be your undoing, so our father would tell you if he were alive."

Always, always, a knife-jab at Hekat. "It is not so simple, Dmitrak," he said, almost sharply. Then he relented. "It is also too late. Lilit is so sweet. Vortka would like her, they share the same kindness. She is gentle with her father, you should see them together. When I am with her, I do not feel old. I do not feel weary. I do not smell the blood."

"Tcha," said Dimmi. "What sadsa-froth is this? You are not *old*."

"No. Not in seasons counted on my fingers. But I tell you, there are times . . ."

Dimmi did not want to hear that. He said, grinning slyly, "Vortka might like the girl, but the Empress won't."

"I know," he admitted, after a moment.

Dimmi laughed. "No, she will hate her. So I say *fuck on*, brother. Hekat is in Mijak, let her stay there and rot. You are the god's hammer, I say fuck who you like, even if it is a piebald bitch. It's your life, Zanda. You don't belong to the Empress."

Zandakar shrugged, and loosened his brother's hand. "Do not call Lilit a piebald bitch."

The hand was withdrawn. "You are the warlord," said Dimmi, no longer smiling. "Your word is your word." With a sharp nod, he disappeared into his tent.

Zandakar sighed, and withdrew to his own.

A tensun later, after newsun sacrifice at the village god-post, Radeet godspeaker pulled him aside and said, "Warlord, the god has spoken. There are omens and the godbones agree. The warhost has rested long enough in Harjha. It is time to ride upon Na'ha'leima."

Zandakar felt his heart thud. The other godspeakers were cleaning up the blood and carcasses, the villagers were gone about their business, Lilit sat with her dying father, and the warriors in camp walked to the cleared training field for knife-dance practice with Dimmi.

He wished with his whole heart he could be with Lilit, but he was the warlord. It would not be wise.

He said, "If that is the god's desire, godspeaker, then it

must be mine also. But do not forget I am the warlord and the hammer, the warhost is my business. It will ride when I say it is ready to ride. When you say now, that means within a godmoon. You know what must be done for the warhost to ride."

Radeet nodded. "Warlord, I do."

"Very well, then." He turned back for the warcamp, but the godspeaker took his arm, restraining him. "*Radeet?*" he demanded, his voice a whip.

There was no apology in the godspeaker's face. It was cold and unflinching. They were nearly the same age. "Warlord, I am given a private omen, I received it in the last quiet time when the god moved me to pray. The woman you fuck with has conceived a son."

A son? "What woman?" Zandakar said, after a shuddering moment. "Who says I have—"

"Tcha," said Radeet. "You thought it secret, you were wrong, Zandakar." He frowned. "I should have stopped you, I should have tasked you for lewdness and forbade you her flesh."

"Why did you not?"

"I have eyes, warlord. I see your burden," Radeet said simply. "I asked the god should I task you for fucking her, the god did not answer. I took that as an answer in itself. In six warring seasons you have not looked at a woman. You looked at this one, it must be the god's plan. You do not shun your taskings, you are not a sinful man. You are its hammer, its chosen in the world."

He hardly heard the godspeaker's reply. *Lilit, Lilit, she carries my son.* He said, "Your wisdom is appreciated, Radeet godspeaker. If this matter remains between us do not speak of it further, not even to your fellow godspeakers. I will ask the god in solitude for its guidance in this business."

Radeet nodded. "And you will also prepare the warhost for war. That answer I did receive, warlord, there was no room for dispute."

Aieee, more blood and smiting, it was his purpose. "No dispute, godspeaker. The warhost will ride."

Of course, he told Dimmi.

"*Pregnant*?" his brother echoed. "Aieee, Zandakar, that is disaster. How could you not make sure she was sealed against your seed? The warlord of Mijak cannot breed with a *piebald*. Fucking is one thing, but her blood is not pure. The dregs of her people are slaves in Mijak, would you raise a slave and call it your *equal*?"

"Do not speak like that!" he commanded his brother. "This is the god's will, Dmitrak. You speak against the god."

"Oh, so the *god* told you to plant your son in her belly? Zanda, what if he's *piebald*? You think *Hekat* will accept a piebald grandson? You think Mijak will follow a piebald warlord? If you do, you are *mad*! You were mad to fuck her!"

Zandakar stared. Dimmi was his little brother, little shadow at his heels, he did not raise his voice like this, he did not disrespect his warlord brother. They were alone in a woodland some distance from the village, he had invited Dimmi to ride with him as he looked at a possible site for a new Mijaki city. Their horses' reins were hitched to a sapling, the horses tossed their heads at the sound of raised voices.

"How can you say that? You *encouraged* me to fuck her!"

"Yes, I did, but I *never* said get her pregnant!"

Zandakar felt his fists clench. "I am the god's hammer, Dmitrak. I live in its eye. Do you think this could happen without its will?"

"You are so certain," spat Dimmi. "*I* say this is the work of demons. I say the piebald is demon-touched, she has poisoned your heart. She has stopped your ears so you're deaf to the god, and me."

Zandakar struck him, he knocked his brother to the ground. "That is a *lie*! You lie with your tongue! She is gentle and precious, there is *no* demon in her!"

Speechless, Dimmi sprawled on the grass.

Zandakar cursed and fell to his knees. Never in his life had he struck his brother. "Aieee, Dimmi, forgive me. I am not myself. I am turned about with this news of a son. I want you to be pleased for me, I want you to understand—"

Dimmi struck his outstretched hand aside. "I understand, Zanda." With a grunt, he bounced to his feet. "What is a brother, compared to a son? Even a son who looks like a slave."

"*Dmitrak!*" he shouted, but it was no use, Dimmi would not listen, he vaulted into his saddle and rode his stallion away.

Disconsolate, Zandakar mounted his own horse and followed his brother back to the village.

Speak to him, god. Tell him the truth, that I still love him, I will always love him, he is my brother. No son can change that.

*   *   *

In the village he found Lilit in her mud-and-sapling home, weeping beside her dead father's body.

"He is gone, Zandakar, his spirit is fled," she sobbed, falling against him.

"Not his spirit, his godspark," he said, and kissed her brow. "Lilit, dry your tears. Weeping will not bring him back, do I not know it, who also watched a father die?"

She rubbed her hands across her face. "Yes. You are right. And he was ready to go. His eyes told me he was ready, I could not keep him."

He gazed at her belly, still flat beneath her shift. "I have something to tell you, Lilit. Two things I must tell you, both from the god."

"Then tell me, Zandakar. I learn from the godspeakers, I know the god's will is first in all things."

He framed her face with his hands. "You carry my son. The god has seen you quicken with my seed, you will be the mother of the god's warlord in the world."

She gasped. "The god has told you? It has told me too!"

"When? How?"

"In a dream, three nights ago."

"And you did not *tell* me?"

"I am sorry, Zandakar," she whispered. "I was not certain. I thought it might be only a wanting dream." Tears welled in her beautiful eyes. "I was not keeping secrets, I swear to you, I swear! Please don't be angry."

He kissed her lips. "I am not angry."

"And you are pleased, about the baby?"

"Pleased?" He pulled her to him. "Aieee, god. I am pleased. This son is the god's gift, I will ride my smiting way through the world undefeated because of the son sleeping under your heart."

"Oh, Zandakar," she breathed, and slid her arms around him. "I am glad too. What else does the god tell you, that I must know?"

He rested his cheek upon her head. "It is time for the warhost to ride out of Harjha. Between here and the Great Desert there are lands yet unconquered. I must reclaim them for the god. I must make them part of Mijak's empire. That is my purpose, and the Empress's desire. Once those lands are conquered, we will divine our way across that desert, the god will guide us and see us through safely, its godposts will spread over the face of the world."

"A fearsome thing, Zandakar," she said softly. "I do not know what lies beyond the desert. Perhaps many countries, many people, many cities. Will you smite them all, warlord? Must they all kneel, or die?"

He kissed her. "You know they must." He kissed her again. "And you must leave Harjha and ride to Et-Raklion. To the Empress, my mother, where you will be safe."

"Leave Harjha?" she said, and pulled away. "Leave *you*? No, Zandakar, I do not want to!"

"What you want cannot matter to me, Lilit," he said. "All that can matter is our son. Will I see him born here, in the godless wilderness? I think I will not. He must be born in Et-Raklion, the place of my birth. Vortka high godspeaker must sacrifice for him with his own hands. My son will be the warlord of Mijak, he will one day wield the god's gold-and-crystal hammer. You and he *must* go to Et-Raklion, Lilit."

She wept, her tears burned him. "Aieee, Zandakar,

how will I live in that faraway city? I want to be with you,
I want—"

"Even if you stayed here we would not be together," he
said, his voice harsh. "Have I not told you? I ride for the
god. I ride to smite first Na'ha'leima."

"Not Na'ha'leima!" she cried in protest. "It is a quiet
land, not like Targa, demons do not possess it, those people are *good*."

He shook his head. "They are not good if they do not
know the god, Lilit. They must be smitten, it is the god's
will."

Now her eyes were angry. "Will you smite the children, warlord? Will you smite the women with babies in
their bellies? Zandakar—"

He flung her from him and turned away. Was Dmitrak
right, did a demon live in her tongue? "*No more, Lilit*! Do
not tempt me from my purpose! That is a sin and the godspeakers will know!"

She moaned, and pressed her hands against his back.
"If you do this you will suffer, Zandakar. Do I not hear
the weeping in your heart? Do I not know your sorrow,
I—"

"*I have no sorrow! The god's hammer does not weep*!"
He turned on her, desperate, and caught her hands in his.
"I was weary when I came here, Lilit. Six long seasons of
constant war, what man would not be tired? But I am
rested now, I am strong in the god's eye. The god has
given me you and a son, will I thank it with a sinning
heart? Will I thwart its desire in the world? I will not do
that, and you will not ask me."

Tears and tears washed down her face. "I am afraid,

Zandakar. I am afraid to leave you. I fear what will happen in Et-Raklion city."

"Nothing will happen, Lilit," he soothed her. "The god will protect you, and so will my mother. I promise. I *promise*. You will be safe."

He wrote a letter to his mother and one to Vortka. He dried the damp clay tablets overnight in his hot tent and after newsun sacrifice gave them to Akida, wrapped in thick protecting cloths.

"Here are important messages for the Empress and her high godspeaker. Here is a woman, Lilit, she lives in my eye. You and your shell must deliver her and the messages unharmed to Mijak, to Et-Raklion's palace. If you fail in this the god will strike you down."

Akida looked disappointed. "We do not ride with you to smite Na'ha'leima?"

He shook his head. "I have a warhost full of warriors, but here is something precious. Only Akida is trusted to guard it."

She banged her fist above her heart, pleased by his praise and trust. "Warlord."

He put Lilit on her horse. "Do not forget me, beloved. I will come home to see our son born. That is my promise, my word is my word."

"Warlord," she whispered. Her eyes were full of tears and love. "Remember me, and think of this. If it is possible, do not be cruel to Na'ha'leima."

He watched her ride away, surrounded by his warriors. He thought he felt his heart tear, and bleed. When she was gone from his eye he turned to Dimmi, silent and unsympathetic by his side. They had hardly spoken since their fight in the woodland.

"It is time for the warhost to ride for the god, brother. We must smite Na'ha'leima in its conquering eye."

"Tcha," said Dimmi. He did not smile. "It is past time we did this. You are come to your senses, warlord. Let us pray it is not too late."

Aieee, Dimmi. Dimmi. He was still angry.

He will forgive me. We are brothers. He must.

Two warbands rode out of Harjha, one led by Zandakar, the other by his brother. They swept into Na'ha'leima like the fiery breath of god. Its people were peaceful, as the Harjhans were peaceful, but they said they had a god already, they had no need of Mijak's god.

The villages of Na'ha'leima were smitten for their sins.

As his warriors took their ease amid the death and ruins of another village, Zandakar stared at the body of the village's elder, sprawled at his feet and dead by his hand. Her tattooed face was smeared with blood and brains, her nose-ring dulled with slime. Planting a foot on her smashed chest, he grasped the long single braid of her orange hair and deftly severed her head from her neck. His snakeblade snagged on gristle. A practiced flick of his wrist, a small grunt of effort, and the spinal cord surrendered. A little blood pooled sluggishly, thickened now, with no beating heart to pump it freely.

I am sorry, Lilit. She had to die.

His stallion was too well trained to pull away, flattened black ears were its only protest as he tied the head to his saddle and prepared to remount. A small noise stopped him, breathy, shocked. He looked around. He and the horse stood at the entrance to the elder's dwelling. Behind them, six dead dogs and four hacked bodies, two men, two women. They'd perished trying to protect the elder. One severed hand still clutched a kitchen knife, scant protection against the god's warlord. No more sound from those slashed throats, no cries of pleasure or pain, no laughter, no tears, no jokes, complaints, railings, compliments or accusations. They had died in sin, abandoned by the god.

The noise came again. Louder, this time. A baby. Crying.

Zandakar wiped his snakeblade clean, he sheathed it and ducked into the dwelling. They were a short people, these Na'ha'leimans. Short and peaceful and unprepared. Inside the small house oil-lamps burned, stinking the air, dispelling gloom. Woven rush mats on the floor deadened his footfalls. Fresh flowers spilled red and orange and blue from an earthenware vase. A loved house, this. Poor by palace standards, no bright jeweled columns, no intricate mosaics beneath his boots, no hand-seamed silken curtains to flutter in slave-made breezes . . . but it had a rough charm, all the same.

The baby wailed again. More demanding this time, the fear ebbing, crossness growing in its stead. He ducked through a threadbare curtain into an adjoining room. The kitchen. Eggs in a bowl, brown and cream and speckled. A knob of butter. Kneaded bread on a windowsill, rising for no-one now. High in one corner a small cage, and in it a blue and green bird that cocked a suspicious eye and fluttered its striped wings in warning.

He set it free, balancing the cage at the open window and rattling the bars until it darted through the unlatched

door into the freedom beyond. Eight determined strokes
of the air and it was vanished from sight.

"Won't last till newsun, most like," said a respect-
fully disparaging voice. "Perish of cold, or get eaten by
crows."

He turned. Vanikil shell-leader, reeking of blood.

"Sun's fast sinking, warlord. We need to ride."

"Yes. I know." He turned back to the window, stared
into the sky, hoping for a glimpse of the bird. It might not
die. It might survive. Not all things ended in death. Not
so swiftly, at least.

The baby wailed again, resentment echoing through
the still cottage. "A brat?" said Vanikil, and scowled. "I'll
see to it, warlord." He ducked out of the kitchen.

Zandakar opened his mouth to stop him, but there was
no point. It had no mother, its people were dead. In the
next room the baby screeched on an upward sliding scale
that ended abruptly with a sharp crack as the thin wall beside him vibrated. Then Vanikil was standing in the doorway, dead dripping flesh dangling from one large fist,
limp as a neck-wrung chicken.

"There was only this one, warlord," he said.

Zandakar stared at the baby. It was dressed in soft
brown wool. The side of its head was flattened, scarlet
slowly soaking scant orange hair. An echo of the elder's
flaming braid. Daughter? Son? At this age they were sexless. Its eyes were open. Staring.

I am sorry, Lilit. It had to die.

Vanikil stepped back. "Warlord?" He tossed the dead
child away, it struck the edge of the kitchen bench and
fell to the floor. "It was your place to kill it." He dropped
to his knees, and waited for smiting.

Zandakar heard himself say, "Stand, warrior. The brat is dead, the god is served. We must ride before it is dark."

He and his warriors released the village animals before leaving, so they might survive and service the settlers from Mijak when at last they arrived. The only sound as they rode away from the village was the excited cawing and pecking of carrion birds, who lined the branches of the surrounding trees and eagerly eyed the feast spread below.

CHAPTER FORTY-FOUR

Zandakar and his warriors reached their camp site two fingers later on horses stumbling with weariness. Cook-fires were already smoking, godspeakers prepared the lowsun sacrifice. One of Dimmi's warriors came to take his horse. There was blood on her face, she had not cleaned herself since returning with his brother and their warband. Fresh fingerbones dangled round her neck, fleshed and gristled still.

"The god sees you, warlord. How was its business, in the wild?"

A cry, a screech, a crack. Silence. Soft brown wool. Dead, open eyes.

"Its business was its business," he said, and tossed her the reins. "See to my horse, it will be sacrifice soon. Give the head to the godspeakers." To discourage demons they would bind it with charms and burn it in a sacred fire. No settlers could come here until the land was cleansed of evil and the memory of its former inhabitants. One head taken from every cleansed city and village. How many heads since leaving Et-Raklion? He had lost count of that, too. He did not want to know.

The warrior—his mind was empty, he could not recall her name—nodded. A shadow of hurt touched her eyes, he was not usually curt with his warhost. "Yes, warlord."

"Where is my brother?"

"At his ease," she said, pointing to a break in the trees, where smoke was rising.

He nodded, her gaze was on him as he walked away. His skin crawled, even though he had hurt her there was adoration in her eyes. He was the warlord, the hammer, the god was in him. Her favor made him feel old and tired and unclean.

Dimmi sat on the grass by a cheerful fire, chewing on dried goat meat. He looked up and nodded. Since leaving Harjha his mood had sweetened, they spoke again now as though nothing were different. On the surface nothing was, beneath it all had changed.

Lilit, Lilit, do you travel safely?

"The god see you, brother," said Dimmi. "You hunted well today?"

"I hunted," he said, folding to the ground. "What of you?"

Dimmi shrugged. "I hunted also. It will not take long to cleanse this land. Did you wield the hammer?" His eyes were avaricious, he loved the gold-and-crystal weapon, he loved to watch it burn and destroy.

Zandakar shook his head, frowning. The fire was

small, were it as large as Et-Raklion itself it would not warm him. "No."

"Why not? It is the god's weapon, the god's power must be seen in the world."

"The god's power is its power, in a blade of grass and a flower in the field. There was no need to wield the weapon, the village was small and undefended. I was a warrior before I was the god's hammer. If I do not dance with my snakeblade the god will take my *hotas* from me."

"*Tcha!* The god will never take your *hotas*," said Dimmi, scornfully. He picked up a goatskin and drank from it, then held it out. "Drink. You look like you are come from a godmoon's tasking in the godhouse."

Zandakar took the goatskin and drank the sour wine. If he drank enough, would he forget his day's work for the god?

Children playing, chickens scratching through the dirt. Men in the grain field, women picking fruit. The music of laughter, small lives unlived in the god's eye. Blood, screaming, terror, death . . .

Aieee, if Lilit had seen his work this highsun, if she had seen him dancing with his snakeblade. If she had seen the blood he spilled . . .

If she had seen that slaughtered baby.

"Stop thinking of that woman, Zanda," Dimmi said curtly. "And do not deny your thoughts to me, you know I know when she eats your heart."

I am the only person who has ever loved him. He is a man, he is still afraid.

"I have told you and told you, Dmitrak," he said, with patience. "I love her, I must think of her. You are my brother, I love you no less."

Dimmi's face twisted. "Love," he spat. "Do I speak of love, that milkish thing? I speak of the god, Zandakar, I speak of your godspark. The godspeakers sit in their god-houses and under the stars, they sacrifice and read the omens, that is their purpose, they ponder the god. You are its hammer, your purpose is *killing*. Kill these maggot thoughts, brother, before they eat you and you die!"

He sighed. "I do think of Lilit, I think of my son growing in her belly. You are right, I should forget them. They ride to Mijak and I am here, the god's chosen hammer. Dmitrak, forgive me. I do not mean to worry you, little brother."

"Tcha! Not so little anymore!" growled Dimmi, and caught him in a fierce embrace. "It pleases me you are returned from hunting, untouched in the god's eye," he whispered. "You may be the god's hammer, and these slaves of Na'ha'leima no more than pitiful earth-grubbers, but there is such a thing as demonstrike. When you ride to war without me I am always afraid."

Zandakar returned the gesture, feeling Dimmi's hard adult muscle beneath his hands, remembering the baby who once fitted so neatly in the curve of his arms.

A cry. A screech. A vulnerable skull meeting unforgiving wall. Pale orange hair, drenched in blood.

"No need for fear, little brother. Am I not in the god's eye?"

Dimmi released him. "You are. Do not forget it."

The godbell sounded, it was time for sacrifice.

More blood. More death. I am sick of bloodshed . . .

"Come, Zandakar hammer," said Dimmi, smiling. "Let us worship the god."

Heartsick and weary, Zandakar followed his lead.

*   *   *

For newsun sacrifice there was a brown goatkid, brought back by Dimmi from a slaughtered village. A meek thing, it bleated once as the godspeaker drew her curved knife across its upstretched throat. Hot blood splashed scarlet into the golden sacrifice bowl.

As a child of three seasons, Zandakar had learned to hide his revulsion at the taste of hot blood. *I am Hekat, I am not disgraced in public,* his mother had hissed as she dragged him to the godhouse taskmaster, all flaming eyes and pinch-lipped fury. *You are a warlord! You will drink the blood, you will glory in the blood, you will thirst for the blood!* The taskmaster had beaten him, she had watched every stroke, unmoved by his cries of pain.

He'd forgiven her, of course. How could he not, when she'd eased the burning weals herself? Held his hand as he swallowed his tears, whispering, *There, there, my little warlord. I do this because you are godchosen and precious, the god sees you in its eye. In its time you will lead the warhost, you must be strong for the god.*

The pain faded, eventually. The weals disappeared. He never again betrayed his disgust when a sacrifice bowl filled with blood touched his lips.

He drank now, the merest touching to his tongue, then passed the bowl to Dimmi, who swallowed with evident enjoyment and passed it to the next man. And so sacrifice proceeded, until every last warrior had tasted of the sacred blood. Then the godspeaker read the omens, taking a long time to do so. After that she threw the godbones. At last she turned and said, "Zandakar warlord, the god shows me a sinning city. The warhost must ride to it, it must be subdued."

He added. "What is this city's name?"

"What does it matter?" said Dimmi. "It will soon be destroyed."

A city. That meant the hammer, no knife-dancing with his snakeblade. He must unwrap the gold-and-crystal weapon, he must draw it onto his hand and arm, summon the god's power and let it scour him with fire.

"Aieee!" said Dimmi. "That is good to hear!"

Of course Dimmi would think so. His warriors thought so too, they were smiling and nodding, they gloried in the power of his smiting fist. The people of the sinning city might fight but they would still die. The crows and the wild dogs, the carrion eaters of this place, they would feast well after, until the maggots reduced succulent flesh to greasy putrefaction.

Lilit's tear-filled eyes, her beseeching whisper. *Do not be cruel to Na'ha'leima.*

He shook his head. *Lilit, leave me.* He said, "The god sees you, godspeaker. It sees you in its eye. Dmitrak—" He turned. "Prepare the warhost for riding."

Dimmi grinned, and struck a fist to his breast. *"Warlord!"*

As his brother and the warhost withdrew to break camp, Zandakar turned back to the godspeaker, making certain she would not see the sorrow in his eyes. "I am the god's hammer, you know my purpose. Tell me where the warhost must ride, so I might smite this sinning city to its knees."

*   *   *

They rode for a finger towards the rising sun, they saw no living creatures, all the villages were dead. The fat land was quiet, it was holding its breath. The god guided Zandakar and his warriors, they rode deep inside its eye, they would not be seen or heard until the god desired it. The god whispered in Zandakar's heart, he surrendered to its ravenous will. The warhost trotted down rocky slopes, through shallow streams, up tree-studded inclines, along the spines of craggy ravines and back down to flat lands, where they rode fast.

As they reached the peak of a slow-rising hill, he raised his fist in the air, slowing his warhost. They spread around and behind like a shadow on the land, like the god's black breath extinguishing the light.

The nameless city, too small to be called that by Mijaki standards, nestled undefended at the foot of the hill. Through the thin morning air came a cockerel's self-important gurgle. The rattle of a metal pail. Above several houses, smudges of smoke. The township was waking. All unknowing, making preparations for the final sleep of death.

Zandakar put on his hammer. Fractured scarlet sunlight flashed, a shiver of power thrummed his bones. Beneath him, his knowing, eager stallion half-reared. He raised his arm above his head, fingers fisted tighter than rock. Summoning the god, he cried "*It is time!*" and sent a column of blue-white fire towards the sun.

His brother and his warhost screamed. "*Mijaaaaaaak! Ai-ai-ai-ai-ai-ai-aieeeeee!*"

As one ravening beast Zandakar and his warhost launched from the crest of the hill towards the walking dead below.

Pounding hooves. Flashing blades. War cries, shrill

and loud and chilling. Shrieks of alarm. Men running.
Dogs howling. Women screaming. Cattle lowing. Children sobbing. Panic. Terror.

Breathless with laughter, Dimmi galloped beside
Zandakar down the hard-earth streets, between dingy
mud-brick houses and shops, knocking the people down,
galloping over them, smashing them to pieces beneath
iron-hard hooves. Dimmi swung his longblade and took
two heads with one blow. His familiar face disappeared
beneath the fountaining blood. Steaming, dripping, fragrant with death, he pivoted his horse on its haunches and
killed two more.

"Kill them, Zandakar!" he bellowed. "Smite them for
the god! Kill them before they draw our blood!"

There was no need. These people had no defenses. No
weapons. No god to save them. The victory had been his
before the first blow was struck. It was show and gaud, to
annihilate them with the hammer.

"Zandakar!" cried Dimmi, "What are you waiting for?
Use the hammer, wield it for the god!"

*It is my purpose. I am the god's hammer, the hammer
smites. It destroys the godless, it throws demons down.*

His arm was so heavy. He raised it high and summoned his power. Blood-red crystals blazed in the light.
Like every sinning city before this one, the dwellings before him disappeared in shards and lumps and flying
spars of burning timber. He struck again, he killed buildings, people, anything that moved. He lost his mind in an
orgy of bloodshed, in blood he drowned Lilit's beautiful
voice.

Do not be cruel to Na'ha'leima.

The screams of the dying were ferocious, they were

claws in his belly, tearing him wide. He lost sight of Dmitrak in the smoke of his burnings, he could still hear his brother, laughing as he killed. His horse plunged beneath him, maddened with bloodlust.

A flicker of movement caught his eye. A woman sobbing, stumbling, a meager length of firewood in her hands. She thought it was a weapon. Clutching her skirts, a small girl-child. Zandakar summoned the god, felt it boil in his veins. Ripple and curdle and batter and blind, tremble him, fill him, hollow him, devour him.

Blue-white fire shot from his fist. Woman and child transfixed now, twin pillars of flame. Within the azure incandescence, silhouettes of suffering. Eyes wide. Mouths open. No sound but burning. The stench of scorched flesh.

"Zandakar! Warlord! Hammer of the god!" Dimmi, his brother, raucous with pride. Eyes blazing in a wet, crimson mask.

Warriors paused in their slaughter to echo the cry. The hammer's blue flame spurred them on. A city man, running, contorted with grief. Pitchfork in his hand, hatred in every straining muscle.

And now there were three columns of flame.

Dimmi howled his triumph, he sounded like a dog. A cheer went up from the warhost, wails of fear from the doomed.

Three piles of ash. Big. Smaller. Smallest.

A boy running. A warrior hunting. Four strides. Three. Two. One. Her swinging longblade sliced the child's head from his shoulders. Blood flew through the air, his head struck a smashed wall, his body skidded across the ground.

Do not be cruel to Na'ha'leima.

Time stopped. Zandakar stopped with it.

Blind, he saw everything.

Deaf, he heard all.

Dumb, he said: *No more.*

He heard a whispering voice inside him: *Enough killing, Zandakar. That was your purpose, it is ended now. Return to Mijak, and be what you are.*

It was the sad voice he'd heard so long ago, in the god-house godpool, in Et-Raklion. The voice he remembered now, from his haunted dreams.

A scream sounded behind him, he wheeled his horse. A family, running. The warrior pursuing them struck down three, three more remained. The warrior's horse stumbled, throwing its rider.

"Mine!" shouted Dimmi, and started forward.

"No!" cried Zandakar. "Dmitrak, *stop*!"

Dimmi ignored him. He sent a stream of godfire into the ground before his brother's cantering horse, the beast swerved wildly, Dimmi nearly fell.

"*Zandakar*? What are you *doing*?" he demanded, incredulous, wrenching his stallion under control.

He felt so peaceful. So completely at ease. *I am ending this, the slaughter is done. I am gorged on blood, my belly is full.* "Conquest is over, Dmitrak. We will kill no-one else."

An eerie silence fell. Warriors milled, discipline deserted. Terrified sinners huddled in doorways, in the shelter of each other's arms.

"*Zandakar*! You are the *hammer*. You are the god's warlord in the world!" A terrible despair was in Dimmi's face, his voice. Beneath despair, a rising anger. "*You must finish this!*"

"It is finished," he said calmly. "We are going home."

"To *Mijak*?" said Dimmi. "Zandakar, no. Conquest is not over, it will *never* be over, not till Mijak is the world!"

Zandakar shook his head. "The god has spoken, Dimmi. We must obey."

"Don't *call* me that, my name is *Dmitrak!*"

"Of course. Forgive me. Dmitrak."

Beneath its mask of drying blood, Dimmi's face was rock hard with rage. "You say the god has spoken? I say you hear that bitch, that piebald bitch, she is a *plague* in you, Zandakar! She is a *disease!*"

Blue-white fire shimmered over his fist. "Dmitrak . . . I warn you, do not—"

Now there was fear in Dmitrak's eyes. Sick disappointment. Shattered belief.

I am sorry. I am sorry. I must obey the god.

"Gather the warhost, Dmitrak," he said, suddenly exhausted. "We ride for Harjha, then for home."

When they stopped for a brief rest halfway back to Lilit's village, so the horses would not founder, his brother confronted him beneath the hot sun. The discreetly distanced warhost took its ease on the ground, mostly silent, exchanging long looks.

Dimmi stabbed a finger into his chest. "The Empress will not stand for this, Zandakar. She will not let you abandon the world."

Zandakar braced his aching back. In his life he had often been tired, but never like this. Not so that lifting his ribs to breathe was almost impossible. "She will have no choice. This is the god's desire."

"No, it is *your* desire," hissed Dimmi, vicious. "Since you fucked that piebald bitch you have not been yourself, your bones have turned soft, you have lost your thirst for blood. Am I blind, Zandakar? Am I not your brother? I know it is so, do *not* deny me."

He rested his hand on Dimmi's shoulder. "A man's desire and the god's can be one and the same."

Dimmi shrugged him away. "I think you are demon-struck! You fucked with a demon and it rotted your godspark, the bitch has blighted you in the god. That thing in her belly, it is a demon unborn! Your seed is curdled, Zanda, you have sired a monster like its mother before it!"

Fury filled him, his snakeblade bit into Dmitrak's throat. "Hold your tongue, *brother*, or I will cut it out. The god sent me Lilit, it desired her quickened with my seed. My son will be beautiful. He will be a man."

Dmitrak touched his neck, beside the snakeblade. His fingers came away red, he stared at the blood. "You've cut me," he said. His voice was small. Uncertain. "Zandakar, you've made me bleed."

Drowning in anguish, he dropped his snakeblade. "Aieee, Dimmi, little brother! I am sorry, I am *sorry*—"

Dimmi fended him off, he backed away. "You are *sorry*, Zandakar? What use is *sorry*? You abandon the god!"

"I do not abandon it! How often must I tell you? The god stayed my hand, it told me to stop!"

"*I don't believe you!*" Dimmi shouted. His face was so stark, he looked almost a stranger.

"You *must* believe me. When have I ever lied to you?"

Now Dimmi laughed, a bitter sound. "Every time you said the Empress loved me."

Silence.

Zandakar felt sweat trickle down his spine, he heard a terrible roaring in his ears. The sun was hot against his skin. His witnessing warriors were on their feet.

"Dimmi . . ." His voice sounded odd, not like his voice.

"*No*," said his brother. "You have said enough. Now *I* say this will be settled in the godhouse, in the god's eye. I will ride back with you to Et-Raklion, the warhost and the godspeakers will stay behind. They will hold these lands for the god in the world. You will tell the Empress and Vortka what you *claim* the god whispers in your heart. And *I* will tell them what it has shown *me*."

Zandakar could see in Dimmi's eyes his brother would not be dissuaded. *Aieee, god. God. Heal this breach between us.* Letting out his breath, Zandakar nodded. "As you say. We will ride to Et-Raklion. The god will speak for itself. You will see I am not lying, Dmitrak. You will see I am telling you the truth."

Risen at newsun, Hekat slid naked from her bed and wandered to her palace balcony. In the garden below her blue and gold godbirds flitted among the small trees, drunk with song, and flower perfumes. A spring bubbled endlessly from an underground river. Her belly gurgled, she was hungry for cornmush and sadsa with honey. She would just have time to eat and bathe before she must present herself to the people in the godtheater, where Vortka would have a white bull-calf decked with garlands and breathing its last moments in cudding ignorance, and the people of Mijak would chant her name.

In her hands she held Zandakar's letter, her fingers caressed it as though clay were flesh, she did not need to read the symbols to know what he had written there. She missed him so much it was hard to breathe. Who would have thought six seasons could feel like a lifetime?

His letter said: *Yuma, my mother, Empress of Mijak. Once you said to me, I am your weakness. You always forgive me. Please, surrender your strength and forgive me now. Here is Lilit, the god's gift to your son. Did I not tell you it would send me a wife? Look past her outside and see her pure heart. She came to me virgin, she carries my son. If ever you believed the god has a purpose, if ever you believed I live in its eye, believe that Lilit is godchosen for me, believe when I took her I obeyed the god. Yuma, I love you. For my sake, love Lilit.*

Aieee, Zandakar, Zandakar. Such a sharp snakeblade in his smile. His love was a whip, she bled from its beating. Of course she forgave him. What else could she do?

Vortka had told her: *I have a letter, too, Hekat. You cannot reject this girl, she bears Zandakar's son. This is the god's will, you must not interfere.*

He would not tell her what his letter said.

As the newsun sky brightened she returned to her chamber, tossed the clay tablet on the bed, and dressed so she might eat her breakfast with her son's piebald woman.

Do you see my devotion, god? I hope you are pleased.

Slaves threw themselves to the floor as she passed, burying their chanting faces in the stone. "The Empress comes, the earth trembles beneath her feet, the sky blushes at her beauty, with my body and my voice shall I worship the Empress, she lives in the god's eye, she is precious and beautiful. My blood shall spill for the Empress's glory."

And so it would. And so it did.

When she entered the bitch's apartments, Zandakar's mistake was ogling herself in front of the mirror, hands spread over the nauseating thrust of her belly. Her piebald face flushed as she lurched away from the polished silver disc and dipped her knees in a travesty of obeisance.

"Empress—you honor me—the glory of your presence—your glory—I—you honor—" Scarlet and brown, she pressed her fingers to her lips and dripped tears.

Wrong. As usual, the stupid slut got the ritual greeting wrong. Hekat's palms itched to sting themselves against that mottled hide. *Tcha*, how could Zandakar find her attractive, with her milk and mud skin and her long, thin legs and dugs like melons over-ripened on the vine! An ugly people, the Harjha, fit for nothing save conquering and chains.

Zandakar, Zandakar, how could you do this to me?

She made herself smile. "The god see you, Lilit. Are you ready for breakfast?"

"Empress, the table is laid and waiting."

Her smile tightened. That accent, warping the pure tongue of Mijak like mold on honey. What had she been thinking, allowing Zandakar to keep this bitch?

She heard his voice in the letter he sent her: *Yuma, I love you, for my sake love Lilit.*

Aieee, love. What stupid fools it had made of them both.

The piebald was staring. "Empress? Are you all right?"

No. She was not. "Let us eat, quickly. We are expected in the godtheater for the public sacrifice."

The piebald nodded, looking away. She was pathetic, squeamish, she hated the blood.

Zandakar, Zandakar, what have you done?

They ate, they dressed, Vortka joined them. They traveled to the godtheater where the people and warriors and god-speakers gathered. The bull-calf was sacrificed, she plunged her snakeblade through the throat of the custom-ary godforsaken criminal. It hurt her body as much as ever, it was expected, she had no choice. Lilit stood watching like a lump of fat, hands pressed against her thrusting belly.

A godspeaker came running as the sacrifice ended, he ran to Vortka and whispered in his ear. Vortka straight-ened, and came to her side. After so long as high god-speaker his face remained guarded, his eyes were alive and filled with feeling.

"Empress, Zandakar warlord approaches the city. His brother Dmitrak rides by his side."

She stared at him, shocked. "What? What do you say?"

"Zandakar is sighted," said Vortka. His clasped hands were trembling. "He will soon ride through Et-Raklion's gates."

The piebald heard him. She gasped. "Zandakar? He comes? He comes for our son?"

Oh, how she wanted to cut out that tongue. "Be quiet. I do not know why Zandakar comes." Her heart was beating, she was burning with love. *My son, my son, there is time to undo this. Cast this bitch aside, you will have a new wife.* She said, "Vortka? Did you know? Did the god tell you he was coming home?"

Vortka frowned. "No. If it had, I would have said so, Empress."

She felt her mouth suck dry with fear. Her fingers touched her scorpion amulet, it was cool, it did not wake. "I am sure there is no trouble. The god would have warned you if there was trouble." *It would have warned me.*

He did not touch her, his look was a touch. "Yes, Empress. The god would have warned me."

Zandakar, Zandakar, my beautiful son . . . "Send your godspeaker to greet him, Vortka. Have the warlord ride here to the godtheater, that his people might see him in his pride."

"Empress," said Vortka, and sent the godspeaker back, running harder.

Waiting for Zandakar to arrive was agony. Sitting still upon her cruel scorpion throne, remaining composed and indifferent when she longed to run to him like that godspeaker, she would rather return to the scorpion pit.

At last, he came.

Aieee, my son, my beautiful son. My heart is returned, I can breathe again.

The godspeakers in the shouting crowd had cleared a pathway for him, he rode like a warlord towards her throne with his gold-and-crystal weapon on his arm. The other one, Dmitrak, rode behind him.

Her heart beat harder. As he approached she studied his face, tcha, he looked older and worn with care. The crowd in the godtheater stopped its shouting, it slowly fell silent. All tongues were stilled.

Something was wrong.

Zandakar drew rein at the foot of the steps leading up to her throne. He slid from his horse, he climbed those stairs. Dmitrak, uninvited, unwanted, climbed them behind him, he drove his heels into the smooth stone as though he were the god.

Hekat watched them come, her blood was surging. The god was in her, it whispered *beware*. Zandakar did not look at her first. First he looked at the piebald bitch.

Just for that, she ached to strike him.

"The god sees you, Empress," her son said, his voice soft. "Godtouched and precious, it sees you in its merciful eye."

The god was not *merciful*. And neither was she. He brought trouble with him, it stank in the air.

"I did not look to see you here, warlord," she said, all her love fled, her voice was stone. "Tell me of your prowess in battle. Tell me of the new lands you give me, making great the god's Empire of Mijak."

Zandakar rested his gaze on her face. In silence he removed the gold-and-crystal weapon from his arm. He gave it to her, his fingers were cold. "Empress, that is not why I am come."

"Zandakar?" said the piebald bitch. "You have spared Na'ha'leima?"

In the dreadful silence, which was Zandakar's answer,

Dmitrak said, "He would not smite their godforsaken city. He says the god spoke to him. I say he lies." His voice was vicious, his eyes full of rage.

Zandakar's weapon slid from Hekat's grasp. Vortka caught it before it hit the dais. She did not believe Dmitrak. He was Nagarak's son, *he* was the liar. "*Zandakar?*"

Her son kissed her with his eyes. "Empress, I tell you, it is no lie. The god spoke in my heart, it told me conquest was over. It told me to come home. It has had its fill of blood."

She looked at Vortka, whose eyes had gone blank. "*High godspeaker?*"

"Empress . . ." He shook his head. "The warlord's purpose remains unchanged. The god sees him in its conquering eye. He *is* the warlord, the god's smiting hammer. His purpose is to reshape the world."

Zandakar said nothing. The other one, Dmitrak, shoved him with hard fists. "I *knew* it! You liar, you deceiver! You sinning betrayer of the god!"

"Empress," said Zandakar. His voice was low and steady. "Yuma. I would have words with you alone."

Her heart was shriveled, a scorpion had stung it. "We are alone," she said coldly. "If you have words for me, speak them."

Incredibly, the piebald bitch opened its mouth again. "Zandakar, beloved, tell us what happened. Everything will be all right."

Hekat slid her snakeblade out of its sheath. Held it up, so the light flashed on its edge. "One more word, you will not speak another."

"*Yuma!*" said Zandakar, and reached out his hand.

"*I am not Yuma! I am the Empress!*"

He dropped to his knees like a slaughtered bull. "You are the Empress," he said, his head meekly bowed. "Empress, forgive me. I *did* hear the god. In my heart it told me, *enough.*"

She looked at Vortka. There were tears in his eyes. His scorpion pectoral weighed him down. "Hekat . . ." The tears were on his cheeks now. Vortka was weeping. "It was not the god."

Dmitrak said, "*Tcha*. I *knew* it. He has turned from you, Empress, as he turned from me. All he cares for is that piebald bitch. You should taste her blood, Vortka. I think she is a demon."

Hekat caught her breath. Betrayal was a hot knife, plunged hard and deep between her ribs. She was a slave again, a bratty child, she stood in the chamber of Abajai's villa and learned that all she thought was true were lies.

Dmitrak said, "I tried to reason with him, Empress. I tried to make him listen to the god. He cut me with his snakeblade! He tried to *kill* me with the hammer!"

She would not care if he had killed Dmitrak. She would not care if he had killed himself. She wished he was dead now. She wished that she was.

I am Hekat, godtouched and precious. How can this be happening to me?

"Is this so, warlord?" she whispered. "Did you turn the god's hammer on your brother?"

Zandakar swallowed, his godbells cried. "Not to hurt him. Only to stop him. Yuma, I swear, I heard the god. I am not meant to make Mijak the world. I am meant for another purpose."

His words struck her like blows. Annihilating. Numbing. Dimly she was aware of the watching crowd. Of Vortka beside her, his robes brushing her arm. She could hear the piebald bitch, breathing. That was offensive. This was her fault.

She tipped her face towards the sun. Breathed in deep the searing air. Around her neck, the scorpion amulet burned.

"*Aieeeeeeee! The god see me! My son Zandakar is dead!*"

She leapt from her stone throne, she brought up her snakeblade, she dragged its sharp point through her left cheek, her right. She severed her silver scars, she turned them scarlet, she bled for the god and the pain in her heart. With her sharp snakeblade she cut her breasts, her arms, she soaked the hot air with her acrid blood.

The piebald bitch screamed. The crowd was screaming. Vortka was shouting, Zandakar too, even Dmitrak shouted, though he could not care.

Zandakar reached for her. "Yuma! *Yuma!*"

She could not hear him, her son was dead.

The piebald bitch screamed again, even louder. Hekat turned, blood pouring down her face. "Be silent, you patched slut! Did you not *hear* me, there *is* no Zandakar! *Zandakar is dead!* Dead in the god's eye, dead in mine!"

"No, no, he kneels before you!" the piebald bitch cried. "Do not disown him, forgive him, Empress. Whatever he did, he did for me! For his son in my belly, for the love between us!"

Forgive him? *Forgive* him?

He is unforgivable.

There was a roaring in her head, it was the god, the god was screaming. She lifted her snakeblade, the world was turned scarlet.

A dead man howled at her, "*Yuma, no!*"

With five slashing strikes of her snakeblade she opened the piebald's bulging belly. Watched, immobile, as the bitch's ugly mouth widened, as her body went rigid, as something brown and white and covered in blood slid from that slashed place and fell to the ground. It writhed feebly for two heartbeats, then was still.

Slowly, the piebald's stunned eyes lifted, then she began screaming. Dmitrak's snakeblade plunged into her throat. The piebald thudded to the blood-slicked stone dais.

Silence, but for a dead man's weeping.

Hekat looked at Dmitrak, saw Nagarak inside him. Saw the flash of the god's power and snatched the hammer from Vortka. She gave it to Dmitrak, he put it on. In his face a riot of triumph, a hunger for power finally assuaged.

He raised his arm, and crimson power surged into the sky.

"Behold the god's chosen!" she screamed for the crowd. "Dmitrak warlord, hammer of the god!"

It was the watching warriors who broke the dreadful silence. They yelled, they shouted, they surged for the stairs.

"*Dmitrak! Dmitrak! Behold the god's hammer!*"

The crowd took up their frantic chant.

"*Dmitrak! Dmitrak! The god's mighty hammer!*"

Dmitrak bared his teeth at her, it was almost a smile.

With the power still surging, he turned to her people, he swam in their chanting, he grew in their eyes.

Hekat could not bear it. She looked at dead Zandakar, slumped over the piebald. He was oblivious, weeping, groaning like a man strapped to the scorpion wheel. She seized his godbraids, she wrenched his head back, she raised her snakeblade—

"*No, Hekat!*" cried Vortka, and took hold of her wrist.

"Do not dare to stop me!" she cried, her voice was a stranger's. "He is dead already, I but finish my task!"

Vortka's face was running with water. "Hekat, *don't*. When your anger cools you will *hate* yourself!"

Was she weeping also? She could not tell. "I have given *him* all my hatred, I have none left, not even for *that*!" She kicked the piebald's flaccid body.

"You think so now, you will not think it forever!"

"You try to save him because he is yours!" she hissed. "Release me, Vortka, or lose your hand!"

Vortka pulled her close, he pressed his cheek to hers. He did not care who might be watching. Truly, to Vortka, they were alone.

"Hekat, spare him, I beg you. For what was between us, for how he was made." He was weeping so hard, he was almost incoherent. "You will never see him again, you have my word. But *do not kill him*. I ask on my life."

She looked again at her dead breathing son. *Why should I spare him, this wicked sinner? For his sinning betrayal, god, he should die.*

A flicker of memories crossed her inner eye:

Zandakar, bloody and slimed with mucus, still roped to her sweaty, exhausted body . . . Zandakar, two teeth revealed in his triumphant smile as he stood alone for the very first time . . . Zandakar, kissing her, saying, *Yuma, I love you* . . . Zandakar, brown and gold and gleaming, galloping his pony ahead of Raklion and the warhost . . . Zandakar, riding to conquer the world . . .

Zandakar . . . Zandakar . . . Zandakar . . .

She released his godbraids. Stepped away from his body. Wrenched her wrist free from Vortka's desperate grasp. With her cold gaze resting upon the face of Dmitrak warlord, the god's mighty hammer, her only living son, she said:

"Then take him, Vortka. Get him out of my sight. The next time I see him I swear, he will die."

ACKNOWLEDGMENTS

Well, this was an adventure! Kind of like trying to nail smoke to a wall, only harder.

First and foremost, heartfelt thanks to my long-suffering editor Stephanie Smith, who bore with patience above and beyond my extraordinary cluelessness through the writing of this book.

The entire Voyager team in Australia for their hard work and support: you guys rock every casbah on the planet.

My esteemed and invaluable guinea-pig readers, who must have qualified for some kind of purple heart: Glenda Larke, Mark Timmony, Elaine and Peter Shipp and Mary Webber.

My agent, Ethan Ellenberg, who scared the you-know-what out of me with a last-minute critique that *really* put the cat among the pigeons and the grey hairs on my head. Thanks, Ethan. I think. *g*

Those mad, mad puppies at Voyager Online (aka The Purple Zone) for—well—being mad, mad puppies.

Les Petersen, for his beautiful cover illustration, and Darren Holt, for the spectacular design.

The booksellers, who help spread the word.

extras

orbit

meet the author

KAREN MILLER was born in Vancouver, Canada, and moved to Australia with her family when she was two. She started writing stories while still in primary school, where she fell in love with speculative fiction after reading *The Lion, the Witch and the Wardrobe*. Over the years she has held down a wide variety of jobs, including horse stud groom in Buckingham, England. She is working on several new novels. Visit the official Karen Miller website at www.karenmiller.net.

interview

Your first series—Kingmaker Kingbreaker—was a two-book series which is quite unusual. Why did you decide to do this and do you plan to make it into a trilogy at a later date?

Funny you should ask that . . . originally, it was a stand-alone novel. Why? Because I honestly couldn't imagine writing a trilogy. I never believed I had that many words in me. The idea of writing a single novel was daunting enough. Thoughts of a trilogy had me crawling under the blankets! As it was I struggled for a long, long time to get that single novel written. In the end I wrote it as a film script—I've always found dialogue fun and narrative prose more challenging. The only way to reach The End was to do it all in dialogue. After that I went back and novelized my script (you'd have to think there's an easier way, wouldn't you?) and—making the classic new writer's mistake—submitted it to a publisher way before it was ready to be seen. But the editor liked it enough to include a list of rewrite suggestions with the rejection letter, and invited me to resubmit after having another try. Of course when I re-read it I saw all the mistakes—the biggest one being I'd massively shortchanged the story. So I looked for the natural breakpoint, cut the manuscript in two, making it a two book series . . . and got published.

Having said that, though, I do like the two-act structure. I do a lot of theater stuff, so it seems to be quite comfortable. As for expanding the series from two to more . . . well, there is something in the pipeline. No official announcements yet but stay tuned!

Kingmaker Kingbreaker is about the arduous coming of age of your protagonists. What is it about this situation that you think fascinates fantasy authors and readers? Is it also the sort of theme you enjoy coming across in books as a reader?

Well, it's about a lot of things—love, hate, revenge, sacrifice—but certainly coming of age is a major factor in the story. It's a theme that resonates through all literary genres, I think, and has done for as long as there have been stories. Because "coming of age" can be a great many things. As complicated human beings I think it's possible that we never stop coming of age. Every time we grow in our lives, every time we take a chance, meet a challenge, survive something dangerous or frightening, we've come of age. We've reinvented ourselves. We've found a new way to live in the world. That's where the appeal lies, I think. Because change is frightening. It's confronting. Experiencing it vicariously through characters in a story can be helpful—but it's also a lot of fun! All the emotional payoff without the actual scary of real life. It works for me!

Your books are very character-driven. Do you have a favorite among your characters? Are they based on people you know? (You're allowed to say!)

It does seem to be working out that way, I think—that my books are more about the characters than they are about anything else. Certainly in my own reading and drama diet I gravitate towards stories that are about people more than stuff. I think people are fascinating. What makes us tick is a never-ending source of interest. The characters in my books are a kind of patchwork quilt, made up of aspects of myself and of people I've met in the real world. I've never based a character on a totally real person, but I've certainly been inspired by one. There's an upcoming character, a psychic named Ursa, who was inspired by a doctor I know.

As for having favorites, well . . . if I admit to a sneaking affection for Hekat are you going to call for the men in white jackets? And of course I'm very fond of Asher—so brave and bloody-minded! I think he's a doll.

The scenario you created for **Empress** *is more expansive than your previous series. Is it inspired by anything or did you just feel you wanted to stretch your wings a bit further? Did the greater scope of the new series bring any new challenges to your writing?*

With the Godspeaker trilogy I certainly did want to challenge myself. I wanted to shake things up a bit to make sure I didn't let the fear of pushing the envelope keep me in the same place. The story idea had been sitting around for a long time—I had part of it written while I was still working on the Kingmaker, Kingbreaker books. When I came back to it I realized I'd made the same mistake as before—I was keeping the story too small. So I took a very deep breath, committed to a trilogy (a story in three acts, see, the theater will out!) and realized that I had to go back in time and start with Hekat's story. So that's what I did, with much trepidation! So I guess I'd have to say that the expansion grew naturally out of discovering the story I was trying to tell.

As for that providing challenges—yikes! Talk about growing pains. It's proving to be an arduous journey. I've discovered my story ideas are like the Tardis: they're bigger on the inside. And they take a lot of wrangling to make them behave! It's not only keeping the various story threads neat and untangled, it's remembering who said what to whom and when and how many times, and not falling into the trap of repeating myself with certain words and phrases, and remembering the big picture while I'm focusing on a small, intimate scene. Sheesh! It's like trying to juggle twenty-seven balls at once without dropping any. It's been a huge learning curve, but a fantastic one. I am in awe of writers who do big multi-volume series. I don't understand how they keep everything straight!

Unlike your first series, the gods play a large part in **Empress.** *Can you tell us a bit about the thinking behind that?*

Philosophically, I wanted to have a look at the nature of divinity. We seem to fall so short of measuring up to certain religious ideals in our own world. People who claim to be religious do terrible things, and others who say they believe in no God at all routinely perform acts of great kindness and charity in ways that seem to fit a religious framework. That's such an odd contradiction. And the exact nature of God is so elusive. I'm intrigued by those things, and wanted to explore some thoughts and ideas. Of course there's not necessarily a direct parallel between the divine in the books and in the real world, but hopefully it's interesting.

Do you have a personal theory on why Fantasy is so popular?

Fantasy is a really romantic genre. And I don't just mean the hearts-and-flowers true love romantic—it's sweeping and exotic and breathtaking. It has the power to whisk you away into amazing new worlds where romantic ideals like truth and love and justice and sacrifice and redemption and courage—ideals that are so often sneered at in our modern society—are celebrated and seen as something true and wonderful to aspire to. And I like that. I really enjoy a lot of science fiction, but often it's very bleak and cynical. Mostly I think fantasy celebrates being human, it celebrates big emotions, it wears its heart on its sleeve—and it's not ashamed of that. And while it can be down and dirty and gritty at times, still at the core it's about hope and the triumph of the best of human nature—which is why I think it has such a strong and broad appeal.

Do you read mainly fantasy fiction yourself, or do you prefer a change of genre after a hard day of writing? What are you currently reading?

Overall I read a great deal less than ever I used to—not because there aren't brilliant books out there, but because after eight hours in front of the computer thinking up words my brain is cactus and I can't cope with any more! When I do read, I tend to switch genres so I'm using a different part of my imagination. I love crime, mystery and some romance. I can read those without exploding my head. I do still read fantasy and science fiction—I have a massive pile now waiting for my attention. I'll get to them when I've made my current deadline. I also read non-fiction stuff, books on history mainly, for research. They're always fun and quite relaxing. And I watch a lot of drama on DVD. TV dramas give me my story fix without words coming into the picture.

Currently I'm reading an older JD Robb thriller, the new Rachel Caine and a book about ancient imperial China.

Do you have any particular favorite authors who have influenced your work?

Probably the most influential writer in my life so far has been Dorothy Dunnett. Sadly she's dead now, but she wrote historical fiction. Her most famous work is a six-book series called The Lymond Chronicles. It's about a sixteenth-century Scots nobleman called Francis Crawford, and it follows his life for some fifteen years as he intrigues his way around most of the known world as a mercenary and a courtier trying to uncover the truth of his heritage.

The series is sheer magic. Breathtaking prose, immaculate worldbuilding, magnificent characters. Basically I want to be Dorothy when I grow up. I suspect that's a tall order, but it's something to aspire to!

What do you do when you're not writing or reading?

The little time left over when I'm not unconscious, I spend at my local theater as an actor, director and public relations officer, or watching DVD dramas. It's a sad little life but someone has to live it.

Can you tell us a little about where the story goes after Empress?

Well, there's a change in location, for a start, to an island kingdom called Ethrea. We don't lose touch with Mijak entirely—and one character in particular returns with an important role to play—but in the next book we meet the people who must stand in the way of Hekat and her warhost as she seeks to conquer the world. Unfortunately these new characters are dealing with their own major crisis—and if they don't resolve it they'll have no hope of saving themselves from Hekat. Things are about to get very interesting . . .

And, lastly, for those writers who have yet to see their books appearing in the shops, how did it feel to see your first novel in print?

Totally surreal. It's the oddest feeling, having a dream come true. I've wanted to be a writer since I was a little girl in school. Having that happen now, holding the books in my hand, it's exhilarating and terrifying at the same time. I frequently wonder when I'm going to wake up . . . but of course you know I'm praying I don't!

introducing

If you enjoyed **EMPRESS**,
look out for

THE RIVEN KINGDOM

Book 2 of the Godspeaker Trilogy
by Karen Miller

The king of Ethrea was dying.

Rhian sat by her father's bedside, holding his frail hand in hers and breathing lightly. Her world was a glass bubble; if she breathed too deeply it would shatter, and her with it.

This isn't fair, this isn't fair, this isn't fair . . .

Droning in the privy bedchamber corner, the Most Venerable Justin. One of Prolate Marlan's senior clergy, sentenced to praying for her father's soul. His shaved head was bowed over his prayer-beads, click-click-clicking through his fingers till she thought she would scream.

I wish you'd get out. I wish you'd go away. We don't

want you here. This is our time, we don't have so much that we can share.

She had to bite her lip, hard, to quell fresh tears. She'd wept so often lately she felt soggy, like moss. And what was the point of weeping anyway? Weeping wouldn't save her father, he was broken, he was slipping away.

I will be an orphan soon.

She'd been half an orphan for ten years, now. Without the portraits on the castle walls she might not even remember Queen Ilda's sweet face. A frightening thought, to lose her mother twice. Was she destined to lose her brothers twice as well? Ranald and Simon were dead only two months, she still heard their voices on the edge of sleep. She thought it was likely, and after them her father twice. All these double-bereavements. Where was God in this? Was he sleeping? Indifferent?

Mama, the boys, and now dear Papa. I know I'm the youngest, nature's law dictates I'd be the last one left . . . but not this soon! Do you hear me, God? It isn't fair!

As though sensing her rebellion, the venerable paused in his bead-clicking and droning and said, "Highness, the king will likely sleep for hours. Perhaps your time would be better spent in prayer."

She wanted to say, *I think you're praying enough for both of us, Ven'Justin.* But if she said that he'd tell her chaplain, Helfred, and Helfred would tell Prolate Marlan, and Marlan would be unamused.

It wasn't wise, to stir Marlan to anger.

So she said, her heart seething, "I do pray, Ven'Justin. Every breath I take is a prayer."

Ven'Justin nodded, not entirely convinced. "Admirable, Highness. But surely the proper place for your prayers is the castle chapel."

He may be a Most Venerable, but still he lacked the authority to command a king's daughter. She looked again at her father's cadaverous face, with its jaundiced skin pleated over fleshless bone, so he would not see her anger. Her voice she kept quiet, sweet and unobjectionable. *Be a lady, be a lady, be always a lady.*

"I will go to the chapel, by and by. For now, Ven'Justin, even if he is asleep, I know His Majesty takes comfort from my presence."

Click-click-click went Most Venerable Justin's prayer-beads. He picked up his droning where he'd left off.

On his mountain of pillows, her father stirred. Beneath his paper-thin eyelids his eyes shifted, restless. The pulse in his throat beat harder. "Ranald," he muttered. "Ranald, my boy . . . I'm coming. I'm coming." His voice, once treacle-dark and smooth as silk, rasped in his throat like ugly rusted wire. "Ranald, my good son . . ." His exhaled breath became a groan.

A basin of water and a soft cloth sat near at hand, on the bedside cabinet. Gently, Rhian moistened her father's cheeks and lips. "It's all right, Papa. Don't fret. I'm here. Please, try to rest."

"Ranald!" said her father, and opened his eyes. So recently the deepest blue, clear and clean as a summer sky, now they were rheumy, their whites stained yellow with the failing of his liver. For a horrible moment they were clouded, confused. Then he remembered her, and sighed. "Rhian. I thought I heard Ranald."

She dropped the cloth back in the basin and took his hand again. His fingers felt so brittle. Hold him too tightly and he'd break into pieces. "I know, Papa. You were dreaming."

A single tear trailed through his grey stubble. "I never should have let Ranald go voyaging with Simon," he whispered. "I was selfishly indulgent, I cared more for Ranald loving me than I did what was best, and now they are dead. My heir is dead and so is his brother. I have failed the kingdom. I am a bad king."

It was, by now, a familiar refrain. Rhian kissed his cold hand. "That's nonsense, Papa. You have been the very best of kings. Every great man's sons go abroad to see the world. Not a lord in your kingdom has once told his sons, 'No, you must stay at home.' Your own father didn't forbid you the world, even though you were the heir. You could never have denied your sons that adventure. Ranald and Simon had bad luck, that's all. It's not your fault. You aren't to blame."

In the corner, Ven'Justin's beads clicked louder. The church frowned on superstitious beliefs like luck. She spared the man a warning, glaring glance. Venerable or not, she wouldn't have him upsetting her father.

"Rhian."

"Yes, Papa?"

His fingers tried to squeeze hers. "My good girl. What will become of you when I'm gone?"

She could answer that, but not in front of Most Venerable Justin. Not in front of anyone who would carry her words straight back to Helfred, and Marlan. "Hush, Papa," she said, and smoothed her other hand over his thinning hair. "Don't tire yourself talking."

But he was determined to fret. "I should have seen you betrothed, Rhian. I have failed you as I failed your brothers."

A single name rang like a bell in her heart. Alasdair. But there was no point considering him, returned to duchy Linfoi and his own ailing father. Besides, a husband would only complicate things.

"Papa, Papa, do not excite yourself," she soothed. "You need to rest. God will take care of me." Another glance, over her shoulder. "Isn't that so, Ven'Justin?"

Grudgingly, the Most Venerable nodded. "God takes care of all his children, to the length and breadth of their deserving."

"There," she said. "You see? Ven'Justin agrees." Then added, even as she felt the hot tears rise, "Besides, you're not going anywhere. Do you hear me, Papa? You're going to get well."

"Throughout my life I have not been the most reverent of men," her father said, his voice reduced to a whisper. Then he smiled, a gummy business now, with all his teeth rattled loose in their sockets. "But even I know, Rhian, that God does as God wills. I will leave when I am called and not even you, my bossy minx, can dictate I'll stay."

My bossy minx. It was one of his pet phrases for her. She hadn't heard him use it in the longest time. "Yes, Papa," she said, and again kissed his cold fingers.

Soon after he drifted back to sleep. Ignoring the Most Venerable Justin and his pointed sighs, she held her father's fragile hand and, defiant in the face of God's apparent decision, willed him to live, live, live.